Praise for Amanda Hocking

"There is no denying that Amanda Hocking knows how to tell a good story and keep readers coming back for more. More is exactly what they will be looking for once they've turned the last page." —*Kirkus Reviews*

"Hocking hits all the commercial high notes . . . She knows how to keep readers turning the pages."
—*The New York Times Book Review*

"Wendy is a flawed antihero, which helps differentiate her from the throng of paranormal-romance heroines, and the potential for development, both dramatic and romantic, should make readers anxious for the next installment of the Trylle trilogy." —*Booklist*

"The romance is smoldering, the action is suspenseful, and the characters are quirky, likeable, and original. Amanda Hocking has a gift for storytelling that will grip readers and keep them wanting more. . . . Entrancing." —*LibraryThing*

"You can't beat the story line for *Switched*, the book that starts off the series with a bang . . . full of mysteries, dangers, and untapped powers that Wendy never knew she had."
—*MTV.com*

"*Switched* is written so wonderfully that it is not hard to imagine you are in this fantastic world! Readers will love the exhilarating roller-coaster ride of Wendy's life as she adapts to . . . a frightening and exciting life." —*RT Book Reviews*

Trylle: The Complete Trilogy

Switched, Torn, and Ascend

Amanda Hocking

St. Martin's Griffin ✿ New York

TRYLLE: THE COMPLETE TRILOGY. SWITCHED Copyright © 2010 by Amanda Hocking. TORN Copyright © 2010 by Amanda Hocking. ASCEND Copyright © 2011 by Amanda Hocking. All rights reserved. Printed in the United States of America. For information, address St. Martin's Press, 175 Fifth Avenue, New York, N.Y. 10010.

www.stmartins.com

ISBN 978-1-250-06708-1 (trade paperback)

St. Martin's Griffin books may be purchased for educational, business, or promotional use. For information on bulk purchases, please contact the Macmillan Corporate and Premium Sales Department at 1-800-221-7945, extension 5442, or write to specialmarkets@macmillan.com.

First Edition: January 2015

10 9 8 7 6

switched

To Pete—fellow Aardvark, comrade,
and original cover model

ACKNOWLEDGMENTS

First and foremost, I have to thank the readers and book bloggers. I've said it before but it bears repeating—I could never have gotten this far without all your support and encouragement. I want to thank you all by name, but if I did that, the acknowledgments would become a novel itself. So I just want to say thank you to every person who read *Switched,* told their friends about it, left a review, tweeted about it, blogged about it, or liked it on Facebook, thank you a million times over.

I want to thank my mom for being ridiculously supportive and understanding in all my endeavors, no matter how insane or far out they might be. The actions of the mothers in this book—namely, Kim and Elora—in no way reflect my experiences with my own mother or my stepmom. Both of them are caring, intelligent, strong women who have always had my back and loved me even when I didn't deserve it.

I need to thank my platonic lifemate/roommate Eric

Goldman for being the only person in the whole world who can tolerate my random but frequent obsessions, the sheer volume of my voice, and the fact that I spend more time with people I make up in my head than with people in the real world.

I can't forget the rest of the Clique—Fifi, Valerie, Greggor, Pete, Matthew, Bronson, and Baby Gels. You guys are the greatest friends in the whole world. Seriously. I have no idea why you're friends with me, but I'm grateful for it every day.

The whole writing process I've gone through to get here has allowed me to meet other fantastic authors, including the Indie Author Mafia: Daniel Arenson, David Dalglish, David McAfee, Robert Duperre, Sean Sweeney, Mike Crane, and Jason Letts. Not only are these guys awesome writers (and if you haven't checked out their books, you definitely should), but they are funny, smart, fiercely loyal, and incredibly nice. They've definitely helped me keep a saner head in times of insanity. I have to give a shout-out to the rest of my author support team: Stacey Wallace Benefiel and Jeff Bryan, and to everyone over at the Kindleboards.

Last but not least, I have to thank my current writing team. People often ask me if I feel bitterness or resentment toward all the agents who passed on my work before, and to that I say a resounding no. It wasn't the right time or the right place, and I needed all those no's to get to the right agent and the right publisher.

From day one, my agent, Steve Axelrod, has been working hard for my books and for me. I daresay he's the greatest agent on the planet. My new publishers at St. Martin's Press, namely, my editor, Rose Hilliard, and the SVP Matthew Shear are so tremendous. Rose has believed in me since long before I signed with them.

And finally, I want to thank you for reading this. Without the support of readers like you, I'd just be a dreamer. You're the ones who make my dreams come true every day.

eleven years ago

A couple things made that day stand out more than any other: it was my sixth birthday, and my mother was wielding a knife. Not a tiny steak knife, but some kind of massive butcher knife glinting in the light like in a bad horror movie. She definitely wanted to kill me.

I try to think of the days that led up to that one to see if I missed something about her, but I have no memory of her before then. I have some memories of my childhood, and I can even remember my dad, who died when I was five, but not her.

When I ask my brother, Matt, about her, he always answers with things like, "She's batshit, Wendy. That's all you need to know." He's seven years older than I am, so he remembers things better, but he never wants to talk about it.

We lived in the Hamptons when I was a kid, and my mother was a lady of leisure. She'd hired a live-in nanny to deal with me, but the night before my birthday the nanny had left for a family emergency. My mother was in charge of me, for the first time in her life, and neither of us was happy.

I didn't even want the party. I liked gifts, but I didn't have any friends. The people coming to the party were my mother's friends and their snobby little kids. She had planned some kind of princess tea party I didn't want, but Matt and our maid spent all morning setting it up anyway.

By the time the guests arrived, I'd already ripped off my shoes and plucked the bows from my hair. My mother came down in the middle of opening gifts, surveying the scene with her icy blue eyes.

Her blond hair had been smoothed back, and she had on bright red lipstick that only made her appear paler. She still wore my father's red silk robe, the same way she had since the day he died, but she'd added a necklace and black heels, as if that would make the outfit appropriate.

No one commented on it, but everyone was too busy watching my performance. I complained about every single gift I got. They were all dolls or ponies or some other thing I would never play with.

My mother came into the room, stealthily gliding through the guests to where I sat. I had torn through a box wrapped in pink teddy bears, containing yet another porcelain doll. Instead of showing any gratitude, I started yelling about what a stupid present it was.

Before I could finish, she slapped me sharply across the face.

"You are not my daughter," my mother said, her voice cold. My cheek stung from where she had hit me, and I gaped at her.

The maid quickly redirected the festivities, but the idea percolated in my mother's mind the rest of the afternoon. I think, when she said it, she meant it the way parents do when their child behaves appallingly. But the more she thought, the more it made sense to her.

After an afternoon of similar tantrums on my part, someone decided it was time to have cake. My mother seemed to be taking forever in the kitchen, and I went to check on her. I don't even know why she was the one getting the cake instead of the maid, who was far more maternal.

On the island in the kitchen, a massive chocolate cake covered in pink flowers sat in the middle. My mother stood on the other side, holding a gigantic knife she was using to cut the cake to serve on tiny saucers. Her hair was coming loose from its bobby pins.

"Chocolate?" I wrinkled my nose as she tried to set perfect pieces onto the saucers.

"Yes, Wendy, you like chocolate," my mother informed me.

"No, I don't!" I crossed my arms over my chest. "I hate chocolate! I'm not going to eat it, and you can't make me!"

"Wendy!"

The knife happened to point in my direction, some frosting stuck to the tip, but I wasn't afraid. If I had been, everything might've turned out different. Instead, I wanted to have another one of my tantrums.

"No, no, no! It's my birthday, and I don't want chocolate!" I shouted and stomped my foot on the floor as hard as I could.

"You don't want chocolate?" My mother looked at me, her blue eyes wide and incredulous.

A whole new type of crazy glinted in them, and that's when my fear started to kick in.

"What kind of child are you, Wendy?" She slowly walked around the island, coming toward me. The knife in her hand looked far more menacing than it had a few seconds ago.

"You're certainly not my child. What are you, Wendy?"

Staring at her, I took several steps back. My mother looked maniacal. Her robe had fallen open, revealing her thin collarbones and the black slip she wore underneath. She took a step forward, this time with the knife pointed right at me. I should've screamed or run away, but I felt frozen in place.

"I was pregnant, Wendy! But you're not the child I gave birth to! Where is my child?" Tears formed in her eyes, and I just shook my head. "You probably killed him, didn't you?"

She lunged at me, screaming at me to tell her what I had done with her real baby. I darted out of the way just in time, but she backed me into a corner. I pressed up against the kitchen cupboards with nowhere to go, but she wasn't about to give up.

"Mom!" Matt yelled from the other side of the room.

Her eyes flickered with recognition, the sound of the son she actually loved. For a moment I thought this might stop her, but it only made her realize she was running out of time, so she raised the knife.

Matt dove at her, but not before the blade tore through my dress and slashed across my stomach. Blood stained my clothes as pain shot through me, and I sobbed hysterically.

My mother fought hard against Matt, unwilling to let go of the knife.

"She killed your brother, Matthew!" my mother insisted, looking at him with frantic eyes. "She's a monster! She has to be stopped!"

ONE

home

Drool spilled out across my desk, and I opened my eyes just in time to hear Mr. Meade slam down a textbook. I'd only been at this high school a month, but I'd quickly learned that was his favorite way of waking me up from my naps during his history lecture. I always tried to stay awake, but his monotone voice lulled me into sleeping submission every time.

"Miss Everly?" Mr. Meade snapped. "Miss Everly?"

"Hmm?" I murmured.

I lifted my head and discreetly wiped away the drool. I glanced around to see if anyone had noticed. Most of the class seemed oblivious, except for Finn Holmes. He'd been here a week, so he was the only kid in school newer than me. Whenever I looked at him, he always seemed to be staring at me in a completely unabashed way, as if it were perfectly normal to gawk at me.

There was something oddly still and quiet about him, and I had yet to hear him speak, even though he was in four of my classes. He wore his hair smoothed back, and his eyes were a matching shade of black. His looks were rather striking, but he weirded me out too much for me to find him attractive.

"Sorry to disturb your sleep." Mr. Meade cleared his throat so I would look up at him.

"It's okay," I said.

"Miss Everly, why don't you go down to the principal's office?" Mr. Meade suggested, and I groaned. "Since you seem to be making a habit of sleeping in my class, maybe he can come up with some ideas to help you stay awake."

"I am awake," I insisted.

"Miss Everly—now." Mr. Meade pointed to the door, as if I had forgotten how to leave and needed reminding.

I fixed my gaze on him, and despite how stern his gray eyes looked, I could tell he'd cave easily. Over and over in my head I kept repeating, *I do not need to go the principal's office. You don't want to send me down there. Let me stay in class.* Within seconds his face went lax and his eyes took on a glassy quality.

"You can stay in class and finish the lecture," Mr. Meade said groggily. He shook his head, clearing his eyes. "But next time you're going straight to the office, Miss Everly." He looked confused for a moment, and then launched right back into his history lecture.

I wasn't sure what it was that I had just done exactly—I tried not to think about it enough to name it. About a year ago, I'd discovered that if I thought about something and looked at somebody hard enough, I could get that person to do what I wanted.

As awesome as that sounded, I avoided doing it as much as possible. Partially because I felt like I was crazy for really believing I could do it, even though it worked every time. But mostly because I didn't like it. It made me feel dirty and manipulative.

Mr. Meade went on talking, and I followed along studiously, my guilt making me try harder. I hadn't wanted to do that to him, but I couldn't go to the principal's office. I had just been expelled from my last school, forcing my brother and aunt to uproot their lives again so we could move closer to my new school.

I had honestly tried at the last school, but the Dean's daughter had been intent on making my life miserable. I'd tolerated her taunts and ridicules as best I could until one day she cornered me in the bathroom, calling me every dirty name in the book. Finally, I'd had enough, and I punched her.

The Dean decided to skip their one-strike rule and immediately expelled me. I know in large part it was because I'd resorted to physical violence against his child, but I'm not sure that was it entirely. Where other students were shown leniency, for some reason I never seemed to be.

When class finally ended, I shoved my books in my book bag and left quickly. I didn't like hanging around after I did the mind-control trick. Mr. Meade could change his mind and send me to the office, so I hurried down to my locker.

Bright-colored flyers decorated battered lockers, telling

everyone to join the debate team, try out for the school play, and not to miss the fall semiformal this Friday. I wondered what a "semiformal" consisted of at a public school, not that I'd bothered to ask anyone.

I got to my locker and started switching out my books. Without even looking, I knew Finn was behind me. I glanced over my shoulder and saw him getting a drink from the fountain. Almost as soon as I looked at him, he lifted his head and gazed at me. Like he could sense me too.

The guy was just looking at me, nothing more, but it freaked me out somehow. I'd put up with his stares for a week, trying to avoid confrontation, but I couldn't take it anymore. *He* was the one acting inappropriately, not me. I couldn't get in trouble for just talking to him, right?

"Hey," I said to him, slamming my locker shut. I readjusted the straps on my book bag and walked across the hall to where he stood. "Why are you staring at me?"

"Because you're standing in front of me," Finn replied simply. He looked at me, his eyes framed by dark lashes, without any hint of embarrassment or even denial. It was definitely unnerving.

"You're *always* staring at me," I persisted. "It's weird. You're weird."

"I wasn't trying to fit in."

"Why do you look at me all the time?" I knew I'd simply rephrased my original question, but he still hadn't given me a decent answer.

"Does it bother you?"

"Answer the question." I stood up straighter, trying to make my presence more imposing so he wouldn't realize how much he rattled me.

"Everyone always looks at you," Finn said coolly. "You're very attractive."

That sounded like a compliment, but his voice was emotionless when he said it. I couldn't tell if he was making fun of a vanity I didn't even have, or if he was simply stating facts. Was he flattering me or mocking me? Or maybe something else entirely?

"Nobody stares at me as much as you do," I said as evenly as I could.

"If it bothers you, I'll try and stop," Finn offered.

That was tricky. In order to ask him to stop, I had to admit that he'd gotten to me, and I didn't want to admit that anything got to me. If I lied and said it was fine, then he would just keep on doing it.

"I didn't ask you to stop. I asked you why," I amended.

"I told you why."

"No, you didn't." I shook my head. "You just said that everyone looks at me. You never explained why *you* looked at me."

Almost imperceptibly the corner of his mouth moved up, revealing the hint of a smirk. It wasn't just that I amused him; I sensed he was pleased with me. Like he had challenged me somehow and I had passed.

My stomach did a stupid flip thing I had never felt before, and I swallowed hard, hoping to fight it back.

"I look at you because I can't look away," Finn answered finally.

I was struck completely mute, trying to think of some kind of clever response, but my mind refused to work. Realizing that my jaw had gone slack and I probably looked like an awe-struck schoolgirl, I hurried to collect myself.

"That's kind of creepy," I said at last, but my words came out weak instead of accusatory.

"I'll work on being less creepy, then," Finn promised.

I had called him out on being creepy, and it didn't faze him at all. He didn't stammer an apology or flush with shame. He just kept looking at me evenly. Most likely he was a damn sociopath, and for whatever reason, I found that endearing.

I couldn't come up with a witty retort, but the bell rang, saving me from the rest of that awkward conversation. Finn just nodded, thus ending our exchange, and turned down the hall to go to his next class. Thankfully, it was one of the few he didn't have with me.

True to his word, Finn wasn't creepy the rest of the day. Every time I saw him, he was doing something inoffensive that didn't involve looking at me. I still got that feeling that he watched me when I had my back to him, but it wasn't anything I could prove.

When the final bell rang at three o'clock, I tried to be the first one out. My older brother, Matt, picked me up from school, at least until he found a job, and I didn't want to keep him waiting. Besides that, I didn't want to deal with any more contact with Finn Holmes.

I quickly made my way to the parking lot at the edge of the school lawn. Scanning for Matt's Prius, I absently started to chew my thumbnail. I had this weird feeling, almost like a shiver running down my back. I turned around, half expecting to see Finn staring at me, but there was nothing.

I tried to shake it off, but my heart raced faster. This felt like something more sinister than a boy from school. I was still staring off, trying to decide what had me freaked out, when a loud honk startled me, making me jump. Matt sat a few cars down, looking at me over the top of his sunglasses.

"Sorry." I opened the car door and hopped in, where he looked me over for a moment. "What?"

"You looked nervous. Did something happen?" Matt asked, and I sighed. He took his whole big brother thing way too seriously.

"No, nothing happened. School sucks," I said, brushing him off. "Let's go home."

"Seat belt," Matt commanded, and I did as I was told.

Matt had always been quiet and reserved, thinking everything over carefully before making a decision. He was a stark contrast to me in every way, except that we were both relatively short. I was small, with a decidedly pretty, feminine face. My brown hair was an untamed mess of curls that I kept up in loose buns.

He kept his sandy blond hair trim and neat, and his eyes were the same shade of blue as our mother's. Matt wasn't overtly muscular, but he was sturdy and athletic from working out a lot. He had a sense of duty, like he had to make sure he was strong enough to defend us against anything.

"How is school going?" Matt asked.

"Great. Fantastic. Amazing."

"Are you even going to graduate this year?" Matt had long since stopped judging my school record. A large part of him didn't even care if I graduated from high school.

"Who knows?" I shrugged.

Everywhere I went, kids never seemed to like me. Even before I said or did anything. I felt like I had something wrong with me and everyone knew it. I tried getting along with the other kids, but I'd only take getting pushed for so long before I pushed back. Principals and deans were quick to expel me, probably sensing the same things the kids did.

I just didn't belong.

"Just to warn you, Maggie's taking it seriously," Matt said. "She's set on you graduating this year, from this school."

"Delightful." I sighed. Matt couldn't care less about my schooling, but my aunt Maggie was a different story. And since she was my legal guardian, her opinion mattered more. "What's her plan?"

"Maggie's thinking bedtimes," Matt informed me with a smirk. As if sending me to bed early would somehow prevent me from getting in a fight.

"I'm almost eighteen!" I groaned. "What is she thinking?"

"You've got four more months until you're eighteen," Matt corrected me sharply, and his hand tightened on the steering wheel. He suffered from serious delusions that I was going to run away as soon as I turned eighteen, and nothing I could say would convince him otherwise.

"Yeah, whatever." I waved it off. "Did you tell her she's insane?"

"I figured she'd hear it enough from you." Matt grinned at me.

"So did you find a job?" I asked tentatively, and he shook his head.

He'd just finished an internship over the summer, working with a great architecture firm. He'd said it didn't bother him, moving to a town without much call for a promising young architect, but I couldn't help feeling guilty about it.

"This is a pretty town," I said, looking out the window.

We approached our new house, buried on an average suburban street among a slew of maples and elms. It actually seemed like a boring small town, but I'd promised I'd make the best of it. I really wanted to. I didn't think I could handle disappointing Matt anymore.

"So you're really gonna try here?" Matt asked, looking over at me. We had pulled up in the driveway next to the butter-colored Victorian that Maggie had bought last month.

"I already am," I insisted with a smile. "I've been talking to this Finn kid." Sure, I'd talked to him only once, and I wouldn't even remotely count him as a friend, but I had to tell Matt something.

"Look at you. Making your very first friend." Matt shut off the car's engine and looked at me with veiled amusement.

"Yeah, well, how many friends do you have?" I countered. He just shook his head and got out of the car, and I quickly followed him. "That's what I thought."

"I've had friends before. Gone to parties. Kissed a girl. The whole nine yards," Matt said as he went through the side door into the house.

"So you say." I kicked off my shoes as soon as we walked into the kitchen, which was still in various stages of unpacking. As many times as we'd moved, everyone had gotten tired of the whole process, so we tended to live out of boxes. "I've only seen one of these alleged girls."

"Yeah, 'cause when I brought her home, you set her dress on fire! While she was wearing it!" Matt pulled off his sunglasses and looked at me severely.

"Oh, come on. That was an accident and you know it."

"So you say." Matt opened the fridge.

"Anything good in there?" I asked and hopped onto the kitchen island. "I'm famished."

"Probably nothing you'd like." Matt started sifting through the contents of the fridge, but he was right.

I was a notoriously picky eater. While I had never purposely sought out the life of a vegan, I seemed to hate most things that had either meat in them or man-made synthetics. It was odd and incredibly irritating for the people who tried to feed me.

Maggie appeared in the doorway to the kitchen, flecks of paint stuck in her blond curls. Layers of multicolored paint covered her ratty overalls, proof of all the rooms she had redecorated over the years. She had her hands on her hips, so Matt shut the fridge door to give her his full attention.

"I thought I told you to tell me when you got home," Maggie said.

"We're home?" Matt offered.

"I can see that." Maggie rolled her eyes, and then turned her attention to me. "How was school?"

"Good," I said. "I'm trying harder."

"We've heard that before." Maggie gave me a weary look.

I hated it when she gave me that look. I hated knowing that I made her feel that way, that I had disappointed her that much. She did so much for me, and the only thing she asked of me was that I at least *try* at school. I had to make it work this time.

"Well, yeah . . . but . . ." I looked to Matt for help. "I mean, I actually promised Matt this time. And I'm making a friend."

"She's talking to some guy named Finn," Matt said corroborating my story.

"Like a *guy* guy?" Maggie smiled too broadly for my liking.

The idea of Finn being a romantic prospect hadn't crossed Matt's mind before, and he suddenly tensed up, looking at me with a new scrutiny. Fortunately for him, that idea hadn't crossed my mind either.

"No, nothing like that." I shook my head. "He's just a guy, I guess. I don't know. He seems nice enough."

"Nice?" Maggie gushed. "That's a start! And much better than that anarchist with the tattoo on his face."

"We weren't friends," I corrected her. "I just stole his motorcycle. While he happened to be on it."

Nobody had ever really believed that story, but it was true, and it was how I figured out that I could get people to do things just by thinking it. I had been thinking that I really wanted his bike, and then I was looking at him and he was listening to me, even though I hadn't said anything. Then I was driving his motorcycle.

"So this really is gonna be a new start for us?" Maggie couldn't hold back her excitement any longer. Her blue eyes started to well with happy tears. "Wendy, this is just so wonderful! We can really make a home here!"

I wasn't nearly as excited about it as she was, though I couldn't help but hope she was right. It would be nice to feel like I was home somewhere.

"if you leave"

O ur new house also supplied us with a large vegetable garden, which thrilled Maggie endlessly. Matt and I were much less thrilled. While I loved the outdoors, I'd never been a big fan of manual labor.

Autumn was settling in, and Maggie insisted that we had to clear the garden of its dying vegetation to prepare it for planting in the spring. She used words like "rototiller" and "mulch," and I hoped Matt would deal with them. When it came to work, I usually just handed Matt the necessary tools and kept him company.

"So when are you hauling out the rototiller?" I asked, watching as Matt tore up dead vines. I'm not sure what they used to be, but they reminded me of grapevines. While Matt pulled things up, my job was to hold the wheelbarrow so he could throw them in.

"We don't have a rototiller." He gave me a look as he tossed the dead plants into the wheelbarrow. "You know, you could be helping me with this. You don't need to physically hold that at all times."

"I take my job very seriously, so I think it'd be better if I did," I said, and he rolled his eyes.

Matt continued grumbling, but I tuned him out. A warm fall breeze blew over us, and I closed my eyes, breathing it in. It smelled wonderfully sweet, like fresh-cut corn and grass and wet leaves. A nearby wind chime tinkled lightly, and it made me dread winter coming and taking this all away.

I'd been lost in the moment, enjoying the perfection, but something snapped me out of it. It was hard to describe exactly what it was, but the hair on the back of my neck stood up. The air suddenly felt chillier, and I knew somebody was watching us.

I looked around, trying to see who it was, and this weird fear ran over me. We had a privacy fence at the back of the yard, and a thick row of hedges blocking our house on either side. I scanned them, searching for any signs of crouching figures or spying eyes. I didn't see anything, but the feeling didn't go away.

"If you're gonna be out here, you should at least wear shoes," Matt said, pulling me from my thoughts. He stood up, stretching his back, and looked at me. "Wendy?"

"I'm fine," I answered absently.

I thought I saw movement around the side of the house, so I went over there. Matt called my name, but I ignored him. When I rounded the house, I stopped short. Finn Holmes stood on the sidewalk, but oddly enough, he wasn't looking at me. He was staring at something down the street, something out of my sight.

As strange as it sounds, as soon as I saw him, the anxiety I'd felt started to subside. My first thought should've been that it was him causing my uneasiness, since he was the one who always stared at me in such a creepy fashion. But it wasn't.

Whatever I'd felt in the backyard, it wasn't because of him. When he stared, he made me self-conscious. But this . . . this made my skin crawl.

After a second, Finn turned to look back at me. His dark eyes rested on me a moment, his face expressionless as always. Then, without saying a word, he turned and walked off in the direction he'd been staring.

"Wendy, what's going on?" Matt asked, coming up behind me.

"I thought I saw something." I shook my head.

"Yeah?" He looked at me hard, concern etched on his face. "Are you okay?"

"Yeah. I'm fine." I forced a smile and turned to the back-yard. "Come on. We've got a lot of work to do if I'm gonna make it to that dance."

"You're still on that kick?" Matt grimaced.

Telling Maggie about the dance may have been the worst idea I've ever had, and my life is made up almost entirely of bad ideas. I hadn't wanted to go, but as soon as she'd heard about it, she decided it would be the most fantastic thing ever. I'd never gone to a dance before, but she was so excited about it, I let her have this small victory.

With the dance at seven, she figured she had enough time to finish the coat of paint in the bathroom. Matt had started to voice his complaints, mostly about my interacting with the opposite sex, but Maggie shut him down. To keep him from getting in her way, she ordered him to finish the yardwork. He complied only because he knew that there was no stopping Maggie this time.

Despite Matt's attempts to slow us down, we finished the garden pretty quickly, and I went inside to get ready. Maggie sat on the bed and watched me as I rummaged through my closet, offering suggestions and comments on everything. This included an endless stream of questions about Finn. Matt would grunt or scoff every now and then at my answers, so I knew he was listening nearby.

Once I had decided on a simple blue dress that Maggie insisted looked amazing on me, I let her do my hair. My hair refused to cooperate with anything I tried to do it, and while it wasn't exactly obedient for Maggie, she outwitted it. She left some of it down, so the curls framed my face, and pulled the rest of it back.

When Matt saw me, he looked really pissed off and a little awed, so I knew that I must look pretty awesome.

Maggie gave me a ride to the dance, because we both weren't convinced that Matt would let me out of the car. He kept insisting on a nine o'clock curfew, even though the dance went until ten. I thought I'd be back well before that, but Maggie told me to take all the time I wanted.

My only experience with dances was what I had seen on

TV, but reality wasn't that far off. The theme appeared to be "Crepe Paper in the Gymnasium," and they had mastered it perfectly.

The school colors were white and navy blue, so white and navy blue streamers covered everything, along with matching balloons. For romantic lighting, they had strung everything with white Christmas lights.

Refreshments covered a table on the side, and the band playing on the makeshift stage under the basketball hoop wasn't that bad. Their set list appeared to include only songs from the films of John Hughes, and I arrived in the middle of a "Weird Science" cover.

The biggest difference between real life and what films had taught me was that nobody actually danced. A group of girls stood directly in front of the stage swooning over the lead singer, but otherwise the floor was mostly empty.

People sat scattered all over the bleachers, and, attempting to fit in, I sat in the first row. I kicked off my shoes immediately, because for the most part I hate shoes. With nothing else to do, I resorted to people-watching. As the night wore on, I found myself feeling increasingly lonely and bored.

Kids actually started dancing as the gymnasium filled up, and the band moved on to some kind of Tears for Fears medley. I decided that I'd been here long enough, and I was planning my escape when Finn pushed through the doors.

Wearing a slim-fitting black dress shirt and dark jeans, he looked good. He had the sleeves rolled up and an extra button undone on his shirt, and I wondered why I never realized how attractive he was before.

His eyes met mine, and he walked over to me, surprising me with his direct approach. As often as he seemed to be watching me, he'd never initiated contact before. Not even today, when he'd walked past my house.

"I didn't peg you for the dancing kind," Finn commented when he reached me.

"I was thinking the same thing about you," I said, and he shrugged.

Finn sat down on the bleachers next to me, and I sat up a bit straighter. He glanced over at me but didn't say anything. Already he looked annoyed, and he'd just gotten here. An awkward silence settled over us, and I hurried to fill it.

"You arrived awfully late. Couldn't decide what to wear?" I teased.

"I had stuff with work," Finn explained vaguely.

"Oh? Do you work somewhere near my house?"

"Something like that." Finn sighed, clearly eager to change the subject. "Have you been dancing?"

"Nope," I said. "Dancing is for suckers."

"Is that why you came to a dance?" Finn looked down at my bare feet. "You didn't wear the right shoes for dancing. You didn't even wear the right shoes for walking."

"I don't like shoes," I told him defensively. My hem landed above my knees, but I tried to pull it down, as if I could get it to cover my bare-feet embarrassment.

Finn gave me a look I couldn't read at all, then went back to staring at the people dancing in front of us. By now the floor was almost entirely covered. Kids still dotted the bleachers, but they were mostly the headgear kids and the ones with dandruff.

"So this is what you're doing? Watching other people dance?" Finn asked.

"I guess." I shrugged.

Finn leaned forward, resting his elbows on his knees, and I moved so I was sitting up straighter. My dress was strapless, and I rubbed at my bare arms, feeling naked and uncomfortable.

"You cold?" Finn glanced over at me, and I shook my head. "I think it's cold in here."

"It's a little chilly," I admitted. "But nothing I can't handle."

Finn would barely look at me, which was a complete 180 from his constant creepy staring. Somehow, I found this worse. I don't know why he had even come to the dance if he hated it so much, and I was about to ask him that when he turned to look at me.

"You wanna dance?" he asked flatly.

"Are you asking me to dance with you?"

"Yeah." Finn shrugged.

"Yeah?" I shrugged sarcastically. "You really know how to sweet-talk a girl."

His mouth crept up in a hint of a smile, and that officially won me over. I hated myself for it.

"Fair enough." Finn stood up and extended his hand to me. "Would you, Wendy Everly, care to dance with me?"

"Sure." I placed my hand in his, trying to ignore how warm his skin felt and the rapid beating of my own heart, and got to my feet.

Naturally, the band had just started playing "If You Leave" by OMD, making me feel like I had walked into a perfect movie moment. Finn led me to the dance floor and placed his hand on the small of my back. I put one hand on his shoulder while he took my other hand in his.

I was so close to him I could feel the delicious heat radiating from his body. His eyes were the darkest eyes I had ever seen, and they were looking at only me. For one unspoiled minute, everything in life felt perfect in a way that it never had before. Like there should be a spotlight on us, the only two people in the world.

Then something changed in Finn's expression, something I couldn't read, but it definitely got darker.

"You're not a very good dancer," Finn commented in that emotionless way of his.

"Thanks?" I said unsurely. We were mostly just swaying in a small circle, and I wasn't sure how I could screw that up, plus we seemed to be dancing the exact same way as everyone else. Maybe he was joking, so I tried to sound playful when I said, "You're not that great yourself."

"I'm a wonderful dancer," Finn replied matter-of-factly. "I just need a better partner."

"Okay." I stopped looking up at him and stared straight ahead over his shoulder. "I don't know what to say to that."

"Why do you need to say anything to that? It's not necessary for you to speak incessantly. Although I'm not sure you've realized that yet." Finn's tone had gotten icy, but I still danced with him because I couldn't come up with enough sense to walk away.

"I've barely said anything. I've just been dancing with you." I swallowed hard and didn't appreciate how crushed I felt. "And you asked me to dance! It's not like you're doing me a favor."

"Oh, come on," Finn said with an exaggerated eye roll. "The desperation was coming off you in waves. You were all but begging to dance with me. I *am* doing you a favor."

"Wow." I stepped back from him, feeling confused tears threatening and this awful pain growing inside of me. "I don't know what I did to you!" His expression softened, but it was too late.

"Wendy—"

"No!" I cut him off. Everyone nearby had stopped dancing to stare at us, but I didn't care. "You are a total dick!"

"Wendy!" Finn repeated, but I turned and hurried through the crowd.

There was nothing in the world I wanted more than to get out of here. Patrick, a kid from biology class, stood by the punch bowl, and I rushed over to him. We weren't friends, but he'd been one of the few kids here who had been nice to me. When he saw me, he looked confused and concerned, but at least I had his attention.

"I want to leave. *Now*," I hissed at Patrick.

"What—" Before Patrick could ask what had happened, Finn appeared at my side.

"Look, Wendy, I'm sorry," Finn apologized sincerely, which only pissed me off more.

"I don't wanna hear anything from you!" I snapped and refused to look at him. Patrick looked back and forth between the two of us, trying to decipher what was going on.

"Wendy," Finn floundered. "I didn't mean—"

"I said I don't want to hear it!" I glared at him, but only for a second.

"Maybe you should let the guy apologize," Patrick suggested gently.

"No, I shouldn't." Then, like a small child, I stomped my foot. "I want to go!"

Finn stood just to the side of us, watching me intently. I clenched my fists and looked at Patrick directly in his eyes. I didn't like doing this when people watched, but I had to get out of here. I kept chanting what I wanted over and over in my head. *I want to go home, just take me home, please, please, just take me home. I can't be here anymore.*

Patrick's face started to change, his expression growing relaxed and faraway. Blinking, he stared blankly at me for a minute.

"I think I should just take you home," Patrick said groggily.

"What did you just do?" Finn asked, narrowing his eyes.

My heart stopped beating, and for one terrifying second

I was certain he knew what I'd done. But then I realized that'd be impossible, so I shook it off.

"I didn't do anything!" I snapped and looked back at Patrick. "Let's get out of here."

"Wendy!" Finn said, giving me a hard look. "Do you even know what you just did?"

"I didn't do anything!" I grabbed Patrick's wrist, dragging him toward the exit, and, much to my relief, Finn didn't follow.

In the car, Patrick tried to ask me what had happened with Finn, but I wouldn't talk about it. He drove around for a while, so I was reasonably calm by the time he dropped me off, and I couldn't thank him enough for it.

Matt and Maggie were waiting by the door for me, but I barely said a word to them. That freaked out Matt, who started threatening to kill every boy at the dance, but I managed to reassure him that I was fine and nothing bad had happened. Finally, he let me go up to my room, where I proceeded to throw myself onto the bed and not cry.

The night swirled in my head like some bizarre dream. I couldn't get a read on the way I felt about Finn. Most of the time he seemed weird and bordering on creepy. But then we had that glorious moment when we danced together, before he completely shattered it.

Even now, after the way he'd treated me, I couldn't shake how wonderful it had felt being in his arms like that. In general, I never liked being touched or being close to people, but I loved the way I had felt with him.

His hand strong and warm on the small of my back and the

soft heat that flowed from him. When he had looked at me then, so sincerely, I had thought . . .

I don't know what I had thought, but it turned out to be a lie.

Strangest of all, he seemed to be able to tell that I had done something to Patrick. I didn't know how anyone could know. I wasn't even sure that I was doing it. But a normal, sane person wouldn't even suspect that I could do that.

I could suddenly explain all Finn's odd behavior: he was completely insane.

What it came down to was that I knew nothing about him. I could barely tell when he was mocking me and when he was being sincere. Sometimes I thought he was into me, and other times he obviously hated me.

There wasn't anything I knew about him for sure. Except that despite everything, I was starting to like him.

Sometime in the night, after I had changed into sweats and a tank top, and after I had spent a very long time tossing and turning, I must've finally fallen asleep. When I woke up, it was still dark out, and I had drying tears on my cheeks. I had been crying in my sleep, which seemed unfair, since I never let myself cry when I was awake.

I rolled over and glanced at the alarm clock. Its angry numbers declared it was a little after three in the morning, and I wasn't sure why I was awake. I flicked on my bedside lamp, casting everything in a warm glow, and I saw something that scared me so badly, my heart stopped.

stalker

A figure was crouched outside my window, my *second-story* window. Admittedly, a small roof was right outside of it, but a person standing on it was about the last thing I expected to see. On top of that, it wasn't just anybody.

Finn Holmes looked hopeful, but not at all ashamed or frightened at having been caught peeping into my room. He knocked gently at the glass, and belatedly I realized that's what had woken me up.

He hadn't been peeping intentionally; he'd been trying to get my attention so I could let him into my room. So that was *slightly* less creepy, I supposed.

For some reason, I got up and went over to the window. I caught sight of myself in my mirror, and I did not look good. My pajamas were of the sad, comfy variety. My hair was a total mess, and my eyes were red and puffy.

I knew I shouldn't let Finn in my room. He was probably a

sociopath and he didn't make me feel good about myself. Besides, Matt would kill us both if he caught him in here.

So I stood in front of the window, my arms crossed, and glared at him. I was pissed off and hurt, and I wanted him to know it. Normally I prided myself on not getting hurt, let alone telling people they had hurt me. But this time I thought it would be better if he knew that he was a dick.

"I'm sorry!" Finn said loud enough so his voice would carry through the glass, and his eyes echoed the sentiment. He looked genuinely remorseful, but I wasn't ready to accept his apology yet. Maybe I never would.

"What do you want?" I demanded as loudly as I could without Matt hearing me.

"To apologize. And to talk to you." Finn looked earnestly at me. "It's important."

I chewed my lip, torn between what I knew I should do and what I really wanted to do.

"Please," he said.

Against my better judgment, I opened the window. I left the screen in place and took a step back so I was sitting on the end of my bed. Finn pulled the screen out easily, and I wondered how much experience he had sneaking in girls' windows.

Carefully, he climbed into my room, shutting the window behind him. He glanced over my room, making me feel self-conscious. It was rather messy, with clothes and books strewn about, but most of my stuff sat in two large cardboard boxes and a trunk on one side of my room.

"So what do you want?" I said, trying to drag his attention back to me and away from my things.

"I'm sorry," Finn repeated, with that same sincerity he had demonstrated outside. "Tonight I was cruel." He looked away thoughtfully before continuing. "I don't want to hurt you."

"So why did you?" I asked sharply.

Licking his lips, he shifted his feet and exhaled deeply. He had intentionally been mean to me. It wasn't some accident because he was cocky or unaware of how he treated people. Everything he did was meticulous and purposeful.

"I don't want to lie to you, and I promise you that I haven't," Finn answered carefully. "And I'll leave it at that."

"I think I have a right to know what's going on," I snapped and then remembered that Matt and Maggie were sleeping down the hall and hastily lowered my voice. "And what you're doing at my window in the middle of the night."

"I came here to tell you," Finn assured me. "To explain everything. This isn't the way we normally do things, so I had to make a phone call before I came to see you. I was trying to figure things out. That's why it's so late. I'm sorry."

"Call who? Figure out what?" I took a step back.

"It's about what you did tonight, with Patrick," Finn said gently, and the pit in my stomach grew.

"I didn't do anything with Patrick." I shook my head. "I have no idea what you're talking about."

"You really don't?" Finn eyed me suspiciously, unable to decide if he believed me or not.

"I—I don't know what you're talking about," I stammered. A chill ran over me and I started feeling vaguely nauseous.

"Yeah, you do." Finn nodded solemnly. "You just don't know what it is."

"I'm just very . . . convincing," I said without any real confidence. I didn't want to keep denying it, but talking about it, giving credibility to my own private insanity, scared me even more.

"Yeah, you are," Finn admitted. "But you can't do that again. Not like you did tonight."

"I didn't do anything! And even if I did, who are you to try and stop me?" Something else flashed in my mind, and I looked at him. "Can you even stop me?"

"You can't use it on me now." Finn shook his head absently. "It's really not that major, especially the way you're using it."

"What is it?" I asked quietly, finding it hard to make my mouth work. I let go of any pretense I had that I didn't know what was going on, and my shoulders sagged.

"It's called *persuasion*," Finn said emphatically, as if that were somehow much different from what I had been saying. "Technically, it would be called psychokinesis. It's a form of mind control."

I found it disturbing how matter-of-factly he talked about all of this, as if we were talking about biology homework instead of the possibility that I possessed some kind of paranormal ability.

"How do you know?" I asked. "How do you know what I have? How did you even know I was doing it?"

He shrugged. "Experience."

"What does that mean?"

"It's complicated." He rubbed the back of his head and stared at the floor. "You're not going to believe me. But I haven't lied to you, and I never will. Do you believe that, at least?"

"I think so," I replied tentatively. Considering we'd only spoken a handful of times, he hadn't had much of an opportunity to lie to me.

"That's a start." Finn took a deep breath, and I nervously pulled at a strand of my hair as I watched him. Almost sheepishly, he said, "You're a changeling." He looked expectantly at me, waiting for some kind of dramatic reaction.

"I don't even know what that is. Isn't it like a movie with Angelina Jolie or something?" I shook my head. "I don't know what it means."

"You don't know what it is?" Finn smirked. "Of course you don't know what it is. That would make it all too easy if you had even the slightest inkling about what is going on."

"It would, wouldn't it?" I agreed.

"A changeling is a child that has been secretly exchanged for another."

The room got this weird, foggy quality to it. My mind flashed to my mother, and the things she had screamed at me. I had always felt I didn't belong, but at the same time I'd never consciously believed it was true.

But now, suddenly, Finn confirmed all the suspicions I had been harboring. All the horrible things my mother had told me were true.

"But how . . ." Dazedly, I shook my head, then one key question sprang to mind. "How would you know that? How could you possibly know that? Even if it were true?"

"Well . . ." Finn watched me for a moment as I struggled to let everything sink in. "You're Trylle. It's what we do."

"Trylle? Is that like your last name or something?" I asked.

"No." Finn smiled. "Trylle is the name of our 'tribe,' if you will." He rubbed the side of his temple. "This is hard to explain. We are, um, trolls."

"You're telling me that I'm a *troll?*" I raised one eyebrow, and finally decided that he must be insane.

Nothing about me resembled a pink-haired doll with a jewel in its stomach or a creepy little monster that lived under a bridge. Admittedly, I was kind of short, but Finn was at least six feet tall.

"You're thinking of trolls the way they've been misrepresented, obviously," Finn hurried to explain. "That's why we prefer Trylle. You don't get any of that silly 'Billy Goats Gruff' imagery. But now I have you staring at me like I have totally lost my mind."

"You have lost your mind." I trembled in shock and fear, not knowing what to think. I should've thrown him out of my room, but then again, I never should've let him in.

"Okay. Think about it, Wendy." Finn moved on to trying to reason with me, as if his idea had real merit. "You've never really fit in anywhere. You have a quick temper. You're very intelligent and a picky eater. You hate shoes. Your hair, while lovely, is hard to control. You have dark brown eyes, dark brown hair."

"What does the color of my eyes have to do with anything?" I retorted. "Or any of those things—"

"Earth tones. Our eyes and hair are always earth tones," Finn answered. "And oftentimes our skin has almost a greenish hue to it."

"I'm not green!" I looked at my skin anyway, just to be sure, but there was nothing green about it.

"It's very faint, when people do have it," Finn said. "But no, you don't. Not really. Sometimes it gets more predominant after you've been living around other Trylle for a while."

"I am not a troll," I insisted fiercely. "That doesn't even make any sense. It doesn't . . . So I'm angry and different. Most teenagers feel that way. It doesn't mean anything." I combed through my hair, as if to prove it wasn't that wild. My fingers got caught in it, proving his point rather than mine, and I sighed. "That doesn't mean anything."

"I'm not just guessing here, Wendy," Finn informed me with a wry smile. "I know who you are. I know you're Trylle. That's why I came looking for you."

"You were looking for me?" My jaw dropped. "That's why you stare at me all the time in school. You're stalking me!"

"I'm not *stalking*." Finn raised a hand defensively. "I'm a tracker. It's my job. I find the changelings and bring them back."

Of all the major things that were wrong with this situation, the thing that bothered me most was when he said it was his job. There hadn't ever been any attraction between us. He had just been doing his job, and that meant following me.

He was stalking me, and I was only upset about it because he was doing it because he had to, not because he wanted to.

"I know this is a lot to take in," Finn admitted. "I'm sorry. We usually wait until you're older. But if you're already using persuasion, then I think you need to head back to the compound. You're developing early."

"I'm what?" I just stared up at him.

"Developing. The psychokinesis," Finn said as if it should be obvious. "Trylle have varying degrees of ability. Yours are clearly more advanced."

"They have *abilities*?" I swallowed "Do you have abilities?" Something new occurred to me, twisting my insides. "Can you read my mind?"

"No, I can't read minds."

"Are you lying?"

"I won't lie to you," Finn promised.

If he hadn't been so attractive standing in front of me in my bedroom, it would've been easier to ignore him. And if I hadn't felt this ludicrous connection with him, I would've thrown him out right away.

As it was, it was hard to look into his eyes and not believe him. But after everything he had been saying, I couldn't believe him. If I believed him, that meant my mother was right. That I was evil and a monster. I had spent my whole life trying to prove her wrong, trying to be good and do the right things, and I wouldn't let this be true.

"I can't believe you."

"Wendy." Finn sounded exasperated. "You know I'm not lying."

"I do." I nodded. "Not intentionally anyway. But after what I went through with my mother, I'm not ready to let another crazy person into my life. So you have to go."

"Wendy!" His expression was one of complete disbelief.

"Did you really expect any other reaction from me?" I stood up, keeping my arms crossed firmly in front of me, and I tried to look as confident as I possibly could. "Did you think you could treat me like shit at a dance, then sneak into my room in the middle of the night and tell me that I'm a troll with magical powers, and I'd just be like, yeah, that sounds right?

"And what did you even hope to accomplish with this?" I asked him directly. "What were you trying to get me to do?"

"You're supposed to come with me back to the compound," Finn said, defeated.

"And you thought I would just follow you right out?" I smirked to hide the fact that I was really tempted to do that. Even if he was insane.

"They usually do," Finn replied in a way that completely unnerved me.

Really, that answer was what completely lost me. I might have been willing to follow his delusions because I liked him more than I should, but when he made it sound like there had been lots of other girls willing to do the same thing before me, it really turned me off. Crazy, I could deal with. Slutty, not so much.

"You need to go," I told him firmly.

"You need to think about this. This is obviously different for you than it is for everyone else, and I understand that. So I'll give you time to think about it." He turned and opened the window. "But there is a place where you belong. There is a place where you have family. So just think about it."

"Definitely." I gave him a plastic smile.

He started to lean out the window, and I walked closer to him so I'd be able to shut the window behind him. Then he stopped and turned to look at me. He felt dangerously close, his eyes full of something smoldering just below the surface.

When he looked at me like that, he took all the air from my lungs, and I wondered if this was how Patrick felt when I persuaded him.

"I almost forgot," Finn said softly, his face so close to mine I could feel his breath on my cheeks. "You looked *really* beautiful tonight." He stayed that way a moment longer, completely captivating me, then he turned abruptly and climbed out the window.

I stood there, barely remembering to breathe, as I watched him grab a branch of the tree next to my house and swing down to the ground. A cool breeze fluttered in, so I closed the window and pulled my curtains shut tightly.

Feeling dazed, I staggered back to my bed and collapsed on it. I had never felt more bewildered in my entire life.

I barely got any sleep. What little I had was filled with dreams of little green trolls coming to take me away. I lay in bed for a while after I woke up. Everything felt muddled and confusing.

I couldn't let myself believe that anything Finn had said

made sense, but I couldn't discount how badly I wanted it to be true. I had never felt like I belonged anywhere. Until recently, Matt had been the only person I ever felt any connection with.

Lying in bed at six-thirty in the morning, I could hear the morning birds chirping loudly outside my window. Quietly, I got up and crept downstairs. I didn't want to wake Matt and Maggie this early. Matt got up early every school day to make sure I didn't oversleep and then drove me to school, so this was his only time to sleep in.

For some reason, I felt desperate to find something to prove we were family. All my life I had been trying to prove the opposite, but as soon as Finn had mentioned that it might be a real possibility, I felt oddly protective.

Matt and Maggie had sacrificed everything for me. I had never been that good to either of them, yet they still loved me unconditionally. Wasn't that evidence enough?

I crouched on the floor next to one of the cardboard boxes in the living room. The word "memorabilia" was scrawled across it in Maggie's pretty cursive.

Underneath Matt's and Maggie's diplomas and lots of Matt's graduation pictures, I found several photo albums. Based on the covers, I could tell which ones had been Maggie's purchases. Maggie picked albums covered in flowers and polka dots and happy things.

My mother only had one, and it was adorned with a faded brown, nondescript cover. There was also a damaged blue baby book. Carefully, I pulled it out, along with my mom's photo album.

My baby book had been blue because all the ultrasounds had said I was a boy. Tucked in the back of the book there was even a cracked ultrasound photo where the doctor had circled what they had incorrectly assumed was my penis.

Most families would have made some kind of joke about that, but not mine. My mother had just looked at me with disdain and said, "You were supposed to be a boy."

Most mothers start out filling the beginning of a baby book, but then forget as time goes on. Not mine. She'd never written a thing in it. The handwriting was either my father's or Maggie's.

My footprints were in there, along with my measurements and a copy of my birth certificate. I touched it delicately, proving that my birth was real and tangible. I had been born into this family, whether my mother liked it or not.

"What are you doing, kiddo?" Maggie asked softly from behind me, and I jumped a little. "Sorry. I didn't mean to scare you." Wrapped in her housecoat, Maggie yawned and ran a hand through her sleep-disheveled hair.

"It's okay." I tried to cover up my baby book, feeling as if I had been caught doing something naughty. "What are you doing up?"

"I could ask you the same thing," Maggie replied with a smile. She sat down on the floor next to me, leaning against the back of the couch. "I heard you get up." She nodded at the pile of photo albums on my lap. "You feeling nostalgic?"

"I don't know, really."

"What are you looking at?" Maggie leaned over so she

could peer at the photo album. "Oh, that's an old one. You were just a baby then."

I flipped open the book and it went chronologically, so the first few pages were of Matt when he was little. Maggie looked at it with me, making clucking sounds at my dad. She gently touched his picture once and commented on how handsome her brother was.

Even though everyone agreed that my father had been a good guy, we rarely talked about him. It was our way of not talking about my mother and not talking about what had happened. Nothing before my sixth birthday mattered, and that just happened to include every memory of Dad.

Most of the pictures in the album were of Matt, and there were many with my mother, my dad, and Matt looking ridiculously happy. All three of them had blond hair and blue eyes. They looked like something out of a Hallmark commercial.

Toward the end of the book, everything changed. As soon as pictures of me started to appear, my mother began looking surly and sullen. In the very first picture, I was only a few days old. I wore an outfit with blue trains all over it, and my mother glared at me.

"You were such a cute baby!" Maggie laughed. "But I remember that. You wore boys' clothes for the first month because they were so sure you were going to be a boy."

"That explains a lot," I mumbled, and Maggie laughed. "Why didn't they just get me new clothes? They had the money for it."

"Oh, I don't know." Maggie sighed, looking faraway. "It

was something your mother wanted." She shook her head. "She was weird about things."

"What was my name supposed to be?"

"Um . . ." Maggie snapped her fingers when she remembered. "Michael! Michael Conrad Everly. But then you were a girl, so that ruined that."

"How did they get Wendy from that?" I wrinkled my nose. "Michelle would make more sense."

"Well . . ." Maggie looked up at the ceiling, thinking. "Your mother refused to name you, and your father . . . I guess he couldn't think of anything. So Matt named you."

"Oh, yeah." I faintly remembered hearing that before. "But why Wendy?"

"He liked the name Wendy." Maggie shrugged. "He was a big *Peter Pan* fan, which is ironic because *Peter Pan* is the story of a boy who never grows up, and Matt was a boy who was always grown up." I smirked at that. "Maybe that's why he's always been so protective of you. He named you. You were his."

My eyes settled on a picture of me from when I was about two or three with Matt holding me in his arms. I lay on my stomach with my arms and legs outstretched, while he grinned like a fool. He used to run me around the house like that, pretending that I was flying, and call me "Wendy Bird," and I would laugh.

As I got older, it became more and more apparent that I looked nothing like my family. My dark eyes and frizzy hair contrasted completely with theirs.

In every picture with me, my mother looked utterly exasperated, as if she had spent the half hour before the picture was taken fighting with me. But then again, she probably had. I had always been contrary to everything she was.

"You were a strong-willed child," Maggie admitted, looking at a picture of me covered in chocolate cake at my fifth birthday. "You wanted things the way you wanted them. And when you were a baby, you were colicky. But you were always an adorable child, and you were bright and funny." Maggie gently pushed a stray curl back from my face. "You were *always* worthy of love. You did nothing wrong, Wendy. She was the one with the problem, not you."

I nodded. "I know."

But for the first time, I truly believed that this all might be entirely my fault. If Finn was telling the truth, as these pictures seemed to confirm, I wasn't their child. I wasn't even human. I was exactly what my mother had accused me of being. She was just more intuitive than everybody else.

"What's wrong?" Maggie asked, looking concerned. "What's going on with you?"

"Nothing," I lied and closed the photo album.

"Did something happen last night?" Her eyes were filled with love and worry, and it was hard to think of her as not being my family. "Did you even sleep?"

"Yeah. I just . . . woke up, I guess," I answered vaguely.

"What happened at the dance?" Maggie leaned back against the couch, resting her hand on her chin as she studied me. "Did something happen with a boy?"

"Things just didn't turn out the way I thought they would," I said honestly. "In fact, they couldn't have turned out more different."

"Was that Finn boy mean to you?" Maggie asked with a protective edge to her voice.

"No, no, nothing like that," I assured her. "He was great. But he's just a friend."

"Oh." Understanding flashed in her eyes, and I realized she'd probably gotten the wrong idea, but at least it kept her from asking more questions. "Being a teenager is hard, no matter what family you come from."

"You're telling me," I muttered.

I heard Matt getting up and moving around upstairs. Maggie shot me a nervous look, so I hurried to pack up the photo albums. He wouldn't exactly be mad at me for looking at them, but he definitely wouldn't be happy either. And first thing in the morning, I did not want to deal with a fight with my brother, on top of worrying about whether or not he was really even my brother.

"You know, you can talk to me about this stuff whenever you want," Maggie whispered as I slipped the albums back in the cardboard box. "Well, at least whenever Matt isn't around."

"I know." I smiled at her.

"I suppose I should make you breakfast." Maggie stood up and stretched, then looked down at me. "How about plain oatmeal with fresh strawberries? Those are things you eat, right?"

"Yeah, that sounds great." I nodded, but something about her question pained me.

There were so many things I wouldn't eat, and I was constantly hungry. It had always been a struggle just to feed me. When I was a baby, I wouldn't even drink breast milk. Which only added more fuel to the idea that I wasn't my mother's child.

Maggie had turned to walk into the kitchen, but I called after her. "Hey, Mags. Thanks for everything. Like . . . making me food and stuff."

"Yeah?" Maggie looked surprised and smiled. "No problem."

Matt came downstairs a minute later, deeply confused by the fact that both Maggie and I were up before him. We ate breakfast together for the first time in years, and Maggie was overly happy, thanks to my small compliment. I was subdued, but I managed to play it off as something resembling happiness.

I didn't know if they were my real family or not. There were so many signs pointing to the contrary. But they had raised me and stood by me the way no one else had. Even my supposed mother had failed me, but not Matt or Maggie. They were unfailing in their love for me, and most of the time they had gotten next to nothing in return.

Maybe that last part was the proof that my mother was right. They only gave, and I only took.

FOUR

changeling

The weekend was turbulent. I kept expecting Finn to appear at my window again, but he didn't, and I wasn't sure if that was good or bad. I wanted to talk to him, but I was terrified. Terrified he might be lying, and terrified he might be telling the truth.

I kept looking for clues in everything. Like, Matt is pretty short and so am I, so he must be my brother. Then a minute later, he would say he prefers winter to summer, and I hate winter, so he must not be my brother.

These weren't clues one way or another, and deep down I knew that. My whole life was now one giant question, and I was desperate for answers.

There was also that burning unanswered question about what exactly Finn wanted with me. Sometimes he treated me like I was nothing more than an irritant. Then there were other times when he looked at me and took my breath away.

I hoped that school would bring some kind of resolution to all of this. When I got up Monday morning, I took extra care to look nice, but I tried to pretend it wasn't for any particular reason. That it wasn't because this was the first time I'd see Finn since he had come into my room, and that I still wanted to talk to him. I still wanted to impress him.

When the first-period bell rang and Finn still hadn't taken his place a few rows behind me, a knot started growing in my stomach. I looked around for him all day, half expecting him to be lurking around some corner. He never was, though.

I barely paid attention to anything all day in school, and I felt incredibly defeated when I walked to Matt's car. I had expected to gain some knowledge today, but in the end I was left with even more questions.

Matt noticed my surly demeanor and tried to ask about it, but I just shrugged him off. He had been growing increasingly concerned since I had come home from the dance, but I had been unable to put his mind at ease.

I already felt the sting of Finn's absence. Why hadn't I gone with him? I was more attracted to him than I had ever been to anyone, and it was more than just physical. In general, people didn't interest me, but he did.

He promised me a life where I fit in, where I was special, and, maybe most important, a life with him. Why was I staying here?

Because I still wasn't convinced that I was evil. I wasn't ready to give up on the good I had worked so hard for in my life.

I knew of one person who had always seen through my

façade and known exactly what I was. She'd be able to tell me if I had any good in me, or if I should just give in, give up, and run off with Finn.

"Hey, Matt?" I stared down at my hands. "Are you busy this afternoon?"

"I don't think so . . ." Matt answered tentatively as he turned on the block toward our house. "Why? What's on your mind?"

"I was thinking . . . I'd like to go visit my mother."

"Absolutely not!" Matt cast me a livid glare. "Why would you even want that? That's so completely out of the question. No way, Wendy. That's just obscene."

He turned to look at me again, and in that moment, staring directly into his eyes, I repeated the same thoughts over and over. *I want to see my mother. Take me to see her. Please. I want to see her.* His expression was hard, but eventually it started to soften around the edges.

"I'll take you to see our mother." Matt sounded like he was talking in his sleep.

I instantly felt guilty for what I was doing. It was manipulative and cruel. But I wasn't just doing it to see if I could. I needed to see my mother, and this was the only way I could do that.

I felt nervous and sick, and I knew Matt would be irate once he realized what he was doing. I didn't know how long this persuasion would last. We might not even make it to the hospital where my mother lived, but I had to try.

It would be the first time I'd see my mother in over eleven years.

There were several times throughout the long car ride when Matt seemed to become aware that he was doing something he would never normally do. He would start ranting about how terrible my mother was and that he couldn't believe he'd let me talk him into this.

Somehow it never occurred to him to turn around, but maybe it *couldn't* occur to him.

"She's a horrible person!" Matt said as we approached the state hospital.

I could see the internal battle waging underneath his grimace and tortured blue eyes. His hand was locked on the steering wheel, but something about the way he gripped it looked like he was trying to let go but couldn't.

Guilt flushed over me again, but I tried to push it away. I didn't want to hurt him, and controlling him like this was reprehensible.

The only real comfort I had was that I wasn't doing anything wrong. I wanted to see my mother, and I had every right to. Matt was just being overzealous about his protective duties once again.

"She can't do anything to hurt me," I reminded him for the hundredth time. "She's locked up and medicated. I'll be fine."

"It's not like she's going to strangle you or anything," Matt allowed, but there was an edge to his voice hinting that he hadn't completely ruled out the possibility. "She's just . . . a bad person. I don't know what you hope to gain from seeing her!"

"I just need to," I said softly and looked out the window.

I had never been to the hospital, but it wasn't exactly as I'd imagined. My entire basis for it was Arkham Asylum, so I had always pictured an imposing brick structure with lightning perpetually flashing just behind it.

It was raining lightly and the skies were overcast as we pulled up, but that was the only thing similar to the psychiatric hospital of my fantasies. Nestled in thick pine forest and rolling grassy hills, it was a sprawling white building that looked more like a resort than a hospital.

After my mother had tried to kill me and Matt tackled her in the kitchen, someone had called 911. She was hauled off in a police car, still screaming things about me being monstrous, while I was taken away in an ambulance.

Charges were brought against my mother, but she pleaded guilty by reason of insanity, and the case never went to trial. They had originally given her a cross-diagnosis of latent postpartum depression and temporary psychosis brought on by the death of my father.

With medication and therapy, there had been the general expectation that she would be out in a relatively short amount of time.

Cut to eleven years later when my brother is talking to the security guard so we can get clearance to get inside the hospital. From what I understood, she refused to admit any remorse for what she'd done.

Matt went to visit her once, five years ago, and what I got out of it was that she didn't know she'd done anything wrong. It was inferred, though never actually spelled out, that if she got out, she'd do it again.

There was a great deal of bustling about once we finally got inside. A nurse had to call a psychiatrist to see if I would even be able to see her. Matt paced anxiously around me, muttering things about everyone being insane.

We waited in a small room filled with plastic chairs and magazines for forty-five minutes until the doctor came to meet with me. We had a brief conversation in which I told him that I only wished to speak with her, and even without persuasion he seemed to think it might be beneficial for me to have some closure.

Matt wanted to go back with me to see her, afraid that she would damage me in some way, but the doctor assured him that orderlies would be present and my mother hadn't had a violent outburst in eleven years. Matt eventually relented, much to my relief, because I had just been about to use persuasion on him again.

He couldn't be there when I talked to her. I wanted an honest conversation.

A nurse led me to an activity room. A couch and a few chairs filled the room, along with a few small tables, some with half-completed puzzles on them. On one wall, a cabinet overflowed with beat-up games and battered puzzle boxes. Plants lined the windows, but otherwise it was devoid of life.

The nurse told me that my mother would be there soon, so I sat down at one of the tables and waited.

A very large, very strong-looking orderly brought her into the room. I stood up when she came in, as some kind of misplaced show of respect. She was older than I had expected her to be. In my mind she had stayed frozen the way I'd seen her last, but she had to be in her mid-forties by now.

Her blond hair had turned into a frizzy mess thanks to the years of neglect, and she had it pulled back in a short ponytail. She was thin, the way she had always been, in a beautifully elegant borderline-anorexic way. A massive blue bathrobe hung on her, frayed and worn, the sleeves draping down over her hands.

Her skin was pale porcelain, and even without any makeup, she was stunningly beautiful. More than that, she carried this regality with her. It was clear that she had come from money, that she had spent her life on top, ruling her school, her social circles, even her family.

"They said you were here, but I didn't believe them," said my mother with a wry smirk.

She stood a few steps away from me, and I wasn't sure what to do. The way she looked at me was the same way people might inspect a particularly heinous-looking bug just before they squashed it under their shoe.

"Hi, Mom," I offered meekly, unable to think of anything better to say.

"Kim," she corrected me coldly. "My name is Kim. Cut the pretense. I'm not your mother, and we both know it." She gestured vaguely to the chair I had pushed out behind me and walked over to the table. "Sit. Take a seat."

"Thanks," I mumbled, sitting down. She sat down across from me, crossing her legs and leaning back in her chair, like I was contagious and she didn't want to get sick.

"That's what this is about it, isn't it?" She waved her hand in front of her face, then laid it delicately on the table. Her nails were long and perfect, recently painted with clear polish. "You've finally figured it out. Or have you always known? I never could tell."

"No, I never knew," I said quietly. "I still don't know."

"Look at you. You're not my daughter." My mother gave me a contentious look and clicked her tongue. "You don't know how to dress or walk or even speak. You mutilate your nails." She pointed a manicured fingertip at my chewed-down nails. "And that hair!"

"Your hair isn't any better," I countered. My dark curls had been pulled up in their usual bun, but I had actually tried styling my hair this morning when I was getting ready. I thought it looked pretty good, but apparently I was wrong.

"Well . . ." She smiled humorlessly. "I have limited resources." She looked away for a moment, then turned back to rest her icy gaze on me. "But what about you? You must have all the styling products in the world. Between Matthew and Maggie, I'm sure you're spoiled rotten."

"I get by," I allowed sourly. She made it sound like I should feel ashamed for the things I had, like I had stolen them. Although I suppose, in her mind, I kinda had.

"Who brought you here anyway?" Clearly the idea had just occurred to her, and she glanced behind her, as if she expected to see Matt or Maggie waiting in the wings.

"Matt," I answered.

"Matthew?" She looked genuinely shocked. "There is no way he would condone this. He doesn't even . . ." Sadness washed across her face and she shook her head. "He's never understood. I did what I did to protect him too. I never wanted you to get your claws into him." She touched her hair, and tears welled in her eyes, but she blinked them back and her stony expression returned.

"He thinks he has to protect me," I informed her, mostly because I knew it would bother her. Disappointingly, she didn't look that upset. She just nodded in understanding.

"For all his sense and maturity, Matthew can be incredibly naive. He always thought of you as some lost, sick puppy he needed to care for." She brushed a frizzy strand of hair from her forehead and stared at a spot on the floor. "He loves you because he's a good man, like his father, and that has always been his weakness." Then she looked up hopefully. "Is he going to visit me today?"

"No." I almost felt bad about telling her that, but she smiled bitterly at me and I remembered why she was here.

"You've turned him against me. I knew you would. But . . ." She shrugged emptily. "It doesn't make things easier, does it?"

"I don't know." I leaned in toward her. "Look, M- . . . Kim. I am here for a reason. I want to know what I am." I backtracked quickly. "I mean, what you think I am."

"You're a changeling," she said matter-of-factly. "I'm surprised you didn't know that by now."

My heart dropped, but I tried to keep my expression

neutral. I pressed my hands flat on the table to keep them from shaking. It was just as I had suspected, and maybe I had always known.

When Finn told me, it had instantly made sense, but I don't know why hearing it from Kim made things feel so different.

"How could you possibly know that?" I asked.

"I knew you weren't mine the second the doctor placed you in my arms." She twisted at her hair and looked away from me. "My husband refused to listen to me. I kept telling him that you weren't ours, but he . . ." She swallowed, pained at the memory of the man she'd loved.

"It wasn't until I was in here, when I had all the time in the world, that I found out what you really were," she went on, her eyes hardening and her voice strengthening with conviction. "I read book after book searching for an explanation for you. In an old book on fairy tales, I found out what kind of parasite you truly are—a *changeling*."

"A changeling?" I fought to keep my voice even. "What does that mean?"

"What do you think it means?" she snapped, looking at me like I was an idiot. "Changeling! You were changed out for another child! My son was taken and you were put in his place!"

Her cheeks reddened with rage, and the orderly took a step closer to her. She held up her hand and fought to keep herself contained.

"Why?" I asked, realizing that I should've asked Finn this question days earlier. "Why would anyone do that? Why would they take your baby? What did they do with him?"

"I don't know what kind of game you're playing." She smiled sadly and fresh tears stood in her eyes. Her hands trembled when she touched her hair, and she all but refused to look at me. "You know what you did with him. You know far better than I do."

"No, I don't!" The orderly gave me a hard look, and I knew I had to at least look like I wasn't freaking out. In a hushed voice I demanded, "What are you talking about?"

"You killed him, Wendy!" My mother snarled. She leaned in toward me, her hand clenched into a fist, and I knew she was using all her willpower to keep from hurting me. "First you killed my son, then you drove my husband insane and killed him. You *killed* them both!"

"Mom . . . Kim, whatever!" I closed my eyes and rubbed my temples. "That doesn't make any sense. I was just a baby! How could I kill anyone?"

"How did you get Matthew to drive you here?" she demanded through gritted teeth, and an icy chill ran down my spine. "He would never drive you here. He would never let you see me. But he did. What did you do to him to make him do it?" I lowered my eyes, unable to even pretend to be innocent. "Maybe that's exactly what you did to Michael!" Her fists were clenched, and she breathed so hard, her delicate nostrils flared.

"I was just a baby," I insisted without any real conviction. "I couldn't have . . . Even if I did, there had to be more people involved. It doesn't explain anything! Why would anybody take him or hurt him and put me in his place?"

She ignored my question. "You were always evil. I knew it

from the moment I held you in my arms." She had calmed herself a bit and leaned back in her chair. "It was in your eyes. They weren't human. They weren't kind or good."

"Then why didn't you just kill me then?" I asked, growing irritated.

"You were a baby!" Her hands shook, and her lips had started to quiver. She was losing the confidence she had come in with. "Well, I thought you were. You know I couldn't be sure." She pressed her lips together tightly, trying to hold back tears.

"What made you so sure?" I asked. "What made you decide that day? On my sixth birthday. Why that day? What happened?"

"You weren't mine. I knew you weren't." She brushed at her eyes to keep the tears from spilling over. "I had known forever. But I just kept thinking about what the day should've been like. With my husband, and my son. Michael should've been six that day, not you. You were a horrible, horrible child, and you were alive. And they were dead. I just . . . it didn't seem right anymore." She took a deep breath and shook her head. "It still isn't right."

"I was six years old." My voice had started quavering. Whenever I'd thought of her or what happened, I'd only ever felt numb. For the first time, I really felt hurt and betrayed.

"*Six years old.* Do you understand that? I was a little kid, and you were supposed to be my mother!" Whether she really was or not was irrelevant. I was a child, and she was in charge of raising me. "I had never done anything to anyone. I never even *met* Michael."

"You're *lying*." My mother gritted her teeth. "You were always a liar, and a monster! And I know you're doing things to Matthew! Just leave him alone! He's a good boy!" She reached across the table and grabbed my wrist painfully. The orderly came up behind her. "Take what you want, take anything. Just leave Matthew alone!"

"Kimberly, come on." The orderly put his strong hand on her arm, and she tried to pull away from him. "Kimberly!"

"Leave him alone," she shouted again, and the orderly started pulling her up. She fought against him, screaming at me. "Do you hear me, Wendy? I will get out of here someday! And if you've hurt that boy, I will finish the job I started!"

"That's enough," the orderly bellowed, dragging her out of the room.

"You're not human, Wendy! And I know it!" That was the last thing she yelled before he carried her out of my sight.

The staff let me sit there for a minute, trying to catch my breath and get myself under control. Matt couldn't see me like this. I really, really thought I was going to throw up, but I managed to keep it down.

Everything was true. I was a changeling. I wasn't human. She wasn't my mother. She was just Kim, a woman who had lost her grasp on reality when she realized I wasn't her child. I had been switched for her son, Michael, and I had no idea what happened to him.

Maybe he was dead. Maybe I really had killed him, or someone else had. Maybe someone like Finn.

She was convinced that I was a monster, and I couldn't argue that I wasn't. In my life, I had caused nothing but pain. I had ruined Matt's life, and I still was doing that.

Not only did he constantly have to uproot himself for me and spend every minute worrying about me, but I was manipulating and controlling him, and I couldn't say for sure how long that had been going on. I didn't know the long-term effects of it either.

Maybe it would've been better if she had killed me when I was six. Or better yet, when I was still a baby. Then I wouldn't have been able to hurt anybody.

When the staff finally led me back to the waiting room, Matt rushed over to hug me. I stood there, but I didn't hug him back. He inspected me to make sure I was all right. He had heard there was some kind of scuffle and was petrified that something had happened to me. I just nodded and got out of there as fast as I could.

insanity

So . . ." Matt began on the drive home. I rested my fore-head against the cold glass of the car window and refused to look at him. I had barely spoken since we'd left. "What did you say to her?"

"Things," I replied vaguely.

"No, really," he pressed. "What happened?"

"I tried talking to her, she got upset." I sighed. "She said I was a monster. You know, the usual."

"I don't know why you even wanted to see her. She's a ter-rible person."

"Oh, she's not that bad." My breath fogged up the window, and I started drawing stars in the mist. "She's really worried about you. She's afraid I'm going to hurt you."

"That woman is insane," Matt scoffed. "Literally, since she lives there, but . . . you can't listen to her, Wendy. You aren't letting anything she said get to you, are you?"

"No," I lied. Pulling my sleeve up over my hand, I erased my drawings on the window and sat up straighter. "How do you know?"

"What?"

"That she's insane. That . . . I'm not a monster." I twisted my thumb ring nervously and stared at Matt, who just shook his head. "I'm being serious. What if I am bad?"

Matt suddenly put on his turn signal and pulled the car over to the shoulder. Rain pounded down on the windows as other cars sped by us on the freeway. He turned to face me completely, putting an arm across the back of my seat.

"Wendy Luella Everly, there is nothing bad about you. *Nothing*," Matt emphasized solemnly. "That woman is completely insane. I don't know why, but she was never a mother to you. You can't listen to her. She doesn't know what she's talking about."

"Be serious, Matt." I shook my head. "I've gotten expelled from every school I've ever gone to. I'm unruly and whiny and stubborn and so picky. I know that you and Maggie struggle with me all the time."

"That doesn't mean you're bad. You've had a *really* traumatic childhood, and yeah, you're still working through some things, but you are not bad," Matt insisted. "You are a strong-willed teenager who isn't afraid of anything. That's all."

"At some point that has to stop being an excuse. Sure she tried to kill me, but I have to take responsibility for who I am as a person."

"You are!" Matt said with a smile. "Since we've moved

here, you have shown so much promise. Your grades are going up, and you're making friends. And even if that makes me a little uncomfortable, I know it's a good thing for you. You're growing up, Wendy, and you're going to be okay."

I nodded, unable to think of an argument for that.

"I know I don't say it enough, but I'm proud of you, and I love you." Matt bent over so he could kiss the top of my head. He hadn't done that since I was little, and it stirred something inside me. I closed my eyes and refused to cry. He straightened back up in his seat and looked at me seriously. "Okay? Are you okay now?"

"Yeah, I'm fine." I forced a smile.

"Good." He pulled back into traffic, continuing the drive home.

As much as I inconvenienced Matt and Maggie, it would break their hearts if I left. Even if going with Finn would be more promising, it would hurt them too much. Leaving would put my needs in front of theirs. So if I stayed, I put them before me.

Staying would be my only proof that I wasn't evil.

When we got home, I went up to my room before Maggie could try to talk to me. My room felt too quiet, so I went over to my iPod and started scrolling through songs. A light tapping sound startled me from my search, and my heart skipped a beat.

I walked over to my window, and when I pulled back the curtain, the rain had stopped, and there was Finn, crouched on the roof outside. I considered closing the curtain and ignoring him, but his dark eyes were too much. Besides, this would give me a chance to say a proper good-bye.

"What are you doing?" Finn asked as soon as I opened the window. He stayed out on the roof, but I hadn't moved back so he could come in.

"What are *you* doing?" I countered, crossing my arms.

"I came to make sure you're all right," he said, concern in his eyes.

"Why wouldn't I be all right?" I asked.

"It was just a feeling I had." He avoided my gaze, glancing behind him at a man walking his dog on the sidewalk before turning back to me. "Mind if I come in so we can finish this conversation?"

"Whatever."

I took a step back and tried to seem as indifferent as possible, but when he slid through the window past me, my heartbeat sped up. He stood in front of me, his dark eyes burning into mine, and he made the rest of the world disappear. I shook my head and stepped away from him, so I wouldn't let myself get mesmerized by him anymore.

"Why did you come in the window?" I asked.

"I couldn't very well come to the door. That guy would never let me in here to see you." Finn was probably right. Matt had hated him ever since the dance.

"That *guy* is my brother, and his name is Matt." I felt incredibly defensive and protective of him, especially after the way he supported me after we saw Kim.

"He's not your brother. You need to stop thinking of him

like that." Finn cast a disparaging look around my room. "Is that what this is all about? This is why you won't leave?"

"You couldn't possibly understand my reasons." I went over and sat on my bed, making a point of laying physical claim to this space.

"What happened tonight?" Finn asked, ignoring my attempts at defiance.

"How are you so certain something happened?"

"You were gone," he said, without any fear that I might find it disturbing that he knew about my comings and goings.

"I saw my mother. Er, well . . . the woman who is supposed to be my mother." I shook my head, hating the way this all sounded. I considered lying to him, but he already knew more about all of this than anyone. "What do you call her? Is there a name for her?"

"Usually her name will suffice," Finn replied, and I felt like an idiot.

"Yeah. Of course." I took a deep breath. "Anyway, I went and saw Kim." I looked up at him. "Do you know about her? I mean . . . how much do you really know about me?"

"Honestly, not that much." Finn seemed to disapprove of his own lack of knowledge. "You were incredibly elusive. It was rather disconcerting."

"So you don't . . ." I realized with dismay that I was on the verge of tears. "She knew I wasn't her daughter. When I was six, she tried to kill me. She had always told me that I was a monster, that I was evil. And I guess I had always believed her."

"You're not evil," Finn insisted earnestly, and I smiled thinly at him, swallowing back my sadness. "You can't possibly stay here, Wendy."

"It's not like that anymore." I shook my head, looking away from him. "She doesn't live here, and my brother and my aunt would do anything for me. I can't just leave them. I won't."

Finn eyed me carefully, trying to decide if I was serious. I hated how attractive he was and whatever power it was he held over me. Even now, with my life in complete shambles, the way he looked at me made it hard to focus on anything besides my racing heart.

"Do you realize what you're giving up?" Finn asked softly. "There is so much that life has to offer you. More than anything they can give you here. If Matt understood what was in store for you, he would send you with me himself."

"You're right. He would, if he thought it was what's best for me," I admitted. "Which is why I have to stay."

"Well, I want what's best for you too. That's why I found you, and why I've been trying to bring you home." The underlying affection in his voice shivered through me. "Do you really believe I would encourage you to return home if it would adversely affect you?"

"I don't think you know what's best for me," I replied as evenly as I could.

He had thrown me off guard by hinting at caring about me, and I had to remind myself that that was part of his job. All of this was. He needed to make sure I was safe and convince me to return home. That wasn't the same as actually caring about *me*.

"You're sure this is what you want?" Finn asked gently.

"Absolutely." But I sounded more confident than I really was.

"I'd like to say that I understand, but I don't." Finn sighed resignedly. "I can say that I'm disappointed."

"I'm sorry," I said meekly.

"You shouldn't be sorry." He ran a hand through his black hair and looked at me again. "I won't be going to school anymore. It seems unnecessary, and I don't want to disturb your studies. You should at least get an education."

"What? Don't you need one?" My heart dropped to the pit of my stomach as I realized that this might be the last time I saw Finn.

"Wendy." Finn gave a small humorless laugh. "I thought you knew. I'm twenty years old. I'm done with my education."

"Why were you . . ." I said, already figuring out the answer to my question.

"I was only there to keep track of you, and I have." Finn dropped his eyes and sighed. "When you change your mind . . ." He hesitated for a moment. "I'll find you."

"You're leaving?" I asked, trying to keep the disappointment from my voice.

"You're still here, so I am too. At least for a while," Finn explained.

"How long?"

"It depends on . . . things." Finn shook his head. "Everything about your situation is so different. It's hard to say anything with certainty."

"You keep saying that I'm different. What does that mean? What are you talking about?"

"We usually wait until changelings are a few years older, and by then you've already figured out that you're not human," Finn explained. "When the tracker comes to find you, you're relieved and eager to go."

"So why did you come for me now?" I asked.

"You moved so much." Finn gestured to the house. "We were afraid that something might be the matter. So I was here monitoring you until you were ready, and I thought you might be." He exhaled deeply. "I guess I was wrong."

"Can't you just 'persuade' me to go along?" I asked, and some part of me that wanted to go with him hoped he could.

"I can't." Finn shook his head. "I can't force you to come with me. If this is your decision, then I'll have to respect it."

I nodded, knowing full well that I was turning down any chance of getting to know my real parents, my family history, and spending more time with Finn. Not to mention my abilities, like persuasion, which Finn had promised there would be more of as I got older. On my own, I'm sure I'd never be able to master or understand them.

We looked at each other, and I wished he wasn't so far away from me. I was wondering if it would be appropriate if we hugged when the door to my bedroom opened.

Matt had come in to check on me. As soon as he saw Finn, his eyes burned. Quickly I jumped up, moving in front of Finn to block any attempts by Matt to kill him.

"Matt! It's okay!" I held up my hands.

"It is not okay!" Matt growled. "Who the hell is this?"

"Matt, please!" I put my hands on his chest, trying to push him away from Finn, but it was like trying to push a brick wall. I glanced back at Finn, and he just stared blankly at my brother.

"You have some nerve!" Matt reached over my shoulder, pointing at Finn as he yelled. "She is seventeen years old! I don't know what the hell you think you're doing in her room, but you're never doing anything with her again!"

"Matt, please, stop," I begged. "He was just saying goodbye! *Please!*"

"Perhaps you should listen to her," Finn offered calmly.

I knew his composure must be pissing off Matt even more. Matt's day had been horrible too, and the last thing he needed was some kid in here defiling me. Finn's only reaction was to stand there, cool and collected, and Matt would want him too scared to ever come near me again.

Matt actually knocked me out of the way, and I fell backward onto the floor. Finn's eyes flashed darkly at that, and when Matt pushed him, Finn didn't move an inch. He just glared down at my brother, and I knew that if they fought, Matt would be the one with a serious injury.

"Matt!" I jumped to my feet.

Already I had started chanting, *Leave my room. Leave my room. You need to calm down and get out of my room. Please.* I wasn't sure how effective it was without eye contact, so I grabbed his arm and forced him to turn to me.

He tried to look away instantly, but I caught him. I kept my eyes focused and just kept repeating it over and over in my head. Finally, his expression softened and his eyes glazed.

"I'm going to leave your room now," Matt said robotically.

Much to my relief, he actually turned and walked out into the hall, closing the door behind him. I'm not sure if he walked any farther than that, or how much time I had, so I turned to Finn.

"You have to leave," I insisted breathlessly, but his expression had changed to one of concern.

"Does he do that often?" Finn asked.

"Do what?"

"He pushed you. He clearly has an anger problem." Finn glared at the door Matt had left through. "He's unstable. You shouldn't stay here with him."

"Yeah, well, you guys should be more careful who you leave babies with," I muttered and went to the window. "I don't know how much time we have, so you need to go."

"He probably shouldn't ever be able to come into your room again," Finn said absently. "I'm serious, Wendy. I don't want to leave you with him."

"You don't have much of a choice!" I said, exasperated. "Matt's not usually like that, and he would never hurt me. He's just had a *really* hard day, and he blames you for upsetting me, and he's not wrong." The panic was wearing away, and I realized that I had just used persuasion on Matt again. I felt nauseous. "I *hate* doing that to him. It's not fair and it's not right."

"I am sorry." Finn looked at me sincerely. "I know you did

that to protect him, and it's my fault. I should've just backed down, but when he pushed you . . ." He shook his head. "My instincts kicked in."

"He's not going to hurt me," I promised.

"I'm sorry for the trouble I've caused you."

Finn glanced back at the door, and I could tell he really didn't want to leave. When he looked back at me, he sighed heavily. He was probably fighting the urge to throw me over his shoulder and take me with him. Instead, he climbed out the window and swung back down to the ground.

With that, he turned past the neighbors' hedges and I couldn't see him anymore. I kept looking after him, wishing that this didn't mean we had to say good-bye.

The awful truth was that I was more than a little sad to see Finn go. Eventually, I shut the window and closed my curtains.

After Finn left, I found Matt sitting on the steps, looking bewildered and pissed off. He wanted to yell at me about Finn, but he couldn't seem to understand exactly what had happened. The best I could get out of it was that he vowed to kill Finn if he ever came near me, and I pretended like I thought that was a reasonable thing to do.

The next few days, school dragged on and on. It didn't help that I found myself constantly looking around for Finn. Part of me kept insisting that the last week had been a bad dream, and that Finn should still be here, staring at me like he always had.

On top of that, I kept feeling like I was being watched. My neck got that scratchy feeling it did when Finn stared at me for too long, but whenever I turned around, nobody was there. At least nobody worth noting.

At home, I felt distracted and ill at ease. I excused myself from supper early on Thursday night and went up to my room. I peered out my curtains, hoping to find Finn lurking around somewhere nearby, but no such luck. Every time I looked for him and didn't find him, my heart hurt a little more.

I tossed and turned all night, trying not to wonder if Finn was still hanging around. He'd made it painfully clear that he'd soon have to move on and end this assignment.

I wasn't ready for that. I didn't like the idea of him moving on when I hadn't.

Around five in the morning I gave up entirely on sleep. I looked out the window again, and this time I thought I saw something. Nothing more than a shadowy blur of movement in the corner of my eye, but it was enough to indicate that he was out there, hiding nearby.

I just needed to go out and talk to Finn, to make sure he was still there. I didn't even bother changing out of my pajamas or fixing my hair.

Hastily, I climbed out onto the roof. I tried to grab on to the branch and swing to the ground like Finn had. As soon as my fingers grabbed the branch, they slipped off and I fell to the ground, landing heavily on my back. All the wind had been knocked out of me, and I coughed painfully.

I would've loved to lie on the lawn for ten minutes while the pain subsided, but I was afraid that Matt or Maggie might have heard my fall. I gingerly got to my feet and rounded the hedges toward the neighbors' house.

The street was completely deserted. I wrapped my arms tightly around myself to ward off the cold that seeped in and looked around. I *knew* he had been out here. Who else would be moving around out here just before dawn? Maybe my fall had scared him away; he might have thought it was Matt.

I decided to walk a little farther down the street, investigating everyone's lawn for a hidden tracker. My back ached from the fall, and my knee felt a little twisted and weird. That left me hobbling down the street in my pajamas at five in the morning. I had truly lost my mind.

Then I heard something. Footsteps? Somebody was definitely following me, and based on the dark chill running down my spine, it wasn't Finn. It was hard to explain how I knew it wasn't him, but I knew it just the same. Slowly, I turned around.

monsters

Agirl stood a few feet behind me. In the glow from the streetlamp, she looked ravishing. Her short brown pixie cut spiked up all over. Her skirt was short and her black leather jacket went down to her calves. A wind came up, blowing back her coat a bit, and she reminded me of some kind of action star, like she should be in *The Matrix*.

But the thing that caught my attention the most was that she was barefoot.

She just stared at me, so I felt like I had to say something.

"Okay . . . um, I'm going to go home now," I announced.

"Wendy Everly, I think you should come with us," she said with a sly smile.

"Us?" I asked, but then I felt him behind me.

I don't know where he had been before that, but suddenly I felt his presence behind me. I looked over my shoulder, where a tall man with dark, slicked-backed hair stared down at me. He wore the same kind of jacket as the girl, and I thought it was neat that they had matching outfits, like a crime-fighting duo.

He smiled at me, and that's when I decided that I was in trouble.

"That's a really nice invitation, but my house is like three houses down." I pointed toward it, as if I didn't think they already knew exactly where I lived. "So I think that I should probably just get home before my brother starts looking for me."

"You should've thought of that before you left the house," the guy behind me suggested.

I wanted to take a step forward to get away from him, but I thought that would only encourage him to pounce on me. I could probably take the girl, but I wasn't so sure about him. He was like a foot taller than me.

"You guys are trackers?" I asked. Something in the way they stared at me reminded me of Finn, especially when I'd first met him.

"You're a quick one, aren't you?" The girl smiled wider, and it didn't sit right with me.

They might be trackers, but not the same kind as Finn. Maybe they were bounty hunters or kidnappers or just big fans of chopping up girls into little pieces and disposing of them in a ditch. Fear crept through me, but I tried not to let on.

"Well, this has been a blast, but I have to get ready for school. Big test and all that." I started taking a step away, but the guy's hand clamped painfully on my arm.

"Don't damage her," the girl insisted, her eyes flashing wide. "She's not to be hurt."

"Yeah, ease up." I tried to pull my arm from him, but he refused to let go.

I had already decided that I wasn't going wherever they wanted to take me. Since they were under some kind of instruction not to hurt me, it would give me the advantage in a fight. I only had to get a few houses down, then I'd be at home, where Matt kept a gun under his bed.

I elbowed the guy in the stomach as hard as I could. He made a coughing sound and doubled over but didn't let go of my arm. I kicked him in the shin and moved to bite the hand that was gripping me.

He yowled in pain, and then the girl was in front of me. He had let go of me, and she tried to grab me, so I punched her. She dodged, so my fist just connected with her shoulder.

Then I was off balance, and the guy grabbed me around the waist. I screamed and kicked at him as hard as I could. Apparently he got tired of that, so he dropped me on the ground.

I was on my feet instantly, but he grabbed my arm again and turned me so I was facing him. He raised his hand and slapped me harder than I had ever been hit before. Everything went white, and my ear started ringing. Then he let go of me, and I collapsed backward on the grass behind me.

"I said not to hurt her," the girl hissed.

"I didn't. I was subduing her," the guy growled and looked down at me. "And if she doesn't knock it off, I'll subdue her again, but harder this time."

My neck ached from the force of his hit, and my jaw screamed painfully. A throbbing spread behind my left eye, but I still tried to stagger to my feet. She kicked me then, not hard enough to really hurt, but enough so I'd fall back down.

I lay on my back, staring up at the sky. From the corner of my eye, I could see a light flick on in the window of a house behind me. We were making enough of a ruckus to wake the neighbors, even if we weren't close enough for Matt to hear us.

I opened my mouth to scream and yell for help, but the male tracker must've realized what I meant to do. Little more than a yelp had escaped my lips when I felt his foot press down hard on my throat.

"If you make a sound, I'll make this much harder for you," the guy warned me. "I might not be allowed to snap your neck, but I can make you wish you were dead."

I couldn't breathe, and I clawed at his foot, trying to get it off me. When he asked if I promised to be good, I nodded frantically. I would've agreed to anything that let me breathe again.

He stepped back and I gasped for breath, taking in big gulps of air that burned my throat.

"Let's just get her to the car," the girl said, exasperated.

He bent down to try to pick me up, but I hit away his hands. I was lying on my back, and I lifted up my legs. I wasn't really trying to kick him, but I was going to use my legs to push him back if he came near me.

In response, he hit my calf hard enough to give me a charley horse, which I gritted my teeth through. He put his knee on my stomach, holding me down so I couldn't fight as much.

When he tried to grab me, I pushed him back with my hands, so he grabbed my wrists, pressing them tightly together with one hand.

"Stop," he commanded. I tried to pull my hands free, but he just squeezed tighter and my bones felt like they were about to snap. "Just stop. We're going to take you no matter what."

"Like hell you are!" Finn barked, his voice coming from out of nowhere.

I swiveled my head so I could see Finn. I had never been so happy to see anyone in my life.

"Oh, dammit," the girl said with a sigh. "If you hadn't spent so much time fighting with her, we'd be out of here by now."

"She was the one fighting with me," the guy insisted.

"Now I'm the one fighting with you!" Finn growled, glaring at him. "Get off her! *Now!*"

"Finn, can't we just talk about this?" The girl tried to sound sultry and flirty as she took a step closer to Finn, but he didn't even look at her. "I know how you feel about duty, but there's got to be some kind of agreement we can come to."

She took another step closer to him, and he pushed her back, so hard she stumbled and fell backward.

"I hate fighting with you, Finn." The guy let go of my hands and took his knee off my stomach. I took the opportunity to try to kick him in the nuts, and reflexively he whirled on me and smacked me hard again.

Before I could even curse him for hitting me, Finn was on

him. I had rolled onto my side, cradling my injured face, so I could only see part of what was going on.

My attacker had managed to get to his feet, but I could hear the sounds of Finn punching him. The girl leaped on his back to stop him, but Finn elbowed her in the face. She collapsed to the ground, holding her bleeding nose.

"Enough!" The guy had cowered down, his arms shielding his face against any more blows. "We're done! We'll get out of here!"

"You better fucking get out of here," Finn shouted. "If I see you anywhere near her again, I will kill you!"

The guy walked over to the girl and helped her to her feet, then they both headed down the street to a black SUV parked at the end of the block. Finn stood on the sidewalk in front of me, watching them until they got in and sped off.

A moment later, he knelt down next to me where I was lying on the ground. He placed his hand on my cheek where I had been slapped. The skin was tender, so it stung a little, but I refused to show it. His hand felt too good to push away.

His dark eyes were pained when he looked me over, and as terrible as everything had been up until this moment, I wouldn't have traded it for anything because it led to this, to him touching me and looking at me like that.

"I'm sorry it took me so long." He pursed his lips, clearly blaming himself for not getting here sooner. "I was sleeping, and I didn't wake up until you were completely panicked."

"You sleep in your clothes?" I asked, looking at his usual dark jeans and button-down shirt combo.

"Sometimes." Finn pulled his hand from my face. "I knew something was up today. I could feel it, but I couldn't pinpoint it because I couldn't stay as close to you as I would've liked. I never should've slept at all."

"No, you can't blame yourself. It was my fault for coming out of my room."

"What were you doing out here?" Finn looked at me curiously, and I looked away, feeling embarrassed.

"I thought I saw you," I admitted quietly, and his face went dark.

"I should've been here," he said, almost under his breath, and then he got to his feet. He held out his hand and pulled me to my feet. I grimaced a little but tried not to show it. "Are you all right?"

"Yeah, I'm fine." I forced a smile. "A little sore, but fine."

He touched my cheek again, just with his fingertips, sending flutters through me. He studied my injury intently, and then his eyes met mine, dark and wonderful. It was at that moment that I knew I had officially fallen for him.

"You're going to have a bruise," Finn murmured, dropping his hand. "I'm sorry."

"It's not your fault," I insisted. "It's mine. I was being an idiot. I should've known . . ." I trailed off. I had been about to say that I should've known it was dangerous, but how could I have possibly known that? I had no idea who those people were. "Who were they? What did they want?"

"Vittra," Finn growled, glaring down the road as if they would appear at the sound of their name. He tensed up as he scanned the horizon, then put his hand on the small of my back to usher me away. "Come on. I'll explain more in the car."

"The car?" I stopped where I was, making him press his palm harder on my back until he realized I wasn't going anywhere. His hand stayed there, and I had to ignore the small pleasure of it so I could argue with him. "I'm not going in the car. I have to go home before Matt realizes I'm gone."

"You can't go back there," Finn said, apologetic but firm. "I'm sorry. I know this is directly against your wishes, but it's not safe for you there anymore. The Vittra have found you. I will not leave you here."

"I don't even understand what this Vittra is, and Matt is . . ." I shifted uncomfortably and looked backed toward my house.

Matt was tough, as far as people went, but I wasn't sure what kind of match he would be for the guy who attacked me. And even if he could take him, I didn't want to bring that element into the house. If something happened to Matt or Maggie because of me, I could never forgive myself.

Red and blue lights lit up the neighborhood as a police car drew near. The neighbors must've called the cops when they heard me fighting with the trackers. It apparently hadn't sounded dangerous enough to warrant sirens, but the lights were flashing a block away.

"Wendy, we must hurry," Finn insisted. The police expedited his urgency, so I nodded and let him take me away.

Apparently he'd run to my rescue this morning, because his car was still parked at his house two blocks away. We jogged toward it, but when the cop car got closer, we ducked behind a shed to hide.

"This is going to break Matt's heart," I whispered as we waited for the police to pass us.

"He'd want you to be safe," Finn assured me, and he was right. But Matt wouldn't know I was safe. He wouldn't know anything about me.

Once Finn was certain we were in the clear, we stepped out from behind the shed and hurried on to his car.

"Do you have a cell phone?" I asked.

"Why?" Finn kept glancing around as we approached his car. He pulled his keys from his pocket and used the remote to unlock it.

"I need to call Matt and let him know that I'm okay," I said. Finn held the passenger door open while I got inside. As soon as he got in the driver's seat, I turned to him. "Well? Can I call him?"

"You really want to?" Finn asked as he started the car.

"Yes, of course I do! Why is that so surprising?"

Finn threw the car in gear and sped off down the road. The whole town was still asleep, except for us and the neighbors we'd awoken. He glanced over at me, debating. Finally, he dug in his pocket and pulled out his cell phone.

"Thank you." I smiled gratefully at him.

When I started dialing the phone, my hands shook, and I felt sick. This was going to be the hardest conversation of my life. I held the phone to my ear, listening to it ring, and I tried to slow my breathing.

"Hello?" Matt answered the phone groggily. He clearly hadn't woken up yet, so he must not know I was gone. I wasn't sure if that was a good thing or not. "Hello? Who's there?"

I closed my eyes and took a deep breath. "Matt?"

"Wendy?" Matt instantly sounded alert, panic in his voice. "Where are you? What's going on? Are you all right?"

"Yeah, I'm fine." My cheek still hurt, but I was fine. Even if I wasn't, I couldn't tell him that. "Um, I'm calling because . . . I'm leaving, and I wanted you to know that I'm safe."

"What do you mean, you're leaving?" Matt asked. I could hear him open his door, and then the bang of my bedroom door being thrown open. "Where are you, Wendy? You need to come home right now!"

"I can't, Matt." I rubbed my forehead and let out a shaky breath.

"Why? Does somebody have you? Did Finn take you?" Matt demanded. In the background, I could hear Maggie asking questions. He must have woken her up with all the commotion. "I'll kill that little bastard if he lays one hand on you."

"Yeah, I'm with Finn, but it's not like you think," I said thickly. "I wish I could explain everything to you, but I can't. He's taking care of me, though. He's making sure I'm safe."

"Safe from what?" Matt snapped. "I take care of you! Why are you doing this?" He took a deep breath and tried to calm down. "If we're doing something wrong, we can change it, Wendy. You just need to come home, right now." His voice was cracking, and it broke my heart. "Please, Wendy."

"You're not doing anything wrong." Silent tears slid down

my face, and I tried to swallow the lump in my throat. "You didn't do anything. This isn't about you or Maggie, honest. I love you guys, and I would take you with me if I could. But I can't."

"Why do you keep saying 'can't'? Is he forcing you? Tell me where you are so I can call the police."

"He's not forcing me, Matt." I sighed and wondered if this phone call had been a bad idea. Maybe I just made it worse for him. "Please don't try and find me. You won't be able to, and I don't want you to. I just wanted you to know that I'm safe and that I love you and you never did anything wrong. Okay? I just want you to be happy."

"Wendy, why are you talking like that?" Matt sounded more afraid than I had ever heard him before, and I couldn't be certain, but I think he'd started to cry. "You sound like you're never coming back. You can't leave forever. You . . . Whatever is going on, I can take care of it. I'll do whatever I have to do. Just come back, Wendy."

"I'm so sorry, Matt, but I can't." I wiped at my eyes and shook my head. "I'll call you again if I can. But if you don't hear from me, don't worry. I'm okay."

"Wendy! Stop talking like that!" Matt shouted. "You need to come back here! Wendy!"

"Good-bye, Matt." I hung up to the sound of him yelling my name.

I took a deep breath and reminded myself that this was the only thing I could do. It was the only way that I could keep them safe, and it was the safest thing for me, which was exactly what Matt would want.

If he knew what was going on, he would agree with this completely. It didn't change the fact that it was absolute torture to say good-bye to him like that. Hearing his pain and frustration so evident over the phone . . .

"Hey, Wendy. You did the right thing," Finn assured me, but I just sniffled.

He reached over and took my hand, squeezing it lightly. Ordinarily I would've been delighted by that, but right now it took everything I had to keep from sobbing or throwing up. I wiped at my tears, but I couldn't seem to stop crying.

Finn pulled over to the side of the road. "Come here," he said gently. He put his arm around my shoulders and pulled me closer to him. I rested my head against his shoulder, and he held me tightly to him.

förening

Taking a deep breath, I finally managed to stop crying. Even though Finn no longer had his arm around me, we still sat so close we were practically touching. When I looked at him, he seemed to become aware of this and moved his arm farther away.

"What's going on?" I asked. "Who were those people? Why did we have to run away?"

Finn looked at me for a moment, then pulled back on the road and took a breath. "That is a very long answer, one that is best explained by your mother."

"My mother?" I didn't understand what more Kim would know about this, then I realized he meant my *real* mother. "We're going to see her? Where is she? Where are we going?"

"Förening," Finn explained. "It's where I live—where you'll live." He gave a small smile, meant to ease my concerns, and it did, a little. "Unfortunately, it's about a seven-hour drive."

"Where is it?"

"It's in Minnesota, along the Mississippi River in a very secluded area," Finn said.

"So what is this Förening place we're going to?" I asked, watching him.

"It's a town, sort of," Finn said. "They consider it to be more of a compound, but in the way the Kennedys have a compound. It's just a glorified gated community, really."

"So do people live there too? Humans, I mean." I was already wondering if I could bring Matt along with me.

"Not in the sense you're talking about." He hesitated before he continued, and glanced at me out of the corner of his eye. "It's entirely Trylle, trackers, and mänsklig. There are about five thousand who live there in total, and we have gas stations, a small grocery store, and a school. It's just a very small, quiet community."

"Holy hell." My eyes widened. "You mean there's just a whole town of . . . trolls? In Minnesota? And nobody ever noticed?"

"We live very quietly," Finn reiterated. "And there are ways to make people not notice."

"You sound like you're in the Mafia," I commented, and Finn smiled crookedly. "Do you guys make people sleep with the fishes or something?"

"Persuasion is a very powerful ability," he said, and his smile disappeared.

"So you have persuasion?" I asked carefully. Something seemed to upset him, and as I expected, he shook his head. "Why not?"

‍acker. Our abilities are different." He glanced over
and, sensing that I would just ask more questions, he
‍nt on. "They're more suited for tracking, obviously. Persuasion isn't particularly useful in that arena."

"What is useful?" I pressed, and he sighed wearily.

"It's hard to explain. They're not even real abilities in the
sense of the word." His jaw ticked, and he shifted in his seat.
"It's more instinct and intuition. Like the way a bloodhound
follows a scent, except it's not actually something I can smell.
It's just something I know." He looked over to see if I was getting it, but I just stared at him blankly.

"For example, when you went to visit that woman the other
night"—that woman being someone who I had thought was
my mother my entire life—"I knew you were far away, and I
knew something was distressing you."

"You can tell when I'm upset? Even when you're not around
me?" I asked.

Finn nodded. "As long as I'm tracking you, yes."

"I thought you said you weren't psychic," I muttered. "Being
able to know my feelings sounds awfully psychic to me."

"No, I said I couldn't read minds, and I can't." Then, with
an exasperated sigh, he added, "I never have any idea what
you're thinking.

"I can't even tell everything you're feeling," he went on.
"Just distress and fear. I need to be alert to situations when
you're in danger so I can help you. My job is to keep you safe
and bring you home."

"How do you know how to track people like me? Before you find us, I mean."

"Your mother has things from when you were a baby. A lock of hair usually," Finn elaborated. "I get a vibe from that, and the parents usually have a general idea where you are. Once I'm around you, I start to get a real scent of you, and that's it."

An odd warmth filled my chest. My mother had things from me. Kim had never treasured anything about me, but someone out there had. She had taken a lock of hair when I was born and kept it safe all these years

"Is that why you stared at me all the time? Because you were feeling this . . . this vibe?" I thought of the way his eyes were always on me, and the way I could never make sense of his expression.

"Yes." There was something about his answer—he wasn't lying exactly, but he was holding something back. I thought about pressing him further but there were so many other things I wanted to know.

"So . . . how often do you do this?"

"You are my eleventh." He looked at me to gauge my response, so I kept my face as expressionless as possible.

I was a little surprised by his answer. It seemed like an incredibly time-consuming process, for one thing. And he seemed fairly young to have done it eleven times. Plus, it was unnerving to think there were that many changelings out there.

"How long have you been doing this?"

"Since I was fifteen," Finn answered.

"Fifteen? No way." I shook my head. "So you're trying to tell me that at fifteen years old, your parents sent you out into the world to track and find kids? And these kids, they trusted you and believed you?"

"I'm very good at what I do," Finn replied matter-of-factly.

"Still. That just seems . . . unreal." I couldn't wrap my mind around it. "Did they all come back with you?"

"Yes, of course," he said simply.

"Do they always? With all the trackers, I mean?"

"No, they don't. They usually do, but not always."

"But they always do with you?" I persisted.

"Yes." Finn looked over at me again. "Why do you find it so hard to believe?"

"I find this all hard to believe." I tried to pinpoint what was bothering me. "Wait. You were fifteen? That means that you were never . . . you weren't a changeling. So not all Trylle begin life as changelings? How does this work?"

"Trackers are never changelings." He rubbed the back of his neck and pursed his lips. "I think it's best if your mother explains the changelings to you."

"How come trackers aren't ever changelings?" I questioned.

"We need to spend our lives being trained to be a tracker," Finn said. "And our youth is an asset. It's much easier to get close to a teenager when you are a teenager than it is when you're forty."

"A big part of what you do is building trust." I eyed him with renewed suspicion.

"Yes, it is," Finn admitted.

"So at the dance, when you were being a total dick to me. That was you building trust?"

For a split second he looked pained, then his normal emotionless expression returned. "No. That was me putting a distance between us. I shouldn't have asked you to dance. I was trying to correct the error. I needed you to trust me, but anything more would be misleading."

Everything that had transpired between us had just been because he was trying to get me to the compound. He had been keeping me safe, getting me to like him, and when he noticed my crush developing, he had tried to put me in my place. It stung painfully, so I just swallowed hard and stared out the window.

"I'm sorry if I've hurt you," Finn said quietly.

"Don't worry about it," I replied icily. "You were just doing your job."

"I know that you're being facetious, but I was." He paused. "I still am."

"Well, you're very good at it." I crossed my arms and continued to stare out the window.

I didn't feel much like talking anymore. There were still a million questions I had about everything, but I'd rather wait and talk to somebody else, anybody else. I thought I would be too anxious and excited to sleep, but after about an hour into the drive, I started nodding off. I fought to stay awake until I realized the ride would go quicker if I just slept.

When I opened my eyes, the sun was shining brightly above us. I had curled up on the seat with my knees pressed against my chest, so my whole body felt sore and achy. I looked around, then I sat up and stretched, trying to work the kinks out of my neck.

"I thought you were going to sleep the whole ride," Finn said.

"How far away are we?" I yawned and slouched low in the seat, resting my knees against the dashboard.

"Not far."

The scenery had started giving way to tall tree-lined bluffs. The car rolled up and down through the hills and valleys, and it really was stunningly beautiful. Eventually Finn slowed and we turned, driving to the top of a bluff. Soon the road curved down again, winding among the trees. Through them I could see the Mississippi River cutting through the bluffs.

A large metal gate blocked our path, but when we reached it, a guard nodded at Finn and waved us on. Once we were through, I saw beautiful houses dotting the bluffs.

They were all heavily obscured by trees, which gave me an odd sensation that there were more homes than I could actually see. But every one of them appeared luxurious and perfectly positioned to make the best of the view.

We pulled up in front of an opulent mansion perched precariously on the edge of a bluff. It was pure white, with long vines growing up over it beautifully. The back, which faced the river, was made entirely of windows, but it seemed to be held up by weak supports. While stunningly gorgeous, the house looked as if it could fall off the edge at any moment.

"What's this?" I took a break from gaping at the house to look back at Finn.

He smiled in the way that sent shivers through me. "This is it. Welcome home, Wendy."

I had come from money, but it had never been anything like this. This was aristocratic. Finn walked me to the house, and I couldn't believe that I'd truly come from this. I had never felt so small or ordinary in my entire life.

With a house like this, I had expected a butler to answer the door. Instead, it was just a kid. He looked about my age, with sandy hair cascading across his forehead. He was very attractive, but that made sense, because I couldn't believe that anything ugly ever came from a house like this. It was too perfect.

He seemed confused and surprised at first, but when he saw Finn, an understanding came to him and he smiled broadly.

"Oh, my God. You must be Wendy." He opened the massive front door so we could come in.

Finn let me go in first, which made me nervous, and I felt embarrassed with the way this kid smiled at me, especially considering my pajamas and bruised cheek. He was dressed like any other normal kid I had gone to school with, at least in the private schools, and I found that weird. As if it would be more natural for him to run around in a tuxedo first thing in the morning.

"Um, yeah," I mumbled awkwardly.

"Oh, sorry, I'm Rhys." He touched his chest, gesturing to himself, and turned back to Finn. "We weren't expecting you this soon."

"Things happen," Finn explained noncommittally.

"I'd really love to stay and talk, but I just came home for lunch, and I'm already running late on getting back to school." Rhys glanced around and looked at us apologetically. "Elora is down in the drawing room. You can get yourself there, right?"

Finn nodded. "I can."

"All right. Sorry to rush out like this." Rhys smiled sheepishly and picked up the messenger bag lying by the front door. "It was really nice meeting you, Wendy. I'm sure I'll be seeing a lot more of you."

Once he hurried out the door, I took a moment to take in my surroundings. The floors were marble, and a giant crystal chandelier hung above us. From where I stood, I could see the breathtaking view through the windowed back wall of the house. It was floor-to-ceiling glass, and all I could see were the tops of trees and the river plummeting below us. It was enough to give me vertigo, and I was on the other side of the house.

"Come on." Finn walked ahead of me, turning down a decadently furnished hall, and I scampered after him.

"Who was that?" I whispered, as if the walls could hear me. They were lined with pictures, a few of which I recognized as being painted by master painters.

"Rhys."

"Yeah, I know, but . . . is he my brother?" I asked.

"No," Finn replied. I waited for more, but apparently that was all he would say on the subjet.

Abruptly he turned and entered a room. It was the corner of the house, so two of the walls were entirely glass. One interior wall had a fireplace, and hanging above it was the portrait of an attractive older gentleman. Books lined the other interior wall. Elegant antique furniture filled the room, and a velvet chaise lounge sat poised in front of the fireplace.

A woman sat on a stool in the corner, her back to us. Her dress was dark and flowing, just like the hair that hung down her back. A large canvas was set on the easel before her. The painting was only partially finished, but it appeared to be some kind of fire, with dark smoke filtering over broken chandeliers.

She continued painting for several minutes while we stood there. I glanced over at Finn, but he just shook his head, trying to quiet me before I voiced a complaint. His hands were clasped behind his back, and he stood rigidly straight, reminding me of a soldier.

"Elora?" Finn said cautiously, and I got the sense that she intimidated him. This was as unnerving as it was surprising. He didn't seem like he could be intimidated by anyone.

When she turned to look at us, I forgot to breathe. She was much older than I had expected, in her fifties probably, but there was something stunningly elegant and beautiful about her, particularly her large dark eyes. In her youth she had probably been unbearably attractive. As it was, I could hardly believe that she was real.

"Finn!" Her voice was angelic and clear, and her surprise was endearing. With a graceful move, she swiftly stood up, and Finn did a small bow to her. It confused me, but I clumsily tried to copy it, and this caused her to laugh. She looked at Finn, but gestured to me. "This is her?"

"Yes. It is." There was a hint of pride in his voice. He had brought me here, and I was starting to realize that I must have been a very special request.

When she moved, she looked even more poised and regal. The length of her skirt swirled around her feet, making it seem as if she floated rather than walked.

Once in front of me, she inspected me carefully. She seemed to disapprove of my pajamas, especially the dirt stains on my knees I had sustained during the fight, but it was the bruise on my face that caused her to purse her lips.

"Oh, my." Her eyes widened with surprise, but her expression lacked anything resembling concern. "What happened?"

"Vittra," Finn answered with the same contempt he had used when speaking that term before.

"Oh?" Elora raised an eyebrow. "Which ones?"

"Jen and Kyra," Finn said.

"I see." Elora stared off for a minute, smoothing out the nonexistent wrinkles in her dress. Sighing tiredly, she looked to Finn. "You're sure it was only Jen and Kyra?"

"I believe so," Finn said, thinking hard. "I didn't see any signs of others, and they would've called for backup, had there been any to call. They were quite insistent on taking Wendy. Jen got violent with her."

"I can see that." Elora looked back at me. "Just the same, you are lovely." She sounded almost awed by me, and I felt a blush redden my cheeks. "It's Wendy, isn't it?"

"Yes, ma'am." I smiled nervously at her.

"What an ordinary name for such an extraordinary girl."

She looked displeased for a moment, and then turned to Finn. "Excellent work. You may be excused while I talk to her. Stay close by, though. I'll call when I need you."

Finn did another small bow before leaving the room. His level of reverence made me uncomfortable. I wasn't sure how to act around her.

"I'm Elora, and I won't expect you to call me any different. I know you still have so much to get accustomed to. I remember when I first came back." She smiled and gave a light shake of her head. "It was a very confusing time." I nodded, unsure what else to do as she gestured expansively to the room. "Sit. We have much to talk about."

"Thanks." Uncertainly, I took a seat on the edge of the sofa, afraid that if I really sat down on it I would break it or something.

Elora went to the chaise lounge, where she lay on her side, letting her dress flow around her. She propped her head up with her hand and watched me with intense fascination. Her eyes were dark and beautiful, but there was something familiar about them. They reminded me of a wild animal trapped in a cage.

"I'm not sure if Finn has explained it to you, but I am your mother," Elora said.

EIGHT

family

It was impossible. I wanted to correct her. There must be some mistake. Nothing as stunning and elegant as that could spawn me. I was awkward and impulsive. Her hair was like silk, and as it had been pointed out to me before, my hair was like a Brillo pad. I couldn't be related to her.

"Ah. I see he did not," Elora said. "From your bewildered expression, I take it you don't believe me. But let me assure you, there is no mistaking who you are. I personally chose the Everly family for you and delivered you to them myself. Finn is the best tracker we have, so there is no way you could be anyone else but my daughter."

"I'm sorry." I shifted uncomfortably in my seat. "I didn't mean to question you. I just . . ."

"I understand. You're still used to your normal human way of being. That will all change soon. Did Finn explain anything to you about Trylle?"

"Not really," I admitted carefully, afraid that I might get him in trouble.

"I'm certain you have many questions, but let me explain everything to you, and if you still have questions, you can ask me when I'm done." Elora had a coldness to her voice, and I doubted I'd ever be able to question her on anything.

"Trylle are, to the layman, trolls, but that term is antiquated and demeaning, and as you can tell, it doesn't do us justice at all." Elora gestured to the expanse of the room, with all its grace and luxury, and I nodded. "We are beings closely related to humans, but more in tune with ourselves. We have abilities, intelligence, and beauty that far surpass that of humans.

"There are two important distinctions to our lifestyle as Trylle that separate us from the humans," Elora continued. "We want to live a quiet life communing with the earth and ourselves. We work to strengthen our abilities and use them to better our lives, to protect ourselves and the things around us. We devote our entire lives to this. Förening exists only to preserve and enhance the Trylle way of life.

"The other distinction is how we maintain this lifestyle, although it isn't that different, really." She looked thoughtfully out the window. "Human children have their schools, but these places prepare them for a life of servitude. That's not what we want. We want a life of complete and total freedom. That is why we have changelings.

"The changeling practice dates back hundreds, maybe thousands of years." Elora looked at me gravely, and I gulped back the growing nausea in my belly. "Originally we were forest dwellers, far less . . . industrialized than you see now. Our children were prone to starvation and medical problems, and we did not have an adequate educational system. So we'd leave our babies in place of human children so they would have the benefits that only a human childhood could offer, then when they were old enough they would come back to us.

"That practice evolved because we evolved. Changelings were healthier, more educated, and wealthier than the Trylle counterparts that stayed behind. Eventually, every child born became a changeling. Of course, now we could easily match the benefits of the human population, but to what end? In order to maintain our current level of existence, we'd have to leave the solace of the compound and spend our lives doing menial jobs. That simply would not do.

"And so we leave our children with the most sophisticated, wealthiest human families. The changelings live a childhood that is the best this world has to offer, and then return with an inheritance from their host families that infuses our society with wealth. That, of course, isn't the only goal, but it is a large part of how we can live like this. The money you obtain from your host family will support you for the rest of your life."

"Wait. I'm sorry. I know I'm not supposed to interrupt, but . . ." I licked my lips and shook my head. "I just need to clarify a few points."

"By all means," Elora said, but venom tinged her voice.

"When I was a baby, you gave me to strangers to raise me so I could have a good education, a good childhood, and I would bring money back. Is that right?"

"Yes." Elora raised an eyebrow, daring me to question this.

I wanted to yell so badly I was shaking. But I was still afraid of her. She looked like she could snap me in half with her mind, so I just twisted my thumb ring and nodded. She had dumped me off on a crazy woman who tried to murder me, just because Elora never wanted to work and needed cash.

"Shall I continue?" Elora asked without even trying to mask the condescending tone in her voice. I nodded meekly. "I don't even remember what I was saying." She waved her hand in irritation. "If you have any other questions, I suppose you can ask them now."

"What are the Vittra?" I asked, trying to distract myself from how angry I was with her. "I don't understand who they are or what they wanted with me."

"Förening is populated with Trylle." Elora extended her arm in a wide gesture. "The term Trylle is a distinction similar to a tribe. We are trolls, and over the years, the troll population has been dwindling. Our numbers used to be great, but now there are less than a million of us on the entire planet.

"We are one of the largest tribes left, but we are not the only one," Elora continued. "The Vittra are a warring faction, and they are forever looking to pick off some of us. Either by turning us to their side, or simply by getting rid of us."

"So the Vittra want me to live with them?" I wrinkled my nose. "Why? What could I do for them?"

"I am the Queen." She paused, letting me take this in. "You are the Princess. You are my only child, the last of my legacy."

"What?" I felt my jaw drop.

"You are the Princess," Elora explained with a condescending smile. "You will one day be Queen, and being the leader of Trylle carries great weight."

"But if I'm not here, won't you just find a replacement? I mean, there's going to be a Queen here even if I'm not," I said, scrambling to make sense of this all.

"There is more to it than that. We are not all created equal," Elora went on. "Trylle are far more gifted than the others. You have already tapped into persuasion, and you have the potential for much more. Vittra are lucky to have any abilities. Adding you to their ranks would greatly add to their power and influence."

"You're saying I'm powerful?" I raised a sardonic eyebrow.

"You will be," Elora amended. "That is why you need to live here, to learn our ways so you can take your rightful place."

"Okay." I took a deep breath and ran my hand along my pajama pants.

None of this seemed real or made sense. The idea of myself as a Queen was completely absurd. I barely managed to pass for an awkward teenager.

"Finn will be staying to watch over you. Since they're looking for you, added protection would be prudent." Elora ran her hand over her skirt, not looking at me. "I'm sure you have many more questions, but you'll get the answers over time. Why don't you go get yourself cleaned up?"

"Wait," I said, my voice small and uncertain. She raised her head, looking at me with disdain. "Just . . . um . . . where's my father?"

"Oh." Elora looked away from me and stared out the window. "Dead. I'm sorry. It happened shortly after you were born."

Finn had promised me a different life where I belonged, but really, it seemed to be the exact same life with different trappings. My mother here seemed almost as cold as my fake mom, and in either life, my dad was dead.

"Also, I don't have any money." I shifted uneasily.

"Of course you don't. You probably won't have access to your trust fund until you're twenty-one, but with persuasion, you can get it sooner. Finn tells me you're very advanced with that."

"What?" I shook my head. "No. I don't even have a trust fund."

"I specifically chose the Everlys because of their wealth," Elora said matter-of-factly.

"Yeah, I know you chose them for their money, because it certainly wasn't for their mental health." I lowered my eyes, realizing I had been smart with her, but quickly plowed through it.

"My dad killed himself when I was five, so none of his insurance paid out. My mom never worked a day in her life, and she's been in a mental institution for the past eleven years, which has eaten a lot of her funds. Not only that, we've moved around a lot and wasted tons of money on houses and tuition. We're not poor by any means, but I don't think we're anywhere near the kind of rich you think we are."

"Stop saying 'we.' They're not part of you," Elora snapped

and sat up. "What are you talking about? The Everlys were one of the wealthiest families in the country. You couldn't have bled them completely dry."

"I don't know how much money we—*they*—have, but we don't . . . er . . . I didn't live like they were that rich." I was almost shouting in frustration. "And you weren't listening, I had a *terrible* childhood. My fake mother tried to kill me!"

Elora seemed more shaken by my confession that my family wasn't loaded than she was about Kim trying to kill me. She sat very still for a moment, then took a deep breath.

"Oh. So she was one of those."

"What do you mean by that?" I pressed, and by now I was livid. I couldn't believe the casual, callous air that she had about my attempted murder. " 'One of those'?"

"Oh, well." Elora shook her head as if she hadn't meant to say that. "Every now and again, a mother knows. Sometimes they hurt the child or kill them."

"Whoa, whoa, whoa. You knew there was a chance that she might kill me?" I snapped and stood up. "You knew that I could die but you just left me? You didn't care what happened to me at all!"

"Don't be so melodramatic." Elora rolled her eyes. "This is the way we live. It's a very small risk, and it rarely happens. And you lived. No harm done."

"No harm done?" I pulled up my shirt, showing her the scar that stretched across my belly. "I was six years old, and I had sixty stitches. You call that no harm done?"

"You're being disgusting." Elora stood up and waved me off. "That's not at all how a Princess should behave."

I wanted to protest, but nothing came out of my mouth. Her reaction left me feeling dazed and strange. I let my shirt fall back down over my belly, as Elora glided over to the window. She clasped her hands in front of her and stared outside. She never said a single word, but a minute later Finn appeared in the doorway.

"You need something, Elora?" Finn did a small bow to her back, making me think she probably had ways of seeing him even when she wasn't looking.

"Wendy is tired. Set her up in her room," Elora commanded diffidently. "See that she has everything she needs."

"Of course." Finn looked at me. His dark eyes were comforting, and even though I knew this was just his job, I felt relieved knowing he was there.

He left hastily, and I hurried after him. I wrapped my arms tightly around myself, trying to steady my nerves. I was still reeling from everything, trying to make sense of how I fit into all this.

Elora was right, though. I probably did need to get cleaned up, and maybe if I slept on it, everything would seem better somehow. But I doubted it.

Finn led me up a winding staircase and down another elaborate hall. At the end, he opened a heavy wooden door, revealing what I assumed was my room. It was massive, with high-vaulted ceilings, and one entirely windowed wall that made it seem even larger.

A gigantic four-poster bed sat in the center, and an array of gleaming modern furnishings surrounded it. The room boasted a laptop, flat-screen, gaming systems, iPod, and every other gadget I could possibly want. Finn opened the closet door, which was already stocked with clothing. He opened another door and flicked on the light, revealing my own private bathroom, which more closely resembled a spa.

"How do you know where everything is?" I asked. He seemed to know this house very well, and having him there beside me helped calm me some.

"I stay here from time to time," Finn replied nonchalantly.

"What? Why?" I felt a horrible pang of jealousy, terrified that he was somehow involved with Elora in a perverse fashion. He did seem to revere her more than I thought he should.

"Protection. Your mother is a very powerful woman, but she's not all-powerful," Finn explained vaguely. "Since I'm a tracker, I can tune in to her. I can sense danger and aid her if it's required."

"Is it required?" At that moment I didn't particularly care if a band of raging marauders tried to do her in, but if there were frequent attacks on her "castle," I thought I should know.

"I'll help you get acclimated. Everybody knows this isn't a perfect system. Rhys's room is down the hall. My room, along with Elora's, is on the other wing."

It didn't escape me that Finn had ignored my question entirely, but it had been a long day, so I let it pass. I definitely felt better knowing he would be around. I didn't think I could handle it all if I was left alone in this house with that woman.

While she was clearly stunning and powerful, there wasn't any warmth to her.

I hadn't realized that I even wanted that until now. After all the years of rejecting Maggie's and even Matt's attempts at bonding, I hadn't known how much I'd crave basic human warmth once it was gone.

"So . . . did you do this?" I gestured to my high-tech room.

"No. Rhys decorated it." Finn didn't look that interested in any of the expensive gear I had lying about, so that made sense. "The clothes were all Willa, I believe. You'll meet her later on."

"Rhys isn't my brother?" I asked again. I couldn't figure out how he fit into all of this. We had only met briefly, but he seemed nice and normal.

"No. He's mänsklig," Finn answered, as if I would understand.

"What does that mean?" I furrowed my brow at him.

"It means he's not your brother," Finn replied glibly and made a step toward the door. "Is there anything you need before I go?"

His abrupt decision to leave disappointed me, especially when I felt so isolated and confused, but I had no reason to keep him. Still hugging myself tightly, I shook my head and sat on the bed. Instead of leaving, Finn paused and looked back at me.

"Are you going to be all right with all of this?" Finn asked, eyeing me intently.

"I don't know," I admitted. "This wasn't at all what I had expected." It was far grander and far worse than anything I had envisioned. "I just . . . I feel like I'm in *The Princess Diaries*, if Julie Andrews had been a thief."

"Mmm," Finn murmured knowingly and walked back over to me. He sat on the bed and crossed his arms over his chest. "I know this way of life is a hard concept for some."

"They're grifters, Finn." I swallowed hard. "That's all they are. I'm just a means of swindling money out of rich people. Joke's on her, though. My family's not that rich."

"I can assure you that you are much more than that to her, much more. Elora is a complicated woman, and showing emotion doesn't come easy for her. But she is a good woman. Regardless of whether you have money or not, you will have a place here."

"Do you know how much money they have? The Everlys?" I asked.

"Yes," Finn said almost hesitantly. "Elora had me checking your finances while I tracked you."

"How much?" I asked.

"Do you want to know your trust and what you stand to inherit, or your guardian and brother's total wealth?" Finn's face had gone expressionless. "Do you want net worth? Liquid assets? Are you including real estate, like the house they still own in the Hamptons? Dollar amount?"

"I don't really care." I shook my head. "I was just . . . Elora was convinced that we really did have a lot of money, and I was just curious. I didn't even know I had a trust fund until today."

"Yes. You really do have a lot of money," Finn said. "More

than even Elora had originally thought." I nodded and looked at my feet. "You lived well below your means."

"I think Maggie thought it would be better for me and Matt, and I never really cared that much about money." I kept staring at my feet, and then finally I looked up at Finn. "They would give me anything. They would give me all of it if I asked. But I'm never taking any money from them, not for myself and certainly not for Elora. Make sure you tell her that when you go back to her."

I had expected him to protest in some way, but Finn surprised me. His lips curled into the hint of a smile, and if anything, he looked almost proud of me.

"I will," he promised, amusement tinging his voice. "But right now you should shower. You'll feel better after."

Finn helped me settle into my room. My closet was massive and overstocked, but he knew exactly where my new pajamas were. He taught me how to close the blinds for my windows, which were run by remote control, and how to turn on my overly complicated shower.

Once he left, I sat on the edge of the tub and tried not to let this all get to me. I was starting to think that Matt and Maggie might have been the only people who loved me for me, and now I was supposed to steal from them. Even if it wasn't really stealing. I knew they would freely give me anything I asked for, and that only made it hurt worse.

NINE

homesick

When I came out of my shower, wrapped in a fluffy bathrobe, I was surprised to find Rhys sitting on my bed. He had my iPod, the one that had come with the room, and he was scrolling through it. I cleared my throat loudly, since he apparently hadn't heard me exit the bathroom.

"Oh, hey!" Rhys set aside the iPod and got to his feet, grinning at me in a way that made his eyes sparkle. "Sorry. I didn't mean to interrupt you. I just wanted to see how you were doing, how you liked it here."

"I don't know." My hair had to be terrible mess, and I pulled a hand through the wet tangles. "It's too soon to tell yet."

"You like the stuff?" Rhys asked, gesturing around the room. "I picked out everything that I liked, which I know sounds kind of vain. I asked for some input from Rhiannon, because she's a girl, but it's still so hard to pick out stuff for someone you've never met."

"No, it all looks really good. You did a great job." I rubbed my eyes and yawned.

"Oh, sorry. You're probably exhausted." Rhys stood up. "I just got done with school, and I didn't have a chance to talk to you earlier. But . . . yeah. I'll leave you be."

"Wait. You just got done with school?" I furrowed my brow, trying to understand. "Does that mean you're a tracker?"

"No." It was his turn to look confused. "I'm mänks." When he saw the perplexed look on my face, he corrected himself. "Sorry. It's just short for mänsklig."

"What the hell does that mean?" I demanded. My low energy made it hard to conceal my exasperation.

"They'll explain it to you later." Rhys shrugged. "Anyway, I should let you freshen up. If I'm not in my room, I'll be downstairs, getting some food."

"Are you happy here?" I blurted out before I could think about how rude that sounded. His eyes met mine just for a second, revealing something intense I couldn't quite decipher, but then he quickly dropped them.

"Why wouldn't I be happy?" Rhys asked wryly. He ran his fingers along my silk sheets, staring at the bedspread intently. "I have everything a kid could want. Video games, cars, toys, money, clothes, servants . . ." He trailed off, but then a slow smile returned to his face and he looked up at me. "And now I have a Princess living across the hall from me. I'm ecstatic."

"I'm not really a Princess." I shook my head and tucked my hair behind my ears. "Not in the real sense of the word. I mean . . . I just got here."

"You look like a Princess to me." The way he smiled at me made me want to blush, so I looked down, unsure of what else to do.

"So what about you?" I kept my head down, but I raised my eyes to meet his. The smile playing on my lips felt oddly flirtatious, but I didn't mind. "Are you some kind of Prince?"

"Hardly." Rhys laughed. He plucked at his sandy hair, looking rather sheepish. "I should probably let you finish getting dressed. The chef is off tonight, so supper is on me."

Rhys turned and walked down the hall, whistling a song I didn't recognize. I shut my door, wishing I could understand this all better. I was a Trylle Princess to a grifter empire, and I had a mänsklig living across the hall from me, whatever the hell that meant.

I lived in this amazingly stunning house with these cold, indifferent people, and the price of admission was stealing from the only people who cared about me. Sure, Finn was here, but he had made it perfectly clear that his only interest in me was business.

I went through my closet, looking for something to wear. Most of the clothes seemed too fancy for me. Not that I had grown up wearing rags or anything. In fact, if my mother . . . er, Kim . . . hadn't gone crazy and left, these would be exactly the kind of clothes I'd be expected to wear now. All high-class fashion pieces. Eventually I managed to dig up a simple skirt and shirt that resembled something I'd actually wear.

I was starving, so I headed off to find the kitchen to take Rhys up on his offer. The tile floors were cold under my feet, and strangely, I had yet to see any rugs or carpet in the entire house.

I had never been fond of the feel of carpet on my feet, or really the feel of anything on them. When I thought back to my glimpse of the closet here, as large and full as it had been, there hadn't been any shoes. It must be a Trylle thing, and that thought was oddly comforting. I was part of something.

I passed through the living room, where a fireplace filled the partial wall separating it from an elegant dining room. The furniture appeared to be handcrafted wood and was upholstered in white. The floors were all smooth golden wood, and everything was aimed toward the glass wall, forcing you to admire the view.

"Nice digs, right?" Rhys said, and I whirled around to find him standing behind me, smiling.

"Yeah." I looked around the room appreciatively. "Elora definitely has good taste."

"Yeah." Rhys shrugged. "You gotta be hungry, though. Come on. I'll whip you up something in the kitchen." He started walking out of the room, and I followed him. "You'll probably hate what I make, though. You're into all that health food junk like everybody else, right?"

"I don't know." I had never thought of myself as a health nut, but the things I preferred tended to be organic and vegan. "I like natural things, I guess."

He nodded knowingly as he led me past the ornate dining room into a massive kitchen. There were two professional-grade stoves, two massive stainless-steel fridges, a gigantic island in the center, and more cupboards than the residents in this house could possibly use. Rhys went over to the fridge and pulled out a bottle of Mountain Dew and a bottle of water.

"Water, right?" Rhys held it out to me, and I took it from him. "I'm really not the best cook, but you'll have to settle for my cooking."

"How often do you have a chef?" I asked. In a place like this, they definitely had some kind of staff.

"Part-time." Rhys took a sip from his Mountain Dew, then set it on the island and went to the other fridge to start rooting around. "Just weekends, but that's because it's usually when we entertain. I don't know what Elora eats during the week, but I'm on a fend-for-yourself basis."

I leaned on the island, drinking my water. This kitchen reminded me of the one in our house in the Hamptons, the one Kim had attempted filicide in, but that one had been smaller. If she hadn't left, this was probably how I would've been raised. In fact, I'm sure this was how she had been brought up.

Maggie easily could've lived like this. I thought back to what Finn had told me about Matt and Maggie living well below their means. I wondered why it was so important to them to preserve the family nest egg.

The only explanation that made sense was that they were saving it for me—to make sure I was taken care of for the rest of my life. Which probably seemed all the more necessary given my problems at school.

Funny that the very thing Elora planned to steal from them was precisely what they planned to give.

And Maggie had made it clear through her choices that taking care of me herself was more important than spending money. She had made a choice that my own mother never would have.

"So you like shitake mushrooms, right?" Rhys was saying. He had been pulling things out of the fridge, but I had been too lost in thought to notice. His arms were overflowing with vegetables.

"Uh, yeah, I love mushrooms." I straightened up and tried to see what all he had, and for the most part it looked like things I enjoyed.

"Excellent." Rhys grinned at me and dropped his armload of food into the kitchen sink. "I'm going to make you the best stir-fry you've ever tasted."

He went about chopping things up, and I offered to help him, but he insisted that he could handle it. The whole time, he talked amicably about the new motorcycle he'd gotten last week. I tried to keep up with the conversation, but all I knew about motorcycles were that they went fast and I liked them.

"What are you making in here?" Finn came into the kitchen, his expression vaguely disgusted.

His hair was damp from a recent shower, and he smelled like the grass after a rain, only sweeter. He walked past me without even a glance in my direction and went over to where Rhys had thrown everything into a wok on the stove.

"Stir-fry!" Rhys proclaimed.

"Really?" Finn leaned over his shoulder and peered down at the ingredients in the pan. Rhys moved to the side a little so

Finn could reach in and grab something out of it. He sniffed it, then popped it into his mouth. "Well, it's not terrible."

"Stop my beating heart!" Rhys put his hand over his heart and feigned astonishment. "Has my food passed the test of the hardest food critic in the land?"

"No. I just said it wasn't terrible." Finn shook his head at Rhys's dramatics and went to the fridge to get a bottle of water. "And I'm certain that Elora is a much harsher food critic than I'll ever be."

"That's probably true, but she's never let me cook for her," Rhys admitted, shaking the wok to stir up the vegetables more.

"You really shouldn't let him cook for you," Finn advised, looking at me for the first time. "He gave me food poisoning once."

"You cannot get food poisoning from an orange!" Rhys protested and looked back at him. "It's just not possible! And even if you can, I *handed* you the orange. I didn't even have a chance to contaminate it!"

"I don't know." Finn shrugged. A smile was creeping onto his face, and I could tell he was amused by how much Rhys was getting worked up.

"You didn't even eat the part I touched! You peeled it and threw the skin away!" Rhys sounded exasperated. He wasn't paying attention to the wok as he struggled to convince us of his innocence, and a flame licked up from the food.

"Food's on fire." Finn nodded to the stove.

"Dammit!" Rhys got a glass of water and splashed it in the

stir-fry, and I started to question how good this was going to taste when he was done with it.

"If being picky is a Trylle trait—and it sounds like it is—how come Rhys isn't picky?" I asked. "Is it because he's mänks?"

In a flash, Finn's face changed to a mask of stone. "Where did you hear that word? From Elora?"

"No, from Rhys," I said. Rhys was still bustling around the stove but something about his posture had changed. He appeared almost sheepish. "And I wish one of you would tell me what that means. What's the big mystery?"

Rhys turned around, a nervous glint in his eye, and exchanged a look with Finn that I couldn't read.

"Elora will explain everything in time," Finn said. "But until then, it's not our place to discuss it."

Rhys turned around again, but I knew that the icy edge in Finn's voice hadn't escaped him.

On that note, Finn turned and walked out of the kitchen.

"Well, that was weird," I said to no one in particular.

When Rhys finished cooking, he pulled stools up to the island. Fortunately, the awkward moment had passed and our mood lightened again.

"So what do you think?" Rhys nodded at the plate of food I was trying to eat.

"It's pretty good," I lied. He had obviously worked hard on it, and his blue eyes showed how proud he was of it, so I couldn't let him down. To prove my point, I took a bite and smiled.

"Good. You guys are hard to cook for." When Rhys took a

mouthful of his own food, his sandy hair fell into his eyes, and he brushed it away.

"So . . . you know Finn pretty well?" I asked carefully, stabbing my fork into a mushroom.

Their banter earlier had left me curious. Before things got weird, Finn seemed to genuinely enjoy Rhys, and I had never seen Finn enjoy anybody. The closest he came was respect and obedience for Elora, but I couldn't tell what his true feelings were for her.

"I guess." Rhys shrugged like he hadn't really thought about it. "He's just around a lot."

"Like how often?" I pressed as casually as I could.

"I don't know." He took a bite and thought for a minute. "It's hard to say. Storks move around a lot."

"Storks?"

"Yeah, trackers." Rhys smiled sheepishly. "You know how you tell little kids that a stork brings the babies? Well, trackers bring the babies here. So we call them storks. Not to their faces, though."

"I see." I wondered what kind of nickname they had for people like me, but I didn't think that now was the best time to ask. "So they move around a lot?"

"Well, yeah. They're gone tracking a lot, and Finn is in pretty high demand because he's so good at it," Rhys explained. "And then when they come back, a lot of them stay with some of the more prestigious families. Finn's been here off and on for the past five years or so. But when he's not here, somebody else usually is."

"So he's a bodyguard?"

"Yeah, something like that." Rhys nodded.

"But what do they need bodyguards for?" I thought back to the iron gate and the security guard who had allowed our entrance into Förening in the first place.

When I had looked around the entryway, I remembered seeing a fancy alarm system by the front door. This all seemed like an awful lot of trouble to go to for a small community hidden in the bluffs. I wondered if this was all for the Vittra, but I didn't want to ask.

"She's the Queen. It's just standard procedure," Rhys answered evasively, and he purposely stared down at his plate. He tried to erase his anxiety before I noticed, and forced a smile. "So how does it feel being a Princess?"

"Honestly? Not as awesome as I thought it would be," I said, and he laughed heartily at that.

Rhys kind of straightened up the kitchen after we finished eating, explaining the maid would be in tomorrow to take care of the rest of it. He gave me a brief tour of the house, showing me all the ridiculous antiquities that had been passed down from generation to generation.

One room only held pictures of previous Kings and Queens. When I asked where a picture of my father was, Rhys just shook his head and said he didn't know anything about it.

Eventually we parted ways. He cited some homework he had to get done and having to get to bed because he had school in the morning.

I wandered around the house a bit more, but I never saw

either Finn or Elora. I played around with the stuff in my room, but I quickly tired of it. Feeling restless and bored, I tried to get some rest, but sleep eluded me.

I felt incredibly homesick. I longed for the familiar comfort of my regular-sized house with all my ordinary things. If I were at home, Matt would be sitting in the living room, reading a book under the glow of the lamplight.

Right now he was probably staring at the phone, or driving around to look for me. And Maggie was probably crying her eyes out, which would only make Matt blame himself more.

My actual mother was somewhere in this house, or I assumed she was, anyway. She had abandoned me with a family that she knew nothing about except that they were rich, and she knew there was a risk that I could be killed. It happens sometimes. That's what she said. When I came back, after all these years away from me, she hadn't hugged me, or even been that happy to see me.

Everything felt way too big in this house. With all this vast space between everything, it felt like I was trapped on an island. I had always thought that's what I wanted, to be my very own island. But here I was, and I felt nothing but isolated and confused.

It didn't help that people weren't telling me things. Every time I asked something, there were only half answers and vague responses before the person I'd asked quickly changed the subject. For being set to inherit a kingdom of sorts, I was pretty low on the information ladder.

precognition

After sleeping fitfully, I got up and got ready for the day. I wandered around the house, but not intentionally. I had been trying to get to the kitchen, but I took a wrong turn somewhere and got lost. Rhys had given me an explanation of the palace layout the day before, but not enough, apparently.

The palace was divided into two massive wings, separated by the grand entryway. All official business took place in the south wing, which housed the meeting rooms, ballroom, a massive dining hall, offices, the throne room, as well as staff quarters and the Queen's bedroom.

The north wing was more casual and contained my room, guest bedrooms, a living room, the kitchen, and the sitting parlor.

I was wandering around the north wing, opening doors and investigating. As far as I could tell, this place had almost as many guest rooms as a Holiday Inn, only they were a whole lot fancier. I eventually found Elora's parlor, but she wasn't there, so it didn't help me any.

I moved on and tried to open the door across the hall from Elora's space, but it wouldn't budge. So far, this was the only door I'd found that had been locked, and I found that strange. Especially in this wing. I suppose in the south wing, locking up official business would make sense.

Fortunately, I knew a thing or two about lock-picking. In attempts to keep from being expelled, I had broken into a few school offices and stolen papers. I don't recommend it, and in the end, it was usually ineffective.

I pulled a bobby pin from my hair and looked around. I didn't see anyone, and hadn't so far this morning, so I set about breaking in. After a few unsuccessful twists in the lock, I felt something give, and I turned the knob.

Pushing the door open slowly, I peeked in, half expecting to find the royal bathroom or something. When nobody screamed at me to go away, I pushed the door open wider and stepped inside. Unlike the other rooms, this one was completely dark.

Feeling along the wall, I finally found the light switch and flicked it on. The room reminded me of a large storeroom. It had no windows, and the walls were dark brown. With a bare lightbulb in the ceiling, it held none of the grandeur of the rest of the house, and it had no furniture.

But it was filled to the brim with paintings. Not hanging on the wall. Just stacked and piled around in every available space. At first I assumed they must be leftovers from the King and Queen room, but from what I could see, none of them were portraits.

I picked up the one nearest to me, and it was a lovely picture of a newborn baby wrapped in a blue blanket. I set it aside and picked up another, which appeared to be Elora, looking much younger and even more beautiful, dressed in a gorgeous white gown. Despite the beauty of the picture, her eyes looked sad and remorseful.

Holding the picture at arm's length so I could get a better look at it, I realized something. It had the same brushstrokes, the same technique as the painting of the baby. I picked up another picture to compare, and it was the same too.

These were all painted by the same artist.

I thought back to the drawing room and the painting I had seen Elora working on. Something with dark smoke and chandeliers. I couldn't be certain, but I would guess these were hers.

I sifted through a few more of the paintings, growing even more bewildered, and then I saw one that stopped my heart cold. When I picked it up, I wasn't surprised to see my hands were shaking.

It showed me, looking about the same as I did now, except dressed nicer. I wore a beautiful flowing white gown, but there was a tear in the side of the dress, revealing a thin line of red blood. My hair had been pulled back, but it was starting to come loose, wild strands falling free.

In the painting, I lay on my belly on a marble balcony. The floor around me was covered in pieces of glass that shimmered like diamonds, but I didn't seem to notice. My outstretched hand extended past the balcony, reaching into a dark oblivion.

But my face was what struck me the most. I looked absolutely horrified.

Once I got past that, I realized something even more disturbing. This picture looked *exactly* like me. And I'd only been here for a day. There was no way Elora could've painted something this detailed within twenty-four hours of meeting me.

But how could she paint me with such accuracy if we'd never met?

"I should've known you'd be snooping," Finn said from behind me, startling me so much I dropped the painting.

"I—I got lost." I turned to look at him standing in the doorway.

"In a locked room?" He raised an eyebrow and crossed his arms.

"No, I—" I started to formulate some kind of lame excuse, but decided against it. I picked up the picture, the one of me reaching for nothing, and held it up for him to see. "What's this?"

"It appears to be a painting, and if you hadn't gathered from the locked door, it's also none of your business." It came as a relief that Finn didn't sound very upset. At least not as upset as Elora would be if she found out I was in here, I'm sure.

"This is me." I tapped the picture.

"Maybe." He shrugged, as if he wasn't convinced.

"No, I wasn't asking. This is me," I insisted. "What am I doing?"

"I haven't the faintest idea," Finn sighed. "I didn't paint it."

"Did Elora?" I asked, and when he didn't say anything, I took that as my answer. "Why would she paint this? *How* did she paint this? We'd never met before yesterday."

"She gave birth to you. You'd met before," Finn replied dryly.

"Yeah, when I was a baby. That doesn't count." I raised the picture higher so he couldn't help but look at it. "Why would she paint this? Or any of these?"

"In all your myriad questions about this room, did you ever stop to ask yourself *why* this room is locked?" Finn gave me a hard look. "That Elora might not want people looking at these?"

"Yeah, it did occur to me." I looked back down at the painting, ignoring him. "But this is me. I have a right to know."

"That's not how it works. You don't have the right to know other people's thoughts just because they include you," he said. "Just the same as I don't have the right to yours just because they're about me."

"You presume that I think of you?" I fought the growing blush on my cheeks and shook my head, trying to get back to the point. "Just tell me what's going on. And don't just tell me to wait for Elora to tell me, because that's not good enough. Not after seeing this."

I put the painting down and returned my gaze to Finn.

"Fine. But get out of there before Elora finds you." He moved back from the doorway, making room for me to step out.

I had to climb over all the paintings I had disturbed, but he didn't tell me to put them back in order, which was good because I didn't think I could. The room had no organization, and all the paintings were placed haphazardly.

Once I made my escape, Finn shut the door, making certain it was locked properly.

"So?" I asked, looking at him expectantly. He had his back to me, testing the door again to be sure it wouldn't budge.

"So, that's Elora's private room." He turned to look at me and pointed at the door. "Do not go in there. Do not touch her private things."

"I don't know what's so bad about them. Why does she paint them if she's gonna hide them away?"

He started walking down the hall, so I went after him. "She paints them because she has to."

"What do you mean?" I crinkled my brow. "Like an artist's urge takes hold of her?" I thought about it more, and it made even less sense. "Elora doesn't seem like an artist type."

"She's not, really." Finn sighed. "She has precognition."

"What? Like she can see the future?" I asked dubiously.

"Kind of." He wagged his head, like that wasn't quite right. "She can't see it. She can only *paint* it."

"Wait." I stopped short, and he walked a few more steps before stopping to look back at me. "You're telling me all those paintings were of the future?"

Finn nodded. "At the time they were painted, yes. Some of them are old, and they've already happened."

"But that means the picture of me, that's in the future!" I pointed back at the room. "What does that mean? What am I doing?"

"I don't know." He shrugged, as if he hadn't thought of it. "Elora doesn't know."

"How can she not know? That makes no sense—she painted it."

"Yes, and all she knows is what she paints," Finn explained slowly. "She doesn't see anything. She picks up the brush, and it just . . . comes out. Or at least that's my understanding of the process."

"But why would she just randomly paint me looking so scared?"

"It's just how it is," he said, a note of sadness in his voice. Breathing deeply, he started walking away again. "And that's why the room is locked."

"What do you mean?" I chased after him.

"People want to know more about what she's painted, but she doesn't have the answers," Finn said. "Or they want her to paint a particular spot in the future, and she can't. She has no control over what she sees."

"What's the point of it, then?" I asked. I quickened my pace to keep up with him, staring at his profile while he continued to stare straight ahead.

"She thinks it's a punishment."

"For what?"

"Everybody has something to be punished for." He shook his head vaguely.

"So . . . she has no idea what will happen to me? Or how to prevent it?"

"No."

"That's horrible," I said, more to myself than him. "That's even worse than not knowing anything."

"Precisely." Finn looked at me and slowed down, then stopped completely.

"Will I be able to do that? Have precognitive painting?" I asked.

"Maybe, maybe not." His eyes searched mine, in that soft way they did sometimes, and if I hadn't been worrying about my impending doom, I would've felt my stomach flutter.

"Do you know what my abilities will be?"

"No. Only time will tell for sure." He looked away, staring off at nothing. "Based on your parentage, they'll be very strong."

"When will I know for sure?"

"Later. After your training starts, and maybe when you get a bit older." Finn smiled thinly at me. "You have much to look forward to."

"Like what?"

"Like everything." He smiled more genuinely, and turned to walk away again. "Come on. I want to show you something."

ELEVEN

secret garden

Finn led me through the house and down a hall I didn't know existed. We went out the side door and stepped onto a narrow gravel trail lined with tall hedges. It curved around the house, leading us down the bluffs before it opened into a beautiful garden. The house and balcony hung over part of it, leaving half of it in shadows, but the rest was bathed in the warm bright glow of the sun.

Brick walls covered in thick flowered vines kept the garden blocked off from the rest of the world. Apple, pear, and plum trees blossomed all over the garden, making it more of an orchard than a garden. Flowers of pink and purple and blue sprang out in small beds, and mossy greens like creeping Charlie grew in patches along the ground.

It was on a hillside, so the whole thing tilted down. As we walked down the trail, I slipped a bit, and Finn took my hand to steady me. My skin flushed warmly, but the second I caught my balance, he let go of my hand. Still, I refused to let it dampen my mood.

"How is this possible?" I asked as butterflies and birds flitted about the trees. "None of these things are in season. They shouldn't be flowering."

"They always flower, even in winter," Finn said, as if that made more sense.

"How?" I repeated.

"Magic." He smiled and walked ahead.

I looked up at the house towering above us. From where I stood, I couldn't see any of the windows. The garden had been built in the perfect spot so it wasn't visible from the house, leaving it hidden among the trees. It was a secret garden.

Finn was ahead of me, and I hurried to catch up to him. The sound of the wind in the trees and the river flowing echoed through the bluffs, but over that I heard laughter. I walked around a hedge and saw a pond that inexplicably included a small waterfall.

I found the source of the laughter on two curved stone benches poised around it.

Rhys lay on his back on one bench, laughing and looking up at the sky, and Finn stood next to him, admiring the sparkling pond. A girl looking a little bit older than me sat on the other bench, a Mountain Dew bottle in her hand. Her hair was shiny red, her eyes sparkled green, and she had a nervous smile. When she saw me, she stood up and paled a little.

"You got here just in time, Wendy." Rhys smirked, sitting

up. "We were having a show. Rhiannon was just about to burp the alphabet!"

"Oh, my gosh, Rhys, I was not!" the girl protested, her cheeks flushing with embarrassment. "I just drank the Mountain Dew too fast and I said excuse me!" Rhys laughed again, and she looked apologetically at me. "I'm sorry. Rhys can be such an idiot sometimes. I wanted to make a better first impression than this."

"You're doing okay so far." I wasn't used to the idea of anybody trying to impress me . . . ever, and I couldn't imagine that this girl would have to try too hard. She already had a certain likable quality to her.

"Anyway, Wendy, this is Rhiannon, the girl next door." Rhys gestured from one to the other of us. "Rhiannon, this is Wendy, future ruler of everything around you."

"Hi, nice to meet you." She set down her pop and came over to me so she could shake my hand. "I've heard so much about you."

"Oh, yeah? Like what?" I asked.

Rhiannon floundered helplessly for a minute, looking to Rhys for help, but he just laughed.

"It's okay. I was just kidding," I told her.

"Oh. Sorry." She flashed an embarrassed smile.

"Why don't you come have a seat, Rhiannon, and relax for a bit?" Rhys patted the seat next to him, trying to ease her discomfort. She felt awkward because of me, and I still couldn't wrap my head around the concept.

"Is this new?" Finn asked Rhys and pointed to the pond.

"Uh, yeah." Rhys nodded. "I think Elora had it put in while you were gone. She's getting everything all fancied up, 'cause of everything that's coming."

"Mmm," Finn said noncommittally.

I went over to inspect the pond and waterfall myself. The waterfall should've drained the pond, since the pond had no other water flowing into it. I admired the way it sparkled brightly under the sun, and thought it shouldn't even be possible. But then again, none of this should be possible.

Rhys continued to tease Rhiannon about everything, and she kept blushing and making apologies for him. Their relationship resembled a normal healthy sibling relationship, and I had to push the thought away before I had a chance to think of Matt.

I sat down on the bench across from them, and Finn took a seat next to me. Rhys tended to dominate the conversation, with Rhiannon interjecting when he said things that were categorically untrue or apologizing when she thought he was being rude. He never was, though. He was funny and lively and kept things from ever feeling awkward.

Occasionally Finn would look over at me and make quiet comments when Rhys and Rhiannon were otherwise engaged in some kind of debate. Every time he did, I felt his knee brush against mine.

At first I assumed it was a simple accident because of our close proximity, but he had actually tilted himself toward me, leaning in closer. It was a subtle move, one that Rhys and Rhiannon probably wouldn't catch, but I definitely had.

"You are such a pest!" Rhiannon grumbled playfully after Rhys had flicked an unwanted flower at her. She twirled it in her hands, admiring the beauty of it. "You know you're not even supposed to pick these flowers. Elora will kill you if she finds out."

"So what do you think?" Finn asked me, his voice low. I leaned toward him so I could hear him better, and his dark eyes met mine.

"It's really lovely." I smiled, gesturing to the garden around us, but I couldn't look away from him.

"I wanted to show you that it's not all cold and intimidating," Finn explained. "I wanted you to see something warm and beautiful." A small smile played on his lips. "Although, when you're not around, it's not quite as nice here."

"You think so?" I asked, trying to make my voice sound sexier somehow, but I completely failed. Finn smiled wider, and my heart nearly hammered out of my chest.

"Sorry for interrupting your playtime," Elora spoke from behind us. Her voice wasn't that loud, but somehow it seemed to echo through everything.

Rhys and Rhiannon immediately stopped their fighting, both of them sitting up rigidly and staring down at the pond. Finn moved away from me, at the same time turning around to face Elora, making it look like that had been his intention. The way she looked at me made me feel guilty, even though I was pretty sure I hadn't done anything wrong.

"You weren't interrupting anything," Finn assured her, but I sensed nervousness below his calm words. "Were you planning to join us?"

"No, that'll be quite all right." Elora surveyed the garden with distaste. "I needed to speak with you."

"Would you like us to be excused?" Rhys offered, and Rhiannon promptly stood up.

"That won't be necessary." Elora held up her hand, and Rhiannon blushed as she sat back down. "We will be having guests for dinner." Her eyes went back to Rhys and Rhiannon, and Rhiannon seemed to cower under Elora's gaze. "I trust that you two will find a way to make yourselves useful."

"When they come over here, I'll go over to Rhiannon's," Rhys suggested cheerily. Elora nodded at him, indicating that his response was sufficient.

"As for you, you will be joining us." Elora smiled at me, but couldn't mask the unease behind it. "The guests are very good friends of our family, and I expect you to make a good impression on them." She gave Finn that intense look, staring at him so long I felt uncomfortable, and he nodded in understanding. "Finn will be in charge of preparing you for the dinner."

I nodded, figuring that I had better say something. "Okay."

"That is all. Carry on." Elora turned and walked away, her skirt flowing behind her, but nobody said anything until she was long gone.

Finn sighed, and Rhiannon practically shivered with relief. She was clearly even more terrified of the Queen than I was, and I wondered what Elora had done to make the girl so afraid. Only Rhys seemed to shake it off as soon as she had left.

"I don't know how you can stand that creepy mind-speak

thing she does with you, Finn." Rhys shook his head. "I would freak out if she was in my head."

"Why? There's nothing in your head for her to get into." Finn stood up, and Rhiannon giggled nervously.

"What did she say to you, anyway?" Rhys pressed, looking up at him.

Finn dusted off his pants, ridding them of dirt and leaves from the bench, but he didn't respond.

"Finn? What'd she say?"

"It's nothing to concern yourself with," Finn admonished him quietly, then turned to me. "Are you ready?"

"For what?"

"We have a lot to go over." He glanced warily at the house, then back at me. "Come on. We better get started."

As we walked back to the house, I realized that whenever Elora left, I was able to breathe again. Whenever she was present, it was as if she took all the oxygen from the room. Breathing deeply, I ran my hand up and down my arm to stifle the chill that ran over me.

"Are you holding up all right?" Finn asked, noticing my unease.

"Yeah, I'm great." I tucked some of my curls behind my ears. "So . . . what's going on with you and Elora?"

"What do you mean?" Finn looked at me from the corner of his eye.

"I don't know." I shrugged, thinking of what Rhys had said after she'd left. "It just seems like she looks at you intently a lot, and like you understand exactly what she means." As soon as it came out of my mouth, it dawned on me. "That's one of her abilities, isn't it? Talking inside your head? Kind of like what I can do, but less manipulative. 'Cause she's just telling you what to do."

"Not even telling me what to do. She's just talking," Finn corrected me.

"Why doesn't she talk to me like that?" I asked.

"She wasn't sure if you'd be receptive. If you're not accustomed to it, hearing another person's voice in your head can be unsettling. And she didn't really need to."

"But she needed to with you?" I slowed down, and he matched my pace. "She was talking to you privately about me, wasn't she?"

Finn paused, and I could see that he was considering lying to me. "Some of it, yes," he admitted.

"Can she read minds?" I felt slightly horrified at the thought.

"No. Very few can." When he looked over at me, he smiled crookedly. "Your secrets are safe, Wendy."

We went into the dining room, and Finn set about preparing me for dinner. As it turned out, I wasn't completely socially stunted and had a basic understanding of manners. Most of what Finn said amounted to commonsense things, like always say please and thank you, but he also encouraged me to keep my mouth shut whenever possible.

I think his task had been less about preparing me for the dinner and more about keeping me in line. The secret things

Elora had been telling him had just been a warning to babysit me—or else.

Dinner was at eight, and the company was arriving at seven. About an hour or so before that, Rhys popped in to wish me good luck and let me know he was heading over to Rhiannon's, in case anybody cared. Shortly after I got out of the shower, Finn came in, looking even sharper than usual.

He was clean-shaven for the first time since he'd stopped going to school, and he wore black slacks and a black button-down shirt with a narrow white tie. It should've been too much with all that black, but he managed to pull it off, all the while looking incredibly sexy.

I had on only my bathrobe, and I wondered why nobody here thought it was inappropriate for boys to barge in when I wasn't dressed. At least I was doing something semi-sexy: sitting on the edge of my bed putting lotion on my legs. I did it every time I showered, but since Finn was in the room, I tried to play it off as being sensual when it really wasn't.

Not that Finn even noticed. He knocked once, opened my bedroom door, and only gave me a fleeting glance as he headed straight to my closet. After a little while, I sighed in frustration and hurriedly rubbed the rest of the lotion in while Finn continued to rummage through my clothes.

"I don't think I have anything in your size," I said and leaned farther back on my bed, trying to see what he was doing in there.

"Funny," he muttered absently.

"What are you doing in there?" I asked, watching him, but he didn't even look at me.

"You are a Princess, and you need to dress like one." He went through my dresses and pulled out a long white sleeveless gown. It was gorgeous and much too fancy for me. When he came out of the closet, he handed it to me. "I think this might work. Try it on."

"Isn't everything in my closet suitable?" I tossed the dress on the bed next to me and turned to look at him.

"Yes, but different things are better for different occasions." He came over to the bed to smooth out the dress, making sure it didn't have any wrinkles or creases. "This is a very important dinner, Wendy."

"Why? What makes this one so important?"

"The Stroms are very good friends of your mother's and the Kroners are very important people. They affect the future." Finn finished smoothing the dress and turned to me. "Why don't you continue getting ready?"

"How do they affect the future? What does that mean?" I pressed.

"That's a conversation for another day." Finn nodded toward the bathroom. "You need to hurry if you're going to be ready in time for dinner."

"Fine." I sighed, getting up off the bed.

"Wear your hair down," Finn commanded. My hair was wet, so it was behaving now, but I knew that as soon as it dried, it would turn into a wild thicket of curls.

"I can't. My hair is impossible."

"We all have difficult hair. Even Elora and I. It's the curse of being Trylle," Finn said. "It's something you must learn to manage."

"Your hair is nothing like mine," I said dourly. His hair was short and obviously had some product in it, but it looked smooth, straight, and obedient.

"It most certainly is," Finn replied.

I meant to prove him wrong, so impulsively I reached out and touched his hair, running my fingers through the hair at his temple. Other than being stiff with product, it felt like my hair.

It wasn't until I had done it that I realized there was something inherently intimate about running my fingers through another person's hair. I had been looking at his hair, but then I met his dark eyes and realized exactly how close I was to him.

Since I was short, I was standing on my tiptoes, leaning up to him as if I were about to kiss him. Somewhere in the back of my mind I thought that would be a very good course of action right about now.

"Satisfied?" Finn asked. I retracted my hand and took a step back. "There should be hair products in your bathroom. Experiment."

I nodded my compliance, still too flustered to speak. Finn was unnaturally calm, and at times like that, I really hated how aloof he could be. I barely even remembered to breathe until I was in my bathroom.

Being that near to him made me forget everything but his dark eyes, the heat from his skin, his wonderful scent, the feel of his hair beneath my fingers, the smooth curve of his lips . . .

I shook my head, clearing it of any thoughts of him. That had to be the end of that.

I had a dinner tonight to worry about, and somehow I had to do something with my hair. I tried to remember what Maggie had used in my hair before I went to the dance, but that felt like a lifetime ago.

Thankfully, my hair magically decided to behave itself tonight, making the whole process go easier. Finn seemed to think my hair looked better down, so I left the length of it hanging in the back and pulled the sides back with clips. To top off the ensemble, I got a diamond necklace from my jewelry box.

The dress turned out to be trickier than my hair. It had one of those stupid zippers that refused to move higher than my lower back, and no matter how I contorted myself, I couldn't win. After struggling with it so long my fingers hurt, I had to get help.

Tentatively, I pushed open the bathroom door. Finn had been looking out the window at the sun setting over the bluffs. When he turned, his eyes rested on me for a full minute before he finally spoke.

"You look like a Princess," he said with a crooked smile.

"I need help with the zipper," I said meekly, gesturing to the open slit down my back.

He walked over, and it was almost a relief to have my back to him. The way he looked at me made my stomach swirl with nervous butterflies. One of his hands pressed warmly on my bare shoulder to steady the fabric as he zipped me up, and I shivered involuntarily.

When he had finished, I went over to the mirror to investigate for myself. Even I had to admit that I looked lovely. With the white dress and the diamond necklace, I almost looked too lavish. Maybe it was too much for just a dinner.

"I look like I'm getting married," I commented and glanced back at Finn. "Do you think I should change?"

"No, it's perfect." He looked pensively at me, and if I didn't know better, I'd say he looked almost sad. The doorbell chimed loudly, and Finn nodded. "The guests have arrived. We should greet them."

introductions

We walked down the hall together, but at the top of the stairs, Finn deliberately fell a few steps behind me. Elora and three people I guessed were the Kroners were standing in the alcove as I descended the stairs, and they all turned to look up at me. It was the first grand entrance I had ever made in my life, and there was something wonderful about it.

The Kroners consisted of a stunningly beautiful woman in a floor-length dark green dress, an attractive man in a dark suit, and an attractive boy about my age. Even Elora looked more extravagant than usual. Her dress had more detailing and her jewelry was more pronounced.

I could feel them appraising me as I walked toward them, so I was careful to keep my steps as smooth and elegant as possible.

"This is my daughter, the Princess." Elora smiled in a way

that almost looked loving and held her hand out to me. "Princess, these are the Kroners. Aurora, Noah, and Tove."

I smiled politely and did a small curtsy. Immediately after, I realized that they were probably the ones who should be curtsying to me, but they all continued to smile pleasantly at me.

"It's such a pleasure to meet you." Aurora's words had a syrupy tone that made me wonder whether or not I should trust her. A few dark curls fell artfully from her elegant updo, and her chestnut eyes were large and stunning.

Her husband, Noah, gave me a small bow, as did her son, Tove. Both Noah and Aurora looked appropriately respectful, while Tove looked vaguely bored. His mossy green eyes met mine very briefly, then darted away, as if eye contact made him uncomfortable.

Elora ushered us into the sitting parlor to talk until supper. The conversation was overly polite and banal, but I suspected there were undercurrents that I didn't fully understand. Elora and Aurora did most of the talking, with Noah adding very little. Tove said nothing at all, preferring to look anywhere but directly at anyone.

Finn was more in the background, speaking only when spoken to. He was poised and polite, but from the disdainful way Aurora looked at him, I gathered she didn't approve of his presence.

The Stroms were fashionably late, as Finn had predicted they would be. He'd briefed me extensively on both them and the Kroners earlier in the day, but he was much more familiar with the Stroms and talked of them in much more affectionate tones.

Finn had been a tracker for Willa, so he knew her and her father, Garrett, quite well. Garrett's wife (Willa's mother) had died some years earlier. Finn claimed that Garrett was easy-going, but that Willa was a tad high-strung. She was twenty-one, and prior to living in Förening, she'd been privileged to the point of excess.

When the doorbell rang, interrupting the irritatingly dull conversation between Aurora and my mother, Finn immediately excused himself to answer the door and returned with Garrett and Willa in tow.

Garrett was a rather handsome man in his mid-forties. His hair was dark and disheveled, making me feel better about my own imperfect hair. When he shook my hand with a warm smile, he immediately put me at ease.

Willa, on the other hand, had that snobby look as if she were simultaneously bored and pissed off. She was a waif of a girl with light brown waves that fell neatly down her back, and she wore an anklet covered in diamonds. When she shook my hand, I could tell that her smile was at least sincere, making me hate her a little less.

Now that they had arrived, we adjourned to the dining room for supper. Willa attempted to engage Tove in conversation as we walked into the other room, but he remained completely silent.

Finn pulled my chair out for me before I sat down, and I enjoyed it since I couldn't remember a single time that anyone had ever done that for me. He waited until everyone was sitting before taking a seat himself, and this deference would be the standard for the evening.

As long as at least one person was standing, so would Finn. He was always the first to his feet, and even though the chef and a butler were on staff tonight, Finn would offer to get anyone anything they needed.

The dinner dragged on much more slowly than I had imagined it could. Since I wore white, I barely ate out of fear of spilling anything on my dress. I had never felt so judged in my entire life. I could feel Aurora and Elora waiting for me to screw up so they could pounce, but I wasn't sure how either of them would benefit from my failure.

I could tell that on several occasions Garrett tried to lighten the mood, but his attempts were rebuffed by Aurora and Elora, who dominated the conversation. The rest of us rarely spoke.

Tove stirred his soup a lot, and I became mildly hypnotized by that. He'd let go of his spoon, but it kept swirling around the bowl, stirring the soup without any hand to guide it. I must have started to gape because I felt Finn gently kick me under the table, and I quickly dropped my eyes back to my own food.

"It is so nice to have you here," Garrett told me at one point, changing the entire topic of conversation. "How do you like the palace so far?"

"Oh, it is not a *palace*, Garrett," said Elora with a laugh. It wasn't a real laugh, though. It was the kind of laugh rich people use whenever they talk about new money people. Aurora tittered right along with it, and that quieted Elora down somehow.

"You're right. It's better than a palace," Garrett said, and Elora smiled demurely.

"I like it. It's very nice." I knew I was making bland conversation, but I was afraid to elaborate more.

"Are you adjusting here all right?" Garrett asked.

"Yes, I think so," I said. "I haven't been here that long, though."

"It does take time." Garrett looked at Willa with affectionate concern. His easy smile returned quickly and he nodded at Finn. "But you've got Finn there to help you. He's an expert at helping the changelings acclimate."

"I'm not an expert at anything," Finn said quietly. "I just do my job the best I can."

"Have you had a designer come over to make the dress yet?" Aurora asked Elora, taking a polite sip of wine. It had been a minute since she'd last spoken, so it was time for her to assert herself once more in the conversation. "That dress the Princess has on is very lovely, but I can't imagine that it was made specifically for her."

"No, it was not." Elora gave her a plastic smile and cast a very small but very distinct glare at my dress. Until just that second it had felt like the most beautiful thing I had ever worn. "The tailor is set to come over early next week."

"That is cutting it a bit short for next Saturday, isn't it?" Aurora questioned, and I could see Elora bristling just below the surface of her perfect smile. "That's just over a week away."

"Not at all," Elora said in an overly soothing tone, almost as if she were talking to a small child or a Pomeranian. "I am using Frederique Von Ellsin, the same one who designed Willa's gown. He works very quickly, and his gowns are always impeccable."

"My gown was divine," Willa interjected.

"Ah, yes." Aurora allowed herself to look impressed. "We have him on reserve for when our daughter comes home next spring. He's much harder to get then, since that is the busy season for when the children return."

There was something vaguely condescending in her voice, as if we had done something tacky by having me arrive here when I did. Elora kept on smiling, despite what I now realized was a steady stream of polite barbs from Aurora.

"That is one major benefit of having the Princess come home in the fall," Aurora continued, her words only getting more patronizing as she spoke. "Everything will be so much easier to book. When Tove came home last season, it was so difficult to get everything just right. I suppose you'll have everything you want on hand. That should make for a stunning ball."

Several things were setting off alarms in my head. First, they were talking about both me and Tove as if we weren't even there, although he didn't seem to notice or care about anything going on around him.

Second, they were talking about something going on next Saturday that I apparently needed a specially designed dress for, and yet nobody had bothered to mention it to me. Then again, this shouldn't surprise me. Nobody told me anything.

"I haven't had the luxury of making plans a year in advance the way most people do, since the Princess came home most unexpectedly." Elora's sweet smile dripped with venom, and Aurora smiled back at her as if she didn't notice.

"I can certainly lend you a hand. I just did Tove's, and as I said, I'm already preparing for our daughter's," Aurora offered.

"That would be delightful." Elora took a long drink of her wine.

Dinner continued that way, Elora and Aurora's conversation barely masking how much they detested each other. Noah didn't say much, but at least he managed not to look awkward or bored.

Willa and I ended up watching Tove quite a bit, but for entirely different reasons. She stared at him with unabashed lust, although I couldn't figure out what he'd done to deserve that, other than being attractive. I kept watching because I was certain he was moving things without touching them.

The Kroners didn't linger after dinner, but the Stroms did. I assumed that was because Elora actually liked Garrett and Willa.

Elora, Finn, and I walked the Kroners out, with Finn coming along only to open the doors for them. When saying their good-byes, Aurora and Noah bowed before us, making me feel quite ridiculous. There was absolutely no reason why anyone should bow to me.

To my astonishment, Tove gently took my hand in his, kissing it softly when he bowed. When he straightened up, his eyes met mine, and very seriously he said, "I look forward to seeing you again, Princess."

"And I, you." I was so pleased that I had said something

that sounded completely perfect for the moment. And then I smiled much too wide, I'm sure.

Once they departed into the night, oxygen seemed to return to the house, and Elora let out an irritated sigh. Finn rested his forehead against the door for a moment before turning back around to face us. I felt much better knowing that everyone else had found the evening exhausting too.

"Oh, that woman." Elora rubbed her temples and shook her head, then pointed at me. "*You*. You do not bow to anyone, ever. Especially not that woman. I know you thrilled her endlessly, and she's going to be telling everyone about the little dim-witted Princess who didn't know enough not to bow before a Marksinna." I looked at the floor, feeling any sense of pride vanish. "You don't even bow before me, is that clear?"

"Yes," I said.

"You are the Princess. *Nobody* is higher than you. Have you got that?" Elora snapped, and I nodded. "Then you need to start acting like it. You need to command the room! They came here to see you, to gauge your power, and you need to show them. They need to have confidence that you will be able to lead them all when I am gone."

I kept my eyes locked on the floor, even though I knew that probably offended her, but I was afraid I would cry if I looked at her yelling at me.

"You sit there like some beautiful, useless jewel, and that's exactly what she wants." She sighed disgustedly again. "Oh, and the way you gaped at that boy—"

At that, she abruptly stopped. She shook her head, as if too weary to continue, then turned and walked back to the sitting parlor. I swallowed back my feelings, and Finn gently touched my arm, smiling at me.

"You did just fine," he assured me quietly. "She's upset with Aurora Kroner, not you."

"It sure sounded like she was upset with me," I muttered under my breath.

"Don't let her get to you." He squeezed my arm, sending warming tingles through me, and I couldn't help but return his smile. "Come on. We need to get back to the guests."

In the sitting parlor, Garrett and Willa waited for us, the entire atmosphere far more relaxed than it had been at dinner. Finn even loosened his tie. Her outburst seemed to have calmed Elora completely, and she lounged on the chair next to Garrett. He seemed to capture a disproportionate amount of her attention, but I didn't mind.

Soon a whole other side of Finn emerged. He sat next to me, his leg crossed over his knee, making charming small talk with the group. He was still gracious and respectful, but he chatted easily. I bit my tongue, afraid to say the wrong thing, happy to let Finn entertain Garrett and Willa. Even Elora looked pleased.

Garrett and Elora started talking politics, and Finn became more engaged in the conversation. Apparently, Elora had to appoint a new Chancellor in six months. I didn't even know what that was, and I thought asking would only make me look foolish.

As the night progressed, Elora had to excuse herself because of a migraine. Garrett and Finn offered their sympathy, but neither of them seemed particularly surprised or concerned. When they continued with the whole Chancellor business again, it became clear that Willa had grown bored. She said she needed fresh air and invited me to join her.

We went down a long hall to a small alcove with nearly invisible glass doors. They led out to the balcony that ran from one end of the house to the other, lined with a thick black railing that reached up to my chest.

I froze, remembering the painting I had seen in Elora's locked room. It was this marble balcony I had been lying on, my hand outstretched at nothing, my face contorted in horror. I looked down at my dress, but it didn't feel right. This one was lovely, but the dress in the picture had shimmered. Broken glass had littered the ground also, and I didn't see any.

"Are you coming?" Willa glanced back at me.

"Uh, yeah." I nodded and, taking a deep breath, I followed her out.

Willa went over to the farthest corner and leaned on the railing. Out here, the view was even more intimidating. The balcony hung over a hundred-foot drop. Below us the tops of maples, oaks, and evergreens stretched out as far as the eye could see. The secret garden remained hidden from sight.

Farther down the bluff I could see the tops of houses, and way down at the bottom the turbulent river ran past us. Just then a breeze blew across the balcony, sending a cold chill down my bare arms, and Willa sighed.

"Oh, knock it off!" Willa grumbled, and at first I thought she was talking to me.

I was about to ask what she meant when she lifted her hand and waved her fingers lightly in the air. Almost instantly her hair, which had been blowing back in the breeze, settled on her shoulders. The wind had died away.

"Did you do that?" I asked, trying not to sound as awed as I felt.

"Yeah. That's the only thing I can do. Lame, isn't it?" Willa wrinkled her nose.

"No, actually, I think it's pretty cool," I admitted.

She controlled the wind! Wind was an unstoppable force, and she just wiggled her fingers, and magically it stopped.

"I kept hoping I'd get a *real* ability someday, but my mother only had command over the clouds, so at least I did better than that." Willa shrugged. "You'll see when your abilities start coming in. Everybody hopes for telekinesis or at least some persuasion, but most of us are stuck with basic use of the elements, if we're lucky. The abilities aren't what they used to be, I guess."

"Before you came here, did you know you were something?" I asked, looking over my shoulder at her. She had her back against the railing, and she leaned over it, letting her hair hang down over the edge.

"Oh, yeah. I always knew I was better than everyone else." Her eyes fluttered shut and she waved her fingers again, stirring up a light breeze to flow through her hair. "What about you?"

"Um . . . kind of." Different, yes. Better, not at all.

"You're younger than most of us, though," Willa commented. "You're still in school, aren't you?"

"I was." Nobody had made any mention of school since I got here, and I had no idea what their intentions were for the remainder of my education.

"School sucks anyway." Willa stood up straight and looked at me solemnly. "So why did they get you early, anyway? Is it because of the Vittra?"

"What do you mean?" I asked nervously.

I knew what she meant, but I wanted to see if she'd tell me. Nobody seemed that keen on talking about the Vittra, and Finn hadn't even mentioned their attack since I'd come here. Inside the compound I assumed I was safe, but I didn't know if they still wanted me.

"I've heard stories that the Vittra have been prowling around lately, trying to catch Trylle changelings," Willa said casually. "I figured you'd be a top priority 'cause you're the Princess, and that's kind of a big deal here."

She looked thoughtfully at her bare toes and mused, "I wonder if I'd be a top priority. My dad's not a King or anything like that, but we are kind of royalty. What's lower than a Queen in the human world? Is that a Duchess or something?"

"I don't know." I shrugged. I knew nothing of monarchy and titles, which was ironic, considering that I was now integral to a monarchy.

"Yeah, I think I'm like that." Willa narrowed her eyes in concentration. "My official title is Marksinna, and that's like a Duchess. My dad is a Markis, which is just a male Marksinna.

We're not the only ones, though. There are maybe six or seven other families in Förening alone with the same title. The Kroners were next in line for the crown if you didn't come back. They're real powerful, and that Tove is a catch."

While he was attractive, nothing had impressed me about Tove other than his telekinesis. Still, it felt weird knowing that they were vying for my spot, and we had just eaten dinner with them.

"I don't have to worry that much about it, though." Willa yawned loudly. "Sorry. Boredom makes me sleepy. Maybe we should go inside."

It was getting cold, so I was happy to oblige. As soon as we went back in, Willa lay on the couch and all but fell asleep, so Garrett excused himself shortly after. He went to say good-bye to Elora, and then helped Willa out to the car.

The butler was cleaning everything up, so Finn suggested that we head up to our respective rooms. The night had been surprisingly tiring, so I was eager to comply.

"What's going on?" I asked after the Stroms left. It was the first chance I'd had all evening to really talk to him. "What is this ball or party or whatever that's happening next Saturday?"

"It's the Trylle equivalent of a debutante ball, except that boys go through it too," Finn explained as we climbed the stairs.

Dully, I remembered how grand I had felt coming down the stairs a few hours earlier. For the first time I had felt almost like a Princess, and now I felt like a child playing dress-up.

Aurora had seen through my fancy trappings (which she didn't even find all that fancy) and realized that I wasn't special.

"I don't even know what a debutante ball is." I sighed. I knew nothing of high society.

"It's a coming-out party, your presentation to the world," Finn elaborated. "Changelings aren't raised here. The community doesn't know them. So when they come back, they're given a small amount of time to acclimate, and then they're introduced to society. Every changeling has one, but most are very small. Since you are the Princess, you will have guests from all over the Trylle community. It is quite an ordeal."

I groaned. "I'm not ready for that at all."

"You will be," Finn assured me.

We walked in silence the rest of the way to my bedroom as I fretted and worried about the upcoming party. It hadn't been that long ago that I had gone to my very first dance, and now I was expected to be the center of a formal ball.

I could never pull that off. Tonight had only been a semi-formal dinner, and I hadn't even performed well at that.

"I trust you'll sleep well this evening," Finn said as I opened the bedroom door.

"You need to come in with me," I reminded him, then pointed to my dress. "I can't unzip this thing on my own."

"Of course."

Finn followed me into the darkened room and flipped on the lights. The glass wall worked as a mirror thanks to the black night. In the reflection, I still thought I looked nice, and then I realized that was probably because I had other people picking out my clothes. My judgment was too flawed. I turned away from the glass and waited for Finn to unzip me.

"I really botched things tonight, didn't I?" I asked sadly.

"No, of course not."

Finn's hand pressed warm on my back, and I felt the dress loosen as he pulled the zipper down. I wrapped my arms around myself to keep it up, then turned to look at him. Some part of me was distinctly aware that we were only a few inches apart, my dress was barely on, and his dark eyes were fixed on me.

"You did exactly what I told you," Finn said. "If anyone ruined things, it was me. But the night wasn't ruined. Elora is just sensitive about the Kroners."

"Why? Why does she let them get to her so much? She's the Queen."

"Monarchs have been overthrown before," Finn answered calmly. "If you seem unfit for the position, the next in line can contest it and petition to take the title."

All the color drained from my face. There was suddenly way too much pressure on me to perform. I felt sick, and I swallowed hard. The ball had scared me enough before I knew that, if I failed, my mother could be overthrown.

"Don't worry. You'll be fine." His expression saddened again, and he added quietly, "Elora has a plan to appease them."

"What is it?" I asked.

Instead of answering, his eyes got far away and his expression blanked. His brow furrowed, and then he nodded.

"I am sorry," Finn said. "You're going to have to excuse me. Elora requires assistance in her room."

"Elora called you to her room?" I stumbled over the question, unable to hide my shock.

Somehow it seemed vaguely inappropriate that Finn would be making a late-night visit to her room. Maybe it was because she had just asked him inside his head, and I couldn't get a read on the exact nature of their relationship.

The fact that I was feeling jealous of my own mother was more than a little creepy, and that added a nauseous feeling on top of everything else.

"Yes. Her migraine is quite severe." Finn took a step away from me.

"All right, well, have fun with that," I muttered.

The door closed softly behind him, and I went into the bathroom to take off my jewelry and change into baggy pajamas. Sleep was difficult for me that night. I was too anxious about all the things I was expected to accomplish.

I knew nothing about this world or these people, and yet I was supposed to rule over them someday. That wouldn't have been so bad, except that I was supposed to master everything in less than a week so they would believe that I could rule.

If I didn't, everything my mother had worked so hard for would be taken away. Even though I wasn't that fond of Elora, I was even less fond of Aurora, and I didn't like the idea of ruining my family's entire legacy.

THIRTEEN

being trylle

Lazy Sundays happened even in Förening, thankfully. I woke up late and was happy to learn the chef was still on hand to make breakfast. I saw Finn briefly, passing him in the hall, but it was no more than a nod hello.

I flopped back onto my bed, thinking I would spend the day bored out of my mind. Then Rhys knocked on my door, interrupting my plans for moping, and invited me over to his room to watch movies with him and Rhiannon.

His room was a masculine version of mine, which made sense since he had decorated my room. A huge overstuffed couch sat in front of his TV, the one big difference between our rooms. We ended up watching *The Lord of the Rings* trilogy because Rhys insisted it was much funnier once I'd spent time with actual trolls.

Rhys sat between us on the couch. When the first movie started, he was directly in the middle, but somewhere around three or four hours into the marathon I noticed he'd moved closer to me, not that I minded.

He talked and joked a lot with Rhiannon, and they had a way of making me feel comfortable. After spending the weekend failing to be the perfect little princess Elora wanted me to be, it felt good to just relax and laugh.

Rhiannon left right after the third movie started, saying she had to get up early in the morning. Even after she'd gone, Rhys didn't move away from me. He sat so close to me on the couch that his leg pressed against mine.

I thought about moving away, but I didn't really have any reason to. The movie was fun, he was foxy, and I enjoyed being with him. It wasn't too long before his arm "casually" went around my shoulders, and I almost laughed.

He didn't make my heart race, not the way Finn did, but his arm felt nice. Rhys made me feel normal in a way that I never had before, and I couldn't help but like him for it. Eventually I leaned in to him and rested my head on his shoulder.

What I didn't realize was that watching all three extended-edition versions of *Lord of the Rings* in one sitting ends up being over eleven hours of movie viewing. At one in the afternoon on a boring Sunday, that sounded genius. But by the time midnight rolled around, it became a war on sleep, and I eventually lost.

In the morning, while I slept soundly on the couch in Rhys's room, I had no idea that a commotion was going on in the house. I would've been happy to sleep through it too, but Finn threw open the door in a panic, jolting me awake.

"Oh, my gosh!" I shouted, jumping up off the couch. Finn had scared the hell out of me, and my heart pounded in my chest. "What's going on? Is everything okay?"

Instead of answering, Finn just stood there glaring at me. Behind me, Rhys was waking up much more slowly. Apparently, Finn hadn't terrified him the way he had me.

I glanced back at Rhys, who was dressed in a T-shirt and sweats that somehow managed to look good on him, and it dawned on me how this must have looked to Finn when he first burst in.

I still wore my lazy-day comfy clothes, but Rhys and I had been curled up together. And even if Finn hadn't noticed that detail, there was no denying that I'd spent the night in here. My mind scrambled to think of an excuse, but at that moment even the innocent truth escaped me.

"She's in here!" Finn called out flatly.

Rhys groaned, so I knew things weren't good. He looked completely alert now, and he stood sheepishly next to me. I wanted to ask what was going on and why Finn looked so pissed off, but Elora didn't give me a chance.

She appeared in the doorway, her emerald robe flaring out behind her in a dramatic billow, and her hair hung down her back in a thick braid. She stood behind Finn, but she somehow managed to eclipse everything else.

Several times before I had thought she looked unhappy, but that was nothing compared to the severe expression she had on now. She scowled so deep it looked painful, and her eyes were filled with fury.

"What do you think you're doing?" Elora's voice echoed painfully inside my head, and she had added some of her psychic voice to make it more intense.

"Sorry," I said. "We were just watching movies and fell asleep."

"It was my fault," Rhys added. "I put the—"

"I don't care what you were doing! Do you have any idea how inappropriate this behavior is?" Her eyes narrowed on Rhys, and he shrank back even more. "Rhys, you know this was completely unacceptable." She rubbed her temples as if this were giving her another headache, and Finn looked at her with concern. "I don't even want to deal with you. Get ready for school, and stay out of my sight!"

"Yes, ma'am." Rhys nodded. "Sorry."

"As for you—" Elora pointed a finger at me but couldn't find the words to finish. She just looked so disappointed and disgusted with me. "I don't care how you were raised before you came here. You still know what kind of behavior is ladylike and what isn't."

"I wasn't—" I began, but she held up her hand to silence me.

"But to be honest, Finn, you disappoint me the most." She had stopped yelling, and when she looked at Finn, she just sounded tired. He lowered his eyes in shame, and she shook her head. "I can't believe you allowed this to happen. You know you need to keep your eyes on her at all times."

"I know. I won't let it happen again." Finn bowed apologetically to her.

"You most certainly won't. Now fix this mess by educating

her in the ways of the Trylle. In the meantime, I do not want to see any of you for the rest of the day." She held her hands up, like she was done with the lot of us, and then shook her head and left the room.

"I am so sorry," Rhys apologized emphatically. His cheeks were red with shame, and somehow that only made him cuter.

Not that I was really paying attention to how he looked just then. My stomach was twisted in knots, and I was thankful that I hadn't started to cry. I didn't even fully understand what I'd done. I knew sleeping in a boy's room wasn't ideal, but they were acting like it was a capital offense.

"You need to get ready for school," Finn snapped, glaring at Rhys. Then he pointed to the hall and turned to me. "You. Out. *Now.*"

I gave him a wide berth on my way out the door. Normally I loved being close to him, but not today. My heart pounded erratically, but not for any pleasurable reason. Finn tried to keep his face expressionless, but tension and anger radiated from his body. I slunk across the hall to my room, and Finn barked something at Rhys about behaving himself.

"Where are you going?" Finn demanded when I opened my bedroom door. He had just emerged from Rhys's room and slammed the door behind him, making me jump.

"To my room?" I pointed at my room and looked confused.

"No. You need to come to my room with me," Finn said.

"What? Why?" I asked.

A very small part of me felt excited about the prospect of going to his room with him. That sounded like the start of a fantasy I might have. But the way he was looking at me now, I was afraid he might kill me once we were in private.

"I need to get ready for the day, and I can't very well let you out of my sight." He wore pajama pants and a T-shirt, and his dark hair wasn't as sleek as it normally was.

I nodded and hurried after him. He walked fast and pissed off, and I fell about a step or two behind.

"I really am sorry, you know," I said. "I didn't mean to fall asleep there. We were just watching movies, and it got late. If I had known it would be like this, I would've made sure I was in my room."

"You should've known, Wendy!" Finn exclaimed, exasperated. "You should know that your actions have consequences and the things you do matter!"

"I am sorry!" I repeated. "Yesterday was so boring and I just wanted to do *something*."

Finn whirled on me suddenly, startling me so I took a step backward. My back hit the wall, but he stepped closer to me. He rested an arm against the wall on the side of me, his face only a few inches from mine. His dark eyes were blazing, but somehow his voice remained calm and even.

"You know how it looks when a girl spends the night alone with a boy. I know you understand that. But it is *so* much worse when a *Princess* spends the night alone with a *mänsklig*. It could put everything in jeopardy."

"I-I don't know what that means," I fumbled. "None of you will tell me."

Finn continued to glare at me for another painful minute,

then sighed and took a step back. As he stood there, rubbing his eyes, I swallowed back tears and caught my breath.

When he looked back at me, his eyes had softened a bit, but he didn't say anything. He just walked to his room and, uncertainly, I followed him.

His room was smaller than mine, but a much more comfortable size. Even though the blinds were shut, I could tell one of his walls was made entirely of glass. Dark blankets covered his bed, and books overflowed from several bookshelves. In one corner he had a small desk with a laptop on it.

Like me, he had an adjoining bathroom. When he went in it, he left the door open, and I heard the sound of him brushing his teeth. Tentatively, I sat on the edge of his bed and looked around.

"You must stay here a lot," I commented. I knew that he stayed here on and off, but to have a room full of stuff implied a more permanent living situation.

"I live here when I'm not tracking," Finn said.

"My mother is quite fond of you," I said dimly.

"Not right now she's not." Finn turned off the water and came out, leaning on the doorframe to his bathroom. Sighing, he lowered his eyes. "I'm sorry for yelling at you."

"It's okay." I shrugged. I still didn't understand why he'd been *that* mad, but he had a point. I was a Princess now, and I had to start behaving like one.

"No, you didn't deserve it." He scratched his temple and shook his head. "My anger was misdirected. When you weren't in your room this morning, I panicked. With everything going on with the Vittra . . ." He shook his head again.

"What's going on with the Vittra?" I asked, my heart speeding up.

"It's nothing to concern yourself with," Finn said. "My point is that my emotions were high when I couldn't find you, and I snapped at you. I apologize."

"No, it's my fault. You guys were right," I said. Finn just stood there looking away from me, and then I realized something. "How did you even know I wasn't in my room?"

"I checked on you." Finn gave me a look like I was an idiot. "I check on you every morning."

"You check on me when I'm sleeping?" I gaped at him. "Every morning?"

He nodded.

"I didn't know that."

"Why would you know that? You're sleeping," Finn pointed out.

"Well . . . it just feels weird." I shook my head. Matt and Maggie used to check on me, but it felt strange knowing that Finn would come in and watch me sleep, even if it was only for a second.

"I have to make sure you're safe and sound. It's part of my job."

"You sound like a broken record sometimes," I muttered wearily. "You're always just doing your job."

"What else do you want me to say?" Finn countered, looking at me evenly.

I just shook my head and looked away. My pants suddenly became very fascinating, and I picked lint off them. Finn kept looking at me, and I expected him to finish getting ready. When he didn't, I decided that I had to fill the silence.

"What is a mänsklig?" I looked at Finn again, and he exhaled.

"The literal translation for mänsklig is 'human.'" He tilted his head, resting it against the doorframe, and watched me. "Rhys is human."

I shook my head. "I don't understand. Why is he around?"

"Because of you," Finn said, and that only confused me more. "You're a changeling, Wendy. You were switched at birth. Meaning that when you took the place of another baby, that baby had to go somewhere else."

"You mean . . ." I trailed off, but it was incredibly obvious once Finn said it. "Rhys is Michael!"

Suddenly my crush on him felt very weird. He wasn't my blood brother, but he was my brother's brother, even though Matt wasn't really my brother either. It still felt . . . not right, somehow.

And really, I should've noticed sooner. I couldn't believe I didn't. Rhys and Matt looked so much alike—their sandy hair, blue eyes, even the way their faces were shaped. But Matt's worry had hardened him, while Rhys was quick to smile and laugh.

Maybe that's why I hadn't noticed it. The complete contrast between their personalities had thrown me off.

"Michael?" Finn looked perplexed.

"Yeah, that's what my mother—Kim, my fake mom—named him. She knew she had a son, and that's Rhys." My mind swirled. "But how . . . how did they do it? How did they switch us?"

"It's relatively simple," Finn explained, almost tiredly. "After Rhys was born, Elora induced labor with you, and using persuasion on the family and hospital staff, she switched you out for him."

"It can't be that simple. The persuasion didn't really work on Kim," I pointed out.

"We normally do same-sex exchanges, a girl for a girl, a boy for a boy, but Elora had her mind set on the Everlys. It doesn't work as well when you do a boy-to-girl switch like that. Mothers are more likely to pick up on something being wrong, as was the case with your host mother."

"Wait, wait!" I held up my hands and looked at him. "She knew it was more dangerous, that Kim would be more likely to snap? But she did it anyway?"

"Elora believed that the Everlys would be the best for you," Finn maintained. "And she wasn't completely wrong. Even you freely admit that the aunt and the brother were good to you."

I had always kind of hated Kim. I thought she had been terrible and cruel like so many of my classmates, but she had known that I wasn't her child. Kim had actually been an insanely good mother. She had remembered her son, even when she shouldn't have been able to, and she refused to give up on him. The whole thing was tragic, when I thought about it.

"So that's why they don't want me with the mänsklig? 'Cause he's like a stepbrother?" I wrinkled my nose at the thought.

"He's not your brother," Finn emphasized. "Trylle and mänsklig have absolutely no relation. The problem is that they're human."

"Are we, like . . . physically incompatible?" I asked carefully.

"No. Many Trylle have left the compound to live with humans and have normal offspring," Finn said. "That's part of the reason our populations are going down."

"What happens to Rhys now that I'm back?" I asked, ignoring the clinical way Finn addressed everything. He was nothing if not professional.

"Nothing. He can live here for as long as he wants. Leave if he decides to. Whatever he chooses." Finn shrugged. "Mänsklig aren't treated badly here. For example, Rhiannon is Willa's mänsklig."

"That makes sense." I nodded. Rhiannon seemed so skittish and nervous, but also rather normal, unlike everyone else. "So . . . what do they do with mänsklig?"

"They aren't exactly raised as real children, but they are given everything to keep them happy and content," Finn said. "We have schools set up for the mänsklig, and while they aren't as nice the schools you've gone to, the mänks do get an education. They even have a small trust fund set up for them. When they're eighteen, they're free to do as they please."

"But they're not equals," I realized. Elora tended to talk down to everyone, but she was worse with Rhys and Rhiannon. I couldn't imagine that Willa was much nicer either.

"This is a monarchy. There are no equals." For an instant Finn looked almost sad, then he walked over and sat on the bed next to me. "As your tracker, I am expected to educate you, and as Elora pointed out, I should've started sooner. You need to understand the distinct hierarchy here.

"There is royalty, of which you are at the top." Finn gestured to me. "After Elora, of course. Below you there are the Markis and Marksinna, but they can become Kings and Queens through marriage. Then there are your average Trylle, the common folk, if you will. Below that there are trackers. And at the very bottom, there are mänsklig."

"What? Why are trackers so low?"

"We are Trylle, but we only track. My parents were trackers, and their parents before them, and so on," Finn explained. "We have no changeling population. Ever. That means that we have no income. We bring nothing into the community. We provide a service for other Trylle, and in return we are provided with a home and food."

"You're like an indentured servant?" I gasped.

"Not exactly." Finn tried to smile, but it looked forced. "Until we retire from tracking, we don't need to do anything else. Many trackers, such as myself, will work as a guard for some of the families in town. All of the service jobs, like the nannies, the teachers, the chefs, the maids, are almost entirely retired trackers, and they make an hourly wage. Some are also mänsklig, but they stick around less and less."

"That's why you always bow to Elora," I said thoughtfully.

"She is the Queen, Wendy. Everyone bows to her," Finn corrected me. "Except for you and Rhys. He's rather impossible, and host parents don't usually force their mänks to bow to them."

"It's nice to know that being the Princess has some perks, like not bowing," I said, smirking.

"Elora may seem cold and aloof, but she is a very powerful woman." Finn looked at me solemnly. "*You* will be a very powerful woman. You will be given every opportunity the world has to offer you. I know you can't see it now, but you will have a very charmed life."

"You're right. I can't see it," I admitted. "It probably didn't help that I just got in trouble this morning, and I don't feel very powerful."

"You're still very young," Finn said with a trace of a smile.

"I guess." I remembered how angry he had been earlier and I turned to him. "I didn't do anything with Rhys. You know that, right? Nothing happened."

Finn stared thoughtfully at the floor. I studied him, trying to catch a glimpse of something, but his face was a mask. Eventually he nodded. "Yes. I know that."

"You didn't this morning, though, did you?" I asked.

This time Finn chose not to answer. He stood up and said

he needed to shower. He gathered his clothes and went into the bathroom.

I thought this might be a good time to explore his room, but I suddenly felt very tired. He'd woken me early, and this whole morning had been incredibly draining. Lying back down, I rolled over and curled up in his blankets. They were soft and smelled like him, and I easily fell asleep.

kingdom

Other than the garden out back, I'd seen little of the palace grounds. After breakfast, Finn took me outside to show me around. The sky was overcast and gloomy, and he stared up at it with a skeptical eye.

"Is it going to rain?" I asked.

"You never can tell around here." He sounded annoyed, then shook his head and walked on, apparently deciding to risk it.

We'd gone out the front door of the mansion this time, stepping out on the cobblestone driveway. Trees overshadowed the palace, arching high into the sky. Immediately at the edge of the driveway, lush ferns and plants filled in the gaps between the pines and maples.

Finn walked into the trees, pushing the plants aside gently to make a pathway. He'd insisted I wear shoes today, and as I followed behind him, I understood why. A rough trail had been made, but it was overgrown with moss, and twigs and stones littered the ground.

"Where are we going?" I asked, as the path climbed upward.

"I'm showing you Förening."

"Haven't I already seen Förening?" I stopped and looked around. Through the trees I couldn't see much of anything, but I suspected it all looked about the same.

"You've barely seen anything yet." Finn glanced back at me, smiling. "Come on, Wendy."

Without waiting for my answer, he climbed on. The trail already had a steep incline, and it looked slick with mud and moss. Finn maneuvered it easily, grabbing on to the occasional branch or protruding root.

My climb wasn't anywhere near as graceful. I slipped and stumbled the whole way up, scraping my palms and knees on several sharp rocks. Finn didn't slow and rarely glanced back. He had more faith in my abilities than I did, but I suppose that was nothing new.

If I hadn't been so busy mastering a slippery slope, I might've enjoyed the time. The air smelled green and wet from all the pine and leaves. The river below seemed to echo through everything, reminding me of the time I put a conch shell to my ear. Over it, I heard birds chirping, singing a fevered song.

Finn waited for me next to a giant boulder, and when I reached him, he made no comment about my slow pace. I didn't have a chance to catch my breath before he grabbed a small handhold in the boulder and started pulling himself up.

"I'm pretty sure I can't climb up that," I said, eyeing the slick surface of the rock.

"I'll help you." He had his feet in a crevice, and he reached back, holding his hand out to me.

Logically speaking, if I grabbed on to him, my body weight would pull him back off the boulder. But he didn't doubt his ability to pull us both up, so neither did I. Finn had this way of making me believe anything, and it scared me sometimes.

I took his hand, barely getting a chance to enjoy how strong and warm it felt before he started pulling me up. I squealed, which only made him laugh. He directed me to a crevice, and I found myself hanging on to the boulder for dear life.

Finn climbed up, always keeping one hand out for me to grab if I slipped, but I did most of the actual climbing myself. I was surprised when my fingers didn't give and my feet didn't slide. When I pulled myself up to the top of the boulder, I couldn't help but feel a bit of pride.

Standing up on the massive rock, wiping mud off my knees, I started to make some comment about my amazing agility, but then I caught sight of the view. The top of the boulder had to be the highest point atop the bluffs. From here I could see everything, and somehow it was even more amazing than the view from the palace.

Chimneys stood out like dots among the trees, and I could see the plumes of smoke blowing away in the wind. Roads curved and wound through the town, and a few people walked along them. Elora's palace was masked with vines and trees, but it still looked startlingly large hanging on the edge of its bluff.

The wind whipping through my hair made the whole thing exhilarating. Almost like I was flying, even though I was just standing there.

"This is Förening." Finn gestured to the hidden houses peeking out among the green foliage.

"It is breathtaking," I admitted. "I'm totally in awe."

"It's all yours." His dark eyes met mine, emphasizing the solemnity of his words. Then he looked away, scanning the trees. "This is your kingdom."

"Yeah, but . . . it's not actually mine."

"Actually, it kind of is." He offered me a small smile.

I looked back down. In terms of kingdoms, I knew this one was relatively small. It wasn't as if I'd inherited the Roman Empire or anything, but it still felt strange to me that I might possess any kind of kingdom.

"What's the point?" I asked softly. When Finn didn't answer, I thought my words might have been carried away by the wind, so I asked louder. "Why do I get this? What am I to do with it?"

"Rule over it." Finn had been standing behind me, but he stepped closer, moving next to me. "Make the decisions. Keep the peace. Declare the wars."

"Declare the wars?" I looked at him sharply. "That's really something we do?"

He shrugged.

"I don't understand," I said.

"Most things will already be decided when you take the throne," Finn said, staring down at the houses instead of me.

"The order is already in place. You just have to uphold it, enforce it. Mostly, you live in the palace, attend parties, trivial governmental meetings, and occasionally decide on something substantial."

"Like what?" I asked, not liking the hard tone his voice had taken on.

"Banishments, for one." He looked thoughtful. "Your mother once banished a Marksinna. It hadn't been done in years, but she's entrusted with making the decisions that best protect our people and our way of life."

"Why did she banish her?" I asked.

"She corrupted a bloodline." He didn't say anything for a minute, and I looked at him questioningly. "She had a child with a human."

I wanted to ask him more about that but I felt a drop of rain splash on my forehead. I looked up to the sky to be certain I'd felt rain, and the clouds seemed to rip open, pouring water down before I had a chance to shield myself.

"Come on!" Finn grabbed my hand, pulling me.

We slid down the side of the rock, my back scraping against the rough surface of it, and fell heavily into a thicket of ferns. Rain had already soaked through my clothes, chilling my skin. Still holding my hand, Finn led me to shelter underneath a giant pine tree.

"That came on really suddenly," I said, peering out from under the branches. We weren't completely dry under the tree, but only a few fat drops of rain made their way through.

"The weather is so temperamental here. The locals blame

it on the river, but the Trylle have more to do with it," Finn explained.

I thought back to Willa, and her complaint that she could only control the wind, and her mother, the clouds. The garden behind the palace bloomed year-round thanks to Trylle abilities, so it wouldn't be hard to fathom that they could make it rain too.

The birds had fallen silent, and over the sound of the rainfall I couldn't hear the river. The air smelled thick with pine, and even in the middle of the rainstorm I felt oddly at peace. We stood there watching the rain in companionable silence for a while longer, but soon the growing chill began to affect me, and my teeth started to chatter.

"You're cold."

I shook my head. "I'm fine."

Without further prompting, Finn put his arm around me, pulling me closer to him. The abruptness of it made me forget to breathe, and even though he felt no warmer than I did, the strength of his arm wrapped around me sent warmth spreading through me.

"I suppose I'm not much help," he said, his voice low and deep.

"I've stopped shivering," I pointed out quietly.

"We should get back inside, so you can change into dry clothes." He breathed deeply, looking at me a moment longer.

Just as abruptly as he had grabbed me, he pulled away and started heading back down the bluff. The rain came down fast and cold, and without him to warm me, I had no urge to stay in it longer than I had to. I went down after him, half running half sliding to the bottom.

We ran inside the front doors, skidding on the marble floors, and water dripped off us into rapidly growing puddles. I only had a second to catch myself when I realized we weren't alone in the entryway.

Elora walked toward us, carrying herself with her usual regality. Her gown swam around her, making her appear to float as she moved. With her was an obese balding man, his jowls jiggling as he walked.

"How good of you to arrive now, as I'm showing the Chancellor out," Elora said icily, glaring at both Finn and me. I wasn't sure which of us she was more angry with.

"Your Majesty, I can stay and talk," the Chancellor said, looking up at her with small, fevered eyes. He wore a white suit that I couldn't imagine looking good on anyone, but it made him look like a giant, sweaty snowball.

"Chancellor, I'm sorry we missed your visit," Finn said, doing his best to compose himself. Even dripping wet, he looked collected and eager to please. I, on the other hand, hugged my arms around myself and tried not to shiver.

"No, you've given me much to consider, and I don't want to waste your time further." Elora smiled thinly at the Chancellor, and her eyes burned with contempt.

"You will take it under advisement, then?" He looked up at her hopefully and stopped walking. She'd been trying to usher him to the door, and her smile grew strained when he stopped.

"Yes, of course." Elora sounded too sweet, and I assumed she was lying. "I take all of your concerns very seriously."

"My sources are very good," the Chancellor went on. Elora had gotten him walking again, urging him closer to the door. "I have spies all over, even in the Vittra camps. That is how I got my position."

"Yes, I remember your platform." Elora appeared to suppress an eye roll, but his chest puffed up as if she'd complimented him.

"If they say there's a plot, then there's a plot," the Chancellor said with conviction. Next to me I saw Finn tense up, narrowing his eyes at the Chancellor.

"Yes, I'm sure there is." Elora nodded to Finn, who held the door open for the Chancellor. "I'd love to talk with you more, but you must hurry if you want to beat the worst of this storm. I don't want you to get stranded."

"Oh, yes, quite right." The Chancellor looked at the sheets of rain coming down, and his face paled slightly. He turned back toward Elora. Bowing, he took her hand and kissed it once. "My Queen. I'm at your service, always."

She smiled tightly at him while Finn wished him a safe journey. The Chancellor barely even glanced in my direction before diving out into the rain. Finn shut the door behind him, and Elora let out a sigh of relief.

"What were you doing?" Elora looked at me with disdain, but before I could answer, she waved me off. "I don't care. You're just lucky the Chancellor didn't realize you were the Princess."

I glanced down at my dirty, soaking-wet clothes, knowing I looked nothing like royalty. Somehow Finn still looked high-class, and I had no idea how he managed that.

"What was the nature of the Chancellor's visit?" Finn asked.

"Oh, you know the Chancellor." Elora rolled her eyes and started walking away. "He always has some conspiracy theory brewing. I should really change the laws so I have total say about who is appointed the Chancellor, instead of letting the Trylle vote. The people always fall for idiots like him."

"He mentioned something about a Vittra plot," Finn pressed. He followed her, staying a few steps behind, and I trailed in their wake.

"I'm sure it's nothing. We haven't had Vittra come into Förening in years," Elora said with an eerie confidence.

"Yes, but with the Princess—" Finn began, but she held up her hand, silencing him. She turned to him, and by the look on her face I knew she was speaking in his mind. After a minute he took a deep breath and spoke. "All I am proposing is that we take extra precautions, have extra guards on duty."

"That's why you're around, Finn." She smiled at him, something that almost looked genuine, but with a weird malicious edge to it. "It's not just for your pretty face."

"Your Majesty, you put too much faith in me."

"Now that I can believe." Elora sighed and started walking away. "Go change out of those clothes. You're dripping all over everything."

Finn watched her retreating figure for a minute, and I

waited next to him until I was certain she was out of earshot. Although, if I thought about it, I wasn't sure that Elora was ever out of earshot.

"What was that about?" I whispered.

"Nothing." Finn shook his head. He glanced over at me, almost as if he'd forgotten I was there. "You need to change before you get sick."

"That wasn't nothing. Is there going to be an attack?" I demanded, but Finn only turned and started walking toward the stairs. "What is it with you people? You're always walking away from questions!"

"You're soaking wet, Wendy," Finn said matter-of-factly, and I jogged to catch up to him, knowing he wouldn't wait for me. "And you heard everything I heard. You know what I know."

"That's not true! I know she did that creepy mind-speak with you."

"Yes, but she only told me to keep quiet." He climbed the stairs without looking back at me. "You'll be safe. You're the Princess, the most important asset this kingdom has right now, and Elora won't risk you. She just hates the Chancellor."

"Are you sure I'm safe?" I asked, and I couldn't help but think of that painting in Elora's hidden room. The one that showed me terrified and reaching for nothing.

"I would never do anything to put you at risk," Finn assured me when we reached the top of the stairs. He gestured down the hall to my room. "We still have much to go over. It'd be best if you forgot about this and changed into something warmer."

education

After I had changed, Finn directed me to a sitting room on the second floor, down the hall from my room. The vaulted ceiling had a mural, all clouds and unicorns and angels. Despite that, the furniture looked modern and normal, unlike the expensive antiques that filled most of the house.

Finn explained that this had once been Rhys's playroom. When he'd outgrown it, they had turned it into a room for him, but he rarely used it.

Lying on my back on the couch, I stared up at the ceiling. Finn sat in an overstuffed chair across from me with a book splayed open on his lap. Stacks of texts sat on the floor next to him, and he tried to give me a crash course on Trylle history.

Unfortunately, despite the fact that we were some type of mythical creatures, Trylle history wasn't any more exciting than human history had been.

"What are the roles of the Markis and Marksinna?" Finn quizzed me.

"I don't know. Nothing," I replied glibly.

"Wendy, you need to learn this." Finn sighed. "There will be conversations at the ball, and you need to appear knowledgeable. You can't just sit back without saying anything anymore."

"I'm a Princess. I should be able to do whatever I want," I grumbled. My legs were draped over the arm of the couch, and I swung my feet back and forth.

"What are the roles of the Markis and Marksinna?" Finn repeated.

"In other provinces, where the King and Queen don't live, the Markis and Marksinna are the leaders. They're like governors or something." I shrugged. "In times when the King or Queen can't fulfill their duties, a Markis can step up and take their place. In places like Förening, their title is mostly just a way of saying that they're better than everyone else, but they don't really have any power."

"That is true, but you can't say that last part," Finn said, then flipped a page in the book. "What is the role of the Chancellor?"

"The Chancellor is an elected official, much like the prime minister in England," I answered tiredly. "The monarchy has the final word and wields the most power, but the Chancellor serves as their adviser and helps give the Trylle commoners a voice in the way the government is run.

"But I don't get it," I said, looking at him. "We live in

America, and this isn't a separate country. Don't we have to follow their laws?"

"Theoretically, yes, and for the most part Trylle laws coincide with American laws, except that we have more of them. However, we live in separate pockets unto ourselves. Using our resources—namely, cash and persuasion—we can get government officials to look the other way, and we conduct our business in private."

"Hmm." I twirled a lock of hair on my finger and thought over what he was saying. "Do you know everything about Trylle society? When you were talking with Garrett and Elora, it was like there was nothing you didn't know."

I'm sure he would've easily won the Kroners over if he had tried. Instead he had assumed it was his role to hide in the background when they were around, so he'd kept his mouth shut. But everything about him was more refined than me. Cool, collected, intelligent, charming, and handsome, he seemed much more like a leader than I did.

"A foolish man thinks he knows everything. A wise man knows he doesn't," Finn replied absently, still looking down at the book.

"That's such a fortune-cookie answer," I said with a laugh, and even he smirked at me. "But seriously, Finn. This doesn't make any sense. You should be a ruler, not me. I don't know anything, but you're all set to go."

"I'll never be a ruler." Finn shook his head. "And you are right for the job. You just haven't had the training that I've had."

"That's stupid," I grumbled. "It should be based on your abilities, not lineage."

"It *is* based on abilities," Finn insisted. "They just happen to come with lineage."

"What are you talking about?" I asked, and he shut the book on his lap.

"Your persuasion? That comes from your mother," Finn elaborated. "The Markis and Marksinna are what they are because of the abilities they have, and they are passed down through their children. Regular Trylle have some abilities, but they've faded with time. Your mother is one of the most powerful Queens we've had in a very long time, and the hope is that you will continue the tradition of power."

"But I can barely do anything!" I sat up. "I have mild persuasion, and you said it wouldn't even work on you!"

"Not yet, no, but it will," Finn corrected me. "Once you start your training, it will make more sense to you."

"Training? What training?"

"After the ball this weekend. Then you will begin working on your abilities," Finn said. "Right now your only priority is preparing for the ball. So . . ." He flipped open the book again, but I wasn't ready to go back to studying.

"But *you* have abilities," I countered. "And Elora prefers you to me. I'm sure she'd like it better if you were Prince." I realized sadly that that was true, and I lay back down on the couch.

"I'm sure that isn't true."

"It is too," I said. "What is the deal with you and Elora?

She definitely likes you better than me, and she seems to confide in you."

"Elora doesn't really confide in anyone." Finn fell silent for a moment, and then exhaled. "If I explain this to you, do you promise to get back to studying?"

"Yes!" I answered immediately and looked over at him.

"What I say to you cannot leave this room. Do you understand?" Finn asked gravely, and I nodded, gulping, afraid of what he was going to tell me.

I had been growing more and more preoccupied with Finn and Elora's relationship. She was an attractive older woman, and he was definitely a foxy guy, and I could see her digging her cougar claws into him. That was what I was afraid of, anyway.

"About sixteen years ago, after your father was gone, *my* father came under the employ of your mother. He had retired from tracking, and Elora hired him to guard her and the estate." His eyes darkened and his lips tightened, and my heart raced.

"Elora was in love with my father. No one knew, except for my mother, who is still married to him. Eventually, my mother convinced him to leave. However, Elora remained quite fond of my father and, in turn, rather fond of me." He sighed and continued casually, as if he were talking about the weather. "She has personally requested my services over the years, and because she pays well, I have accepted."

I stared at him, feeling nauseous and nervous. Since his father became involved with my mother after I was born, I could safely assume that we weren't siblings, so at least that was something.

Everything else made it feel rather disturbing, and I wondered if Finn secretly hated me. He had to hate Elora, and he must only be here because of how much she paid him. Then I wondered if he was some kind of glorified gigolo, and I had to fight to keep from vomiting.

"I am not sleeping with her, and she has never made any advances of the sort," Finn clarified, looking at me evenly. "She is fond of me because of her feelings for my father. I don't blame her for what happened between them. It was a long time ago, and my father was the one who had a family to think of, not her."

"Huh." I looked up at the ceiling because it was easier than looking at him.

"I have distressed you. I'm sorry," Finn apologized sincerely. "This is why I was hesitant to say anything to you."

"No, no, I'm fine. Let's just go on," I insisted unconvincingly. "I have a lot to go over and all that."

Finn remained silent for a minute, letting me absorb what he had just told me, but I tried to push it from my mind as quickly as possible. Thinking about it made me feel dirty, and I already had too much on my mind.

Eventually Finn continued on with the texts, and I tried harder to pay attention. If I was thinking about what exactly a Queen's job entailed, I wasn't thinking about my mother crushing on his father.

Frederique Von Ellsin, the dress designer, came over the next day. He was excited and flamboyant, and I couldn't tell for sure whether or not he was Trylle. I wore only a slip as he took my measurements and sketched like mad in a notepad. Finally, he declared that he had the perfect gown in mind, and he dashed out of my room to get working on it.

All day long there was an irritating succession of people. They were all staff of some kind, like caterers and party planners, so most of them ignored me. They just trailed after Elora as she rattled off an inconceivable amount of information about what she expected them to do, and they all scurried to write it down or punch it into their BlackBerrys.

Meanwhile, I had the pleasure of camping out in my sweats all day. Whenever Elora saw me, she glared at my apparel with disgust, but she was always too busy making demands on somebody else to complain about me.

Everything that I managed to overhear only made my coming-out festivities sound even more terrifying. The most horrific thing I heard as she zipped by: "We'll need seating for at least five hundred." Five hundred people were going to be at a party where I would be the center of attention? Splendid.

The only upside of the day was that I got to spend the entire thing with Finn. But that became less enjoyable because Finn refused to talk about anything that wasn't related to my performance at the party.

We spent two hours going over the names and pictures of the more prominent guests. Two whole hours spent poring over a yearbook-type thing trying to memorize the faces, names, and notable facts of about a hundred people.

Then there was the hour and a half spent at the dinner table. Apparently I did not know how to eat properly. There were certain ways to hold the fork, tilt the bowl, lift the glass, and even place the napkin. Up until that time I had never mastered any of those skills, and from what I gathered about the way Finn regarded me, I still hadn't.

Eventually I gave up. Pushing my plate back, I laid my head down and pressed my cheek against the cold wood of the table.

"Oh, my God, has he killed you?" Willa asked, sounding appalled.

I lifted my head to see her standing at the end of the dining room table, hands on her fashionable hips. She wore too much jewelry, her necklaces and bracelets overly adorned and jangly, but perhaps that was part of being a troll. They all seemed to have a fondness for trinkets, something I had somehow missed, other than my obsession with my thumb ring.

"He bored me to death too." Willa smiled at me, and I couldn't believe I felt relieved to see her. No way would she try to drill me about the names of the past three hundred monarchs.

"And yet you look as alive as ever," Finn said dryly, leaning back in his chair. "Perhaps I didn't try hard enough with you."

"Is that some kind of burn, *stork*?" Willa pulled back her lip in some kind of snide grimace, but she didn't completely pull it off.

"If you're feeling a burn, I suggest you look to your former sexual partners." Finn gave her a small smile, and I gaped at him. I'd never heard him speak like that to anyone before.

"Funny." Willa tried to keep a straight face, but I got the impression she was amused. "Anyway, I'm here to rescue the Princess."

"Really?" I asked a little too brightly. "Rescue me how?"

"Fun stuff." She shrugged in a cute way, and I looked to Finn to see if I could leave.

"Go." He waved vaguely at me. "You've worked hard and you need a break."

I didn't think I'd ever be happy to get away from Finn, but I nearly scampered after Willa. She looped her arm through mine, leading me away from the dining room and toward my room. I instantly felt bad about leaving Finn, but I couldn't take another lecture on silverware.

Willa chatted with me the whole way to my room in one endless stream of commentary about how dreadful her first few weeks were. She'd been certain that Finn would stab her with a fork before they even made it through the dining service, or vice versa.

"This is the worst part," she said solemnly as we walked into my bedroom. "The whole boot camp before the ball." She wrinkled her nose. "It's *horrid.*"

"Yeah, I'm not enjoying it," I admitted tiredly.

"But I made it through, so you'll definitely make it through." She walked into my bathroom, and when I didn't follow, she looked back at me. "Are you coming?"

"To the bathroom with you?"

"To practice hairstyles." She gave me a *duh* look, and reluctantly I walked in after her. Out of the frying pan and into the fire.

"Hairstyles?" I asked as Willa ushered me over to the stool in front of the vanity.

"Yeah, for the ball." She sifted through the hair products on the counter and stopped, meeting my eyes in the mirror. "Unless your mother is going to help you with it."

"Not that I know of." I shook my head.

"She's definitely not the nurturing type," Willa agreed, somewhat sadly. Picking a bottle of something and a brush, she turned to me. "Do you want your hair up or down?"

"I don't know." I thought back to when I'd first met Willa, and Finn had told me to wear it down. "Down. I guess."

"Good choice." She smiled and pulled out my hair tie, painfully taking my hair down. "So, did Frederique come today?"

"Uh, yeah, a few hours ago," I said between gritted teeth as she raked a comb through my hair.

"Excellent," Willa said. "When you have your fitting, you should take a picture and send it to me. I'd love to see what it looks like."

"Yeah, sure thing."

"I know how ridiculous and confusing everything is at first." Willa teased and primped my hair, all the while chatting happily. "And Finn knows pretty much everything, but he can be a little . . . cold, at times. And I'm sure the Queen isn't much better."

"Not really," I admitted. But cold wouldn't be how I described Finn. Sometimes he was standoffish, but other times, when he looked at me just so, he was anything but cold.

"I'm just letting you know that I wanna help you." She stopped pulling at my hair long enough to meet my eyes in the mirror again. "And not like that backstabbing bitch Aurora

Kroner, or because my father told me to, although he did. Or even like Finn because it's his job. I just know what it's like to be you. And if I can help, I want to."

She gave me a crooked smile, and the sincerity in it startled me. Underneath her vapid pretense, she was actually a kind person. So few people here seemed to genuinely care about anyone else, and it was nice to have finally found one.

Immediately after that moment, Willa launched into a lengthy monologue about gowns. She could describe every gown she'd seen since coming to Förening three years ago, and she only liked one or two of them.

So my training with Willa didn't turn out to be that much more interesting than that with Finn. She had a lot more gossip, about who dated whom and who was engaged and all that. But since I didn't know who any of the people were, it wasn't that interesting.

Willa was thus far single, and it didn't sit well with her. She kept saying that her father needed to arrange something, and mentioned a few guys she'd had her eye on who'd slipped by. She spoke very fondly of Tove Kroner. Although she did point out that by missing out on him, she'd also miss out on a monster of a mother-in-law.

Still, by the end of the day I had a hairstyle picked out, a makeup "plan" in order, and I felt like I knew a little bit more about Trylle royalty. She made it all sound a lot like high school, which would've been comforting, except I hadn't done that well at high school.

SIXTEEN

further instruction

They had taken an interest in me, and I knew I should feel flattered, but I wished they'd just left me alone. Elora and Aurora Kroner stood on the opposite side of the table. A seating chart stretched across the giant oak surface, and they both leaned over it, staring with intense scrutiny.

I had a feeling Elora had just dragged me with her because misery loves company. As for Aurora, I didn't really get why she was interested in me. The best I could figure was that she hoped to understand me in order to bring about my demise. The too-big way she smiled at me kept making me want to cringe.

Finn had snuck into my room early in the morning, and my initial excitement faded when I saw how frantically he picked out my clothes. He instructed me to get ready with lightning speed and to be on my best behavior all day. I hated the way he treated me like I was five and it was my first day of kinder-garten.

But sitting there, watching them analyze every minute detail of a flippin' seating chart, I really felt like a five-year-old. One who had gotten in trouble and had to sit in a very agonizing time-out. I tried to look studious and interested in all of this, but I didn't know any of these people.

We were in the War Room in the south wing where walls were plastered with maps. Red and green patches speckled all of them, indicating other tribes of trolls. I'd been trying to study them while Elora and Aurora talked, but Elora kept snapping my attention back every time it wandered.

"If we put the Chancellor here, then Markis Tormann will have to move from this table entirely." Aurora tapped the paper.

"I don't see another way around it." Elora smiled as sweetly as she could manage, and Aurora matched it perfectly.

"He's traveling a great distance to be here for this." Aurora batted her eyes at Elora.

"He'll still be near enough where he can hear the christening," Elora said and turned her attention to me. "Are you ready for the christening ceremony?"

"Um, yeah," I said. Finn had mentioned it to me, but I hadn't been paying that much attention. I couldn't say that to Elora, though, so I just smiled and tried to look confident.

"A Princess doesn't say 'um.'" Elora narrowed her eyes at me, and Aurora did a poor job of trying to mask a snicker.

I sighed. "Sorry."

Elora looked like she wanted to chastise me further, but Aurora watched us both like a hawk. Elora pursed her lips, biting her tongue so she wouldn't show any sign of weakness.

I didn't understand what Aurora was doing here or what Elora had to fear from her. She was the Queen, and as far as I could tell, Aurora's only ability seemed to be making backhanded compliments and veiled threats.

The Marksinna looked radiant, wearing a long burgundy gown that made me feel incredibly underdressed in a simple skirt. Aurora's beauty nearly overshadowed Elora's, and that was really saying something, but I don't think that kind of thing mattered to Elora.

"Perhaps you should continue your training elsewhere," Elora suggested, glaring at me.

"Yes. Excellent idea." I jumped to my feet so quickly I almost knocked the chair over behind me. Aurora's amused expression changed to downright disgust, and Elora rolled her eyes. "Sorry. I'm very excited about all of this."

"Contain yourself, Princess."

Using restraint, I left the room as calmly as I could. I wanted to rush out, feeling much like a kid on the last day of school. I wasn't sure that I knew my way back, and I had no idea where Finn was, but as soon as I thought it was safe, I picked up my pace, nearly jogging away.

I'd made it a little ways down the hall, past several closed doors, when somebody stopped me.

"Princess!" a voice called from one of the few open doors.

I stopped, tentatively peering inside the room. It appeared to be more of a den, with a lush red rug in the center surrounded by leather chairs. One wall was made of glass, but the shades had been pulled shut over most of it, leaving the room in shadows.

A heavy mahogany bar sat in the corner, and a man leaned in front of it, holding a glass in his hand. I squinted, trying to get a better look at him. His hair looked disheveled, and he was dressed nice but casual.

"Don't you recognize me, Princess?" He had a smile in his voice, so I thought he might be teasing.

"It's just hard to see," I said, stepping into the room.

"Garrett Strom. Willa's father," he told me, and I could see his grin widening.

"Oh, right. It's good to see you." I smiled back, feeling more at ease. I'd only met him at dinner the other night, but I liked him. "Can I help you with something?"

"Nope. I'm just waiting for your mother, but I'm assuming it'll be a long day, so I got a jump start." Garrett motioned to the drink in his hand.

"Nice."

"Do you want something to drink?" Garrett offered. "I'm sure you need one, with Elora putting you through your paces."

I chewed my lip, thinking. I'd never drank before, other than a glass of wine with dinner, but after the last few days I definitely could use something to take the edge off. However, Elora would kill me if she found out, and Finn would be more than disappointed in me.

"No, I'm good." I shook my head. "Thanks, though."

"Don't thank me. It's your liquor," he pointed out. "You do look worn out. Why don't you take a load off?"

"All right." I shrugged and sat down in one of the chairs. The leather may have looked distressed, but the chair had the hard buoyancy of being brand-new. I moved around, trying to get comfortable, before eventually giving up.

"What is she having you do?" Garrett asked, sitting down across from me.

"I don't know. She's making a seating chart." I leaned my head against the back of the chair. "I don't even know why she wanted me there, except to point out what I was doing wrong."

"She just wants you to feel included in all of this," Garrett said between sips of his drink.

"Well, I'd rather not be included," I muttered. "Between her and Aurora giving me icy glares and judging everything I say and do, I'm perfectly happy to be left out."

"Don't let her get to you," Garrett advised.

"Which one?"

"Both," he said with a laugh.

"Sorry. I don't mean to dump on you."

"Don't be sorry." He shook his head. "I know how hard this can be, and I'm sure Elora isn't making it any easier on you."

"She expects me to know everything and be perfect already, and I haven't been here that long."

"You're strong-willed. You get that from her, you know." Garrett smiled. "And as strange as it sounds, everything she's doing—it's to protect you."

It was the first time anyone had drawn any kind of comparison between Elora and me, and it warmed me in a weird way. I realized that he was one of very few people I'd met who called her "Elora" instead of "Queen," and I wondered exactly how well he knew her.

"Thanks," I said, unsure what else to say.

"I heard Willa visited you last night." His eyes settled on me. My vision had adjusted to the darkness of the room, and I could see the softness in his gaze.

"Yeah, she did. She's been very helpful."

"Good. I'm glad to hear it." Garrett looked relieved at that, and I wondered what he'd been expecting me to say. "I know she can be a little"—he wagged his head, searching for the right word—"*Willa* at times, but she means well."

"Yeah, Finn filled me in."

"I've been working on her to lighten up on the mänks. But it's a work in progress."

"Why is she so hard on Rhiannon?" I hadn't seen Willa talk to her much, but what little she said had been filled with jabs and snide remarks, even worse than Aurora's.

"Rhiannon got to live with me nineteen years before Willa did," Garrett explained. "Willa's always been secretly afraid that I preferred Rhiannon over her, but the fact is, while I love Rhiannon, I only have one daughter."

I had never thought about him loving Rhiannon, or anyone loving the mänsklig left behind. I looked in the direction of the War Room, as if I could see Elora through the wall. I couldn't imagine her loving anyone.

But the only babies among the Trylle elite were mänsklig, and at some point parental instincts had to take over. Certainly not with everyone, but it made sense that some, like Garrett, would feel as if the child they raised was their own.

"Do you think Elora loves Rhys?" I asked.

"I think Elora is an incredibly hard woman to get close to," Garrett allowed carefully, then he smiled at me. "I know she loves you, though."

"Yeah, I can tell," I said dryly, unwilling to even consider what he'd said, let alone believe it. I'd been burned by enough crazy moms already.

"She speaks very fondly of you. When you're not around, of course." He gave a small chuckle. Something about the way he said that, I felt a sense of intimacy in it.

An image flashed before me. Elora sitting at her vanity, wearing a robe, and putting on jewelry. Garrett was behind her, still lying in her bed with the sheets covering him. She made some offhand comment about me being prettier than she expected, and before he could agree, she told him he needed to hurry and get dressed.

I shook my head, clearing it of the thought.

"Are you dating Elora?" I asked directly, even though I already knew the answer.

"I definitely wouldn't call it dating," he scoffed and took a long drink. "Let me put it this way: I'm about as close to her as anyone can get. Well, at least anyone can get *now*."

"'Now'?" I furrowed my brow. "What do you mean by that?"

"Elora wasn't always the cool, collected Queen you know

and fear." There was a bitter edge to his words, and I wondered how long he'd been seeing her. Had it been while she
was married to my father? Or when she was in love with Finn's
father?

"What made her change?" I asked.

"The same thing that makes everyone change: experience."
He turned his glass in his hands, admiring what little liquor
he had left.

"What happened to my father?"

"You're really digging deep, aren't you?" Garrett cocked an
eyebrow at me. "I do not have enough alcohol for this conversation." He knocked back the rest in one swallow.

"Why? What happened?" I pressed, leaning forward in my
chair.

"It was a very long time ago." He took a deep breath, still
looking down. "And Elora was devastated."

"She really loved him, then?" I still found it weird to think
that she'd ever loved anyone. She didn't seem capable of any
emotion deeper than anger.

"I honestly don't know. I didn't know her that well back
then." Garrett abruptly got up from his chair and walked over
to the bar. "My wife was still alive, and we only had a casual
acquaintance with the Queen." He poured himself another
drink, keeping his back to me. "If you want to know more
about all of this, you'll have to talk to Elora."

"She won't tell me anything." I sighed and leaned back in
the chair.

"Some things are better forgotten," Garrett mused. He

took a long drink, still keeping his back to me, and I realized belatedly that I'd upset him.

"Sorry." I stood up. I didn't know how to correct the situation, so I thought leaving might be the best way to fix it.

He shook his head. "No need to be sorry."

"I should get back, anyway." I edged toward the door. "Finn is probably looking for me by now."

Garrett nodded. "Probably." I'd almost made it out the door when he stopped me. "Princess?" He turned his head to the side, so shadows darkened his profile. "Elora's hard on you because she's afraid to care about you. But she'll fight to the death for you."

"Thanks," I mumbled.

The light in the hallway felt too bright after the dimness of the den. I didn't know what I'd said that had upset Garrett so much. Maybe bringing up memories of his dead wife. Or maybe reminding him that while Elora couldn't openly care for him now, she had cared once, for another man.

I tried to push away the confusion Garrett had made me feel. I wasn't sure if I could trust the things he'd said about Elora. I didn't think he was a liar, but he'd wanted to make me feel better. Convincing me that I had a mother who actually loved me probably would help, but I had long since stopped holding out for that dream.

I found Finn in the front hall, directing several of Elora's aides with the planning for the ball. He had his back to me, so he didn't notice me right away. I stood there for a moment, just watching him direct and take control. He knew exactly what do with everything, and I couldn't help but admire him for it.

"Princess." Finn caught sight of me when he glanced over his shoulder, then he turned fully to me with a smile. An aide asked him something, and he gestured vaguely to the dining hall before walking over to me. "How did this morning go?"

I shrugged. "It could've been worse."

"That doesn't sound promising." He raised an eyebrow. "But I suppose you've earned a bit of a reprieve."

"A reprieve?" It was my turn to look skeptical.

"Yeah, I thought we'd do something fun for a while." Finn smiled.

"Fun?" I remembered yesterday, how he'd tried to convince me his mind-numbing training had been fun. "Do you mean fun fun? Or do you mean looking at pictures for two hours fun? Or Using a Fork 101 fun?"

"Something that at least resembles actual fun," Finn answered. "Come on."

SEVENTEEN

jealousy

As Finn led me down a hall to the south wing, I realized that I'd never seen any of this before. When Garrett had teased Elora about this being a palace, he wasn't kidding. There were so many places I had yet to see. It was astounding.

Finn gestured to a few rooms, pointing out the library, meeting halls where business was conducted, the opulent dining hall where we would hold the dinner on Saturday, and then, finally, the ballroom.

Pushing open the doors, which seemed to be two stories high, Finn led me into the grandest room I had ever seen. Massive and exquisite, the ceiling seemed to stretch on forever, thanks in part to the fact that the entire thing was skylight. Gold beams ran across it, holding up glittering diamond chandeliers. The floors were marble, the walls were off-white with gold detailing, and it looked every bit the ballroom from a Disney fairy tale.

The decorators had started bringing things in, and stacked chairs and tables now leaned against one of the walls. Tablecloths, candlesticks, and all sorts of decorations were piled around them. The only other thing in the room was a white grand piano sitting in the opposite corner. Otherwise the room was empty except for Finn and me.

I hated how taken I was with the splendor. I hated even more that the room was so magnificent and I looked like I did. My hair was in a messy bun, and my skirt felt far too plain. Finn wasn't exactly dressed to the nines either, but his standard button-down shirt and dark wash jeans looked much more fitting.

"So what's the fun part?" I asked, and my voice echoed off the walls.

"Dancing." Finn's lip twitched with a smile, and I groaned. "I've danced with you before, and I know that it needs some improvement."

"The slow circles don't cut it?" I grimaced.

"Unfortunately, no. A proper waltz should be enough, though. If you can master that, you'll be set for the ball on Saturday."

"Oh, no." My stomach dropped as I realized something. "I'm going to have to dance with these people, aren't I? Like strangers and old men and weird handsy boys?" Finn laughed at that, but I wanted to curl up in a ball and die.

"I could lie to you, but to be honest, those are probably the only people who will ask you to dance," Finn admitted with a wry smirk.

"You're enjoying this more than I've ever seen you enjoy anything," I said, and that only deepened his smile. "Well, I'm glad you find this funny. Me being felt up by complete strangers and tripping all over them. What a great time."

"It won't be so bad." He motioned for me to come over. "If you learn the basic steps, at least you won't be tripping over them."

I sighed loudly and walked over to him. Most of my trepidation about dancing with strangers melted away the instant Finn took my hand in his. It suddenly occurred to me that before I had to dance with them, I got to dance with *him*.

After a few directions from him and a rough start by me, we were dancing. His arm was around me, strong and reassuring. He instructed me to keep my eyes locked on his so I wouldn't get in the habit of watching my feet while I danced, but I wouldn't have looked anywhere else anyway. His dark eyes always mesmerized me.

We were supposed to keep a certain distance between our bodies, but I found it impossible. His body nearly pressed against mine, and I delighted in the sensation. I was certain we weren't going as fast as we should, but I didn't care. This moment with him seemed entirely too perfect to be real.

"Right, okay." Finn suddenly stopped and took a step away from me. Disappointed, I let my hands fall to the side. "You've got that down pretty well, but there's going to be music. So you should see how you do with that."

"Okay?" I said unsurely.

"Why don't I play the piano, and you count out the steps

yourself?" Finn had already started backing away to the piano, and I wondered what I had done wrong that made him stop so suddenly. "That might be a better way for you to learn."

"Um, okay." I shrugged uncertainly. "I thought I was doing fine before."

"We weren't going fast enough. The music will help you keep time."

I frowned at him, wishing he would just come back and dance with me. I remembered how he once told me I was a terrible dance partner, and wondered if maybe that was the problem.

He sat down at the piano and started playing a beautiful, elaborate waltz. Of course he could play. He could do anything. I just stood there staring at him, until he directed me to start dancing.

I whirled around on the dance floor, but it definitely wasn't as fun as it had been with him. In fact, it wasn't really that fun at all. It might have been if I weren't trying to figure out what I did wrong that always made Finn back away from me.

It was hard to concentrate on that, though, when Finn kept barking out corrections at me. Funny, he hadn't noticed any of my mistakes when we had been dancing together.

"Nope, that's it," I panted after what felt like an eternity.

My feet and legs were getting sore, and a sheen of sweat covered my body. I had had my fill of dancing for the day. I sat down heavily on the floor, then leaned back, sprawling out on the cool marble.

"Wendy, it hasn't even been that long," Finn insisted.

"Don't care. I'm out!" I breathed deeply and wiped the sweat from my forehead.

"Haven't you ever worked at anything?" Finn complained. He got up from the piano bench and walked over to me so he could lecture me up close. "This is important."

"I'm aware. You tell me every second of every day."

"I do not." Finn crossed his arms and looked down at me.

"This is the hardest I've ever worked at anything," I said, staring back up at him. "Everything else I've quit before this, or I never even tried. So don't tell me I'm not putting effort into this."

"You've never tried harder than this? At anything?" Finn asked incredulously, and I shook my head. "That brother you had never made you do anything?"

"Not really," I admitted thoughtfully. "He made me go to school, I guess. But that's about it." Matt and Maggie encouraged me to do many things, but there was very little they actually made me do.

"They spoiled you more than I thought." Finn looked surprised at that.

"They didn't spoil me." I sighed, then quickly amended, "They didn't spoil me rotten. Not the way Willa was spoiled, and I'm sure a lot of the other changelings were. They just wanted me to be happy."

"Happiness is something you work for," Finn pointed out.

"Oh, stop with that fortune-cookie crap," I scoffed. "We worked for it just like anybody else. They were just really careful with me, probably because my mom tried to kill me. It set them up to treat me more gently than they would've otherwise."

"How did your mother try to kill you?" Finn asked, startling me. I hadn't told him much about it, but he rarely wanted to talk about my past.

"It was my birthday, and I was being my usual bratty self. I was angry because she'd gotten me a chocolate cake, and I hated it," I said. "We were in the kitchen, and she snapped. She started chasing after me with this giant knife. She called me a monster, and then she tried to stab me but she just managed to cut my stomach pretty badly. Then my brother Matt rushed in and tackled her, saving my life."

"She cut open your stomach?" Finn furrowed his brow with concern.

"Yeah." I pulled up my shirt, revealing the scar that stretched across it.

Immediately after I'd done that, I regretted it. Lying on the floor and flashing Finn the fattest part of my body did not seem like a good idea.

Finn crouched on the floor next to me, and tentatively his fingertips traced along the mark etched on my belly. My skin quivered underneath his touch, and nervous warmth spread through me. He continued to stare intently at the scar, then he laid his hand flat on my belly, covering it. His skin felt hot and smooth, and inside, my stomach trembled with butterflies.

He blinked and, seeming to realize what he was doing, he pulled his hand back and got to his feet. Quickly I pulled my shirt back down. I didn't even feel that comfortable lying down anymore, so I sat up and fixed my bun.

"Matt saved your life?" Finn asked, filling that semi-awkward silence that had shrouded us. He still had a contemplative look on his face, and I wished I knew what he was thinking.

"Yeah." I got to my feet. "Matt always protected me, ever since I could remember."

"Hmm." Finn looked thoughtfully at me. "You bonded so much more with your host family than the changelings normally do."

"'Host family'?" I grimaced. "You make me sound like a parasite."

Then I realized that I probably was. They had dropped me off with the Everlys so I would use their resources, their money, their opportunities, and bring them back here. That's exactly what a parasite did.

"You're not a parasite," Finn said. "They loved you, and you genuinely loved them in return. It is unusual, but that's not a bad thing. In fact, it's a very good thing. Maybe it's given you a compassion that Trylle leaders have been lacking for a very long time."

"I don't think I'm very compassionate." I shook my head.

"I see how it bothers you the way Elora talks to people. Elora thinks the only way to command respect is to command fear, but I have a feeling that you will have an entirely different way of ruling."

"And how will I rule?" I arched my eyebrow at him.

"That is for you to decide," Finn said simply.

He ended our lesson after that, saying I needed to rest up for tomorrow. The day had exhausted me, and I was eager to curl up in my blankets and sleep until Sunday, straight through the ball and all the angst that accompanied it.

Sleep didn't come easy, though. I found myself tossing and turning, thinking about the way it felt dancing with Finn, and his hand resting warmly on my stomach.

But I would always end up thinking of Matt and how much I still missed him. I had expected that to lessen the longer I was here, but it only seemed to get worse. After all this, I really needed to know that someone had my back and cared about me unconditionally.

I woke up early the next morning. Actually, I'd been waking up all night long, and at six I finally just gave up. I got up with the intention of sneaking downstairs to grab a bite to eat, but when I hit the top of the stairs, Rhys came barreling up them to meet me, chomping on a bagel.

"Hey, what are you doing up?" He grinned, swallowing down his bite.

"Couldn't sleep." I shrugged. "You?"

"Same. I have to get ready for school soon anyway." He pushed his hair out of his eyes and leaned back against the stair railing. "Are you worrying about this Saturday?"

"Kind of," I admitted.

"It is pretty intense," Rhys said, his eyes wide. I nodded

noncommittally. "Is something else bothering you? You look pretty . . . upset, I guess."

"No." I shook my head and sighed, then sat down on the top step. I didn't feel much like standing anymore, and I wanted to cry. "I was just thinking about my brother."

"Your brother?" Something flashed across Rhys's face, and slowly he sat down next to me. He seemed almost breathless. At first I didn't understand, but then it dawned on me.

This must be so weird for Rhys. His whole life he had known that this wasn't his real family, and it wasn't even the same as being adopted. His family hadn't wanted to give him up. He had been stolen, and not even by a family that had wanted him. They had just wanted me to have his life.

"Yeah. I mean . . . *your* brother, actually," I corrected myself, and it felt painful saying that. Matt would always be my brother, no matter what our genetics were.

"What's his name?" Rhys asked quietly.

"Matt. He's pretty much the nicest guy in the whole world."

"Matt?" Rhys repeated in an awed tone.

"Yeah." I nodded. "He's the bravest guy ever. He would do anything to protect the people he cares about, and he's completely selfless. He always puts everybody else first. And he's really, really strong. He's . . ." I swallowed and decided that I couldn't talk about him anymore. I shook my head and looked away.

"What about my mom and dad?" Rhys pressed, and I didn't know how to answer that.

"Dad died when I was five," I said carefully. "My mother took it pretty hard, and, um . . . she's been in the hospital ever since. For psychiatric problems. Matt and my dad's sister, Maggie, they raised me."

"Oh." His face contorted with concern.

I suddenly hated Kim even more. I knew that she had done everything because she loved Rhys, but that didn't make her actions any less inexcusable. I didn't have it in me to tell him what she'd done or that she'd never be able to have a life with him because she'd always be locked up.

"I'm sorry." I placed my hand gently on his, to comfort him. "It's hard to explain how I know it, but your mom really loved you. She really wanted you. And I think she always hated me because she knew I wasn't you."

"Really?" There was something hopeful and sad in his eyes when he looked at me.

"Yeah. It kind of sucked for me, actually." I smiled wanly at him, and he laughed.

"Sorry about that." Rhys smiled back at me. "I guess I'm too hard to forget."

"Yeah, I guess you are," I agreed. Rhys moved his hand so it was actually holding mine.

"So what about this Maggie? What's she like?" Rhys asked.

"She's pretty cool. A little overly attentive sometimes, but cool," I said. "She put up with a lot of crap from me. They both did, really." I thought about how strange this all was, that they weren't my family anymore. "This is so weird. They're your brother and your aunt."

"No, I understand. They're your family too," Rhys said. "They loved you and raised you. That's what family is, right?"

I had needed someone to say that to me for so long, and I squeezed his hand gratefully. I still loved them and always would, and I just needed that to be okay.

"Wendy!" Finn came down the hall, still dressed in his pajamas. Instinctively I pulled my hand back, and Rhys stood up. "What are you doing?"

"I just woke up. We were just talking." I looked up at Rhys, who nodded in agreement.

Finn glared at us both, and I felt like we'd just been caught robbing a bank.

"I suggest you get ready for school," he said icily.

"Yeah, that's what I was doing anyway," Rhys said, then smiled down at me. "I'll see you later, Wendy."

"Yeah, okay." I smiled back at him.

"What are you doing?" Finn hissed, glowering down at me.

"I already told you," I insisted and stood up. "We were just talking."

"About what?" Finn asked.

"My family." I shrugged. "What does it matter?"

"You cannot talk to him about your host family," Finn said. "Mänsklig cannot know where they come from. If they did, they would be tempted to track down their families, and that would completely ruin our entire society. Do you understand that?"

"I didn't really tell him anything!" I said, but I felt stupid that that hadn't occurred to me. "I missed Matt, and I just said stuff about how neat he was. I didn't tell Rhys where he lived or anything like that."

"You have to be more careful, Wendy."

"Sorry. I didn't know." I didn't like the way he was glaring at me, so I turned and started walking down the hall toward my room.

"Wait." Finn grabbed my arm gently so I would stop and look at him.

He took a step closer to me so he was right in front of me, but I was trying to be mad at him, so I refused to look at him. I could still feel his eyes on me and the heat from his body, and it did little to help me maintain my anger.

"What?" I asked.

Finn lowered his voice. "I saw you holding his hand."

"So?" I said. "Is that a crime?"

"No, but . . . you *can't* do that. You cannot get involved with a mänsklig."

"Whatever." I pulled my arm from his grip, irritated that the only thing he ever thought about was his job. "You're just jealous."

"I am not jealous." Finn took a step back from me. "I am watching out for your well-being. You don't understand how dangerous it would be to get involved with him."

"Yeah, yeah," I muttered and started walking back to my room. "I don't understand anything."

"That's not what I said." Finn followed me.

"But it's true, isn't it?" I countered. "I don't know anything."

"Wendy!" Finn snapped, and grudgingly, I turned back to

look at him. "If you don't understand things, it's because I didn't explain them well enough."

He swallowed hard and looked down at the floor, his dark eyelashes falling on his cheeks. There was something more that he wanted to say to me, so I crossed my arms, waiting.

"But you were right." He was clearly struggling with the words, and I watched him carefully. "I was jealous."

"What?" My jaw fell open, and my eyes widened with surprise.

"That does not affect the job I have to do, nor does it change the fact that you absolutely cannot become involved with a mänsklig," Finn said firmly, still looking at the floor instead of at me. "Now go get ready. We have another long day ahead of us." He turned around and started to walk away.

"Wait, Finn!" I called after him, and he paused, half looking back at me.

"The matter is not open for discussion," he replied coolly. "I promised I would never lie to you, so I didn't."

I stood in front of my bedroom door, reeling from his confession. For the first time, he had actually admitted that at least some of his feelings for me had nothing to do with the job at hand. Yet somehow I was supposed to forget all that and go about as if everything were normal.

EIGHTEEN

intimidation

I spent a long time getting ready, still making sense of what Finn had told me. It thrilled me that he cared enough to feel jealous, but I also realized how pointless it was. He'd never do anything that conflicted with his sense of honor and duty.

Even with me taking so much time, Finn never came to get me. Eventually, I perched at the top of the spiral staircase to wait for him. I thought about going down to his room, but I didn't really feel comfortable with that. Besides, he'd probably send me away.

From the top of the stairs, I watched in surprise as Tove Kroner pushed open the front door. He hadn't knocked or anything, and he raked a hand through his messy hair, looking around.

"Can I help you?" I called down. As Princess, I felt like I ought to be hospitable, even if I felt flustered and confused as hell.

"Uh, yeah. I'm looking for you." He shoved his hands in his pockets and walked to the bottom of the steps, but didn't go any farther.

"What for?" I wrinkled my nose, then, realizing I'd sounded rude, shook my head. "I mean, I beg your pardon?"

"Just to help." Tove shrugged.

I walked slowly down the stairs, watching his eyes search the room. He never did seem comfortable looking at me.

As I approached him, I took in the soft natural highlights coursing through his dark hair. It was long and unruly, hitting just above his shoulders.

His tanned skin had a subtle mossy undertone, the green complexion that Finn had told me about. Nobody else had skin like that, except maybe his mother, but hers was fainter than Tove's.

"Help me with what?" I asked.

"What?" He'd taken to chewing on his thumbnail. He glanced up at me, still biting it.

"What are you here to help me with?" I spoke slowly and carefully, my tone bordering on condescending, but I don't think he noticed.

"Oh." He dropped his hand and stared off, as if he'd forgotten why he'd come. "I'm psychic."

"What? You can read minds?" I tensed up, trying to block him from reading any of my thoughts.

"No, no, of course not." He brushed me off and walked away, admiring the chandelier hanging from the ceiling. "I can sense things. And I can move things with my mind. But I can't read your thoughts. I can see auras, though. Yours is a bit brown today."

"What does that mean?" I crossed my arms over my chest, as if I could hide my aura that way. I didn't even really know what an aura was.

"You're unhappy." Tove sounded distracted, and he glanced back at me. "Normally it's orange."

"I don't know what that means either." I shook my head. "I don't know how any of this is supposed to help me."

"It's not really." He stopped moving and looked up at me. "Has Finn talked to you about training?"

"You mean the Princess training I'm doing now?"

"No." He shook his head, chewing the inside of his cheek. "For your abilities. It won't start until after the christening. They think if you had any handle on them *before* you were indoctrinated, you'd run wild." He sighed. "They want you calm and docile."

"This is you calm?" I raised a skeptical eyebrow.

"No." Tove stared off at nothing again, then turned back to me, his green eyes meeting mine. "You intimidate me."

"*I* intimidate you?" I laughed, unable to stop myself, but he wasn't offended. "I'm the least intimidating person ever."

"Mmm." His face hardened in concentration. "Maybe to some people. But they don't see what I see or know what I know."

"What do you know?" I asked gently, startled by his confession.

"Have they told you?" Tove eyed me again.

"Told me what?"

"Well, if they haven't told you, I'm certainly not going to." He scratched at his arm and turned his back to me, walking away and looking around the room again.

"Whatever it is you're doing, it's not helping," I said, growing frazzled. "You're only confusing me more."

"My apologies, Princess." Tove stopped moving and bowed at me. "Finn wanted me to talk to you about your abilities. He knows you can't start your real training until after the ball, but he wants you to be prepared."

"Finn asked you to come over?" My heart thumped in my chest.

"Yes." His brow creased with confusion. "Does this upset you?"

"No, not at all," I lied. Finn had probably asked Tove over so he wouldn't have to deal with me. He was avoiding me.

"Do you have questions?" Tove stepped closer, and I was once again struck by the subtle green tinge to his skin. On a less attractive guy it might've been creepy. But on him it managed to look strangely exotic.

"Tons," I said with a sigh. He cocked his head at me. "You'll have to be more specific."

"You have nothing to be afraid of, you know." Tove watched me closely, and I think I might've preferred it when he was scared to look at me.

"I'm not afraid." It took effort not to squirm under his gaze.

"I can tell when you lie," he said, still watching me. "Not because I'm psychic, but because you're so obvious about it. You should probably work on that. Elora is very good at lying."

"I'll practice," I muttered.

"That's probably for the best." Tove spoke with an intense sincerity that I found disarming. His disjointed insanity even had its own charm. He looked down at the floor, his expression turning sad. "I rather like you this way. Honest and flustered. But it'd never work for a Queen."

"No, I don't suppose it would," I agreed, feeling a bit melancholy myself.

"I'm a bit scattered too, if you hadn't noticed." He gave me a small, crooked smile, but his green eyes stayed sad. With that, he crouched down, picking up a small oval stone off the floor. He flipped it around in his hand, staring down. "I find it hard to stay focused, but I'm working on it."

"So . . . not to sound mean or anything, but why did Finn want *you* to help?" I rubbed my arms, hoping I didn't upset him by asking.

"Because I'm strong." Tove tossed the stone aside, apparently tiring of it. "And he trusts me." He looked back at me. "So let's see what you can do."

"With what?" I asked, confused by the abrupt change of subject.

"Anything." He spread his arms wide. "Can you move stuff?"

"With my hands, yeah."

"Obviously." He rolled his eyes. "You're not a paraplegic, so I assumed you were physically capable."

"I can't do much. Just persuasion, and I haven't used it since I've been here."

"Try." Tove pointed to the chandelier dangling above us. "Move that."

"I don't want to move that," I said, alarmed.

An image flashed in my mind. The painting I had seen in Elora's room, all dark smoke and red fires around broken chandeliers. Except the image in my mind seemed much more vivid, as if I could smell the smoke and see the fire raging, casting new shadows in the painting. The sound of glass shattering echoed in my ear.

I swallowed hard and shook my head, taking several steps back from the chandelier. I hadn't been underneath it exactly, but I wanted to get farther away.

"What was that?" Tove asked, cocking his head at me.

"What?"

"Something happened." He studied me, trying to decipher my reaction, but I just shook my head. It felt like too much to explain, and I wasn't sure that I hadn't imagined it. "Interesting."

"Thanks," I mumbled.

"I hate to do this, since you look so frightened, but I need to get you out of my head." He looked up at the chandelier, and my eyes followed his.

My heart raced in my chest, and my throat felt dry. The crystal shards twinkled and chimed and started to shimmer. I took several steps back, wanting to yell at him to stop, but I didn't even know if he'd listen. Then the whole chandelier started to sway, and I couldn't hold back.

"Stop!" I shouted, my voice echoing through the front hall. "Why are you doing that?"

"I am sorry." He exhaled deeply, and looked back down at me. I kept my eyes locked on the chandelier until I was certain it'd stopped moving. "I had to do something, and there was nothing else in the room I could move, except for you yourself, and I didn't think you'd like that either."

"Why did you have to move anything?" I snapped. My panic had started to fade, replaced by a pulsating anger, and I clenched my fists at my sides.

"When you get frightened like that, you project it so intensely." He held up his hands, pushing them out to demonstrate. "Most people can't hear it or feel it anymore, but I'm particularly sensitive to emotion. And when I move things, it helps focus me. It kinda shuts off the noise for a while. You were too strong. I had to silence it." He shrugged. "I'm sorry."

"You didn't need to freak me out like that." I calmed a bit, but my words still came out hard. "Just don't do that again, please."

"It's such a shame." Tove watched me, looking both bemused and rueful. "They won't even be able to see what you really are. They've all gotten so weak that they won't be able to tell how powerful you are."

"What are you talking about?" I momentarily forgot my anger.

"Your mother is so powerful." Tove sounded almost awed

by it. "Probably not as much as you, and maybe not as much as me, but it's in her blood, crackling like electricity. I feel her walking through a room, and she's almost magnetized. But the rest of them . . ." He shook his head.

"You mean the other Trylle?" I clarified, since Tove insisted on being so cryptic.

"We used to move the earth." He sounded wistful, and his whole demeanor had changed. He was no longer pacing or looking around, and I realized that moving the chandelier really had done something to him.

"Are you speaking literally or metaphorically?" I asked.

"Literally. We could make mountains, stop rivers." He moved his arms dramatically, as if he could do those things now. "We created everything around us! We were magic!"

"Aren't we still magic?" I asked, surprised by the passion in his voice.

"Not the way we were before. Once the humans created their own magic with technology, the dependence switched. They had all the power and the money, and we started to depend on them to raise our children," he scoffed. "Changelings stopped coming back, when they realized we didn't have that much to offer them anymore."

"We came back," I pointed out emptily.

"Your gardener, who makes the flowers bloom, she's a Marksinna!" Tove pointed to the back of the house where the garden lay. "A *gardener*! I'm not one for class, but when one of the most powerful members of your population is the gardener, you know it's a problem."

"Well . . . why is she a gardener, then?" I asked.

"Because. Nobody else can do it." He looked at me, his green eyes burning with something. "Nobody can do anything anymore."

"You can. I can," I said, hoping to alleviate whatever distressed him.

"I know." He sighed and lowered his eyes. "Everyone's just gotten too fixated on the human system of monarchy. With designer dresses and expensive jewels." His lip curled with disgust. "Our obsession with riches has always been our downfall."

"Yeah." I nodded. "But your mother seems to be the worst with it."

"I know." Tove raised his eyebrows with weary acceptance. Something softened, and he looked almost apologetically at me. "I'm not against humans. It sounds like I am, doesn't it?"

"I don't know. It sounds like you're passionate," I said.

When I'd first met him, I'd mistaken his inattention as boredom and arrogance. But I was starting to think his abilities had something to do with it, giving him a kind of power-related ADD. Behind that, he had a fearless honesty that few Trylle seemed to possess.

"Maybe." He smiled and lowered his eyes, looking slightly embarrassed.

"How old are you?" I asked.

"Nineteen. Why?"

"How do you know so much about the past? You talked about the way things were like you were there, like you saw it happen. Or like you're a major history buff or something."

"My mother is keen on me studying, in case I ever get a chance for the throne," Tove said, but the idea seemed to tire him. I doubted he was any more excited about the prospect of ruling than I was. Aurora's scheming for the crown must be entirely her idea.

"What'd you see when you looked at the chandelier?" Tove asked, bringing me back to his reason for being here.

"I don't know." I shook my head. I wanted to answer honestly, but I didn't know how to. "I saw . . . a painting."

"Some people see the future." He stared up at the chandelier, the light twinkling above us. "And some people see the past." He paused, thinking. "In the end, they're not all that different. You can't prevent either of them."

"How profound," I said, and he laughed.

"I haven't helped you at all, have I?"

"I don't know," I admitted.

"You're too much for one afternoon, I'm afraid," Tove said.

"How do you mean?" I asked, but he just shook his head.

"I know you have a lot to go over, and you don't need me wasting your time. I don't know that I can help you much right now." He walked toward the door.

"Hey, wait," I said, and he stopped. "You said that normally they don't want us tapping into our abilities until after the christening. But Finn wanted you to help prepare me now. What for? Is something going on?"

"Finn's a protector. It's his job to worry," Tove explained, and my heart twisted. I hated it when people pointed out that

I was just part of Finn's job. "He needs to know that in any event, you'll be taken care of. Whether he's there or not."

"Why wouldn't he be there?" I asked, feeling fear ripple through me.

"I don't know." Tove shrugged. "But when something really matters to you, you make sure it's safe."

With that, Tove turned and walked out of the house. I was grateful for his help, though I wasn't even sure what he'd done. Other than confuse me more. And now I felt a new sense of dread settling over me.

I had no idea what was going on with Finn, and my thoughts insisted on going back to the painting I'd seen in Elora's secret room. I had been reaching off the balcony, looking horrified. Tove's words echoed through my mind, sending a chill down my spine.

You can't prevent the future.

I looked up at the chandelier. I'd been too terrified to even try to move it, thinking it would collapse and I'd bring Elora's painting into life. But I hadn't, and nothing terrible had come to pass.

Had I changed the future? Or was the worst still to come?

christening

O n Friday, with the party only twenty-four hours away, Elora felt the need to check on my progress, not that I blamed her. Her plan was a dress rehearsal for dinner, testing my ability to converse and eat, apparently.

She didn't want a massive audience to witness my possible failure, so she just invited Garrett, Willa, and Rhiannon over to join her, Finn, Rhys, and me. It was the biggest group she could assemble without risk of embarrassment. Since I had already met these people, I didn't feel all that nervous, even though Elora informed me beforehand that I needed to act the same way I would tomorrow night.

Everyone had been instructed similarly, and they all appeared far more regal than normal. Even Rhys had dressed in a blazer, and he looked rather handsome. As usual, Finn was unnecessarily attractive.

Thanks to Finn's random confession of jealousy, I wasn't

entirely sure how to act around him. He had come into my room before dinner to make sure that I was getting ready, and I couldn't help but feel that he was purposely avoiding looking at me.

When I reached the dining hall, Elora instructed us where to sit, with her at one end of the table and me at the other. Rhys and Finn flanked me, and Rhiannon, Garrett, and Willa, took their places in between.

"Who will I be sitting by tomorrow?" I asked between careful sips of wine.

"Between Tove Kroner and I." Elora narrowed her eyes at the drink in my hand. "Hold the glass by the stem."

"Sorry." I thought I had been, but I moved my fingers, hoping I was holding it more correctly now.

"A Princess never apologizes," Elora corrected me.

"Sorry," I mumbled, then realized what I had just done and shook my head. "That was an accident. It won't happen again."

"Don't shake your head; it's not ladylike," Elora chastised me. "A Princess doesn't make promises either. She might not be able to keep them, and she doesn't want them held against her."

"I wasn't really making a promise," I pointed out, and Elora narrowed her eyes more severely.

"A Princess is never contrary," she said coolly.

"I've only been a Princess for like a week. Can't you give me a little break?" I asked as kindly as I could.

I'd grown frustrated by all the Princess talk. Nearly every

sentence she'd said to me in the past two days had started with "A Princess" and was followed by things that a Princess never or always did.

"You've been a Princess your entire life. It's in your blood." Elora sat up even straighter in her chair, as if she were trying to loom over me. "You should know how to behave."

"I am working on it," I grumbled.

"Speak up. Use a clear strong voice no matter what it is you're saying," Elora snapped. "And you don't have time to work on it. Your party is tomorrow. You must be ready *now*."

I wanted to snap back at her, but both Rhys and Finn were giving me warning stares to keep my mouth shut. Rhiannon stared nervously at her plate, and Garrett just went about munching his food politely.

"I understand." I exhaled deeply and took another drink of my wine. I'm not sure if I held the glass right this time, but Elora didn't say anything.

"So, I got your picture of the dress." Willa smiled at me. "It was really stunning. I'm a little jealous, actually. You only get to be the belle of the ball once, and you definitely will be to-morrow. You're going to look amazing."

She was coming to my aid, changing the subject from things I was doing wrong to something I was doing right. Even if she was a bitch to Finn and Rhiannon, I just couldn't bring my-self to hate her.

"Thank you." I smiled back at her gratefully.

My final fitting had been earlier in the day, and since

Willa had asked me to the other night, I sent her a picture. Finn took it on his camera phone.

I felt very awkward posing for the photo, and it didn't help that he never reassured me that I looked good in the dress. It felt like too much for me to pull off, and I would've liked a little boost just then. But Finn had simply snapped the picture, and that had been the end of that.

"Have you seen the dress?" Willa turned to Elora, who nibbled primly at a piece of broccoli.

"No. I trust Frederique's designs, and Finn has final approval," she answered absently.

"I'm going to insist on being involved in the process when my daughter gets her gown," Willa offered thoughtfully. Elora bristled almost imperceptibly at that, but Willa didn't notice. "But I've always loved dresses and fashion. I could spend my whole life at a ball." She looked wistful for a moment, then smiled at me again. "That's why it's so great that you're here. You're going to have such a monumental ball."

"Thank you," I repeated, unsure how else to respond.

"You had a lovely party yourself," Garrett interjected, slightly defensive about the party he had thrown for his daughter. "Your gown was fantastic."

"I know." Willa beamed immodestly. "It was pretty great." Finn made a noise in his throat, and both Elora and Willa glared at him, but neither of them said anything.

"My apologies. Something caught in my throat," Finn explained, taking a sip of his wine.

"Hmm," Elora murmured disapprovingly, then cast a look

back at me. "Oh, that reminds me. I have been too busy this week to ask you. What were your plans for your name?"

"My name?" I asked, tilting my head to the side.

"Yes. At the christening ceremony." She looked at me for a moment, then turned sternly to Finn. "I thought Finn told you about it."

"Yes, but isn't that name already decided?" I was definitely confused. "I mean, Dahl is the family name, isn't it?"

"Not the surname." Elora rubbed her temples, clearly annoyed. "I meant your first name."

"I don't understand. Why wouldn't my name be Wendy Dahl?"

"That isn't a proper name for a Princess," Elora scoffed. "Everyone changes their names. Willa used to be called something different. What was it, dear?"

"Nikki," Willa said. "I took the name Willa, after my mother."

Garrett smiled at that, and Elora tensed up slightly, then turned her focus back to me.

"So what is it? What name would you like?" Elora pressed, possibly using me to deflect the tension.

"I . . . I don't know."

Irrationally, my heart had started pounding in my chest. I didn't want to change my name, not at all. When Finn had told me that about the christening ceremony, I had assumed it would only be my last name. While I wasn't thrilled about that, I didn't care much. Eventually I would probably get married and change my name anyway.

But Wendy, that was *my* name. I turned to Finn for help, but Elora noticed and snapped my attention back to her.

"If you need ideas, I have some." Elora spoke in a clipped tone, and she was cutting her food with irritated fervor. "Ella, after my mother. I had a sister, Sybilla. Those names are both lovely. One of our longest-running Queens was Lovisa, and I've always thought highly of that name."

"It's not that I don't like any of those," I explained carefully. Although, really, I thought Sybilla was quite terrible. "I like my name. I don't know why I have to change it."

Elora waved off the idea. "Wendy is a ridiculous name. It's entirely improper for a Princess."

"Why?" I persisted, and Elora glared at me.

I flat-out refused to change my name, no matter what Elora said. It's not that I thought Wendy was a particularly fabulous name, but Matt had given it to me. He was one of the only people who had ever wanted me, and I wasn't going to get rid of the one thing that I had left of him.

"It is the name of a mänsklig," Elora said through gritted teeth. "And I have had enough of this. You will find a name to suit a Princess, or I will choose one for you. Is that clear?"

"If I am a Princess, then why can't I decide what is proper?" I forced my voice to stay even and clear, trying not to let it shake with anger and frustration. "Isn't that part of the glory of being a Princess, of ruling a kingdom? Having some say in the rules? And if I want my name to be Wendy, why is that so wrong?"

"No Princess has ever kept her human name, and none

ever will." Her dark eyes glared severely at me, but I met them firmly. "My daughter, the Princess, will not carry the name of a *mänks*."

There was a bitter edge dripping from the word "mänks," and I saw Rhys's jaw tense. I knew what it was like to grow up with a mother who hated me, but I had never been required to sit quietly while she openly made derogatory remarks about me. My heart went out to him, and I had to struggle even harder to keep from shouting at Elora.

"I will not change my name," I insisted. Everyone had taken to looking down at their plates while Elora and I stared each other down. This dinner had to be considered an epic failure.

"This is not the proper place to have this discussion," Elora said icily. She rubbed her temple, then sighed. "It's no matter. There isn't a discussion to be had. Your name will be changed, and clearly I will be picking it for you."

"That's not fair!" Tears welled up in my eyes. "I've done everything you've asked of me. I should at least be able to keep my own name."

"That's not the way things are done," Elora replied. "You will do as I say."

"With all due respect," Finn interrupted, startling every-one. "If it is as the Princess wishes, then perhaps it's as it should be. Her wishes are going to be the highest order of the land, and this is such a simple one that I can't imagine anyone would find offense with it."

"Perhaps." Elora forced a thin smile at him, giving him a hard look, but he stared back at her, his eyes meeting hers unabashedly. "But right now my wishes are still the highest order, and until that has changed, my word will remain final."

Her smile deepened, growing even more menacing as she continued. "With all due respect, *tracker*, perhaps you care too much for her wishes and too little for her duties." His expression faltered momentarily, but he quickly met her eyes again. "Was it not your duty to inform her of the specifics of the christening and have her completely ready for tomorrow?"

"It was," Finn replied without any trace of shame.

"It seems you have failed," Elora surmised. "I'm beginning to question how exactly you've been filling your time with the Princess. Has any of it been spent on training?"

Suddenly Rhys knocked over a glass of wine. The glass shattered and liquid splattered everywhere. Everyone had been too busy staring at Elora and Finn to notice, but out of the corner of my eye I saw him do it on purpose.

Rhys started apologizing and rushing about to clean it up, but Elora had stopped glaring at Finn, and he no longer had to defend himself. Rhys had come to his rescue, and I couldn't be more relieved.

After the mess was cleaned up, Willa, who had never seemed that fond of Rhys, suddenly began chatting incessantly with him, and he eagerly reciprocated. They talked just so that Elora and Finn couldn't.

Elora still managed to squeeze in a few biting comments toward me, such as, "Really, Princess, you must know how to use a fork." But as soon as she finished her sentence, Willa would pipe up with a funny story about this girl she knew or this movie she saw or this place where she went. It was end-less, and in general we were all grateful.

When dinner was over, Elora claimed she had a migraine brewing and a million things to do for tomorrow. She apologized that dessert would not be served tonight, but she didn't leave her seat at the head of the table. Unsure of what else to do, everybody started to excuse themselves. Garrett suggested that they should be heading out, and she nodded non-committally.

"I will see you tomorrow evening," Elora replied hollowly. She stared into space instead of looking at him, and he tried not to look troubled by this.

"Take care of yourself," Garrett said, touching her shoulder gently.

Finn, Rhys, and I rose to see Garrett, Willa, and Rhiannon to the door, but Elora's voice stopped me cold. I think it stopped everyone else too, but they did a better job of playing it off.

"Finn?" Elora said flatly, still staring off at nothing. "Would you escort me to my drawing room? I'd like to have a word with you."

"Yes, of course," Finn replied, giving her a small bow.

I froze and looked to him, but he refused to look at me. He just stood stoically, hands behind his back, and waited for Elora to ask for further assistance.

I might've stood there until Elora dismissed me, but Willa looped her arm through mine and started to drag me away.

Rhys and Rhiannon were just ahead of us, whispering

quietly to each other. Garrett stole one last glance at Elora and walked on to the front door.

"So, I'll come over about ten tomorrow morning," Willa said, purposely keeping her tone light and cheery.

"What for?" I asked, feeling somewhat dazed.

"To help you get ready. There is *so* much to do!" Willa said and then shot a look in the direction of the dining room. "And your mother doesn't seem to be the helpful type."

"Willa, don't talk bad about the Queen," Garrett said without conviction.

"Well, anyway, I'll be over to help you with everything. You'll be fabulous." She gave me a reassuring smile and squeezed my arm right before she left with her father.

Soon Rhys and I were alone, standing in the entryway.

"You okay?" he asked.

"Yeah, I'm fine," I lied.

I felt oddly shaky and ill, and I was pretty sure that I didn't want to be a Princess anymore, if I ever did. There weren't many more dinners like this I could handle. I took a step away, preparing to tell Elora just that, but I felt Rhys's hand warm on my arm, stopping me.

"If you go in there, you'll just make it worse," Rhys insisted gently. "Come on."

He put his hand on the small of my back and ushered me over to the stairs. When we reached them, I expected him to try to push me up the stairs to my room, but he didn't. He knew that I had to wait for Finn to find out what had happened.

I peered in the direction of the dining room, hoping to catch a glimpse of something. I wasn't sure what that would help, but I thought if I could just *see* what was happening, I could somehow make it okay.

"That was a rough dinner," Rhys said with a joyless laugh and sat down on the stairs. I couldn't see anything, so I gave up. Pulling my skirt underneath me, I sat next to him.

"I'm sorry," I said.

"Don't be sorry. It wasn't your fault," Rhys assured me with his lopsided grin. "You just made this house a whole lot more interesting."

Elora had purposely pulled Finn aside to make a public spectacle. Otherwise, she would've lectured him privately, inside his head. For some reason, she had wanted me to witness that. I didn't understand what exactly he had done wrong, except disagree with her. But he had been respectful and hadn't said anything that wasn't true.

"What do you think she's saying?" I asked.

"I don't know," Rhys said. "She's never really yelled at me."

"You've got to be kidding." I stared at him skeptically. Rhys was always flouting the rules, and Elora was about as strict as they came.

"No, seriously." Rhys laughed at my shock. "She's snapped at me to knock stuff off when she's around me, but do you know how often she's even around? I was raised by nannies. Elora made it perfectly clear from day one that she wasn't my mother and she never wanted to be."

"Did she ever want to be a mother at all?" From what little

I knew of her, she seemed to be lacking even the slightest bit of maternal instinct.

"Honestly?" Rhys debated whether or not to tell me, before sadly replying, "No. I don't think she did. But she had a lineage to carry on. A duty."

"I'm just part of her job," I muttered bitterly. "For once, I just wish that somebody actually wanted me around."

"Oh, come on, Wendy," Rhys admonished me softly and leaned in closer. "Lots of people want you around. You can't take it personally that Elora's a bitch."

"It's a little hard not to." I fidgeted with my dress. "She's my mother."

"Elora is a strong, complicated woman that you and I can't even begin to understand," Rhys explained tiredly. "She is a Queen above all else, and that makes her cold and distant and cruel."

"What was it like growing up with that?" I glanced over at him, suddenly feeling guilty for moping about my life when he'd had it even harder. At least I had Matt and Maggie.

"I don't know." He shrugged. "Probably like growing up in a boarding school with a strict headmistress. She was always lurking in the background, and I knew that she had the final say on everything. But her interaction with me was at an absolute minimum." He looked at me again, this time uncertainly.

"What?"

"She's not quite as secretive as she thinks, though. This is a big house, but I was a sneaky little kid." He bit his lip and fiddled with a button on his blazer. "You know she used to sleep with Finn's dad?"

"I do," I said quietly.

"I thought he would tell you." Rhys fell silent for a minute, chewing his lip. "Elora was in love with him. She's strange when she's in love. Her face is different, softer and more radiant." Rhys shook his head, lost in a memory. "It was almost worse seeing her like that, knowing that she's capable of kindness and generosity. It made me feel gypped that all I ever got were icy glares from across the room."

"I'm sorry." I put my hand gently on his arm. "I wish I could say something to make you feel better. But to be honest, I can't imagine how horrible it must have been to grow up like that."

He forced a smile, then shrugged, pushing away the memory.

"Anyway. Finn's father left Elora, for his wife, which was just as well." Rhys looked thoughtful for a moment. "Although I bet she would've thrown it all away to be with him, if he had really loved her. But that's not the point."

"What is the point?" I asked shakily.

"Rumor has it she keeps Finn around because she still loves his old man, even though he never loved her. Nothing's ever happened between Finn and Elora, I'm sure." Rhys let out a heavy sigh. "But . . ."

"But what?"

"Finn's dad never looked at her the way Finn looks at you." He let it hang in the air for a second as I tried to figure out what he meant. "So you've got that strike against you too. She never wanted to be a mother, and you're getting the one thing she never had."

"What are you talking about? I haven't gotten anything she never had, and I definitely don't have Finn. I . . . we never . . . it's just official business."

"Wendy." Rhys looked at me with a sad smile. "I know that I wear my heart on my sleeve, but you're just as bad."

"I-I don't know what you're talking about," I stuttered and looked away from him.

"All right." Rhys laughed. "Whatever you say."

To lighten the moment, Rhys made some joke that I didn't really catch. My mind raced and my heart pounded. Rhys must be imagining things. And even if he wasn't, surely Elora wouldn't punish Finn for that. Would she?

TWENTY

resignation

Finn reached the stairs, and I scrambled to my feet. He had probably only been with Elora for fifteen minutes, but in my mind it seemed like forever. Rhys had been sitting next to me, but he got up much slower than I had. Finn looked over us with disdain, then turned and started walking up the stairs without a word.

"Finn!" I jogged after him, but Rhys rather smartly made his escape to the kitchen. "Wait! Finn! What happened?"

"A conversation," Finn replied glibly. I scurried to keep up with him, but he made no effort to slow down, so I grabbed his arm, stopping him halfway up the stairs. He glanced back over his shoulder as if looking for Rhys, clearly avoiding my gaze. "I thought I told you to stay away from the mänsklig."

"Rhys was just sitting with me while I waited for you," I said. "Get over it."

"It's very dangerous for you to be around him." Finn faced

the top of the stairs but looked at me from the corner of his eye. "It's dangerous for you to be around me." I didn't appreciate the way he wouldn't look at me directly. I missed his dark eyes.

"What's that supposed to mean?" I demanded.

"Let go of my arm," Finn said.

"Just tell me what's going on, and I'll leave you alone," I said, tightening my grip.

"I have been relieved of my duties," Finn answered carefully. "Elora no longer perceives a threat, and I have been insubordinate. I am to pack my things and leave the premises as soon as possible."

The air completely went out of my lungs. It was my worst fear. Finn was going to leave, and it was my fault. He had been defending me when I should've been defending myself. Or I should've just kept my mouth shut.

"What?" I gaped at him. "That's not right. You can't . . . You've been here for so long, and Elora trusts you. She can't . . . It's my fault! I'm the one who refused to listen!"

"No, it's not your fault," Finn insisted firmly. "You didn't do anything wrong."

"Well, you can't just leave! I have the ball tomorrow, and I don't know anything!" I continued desperately. "I'm not a Princess at all, Finn. You have so much left to help me with."

"I wouldn't be helping you after the ball anyway." Finn shook his head. "A tutor will be coming in to help you learn everything you need to know from here on out. You're ready for the ball, no matter what Elora says. You'll do wonderfully tomorrow."

"But you won't be here?"

He turned away from me and quietly said, "You don't need me."

"This is my fault! I'm gonna talk to Elora. You can't leave. She has to see that."

"Wendy, no, you can't—" Finn said, but I had already started back down the stairs.

There was an unbearable panic settling over me. Finn had forced me to leave the only people who had ever made me feel loved, and I had done it because I trusted him. Now he was going to leave me alone with Elora and a monarchy I wanted no part of.

Rhys would still be here, but I knew that it was only a matter of time before she sent him away as well. I was going to be more alone and isolated than I had ever been before, and I couldn't handle it.

Even as I was running down to Elora's drawing room, I knew it was more than that. I couldn't stand to lose Finn, and it didn't matter how Elora or anyone else treated me. A life without him just didn't seem possible anymore. I hadn't even realized how important he had become to me until Elora threatened to take him away.

"Elora!" I threw open the drawing room door without knocking. I knew it would piss her off, but I didn't care. Maybe, if I was insubordinate enough, she would send me away too.

Elora stood in front of the windows staring out at the black night, and she wasn't startled at all by the door slamming open. Without turning to look at me, she calmly said, "That's completely unnecessary, and it goes without saying that that is not at all how a Princess behaves."

"You're always going on about how a Princess should behave, but what about how a Queen should act?" I countered icily. "Are you such an insecure ruler that you can't handle the slightest bit of dissension? If we don't bow instantly to your opinion, you ship us off?"

Elora sighed. "I assume this is about Finn."

"You had no right to fire him! He did nothing wrong!"

"It doesn't matter if he did anything wrong, I can 'fire' anyone for any reason. I am the Queen." Slowly she turned to me, her face stunningly emotionless. "It is not the act of disagreeing that I had a problem with; it was why."

"This is about my stupid name?" I spouted incredulously.

"There is much you still have to learn. Please, sit." Elora gestured to one of the couches, and she lay back on the chaise lounge. "There's no need to get huffy with me, Princess. We need to talk."

"I don't want to change my name," I said as I sat down on the couch across from her. "I don't know why it's such a big deal to you. Names can't be that important."

"It's not about the name." Elora waved it off. Her hair flowed out like silk around her, and she played with it absently. "I know that you think I'm cruel and heartless, but I'm not. I care very deeply for Finn, more than a Queen should care for a servant, and I am sorry that I have been so negligent in the examples that I have set for you. It pains me to see Finn go, but I can assure you that I did it for you."

"You did not!" I yelled. "You did it because you were jealous!"

"My emotions played no part in this decision. Not even the way I feel about you factored into this." Her lips tightened, and she stared emptily at me. "I did what I had to do because it was best for the kingdom."

"How is getting rid of him best for anybody?"

"You refuse to understand that you are a Princess!" Elora paused and took a deep, fortifying breath. "It doesn't matter whether or not you understand the gravity of the situation. Everyone else does, including Finn, which is why he is leaving. He knows this is best for you too."

"I don't understand. How can his leaving possibly help me? I count on him for everything, and you do too. And now you're telling me you let him go, just like that?"

"I know you think this is all about money, but it's about something more powerful than that. Our bloodline is rich with tremendous abilities, far exceeding the general Trylle population." Elora leaned in closer to me as she spoke. "Unfortunately, Trylle have become less interested in our way of life, and the abilities have begun to weaken. It is essential to our people that the bloodline is kept pure, that the abilities are allowed to flourish.

"The titles and positions seem arbitrary," Elora continued. "But we are in power because we have the most power. For centuries, our abilities outshone every other family's, but the Kroners are rapidly overtaking us. You are the last chance for hanging on to the throne and retaining power for our family."

"What does this have to do with Finn?" I demanded, growing tired of political talk.

"Everything," Elora answered with a thin smile. "In order to keep the bloodlines as pure and powerful as possible, certain rules were put into effect. Not just for royalty, but for everyone. It's not merely as a repercussion for behaving outside of societal norms, but also so half-breed spawn won't weaken our bloodlines." Something about the way she said "spawn" sent a chill down my spine.

"Consequences vary in severity," Elora continued. "When a Trylle becomes involved with a mänsklig, they are asked to leave the community."

"There's nothing going on between Rhys and me," I interjected, and Elora nodded skeptically.

"While trackers are Trylle, they don't possess abilities in the conventional sense," Elora went on, and I began to realize what she was getting at. "Trackers are meant to be with trackers. If Trylle are involved with them, they are looked down upon, but it is allowed.

"Unless you are royalty." She looked severely at me. "A tracker can never have the crown. Any Marksinna or Princess caught with a tracker is immediately stripped of her title. If the offense is bad enough, such as a Princess destroying an essential bloodline, then they would both be banished."

I swallowed hard. If anything happened between Finn and me, I wouldn't be able to be a Princess, and I wouldn't even be able to live in Förening anymore. That was shocking at first,

"Yeah." I nodded, swallowing hard. "I'm going with you."

"Wendy . . ." His expression softened, and he shook his head. "You can't go with me. You need to be here."

"No, I don't care about here!" I insisted. "I don't want to be a stupid Princess, and they don't need me. I'm terrible at everything. My leaving is the best thing for everyone."

"They do need you. You have no idea how badly they need you." Finn turned away from me. "Without you, it will completely fall apart."

"That doesn't make any sense! I'm just one stupid girl who can't even figure out which fork to eat with! I have no abilities. I'm awkward and silly and inappropriate, and that Kroner kid is *much* better suited for this. I don't need to be here, and I'm not going to stay if you're not here!"

"There is much you have yet to learn," Finn said tiredly, almost to himself. He had started folding his clothes again, so I walked over to him and grabbed his arm.

"I want to be with you, and . . . I think you want to be with me." I felt sick to my stomach saying it aloud. I expected him to laugh at me or tell me that I was insane, but instead, he slowly looked at me.

In a rare moment of vulnerability, his dark eyes betrayed everything they had been trying to hide from me: affection and warmth, and something even deeper than that. His arm felt strong under my hand, and my heart pounded in my chest. Gently he placed his hand on my cheek, letting his fingers press warmly on my skin, and I stared hopefully at him.

"I am not worth it, Wendy," Finn whispered hoarsely.

"You are going to be so much more than this, and I cannot hold you back. I refuse to."

"But Finn, I—" I wanted to tell him more, but he pulled away.

"You have to go." He turned his back to me completely, busying himself with packing so he wouldn't have to look at me.

"Why?" I demanded, tears stinging my eyes.

"Because." Finn picked up some of his books off a shelf, and I followed right behind him, unwilling to relent in my pursuit.

"That's not a reason!"

"I've already explained it to you."

"No, you haven't. You've just made vague comments about the future."

"I don't want you!" Finn snapped.

I felt like I had been slapped. For a moment I stood in stunned silence, just listening to the sound of my heartbeat echo in my ears.

"You're lying." A tear slipped down my cheek. "You promised you would never lie to me."

"Wendy, I need you to leave!" he growled.

He breathed heavily, with his back to me, but he had stopped moving around. He leaned against the bookshelf, his shoulders hunched forward.

This was my last chance to convince him, and I knew it. I touched his back, and he tried to pull away from me, but I wouldn't move my hand. He whirled on me, grabbing my wrist. He pushed me until my back was against the wall, pinning me there.

His body pressed tightly against mine, the strong contours of his body against the soft curves of mine, and I could feel his heart hammering against my chest. He still gripped my wrist, restraining one of my hands against the wall.

I wasn't sure what he intended to do, but he looked down at me, his dark eyes smoldering. Then suddenly I felt his lips press roughly against mine.

He kissed me desperately, like he couldn't breathe without me. His stubble scraped against my cheeks, my lips, my neck, everywhere he dared press his mouth against me. He let go of my wrist, allowing me to wrap my arms around him and pull him even closer.

Seconds ago I had been crying, and I could taste the salt from my tears on his lips. Tangling my fingers in his hair, I pulled his mouth more eagerly against mine. My heart beat so fast it hurt, and an intense heat spread through me.

Somehow he managed to pull his mouth from mine. His hands gripped my shoulders, holding me to the wall, and he took a step back. Breathing hard, he looked at the floor instead of at me.

"This is why I have to go, Wendy. I can't do this to you."

"To me? You're not doing anything to me." I tried to reach out for him, but he held me back. "Just let me go with you."

"Wendy . . ." He lifted his hand back to my cheek, using his thumb to brush away a fresh tear, and looked at me intently. "You trust me, don't you?"

I nodded hesitantly.

"Then you have to trust me on this. You *need* to stay here, and I need to go. Okay?"

"Finn!"

"I'm sorry." Finn let go of me and grabbed his half-packed suitcase off his bed. "I stayed too long." He started walking to the door, and I ran after him. "Wendy! Enough!"

"But you can't just leave . . ." I pleaded.

He hesitated at the doorway and shook his head. Then he opened the door and left.

I could've followed him, but I didn't have any more arguments. His kiss had left me feeling dazed and disarmed, and I wondered dimly if that had been his plan all along. He knew his kiss would leave me too weak to chase after him and too confused to argue with him.

After he had gone, I sat down on the bed, which still smelled like him, and started to sob.

TWENTY-ONE

the ball

I'm not sure I had slept at all when Willa burst into my room the next day to wake me for the ball. My eyes were red and swollen, but she made very little comment about it. She just started in on getting me ready and talking excitedly about how much fun it was all going to be. I didn't believe her, but she didn't seem to notice.

Almost everything I did required verbal and physical prompts. She even had to remind me to rinse the shampoo from my hair, and I was just lucky that modesty had never been her strong suit.

It was impossible to combine fresh heartbreak with the fervor of a ball. Willa kept trying to get me excited or at least nervous about the whole thing, but her efforts were completely futile. The only way I managed to function was by being completely numb.

I couldn't understand how this had happened. When I

first met Finn, he had seemed creepy, and then he was just irritating. Repeatedly I had rejected him and told him that I didn't need him or want to be around him.

How had it turned into this? I had lived my whole stupid life without him, and now I could barely make it through an hour.

I sat on a stool, wrapped in my robe, while Willa did something to my hair. She had offered to style it in front of a mirror so I could see her progress, but I didn't care. Holding a bottle of spray in her hand, she stopped what she was doing and just looked at me.

"Wendy." Willa sighed. "I know Finn's gone, and you're obviously taking it pretty hard. But he's just a stork, and you are a *Princess*."

"You don't know what you're talking about," I mumbled.

I had considered defending him for a moment, but I was kind of pissed that he had left without me. There was no way that I could've left *him* after that kiss. As it was, it had been torture to stay behind. I just lowered my eyes and tried to close the subject.

"Fine." Willa rolled her eyes and went back to spraying my hair. "But you're still a Princess, and this is your night." I didn't say anything as she yanked and teased. "You're still young. You don't understand how many fish there really are in the sea, especially your sea. The most eligible, attractive men are gonna be all over you, and you're not even gonna remember that stupid stork who brought you here."

"I don't like fishing," I muttered dryly, but she ignored me.

"You know who *is* a catch? Tove Kroner." Willa made a pleased sound. "I wish my dad would set me up with him." She sighed wistfully and jerked on a lock of my hair.

"He's really foxy, really rich," Willa went on, as if I had asked her to tell me more. "He's like the highest Markis in the world, which is so weird. The Marksinna are usually the ones with all the abilities. Guys can do some things, but they pale in comparison to what women can do, yet Tove has more ability than anybody else. I wouldn't be surprised if he could read minds."

"I thought nobody could do that," I said, amazed that I was even following her. A few weeks ago, nothing she said would have made sense.

"No. Only very, very few can. So few it's almost the stuff of legends these days." She gently fluffed my hair. "But Tove is the stuff of legends, so that makes sense. And if you play your cards right, you'll be pretty damn legendary yourself." She whipped me around so I was facing her and smiled at her handiwork. "Now we just need to get you into your gown."

Somehow, while getting me ready, Willa had managed to ready herself. She had on a floor-length light blue gown that swept out at her hips, and she looked so beautiful, I had no hope of topping her.

After she had finally gotten me into my own dress, she forced me in front of the mirror, insisting that I looked too amazing to not see myself.

"Oh, wow." Saying that to my reflection felt egotistical, but

I couldn't help it. I had never looked better in my life, and I doubted that I would ever look this good again.

The gown was a shimmery silver and white that flowed around me. It was strapless in an elegant way, and the diamond necklace Willa had chosen set it off. My dark curls fell perfectly behind me, and subtle diamond clips sparkled in my hair.

"You're gonna rock it tonight, Princess," Willa promised with a sly smile.

That was the last calm moment of the night. As soon as we stepped out of my bedroom, we were swept off by aides and staff that I didn't even know Elora had. They gave me a rundown of the times when everything was set to happen and where I had to be and who I had to meet and what I had to do.

It was already more than I could comprehend, and at least momentarily I was spared the dull heartache I got from thinking of Finn. I looked helplessly at Willa, knowing that I would have to try to make this up to her later on. Without her, it would've been completely impossible for me to make it through.

First, there was some kind of meet-and-greet in the ballroom. Elora stood on one side of me, and thankfully, Willa stayed on my other side, taking on the role of some kind of assistant. The three of us stood at one end of the ballroom, flanked by security. A long line of people waited to meet me.

Willa filled in the names and titles as they approached. Most of them were famous in the Trylle world, but Elora explained that anybody could come meet me today, so the line was absolutely endless. My face hurt from smiling, and there were only so many different ways I could say, "Pleased to meet you" and "Thank you."

After that, we went to the dining hall for a more exclusive function. The table only seated a hundred (that's right—*only* a hundred), and with Willa sitting five places down from me, I felt lost.

Whenever I felt insecure, I instinctively searched for Finn, only to remember that he wasn't there. I tried to concentrate on eating my food properly, which wasn't that easy considering how nauseous I felt and how badly my jaw hurt from the forced smiles.

My mother sat to my right at the head of the table, and Tove Kroner sat next to me on my left. Throughout the dinner, he hardly said a thing, and Elora went about making polite conversation with the current Chancellor.

The Chancellor didn't seem to remember me from the other day when I'd come in drenched from the rain, and I was glad for it. The way he looked at me creeped me out, and I found it impossible to smile at him out of fear I might vomit.

"Drink more wine," Tove suggested quietly. Holding a wineglass in his hand, he leaned in a bit toward me to be heard over the din. His mossy eyes rested on mine briefly before he averted them, staring instead at an empty space across from us. "It relaxes the muscles."

"I beg your pardon?"

"From smiling." He gestured to his own mouth and forced a smile before quickly dropping it. "It's starting to hurt, right?"

"Yeah." I smiled lightly at him, feeling the soreness at the corners of my mouth.

"The wine helps. Trust me." Tove took a long drink from his wine, much longer than was polite, and I saw Elora eyeing him as she chatted with the Chancellor.

"Thanks." I took his suggestion, but I drank much more slowly than he did, afraid of inciting the wrath of Elora. I didn't think she'd do anything publicly, but I knew she wouldn't let me get away with anything either.

As the dinner wore on, Tove grew restless. He leaned back in his seat, laying his hand on the table. His wineglass would slowly slide over to his hand, then it would slowly slide away, without him ever touching it. I'd seen him perform a similar trick with his bowl of soup last week, yet I couldn't help but stare.

"You pretty on edge tonight?" Tove asked, glancing at me. I wasn't sure if he caught me watching his trick or not, but I looked down at my plate anyway.

I nodded. "Mmm, a little."

"Yeah, I can tell." He leaned forward, resting his elbows on the table, and I imagined Elora was livid.

"I'm trying to stay calm." I stabbed absently at some kind of vegetable I had no intention of eating. "I think I've been handling this very well, considering everything."

"No, you're acting fine. I can sense it." He tapped the side of his head. "I can't explain it, but . . . I know how tense you are." He chewed his lip. "You project your emotions so forcefully. Your persuasion is immensely powerful."

"Maybe," I allowed. His gaze was unnerving, and I didn't want to disagree with him.

"Here's a tip: use it tonight." Tove was barely audible over the chatter. "You're trying to please so many people and it's exhausting. You can't be everything to everyone, so I try not to be anything to anyone. My mother hates me for it, but . . ." He shrugged. "Just use it a little bit, and you'll charm everyone. Without really trying."

"It takes effort to use persuasion," I whispered. I could feel Elora listening to us, and I didn't think she'd approve of what we were saying. "It would be just as exhausting."

"Hmm," Tove mused, then leaned back in his seat.

"Tove, the Chancellor was just telling me that you had discussed working for him this spring," Elora interjected brightly. I barely glanced up at her, but in that second she managed to glower at me before returning to her overly cheery expression.

"My mother discussed it," Tove corrected her. "I've never said a word to the Chancellor, and I have no interest in the position."

I was increasingly becoming a fan of Tove, even if he weirded me out and I didn't understand what he meant most of the time. He just said whatever he wanted without fear of repercussion, and I admired it.

"I see." Elora raised an eyebrow, and the Chancellor started saying something about the wine they were drinking.

Tove managed to look bored and irritated the rest of the dinner, chewing his nails and looking at everything except me. There was something very strange and unstable about him. He belonged in this world even less than I did, but I imagined that there really wasn't any place that he'd fit in.

Soon we moved on to the ballroom for dancing. The ballroom looked positively magical when it was all done up, and I couldn't help but think of the brief dance I had shared with Finn a couple days before. That, of course, reminded me of the passionate kiss we had shared last night, making me feel weak and sick. I couldn't even force a smile when I thought of Finn.

Making matters worse, it soon became clear that dancing was by far the worst experience of the evening. The receiving line had been rough, but now I was being forced to make conversation with one weird man after another while they put their hands on me.

Garrett managed to steal a dance with me, and that was a relief. I had been dancing nonstop for an hour because everyone kept cutting in. He complimented me, but not in the creepy perv way everyone else seemed to be going for.

Every now and then I would catch Elora spinning around on the floor, or Willa would sneak me a smile as she twirled around with some foxy young guy. It was unfair that she got to pick who she danced with, but I was stuck with every stranger who asked.

"You're probably the most ravishing Princess we've ever had," the Chancellor told me after he cut in for a dance.

His pudgy cheeks were red from exertion, and I wanted to suggest that he sit down and take a break, but I thought Elora would disapprove. He held me much closer than was neces-

sary, and his hand was like a massive ham on my back, pressing me to him. I couldn't pull away without making a scene,
so I just tried to force a smile.

"I'm sure that's not true," I demurred. He sweated so badly,
it had to be bleeding onto my dress. The beautiful silver and
white fabric would be stained yellow after this.

"No, you really are." His eyes were wide with some kind of
weird pleasure, and I wished someone would hurry up and cut
in. We had just started dancing, but I couldn't take much more
of this. "In fact, I've never seen anyone more ravishing than
you."

"Now, that, I'm certain, cannot be true." I glanced around,
hoping to spot Willa somewhere so I could try to pawn him
off on her.

"I know that you'll be expected to start courting soon, and
I'd just like you to know that I have a lot of things going for
me," the Chancellor went on. "I'm very wealthy, very secure,
and my bloodline is immaculate. Your mother would approve
of this arrangement."

"I haven't made any arrangements yet . . ."

I craned my neck, knowing that if Elora saw me, she would
accuse me of being rude. But I didn't know how else to react.
This blubbery man had grabbed my ass during some kind of
marriage proposal. I had to get out of there.

The Chancellor lowered his voice. "I've been told I'm an
excellent lover, as well. I'm sure that you don't have any experience but I could definitely teach you."

His expression grew hungry, and his eyes had dropped

lower than my face. It was taking all my restraint not to push him off me, and in my head I screamed to get away from him.

"May I cut in?" Tove appeared at my side. The Chancellor looked disappointed at the sight of him, but before he could say anything, Tove had put his hand on the Chancellor's shoulder and taken my hand, pulling me away.

"Thank you," I breathed gratefully as we waltzed away from a very confused-looking Chancellor.

"I heard you calling for help." Tove smiled at me. "You seem to be using your persuasion more than you think." In my mind, I had been begging for a way out, but I hadn't uttered an actual word.

"You heard me?" I gasped, feeling pale. "How many other people heard me?"

"Probably just me. Don't worry. Hardly anybody can sense anything anymore," Tove said. "The Chancellor might've noticed if he hadn't been too busy staring at your chest, or if you were more skilled at it. You'll get the hang of it."

"I don't really care if I get the hang of it. I just wanted to get rid of him," I muttered. "I'm sorry if I'm wet. I'm probably covered in his sweat."

"No, you're fine," Tove assured me.

We danced the appropriate width apart, so he probably couldn't feel my dress to tell if it was soaked or not, but there was something relaxing about being with him. I didn't have to say anything or worry about being felt up or ogled. He barely looked at me and said nothing else at all, but the silence between us felt completely comfortable.

Elora finally interrupted the festivities. The christening ceremony would be happening in twenty minutes, and she noted that I needed a break from all the dancing. The dance floor emptied and everyone took seats at the tables edging the dance floor, or milled around the refreshments table.

I knew that I should sit down while I had the chance, but I was desperate to have a moment to breathe, so I went to a corner hidden behind extra chairs and leaned against the wall.

"Who are you hiding from?" Rhys teased, finding me in the corner. Dressed in a flashy tux, he looked dashing as he sauntered over to me, grinning.

"Everyone." I smiled at him. "You look really good."

"Funny, I was just gonna tell you the same thing." Rhys stood next me, putting his hands in his pockets and smiling even wider. "Although 'good' doesn't even begin to do you justice. You look . . . otherworldly. Like nothing else here can even compare to you."

"It's the dress." I looked down, hoping to keep my cheeks from blushing. "That Frederique is amazing."

"The dress is nice, but trust me, *you* make the dress."

Gently, he reached over and fixed a wayward curl that had fallen out of place. He let his hand linger there a minute, his eyes meeting mine, then dropped his hand.

"So, having fun yet?" Rhys asked.

"A blast." I smirked. "What about you?"

"I can't dance with the Princess, so I'm a little bitter," he said with a sad smile.

"Why can't you dance with me?" I would've loved to dance

with him. It would've been a blessed reprieve after everything I'd been through tonight.

"Mänks." He pointed his thumbs at himself. "I'm lucky I'm even allowed in."

"Oh." I looked down at the floor, thinking about what he'd just said. "Not to sound rude or anything, because I'm glad you're here, but . . . why are you here? Why aren't you banned or something equally ridiculous?"

"Didn't you know?" Rhys asked with a cocky grin. "I am the highest mänks in the land."

"And why is that?" I couldn't tell if he was teasing me or not, so I tilted my head, watching as his expression got more serious.

"Because I'm yours," he replied softly.

He was invited because he was my mänsklig, my opposite, but when he answered, that wasn't what he meant at all. Something in his eyes made me blush for real this time, and I smiled sadly at him.

One of Elora's aides burst into the corner, ruining what was left of the moment, and demanded that I take my seat at the head table with the Queen. The christening ceremony was about to start, and a knot formed in my stomach. I hadn't heard what my name was to be, and I was depressed about the idea of changing it.

"Duty calls." I smiled apologetically at Rhys and started to walk past him.

"Hey." Rhys grabbed my hand to stop me, and I turned to

look at him. "You're gonna be great. Everyone's raving about you."

"Thanks." I squeezed his hand gratefully.

A cracking echoed through the room, followed by a tinkling that I didn't understand. The sound was coming from everywhere, so it was hard to place right away. But then it looked like the ceiling was raining glitter, and the skylights crashed to the floor.

falling

Rhys realized what was happening before I did, and, still holding my hand, he yanked me behind him. We were in the corner, out of the way of most of the glass, but from the agonized screams, I gathered that everyone else wasn't so lucky.

Dark figures fell through the broken skylights, landing on the floor with surprising grace. Blood and broken glass layered the floor. Before I recognized them, I remembered the uniform. Matching long black trench coats, like a crime-fighting team.

The word seemed to swell through the room without anybody saying anything: *Vittra*.

Vittra had broken in, crashing through the ceiling, and Trylle guards circled them. In the very center I saw Jen, the tracker who had been so fond of hitting me, his eyes scanning the room.

"You are not invited. Please leave." Elora's voice boomed above everything else.

"You know what we want, and we're not leaving until we get it." Kyra stepped forward, Jen's accomplice from before. She walked on the glass with bare feet but didn't seem to notice. "She's got to be here. Where are you hiding her?"

Jen turned toward me, and his black eyes met mine over Rhys's shoulder. When he grinned wickedly, Rhys realized we were in trouble. He started to push me toward the door, but before we made it, Jen bolted toward us, and everyone burst into life. The Vittra scrambled, going after the guards and other Trylle.

Elora glared at Kyra, who collapsed on the ground, writhing in pain. Nobody had touched her, and based on the look in Elora's eyes, I figured that Kyra's agony had something to do with Elora's abilities.

I saw Tove bound over the table he was sitting at, using his powers to send Vittra flying without even touching them. People screamed, and I felt a strong wind blow through the room, surely Willa's attempt at helping.

Then Jen was in front of us, blocking out the chaos of the ballroom. Rhys stood his ground in front of me. He moved to defend me in some way, but Jen lunged forward and punched him, throwing him to the ground.

"Rhys!" I reached out for Rhys, but he didn't move. I wanted to make sure he wasn't dead, but Jen grabbed me around my waist, restraining me.

"That's what you have protecting you now?" Jen laughed. "Did we scare off Finn?"

"Let go of me!" I kicked at him and tried to pry his arm off me.

With his arm still gripping me, we both abruptly went flying backward, as if someone had pushed him. He slammed into the wall, and his arm loosened enough that I could scramble away from him on my hands and knees.

Dazed, I got to my feet and tried to figure out what had happened. Tove stood on the other side of a glass-strewn table, holding his hand palm-out at Jen.

I smiled appreciatively at him, but my smile disappeared as soon as I got a look at the room. The Vittra clearly had the upper hand. Even though the Trylle in the room outnumbered the Vittra attackers, most of them weren't fighting back. The trackers were throwing punches and pushing back against the Vittra, but most of the royalty appeared to do little more than cower in fear.

A visiting Trylle on the other side of the room had begun using fire, and I could feel Willa's wind whipping about. Garrett had no real powers of his own, but he was attempting hand-to-hand combat with the Vittra, even though they physically appeared to be much stronger.

Other than Tove, Willa, Elora and the Trylle using fire, none of the other Trylle really seemed to have abilities, or at least they weren't using them. The room was total pandemonium, and it was about to get worse. Even more Vittra streamed in through the ceiling.

"This is why you need to work on your persuasion." Tove looked at me evenly, and another Vittra charged at his back.

"Watch out!" I yelled.

Tove turned, throwing his hand back and tossing the Vittra across the room. I looked around to grab a weapon when I felt Jen's arms around my waist again. I yelled and fought as hard as I could, but his arms felt like granite around me.

Tove turned his attention back to me, but two other Vittra chased after him, so he only had a moment to send Jen flying back into the wall again. We hit even harder this time, and it jostled me painfully, but Jen let go.

My head throbbed from the impact, and I blinked to clear it. A hand took mine, helping me to my feet. I wasn't sure if I should accept it, but I did anyway.

"You've got to be more careful, Tove," he said.

"I was just trying to get her free!" Tove snapped, and another Vittra yelled as Tove sent him flying into a table across the room. "And I'm busy here!"

I turned back to see who had helped me, and all the air went out of my lungs. Wearing a black hoodie under a black jacket, Finn surveyed the mess around me. He stood right next to me, holding my hand, and I couldn't think or move.

"Finn!" I gasped, and he finally looked at me, his dark eyes a mixture of relief and panic.

"This is bedlam!" Tove growled.

A table had been flipped on its side, and it separated Tove from Finn and me. Using his abilities, Tove sent it sailing into a Vittra attacking the Chancellor, and then he rushed over to us. All the Vittra seemed to be busy, so he had a moment to catch his breath.

"It's worse than I thought." Finn pursed his lips.

"We've gotta protect the Princess," Tove said.

I squeezed Finn's hand and watched as Jen started to get up, only to be slammed back into the wall by Tove.

"I'll get her out of here," Finn said. "Can you handle it down here?"

"I don't have a choice." Tove barely had time to answer when Willa started screaming across the room. I couldn't see her, and that scared me even more.

"Willa!" I tried to run to see what was happening, but Finn wrapped his arms around me, pulling me back.

"Get her out of here!" Tove commanded as he took a step in the direction of Willa's screams.

Finn started dragging me out of the ballroom while I strained to see what was going on. Tove had disappeared, and I couldn't see Elora or Willa. As Finn pulled me, my feet hit Rhys's leg, and I remembered that he was lying unconscious, bleeding on the ground. I struggled against Finn's arms, trying to reach Rhys.

"He's fine! They won't touch him!" Finn tried to reassure me. He still had one arm around my waist, and he was much stronger than me. "You've got to get out of here!"

"But Rhys!" I pleaded.

"He'd want you to be safe!" Finn insisted and finally managed to get me to the ballroom doors.

I looked up from Rhys and was stunned to see the chaos of

the room. Then all the chandeliers suddenly crashed to the floor, and the only light came from the things that were in flames. People were screaming and yelling, and the sound was echoing off everything.

"The painting," I murmured, and my mind flashed on the picture I'd seen in Elora's drawing room. This was it. This was the exact scene.

And there was nothing I could have done to prevent it. I couldn't even understand it until it was too late.

"Wendy!" Finn shouted, trying to move me into action.

He let go of my waist and took my hand, yanking me out of the room. Using my free hand, I pulled up my dress to keep from tripping on it as we raced down the hallway. I could still hear the carnage from the ballroom, and I had no idea where we were running to.

I didn't have time to ask him where we were going or to feel thankful that I was with him again. My only consolation was that if I died tonight, I'd at least have spent the last few minutes of my life with Finn.

We rounded the corner toward the entryway, and Finn stopped sharply. Three Vittra were coming in the front doors of the palace, but they hadn't seen us yet. Finn changed direction, darting across the hall into one of the sitting rooms, pulling me with him.

He closed the door quietly behind us, leaving us in near darkness. Moonlight spilled in through the glass, and he ran to a corner between a bookcase and the wall. He pulled me tightly to him, shielding me with his body.

We could hear the Vittra outside. I held my breath, pressing my face into Finn's chest and praying they wouldn't come in the room.

When they finally ran past, Finn still didn't loosen his grip on me, but I could hear his heartbeat slow. Somewhere beneath all my panic and fear I became aware of the fact that Finn held me tightly in his arms. I looked up at him, barely able to make out his features in the light from the windows next to us.

"I saw that before," I whispered, looking up at him. "What happened in the ballroom. Elora painted it. She knew that was going to happen!"

"Shh," Finn said gently.

I lowered my voice. "But why didn't she stop it?"

"She didn't know when it would happen or how," Finn explained. "She just knew, and the only thing she could do to prevent it was to add more protection."

"So then why did you leave?" I asked softly.

"Wendy . . ." He pushed back stray curls from my face, and his hand lingered on my cheek as he looked down at me. "I never really left. I was just down the hill, and I never stopped tracking you. I knew what was happening as soon as you did, and I raced back here."

"Are we gonna be okay?" I asked

"I won't let anything happen to you. I promise."

I looked up at him, searching his eyes in the dim light, and I wanted nothing more than to stay in his arms forever.

The door creaked open, and Finn tensed instantly. He

pushed me back against the wall, wrapping his arms around me to hide me. I held my breath and tried to stop my heart from pounding. We heard nothing for a second, and then the light flicked on.

"Well, well, if the prodigal stork hasn't returned." Jen smirked.

"You won't get her," Finn said firmly.

He pulled away from me just enough so he could face Jen. I peered around him, watching Jen walk in a slow semicircle toward us. He walked in an oddly familiar way, like something I had seen on Animal Planet. And then I realized—Jen was stalking his prey.

"Maybe I won't," Jen allowed. "But getting you out of my way would probably make it easier, if not for me, then for somebody else. Because we won't stop coming for her."

"And we won't stop protecting her."

"You're willing to die to protect her?" Jen raised an eyebrow.

"You're willing to die to get her?" Finn challenged evenly.

In the ballroom, Tove had insisted they had to protect me, and I hadn't thought he even cared for me all that much. Was it just that I was the Princess? Had Elora endured similar attacks when she first came home?

I clenched the back of Finn's jacket and watched the two of them stare each other down. I didn't understand what was so damn important about me that so many Vittra were willing to kill, and, according to Finn, so many Trylle were willing to die.

"Neither one of you has to die," I said. I tried to slip around

Finn's arm, but he pushed me back. "I'll go, okay? I don't want anybody else to get hurt over this."

"Why don't you listen to the girl?" Jen suggested, wagging his eyebrows.

"Not this time."

"Suit yourself." Jen had apparently tired of talking and dove at Finn.

Finn was wrenched from my fingertips, and I screamed his name. They both went flying through the glass out onto the balcony, sending shards flying everywhere. I was barefoot, but I ran forward without regard.

Jen managed to land a few good blows, but Finn was much quicker and seemed to be stronger. When Finn hit him, Jen staggered back several feet.

"You've been working out." Jen wiped fresh blood from his chin.

"You could give up now, and I wouldn't think any less of you," Finn said.

"Nice try." Jen lunged forward, kicking Finn in the stomach, but Finn held his own.

I grabbed a giant shard of glass from off the balcony and moved around them, trying to find an opening to attack. I managed to slice open a finger, but I barely noticed. Jen knocked Finn to the balcony floor. He pounced on top of him and started hitting him in the face. Using all my might, I stabbed the glass into his back.

"Ow!" Jen shouted, but he sounded more irritated than wounded.

I stood behind him, panting. That was not the reaction I had expected and I didn't know what to do.

Jen whirled around, smacking me so hard across the face that I went flying to the edge of the balcony. I only had a moment to notice the dizzying drop below as my head hung over the edge, and then I was scrambling to my feet and gripping the railing.

Finn had already regained his feet and knocked Jen back down. Kicking him as hard as he could, Finn growled through gritted teeth, "Don't. Ever. Touch. Her. Again."

When Finn tried to kick him again, Jen grabbed his foot and yanked him back to the floor. I heard the sound of Finn's head cracking against the heavy concrete of the balcony. He withstood the blow, but it stunned him long enough for Jen to bend over and wrap his hands around Finn's throat. He lifted Finn off the floor by his neck.

I jumped on Jen's back, which wasn't as smart as I'd thought it would be, because Jen had the giant shard of glass sticking out of him. The glass cut through my dress and my side without actually impaling me. It was enough to make me bleed and hurt, but not enough to kill.

"Get off!" Jen growled, then jerked his arm back, elbowing me hard in the stomach and knocking me off him.

I landed on my feet but Jen already had Finn pressed back over the railing. The top half of Finn's body dangled over the edge, and if Jen let go, Finn would plummet to his death hundreds of feet below.

For a moment I couldn't breathe or move. All I could see

was the painting of me. The broken shards of glass glinting in the moonlight. My beautiful dress, which appeared stark white by the light of the moon, with the slit of blood in the side. The vast darkness that went on beyond the balcony, and the horrified look on my face as I reached for it.

"Stop!" I pleaded, tears streaming down my face. "I'll go with you! Please! Just let go of him! *Please!*"

Jen laughed. "I hate to break it to you, Princess, but you're going with me either way!"

"Not if I can help . . ." Finn barely managed to speak through Jen's hand clamped on his throat.

Finn kicked his leg up, planting it squarely between Jen's legs, and Jen groaned but didn't loosen his grip on Finn. Keeping his leg there, Finn started tilting backward. Jen realized what he was doing, but Finn had reached forward and grabbed Jen's jacket.

He had changed the weight ratio, and in a moment that felt oddly slow-motion, Finn went backward over the railing, pulling Jen with him.

"*No!*" I screamed and lunged toward them. I landed on my belly, sliding across the balcony with my hand outstretched, grabbing at empty air.

TWENTY-THREE

aftermath

As soon as I reached the railing, Finn floated up, coughing hoarsely. I gaped at him, too shocked to believe he was real. He drifted over the top of the railing, then dropped heavily onto the balcony.

Lying on his back, he coughed again, and I rushed to his side, kneeling next to him. I touched his face, checking to make sure he was real, and his skin felt soft and warm under my hands.

"That was quite the gamble," Tove remarked from behind me, and I turned to look at him.

Tove had lost his blazer, and his white shirt looked slightly burned and bloody. Other than that, he didn't look that bad as he took a step toward us.

"Nah, you always come through," Finn said. And I realized that when Finn had gone over the balcony, Tove had used his power to catch him and lift him back up, setting him down safely.

I went back to staring down at Finn, unable to believe that he was alive and here with me again. My hand was on his chest, above his heart, so I could feel it pounding. He placed his hand over mine, holding it gently, but he looked past me at Tove.

"What's going on in there?" Finn asked Tove and nodded to the house.

"They're retreating." Tove stood over us. "A lot of people were hurt, but Aurora is working on them. My father broke a few ribs, but he'll live. Unfortunately, that's more than I can say for some of the Trylle."

"Did we lose a lot of people?" Finn asked, his expression grim.

"I can't say yet for sure, but we lost a few." Tove grimaced. "But we could've avoided that completely if the Markis and Marksinna would learn to fight. They leave all of their protection in the hands of the trackers, but if the royalty would just get their hands dirty, they could've . . ." He shook his head. "Nobody needed to die today."

Finn pressed his lips together grimly, then looked at me. "What happened? Are you hurt?" His hand went to my side, where I bled all over my dress. I winced under his touch but shook my head.

"It's nothing. I'm fine."

"Have my mother look at it. She'll patch you both up," Tove said. When I gave him a confused look, he went on, "Aurora's a healer. She can touch you and fix you. That's her ability."

"Come on." Finn gave me a shaky smile and slowly sat up.

He tried to act like he was perfectly fine, but he had taken quite a beating and there was hesitation in his movements. Tove helped him to his feet, then took my hand and pulled me up.

I wrapped my arm around Finn's waist, and Finn put his arm around my shoulders, reluctantly putting some of his weight on me. We walked carefully through the broken glass back into the house, and Tove gave more details about the attack.

Other than the trackers who had been guarding, most of the Trylle had played defenseless, myself included. The Vittra might not have as many abilities, but they had mastered physical combat much better than the Trylle.

Thankfully, a few of the Trylle like Tove and Elora were strong enough and smart enough to fight back. What they lacked in physical prowess, they made up for in overwhelming abilities.

But Tove was quick to point out that if all the Trylle had stood up and used what abilities they had—no matter how weak—or simply fought back with their fists, the Vittra would have hardly stood a chance. We should've won this without any deaths and hardly any injuries.

The Trylle royals had grown too complacent, to the point where they believed that defending themselves was beneath them. They'd become too focused on social class to realize that they needed to handle some things themselves, instead of leaving the trackers and mänks to do all the dirty work.

The ballroom looked even worse than it had when we'd left it. Someone had lit lanterns around the edges of the room, so we could at least see better than before.

Willa ran over when she saw me and threw her arms around me. I hugged her back, feeling tremendous relief that she was alive. Despite a few scrapes and bruises, she looked okay.

She then launched into an excited tale about how she had blown a few Vittra out of the ceiling, and I told her I was proud. I wanted to listen to her talk, but the destruction was too overwhelming.

When Elora saw us, she pulled Aurora from where she was helping a bleeding man. I noted with dark satisfaction that the Chancellor had a nasty cut on his forehead, and I hoped that Aurora couldn't make time to fix him.

Elora didn't look any worse for the wear. If I hadn't known, I never would've thought she'd been here when the fight was going on. Aurora, on the other hand, though she still looked beautiful and regal, did show signs of the battle. Her dress was torn, her hair was a mess, and there was blood all over her hands and arms, though I doubted most of it was hers.

"Princess." Elora looked genuinely relieved when she walked over to us, delicately stepping over broken tables and a Vittra corpse. "I'm glad to see you're all right. I was very worried about you."

"Yeah, I'm fine."

She reached out and touched my cheek, but there was nothing affectionate about it. It was the way I would touch a strange animal that I'd been assured was safe though I didn't really believe it.

"I don't know what I would've done if something happened to you." She smiled wanly at me, then dropped her hand and looked at Finn. "I'm sure a thank-you is in order for saving my daughter."

"No need," Finn replied rather curtly, and Elora gazed at him intently for a moment, saying something in his mind. Then she turned and walked away, apparently to deal with something far more pressing than her daughter.

Aurora squeezed Tove's arms and looked at him warmly, making me feel a horrible pang at my own mother's reaction. Aurora had seemed like an ice queen too, but she could at least show signs of genuine happiness that her son hadn't died.

The moment passed quickly, and she moved on to me. She tore the hole in my dress wider so she could put her hand on my wound, and I gritted my teeth at the pain. Finn tightened his arm around my shoulders, a warm tingling sensation passed over my side, and moments later the pain stopped.

"Good as new." Aurora smiled tiredly at me.

She seemed to have aged since before she'd touched me, and I wondered how much all that healing took out of her. She started to step away, going back to help other people, and Finn leaned on me, clearly in pain.

"What about Finn?" I asked, and she looked back at me, startled. Apparently I had asked something wrong, and she didn't know how to react.

"No, no, I'm fine." Finn waved her off.

"Nonsense." Tove clapped him on the back and nodded at his mother. "Finn saved the day. He deserves a little help. Aurora, wanna take care of him?" She looked uncertainly at her son, then nodded and walked over to Finn.

"Of course," Aurora said.

She looked him over for wounds, trying to pinpoint what needed fixing. I glanced away from them, and I saw Rhys sitting on the edge of a table. He held a bloody cloth to his forehead and stared down at the floor.

"Rhys!" I shouted, and when he looked up and saw me, he smiled.

"Go see him," Finn suggested. Aurora poked at something painful in his side and he winced. "She's taking care of me."

"I got him." Tove took Finn's arm, so he would be leaning on Tove instead of me.

I looked back at Finn, but he nodded at me to go, clearly trying not to let on how much pain Aurora was causing him.

I really didn't want to leave Finn, but I felt like I should at least say hi to somebody who tried to save my life. Especially since Rhys had been the only person all night who had told me I looked beautiful without sounding really creepy about it.

"You're alive!" Rhys grinned. He tried to stand up, but I gestured for him to sit back down. "I wasn't sure what happened to you." He looked past me at Finn, and his expression faltered. "I didn't know Finn was back. If I had, I wouldn't have worried."

"*I* was worried about *you*." I reached out and carefully touched his forehead. "You took quite the punch there."

"Yeah, but I couldn't get one in," Rhys grumbled, looking down at the floor. "And I couldn't stop him from taking you."

"Yes, you did!" I insisted. "If you hadn't been there, they would've hauled me off before anybody had a chance to do anything about it. You kind of saved the day."

"Yeah?" His blue eyes were hopeful when he looked at me.

"Definitely." I smiled back at him.

"You know, back in the day, when a guy saved a Princess's life, she would reward him with a kiss," Rhys commented.

His smile was light, but his eyes were serious. If Finn hadn't been standing a few feet behind me, watching, I probably would've kissed him. But I didn't want to do anything to spoil having Finn back, so I just shook my head and smiled.

"Maybe when I slay the dragon. Then I'll get a kiss?"

"I promise," I agreed. "Would you settle for a hug?"

"A hug from you is never settling."

I leaned over and hugged him tightly. A woman sitting nearby looked aghast at the new Princess openly hugging a mänsklig. Things were really going to have to change when I was Queen.

After Aurora patched up Finn, she suggested we both get some rest. The room was still a disaster, but Tove insisted that he and his mother were taking care of everything. I wanted to protest and help more, but I was exhausted, so I didn't put up a fight.

Using his abilities during the fight had focused Tove. His entire personality shone through, and he took control of the situation with ease. I had a feeling that for the first time I was seeing the real Tove, and not the kid trapped behind the noise of his powers.

In a sense, we worked in opposite ways. I projected intensely, which was why my persuasion was strong, whereas Tove received everything. He could pick up on my emotions and thoughts whether he wanted to or not. But I imagined that he sensed other people too, and his mind had to be a fog of everyone's emotions.

Finn went with me to my room, just in case it wasn't completely safe. Before we even reached the stairs, Finn had taken my hand in his. Most of the way I was silent, but when we got close to my door I felt like I had to say something.

"So . . . are you and Tove like pals or something?" I was teasing, but I was curious. I had never really seen them even speak before, but there seemed to be a kind of familiarity between them.

"I'm a tracker," Finn answered. "I tracked Tove. He's a good kid." He looked over at me, smiling a little. "I told him to keep an eye on you."

"If you were so worried about me, why didn't you stay in the palace?" I asked more sharply than I meant to.

Finn shook his head. "Let's not talk about that now." We had stopped in front of my bedroom door, and there was a playful glimmer in his dark eyes.

"What should we talk about, then?" I looked up at him.

"How beautiful you look in that dress." Finn looked me over appreciatively, and he put his hands on my sides.

I laughed, and then he was pushing me against the door. His body was so tight against me I could barely breathe, and his mouth searched for mine. He kissed me in the same frantic way he had before, and I loved it.

I wrapped my arms around him and pushed myself against him eagerly. He reached around me, opening the door, and we tumbled into my room. He caught me before I actually fell, then lifted me easily into his arms and carried me.

Gently, he tossed me onto the bed, and then lowered himself on top of me. His stubble tickled my neck and shoulders as he covered me in kisses.

Sitting back, he peeled off his jacket and hoodie, and I expected him to take off his T-shirt, but he stopped, looking down at me. His black hair was slightly disheveled, but his expression was completely foreign to me. He just stared at me, making my skin redden with shame.

"What?"

"You're just so perfect," Finn said, but he sounded distressed about it.

"Oh, I am not." I blushed and laughed. "You know I'm not."

"You can't see what I see." He leaned over me again, his face right above mine but not kissing me. After a minute's hesitation, he kissed my forehead and my cheeks, and then, very tenderly, kissed my lips. "I just don't want to disturb you."

"How are you going to disturb me?"

"Mmm." A smile played on his lips and then he sat up, climbing off me. "You should go change into pajamas. That dress can't be comfortable."

"What do I need pajamas for?" I sat up. I tried to sound flirty, but I knew there was a panicked edge to my voice. As soon as we'd come in here, I thought things were going to go much further than pajamas would allow.

"I'll stay with you tonight," Finn tried to reassure me. "But nothing more can happen except for sleep."

"Why?"

"I'm here." Finn looked at me intently. "Isn't that enough?"

I nodded and carefully climbed off of the bed. I stood in front of him so he could unzip my dress, enjoying the way his hands lingered on my skin. I didn't understand what was going on, but I would be happy for anything I could have with him.

I went into the bathroom and changed into my pajamas, then came back and climbed into bed. He continued sitting on the edge for a minute, then, almost reluctantly, he came over to me. I curled up in his arms, burying my head in his chest, and he held me tightly to him.

Nothing had ever felt better than being with him like that, and I tried to stay awake so I could relish every minute, but eventually my body gave in and I passed out.

In the morning, I woke up to Elora coming in my room for the first time ever. She was wearing pants, something I had never seen her in. I was still curled up in Finn's arms, and she didn't seem surprised or offended by that.

"I trust you slept well." Elora looked around the room, but not in a nervous way. She had just never been here before. "And I trust that Finn was a gentleman."

"He always is." I yawned.

He had started pulling away from me and getting out of the bed. I furrowed my brow but didn't say anything. It wasn't that shocking that she'd be upset that we were together, so I didn't think much of it when Finn started to gather up his jacket and sweatshirt.

"Thank you for protecting my daughter," Elora said without looking at him.

Finn paused at the doorway to look back at me, his dark eyes conflicted. He nodded, then turned and walked out of my room, shutting the door behind him.

"Well, you took that much better than I thought you would," I admitted, sitting up.

"He's not coming back."

"What?" I stared at the door in dismay.

"He saved your life, so I gave him last night to say good-bye to you," Elora explained. "I will be transferring him out of here as soon as possible."

"You mean he knew?" I gaped at her.

"Yes. I made the agreement with him last night," Elora said. He had known and hadn't let me in on it, and hadn't tried to steal me away.

"But . . . he saved my life!" I insisted, feeling a terrifying pain growing in my chest. It screamed that I couldn't possibly survive without Finn. "He should be here to protect me!"

"He is emotionally compromised and unsuitable for the job," Elora explained flatly. "Not only that, if he stayed around, you would be banished from Förening. He doesn't want that, and neither do I." She sighed.

"I shouldn't have even given him last night, but . . . I don't want to know what you did with him. Don't tell me. Don't tell anyone. Is that clear?"

"Nothing happened." I shook my head. "But I want him back. He'll protect me better than anyone!"

"Let me put it to you this way: he will do anything to keep you alive, Princess." Elora looked at me evenly. "That means he would die to save you, without hesitation. Do you really want that? Do you really want him to die because of you?"

"No . . ." I trailed off, looking dazedly at my blankets. I knew she was right. Last night he had almost died to save me. If Tove hadn't come out onto the balcony, he would be dead.

"Very well. It's in his best interest that he's not around you either," Elora said. "Now you need to get up and get ready. We have much to go over."

TWENTY-FOUR

good-bye

The next few days were an endless stream of defense meetings. There had never been an attack on Förening this severe. The body count was well into the double digits, including several visiting higher royal Trylle. Any loss of powerful Trylle was devastating for the kingdom.

Elora and Aurora led all the meetings, while Tove and I sat quietly in the back. He was the most powerful and should've had more of a say, but he didn't seem that interested.

The twenty or so other people who always seemed to be in attendance offered advice that was completely pointless. Tove just said that our best defense was to get our abilities under control. Willa took this advice to heart and busied herself with self-defense classes and getting a better control of her wind ability. Elora barely spoke to me, and never uttered a kind word.

The one positive was that I'd been spared the christening ceremony, and Elora decided to allow me to keep my own name.

I wandered around in a fog. I didn't care whether I lived or died. If they attacked again, I would deal with whatever happened.

"You're gonna have to snap out of this one day," Rhys said.

I lay in my bed, staring at the ceiling, while he leaned against the doorway. He still had a nasty cut above his eyebrow, since Aurora wouldn't resort to healing a mänks. The wound was slowly getting better, but it pained me to see it. It was just a reminder that he had gotten hurt for me.

"Maybe." I didn't feel like I ever would, and I hoped I wouldn't.

"Oh, come on." Rhys sighed and came over to sit on the bed next to me. "I know that everything that's happened has really taken its toll on you, but it's not the end of the world."

"I never said it was," I muttered. "I just hate this house. I hate my mother. I hate being a Princess. I hate everything about being here!"

"Even me?" Rhys asked.

"No, of course not you." I shook my head. "You're about the only thing I like anymore."

"I feel privileged." He smiled at me, but when I didn't smile back, his quickly faded. "Look, I hate it here too. It's a hard place to live in, especially this house, with Elora. But . . . what else are we gonna do? Where else can we go?"

That's when it occurred to me. I absolutely did not want this life, and this life truly didn't want Rhys. He had grown up surrounded by a cold indifference that made his childhood even worse than my own, and he deserved so much more.

Since I had been here, Rhys had been one of the few people to show me genuine kindness, and he deserved that in return.

I didn't particularly care whether I lived or died, so I didn't need protection, should anyone decide to come after me again, but I wasn't so sure they would anymore. Tove had explained that the Vittra numbers had been damaged, and another attack anytime soon would be highly unlikely.

But somewhere out there, I knew that my brother Matt was worried sick about me. He and Maggie would welcome me back with open arms, and they would be delighted to have Rhys. I didn't know how I would explain him to them, but I'd figure something out.

I was not a Princess, and I didn't want to be one. It would feel so good to be home again. That wouldn't really fix the Finn thing, but Matt and Maggie would know the best way to mend a broken heart.

Rhys wasn't convinced that leaving was the best thing for me, pointing to the cut on his eye from when he'd been unable to protect me or himself. Reluctantly, I resorted to using my persuasion, but I didn't really have another choice. Besides, I was only convincing him that he didn't need to worry about me.

In the middle of the night, I decided to act. I gathered Rhys and we snuck out of the palace, which was more difficult than I'd expected. Guards and other Trylle walked the grounds in case of another Vittra attack. Even though they thought another one would be unlikely, they weren't taking any chances.

Rhys and I went through the kitchen and out the back door,

to the secret garden that bloomed even in the middle of the night. Scaling the high brick walls that surrounded the palace compound would've been impossible if I didn't have Rhys to give me a boost . Once I pulled him up, we both jumped down on the other side.

Without even brushing the dirt from our clothes, we ran along the wall. Rhys led the way because he knew the area better than I did. We'd nearly made it to the garage when we had to duck behind a bush to wait for a guard to pass.

Once the guard moved on, we hurried to the garage. Rhys found his new motorcycle but didn't start it. He pushed it out of the garage, leaving the engine and lights off so as not to attract attention.

At the edge of town was the gate manned by a guard, and I doubted he'd let the Princess through. Rhys had a plan, though. He knew of a weak spot in the fence a ways down the embankment. He'd heard of other mänks getting through it when they ran away.

I had to help Rhys steady the motorcycle so it wouldn't go tumbling down the hill as we made our way through the trees and the brush. Apparently the hole in the fence was even larger now than it had been before. That's how some of the Vittra had broken in, and the Trylle hadn't fixed it yet. Typical of them, to be more focused on securing the palace than making sure the town of Förening was safe.

We were able to get the motorcycle through without much trouble, and it was then, as we pushed it up the hill, that I started feeling the exhilaration and relief of escape. I ignored any pangs of sadness or longing for some of the people I'd met here, like Willa and Tove, and I just tried to focus on the fact that I was getting away. I was free.

Once we got to the road, Rhys started the motorcycle. We sped off into the darkness, and I sat on the bike behind him, wrapping my arms tightly around his waist and burying my face in his leather jacket.

The sky had that eerie blue glow of very early morning when we pulled up in front of my house. Rhys hadn't even turned off the motorcycle before Matt threw open the front door and came jogging down the porch steps.

Even in the dim light I could see how stricken Matt looked. I jumped off the bike, and, completely oblivious to Rhys, Matt threw his arms around me. He held me so tightly to him, it hurt. I didn't care, though. I buried my face in his shoulder, breathing in his familiar scent and relishing the protection of his arms. I was finally *home*.

torn

For Michael Wincott—the greatest villain of all time

return

When Rhys and I showed up at my "brother" Matt's house at eight in the morning, he was happy . . . in the sense that he was glad I was alive and hadn't disappeared forever. Despite being angry, he listened while I put together a vague explanation, glaring at me the whole time with mystified rage.

At least I only had to face Matt. My aunt Maggie is my legal guardian, but she wasn't there when we arrived. Matt explained that she had gone off looking for me in Oregon. I have no idea why, but for some reason, she thought I'd run off there.

As Rhys and I sat on the shabby-chic couch in Matt's living room, surrounded by the boxes that he had yet to unpack from when we'd moved into the house two months ago, Matt paced back and forth in front of us.

"I still don't understand," Matt said. He stopped in front of us, arms folded over his chest.

"There's nothing to understand," I insisted, gesturing at Rhys. "He's your brother! It's pretty obvious when you look at him."

I have dark, wild, curly hair and mahogany eyes. Matt and

Rhys both have sandy hair and sapphire eyes. They had some-thing much more open in their faces too, and they had the same easy smile. Rhys stared up at Matt with bemused wonderment, his eyes wide with awe.

"How could you possibly know that?" Matt asked.

"I don't know why you can't just trust me." I sighed and laid my head back on the couch. "I never lie to you!"

"You just ran away from home! I had no idea where you were. That's a major trust violation!"

Matt's anger couldn't cover up how hurt he still was, and his body showed signs of the strain he had been under. His face was gaunt and haggard, his eyes red and tired, and he had probably lost ten pounds. When I disappeared, he completely collapsed, I'm sure. I felt guilty, but I hadn't had a choice.

Matt had always been too preoccupied with my safety, a side effect from his mother having tried to kill me and all that. His life revolved around me to the point of being unhealthy. He had no friends, no job, no life of his own.

"I had to run away! Okay?" I ran a hand through my tangled curls and shook my head. "I can't explain it to you. I left for my safety and for yours. I don't know if I should even be here now."

"Safety? What were you running from? Where were you?" Matt asked desperately, not for the first time.

"Matt, I can't tell you! I wish I could but I can't."

I wasn't sure if it was legal for me to tell him anything about the Trylle or not. I assumed everything about them was secret, but nobody had expressly forbidden me from telling outsiders either. Matt would never believe me, though, so I didn't see the point in trying.

"You're really my brother," Rhys said in a hushed tone. He leaned forward to get a better look at Matt. "This is so weird."

"Yeah, it is," Matt agreed. He shifted uncomfortably under Rhys's stare before he turned to me, his expression serious. "Wendy, can I have a word with you? Alone?"

"Uh, sure." I looked over at Rhys.

Taking his cue, Rhys stood up. "Where's your bathroom?"

"Down that way, off the kitchen." Matt pointed to his right.

Once Rhys was gone, Matt sat down on the coffee table in front of me and lowered his voice.

"Look, Wendy, I don't understand what's going on. I have no idea how much of what you've told me is true, but that kid looks like a total weirdo to me. I don't want him in my house, and I don't know what you were thinking bringing him here."

"He's your brother," I said wearily. "Honest, Matt. I would never, ever lie about something this major. I am one hundred percent certain that he is your real brother."

"Wendy . . ." Matt rubbed his forehead, sighing. "I get that you believe that. But how could you actually know? I think this kid is feeding you a story."

"No, he's really not. Rhys is the most honest person I've ever known, except for you. Which makes sense, since you're brothers." I leaned in closer to Matt. "Please. Give him a chance. You'll see."

"What about his family?" Matt asked. "Who has been raising him all these years? Don't they miss him? And aren't they your 'real' family or whatever?"

"Trust me, they won't miss him. And I like you better," I said with a smile.

Matt shook his head as if unable to decide what to make of all this. I knew a large part of him didn't trust Rhys and wanted to throw him out of the house, so I admired him all the more for his restraint.

"I wish you would be straight with me about all of this," he said.

"I'm being as straight with you as I can be."

When Rhys came back from the bathroom, Matt leaned away from me and eyed him warily.

"You don't have any family pictures up," Rhys commented as he looked around the room.

That was true. We didn't really have decorations of any kind up, but we didn't particularly care to remember our family. Matt especially was not fond of our . . . er, his mother.

I had yet to explain to Rhys about his mother being a lunatic locked up in a mental institution. Stuff like that is hard to break to someone, especially someone as awestruck as Rhys.

"Yeah, we're just that way," I said and stood up. "We drove all night to get here. I'm pretty beat. What about you, Rhys?"

"Uh, yeah, I guess I'm tired." Rhys seemed a bit startled by my suggestion. Even though he hadn't gotten any sleep, he didn't look tired at all.

"We should get some sleep, and we can talk more later."

"Oh." Matt got to his feet slowly. "You're both going to be sleeping here, then?" He looked uncertainly at Rhys, then back at me.

"Yeah." I nodded. "He doesn't have anywhere else to go."

"Oh." Matt was clearly against the idea, but I knew he was afraid that if he kicked Rhys out, I'd go after him. "Rhys, I guess you can sleep in my room, for now."

"Really?" Rhys tried to tone down his excitement over staying in Matt's room, but it was obvious.

Matt awkwardly showed us up to our rooms. My room was still

my room, all my stuff the same as I had left it weeks earlier. As I settled in, I listened to Matt and Rhys talking across the hall in Matt's room. Rhys was asking him to explain the simplest things, like how to turn on the bedside lamp, and it made Matt frustrated and uncomfortable.

By the time Matt came into my room, I had already changed into my pajamas. They were worn and comfortable, and I loved them.

"Wendy, what is going on?" Matt whispered. He shut the door behind him and locked it, as if Rhys were some kind of spy. "Who is that kid really? Where did you go?"

"I can't tell you what happened while I was gone. Can't you just be happy that I'm here and I'm safe?"

"No, not really." Matt shook his head. "That kid is not right. He's so amazed by everything."

"He's amazed by *you*," I corrected him. "You have no idea how exciting all this is for him."

"None of this is making any sense." Matt ran a hand through his hair.

"I really do need to get some sleep, and this is a lot for you to process. I get that. Why don't you go call Maggie? Let her know I'm safe. I'll get some rest, and you can think about everything I've been saying."

Matt released a defeated sigh. "Fine," he said, then his blue eyes went hard. "But you better think about telling me what's really going on here."

"All right." I shrugged. I could think about it, but I wouldn't tell him.

Matt's gaze softened again, and his shoulders slackened. "I am glad you're home."

I could see just then how terrible this had all been for him. And I knew I could never disappear like that again. I went over and hugged him tightly.

Matt left me alone in my room, and I crawled into the familiar comfort of my twin bed. I had been sleeping in a giant king-sized bed in Förening, but somehow, my narrow bed felt so much better. I snuggled deeper in the covers, relieved to be somewhere that felt sane again.

I'd always had an inkling that I didn't fit in with my family, despite Matt's devotion to me. My mother had nearly killed me when I was six years old, claiming that I was a monster and not her daughter.

Turns out, she was right.

Less than a month ago, I found out I was a changeling—a child that is exchanged in secret for another child. Specifically, I was switched at birth with Rhys Dahl. It turns out that I'm a Trylle. Trylle are basically glamorous grifters with mild superpowers.

Technically, I'm a troll, but not in the creepy little green monster sort of way. I'm of normal height and fairly attractive. In Trylle culture, the use of changelings is a practice that dates back centuries. The custom's intention is to make sure Trylle offspring have the best childhoods possible.

I'm supposed to be a Princess in Förening—the compound in Minnesota where the Trylle live. My birth mother is Elora, the Trylle Queen. After spending a few weeks in Förening, I decided to head home. I had a falling-out with Elora, who had forbidden me from seeing Finn Holmes simply because he's not royalty.

I escaped and took Rhys with me. In Förening, Rhys had shown me genuine kindness, and I felt he deserved some of that in return.

I brought him here to meet Matt, since he is really Rhys's brother, not mine.

Of course, I couldn't tell Matt all of that. He'd think I was completely insane.

Growing drowsy, I thought again how good it felt to be home. It only took ten minutes for Rhys to shatter that comfort when he crept into my room. I was almost asleep, but the sound of my door opening made me alert. Matt had gone downstairs, presumably to make the phone call I suggested, and if he knew Rhys was in here, he'd kill us both.

"Wendy? Are you asleep?" Rhys whispered, sitting gingerly on the edge of my bed.

"Yes," I muttered.

"Sorry. I can't sleep," Rhys said. "How can you sleep?"

"It's not that exciting for me. I lived here before, remember?"

"Yeah, but . . ." He trailed off, probably because he had no argument for that. Suddenly he tensed and sucked in his breath. "Did you hear that?"

"You talking? Yes, but I've been trying not—" Before I could finish my sentence, I heard it too. A rustling sound outside my bedroom window.

Considering I had just had a horrible run-in with some very bad trolls known as Vittra, I was alarmed. I rolled over and peered at the window, but the curtains were drawn, blocking my view.

The rustling turned into actual banging, and I sat up, my heart pounding. Rhys shot a nervous glance at me. We heard the window slide open, and the curtains billowed out from the wind.

interruptions

He stepped into my room in one graceful move, as if entering through bedroom windows were nothing out of the ordinary.

His black hair was slicked back impeccably, but he had stubble growing along his jaw, making him look even sexier. His eyes were so dark they were nearly black, and he took one discerning look at Rhys before settling them on me, making my heart forget to beat entirely.

Finn Holmes had snuck into my room.

He still managed to stun me the same way he always did. I was so happy to see him that I almost forgot how angry I was with him.

The last time I had seen Finn, he was slinking out of my bedroom in Förening, per his deal with my mother. Elora told him that he could spend one more night with me before leaving. Forever.

We had only kissed, but Finn had failed to let me in on Elora's plan. He didn't even bother to say good-bye. He didn't fight it or try to get me to run away with him. He just crept out of my room, leaving Elora to explain to me exactly what had happened.

"What are you doing here?" Rhys asked, and Finn pulled his eyes off me to glare at Rhys.

"I came to collect the Princess, of course," Finn said, but irritation saturated his words.

"Well, yeah, but . . . I thought Elora reassigned you." Rhys seemed thrown by Finn's anger, and he fumbled for a minute. "I mean . . . that's what people were saying around Förening, that you weren't allowed around Wendy anymore."

Finn tensed noticeably at Rhys's words, his jaw flexing, and Rhys looked down at the floor.

"I'm not," Finn admitted after a moment. "I was preparing to leave when I heard that you two had vanished in the middle of the night. Elora was deciding who would be best suited to track Wendy, and I thought it would be in her best interest if I went after her, what with the Vittra *stalking* her."

Rhys opened his mouth to protest but Finn cut in.

"We all know you did a wonderful job of protecting her at the ball," Finn said. "If I hadn't shown up, you might've protected her right into getting murdered."

"I know the Vittra are a threat!" Rhys shot back. "I just . . . we came here to . . ."

Hearing his confusion, I got up off the bed, moving to intercede before Rhys figured out why he'd let me talk him into coming here.

The truth was, Rhys didn't agree to come here. He wanted to meet Matt, but he was adamant about my safety and had flat-out refused to let me leave the security of the compound. Unfortunately for Rhys, I had *persuasion*. When I looked at people and thought about what I wanted them to do, they would do it, whether they wanted to or not.

That's how I convinced Rhys to go with me when we ran away, and I needed to distract him before he caught on.

"The Vittra lost a lot of trackers in that fight," I interjected. "They're not eager to repeat it anytime soon. Besides that, I'm sure they're sick of trying to get me."

"That's highly unlikely." Finn narrowed his eyes, studying Rhys's bewilderment, and then he looked darkly at me. "Wendy, do you care nothing for your own safety?"

"I probably care more than you do." I crossed my arms firmly over my chest. "You were leaving to go on to another job. If I had waited one more day to leave, you wouldn't have even known I was gone."

"Is this about getting *my* attention?" Finn snapped, his eyes burning. I had never seen his anger directed at me this way before. "I don't know how many times I have to explain this to you! You are a Princess! I mean nothing! You need to forget about me!"

"What's going on?" That was Matt, shouting from the stairs. If he came up here and caught Finn in my room, it would be very, very bad.

"I'll go . . . create a diversion." Rhys glanced at me to make sure that was okay, and I nodded. He darted out the door, saying things to Matt about how awesome the house was, and their voices faded as they went downstairs.

I tucked my curls behind my ears and refused to look at Finn. It was hard to believe that the last time I had been with him, he had been kissing me so passionately, I could barely breathe. I remembered the way his scruff scraped against my cheeks and the way his lips pressed against mine.

I suddenly hated him for that memory, and I hated that all I could think about was how badly I wanted to kiss him again.

"Wendy, you are not safe here," Finn insisted quietly.

"I'm not going with you."

"You cannot stay here. I won't allow it."

"You won't allow it?" I scoffed. "I am the Princess, remember? Who are you to *allow* me to do anything? You're not even my tracker anymore. You're some guy being a creepy stalker."

That sounded much harsher than I'd meant it. Not that anything I said ever really seemed to hurt Finn. He just stared at me, his gaze level and unfazed.

"I knew I would find you faster than anyone. If you don't come home with me, that's fine," Finn said. "Another tracker will be here shortly, and you can go with him. I'll just wait with you until he arrives, to ensure your safety."

"It's not about you, Finn!"

He had played a larger part in my leaving Förening than I would ever admit, but it really wasn't just him. I hated my mother, my title, my house, everything. I wasn't meant to be a Princess.

Finn looked at me for a long moment, trying to understand where this was coming from. I had to fight the urge to squirm as he scrutinized me. His eyes flashed darkly for a second, and his expression hardened.

"Is this about the mänsklig?" Finn asked, referring to Rhys. "I thought I told you to stay away from him."

Mänsklig were the human children taken in exchange for Trylle babies. They were the lowest in the Trylle hierarchy, and if a Princess was caught dating one, they'd both be banished forever. Not that I cared, but I didn't have any feelings for Rhys that weren't purely platonic.

"It has nothing to do with Rhys. I just thought he'd like to see his family." I shrugged. "It has to be better than living in that stupid house with Elora."

"Good. He can stay here, then." Finn nodded. "Matt and Rhys are taken care of. Now you can come home."

"That is not my home. *This* is my home!" I gestured widely to my room. "I'm not going, Finn."

"You are not safe." He took a step closer to me, lowering his voice and staring into my eyes. "You saw what the Vittra did in Förening. They sent an army out to get you, Wendy." He put his hands on my arms, strong and warm on my skin. "They will not stop until they have you."

"Why? Why wouldn't they stop?" I asked. "There's got to be Trylle out there who are easier to get than me. And so what if I'm a Princess? If I don't come back, Elora can replace me. I'm meaningless."

"You are far more powerful than you know."

"What does that even mean?"

Before he could answer, there was a noise on the roof outside my window. Finn grabbed my arm and threw open my closet door, shoving me inside. As a rule, I don't enjoy being tossed into closets and having the door shut in my face, but I knew he was protecting me.

I opened the door a crack, so I could watch what happened and intervene if necessary. Even as mad as I was at Finn, I would never let him get hurt over me. Not again.

Finn stood a few feet from the window, his eyes blazing and his shoulders tense. But when the figure climbed through the window, Finn only scoffed.

The kid coming in tripped on the windowsill. He wore skinny jeans and purple shoes with the laces untied. Finn towered over him, looking down at him wearily.

"Hey, what are you doing here?" The kid flipped his bangs out of his eyes and pulled down his ill-fitting jacket. It was zipped all the way up, and the bottom met the top of his jeans. When he bent over or moved, it rode up.

"Getting the Princess. They sent you after her?" Finn arched an eyebrow. "Elora really thought you'd be able to bring her back?"

"Hey, I'm a good tracker. I've brought in way more people than you have."

"That's because you're seven years older than me," Finn replied. That made the clumsy kid twenty-seven. He looked much younger than that.

"Whatever. Elora picked me. Deal with it." The kid shook his head. "What? Are you jealous or something?"

"Don't be absurd."

"So where is the Princess anyway?" He looked around my room. "She ran away for *this*?"

"This is my room." I walked out of the closet, and the new tracker jumped. "You don't need to be condescending."

"Um, sorry," he stumbled, blushing. "My apologies, Princess." He offered me an unsure smile and did a low bow. "I'm Duncan Janssen, and I'm at your service."

"I'm not the Princess anymore, and I'm not going with you. I just finished explaining that to Finn."

"What?" Duncan looked uncertainly at Finn as he adjusted

his jacket again. Finn sat down on the edge of my bed and said nothing. "Princess, you have to come. It's not safe for you here."

"I don't care." I shrugged. "I'd rather take my chances."

"It can't be that bad at the palace." Duncan was the first person I had ever heard genuinely call Elora's house a palace, even though it sort of was one. "You're the Princess. You have everything."

"I'm not going. You can tell Elora that you tried your best, and I refused."

Duncan once again looked to Finn for help. Finn shrugged at Duncan, and his shift to indifference startled me. I had put my foot down on the subject, but I hadn't really expected him to listen.

"She can't possibly stay here," Duncan said.

"You think I don't agree with you?" Finn raised an eyebrow.

"I don't think you're helping." Duncan fidgeted with his jacket and tried to stare Finn down, a task I knew was impossible.

"What do you expect me to say to her that I haven't already said?" Finn asked, sounding surprisingly helpless.

"So you're saying we simply leave her here?"

"I'm right here, you know," I said. "And I don't really appreciate the way you keep referring to me like I'm not."

"If she wants to stay here, then she'll stay here," Finn said, continuing to ignore me. Duncan shifted and glanced over at me. "We're not going to kidnap her. That leaves little in the way of options."

"Can't you, like"—Duncan lowered his voice and fiddled with the zipper of his jacket—"you know, *convince* her somehow?"

Word of Finn's affection for me must have spread through the compound. Aggravated, I refused to let my feelings for him be used against me.

"Nothing is going to convince me," I snapped.

"Do you see?" Finn motioned toward me. Sighing, he got to his feet. "We should be on our way, then."

"Really?" I couldn't hide the shock in my voice.

"Yeah. Really?" Duncan echoed.

"You said there's nothing I can do to convince you. Has that changed?" Finn turned to me. His voice was hopeful, but his eyes were almost taunting. I shook my head firmly. "Then there is nothing left to say."

"Finn—" Duncan started to protest, but Finn held his hand up.

"It is as the Princess wishes."

Duncan looked skeptically at Finn, probably thinking that this was some sort of trick, much as I was. There had to be something I wasn't getting, because Finn wouldn't just leave me here. Sure, that's exactly what he had done a few days ago, but that's when he thought leaving was what was best for me.

"But Finn—" Duncan tried again, but Finn waved him off.

"We must go. Her 'brother' will notice us soon," Finn said.

I glanced at my closed bedroom door, as if Matt would be lurking right there. The last time Matt and Finn had a run-in it had not gone well, and I was not eager to repeat the experience.

"Fine, but . . ." Duncan trailed off, realizing too late that he had nothing to threaten either of us with. He gave me another quick bow. "Princess. I'm sure we'll meet again."

I shrugged. "We'll see."

Duncan climbed out my bedroom window, practically falling onto the roof. After he was out, he half jumped, half fell off the roof. Finn watched him apprehensively for a moment, holding my curtain open, but he didn't follow after immediately.

Instead, he straightened up, looking over at me. My anger and resolution were fading, leaving me hopeful that Finn wouldn't really leave things this way.

"Once I'm out this window, lock it behind me," Finn commanded. "Make sure all the doors are locked, and never go anywhere alone. Never go anyplace at night, and if at all possible, always take Matt *and* Rhys with you." He looked past me for a moment, thinking of something.

"Although neither of them are really good for much of anything . . ." His dark eyes rested on mine once again. His expression was imploring, and he raised his hand as if he meant to touch my face, but he lowered it again. "You *must* be careful."

"Okay," I promised him.

With Finn standing right in front of me, I could feel the warmth of his body and smell his cologne. His eyes were locked on mine, and I remembered the way it felt when he tangled his fingers in my hair and held me so close to him I couldn't breathe.

He was so strong and controlled. In the brief moments he allowed himself to let go of his passion with me, it was the most wonderfully suffocating feeling I'd ever had.

I didn't want him to leave, and he didn't want to leave. But we had both made choices we were unwilling to change. He nodded once more, breaking eye contact, and then turned and slid out the window.

Duncan waited at the bottom of the tree, and Finn dropped gracefully to the ground. From the window, I watched Finn coax a hesitant Duncan away from the house.

When they reached the hedges separating my lawn from the neighbors', Finn looked around, checking to make sure no one was there. Without even looking at me, he and Duncan turned and disappeared.

I closed the window, locking it securely the way he'd said to. I felt a terrible ache watching him go. Even though he had done this kind of thing before, I couldn't wrap my mind around Finn really leaving and convincing Duncan to leave me too. If he was so concerned about the Vittra, why would he leave me so unprotected?

It finally dawned on me. Finn had *never* left me unprotected, no matter what I or anybody else wanted. As soon as he had realized I wasn't going with him, he hadn't wanted to waste any more time arguing. He would wait in the wings until I changed my mind or . . .

I shut the curtains tightly. I hated being spied on, but I also found it strangely comforting that Finn was watching over me. After having my window open for so long, my room felt chilly, so I went over to my closet and pulled on a heavy sweater.

The adrenaline rush from seeing Finn had left me wide awake, but I was looking forward to curling up in bed, even if I wouldn't be able to sleep.

I settled into my bed, trying futilely to forget about Finn. Within minutes, I heard a loud banging downstairs. Matt let out a yell, but it was cut short, leaving the house in total silence.

I jumped and ran to my bedroom door. With shaking hands, I opened it, hoping that Finn had tried to sneak back in and had a misunderstanding with Matt.

Then I heard Rhys screaming.

insentient

Rhys suddenly went silent. I barely took a step out of my room when I heard footsteps pounding up the stairs, and before I could react, she was there.

Kyra, a Vittra tracker I had dealt with before, appeared at the top of the landing. Her dark hair was in a pixie cut, and she wore a long black leather jacket. She hung on to the railing, crouching down. As soon as she saw me, she sneered, showing more teeth than any human would.

I rushed toward her, hoping for the element of surprise, but I was out of luck.

She dodged before I got close and sent a swift kick into my abdomen. I stumbled backward, gripping my stomach dramatically, and when she came at me again, I punched her in the face.

Unfazed, Kyra lunged at me and returned the blow much harder. When I fell down, she stood over me, smiling, with blood dripping from her nose.

I scrambled to my feet, and she grabbed my hair, yanking me up. I kicked at her as she lifted me, and she rewarded my moxie by kicking me in the side so hard I cried out. Kyra laughed at that and kicked me again.

This time I saw white and everything faded out for a moment. My hearing got wonky, and I barely hung on to consciousness.

"Stop!" a strong voice shouted.

When I blinked open my swollen eyes, I saw a man running up the stairs toward Kyra. He was tall, and beneath his black sweater he was well muscled. Kyra dropped me to the floor when he reached the top of the stairs.

"It's not like I can *really* hurt her, Loki," Kyra said, her voice bordering on whining.

I tried to get to my feet again, even though I felt dizzy, and she kicked me down.

"Knock it off," he snapped at her. She grimaced and took a step back.

He stood in front of me, towering above me, and then knelt down. I could scramble away from him, but I wouldn't get far. He cocked his head, looking at me curiously.

"So you're what all the fuss is about," he mused.

He reached forward, taking my face in his hands. Not painfully, but he was forcing me to look at him. His caramel eyes fixed on mine. I wanted to look away, but I couldn't.

This strange fog settled over me, and as terrified as I was, I felt my body relaxing, losing its ability to fight. My eyelids were too heavy to keep open, and, unable to stop it, I fell asleep.

I was dreaming of water. But anything more specific than that I couldn't remember. My body felt cold, like it should be shivering but wasn't. My cheeks were warm, though, resting against something soft.

"You're telling me that she's a *Princess*?" Matt asked, his voice a deep rumble above me. My head lay against his leg, and the more I woke up, the more I realized how terrible my body felt.

"It's not that hard to believe, really," Rhys said. His voice came from somewhere on the other side of the room. "Once you get all the Trylle stuff, the Princess part is pretty easy to take."

"I'm not sure what to believe anymore," Matt admitted.

I opened my eyes with a struggle. My lids felt unnaturally heavy, and my left eye was swollen from where Kyra had punched me. The room swayed, and I blinked it into focus.

When my vision finally cleared, I still didn't understand what I was seeing. The floor appeared to be dirt, and the walls were brown and gray stones, looking damp and weathered. It reminded me of an old cellar . . . or a dungeon.

Rhys paced the other side of the room, fresh bruises on his face. I tried to sit up, but my entire body hurt and my head felt woozy.

"Hey, take it easy," Matt said, putting his hand on my shoulder, but I didn't listen.

I pushed myself up until I was sitting, which took a lot more effort than it normally required. I grimaced and leaned against the wall next to him.

"You're awake!" Rhys grinned. He was probably the only person in the world who could look happy in this situation.

"How are you feeling?" Matt asked. For his part, he didn't have any visible bruises, but he was a better fighter than Rhys and me.

"Great." I had to lie through gritted teeth because it hurt to breathe. Based on the intense shooting pain in my diaphragm, I guessed I had a cracked rib, but I didn't want to worry Matt. "What's going on? Where are we?"

"I was hoping you could shed some light on that," Matt said.

"I already told him, but he won't believe me," Rhys said.

"Where are we, then?" I asked Rhys, and Matt scoffed.

"I'm not sure exactly." Rhys shook his head. "I think we're in the Vittra palace in Ondarike."

"Ondarike?" I asked.

"The Vittra capital," Rhys explained. "But I don't know exactly how far it is from Förening."

"I figured as much," I said, sighing. "I recognized the Vittra who attacked the house. Kyra went after me before."

"What?" Matt's eyes were wide and disbelieving. "These people went after you before?"

"Yeah, that's why I had to leave." I closed my eyes because it hurt too much to keep them open. The world wanted to spin out from under me.

"Told you," Rhys said to Matt. "I'm not lying about this stuff. After what happened, you would think you'd cut me a little slack."

"Rhys isn't lying," I said, wincing. It was getting harder to breathe, and I had to take very shallow breaths, which only made me more light-headed. "He knows more about all of this than I do. I wasn't there very long."

"Why are these Vittra people coming after you?" Matt asked. "Why do they want you?"

I shook my head, unwilling to risk the pain of speaking.

"I don't know," Rhys answered when I didn't. "I've never seen them go after anyone this way before. Then again, she's the first Princess I've been around, and they've foretold of her for a while."

I'd wanted to know what they were foretelling, but everyone gave me vague responses, so all I knew was that I'd be powerful someday. But I didn't feel very powerful, especially right now. It hurt too much to speak, and I was locked up in a dungeon.

And even worse, not only had I failed to save myself, but I'd gotten Rhys and Matt dragged into this mess along with me.

"Wendy, are you okay?" Matt asked.

"Yeah," I lied.

"You don't look okay," Rhys said.

"All your color is gone, and you're barely even breathing," Matt said, and I heard him getting to his feet next to me. "You need a doctor or something."

"What are you doing?" Rhys asked.

I opened my eyes to see what Matt was up to. His plan was simple and obvious—he went to the locked door and pounded on it.

"Help! Somebody! Wendy needs a doctor!"

"What makes you think they'd even want to help her?" Rhys asked, echoing my exact thoughts. Kyra had gone out of her way to hurt me when she captured me.

"They haven't killed her yet, so they probably don't want her dead." Matt had stopped pounding long enough to answer Rhys, then went back to hitting the door and yelling for help.

The sound of it echoed through the room, and I couldn't take it anymore. My head throbbed too much already. I was about to tell Matt to knock it off when the door opened.

This was the perfect time for Matt and Rhys to launch a counterattack, but it didn't occur to either of them. They both just moved away.

The Vittra from the house walked into the room, the one who had rendered me unconscious, and I dimly remembered Kyra calling him Loki. His shaggy hair was surprisingly light for a Vittra, almost blond.

Walking next to him was a troll, like an actual troll. All short and gobliny. His features were humanoid, but his skin was slimy and brown. He wore a hat, and tufts of grayish hair stuck out around the edge. He barely came up to Loki's hip, but the fact that he was an actual troll made him more intimidating somehow.

Rhys and Matt both gaped at the hobgoblin, and I probably would've too, if I'd been capable of gaping. I could barely keep my head up.

"You say the girl is in need of a doctor?" Loki asked, his eyes resting on me. He regarded me with the same mild curiosity he had before.

"Kyra did that?" the hobgoblin asked, his voice unexpectedly deep for such a small creature. He looked to Loki for confirmation, shaking his head at the damage she'd inflicted on me. "She needs to be put on a leash."

"I don't think Wendy can breathe," Matt said, his features hardening with self-restraint.

I was sure my condition was the only thing keeping him from attacking Loki. If he hurt them, they wouldn't be able to help me.

"Well, let me have a look." Loki walked over to me, his strides long and purposeful.

The hobgoblin stayed by the door, guarding it from Matt and Rhys, but they were too focused on me to consider escape.

Loki crouched down in front of me, looking me over with something that resembled concern. I was in too much pain to feel real fear, but I'm not sure I would have been afraid of him. Physically he was much stronger than me, and he had some kind of ability that could knock me out, maybe even more than that. But somehow, I knew he'd help me.

"What hurts?" Loki asked.

"She can barely breathe, let alone talk!" Matt snapped. "She needs immediate medical attention."

Loki held up his hand to silence him, and Matt sighed heavily. "Can you talk?" Loki kept staring at me.

When I opened my mouth, instead of speaking, an excruciating cough rose up in me. Closing my eyes, I tried to fight it. I coughed so hard, tears streamed down my cheeks, and I felt something wet. I opened my eyes to see bright red splattered all over my legs and Loki's feet. I was coughing up blood, and I couldn't stop.

"Ludlow!" Loki shouted at the hobgoblin. "Get Sara! Now!"

FOUR

vitriol

Loki crouched in front of me, keeping Matt back. He probably knew Matt's inclination would be to hold me, and Loki didn't want me moved, afraid that it might rupture something. Matt shouted frantically, but Loki kept insisting that everything would be all right.

Within moments a woman appeared in the room. Her long dark hair was pulled back in a ponytail, and she knelt down in front of me, pushing Loki to the side. Her eyes were almost as dark as Finn's, and I found something comforting in that.

"My name is Sara, and I'm going to help you." She pressed her hand hard against my abdomen, and I winced.

It hurt so bad I wanted to scream, but then the pain began to fade. A weird numbing tingle ran through me. It took me a second to figure out where I had felt the sensation before.

"You're a healer," I mumbled, slightly dismayed that she was helping me. The pain in my chest and stomach had disappeared, and she put her hand on my face, fixing my black eye.

"Does it hurt anywhere else?" Sara asked, ignoring my statement. She looked worn out, a temporary side effect from healing, but otherwise she was incredibly beautiful.

"I don't think so." I sat up, still a little unsteady, but that was lessening by the moment.

"Kyra went way overboard," Sara said, more to herself than me. "Are you okay now?"

"Yeah." I nodded.

"Excellent." Sara stood up and turned to Loki. "You need to control your trackers better."

"They're not *mine*." Loki crossed his arms over his chest. "If you have a problem with how they do their job, take it up with your husband."

"I'm certain my husband wouldn't like how this situation was handled." Sara looked at him severely, but he didn't back down.

"I was doing you a favor," Loki replied evenly. "If I hadn't been there, it would've been worse."

"I'm not having this discussion now." She glanced in my direction, then walked out of the room.

"Is that everything, then?" Loki asked us once she'd gone.

"Not even close." Matt had been sitting next to me but he got to his feet. "What do you want with us? You can't just keep us here!"

"I'll take that as a yes." Loki smiled emptily at me and turned to leave the room.

Matt tried to rush him, but Loki was already out the door before he got to him. He slammed the door and Matt flew into it. There was a loud clicking as bolts locked, and Matt sagged against the door.

"What is going on here?" Matt shouted and turned to look at me. "How come you're not dying anymore?"

"Would you rather I be dying?" I pulled the sleeve of my sweater down and wiped the blood away from my face. "I could get Kyra in here to finish the job."

"Don't be ridiculous." Matt rubbed his forehead. "I want to know what's happening. I feel like I'm in a bad dream."

"It gets easier," I said and turned to Rhys. "What the hell was that hobgoblin thing that came in? Was that an actual troll?"

"I don't know." Rhys shook his head, looking just as bewildered as I felt. "I've never seen one before, but everyone goes out of their way to make sure mänks don't know anything."

"I didn't think there were real trolls." I furrowed my brow, trying to remember what Finn had told me about trolls before. "I thought they were just myths."

"Really?" Matt asked. "After everything that's happened? So you pick and choose what mythology you believe in?"

"I'm not picking and choosing anything." I got to my feet. I still felt sore all over, but it was light-years better than I'd felt when I woke up. "I believe what I can see. I hadn't seen this before. That's all."

"Are you okay?" Matt watched me as I hobbled around the room. "Maybe you should take it easy."

"No, I'm fine." I brushed him off. I wanted to get my bearings in the space, maybe see if there was a way that we could get out. "How did we get here anyway?"

"They broke into the house and attacked us." Matt gestured to the door, referring to Loki and the Vittra. "That guy knocked us out somehow, and we woke up here. We hadn't been awake very long before you woke up."

"Lovely." I pressed my palms against the door, pushing on it as if I thought it would open. It didn't, but I had to try.

"Hey, where's Finn?" Rhys asked, echoing thoughts I was starting to have. "Why didn't he stop this?"

"What does Finn have to do with this?" Matt asked with an edge to his voice.

"Nothing. He used to be my tracker. It's sorta like a bodyguard." I took a step back, staring at the door and willing it to open. "He tried to protect me from all of this."

"That's why you ran away with him?" Matt asked. "He was protecting you?"

I sighed. "Something like that."

"Where is he?" Rhys repeated. "I thought he was with you when the Vittra came."

Matt started yelling about Finn being in my room, but I ignored him. I didn't have the energy to fight with Matt about propriety or his feelings for Finn.

"Finn left before they broke in," I said, once Matt had finished his tirade. "I don't know where he's at."

I wouldn't admit it, but I was surprised that Finn hadn't protected me. Maybe he had really left. I thought it had all been a bluff, but if it was, Finn would've been there when we were attacked.

Unless something bad had happened to him. The Vittra could have gotten to him before they came after me. He cared too much for duty, even if he didn't care enough for me. The only way he wouldn't keep me safe was if he *couldn't*.

"Wendy?" Rhys asked.

I think he'd been talking before that, but I hadn't heard anything he'd said. I'd been too busy thinking of Finn and staring at the door.

"We have to get out of here," I said and turned to Rhys and Matt.

Matt sighed. "Obviously."

"I have an idea." I bit my lip. "But it's not a great one. When they come back, I can use my persuasion. I can convince them to let us go."

"Do you really think it's strong enough?" Rhys voiced the concern I'd had myself.

So far, I'd only used persuasion on unsuspecting humans, like Matt and Rhys, and Finn had told me that without training, my abilities weren't as strong as they could be. I hadn't begun my training yet in Förening, so I had no clue how powerful or weak I might be.

"I really don't know," I admitted.

"Persuasion?" Matt raised an eyebrow and looked at Rhys. "Is that the thing you were telling me about? That mind thing she can supposedly do?" Rhys nodded, and Matt rolled his eyes.

"It's not *supposedly*." I bristled at his skepticism. "I can do it. I've done it to you before."

"When?" Matt asked dubiously.

"How do you think I got you to take me to see Kim?" I asked, referring to when he'd taken me to see his mother, my "host" mother, in the institution.

He hated her and didn't want me to have anything to do with her. I'd used persuasion on him, even though I'd felt guilty about it, but it was the only way I could talk to her.

"You did that?" The shock and hurt in his eyes was instantly replaced by anger. He looked like he'd been slapped in the face. I lowered my eyes and turned away. "You tricked me? How could you do that, Wendy? You always say you never lie to me, then you go and do something like that!"

"It wasn't a lie," I said sheepishly.

"No, it's worse!" Matt shook his head and stepped away from

me, as if he couldn't stand to be near me. "I can't believe you did that. How often did you do that?"

"I don't know," I admitted. "For a long time, I didn't know I was doing it. But once I figured it out, I tried not to do it at all. I don't like doing it, especially to you. It's not fair, and I know it."

"Damn right it's not fair!" Matt snapped. "It's cruel and manipulative!"

"I'm really sorry." I met his eyes, and the hurt in them stung painfully. "I promise I won't ever do it again, not to you."

"I hate to break up this moment, but we need to figure a way out of here," Rhys interrupted. "So what is the plan?"

"We call someone," I said, happy for the reprieve from thinking about how much Matt must hate me.

"What do you mean, 'call someone'? Do you have your cell phone?" Rhys asked excitedly.

"No, I mean, summon someone. The way Matt did before." I pointed to the door behind me. "Knock on the door, say we're hungry or cold or dead or whatever. When they come, I can use my persuasion on them to get them to let us out."

"You think that will really work?" Matt asked, but the disbelief had dropped from his voice. He was only asking my opinion now.

"Maybe." I looked at Rhys. "But I have a favor to ask. Can I practice on you?"

"Sure." Rhys shrugged, trusting me immediately.

"What do you mean, 'practice'?" Matt asked with a concerned edge.

He moved a bit closer to Rhys, and I realized with some surprise that he finally believed Rhys was his brother. He wanted to protect Rhys from me. I felt some relief and happiness knowing that he'd started accepting him, but it hurt a little—okay, *a lot*—to know that Matt thought of me as a threat.

"I haven't done it very much." I didn't like the way Matt scrutinized me with his gaze, so I paced the room, as if that could deflect his attention somehow. "And it's been a while since I've done it at all."

That last part wasn't entirely true, since I'd just used it on Rhys the day before, but I didn't want him reacting the way Matt had. This whole process would go a lot easier the less people hated me.

"So what do you want to do?" Matt asked.

"I don't know yet." I shrugged. "But I just need to practice. It's the only way I can get stronger."

Despite Matt's obvious reservations, Rhys went along with it. It felt very odd to have someone witnessing persuasion, especially someone clearly against it, but I had no choice. It wasn't like I could send Matt into the next room or something.

I could see Matt watching me intently out of the corner of my eye. It was distracting, but that was probably better practice for me. I doubted I could get any of the Vittra to step aside to a quiet place while I tried to use a bit of mind control on the guard.

I decided to start simple. Rhys and I were standing, facing each other, so I started repeating in my head, *Sit down. I want you to sit down.*

His blue eyes met mine evenly at first, then a fog passed over them. His face seemed to slacken, and his expression went completely blank. Without a word, he sat down on the floor.

"Is he okay?" Matt asked nervously.

"Yeah, I'm fine." Rhys sounded like he'd just woken up. He looked up at me, his eyes dazed. "So, are you gonna do it or what?"

"I already did it." I had never talked to anybody about it after using persuasion on them, and it felt strange to be open about it.

"What are you talking about?" Rhys's brow furrowed, and he looked back and forth between Matt and me, trying to understand.

"You got all spaced out, then you sat on the floor," Matt said.

"Why did you sit down?" I asked.

"I . . ." His face scrunched up in concentration. "I don't know. I just . . . I sat down." He shook his head and looked up at me. "You did that?"

"Yeah. You didn't feel anything or sense anything?" I asked.

I had never known if what I did hurt people. They never complained of pain or anything, but maybe they couldn't because they didn't understand what was happening.

"No. I didn't even . . ." He shook his head again, unable to articulate what he meant. "I expected there to be a blackout or something. But . . . I knew that I was sitting. It was more like a reflex. Like, I breathe all the time, but I don't think about it. This was the same."

"Hmm." I looked at him thoughtfully. "Stand up."

"What?" Rhys asked.

"Stand up," I repeated. He stared up at me for a second, then looked around. His eyes hardened and his eyebrows pinched up.

"What's going on?" Matt asked, moving closer to us.

"I . . . I can't stand up."

"Do you need me to help you up?" Matt offered.

"No. It's not like that." Rhys shook his head. "I mean, you could pull me up. You're stronger than me, and I'm not physically pinned to the floor. I just . . . forgot how?"

"Weird." I watched him with fascination.

Once before, I had made Matt get out of my room, and it'd been a while before he'd been able to go in there again. Which meant my persuasion had lingering effects, but it did eventually wear off.

"'Weird'?" Matt scoffed. "Wendy, fix him!"

"He's not broken," I said defensively, but Matt glared at me in a way that made me want to crawl under a rock. I crouched down in front of Rhys. "Rhys, look at me."

"Okay?" He met my eyes uncertainly.

I wasn't even sure if I could reverse the process. I had never tried to undo persuasion before, but I didn't think it'd be that hard. And if I couldn't, then he'd just have to sit down for a week or two. Maybe.

Instead of worrying about the possible repercussions, I focused all my energy on him. I just said, *Stand up*, in my head over and over again. It took longer than it did last time, but eventually his face started to fog over. He blinked at me a few times and got to his feet.

"I am so glad that worked." I let out a sigh of relief.

"Are you sure it worked?" Matt asked me, but his eyes were on Rhys. Rhys stared blankly at the floor, looking more out of it than he had last time. "Rhys? Are you okay?"

"What?" Rhys lifted his head. He blinked at us, as if he'd just noticed we were there. "What? Did something happen?"

"You're standing up." I pointed to his legs, and he looked down.

"Oh." He lifted one of his legs, making sure it still worked, and didn't say anything for a minute. Then he looked up at me. "I'm sorry. Were we talking about something?"

"You couldn't stand up. Remember?" I asked, but my stomach twisted. I might really have broken Rhys.

"Oh. Yeah." He shook his head. "Yeah, I remember. But I can stand now. Did you do that?"

"Wendy, I don't like you playing with him like this," Matt said quietly.

Matt faced Rhys, but he gave me a sidelong glance. He tried to keep his face hard, but his eyes betrayed his fear.

I had scared Matt, and not in the same way as when I'd run away. Then he'd been scared for me, but now he seemed scared *of* me, and it created a painful knot in my chest.

"I'm done now." I stepped away from Rhys.

My dark hair hung around my face. I had a tie around my wrist, so I pulled my hair up into a loose bun.

"What?" Rhys asked, sounding alert.

He had fully come out of the trance I'd had him under, but I didn't want to look at him. Matt made me feel ashamed about using persuasion, even if Rhys was aware of what I had done.

"Sit down," Matt suggested.

"Why? I don't wanna sit down."

"Sit down anyway," Matt said, more firmly this time. When Rhys didn't respond, Matt repeated his command. "Rhys, sit down."

"I don't get why it's so important to you that I sit down." Rhys grew more agitated as Matt pressed him, which was strange, since I'd never really heard him sound irritated with anyone. "I'm fine standing up."

"You can't sit down." Matt sighed, looking over at me. "You broke him a different way, Wendy."

"Wendy did this?" Rhys furrowed his brow. "I don't understand. What did you do? You told me not to sit?"

"No, I told you to sit, and you couldn't stand. Then I told you to stand, and you can't sit." I sighed in frustration. "Now I don't know what to say! I don't really wanna say anything anymore. I might make it so you stop breathing or something."

"Can you do that?" Matt asked.

"I don't know!" I threw my hands up. "I have no idea what I'm capable of."

"I can't sit down for a while." Rhys shrugged. "Big deal. I don't even wanna sit down."

"That's probably a side effect of the persuasion," I told him as I paced our cell.

"Whatever, I don't care if it is," Rhys said. "It doesn't matter. I'm not in a situation that calls for sitting down, anyway. The important thing is that you know that you can do this. You can use this, we can get out of here, and somebody in Förening can fix me. Okay?"

I stopped pacing and looked uneasily at Matt and Rhys. Rhys was right. I needed to get us out of here. It wasn't safe here, and Rhys's inability to sit was a secondary concern. If anything, it just made me want to get us out of here quicker.

"Are you guys ready?"

"For what?" Matt asked.

"To run. I don't know what's on the other side of the door, or how long I can hold them off," I said. "As soon as they open the door, you have to be ready to run as fast as you can, as far as you can."

"Aren't you just gonna *Star Wars* them?" Rhys asked, completely unfazed by the idea. "When Obi-Wan's like, 'These aren't the droids you're looking for.'"

"Yeah, but I don't know how many guards there are, or how dangerous they might be." My thoughts flashed back to Finn and how he hadn't been at my house during the attack. I shivered involuntarily and shook my head.

"Let's just get out of here, okay? There's no way to know what we're up against, so let's deal with it as it comes. Anything's better than sitting around waiting for them to figure out what they want to do with us. Because when they do decide, I have a feeling it won't be good."

Matt didn't look convinced, but I doubted anything could've convinced him. This whole thing had turned into a giant horrible mess, all because I hadn't wanted to stay in Förening and be a stupid Princess.

If I had, none of this would've happened. Matt and Rhys would be at their respective homes, safe and sound, and Finn would be . . . well, I didn't know where he'd be, but it had to be better than where he was now.

With that thought burning in my mind, I pounded on the door, knocking as loudly as I could. My fist hurt from how hard I hit, but I didn't care.

hobgoblin

W hat?" a deep, craggy voice asked, and a slot slid open in the middle of the door.

I bent over to peer through, and I saw the hobgoblin that had come in with Loki. His eyes were buried under bushy eyebrows, and I wasn't sure if I had a good enough view to persuade him. Or if it even worked on actual trolls. They appeared to be an entirely different species.

"Ludlow, is it?" I asked, remembering the name Loki had shouted when sending for help.

"Don't try to sweet-talk me, Princess." The hobgoblin coughed, retching up phlegm and spitting it on the ground. He wiped his face on the back of his sleeve before turning back to me. "I've turned down far prettier girls than you before."

"I need to go to the bathroom." I dropped any pretense of being friendly. I had a feeling that honesty and cynicism would go further with him.

"So go. You don't have to ask me for permission." Ludlow laughed, but it wasn't a pleasant sound.

"There's no bathroom in here. I'm not gonna squat on the ground," I said, genuinely disgusted by the idea.

"Then hold it." Ludlow started to shut the slot, but I put my hand out, blocking it.

"Can't you get a guard or something to take me to the bathroom?" I asked.

"I am the guard," Ludlow snapped, sounding huffy.

"Oh, really?" I smirked at him, realizing this might be far easier than I thought.

"Don't underestimate me, Princess," Ludlow growled. "I eat girls like you for breakfast."

"So you're a cannibal?" I wrinkled my nose.

"Ludlow, are you harassing the poor girl?" came a voice from behind Ludlow. He moved to the side, and through the slot I saw Loki swaggering toward us.

"She's harassing *me*," Ludlow complained.

"Yes, talking to a beautiful Princess—what a rough lot you have in life," Loki said dryly, and Matt snorted behind me.

Ludlow muttered something, but Loki held up his hand, silencing him. Then he was too close to the door for me to see his face. The slot was at Ludlow's eye level, which came up to Loki's waist.

"What seems to be the problem?" Loki asked.

"I need to go to the bathroom." I leaned in closer to the slot, peering up at him. I wanted to catch his eyes, but they remained out of my vision.

"And I told her to go inside the cell," Ludlow said with pride.

"Oh, come, now. She's not a common mänks. We can't leave her in squalor!" Loki chastised the troll. "Open the door. Let her out."

"But sir, I'm not to let her out until the King calls for her." Ludlow looked up at him nervously.

"You think the King would want her treated this way?" Loki asked, and the hobgoblin wrung his hands. "You can explain to the Majesty that this is all my fault, if it comes to it."

Ludlow nodded reluctantly. He slid the slot shut, and I let him this time. I stood up and listened to the sounds of the bolts and locks clicking and turning.

"I don't like this," Matt said in a low voice.

"We don't have much of a choice," I whispered. "I got us into this, and I'll get us out."

The door opened a bit, and I stood back, expecting it to open farther. I thought Loki would step in, I would use persuasion, and we would be off. But he and Ludlow remained hidden outside.

"Well?" Ludlow asked. "I'm not holding this door open all day."

Ludlow had left the door open a few inches, giving me barely enough room to slide my body through. I squeezed my way out, and as soon as I had, Ludlow slammed the door shut. I stared down at him, already busying himself with locking it up.

"The bathroom is this way," Loki said.

He gestured down the hall, which was made of the same dank bricks as the cell I'd been in. The floors were dirt, and torches on the wall lit the way.

"Thanks." I smiled at Loki and caught his eyes easily. They were really quite beautiful, a dark golden color, but I pushed that thought from my mind.

Concentrating as hard as I could, I started chanting silently, *Let them go. Let us go. Open the cell and let us go.* It took a few seconds before I saw any response, but the one I got wasn't at all what I was expecting.

A bemused smile crossed his lips, and his eyes sparkled with wicked pleasure.

"I bet you don't even have to go to the bathroom, do you?" Loki smirked at me.

"I—what?" I fumbled, startled that nothing had happened.

"I told you we shouldn't let her out!" Ludlow shouted.

"Relax, Ludlow," Loki said but kept his eyes on me. "She's fine. Harmless."

I redoubled my efforts, thinking I hadn't tried hard enough. Maybe I'd weakened myself by using persuasion on Rhys so recently. Healers were tired and aged after they used their abilities. I was probably the same way, even though I didn't feel tired.

I started repeating it in my mind again when Loki waved his hand, stopping me.

"Easy, Princess, you're going to hurt yourself." He laughed. "You're persistent, though. I'll give you that."

"So, what? You're immune or something?" I asked.

No point in pretending I hadn't been trying to use persuasion on him. He obviously knew what I was doing.

"Not exactly. You're far too unfocused." He crossed his arms over his chest, watching me with that same curious expression he always seemed to have. "You're quite powerful, though."

"I thought you said she was harmless," Ludlow interjected.

"She is. Without training, she's almost useless," Loki clarified. "Someday she'll be a great asset. Right now she's little more than a parlor trick."

"Thanks," I muttered.

I hurried to rethink the plan. I could probably take down Ludlow, but I didn't understand how all the locks worked. Even if I got him out of the way, I wasn't sure that I could open the door to Matt and Rhys's cell to free them.

But Loki was my biggest problem, since I already knew how well I'd fare against him. Besides being taller and stronger than me, he had the ability to knock me out just by looking at me.

"I can see your mind spinning," Loki said, almost in awe. I tensed up, afraid he might be able to read my mind, and I tried to think of nothing. "I can't see what's *on* your mind. If I had, I wouldn't have let you out. But now that you are, we might as well make the best of it."

"What do you mean?" I asked warily, moving away from him.

"You overestimate my interest in you." Loki grinned broadly. "I prefer my Princesses in unsoiled pajamas."

My clothes would've been relatively clean if it weren't for the blood on my sweater and some dirt on my knees. I was sure I was a mess, but it wasn't my fault.

"I'm sorry. I usually look much nicer after I take a beating," I said, and his smile faltered.

"Yes, well, I don't think you'll have to worry about that now." Loki recovered quickly, his cocky edge returning. "I think it's time you went and saw Sara."

"Sir, I really think that's unwise—" Ludlow interrupted, but Loki glared at him and he shut up.

"What about my friends?" I pointed at the cell.

"They're not going anywhere." Loki smiled at his own joke, and I resisted the urge to roll my eyes.

"I know that. But I'm not leaving without them."

"You're in luck. You're not leaving." Loki took a step back, still facing me. "Don't worry, Princess. They're perfectly safe. Come on. Talking to Sara is in your best interest."

"I've already met Sara," I said, attempting some kind of a protest.

I looked apprehensively back at the cell door, but Loki took another step away. I sighed, deciding that talking to higher-ups would probably be the only way I could barter for Matt and Rhys's release. Even if I couldn't ensure my own.

"How did you know?" I asked as I fell into step with him.

We walked side by side down the hall, passing several more doors like the one on my cell. I didn't hear much of anything or see any other hobgoblins standing guard, but I wondered how many other prisoners were here.

"Know what?"

"That I was . . . you know, trying to persuade you," I said. "If it wasn't working, how did you know?"

"Because you're powerful," Loki reiterated and gestured to his head. "It's like a static. I could feel you trying to push your way inside my head." He shrugged. "You'll feel it too, if anyone tries it on you. I'm not sure if it'd work, though."

"So it doesn't work on Trylle or Vittra?" I asked, doubting he would give me a straight answer. I wondered why he was telling me anything in the first place.

"No, it does. And if you were doing it well, I wouldn't have felt anything at all," Loki explained. "But we're harder to control than mänks. If you do a sloppy job of digging around in our heads, we'll feel it."

We reached some concrete steps, and Loki bounded up them, barely waiting for me. He showed no concern for me escaping, and he had divulged more information than he needed to. As far as I could tell, Loki was a really terrible guard. Ludlow should've had more authority over him.

He pushed through the massive doors at the top of the stairs, and we stepped out into a grand hall. Not a hallway kind of hall, but hall as in a large room with vaulted ceilings. The walls were dark wood with red accents, and an ornate red rug lay in the center of the floor.

It had the same kind of opulence as the palace in Förening, but the tones were deeper and richer. It felt more like a luxurious castle.

"This is really nice," I said, not hiding the surprise and awe in my voice.

"Yes, of course it is. It's the King's home." Loki looked at me, bemused by how stupefied I appeared. "What else would you expect?"

"I don't know. After being downstairs, I assumed something creepier and dirtier." I shrugged. "You didn't even have electricity down there."

"It's for dramatic effect. It's a dungeon." He led the way down a corridor decorated the same as the hall.

"What would happen if I tried to escape?" I asked.

I didn't see anyone else. If I outran Loki, I could probably get away. Not that I knew where to go, and I still wouldn't be able to free Matt and Rhys.

"I would stop you," he replied simply.

"The same way Kyra did at my house?" A pain flared up in my rib, as if reminding me of the damage she'd caused.

"No." Something dark flickered across his face for a second. He quickly erased it and smiled at me. "I would simply take you in my arms and hold you there until you swooned."

"It sounds romantic when you say it that way." I wrinkled my nose, remembering how he'd made me pass out by staring into my eyes. It hadn't been painful, but it hadn't exactly been pleasant either.

"It is when I envision it."

"That's a little twisted," I said, but he shrugged in response. "Why did you kidnap me and take me here?"

"I fear you have too many questions for me, Princess," Loki said, almost tiredly. "You'd do better saving them all for Sara. She's the one with the answers."

We walked the rest of the way without saying anything. He led me down the hall, up a flight of stairs carpeted in red velvet, and down another hall before stopping at ornate wooden double doors. Vines, fairies, and trolls were carved into them, depicting a fantasy scene in the vein of Hans Christian Andersen.

Loki knocked once with dramatic flair, then opened the doors without waiting for a response. I followed behind him.

"Loki!" Sara shouted. "You are to wait to be let into my chambers!"

Her room was much the same as the rest of the house. A large four-poster bed sat in the center, with unmade crimson sheets on top of it.

A dressing table sat on one side of the room, and she was perched on a small stool in front of it. Her hair was pulled up in the same tight ponytail as before, but she'd changed out of her clothes. A long black satin robe hung about her.

When she turned to look at us, the fabric moved as if it were liquid. Her brown eyes widened with shock at the sight of me, but she hurried to compose herself.

A hobgoblin stood next to her, the same kind as Ludlow. He

had attempted to dress up, wearing a small butler's uniform, but he had the same horrible skin and haggard appearance. Long necklaces, layered in diamonds and pearls, hung from his hands. At first I didn't understand why, but soon I realized he was holding them for her, like a living jewelry box.

A yapping ball of fur jumped off the bed when we came into the room. It stopped just short of us, and I saw it was only a Pomeranian. The majority of its rage seemed directed at me, and when Loki told it to be quiet, it fell silent. Eyeing me warily, the dog walked toward Sara.

"I didn't expect to see you so soon." Sara forced a smile at me, and her eyes turned icy when she looked at Loki. "I would've dressed if I had known you were coming."

"The Princess was getting restless." Loki lounged on a velvet couch near the end of the bed. "After the day she's had, I thought she deserved a break."

"I understand that, but I'm a tad unprepared at the moment." Sara continued glaring at him and gestured to her robe.

"Well, then you shouldn't have sent me to retrieve her so soon," Loki said, returning her stare evenly.

"You know that we had to do—" Sara cut herself off and shook her head. "Never mind. What's done is done, and you're absolutely right."

She smiled at me, her expression leaning toward something warm. Or at least something far warmer than my mother Elora ever managed.

"What's going on?" I asked.

Even after all they'd done, I still had no idea what the Vittra really wanted with me. I knew only that they refused to stop coming after me.

"Yes, we should talk." She tapped her fingers on the table for a minute while she thought. "Can you give us a minute, please?"

"Fine." Loki sighed and got to his feet. "Come on, Froud." The little dog ran happily to him, and Loki scooped him up. "The grown-ups need to talk."

The hobgoblin carefully set the jewelry on the table, and then headed toward the door. He walked slowly, his gait wobbly thanks to his stature, but Loki loitered so that the troll made it out of the room before him.

"Loki?" Sara said when he reached the doors, but she didn't look at him. "Make sure my husband is ready for us."

"As you wish." Loki made a small bow, still carrying the dog. When he walked out, he shut the doors behind him, leaving me alone with Sara.

"How are you feeling?" Sara offered a smile.

"Better. Thank you." I wasn't certain that I should be thanking her. She had healed me, but she had something to do with me getting hurt in the first place.

"You'll want to get changed." Sara nodded at my clothes as she stood up. "I might have something in your size."

"Thanks, but I don't really care about my clothes. I want to know what's going on. Why did you kidnap me?" I felt exasperated, and I knew it came out in my tone, but she didn't seem to notice.

"I'm sure I have something," Sara continued, as if I hadn't said anything. She walked over to a large closet in the corner and opened the door. "It might be a little big on you, but I'm sure it'll work." After looking for a matter of seconds, she pulled out a long black dress.

"I really don't give a damn about the clothes!" I snapped. "I want to know why you keep chasing after me. I can't give you what you want if I don't know what it is."

As she walked to the bed, I realized she was uncomfortable looking at me. Her eyes seemed to go everywhere but to me. And anytime they did land on me, she was quick to look away. She went over to the bed, laying my dress on it.

"You sent them out so we can talk and now you won't say anything?" I asked, growing even more frustrated.

"I've imagined this day for a long time." Sara lovingly touched the dress, smoothing it out on the bed. "Yet here it is, and I feel so unprepared."

"Seriously, what does that mean?"

Her expression grew pained for a minute, then returned to the same blank, serene look she'd worn before.

"I hope you don't mind, but I'm going to get dressed." She turned her back to me, walking over to a folding screen in the corner.

A fantasy scene similar to the one on the doors had been painted on it, and a black-and-red ball gown hung from the edge. Sara took the dress and went behind the screen to change in private.

"Do you know where Finn is?" I asked with a painful ache in my chest.

"That's your tracker?" Sara asked, draping the robe over the screen. I could only see the top of her head above it.

"Yes." I swallowed hard, fearing the worst.

"I'm not sure where he is. We don't have him, if that's what you're asking."

"Then why hasn't he come for me? How did he let you take me away?" I demanded.

"I assumed they detained him until they got away with you." She slipped the dress over her head, so her words were muffled for a moment. "I'm not certain of the specifics, but they had orders not to hurt anyone unless it was absolutely necessary."

"Yeah, and Kyra's orders were not to hurt me, right?" I asked wryly, but Sara didn't say anything. "Can you just tell me if he's okay?"

"Loki didn't report any fatalities," Sara said.

"He was in charge of bringing me here?" I looked at the closed doors behind us, realizing too late that I should've been asking him these questions. I thought about going after him, but then Sara came out from behind the screen.

"Yes. And other than Kyra's . . . outburst, Loki recounted that everything went well." She ran her hands along her skirt, then pointed to the dress on the bed. "Please. Get dressed. We're going to see the King."

"And he'll answer my questions?" I raised my eyebrow.

"Yes. I'm certain he'll tell you everything." Sara nodded, keeping her eyes locked on the floor.

I decided to go along with it. If he tried to give me the run-around, I would bolt. I didn't have time to waste on vague answers and evasive language. Matt and Rhys were captive, and Rhys couldn't even sit down.

But I also needed them to like me so that maybe I could talk them into letting Matt and Rhys go. If that meant I had to put on a silly little dress, so be it.

I went behind the screen and changed, while Sara continued getting ready. She put on one of the necklaces that the hobgoblin had left on the table and let down her hair. It was black and straight, shining like silk down her back. It reminded me of Elora's.

I wondered what Elora would make of all this. Would she send out a rescue mission to get me? Did she even know I was gone?

After I put on the dress, Sara tried to tie a loose ribbon on the back, but I wouldn't let her. She had reached out to touch it, and when I snapped at her to leave it alone, her expression fell into something tragic. Her hands hovered in the air for a moment, as if she couldn't believe what had just happened. Then she let them fall to her side and nodded.

Without saying anything, she led me down the hall. At the end, we came to another set of doors that mirrored the ones on her chamber. She knocked, and while we waited for a response, she smoothed down her crimson and black lace skirt again. It already lay perfectly flat, so I suspected this was some kind of nervous habit.

"Come in," a strong gravelly voice boomed from the other side of the doors.

Sara nodded, as if he could see her, then pushed open the doors.

The room was windowless, as had been every room I'd seen, and the walls were dark mahogany. Despite its massive size, the room had a cavelike quality. One wall was covered floor-to-ceiling with bookcases, and a heavy wooden desk sat nearby. Several elegant red chairs were the only other furniture.

The largest one, with intricate designs on the wooden feet, sat directly across from us, and a man sat in it. His dark brown hair ran long, past his shoulders. He wore all black—pressed pants, a dress shirt, and a long jacket that resembled a robe. He was handsome, in a battled kind of way, and he appeared to be in his forties.

Loki had been sitting in a chair, but he stood up when we came in. Froud the small dog had disappeared entirely, and I hoped they hadn't eaten it or something equally horrible.

"Ah, Princess." The King smiled when he saw me but didn't get up. His gaze flitted over to Loki for the briefest of seconds. "Loki, you are dismissed."

"Thank you, sire." Loki bowed and hastily departed. He left me with the impression that he didn't enjoy the company of the King, and that made me all the more nervous.

"So are you gonna tell me what's going on?" I asked the King directly, and his smile widened.

"I suppose we should start with the basics," he said. "I'm the King of the Vittra. My name is Oren, and I am your father."

kings & pawns

My first thought was the most obvious: *He's lying.*

This was quickly followed by: *What if he isn't lying?*

Elora, by all accounts, had been a horrible mother who cared very little for me. I thought of the encounter I'd had a few minutes earlier with Sara. She had lovingly caressed my dress, saying, *I've imagined this day for a very long time.*

Sara stood nearby, wringing her hands. She met my eyes for the first time and smiled hopefully at me, but there still seemed to be a sadness in her face that I didn't understand.

I didn't look like her, not any more than I looked like Elora. They both far surpassed me in beauty, but Sara appeared much younger, only in her early thirties.

"So . . ." I swallowed, forcing my mouth to work, and turned to Oren. "You're saying that Elora isn't my mother?"

"No, unfortunately, Elora is your mother," he said with a heavy sigh.

This confused me even more. His admission gave more credence to his words, though. It would be simpler for him to lie to me. He could've told me that he and Sara were my parents, if his plan was to entice me into staying and taking his side.

But he'd told me that Elora was my mother, which left me with an alliance to her, which couldn't possibly benefit him.

"Why are you telling me this?" I asked.

"You need to know the truth. I know how fond of games Elora is." Every time Oren said her name, it came out bitterly, as if it hurt to speak it. "If you have all the facts, it will be easy for you to make a decision."

"And what decision is that?" I asked, but I thought I knew.

"The only decision that matters, of course." His lips twitched with a strange smile. "What kingdom you will rule."

"To be perfectly honest, I don't want to rule any kingdom." I twisted a stray curl that had come loose from my hair tie.

"Why don't you sit down?" Sara gestured to a chair behind me. After I sat, she took a seat nearer to the King.

"So . . ." I looked at her smiling sadly at me. "You're my step-mother?"

She nodded. "Yes."

"Oh." I sat in silence for a minute, taking it all in. "I don't understand. Elora told me my father was dead."

"Of course she did." Oren laughed darkly. "If she told you about me, she'd have to give you a choice, and she knew you'd never choose her."

"So how did you . . ." I floundered for the right word. "How exactly did the two of you . . . get together to . . . you know, conceive me?"

"We were married," Oren said. "This was long before I married Sara, and it was a rather brief union."

"You married Elora?" I asked and anger boiled up.

Initially, when he'd told me he was my father, I'd thought it was an illicit affair, like the one Elora had had with Finn's father. I didn't imagine that it'd be something of public record, something that every single person I'd met in Förening would've known about.

Including Finn. When he'd been going over the Trylle history, giving me a crash course on everything I needed to know about being a Princess, he'd failed to mention that my mother had been married to the Vittra King.

"Yes, briefly," Oren said. "We were wed because we thought it would be a good way to combine our respective kingdoms. Vittra and Trylle have had their disagreements over the years, and we wanted to create peace. Unfortunately, your mother is the most impossible, irrational, horrible woman on the planet." He smiled at me. "Well, you know. You've met her."

"Yes, I'm aware of how impossible she can be." I felt a strange urge to defend her, but I bit my tongue.

Elora had been cold, bordering on cruel at times, but for some reason, when Oren put her down, it offended me. But I nodded and smiled like I agreed completely.

"It's amazing I even managed to conceive a child with her," he said, more to himself than to me, and I cringed at the thought of it. I didn't need to picture Oren and Elora being intimate. "Before you were even born, the marriage was over. Elora took you, hid you, and I've been searching for you all these years."

"You did a horrible job of it," I said, and his expression hardened. "You do realize that your trackers have beaten me up on three separate occasions? Your wife had to come in and heal me so I didn't die."

"I am terribly sorry about that, and Kyra is being dealt with,"

Oren said, but he didn't sound apologetic. His words were hard and angry, but I hoped that was directed more at Kyra than at me. "But you wouldn't have died."

"How do you know that?" I asked sharply.

"Call it a King's intuition," Oren answered vaguely. I would've pressed further, but he continued, "I don't expect you to greet us with open arms. I know Elora's already had a chance to brainwash you, but I'd like you to take a few days to get to know our kingdom before making a decision to rule here."

"And what if I decide not to stay?" I asked, meeting his eyes evenly.

"Look around our kingdom first," Oren suggested. He smiled, but the edge to his voice was unmistakable.

"Let my friends go," I blurted out. That had been my motivation for speaking to him in the first place, but all this talk of parentage had gotten me sidetracked.

"I'd rather not," he said with that same weird smile.

"I won't stay here if you don't let them go," I said as firmly as I could.

"No, you won't leave if they're here." The gravel in his voice made his words carry greater severity. "They're insurance, so I can be sure that you take my offer *very* seriously."

He smiled at me, as if that would counteract the veiled threat, but the wicked edge to his smile made it worse somehow. The hair on the back of my neck stood up, and I was finding it harder to believe this man was my father.

"I promise you, I won't go anywhere." I struggled to hide the tremor in my voice. "If you let them go, I will stay as long as you want."

"I'll let them go when I believe you," he countered reasonably.

I swallowed hard, trying to think of another way to barter. "Who are these people that you have such concern for?"

"Um . . ." I considered lying to him, but he already knew I cared for them. "It's my brother, er, my . . . host brother or whatever, Matt, and my mänsklig, Rhys."

"They're still doing that practice?" Oren frowned in disapproval. "Elora absolutely despises change. She refuses to break from tradition, so this shouldn't come as a shock. But it's so outdated."

"What?" I asked.

"The whole mänsklig business. It's a total waste of resources." Oren gave a dismissive wave at the whole idea of it.

"What do you mean?" I asked. "What do you do with the baby you take when you leave a changeling?" When a baby is left with the host family then the family's original baby has to be taken.

"We don't take a baby," he said. My stomach twisted when I imagined them killing the infant, the way I had once feared the Trylle did. "We simply leave them behind, at human hospitals or orphanages. It's none of our concern what happens to them."

"Why don't Trylle do that?" I asked. Once he said it, it made sense, and I wondered why everyone didn't do that. It would be easier and cheaper.

"At first they took them as slave labor. Now they do it out of tradition." He shook his head, as if he thought nothing of it.

"It's a moot point, anyway." Oren exhaled deeply. "We rarely even practice changelings anymore."

"Really?" I asked. For the first time since I'd met him, it felt like I might actually agree with him about something.

"Changelings can get hurt, lost, or simply refuse us," Oren said. "It's a waste of a child, and it's killing our lineage. We're far more powerful than the humans. If we want something, we can take it. We don't need to risk our progeny in their clumsy hands."

He had a point, but I wasn't sure it was much better than Elora's. She worked more of a con job, and Oren proposed outright theft.

"She was unwilling to change the old ways." His face grew darker when he spoke of her. "She was so set on keeping the humans and trolls separate that she made their lives irrevocably tied, but she couldn't see the hypocrisy of it. She saw it as nothing more than having your children raised by nannies."

"It's entirely different," I said.

I thought of my childhood with the host mother who had tried to kill me, and my bond with Matt. I couldn't imagine any nanny taking care of a child in the same way.

"Exactly." He shook his head. "And that's why our marriage didn't work. I wanted you. She gave you away."

I knew his reasoning was twisted by some sort of flawed logic I couldn't quite pinpoint. But I felt myself surprisingly moved, even if I didn't entirely believe him. This was the first time any of my parents, host or real, had ever said they wanted me.

"Do I . . ." I said, refusing to let myself be overcome by emotion. "Do I have any siblings?"

Oren and Sara exchanged a look I couldn't read, and Sara stared down at her hands folded in her lap. She was the opposite of Elora in almost every way. Physically they were strikingly similar, with long black hair and beautiful dark eyes, but that's where the parallels ended. Sara spoke little, but conveyed a warmth and submissive nature that Elora would be incapable of.

"No. I have no other children, and Sara has no children at all," Oren said.

This fact seemed to sadden Sara further, so I had a feeling the lack of children had not been her choice.

"I'm sorry," I said.

"She's infertile," Oren announced without provocation, and Sara's cheeks reddened.

"Um . . . I'm sorry. I'm sure it's not her fault," I fumbled.

"No, it's not," Oren agreed heartily. "It's the curse."

"Pardon?" I asked, hoping I'd misheard him.

I didn't think I could take any more of the supernatural. Trolls and abilities were enough without adding curses on top of it.

"Legend has it that a spurned witch cursed the Vittra after we stole her child for a changeling." He shook his head as if he didn't believe it, which gave me some relief. "I don't give much credence to that. It is all part of the same thing that gives us abilities, the thing that we're descended from."

"What is?" I asked.

"We're all trolls. The Vittra, the Trylle, you, me, Sara. All of us are trolls." He gestured around. "And you've seen the trolls that live around here, the ones that look like hobgoblins?"

"You mean Ludlow?"

"Exactly. They're trolls, Vittra, the same as you and me," Oren explained. "But they're an abnormality that only seems to plague our colony."

"I don't understand. Where do they come from?"

"Us." He said it as if it made sense, and I shook my head. "Infertility runs rampant among us, and of the few births we have, over half of them are born as hobgoblins."

"You mean . . . ." I wrinkled my nose, feeling a bit grossed out. "Vittra like you and Sara give birth to trolls like Ludlow?"

"Precisely," Oren said.

"That's actually kinda creepy," I said, and Oren wagged his head like he didn't entirely disagree.

"It's a curse of our longevity, not a bitter old woman's spell, but here we are." He sighed and smiled. "You, obviously, are far lovelier than anything we could've hoped for."

"You can't imagine how pleased we are to have you with us," Sara agreed.

Looking at her hopeful face, it finally dawned on me. I understood why the Vittra had been coming after me so aggressively and so relentlessly. They didn't have a choice. I was their only hope.

"You didn't marry Elora to unite your people," I said, sizing Oren up. "You did it because you couldn't have kids with a member of your own tribe. You needed an heir to the throne."

"You are my daughter." He raised his voice, not so he was shouting, but enough to make it boom through the room. "Elora has no more right to you than I do. And you will stay here because you are the Princess, and it is your duty."

"Oren. Your Majesty," Sara said, imploring him. "She has been through a tremendous amount today. She needs to rest and recuperate. It's impossible to have a reasonable conversation when she hasn't fully healed."

"Why hasn't she fully healed?" Oren gave her an icy glare, and she lowered her gaze.

"I did everything I could for her," Sara said quietly. "And it was not my fault she was injured in the first place."

"If Loki could keep the damn trackers in line," Oren growled. His temper didn't come as a surprise. I'd sensed it lying just below the surface.

"Loki did you a favor, Your Majesty," Sara argued politely.

"This is far beyond what his title dictates. If he hadn't been there, I'm certain things would've gone much worse."

"I'm done arguing with you about that idiot," he said. "If the Princess needs to rest, then show her to her room and leave me be."

"Thank you, sire." Sara stood up, doing a curtsy before him, and turned her attention to me. "Come, Princess. I'll show you to your room."

I wanted to protest, but I knew this wasn't the best time. Oren was ready to strike out against someone simply because he could, and I didn't want to give him any reason for it to be me.

Once we left the King's chambers and the doors were safely shut behind us, Sara began making apologies for him. All of this had been so trying for him. He'd spent nearly eighteen years trying to reach me, and Elora had made it as hard on him as she could. It had all come to a head tonight.

Sara wanted me to believe that he wasn't always this way, but I had a feeling that couldn't be further from the truth. Oren had given me the impression that this was him in a good mood.

When we reached a room nearer to hers, Sara let me in. It was a smaller, more sparsely furnished version of hers, and she expressed regret for the lack of clothing. So their home wasn't stocked the way Förening had been for me. Not that I minded. Clothing and accommodations weren't my priority.

"You don't really expect me to stay here, do you?" I asked. She went about my room, turning on the lights and showing me where things were. "Not when my friends are being held prisoner in the dungeon."

"I expect that you don't have a choice," Sara said carefully. Her words didn't carry the same threat as Oren's. Rather, she was stating a fact.

"You have to help me." I went over to her, appealing to her obvious maternal instinct. "They're down there without food or water. I can't let them stay that way."

"I can assure you that they are safe and will be taken care of." She met my eyes, impressing upon me that she told the truth. "As long as you are here, they will be fed and clothed."

"That's not good enough." I shook my head. "They don't have a bed or a bathroom." I didn't mention that Rhys couldn't sit, and I had no clue how to break the spell I'd accidentally put him under.

"I am sorry," Sara said sincerely. "I can promise you that I will check on them myself to ensure they are being properly cared for, but that's the best I can do."

"Can't you put them in another room or something? Lock them in a spare bedroom." I wasn't thrilled about them being captive no matter what, but getting them out of the dungeon would be a step in the right direction.

"Oren would never allow it." She shook her head. "It'd pose too great a risk. I'm sorry." She looked helplessly at me, and I realized that was the best I could get from her. "I'll get you some appropriate clothing to sleep in."

I sighed and sat on the bed. Once she left, I let my body sag from exhaustion. The emotional roller coaster I'd been on had left me depleted and worn out.

But as tired as I was, I knew I couldn't sleep. Not until I knew that Matt and Rhys were safe.

dungeons & heroes

It's not as if I had a plan or even knew where I was going. Sara had brought me clothes—yoga pants and a tank top, both in black. I changed because sneaking around in a dress didn't sound like much fun, and then I crept out into the hall.

I tried to remember the way Loki had led me up here, but they had dimmed the lights, making it even harder for me to recognize my unfamiliar surroundings. As I recalled, we didn't take that many turns. It should be fairly simple.

The hardest part would be figuring out what to do once I found the dungeon. Maybe I could use persuasion on the guard. Or if it was another hobgoblin, I could overpower him and get him to open the door.

I found the winding staircase. It only led down to the main floor, so I still had to find the rest of the route to the dungeon.

When I reached the bottom of the steps, I heard voices. I froze, debating whether I should run or hide, before deciding that staying in the shadows would be the way to go. I hurried behind the staircase and crouched down, making myself as small as possible.

The voices got louder as they came closer, and they appeared to be arguing about how to make the best squash. My heart pounded so loudly I was certain they could hear it, and I held my breath. Moments later, I saw the feet of two hobgoblins walking past.

One of them appeared to be female, with long ratty hair in a braid down her back. They really were unattractive creatures, but based on the way they talked, they seemed harmless. They sounded more human and normal than some of the Trylle I'd encountered in Förening.

I waited a few minutes until I was sure that the hobgoblins had disappeared down the hall before I started breathing again. I figured I could take them, but I didn't want to beat up random strangers. Besides that, they could make noise and alert everyone else in the palace, including Oren.

I stepped out from underneath the staircase and almost ran into Loki. He leaned casually against the stairs, his elbow resting on the railing and his legs crossed at the ankles. I nearly screamed, but I caught myself, knowing that drawing further attention would only make things worse.

"Hello, Princess." Loki grinned at me. "Couldn't sleep?"

He and Ludlow had been calling me "Princess" from the beginning, and I thought they were taunting me about my standing with the Trylle. But I realized I was their Princess too, and he was actually giving me some form of reverence.

Unfortunately, I knew that my title pulled no weight with him. Right now I was a prisoner too.

"Yeah, I just . . . I needed something to eat," I fumbled.

"A likely story," he said, and his expression became skeptical. "If only I could believe you."

"I haven't had anything to eat all day." While that was actually the truth, my nerves had my stomach too racked to even think about eating.

"What do you plan to do?" Loki asked, ignoring my feeble excuse. "Even if you find the dungeon, how will you get them out?"

"I won't, now. You're gonna run and tell on me, aren't you?" I studied his eyes, trying to get a read on him, but he looked as amused as he always did.

"Maybe." He shrugged as if he hadn't decided yet. "Let me hear your plan. It's probably not even worth bothering anyone with."

"What makes you say that?" I asked.

"You seem like a self-saboteur," he said. I opened my mouth to protest, and he laughed at my obvious indignation. "Don't take it personally, Princess. It happens to the best of us."

"I'm not going to stop until I get my friends out of here."

"Now that I believe." He leaned in toward me. "This all goes so much easier when you're honest."

"Like I'm the one being devious," I scoffed.

"I haven't lied to you yet," he said, sounding oddly serious.

"All right, then," I said. "How do I break my friends out of the dungeon?"

"Just because I don't lie doesn't mean I'll answer you." Loki smiled.

"Fine. I'll find them myself."

I felt confident he wouldn't stop me, although I didn't know why he wouldn't. If Oren found out that he was even indulging my plans for escape, I'm sure it wouldn't bode well for him.

When I brushed past him, walking down the corridor to where I thought the main hall was, he followed me. I tried to walk quickly, but he matched my pace with ease.

"You think it's this way, do you?" Loki asked, a teasing lilt in his voice.

"Don't try to confuse me. I know my directions. I don't get lost," I lied. I got lost a lot. "Isn't that a Trylle affinity or something?"

"I don't know. I'm not Trylle," he replied. "And neither are you."

"I'm half Trylle," I said defensively.

Why was I defending it? I didn't even want to be Trylle, or Vittra, or anything. Plain ordinary human had suited me just fine my whole life. Now that I found myself in this ethnic quagmire, I felt strangely protective of the Trylle and Förening. Apparently, I cared more than I thought I did.

"You're rather feisty for a Princess," Loki remarked, watching me as I walked purposefully down the hallway.

"How many Princesses have you met?" I countered.

"None." He tilted his head thoughtfully. "I suppose I thought you'd be more like Sara. She isn't feisty at all."

"Sara's not my mother," I said.

When we reached the main hall, I wanted to jump up and down, but it didn't seem appropriate. Besides, I'd only found the doorway to the dungeon. I still had to actually rescue Matt and Rhys.

"Now what?" Loki asked, pausing in the center of the hall.

"I go down and get them." I pointed to the large doors leading down to the basement.

"No, I don't very much care for that idea." He shook his head.

"Of course you don't. You don't want me to get them out," I said. My heart beat rapidly, and I wondered exactly how far Loki would let me take this.

"That's not why. It just doesn't seem very interesting." He pushed up the sleeves of his sweater, revealing his tanned forearms. "In fact, I'm rather bored with the whole thing. Why don't we do something else?"

"No, I'm getting them out," I said. "I won't let you keep us prisoner here."

He laughed darkly at that and shook his head.

"Why is that funny?" I demanded, crossing my arms over my chest.

"You say that as if *I'm* the one holding you captive." He'd glanced away from me, but when he looked back, he smiled bitterly and his eyes were sad. "This is Ondarike. We're all prisoners here."

"You expect me to believe that you're being held against your will?" I raised a skeptical eyebrow. "You're roaming around the castle freely."

"As are you." He turned away from me then. "Not all prisons have bars. You should know that better than anyone, Princess."

"So you're not the King's head henchman?" I asked.

"I didn't say that either." Loki shrugged, apparently tiring of the conversation. "I'm saying that since I can't help you with your friends, we ought to find something else to do."

"I'm not doing anything else until I get them," I insisted.

"But you haven't heard what I'd like to do instead." His expression changed from morose to playful, and there was something in his eyes that made me feel funny.

Not bad, and not the same as when he made me pass out. It wasn't a magic Vittra power or anything. It was just a look that made me feel sort of . . . fluttery inside.

Before I had time to analyze what I felt or what he meant, a loud banging at the main doors interrupted us. The hall where we stood contained two sets of doors—the ones leading to the lower level, and the massive ones leading outside. These dwarfed the ones in the King's and Queen's chambers.

The banging came again, making me jump, and Loki moved in front of me. Was he protecting me? Or hiding me?

The doors flew open, and joy surged through me.

Tove had blown the doors open with his abilities, and he stood on the other side of them, looking astonishingly badass. Tove was a rather foxy and very powerful Trylle I'd known in Förening. His quirky, antisocial personality had endeared him to me, but he was also the last person I'd expected to see here. His abilities did allow him to move objects with his mind, though, so he was a very powerful ally to have.

Then I caught sight of who he had with him. Duncan and Finn stood behind him, letting him throw open the doors while they waited to rush in. As soon as I saw Finn, my heart wanted to explode.

I'd been so afraid he had been hurt or I might never see him again, and there he was.

"Finn! You're okay!" I rushed past Loki and ran to Finn.

I threw my arms around him, and for a brief second he hugged me. The strength of his embrace let me know how worried he had been about me. But almost as soon as I felt it, he cut it short, and pushed me away.

"Wendy, we have to get out of here," Finn said, as if I'd suggested that we vacation here.

"Matt and Rhys are here. We have to get them first."

I turned to start telling Finn about the dungeon, and I saw that Tove had Loki pinned up high on the wall. Tove stood several feet back, holding his hand out at Loki, and Loki hung suspended in the air, his face grimacing in pain.

"No, Tove! Don't hurt him!" I yelled.

Tove glanced at me but didn't question my command. He lowered Loki to the floor and released him, leaving Loki gasping for breath. Loki held his side, bending over.

Tove wasn't a violent guy by nature, but after the horrible battle he'd had with the Vittra a few days ago, I didn't blame him for being a little preemptive.

"Let's get you out of here," Duncan said, grabbing my arm as if he meant to drag me out. I glared at him, and he instantly dropped his hand. "Sorry, Princess. But we need to hurry."

"I'm not leaving without Matt and Rhys," I reiterated, and turned to Loki. "Will you help me get them?"

His eyes met mine, and his cocky demeanor had completely disappeared. He looked conflicted and pained, and I knew it wasn't just from Tove hurting him. A few moments ago, he'd seemed to understand what I was going through, but he'd felt unable to help. Now he had a chance, an excuse, and I hoped he would take it.

"We can come back for them," Finn said.

Nobody had rushed to the hall yet to investigate the commotion, but it was only a matter of time before someone did. And I knew it would serve us well not to tangle with Oren.

"No. We can't leave. If we do, he'll kill them." I kept my eyes on Loki, pleading with him. "Loki, please."

"Princess . . ." Loki let his voice trail off.

"Tell the King we overpowered you. Blame it all on us," I said. "He never needs to know you helped us."

Loki didn't answer immediately, and that was too long for Finn. He left my side and went over to Loki, grabbing his arm roughly.

"Where are they?" Finn demanded, but Loki didn't respond.

Knowing we had to hurry, I ran toward the dungeon and everyone followed, Finn dragging Loki along with us. "This way," I said with anxious fervor.

I threw open the basement door and almost tumbled down the stairs in my hurry, but Finn caught my arm before I fell. Duncan actually did trip, thanks to his shoelaces, and I rolled my eyes as I waited for him to catch up.

"What the heck is that?" Duncan asked when he saw the hobgoblin guarding Matt and Rhys's cell. It wasn't Ludlow, but a hobgoblin just like him.

They all stopped short at the sight of him. The shocked reaction of Duncan, Finn, and Tove pleased me. Apparently I wasn't the only one unfamiliar with this particular type of Vittra. I wasn't sure if that meant Oren was very good at keeping secrets or if Elora was, but I had a feeling it was probably both.

"Never mind him." I walked over to the door, pushing the troll out of my way easily.

He didn't put up much of a fight. At the sight of the four of us, with Loki as a hostage, he knew he didn't stand a chance. He started to take off, but Tove stopped him, pinning him against a wall and preventing him from alarming anyone.

"This is pretty weak security," Duncan said. He watched the hobgoblin wiggle against the wall, while I went over to unlock the door.

"We didn't really expect anyone to break in," Loki said. He enunciated his words more than he needed to, as if he were in pain or talking to a small child, but he made no attempt to free himself from Finn's grip.

"Well, that was pretty stupid." Duncan laughed. "I mean, she's the Princess. It's not rocket science that we'd come after her."

"No, I suppose not," Loki said tightly.

"I don't understand this!" I said after futilely twisting at things that did nothing. It had to be the most labyrinthine system of locks I'd ever encountered. I looked to Loki. "Can you do this?"

He sighed, and Finn jerked on his arm. Both Loki and I glared at him, but Finn only acknowledged mine.

"Just help her," Finn said, reluctantly releasing him.

Wordlessly, Loki went over to the door and began unlocking it. I watched him, and I still didn't completely understand what he did. The bolts clicked loudly, and I could hear Rhys shouting something from inside the cell. Finn kept his eyes on Loki, watching for a wrong move, and Duncan looked around, commenting on the dankness of the dungeon.

As soon as the door opened, Matt and Rhys shot out, nearly knocking over Loki in the process. Rhys hugged me in his enthusiasm, and while I couldn't see the angry look I'm sure Finn gave him over that, I could see the way Matt glared at Finn.

This whole situation could become an awful mess, but we didn't have time for it.

"You had something to do with this, didn't you?" Matt asked, his eyes locked on Finn.

"Matt, knock it off," I said, untangling myself from Rhys's hug. "He's here to rescue us, and we have to get out of here. So shut up, and let's go."

"Somebody has to come after us soon, right?" Duncan asked, bewildered by the lack of a counterattack.

"Let's just get out of here," Matt said, taking the cue.

Tove released the hobgoblin pinned to the wall, and the guys all rushed ahead, leading our escape from the dungeon.

I paused, looking back at Loki. He stood in front of the cell door, looking weirdly forlorn. His earlier bravado had completely disappeared, and his golden eyes settled on me.

"Wait a few minutes to tell Oren we're gone, okay?" I asked.

"As you wish," Loki said simply. Something in the way he looked at me stirred up that fluttery feeling I'd had upstairs.

"Thank you for letting us go," I said, but he didn't say anything to that. After hearing what he'd said earlier, I considered asking him to come with us. In fact, I almost did, but then Finn jarred me from the idea.

"Wendy!" Finn snapped.

I ran to catch up, then Finn took my hand. That small touch felt strong and safe, and sent warm tingles running through me. As we raced up the stairs, holding his hand almost made me forget that he'd hurt me or that we were escaping from an enemy prison.

The cold night air hit me when we ran outside. Duncan led the way, stumbling through the dark with Rhys at his heels. Both Tove and Matt kept stopping to make sure that Finn and I were coming, with Matt's gaze particularly wary.

The ground felt icy, and branches and rocks stung my bare feet. Whenever I slowed down, Finn squeezed my hand, and that spurred me on. The air smelled of winter, like ice and pines, and I heard an owl hooting in the distance.

I glanced behind me once, but since the palace had no windows to light it up, I could hardly make out its dark shape looming behind us.

Finn's silver Cadillac waited for us at the edge of the trees. The moon filtered through the branches, glinting on the car, and I quickened my pace. I didn't have the stamina to run all the way to Förening, and I had become a little afraid I might have to.

When we reached the car, Duncan had already jumped in back, and Matt stood next to the open car door, waiting for me to get there. Rhys stood next to him, but he was far more anxious, shifting his weight from one leg to the other.

"Get in the car! Let's go!" Finn commanded, looking at them like they were idiots. Tove was the only one who complied, climbing in the front passenger's side.

"Wendy," Rhys said. "I can't sit down."

"What?" Finn looked irritated, his eyes bouncing between Rhys and me.

"I used my persuasion on him, and I got him stuck—" I tried to explain lamely, but Finn cut me off.

"Just tell him to get in the damn car," Finn said. I didn't understand, so he elaborated. "Use the persuasion. Make him sit in the car. We'll sort it out when we get home."

I looked at Rhys, barely able to make out his eyes in the moonlight, but I didn't know if seeing him actually mattered. Using all my concentration, I told him to get in the car. A few seconds later, he got in the car and let out a massive sigh of relief.

"It feels sooo good to sit down!" Rhys said, and a fresh guilt washed over me.

Matt got in the car after him, but he didn't close the door. He was waiting for me to get in back with him, but Finn still had my hand. He led me around the front of the car, and I got in the driver's side. I slid over so he could drive and sat on the armrest hump in the middle.

Matt started to voice his complaints, but Finn put the car in drive. Matt swore, slamming the car door shut as Finn sped off down the road. The rest of us settled into a tense silence. I think we all had expected the Vittra to put up more of a fight, especially after the way they'd pursued me. This felt almost . . . too easy.

"That's weird," Duncan said. "They didn't do anything. They didn't even try to stop us."

"We did just damage their army," Tove said, offering some kind of an explanation. "I'm sure most of their people are recuperating or . . ." He trailed off, unwilling to verbalize that the Trylle had been forced to kill some of the Vittra in the attack.

Duncan made a few more comments about how strange it was and how Ondarike was different from how he'd thought it'd be. Nobody said anything in response, so eventually he stopped talking.

I got as comfortable as my seat would allow. Once I felt safe, my exhaustion really had a chance to take hold, and it no longer mattered where I was sitting.

I rested my head on Finn's shoulder, taking a small, private glee in being close to him. As I drifted off to sleep, I could hear him breathing, and that definitely helped me relax.

predictions

I t may have felt good falling asleep next to Finn, but it did not feel good waking up. My body still felt sore from Kyra's recent attack, and the uncomfortable way I'd slept had left me full of kinks and aches.

When Finn pulled up in front of the house, I stretched, and my neck screamed at me. I got out of the car, rolling my shoulders, and Matt stared up at the mansion with shock.

Opulent and gorgeous, it really was a palace, resting on the bluffs of the Mississippi River, vines covering the white exterior. It hung off the edge, held up by thin pillars, and the entire wall facing the river was made of glass. I remembered how the mansion's elegance had hit me when I first arrived, but now I was too angry to even look at it.

I wanted to talk to Matt about everything, but I had to talk to Elora first. She had lied to me, again. If I had known that the Vittra King was my father, I never would've taken Rhys to see Matt. I would never have put them in danger that way.

When we went into the house, I left Rhys to help show Matt

around. I hadn't figured out how to fix him yet, so I'd settled for telling him to stand up, and leaving Finn and Tove to help him sort it out.

Finn told me I should calm down first, but I ignored him and stormed down the hall to see Elora. She didn't scare me anymore, not in the slightest. Oren would actually hurt me. At her worst, Elora would just humiliate me.

The palace was divided into two massive wings, separated by a rotunda that served as the front hall. All of the official business took place in the south wing, where there were meeting rooms, a ballroom, a massive dining hall, offices, the throne room, as well as staff quarters and the Queen's bedroom.

The north wing held the more casual rooms in the house, like my room, guest bedrooms, and the kitchen. Elora's sitting parlor was at the far end of the north wing. It was a corner room, so two walls were made entirely of windows. She spent most of her free time there, painting and reading, and whatever else she did to relax.

"When were you gonna tell me that Oren is my father?" I demanded, throwing open the door.

Elora lay on her chaise lounge, her dark gown flowing out around her. Even in repose, she had an innate elegance to her. Her poise and beauty were qualities I'd been envious of when I first met her, but now I saw them as nothing more than a weak façade. Everything she did was for appearance, and I doubted that anything went deeper than that with her.

I stood just inside her parlor, my arms crossed over my chest. She held her arm over her eyes, as if the light were too painful to deal with. She was plagued by regular migraines, so that might have been the case now. Or maybe not, since she left the blinds open on the glass walls, letting the morning light stream in.

"I'm glad to see you're safe," she said but didn't move her arm so she could actually see me.

"I can tell." I walked over and stood directly in front of her. "Elora. You need to tell me the truth. You can't keep hiding stuff from me this way, not if you want me to rule someday. I'd make a very horrible Queen if I was ignorant to everything."

I decided to play it reasonable, instead of shouting all the things I really wanted to say.

"And now you know the truth." She sounded tired of the conversation already, and it'd only just begun. She finally lowered her arm, wearily meeting my angry stare with her dark eyes. "Why are you looking at me that way?"

"That's all you have to say to me?" I asked.

"What more do you want me to say?" Elora sat up in one smooth, graceful move. When I didn't back down, she stood up, apparently not fond of the idea of me looking down on her.

"I was just kidnapped by the Vittra, the King of whom is my father, and you have *nothing* to say to me?" I stared at her incredulously, and she walked away, putting her back to me as she went over to the window.

"I'd feel more sympathetic to your plight if you hadn't run away." She folded her arms over her chest, almost hugging herself as she stared out at the river flowing below. "I specifically forbade you from leaving the compound, and we all told you it was for your own protection. After the attack, you knew firsthand the dangers of leaving, and you left. It's not my fault you put yourself in that situation."

"Because of the attack I thought they'd be too injured and afraid to try anything like that again!" I yelled. "I didn't think the Vittra would have any reason to keep coming after me, but I would've if I had known about my father."

"You took your life into your own hands when you left, and you knew it," Elora said simply.

"Dammit, Elora!" I shouted. "This isn't about placing blame, okay? I want to know why you lied. You told me my father was dead."

"It was far simpler and cleaner than telling you the truth." She said that like it would make everything okay. It was easier lying to me, so that's fine. I wouldn't want to make her life complicated or anything.

"What is the truth?" I asked her directly.

"I married your father because it was the right thing to do." She didn't say anything more for so long I thought she might not continue, but then she said, "The Vittra and Trylle have been fighting for centuries, maybe forever."

"Why?" I stepped closer to her, but she didn't look at me.

"Various reasons." She gave a slight shrug. "The Vittra have always been more aggressive than we, but we're more powerful. It led to an odd power structure, and they were always jostling for more control, more land, more people."

"So you thought marrying Oren would end centuries of fighting?"

"My parents thought so. They had arranged it before I even came to Förening." Elora had been a changeling, like I had, though she rarely spoke of it. "I could've contested it, of course, the way you contested your name."

She said that last part somewhat bitterly. As part of returning to the Trylle, I was supposed to undergo a christening ceremony and change my name to something more fitting. I hadn't wanted to, and thanks to the Vittra busting up the ceremony, I hadn't had to. Elora had relented and allowed me to keep my own name, and I'd been the first Princess to do so in our history.

"But you didn't contest it?" I asked, ignoring her little jab at me.

"No. I had to put my own wants behind the greater good of the people. That's something you'll have to learn to do." The light shone on her hair as if she had a halo. She turned back to the window, and it was gone.

"If a simple wedding would end the abhorrence, then I had to do it," Elora continued. "I had to think of the lives and wasted energy of both the Trylle and Vittra."

"So you married him," I finished for her. "Then what happened?"

"Not a lot. We weren't married for very long." She rubbed her arm, stifling a chill only she felt. "I'd met him a handful of times before the wedding, and he'd been on his best behavior. I hadn't loved him, but . . ."

She didn't finish her thought, and the way she let it hang in the air led me to believe that she had cared for him.

I couldn't imagine Elora caring for anyone. When she flirted with Garrett Strom, it seemed like a show. I'm not sure if they were actually dating or not, but he seemed to like her and hung around a lot. Plus, he was a Markis, so she could marry him if she wanted.

Both Finn and Rhys had told me of a secret, long-standing affair that Elora had had with Finn's father, after my own father was gone. He'd been a tracker and was married to Finn's mother, so they could never be together openly, but Rhys claimed that she truly loved him.

"What happened after you were married?" I asked.

Elora had been lost in thought for a moment, and when I brought her out of it, she shook her head.

"It didn't go well," she said simply. "He wasn't outright cruel, which made things harder. I couldn't leave him, not without just cause. Not with so much riding on it."

"But you did eventually?"

"Yes. After you were conceived, he . . ." She paused, searching for the right word. "He became too much for me to bear. Right before you were born, I left him, and I hid you. I wanted a strong family to protect and shelter you, should he come looking."

"Is that why Finn started tracking me so early?" I asked.

Trackers usually waited to retrieve changelings until they were eighteen or so, once they were legal adults with access to trust funds. Finn had been following me around since the beginning of my senior year, making me one of the youngest changelings ever to return.

He'd claimed it was because I moved around so much, they were afraid of losing me, but now I suspected that they'd been afraid the Vittra would get to me first.

"Yes." Elora nodded. "Thankfully, I wasn't yet Queen of the Trylle when we separated. Oren may have been King of the Vittra, but he was only a prince here. He had no standing over the kingdom. Otherwise things could've gone a lot differently."

"When did you become Queen?" I asked, momentarily distracted from information about Oren.

I couldn't imagine Elora as a Princess. I knew she must've been young and inexperienced at one time, but she had the regality of someone who had always been Queen.

"Not long after you were born." Elora turned to me. "But I am glad that you're here."

"I almost didn't make it back," I said, trying to elicit some concern from her. She raised an eyebrow but said nothing. "Their tracker, Kyra, beat the crap out of me. I would've died if Oren wasn't married to a healer."

"You wouldn't have died." She brushed me off, the same way everybody seemed to when I told them of Kyra hurting me.

"I was coughing up blood! I think a broken rib punctured a lung or something." My ribs still ached, and I'd been certain that I would die in that dungeon.

"Oren would never let you die," Elora said dismissively. She stepped away from the window and sat down on the chaise lounge, but I stayed standing.

"Maybe not," I admitted. "But he could've killed Matt and Rhys."

"Matt?" She was confused for a minute, an expression that looked unusual on her.

"My brother. Er, my host brother, or whatever you wanna call him." I grew tired of trying to explain him as anything else and decided that from here on out, I'd just call him my brother. As far as I was concerned, he still was.

"Are they here now?" Her expression shifted from confusion to irritation.

"Yeah. I wasn't going to leave them there. Oren would kill them to spite me." I wasn't sure if that was true or not, but it felt true.

"You all made it out of there, then?" For a second she sounded and looked as if she actually cared. It was nowhere near Matt's level of concern, but at least it resembled something human and loving.

"Yeah. We did. Finn and Tove got us out of there without any problem." I furrowed my brow, remembering how easy it had been to escape.

"Did something happen?" Elora asked, homing in on my unease.

"No." I shook my head. "And that's just it. *Nothing* happened. We practically walked right out of there."

"Well, that is Oren for you." She rolled her eyes. "He's too arrogant, and that's always been his downfall."

"What do you mean?"

"He's powerful, *very* powerful." Elora's tone held a sense of awe I hadn't witnessed from her before. "But he's always thought that he could take anything he wanted and no one would stop him. It's true most trolls are too afraid to cross him. He incorrectly assumed I would fall into that category."

"But I'm your daughter. He didn't think you'd even try?" I asked dubiously.

"Like I said, he's too arrogant." She rubbed her temple and settled back on the chaise.

Elora had the gift of precognition, as well as some other telekinetic powers. I didn't know the extent of them all, but I hoped to get a better grasp soon.

I turned to look at her paintings more closely, which she used to predict the future. She only had two completed in the room, and one she'd recently started. The new one only had a swatch of blue painted in the corner, so I couldn't get anything from that.

The first finished one showed the garden behind the house. It started under the balcony and ran down the bluff, surrounded by a brick wall. I'd only been in it once, and it had been idyllic, thanks to the Trylle magic that kept it perpetually in bloom.

In her painting, the garden was covered in a light snow that glimmered and sparkled like diamonds. But the stream, flowing like a waterfall to a fountain in the center, hadn't frozen over. Despite the wintry scene, all the flowers were still in full bloom. Petals of pink and blue and purple glistened with a light frost, making it all look like an exotic fairyland.

Elora had a breathtaking skill for painting, and I would've commented on it if I'd thought my opinion mattered to her. The beauty of the garden painting enraptured me so much it took me a moment to realize there was something dark lurking in it.

A figure stood by the hedge. It appeared to be a man with hair far lighter than my own, but the shadows made it hard to tell. He stood in the distance, making his face too blurry to be distinguishable.

Even though I couldn't see much, there was something menacing about him. Or at least Elora thought so when she painted him. I got that vibe from the canvas.

"When did you know the Vittra had gotten me?" I asked, realizing she might've known all along.

"When Finn told me," she answered absently. "He came and retrieved Tove, and then left to get you."

"And you just . . ." I was about to ask why she let them go without sending along help, like an army, perhaps. But my gaze had moved on to the other painting and I stopped.

This one showed me, a close-up from my waist up. The background was a blur of blacks and grays, giving no indication of where I stood. I appeared much the same as I did now, except dressed much better. My hair was down and the dark curls were arranged beautifully. I had on a gorgeous white gown, decorated with diamonds that matched my necklace and the ones in my earrings.

But what was most striking was that on my head I wore a crown, ornately twisted silver adorned with diamonds. My face looked expressionless, and I couldn't tell if I was pleased or upset to be crowned, but there it was. A picture of me as Queen.

"When did you paint this?" I pointed to the picture and turned to Elora. She had her arm draped over her eyes, but she lifted it up to see what I was asking about.

"Oh, that." She dropped her arm. "Don't concern yourself with that. You'll drive yourself mad trying to discern and prevent the future. It's much better letting things unfold."

"Is this why you never seemed worried about me dying?" I asked, surprised at how angry I felt.

She knew I wouldn't die. She had proof that I'd someday be Queen, and she hadn't bothered letting me in on that.

Elora sighed. "Among other things."

"What does that mean?" I snapped. "Why do you always have to be so damn cryptic all the time?"

"It doesn't mean anything!" She sounded exasperated. "For all I know, that painting means you'll be the Vittra Queen. The future is far too fluid to ever understand or change. And just because I paint something doesn't mean it'll come true."

"But you predicted the attack at my christening ceremony," I countered. "I saw the painting. You painted the ballroom on fire."

"Yes, and I couldn't stop it," she said icily.

"You didn't even try! You didn't warn me or cancel the ceremony!"

"I tried to stop it!" She shot me an angry glare that would've made me cringe before, but not anymore. "I met with people. I discussed it with everyone. I told Finn and all the trackers. But I had nothing to go on. I only saw fire and chandeliers and smoke.

No people. Not the room. Not even a time frame. Do you know how many chandeliers there are in the south wing alone? What was I supposed to do? Tell everyone to avoid chandeliers forever?"

"No. I don't know," I stammered. "You could've done . . . something."

"It's not until after that I understand what the vision means," Elora said, more to herself than me. "It's that way with all of them. It's almost worse being able to see the future. I don't know what it means, and I can't stop it. Only after, it all seems so obvious."

"So then what are you saying?" I asked. "I won't be Queen?"

"No. I'm saying that the painting doesn't mean anything." She closed her eyes and rubbed the bridge of her nose. "I'm getting a terrible migraine. I'd rather not continue this conversation."

"Fine. Whatever." I threw my hands up in the air, knowing I couldn't force things with Elora. I was lucky she hadn't summoned Finn to drag me out of here.

Then I remembered him, Finn. I hadn't been able to say much of anything in the car ride to Förening, but I definitely still had a lot to say to him.

I left the parlor to go track down Finn. I should have been more concerned with other things, but right then I only wanted to find a moment alone with him. A moment when we could really talk and I could . . . I don't know. But I had to see him.

Instead of Finn, I found Duncan waiting a little ways down the hall. He'd been leaning against the wall, playing with his phone, but when I came out of the room he straightened up. He offered a sheepish smile, and his attempt at quickly shoving his phone in his pocket only made him drop it.

"Sorry." Duncan scrambled to pick it up as I approached. "I just wanted to give you alone time with your mother."

"Thanks." I continued down the hall, and he followed along. "Why were you waiting for me? Did you need something?"

"No. I'm your tracker now. Remember?" He looked embarrassed. "And the Vittra are really after you, so I'm on guard all the time."

"Right." I nodded. I'd been hoping that since Finn had saved my life—again—he'd be reinstated as my tracker. "Where's Finn? I need to talk to him."

"Finn?" Duncan's steps faltered. "Um, he's not your tracker anymore."

"No, I know that. And it's not a condemnation of your ability." I forced a smile. "I wanted to talk to Finn for a minute."

"No, yeah." He shook his head. "It's just that . . ." Unsure why he was so flustered, I stopped walking. "I mean, he's not your tracker. So . . . he left."

"He left?" I felt that familiar pang shoot through my heart.

I shouldn't be surprised, and I shouldn't let it hurt me anymore. But the wound sprang open fresh, just like when he'd left before.

"Yeah." Duncan stared at his feet and fiddled with the zipper on his jacket. "You're safe and everything. His job's done, right?"

"Right," I said numbly.

I could've asked where Finn had gone, and maybe I should've. He couldn't have gotten too far that fast. I was sure Finn would say he left to protect me, or protect my honor, or something like that. But I didn't care.

Right then, it didn't matter what his reasons were. All I knew was that I was sick of him breaking my heart.

underrated

Tove couldn't fix Rhys because that wasn't how his abilities worked. When I went upstairs after my talk with Elora, I had to send Rhys down for her to fix him. I could've gone with him, but I figured Elora had had her fill of me for the day.

Tove went to his house to get some rest, and I thanked him for everything he'd done. Without him, I'm not entirely sure we could've gotten out. Even though Oren's security was lax, it was Tove who had gotten in and kept the trolls at bay.

Rhys had started getting Matt settled in one of the spare rooms down the hall from mine. I went to see how he was doing, and Duncan seemed far too content to follow at my heels. It took a lot of convincing, but I managed to get him to wait outside. Duncan didn't trust Matt because he was human, but if he was going to be my tracker, he had to learn to deal with it.

Matt stood in the middle of the room looking lost, and he'd never been the kind of guy who got lost. He'd changed into a pair of sweatpants that fit okay, but his T-shirt was snug, so I assumed he'd borrowed them from Rhys.

"How are you doing with all of this?" I asked, closing the bedroom door quietly as I came in. I knew Duncan was keeping his post outside, and I didn't want him listening. Not that I planned on saying anything secret. I just wanted a moment alone with my brother.

"Um . . . great?" He gave me a sad smile and shook his head. "I don't know. How am I supposed to be doing?"

"About like this."

"None of this seems real, you know?" Matt sat down on the bed and sighed. "I keep thinking I'll wake up and this will all be a very strange dream."

"I know the feeling *exactly*." I remembered how confusing and scary everything had seemed when I first got here. It still seemed that way most of the time.

"How long am I staying here?" Matt asked.

"I don't know. I hadn't really thought about it." I came over and sat on the bed next to him. Honestly, I wanted him to stay here forever, but that'd be selfish. "I guess until this all blows over. When the Vittra stop being a threat."

"Why are they coming after you?"

"It's a very long story, and I'll tell you later." I wanted to tell him, but I didn't have the strength for a lengthy explanation. At least not right now.

"But they will stop, won't they?" Matt asked, and I nodded as if I actually believed it.

"Until then, I want you to stay here. I need to know you're safe," I said. I wasn't sure how Elora would feel about that, but I didn't care.

"Yeah, I know the feeling," he said with an edge to his voice, and guilt tightened my heart.

"I'm really sorry, Matt."

"You could've told me about all of this."

"You wouldn't have believed any of it."

"Wendy. This is me, okay?" He turned to face me, and I finally looked at him. "Yeah, this is really hard to believe, and I know that if I hadn't seen it for myself, I'd find it even harder. But I've *always* been on your side. You should've trusted me."

"I know. I'm sorry." I lowered my eyes. "But I'm glad you're here and that I'm telling you stuff now. It was hard for me, keeping things from you. I don't wanna do it again."

"Good."

"But you should call Maggie," I said. "She needs to know where we are, and she can't go home. Not now. I don't know if they would take her to get at me."

"Are you safe here?" Matt asked. "Like, really safe?"

"Yeah, of course I am." I said it with more conviction than I really had. "Duncan's outside standing guard right now."

"That kid's an idiot," Matt said seriously, and I laughed.

"No, we're safe. Don't worry," I assured him as I stood up. "But you should call Maggie, and I should shower and put on my own clothes."

"What should I tell her?"

"I don't know." I shook my head. "Just make sure she doesn't go home."

I promised Matt I'd see him later and explain more to him then, but now I needed a moment to decompress. Duncan tried to follow me down the hall into my room, but I wouldn't let him in.

It wasn't until I was in the shower, with the sound of the water drowning me out, that I let myself cry. I don't even really know why I was crying. Part of it had to do with Finn, leaving me that way again, but mostly it was because it was all just too much.

After I got dressed, I felt better. Everything had turned out all right, as in we all survived with only minor injuries. On top of that, I got to have Matt around again. I didn't know for how long, but at least he knew the truth now.

And I finally knew why the Vittra were so fixated on me. Sure, the answer didn't make things any easier, but I understood, and that was something.

When I thought about it, the only real dark spot was Finn's absence. It left a dull ache inside my chest, but I had to ignore it. There were too many other things going on for me to sit around missing him.

I hated that he'd even come at all. It would've been easier if he'd just left me alone and I'd never seen him again.

I went over to Matt's room and discovered Rhys keeping him company. Elora had fixed him, much to my relief, and Rhys said that I'd have to begin my "training" soon to harness my abilities. I didn't know exactly what that would entail, but I didn't want to pump him for information.

I sat down in an overstuffed chair in Matt's room and decided to tell him everything. Rhys had told him some in the Vittra dungeon, but I wanted to fill in the blanks. More important, I thought Matt needed to hear it from me.

I started from the beginning, explaining how Elora had switched me for Rhys. I told him how Finn had been sent to track me and bring me here, about what it meant to be a Princess, and about the Trylle and their abilities.

The whole time I talked, Rhys said nothing, but watched with rapt interest. I'm not sure how much of this he already knew.

Matt didn't say much of anything either, only asking the occasional question. He began pacing when I started talking, but he didn't seem anxious or confused. When I finished, he stood silently for a minute, absorbing it all.

"So?" I asked when he still didn't say anything.

"So . . . do you guys still eat?" Matt looked over at me. " 'Cause I'm starving."

"Yeah, of course we do." I smiled, feeling relieved.

"I wouldn't call what they eat *food*," Rhys scoffed. He'd been sitting on the bed, but now he stood, since the conversation appeared to be wrapping up.

"What do you mean?" Matt asked.

"Well, you lived with Wendy. You have to know how she eats." Rhys seemed to realize he might have said something wrong, and he hurried to correct it. "Trylle are more careful eaters than us. They don't drink pop or eat meat, really."

Matt stared at Rhys for a moment longer, then glanced at me. There was something new in Matt's eyes, something I was feeling for the first time myself. Rhys had just put Matt and himself into an "us," a club I didn't belong to.

I had never and *could* never think of Matt as less than me, but we were different. We were separate. And despite all the differences between us that had been so obvious, it felt weird to know just how different we actually were, to have someone articulate that we weren't even the same species.

"Fortunately, I have a fridge stocked with real food," Rhys pushed on, trying to change the mood in the room. "And I'm a pretty decent cook. Ask Wendy."

"Yeah, he's pretty good," I lied, but I wasn't that hungry anymore. My stomach had tightened, and I was amazed that I could even force a smile at them both. "Come on. Let's get some food."

Rhys thought that talking nonstop would make up for his small blunder, and neither Matt nor I contradicted him. We walked down to the kitchen, with Duncan tagging along as soon as we'd left Matt's room.

Duncan's constant presence irritated me far more than Finn's ever had, even though Duncan hadn't really done anything. Maybe it was simply because he was there and Finn wasn't.

I pulled up a stool at the kitchen counter and watched Matt and Rhys interact. Rhys kept playing up his cooking skills, but once Matt saw him in action, he realized that he'd better take the lead. I propped my chin up on my hand, feeling all sorts of conflicting emotions as they talked and laughed and teased each other.

Part of me was thrilled that they got to have each other in their lives, the way they should've from the beginning. Depriving Rhys of a wonderful big brother like Matt had been a very cruel side effect of the changeling process.

But part of me couldn't help but feel like I was losing my brother.

"Do you mind if I have a water?" Duncan asked, pulling me from my thoughts.

"Why would I care if you had a water?" I looked at him like he was an idiot, but he didn't notice. Or maybe he got it so often, he thought that was just how people looked at him.

"I don't know. Some Trylle don't like when trackers use their stuff." Duncan went over to the fridge to get a bottled water, while Matt attempted to teach Rhys how to flip blueberry flapjacks.

"Well, how do you eat and drink if you don't use their stuff?" I asked Duncan.

"Buy our own." With the fridge still open, Duncan held a water toward me. "Do you want one?"

I shrugged. "Yeah, sure." He walked over and handed it to me. "You've been doing this for a long time?"

"Almost twelve years, I think." Duncan unscrewed his bottle and took a long drink. "Wow. It's weird it's been that long."

"Are you really the best they have?" I asked, trying to keep the skepticism out of my voice.

He seemed a little too amazed by Matt's ability to make pancakes. He didn't exude any of the confidence or formality that Finn had, but then again, it was probably better for him to be as different from Finn as possible.

"No," Duncan admitted, and if my question shamed him, he didn't show it. He just played with his bottle cap. "But I'm pretty close. My appearance is deceiving, but that's part of why I'm good. People underestimate me."

Something about the way he said that made me flash on to *Scream*. Maybe Duncan had a bit of that clumsy, unassuming boyish charm.

"Did anybody ever tell you that you remind them of Deputy Dewey from the *Scream* movies?" I asked.

"You mean David Arquette?" Duncan asked. "But I'm better-looking, right?"

I nodded. "Oh, yeah, definitely." I could never see myself being attracted to him, but he was kinda foxy. In his own way.

Rhys swore as a flapjack landed on the floor with a splat. Matt patiently tried to explain what he'd done wrong and how to correct it, using the same tone of voice he'd used to teach me how to tie my shoes, ride a bike, and drive a car. It was so strange seeing him be the older brother to somebody else.

"Wendy!" Willa shouted from behind me, and I'd barely turned around when she came running over. She threw her arms around me, shocking me with a fierce hug. "I'm so glad you're all right!"

"Um, thanks," I said, untangling myself from her hug.

Willa Strom was a few years older than me, and the only Trylle other than Finn who actually called me "Wendy" instead of "Princess," so I guess that made us friends. Her father, Garrett, was Elora's only friend, and Willa had been insanely helpful and kind after Finn left the first time. Without her, the christening ceremony would've been a disaster even before the Vittra broke in.

"My dad was telling me that the Vittra had kidnapped you, and nobody knew for sure what was going on." Willa could be snobby, but the concern on her face was sincere. "I rushed over here as soon as I heard you were back. I'm so glad you're here."

"Yeah, me too," I said, but I wasn't sure if that was true or not.

"Duncan?" Willa looked at him, as if noticing he was here for the first time. "You've got to be kidding me. There is no way Elora would let you be her tracker."

"See? Underrated." Duncan smiled. He seemed to take some pride in it, so I let him have it.

"Oh, my god. I'm gonna talk to my dad." Willa shook her head, tucking her perfectly tamed light-brown waves of hair behind her ears. "There's no way he can do this."

"It's fine. I'm fine." I shrugged. "I'm in the palace. What can happen here?"

Willa gave me a knowing look, but thankfully, before she could say something, Matt announced breakfast was done. When I had been regaling him with the tales of being Trylle, I had conveniently left out the part about the Vittra busting in here and Oren being my father. I thought it would freak him out too much.

"Are you gonna eat some too?" Matt asked Willa. He dished up the flapjacks, and, polite as ever, he included her. "We've got plenty to go around."

"Are those blueberry?" Willa wrinkled her nose, looking totally disgusted by the prospect of eating them. "Eww. No way."

"They're really good." Matt slid a plate toward her.

For reasons I didn't completely understand, there were few foods we actually enjoyed. We mostly ate fresh fruits and vegetables. I didn't like juice of any kind, although I did like some wine. Pancakes were made with processed flour and sugar, so they were never that appealing, although I had been eating them for years to appease Matt.

"You're not gonna eat those, are you?" Willa was completely aghast as I picked up my fork and prepared to dig in.

Matt had given Duncan a plate too. I'm sure the pancakes sounded as appealing to him as they did to Willa and me, but Duncan followed suit and picked up his fork.

"They're pretty good," I said.

I had been assured by many people over the years that they were really good, although I'm not sure how anyone could taste them after they drowned them in syrup the way Matt and Rhys were doing. Duncan and I declined syrup. There was no way we could ever force them down like that.

"I've cooked for Wendy for years," Matt said, unfazed by Willa's reaction. "I know how to make food that she likes."

In general, he had gotten pretty good at it, but there were a lot of times when I ate things just to make him happy. And also, I'd starve if I didn't.

"Oh, yeah, right," Willa scoffed. "Like I'm gonna trust a mänks in sweats and a baby tee to make me *pancakes*."

"Willa," I said. "He's my brother, okay? So lay off."

"What?" She tilted her head, not fathoming what I meant. "Oh. You mean he's your host brother?"

"Yeah." I took a big forkful of the pancake and shoved it in my mouth.

"You know he's not your *real*—"

"Willa!" I snapped with a mouthful of food, and I choked it down. "I understand the semantics. Now drop it."

"I can understand how that dweeb Duncan can eat that." Willa smoothed out her designer outfit, trying not to look offended that I'd snapped at her. "But you're a Princess. He's too stupid to—"

"Hey!" Matt said. He had been sitting next to Duncan, eating, but he stopped and glared at her. "I get it. You're fancy and pretty and rich. Good for you. But unless you wanna go over there and make us all breakfast, then I suggest you quit your bitching and sit down."

"Whoa!" Rhys laughed. He loved seeing her put in her place.

Willa made a face at Rhys but didn't say anything. When Matt went back to eating his pancakes, she sat down on the stool next to me.

Since I'd first met Willa, it was clear she walked around with a sense of entitlement. She was nice to me because she thought we were equals, but she definitely didn't feel the same way about everyone else.

"I am thirsty," Willa said after a minute, sounding pouty.

Automatically, Duncan stood to get water for her, but Matt shook his head, stopping him. Uncertainly, Duncan sat back down. As a tracker, he spent a lot of his life waiting on changelings. Trackers were considered staff and treated as such by royalty.

"You know where the fridge's at," Matt said between bites.

Willa opened her mouth but didn't say anything. She turned to me, hoping I would come to her aid, but I only shrugged. She did know where the fridge was at, after all.

After a minute of deliberating, she got up and went over to the fridge. Rhys snickered under his breath, but Matt shushed him.

I found the whole thing kind of amazing. Finn had been Willa's tracker, and a strict one at that. But she never listened to him or treated him with as much respect as she did Matt, who by Trylle standards was much lower in rank than Finn.

In the five minutes he'd known her, Matt had managed to whip her into shape better than anyone else ever had.

Willa hung around me for the rest of the afternoon, and she seemed relieved when we split off from Matt and Rhys. Rhys wanted to play some war video game or something, and I didn't feel like it.

Instead, Willa and I stayed in my room. Duncan stood outside my door for a bit, but eventually I felt sorry for him, so I had him come in and sit down.

She sorted my clothes because she liked doing that, and I lay on the floor, watching Willa and thinking about how weird it was that this was my life. She organized them in some way that I didn't understand, even after she'd explained it to me.

All the while, she talked about how great her training had been going. Willa had power over the wind, and she hadn't thought anything of it before the attack.

Now she wanted to be as prepared and strong as she possibly could. She figured that my training would start right away too, since I needed to be more prepared than anyone else here.

The night went on much the same way, and I was surprised when she joined us for supper. This time she even ate what Matt cooked, and I felt as if the whole world were turning upside down.

I went to bed shortly after, but I tossed and turned all night. My mind raced too much to really sleep. It felt like I'd only just fallen asleep when someone shook me awake. I pushed the person off, snuggling deeper in my covers.

It wasn't until I had buried my face in my pillow that I realized I should probably be alarmed that someone was in my room. What with evil trolls trying to kidnap me and all that.

repositioning

H oly hell!" Tove Kroner shouted and jumped back from the side of my bed.

I'd sat up, almost leaping out of bed, preparing to attack whoever had just woken me up. It turned out to be Tove, and I didn't understand what I'd done to him.

As far as I knew, I hadn't even reacted yet, other than sitting up. But Tove stood off to the side of the room, pressing his palms to his temples. He was bent over, his dark hair falling over his face.

"Tove?" I swung my feet over the edge of the bed and stood up. He didn't respond, so I stepped closer to him. "Tove? Are you okay? Did I do something?"

"Yeah." He shook his head and straightened up. His eyes were closed, but he'd dropped his hands from his head.

"I'm sorry. What did I do?"

"I don't know." Tove opened his mouth wide and stretched his jaw, reminding me of someone who had just been slapped in the face. "I came in to wake you up for your training. And you . . ."

"Did I hit you?" I supplied when he trailed off.

"No, it was in my head." Tove stared ahead thoughtfully for a minute. "No, you were right. It was like you slapped me inside my head."

"What are you talking about?"

"Have you ever done anything like that before? Maybe when you were scared?" He turned to look at me, ignoring my confusion to satisfy his.

"Not that I know of, but I don't even know what I did."

"Hmm." He sighed and ran his hand through his hair. "Your abilities are still developing. They should fully present themselves soon, and maybe this is part of that. Or maybe it's just because I'm me."

"What?"

"Because I'm psychic," Tove reminded me. "Your aura is very dark today."

He couldn't read minds or anything, but he could sense things. I projected, so I could get in people's minds like Elora could and use persuasion, and Tove received, so he could see auras and was more sensitive to emotion.

"What does that mean?" I asked.

"You're unhappy." Tove sounded distracted, and he made for the door. "Hurry. Get dressed. We have much to do."

He left my room before I could ask him more, and I didn't understand what Willa saw in him. I wasn't sure if she really had a crush on him, or if her interest only stemmed from the fact that his family was powerful. The Kroners were next in line for the crown, Tove specifically, if I couldn't fulfill my duties.

Tove was attractive, though. His dark hair had soft natural highlights coursing through it, although it was longish and unruly, settling below his ears. His skin had a distinct mossy undertone, the green complexion that occurred in some powerful Trylle. Nobody here had skin like that, except maybe his mother, but hers was even fainter than Tove's.

I didn't know why Tove would be training me. I'm not sure that Elora approved of him, even if he had connections. Besides that, he was scatterbrained and a little strange.

Tove did have the strongest abilities out of any of the Trylle I'd met. This was particularly weird since men usually had weaker abilities than their female counterparts.

But I wanted to get a handle on my abilities, so I figured it'd do me good to spend the day doing something other than moping around. I dressed quickly and left my room to find Tove chatting with Duncan.

"Ready?" Tove asked without looking at me. He started walking before I answered.

"Duncan, you don't need to come with us," I told him as I hurried after Tove. Duncan followed me the way he always did, but he slowed.

"It's probably best if he does," Tove said, tucking his hair behind his ears.

"Why?" I asked, but Duncan smiled, excited to be included.

"We need someone to test on," Tove replied matter-of-factly, and Duncan's smile instantly faded.

"Where are we going?" I nearly jogged to keep up with Tove, and I wished he would slow down.

"Did you hear that?" Tove stopped abruptly, and Duncan almost ran into him.

"What?" Duncan looked around, as if expecting an attacker to be waiting behind a closed door.

"I didn't hear anything," I said.

"No, of course you didn't." Tove waved me off.

"Why wouldn't I? What's that supposed to mean?"

"Because you're the one that made the sound." Tove sighed, still focused on Duncan. "Are you sure you didn't hear anything?"

"No," Duncan said. He looked over at me, hoping I could shed light on Tove's random behavior, but I shrugged. I had no idea what he was talking about.

"Tove, what's going on?" I asked, speaking loudly so he'd pay attention to me.

"You need to be careful." Tove cocked his head, listening. "You're quiet now. But when you're upset, angry, scared, irritated, you send things out. You're not controlling it, I don't think. I can pick it up, because I'm sensitive. Duncan can't and the average Trylle can't, because you're not directing it at them. But if I can hear it, others might too."

"What? I didn't say anything," I said, growing more frustrated with him.

"You thought, *I wish he'd slow down,*" Tove said.

"I wasn't using persuasion or anything." I was dumbfounded.

"I know. You'll get a handle on it, though," he assured me, and then started walking again.

He led us downstairs. I'm not sure where I thought he'd take us, but I was definitely surprised by where we ended up—the ballroom that had been devastated by the Vittra attack. It had once been luxurious, very much like a ballroom from a Disney fairy tale. Marble floors, white walls with gold detailing, skylights, diamond chandeliers.

After the attack, it looked very different. The glass ceiling had been crashed in, and to keep the elements out, blue and clear tarps had been laid over it, giving the room an odd glow. Shattered chandeliers and glass were still on the floor, as well as broken chairs and tables. The floor and walls were blackened with damage from the fire and smoke.

"Why are we here?" I asked. My voice still echoed, thanks to the room's massive size, but it wasn't as crisp thanks to the tarps.

"I like it here." Tove held his hands out, using his telekinesis to push the debris to the sides of the room.

"Does the Queen know where we are?" Duncan asked. He was uncomfortable being here, and I tried to remember if he'd been present during the attack. I hadn't been paying that much attention, and I'd met far too many people that night to say for certain.

Tove shrugged. "I'm not sure."

"Does she know you're training me?" I asked. He nodded, looking around with his back to me. "Why are you training me? Your abilities aren't the same as mine."

"They're similar." Tove turned around to face me. "And no two people are exactly alike."

"Have you trained anyone before?"

"No. But I'm the best suited to train you," he said and started rolling up the sleeves of his shirt.

"Why?" I asked, and I could see Duncan wearing the same dubious expression I was.

"You're too powerful for everyone else. They wouldn't be able to help you tap into your potential because they don't understand it the way I do." He'd finished rolling up his sleeves and put his hands on his hips. "Are you ready?"

"I guess." I shrugged, unsure what I needed to be ready for.

"Move this stuff." He gestured vaguely to the mess around the room.

"You mean with my mind?" I shook my head. "I can't do that."

"Have you tried?" Tove countered, his eyes sparkling.

"Well . . . no," I admitted.

"Do it."

"How?"

He shrugged. "Figure it out."

"You're really good at this training thing," I said with a sigh.

Tove laughed, but I did as I was told. I decided to start small, so I picked a broken chair nearby. I stared at in concentration. The only thing I knew how to use was persuasion, so I thought I'd go that way. In my mind, I repeated, *I want the chair to move, I want—*

"Nope!" Tove said, snapping me out of it. "You're thinking about it wrong."

"How am I supposed to think about it?"

"It's not a person. You can't tell it what to do. *You* have to move it," Tove said, as if that clarified his point.

"How?" I asked again, but he didn't say anything. "It'd be easier if you told me."

"I can't tell you. That's not how it works."

I grumbled a few unseemly remarks under my breath then I turned to the chair, preparing to get down to business.

So I couldn't tell the chair to move. *I* had to move it. How did that translate to thought? I squinted, hoping that might help somehow, and repeated, *Move the chair, move the chair.*

"Now look what you've done," Tove said.

I didn't think anything at all had happened, and then I saw Duncan walking toward the chair.

"Duncan, what are you doing?" I asked.

"I, uh . . . moving the chair. I guess." He seemed confused but coherent, and once he picked up the chair, he gave me an even more bewildered look. "I don't know where to, though."

"Set it anywhere," I told him absently and turned to Tove. "I did that?"

"Of course you did that. I could hear you chanting loud and clear, and if you'd harnessed it better, I'd be the one picking up the chair." He crossed his arms over his chest, giving me a look that bordered on disapproving.

"I didn't try to do that. I wasn't even looking at him."

"That makes it even worse, doesn't it?" Tove asked.

"I don't understand," Duncan said. He'd set down the chair, and, now free of his duty, walked over to us. "What are you expecting her to do?"

"You need to control your energy before someone gets hurt." Tove looked at me solemnly, his mossy eyes bravely meeting mine for almost a minute before he turned away. He gestured around his head, in much the same way Loki had when he explained how he knew I had persuasion. "You have so much going on. It comes off like a . . ."

"Static?" I suggested.

"Exactly!" He snapped his fingers and pointed at me. "You need to tune it, get your frequencies in check, like a radio."

"I would love to. Just tell me how."

"It's not a matter of turning a dial. You have no on or off switch." He walked around in a large lazy circle. "It's something you have to practice. It's more like being potty-trained. You have to learn when to hold it and when to release."

"That's a pretty sexy analogy," I said.

"You can move the chair." Tove stopped suddenly. "But that can wait. You need to learn to rein in your persuasion." He looked at Duncan. "Duncan, you don't mind being experimented on, do you?"

"Um . . . I guess not?"

"Tell him to do something. Anything." He tilted his head, still watching Duncan, then turned to me. "But make sure I can't hear."

"How? I don't even know how you're hearing," I pointed out.

"Focus. You have to focus your energy. It's imperative."

"How?" I repeated.

He kept telling me to do things without giving me any clue how. He might as well have been telling me to build a damn rocket ship. I had no idea what to do.

"You were more focused when you were around Finn," Tove said. "You were more grounded, in the way electricity is grounded."

"Well, he's not here," I snapped.

"It doesn't matter. *He* didn't do anything," Tove continued, unfazed. "You're the one with the power. You grounded yourself around him. You tell me how."

I didn't want to think about Finn or the way I had been around him. One of the reasons I had been excited for this training was because it would distract me from thoughts of him. Now Tove was telling me that Finn was the key to my success. Perfect.

Instead of yelling at Tove, I walked away. I hated the way he seemed to know everything, but lacked the ability to articulate anything. I stretched my arms and rolled my neck, working out the tension. Duncan started to say something, but Tove shushed him.

Finn. When I was around Finn, what did I do differently? He made me crazy. He made my heart beat too fast and my stomach swirl, and it was hard to take my eyes off him. Whenever he was around, I'd hardly been able to think of anything.

And that was it. It was almost too simple.

When Finn was around, my focus had been on him. That restrained my energy somehow. If my conscious mind focused on something, the rest of my mind would pull itself in. Maybe my energy was going crazy now because I was trying *not* to think of Finn.

Finn wasn't the key. But when he'd been around, I had let my mind focus. When he wasn't, I tried not to think of anything, because everything reminded me of him. Everything scattered all over, latching on to anything it could.

I closed my eyes. *Think of something. Focus on anything.*

Finn came to my mind first, the way he always did, but I pushed him away. I could think of something else. The first thing I thought of after him was Loki, and that shocked me, so I discounted him instantly. I didn't want to focus on him. Or anyone, for that matter.

I thought of the garden behind the palace. It was gorgeous, and I loved it. Elora had painted a beautiful picture of it, but it didn't really do the place justice. I remembered the way the flowers smelled, and the way the grass felt cool on my bare feet. Butterflies had flown about, and I could hear the stream babbling past me.

"Try it now," Tove suggested.

I turned to look at Duncan. He had his hands shoved in his pockets, and he gulped, as if he were afraid I might slap him. Keeping the image of the garden in my mind, I started repeating, *Whistle "Twinkle, Twinkle, Little Star."* It seemed mundane, but that was the point. I didn't want to hurt him.

His face relaxed, his eyes went blank, and then he started whistling. Feeling pleased with myself, I looked over at Tove.

"Well?" I asked hopefully.

"I didn't hear it." Tove smiled. "Excellent work."

I continued trying things out on Duncan the rest of the day. After the first few didn't turn out painful, Duncan became more at ease with the whole thing. He was a terrific sport about it, considering I made him whistle, dance, clap, and do a whole number of silly things.

Tove went on to explain what had gone wrong with Rhys and his inability to sit. Apparently, the more focus and intensity I used when trying to persuade people, the more permanent the command would become.

Rhys was human, so his mind was already more malleable than a Trylle's, and he was open to persuasion. I'd barely have to try to get it to work on him. I'd used far more energy than I needed to. I needed to learn to control the doses of my persuasion to match my target.

Of course, I could undo any command I made, like how I redirected Rhys from sitting to standing, and vice versa. But with unfocused energy, it was possible I could persuade people without even trying, the way I had gotten Duncan to move the chair.

I spent the rest of the day trying to restrain my energy, since it was potentially very dangerous. By the end of the day, I felt completely drained. It didn't help matters that I hadn't stopped for a lunch break, not that I felt like eating anyway.

Tove tried to assure me that eventually this would all be second nature, like breathing or blinking. But the way I felt right now, I didn't believe him.

I walked Tove to the front door, then I headed up to my room for a shower and a nap. Duncan went down to his quarters, daring to leave me alone so he could get in a nap himself. Being the guinea pig had been tiring for him too.

On the way to my room, I got sidetracked.

"This is Queen Sybilla," Willa was saying, pointing to a painting on the wall. Matt stood next to her, admiring the artwork as she explained it. "She's one of the most revered monarchs. I think she ruled over the Long Winter War, which I guess is much worse than it sounds."

"A long winter?" Matt smirked, and she laughed. It was a nice sound; I don't think I'd heard her laugh that way before.

"I know. It's silly." She had her hair up in a ponytail, making her look more playful, and she smoothed out a flyaway hair. "To be honest, most of this stuff is rather silly."

"Yeah, I can tell." Matt smiled.

"Hey, guys," I said tentatively, walking toward them.

"Oh, hey!" Willa smiled wider, and they both turned to face me.

As usual, she was dressed to the nines and looked stunning. Her top was low cut, and a diamond pendant rested just above her cleavage. She wore lots of jewelry—a charm bracelet, anklet, earrings, and rings—but that was all part of being Trylle. We had a fascination with trinkets. I wasn't as bad as Willa, but I'd always had a penchant for rings.

"Where have you been?" Matt asked, but he didn't sound concerned or angry. Merely curious.

"Training with Tove." I shrugged, downplaying the event. I expected Willa to squeal and press me for details about him, but she didn't register any excitement. "What are you guys doing?"

"I came to see if you wanted to do anything, and your brother was wandering around here like a lost puppy." She laughed a little, and he shook his head and rubbed the back of his neck.

"I was not a lost puppy." He grinned, but his cheeks reddened. "I had nothing to do here."

"Right. So I thought I'd show him around." Willa gestured to the halls. "I've been trying to explain your formidable ancestry."

"I really don't get it," Matt said almost wearily.

"I don't really either," I admitted, and they both laughed.

"Are you hungry?" Matt asked, and I was pleased to see him returning to a subject that felt more normal. Like worrying if I'd eaten. "I was about to go downstairs and make supper for me and Rhys and that girl with a weird name."

"Rhiannon?" Willa suggested.

"Yeah, that's her." Matt nodded.

"Oh, she's real nice," Willa said, and my jaw dropped.

Rhiannon was Willa's mänsklig, meaning she was the girl that Willa had been switched at birth with. Rhiannon was friends with Rhys and incredibly sweet, but I'd never heard Willa talk about her that way.

"Are she and Rhys dating or something?" Matt asked, looking at Willa.

"I don't know. She has a big crush on him, but I'm not sure how he feels about her." Willa sounded happy about the prospect. Normally, when she talked about Rhys or any mänks, she sounded bored.

"So what do you think?" Matt turned to me. "Are you gonna eat supper?"

"No, thanks." I shook my head. "I'm pretty beat. I need a shower and a nap."

"Are you sure?" Matt asked, and I nodded. "What about you, Willa? Do you have dinner plans?"

"Um, no." She smiled at him. "I'd love to eat here."

"Awesome," Matt said.

I extricated myself from the conversation as quickly as possible.

It was too weird for me to handle. Willa was being way too nice, and now she was willingly eating food prepared by a mänks.

That said nothing for the way Matt acted, which felt . . . not quite right. It was hard to put my finger on what exactly was going on, but I was relieved to be away from them.

little star

Another long day of training did nothing to improve my mood. My control was getting better, and that was good. But it was getting harder not to think of Finn. I thought time would make it easier, but it didn't. The ache only seemed to grow.

We spent the morning in the throne room, where I'd never been before. It was really an atrium, with a domed skylight stretching high above. The room was circular, the rounded wall behind the throne made entirely of glass. Vines grew over the ornate silver and gold designs etched on the walls, reminding me of the outside of the palace.

Given the height of the ceiling, the room itself didn't seem that large, but it didn't need to be. Tove offhandedly said it was only used for meeting dignitaries.

A solitary throne sat in the center of the room, padded with lush red velvet. Two smaller chairs sat on either side, but they weren't as elegant. Instead of wood, the throne was made of platinum that wove itself into lacy designs. Diamonds and rubies were inlaid into the metal.

I walked over to it, gingerly touching the soft velvet. It felt brand-new, too plush to have ever been used. The heavy metal arms were surprisingly smooth under my fingertips. I ran my hand over it, tracing the swirling patterns of the latticing.

"Unless you plan to move that with your mind, I suggest you get practicing," Tove said.

"Why are we practicing in here?" I turned to look at him, pulling myself away from the chair. I don't know why, but something about it captivated me, made this all the more real.

"I like the space." He gestured vaguely at the airiness of the room. "It helps my thoughts. The ballroom is being worked on today, so we had to move."

Almost reluctantly, I walked away from the throne and went over to Tove to see what cryptic lesson he had in store for me. Duncan stood off to the side of the room for most of the morning, getting a reprieve from being my test subject. Tove wanted me to work on restraining my thoughts again, this time using tactics that made even less sense to me.

I stood facing a wall, and while I counted up to a thousand, I was supposed to picture the garden and use my persuasion. Since I wasn't using it on anyone, I wasn't exactly sure how I'd be able to tell if it was working or not, but Tove said the point was that I learn to flex my psychic muscles. My mind would have to learn to juggle a lot of ideas, some of them conflicting, in order for me to get control over this.

While I practiced, he sprawled on the floor, lying on the cold marble. Duncan eventually tired and went over to the throne, sitting in it with one of his legs draped over the side. I felt a little irritated by that, but I wasn't sure why, so I didn't say anything. I didn't support aristocracy, and I wasn't going to enforce it on Duncan.

"How are you doing?" Tove asked, speaking for the first time in about a half hour. We'd all been silent as I tried to master whatever it was I was supposed to master.

"Fantastic," I muttered.

"Great. Let's add a song." He stared up at the skylight, watching the clouds roll over us.

"What?" I stopped counting and let go of my persuasion so I could turn to face him. "Why?"

"I can still hear you," Tove said. "It's getting fainter, but it's like the hum you hear from power lines. You need to quiet the noise in your head."

"And doing a million things at once will do that?" I asked skeptically.

"Yes. You're getting stronger, which means you're learning to hold things in." He lay down, closing the matter. "Now add a song to it."

"What should I sing?" I sighed, turning to face the wall.

"Not 'Twinkle, Twinkle, Little Star.'" Duncan grimaced. "I've had that stuck in my head for some reason."

"I've always been partial to the Beatles," Tove said.

I glanced over at Duncan, who smirked with surprise. Sighing again, I started singing "Eleanor Rigby." I messed up the words a couple times, but Tove didn't complain, which was good. It was hard enough trying to do this *and* remember the lyrics to a song I hadn't heard in years.

"I hope I'm not interrupting." Elora's voice ruined any semblance I had of concentration, so I stopped singing and turned to face her.

Duncan scrambled out of the chair, but not before I caught

sight of the nasty glare she shot him. He looked down so his hair would cover the crimson blush on his cheeks.

"Not really." I shrugged. For once, I was actually happy to see Elora, since her arrival meant a reprieve from all of this.

Elora surveyed the room with disdain, but I wasn't sure what met her disapproval, since she had to at least have had a hand in the design. She stepped into the room, her long gown pooling around her feet. Tove didn't get up and watched her with offhanded interest.

"Can I have a moment alone with the Princess?" Elora asked without looking at anyone. She managed to stand in such a way that her back was to all three of us.

Duncan mumbled apologies as he hurried out of the room, stumbling over his own feet. Tove left more slowly, always content to do things at his own pace. He ran a hand through his disheveled hair and made a vague comment about coming to find me when I was done.

"I've never cared for this room," Elora said once they'd gone. "It always felt more like a greenhouse to me than a throne room. I know that was the idea behind it, helping us maintain our more organic roots, but it never felt right to me."

"I think it's nice." I understood what she meant, but it was still a beautiful room. All the glass gave it a sleek yet opulent feel.

"Your 'friend' is staying with us." She chose her words carefully and walked over to the throne. She ran her fingers along the arms much the same way I had, letting her black manicured nails linger on the details.

"My friend?"

"Yes. The . . . boy. Matt, is it?" Elora lifted her head, meeting my eyes to see if she was correct.

"You mean my brother," I said deliberately.

"Don't call him that. Think of him however you'd like, but if someone hears you say that . . ." She trailed off. "How long will he be staying with us?"

"Until I feel it's safe for him to leave." I stood up straighter, steeling myself for another fight, but she didn't say anything. She simply nodded once and looked out the window. "You're not gonna try to stop me?"

"I've been Queen for a while, Princess." She smiled thinly at me. "I know how to pick my battles. This is one I suspect I couldn't win."

"So you're okay with it?" I asked, unable to hide the shock in my voice.

"You learn to tolerate the things you cannot change," Elora told me simply.

"Do you want to meet him or anything?" I felt unsure about what I should do.

I didn't know why she'd come to talk to me, if it wasn't to stop me from doing something or tell me I'd done something wrong. That seemed to be the only time she sought me out.

"I'm certain I'll see him in due time." She smoothed her black hair and walked a bit closer to me. "How is your training going?"

"Fine." I shrugged. "I don't get it, really, but it's okay. I guess."

"You're getting along all right with Tove?" Her dark eyes met mine again, as if studying me.

"Yeah. He's fine."

Whatever she saw in me must've pleased her, because she nodded and smiled. Elora stayed and chatted with me a few minutes longer, asking more about the training, but her interest waned almost immediately. She excused herself, citing business to attend to.

Once she had gone, Tove returned to continue the training, but I suggested we get lunch instead. We went down to the kitchen to discover Matt making something for him and Willa. Rhys was at school, so it was just the two of them.

Willa threw a grape at Matt, and when he tossed it back, she giggled. If Tove noticed anything unusual about their banter, he didn't say anything, but he hardly looked up from his plate. He ate in total silence, while I watched Matt and Willa with confused fascination.

I ate in a hurry, then Tove and I went back to training while Matt and Willa were still eating. Not that either of them really seemed to notice or care about our departure.

The rest of the day didn't afford me much time to think about how strange Matt and Willa were acting. Training went on in the throne room much the way it had in the morning. Toward the end of the day I began feeling tired, but I didn't stop until Tove called it quits.

After Tove left, Duncan followed me upstairs, because I couldn't seem to ditch him no matter what I said. I wanted to be alone, but I let Duncan in my room. I felt weird and mean making him stand out in the hall all the time.

I know he supposedly was a bodyguard, but he wasn't some stiff in a suit with an earpiece. He was a kid in skinny jeans, which made it hard for me to treat him like staff.

"I don't understand why you hate it here so much," Duncan said, admiring my room.

"I don't hate it here," I said, but I wasn't sure if that was true.

My hair had been up in a messy bun, and I took it down, running my fingers through the kinks and curls. Duncan looked at the stuff on my desk, touching my computer and CDs. I would've been mad, if any of it were really mine. Everything had come with the place when I moved in. Even though this was my room, very little in it felt like it actually belonged to me.

"Why'd you run away?" Duncan picked up a Fall Out Boy CD and investigated the track list.

"I thought you knew why." I got into my bed, immersing myself in the overflow of blankets and pillows. I folded a pillow under my head so I could see him better. "You seemed to have it all figured out."

"When?" He set the CD down and turned to look at me. "I never seem like I have anything figured out."

"That's true," I said, pushing a dark curl off my forehead. "But at my house, when you came to get me. I thought you knew."

When I'd first met him, he'd said something. I couldn't remember exactly what it was, but he'd implied he knew what had happened between Finn and me. Or at the very least, he'd known why Finn had been dismissed, which was because of the way Finn felt about me.

Although I wasn't so sure about Finn's feelings anymore. I doubted they were real now, if they had ever been. We had lain in this very bed, kissing and holding each other. I'd wanted to do more, but Finn had stopped things, saying he didn't want to disturb me. But maybe he'd never really wanted me at all.

If he had, he wouldn't have just left that way. He couldn't have.

"I don't know what you're talking about." Duncan shook his head. "I don't think I ever understood why you left."

"I must've imagined it, then." I rolled onto my back so I could stare up at the ceiling. Before he could ask me more about it, I changed the subject. "What happened to you guys anyway?"

"When?" He'd moved on from the CDs to perusing the small book collection I had.

They weren't terrible, but they'd all been Rhys's and Rhiannon's choices, so they weren't really my tastes. Other than a book by Jerry Spinelli, there was nothing I would have picked out for myself.

"Back at my house. You guys left, and the Vittra kidnapped me. What'd you do? Where'd you go?"

"We didn't get very far. Finn planned on sticking around. He thought you'd come around eventually." Duncan picked up a book and absently flipped through it. "But we only made it a block away, and they jumped us. This guy with scraggly blondish hair, he just looked at us, and we were out."

"Loki," I said with a sigh.

"Who?" Duncan asked, and I shook my head.

The Vittra must have been watching, waiting for the opportunity to surprise Finn and Duncan. They snuck up on them, and Loki took care of them. Finn was lucky that they'd only knocked him out. Kyra seemed way too keen on destroying me.

She must've been sent ahead to get me, leaving Loki behind to neutralize Finn and Duncan. Loki hadn't seemed that big into violence. In fact, if he hadn't intervened, Kyra might've actually killed me.

"Wait." Duncan narrowed his eyes at me, as if figuring something out. "Did you think we left you there?"

"I didn't know what to think," I said. "You just left, and I hadn't expected you to. I didn't want to go with you, but you left without much of a fight. I thought maybe—"

"Is that why you've been so mopey?"

"I have not been mopey!" I had been a little depressed since I'd gotten back. Well, since before then, really, but I didn't think I'd been *mopey*.

"No, you have," he assured me with a smile. "There's no way we'd leave you that way. You were an easy target. Finn would never let anything happen to you." He'd turned to my stuff and picked up my iPod. "I mean, he can't even leave you now, and you're completely safe here."

"What?" My heart raced in my chest. "What are you talking about?"

"What?" Duncan belatedly realized he'd said too much, and his skin paled. "Nothing."

"No, Duncan, what do you mean?" I sat up, knowing I should at least pretend not to care so much, but I couldn't help it. "Finn's here? You mean like *here* here?"

"I shouldn't say anything." He shifted uneasily.

"You have to tell me," I insisted, scooting to the edge of the bed.

"No, Finn would kill me if he knew I said anything." Duncan stared down at his feet and fiddled with a broken belt loop. "I'm sorry."

"He told you not to tell me he's here?" I asked, once again feeling a painful stab in my heart.

"He's not here, like in the palace." He groaned and looked sheepishly at me. "If I get mixed up in whatever sordid thing it is you have with him, I'll never get a job again. Please, Princess. Don't make me tell you."

It wasn't until the words were out of his mouth that I realized I *could* make him tell me. While my persuasion might not be strong enough for the likes of Tove and Loki, I'd been practicing on Duncan. He was easily susceptible to my charms.

"Where is he, Duncan?" I demanded, looking directly at him.

I didn't even have to chant it in my head. As soon as I'd said it, his jaw sagged and his eyes glassed over. His mind was awfully pliable, and I felt bad. Later on, I'd have to make this up to him somehow.

"He's in Förening, at his parents' house," Duncan said, blinking hard at me.

"His parents?"

"Yeah, they live down the road." He pointed south. "Follow the main road towards the gate, then take the third left on a gravel road. Go down the side of the bluff a little ways, and they live in a cottage. It's the one with goats."

"Goats?" I asked, wondering if Duncan was pulling my leg.

"His mother raises a few angora goats. She makes sweaters and scarves from the mohair and sells them." He shook his head. "I've said way too much. I'm gonna be in so much trouble."

"No, you'll be fine," I assured him as I jumped out of bed.

I ran to the closet to change my clothes. I didn't look bad, but if I was gonna see Finn, I had to look good. Duncan kept groaning about what an idiot he was for telling me anything. I tried to calm him, but my mind raced too much.

I couldn't believe how stupid I was. I'd imagined that as soon as he was unassigned from me, Finn had been sent to track someone else. But now I realized he had to have some turnaround time before his next job, and he had to stay somewhere. If he wasn't living at the palace, his parents were the next logical choice. He'd spoken very little of them, and it never occurred to me that they might be neighbors.

"Elora will find out. She knows everything," Duncan muttered as I exited the closet.

"I promise. I won't tell anyone." I looked at myself in the mirror. I was pale, scattered, and terrified. Finn liked my hair better when it was down, so I left it that way, even though it was messy.

"She'll still find out," Duncan insisted.

"I'll protect your job," I said, but he still looked skeptical. "I'm the Princess. I have to have some pull around here." He shrugged, but I could tell I'd managed to alleviate some of his fears. "I've gotta go. You can't tell anyone where I am."

"They'll freak out if they don't know where you're at."

"Well . . ." I looked around, thinking. "Stay here. If anyone comes looking for me, tell them I'm in the bath and can't be disturbed. We're each other's alibis."

"You sure?" He raised an eyebrow.

"Yes," I lied. "I have to go. And thank you."

Duncan still didn't seem convinced this was a good idea, but I'd left him with little choice. I raced out of the palace, trying to be as inconspicuous as possible. Elora had a few other trackers wandering around to keep watch on things, but I slid past them without any notice.

When I pushed open the front doors, I realized I didn't even know why I was in such a hurry to see Finn. What did I plan on doing once I saw him? Convince him to come with me? Did I even want that?

After the way things had been left between us, what was I going after?

I couldn't answer that for sure. All I knew was I had to see him. I hurried down the winding road, going south, and tried to remember Duncan's directions.

kinfolk

The gravel road wound down at a steep incline. I wouldn't have known I was going the right way if I hadn't heard the goats bleating.

When I rounded the bend, I saw the small cottage nestled into the side of the bluffs. Vines and bushes covered it so much that I might not have noticed it if it weren't for the smoke coming out of the chimney.

The pasture for the goats leveled out a bit more than the rest of the bluff, so it was sitting on a plateau. A wooden fence kept them enclosed. The long fur on the goats was dingy white.

The overcast sky and the chill in the air didn't help bring out the color, though. Even the leaves, which had turned golden and red, appeared faded as they littered the yard around Finn's house.

Now that I was here, I wasn't sure what I should do. I wrapped my arms around myself and swallowed hard. Did I go knock on the door? What did I even have to say to him? He left. He made his choice, and I already knew that.

I looked toward the palace, deciding it might be better if I went home without seeing Finn. A woman's voice stopped me, though, and I turned to Finn's house.

"I've already fed you," a woman was telling the goats.

She walked through the pasture, coming from the small barn on the far side of the field. Her worn dress dragged on the ground, so the hem was filthy. A dark cloak hung over her shoulders, and her brown hair had been pulled up in two tight buns. The goats swarmed around her, begging for a handout, and she'd been too busy gently pushing them back to notice me right away.

When she saw me, her steps slowed so much, she nearly stopped. Her eyes were as black as Finn's, and while she was very pretty, her face was more tired than any other I had seen here. She couldn't be more than forty, but her skin had the worn, tanned look that came from a lifetime of hard work.

"Can I help you?" she asked, quickening her pace as she came toward me.

"Um . . ." I hugged myself more tightly and glanced up the road. "I don't think so."

She opened the gate, making a clicking sound at the goats to get them to back off, and stepped outside of it. She stopped a few feet in front of me, sizing me up in a way that I knew wasn't approving, and she wiped her hands on her dress, cleaning them of dirt from the animals.

Nodding once, she let out a deep breath.

"It's getting cold out here," she said. "Why don't you come inside?"

"Thank you, but I—" I started to excuse myself, but she cut me off.

"I think you should come inside."

She turned and walked toward the cottage. I stayed back for a minute, debating whether or not I should escape, but she left the cottage door open, letting the warm air waft out. It smelled deliciously of vegetable stew, something hearty and homemade and enticing in a way that food hardly ever smelled.

When I stepped inside the cottage, she'd already hung up her cloak and gone over to the large potbellied stove in the corner. A black pot sat on top of it, bubbling with that wonderful-smelling stew, and she stirred it with a wooden spoon.

The cottage looked as quaint and humble as I'd expect a troll's cottage to look. It reminded me of the one where the seven dwarves lived with Snow White. The floors were dirt, packed down into a smooth black from wear.

The table sitting in the center of the kitchen was made of thick, scarred wood. A broom sat propped in one corner, and a flower box sat below each of the small round windows. Like the flowers in the garden at home, these bloomed bright purple and pink, even though it was way past the season for them.

"Will you be staying for supper?" she asked, sprinkling something into the pot on the stove.

"What?" I asked, surprised by her invitation.

"I need to know." She turned to face me, wiping her hands on her dress to clear them of spices. "I'll have to make rolls if I'm feeding another mouth."

"Oh, no, I'm okay." I shook my head, realizing it wasn't an invitation. She was afraid that I would impose myself on her meal and her family, and my stomach twisted sourly. "Thank you, though."

"What is it that you want, then?" She put her hands on her hips, and her eyes were as dark and hard as Finn's when he was upset.

"What? You . . ." I floundered, surprised by the directness of her question. "You invited me in."

"You were lurking around. I know you want something." She grabbed a rag from the metal basin that served as a sink and began washing the table off, even though it didn't appear dirty. "I'd rather you come out and be done with it."

"Do you know who I am?" I asked softly.

I didn't want to tout any superiority, but I didn't understand why she was reacting this way. Especially if she knew that I was the Princess, I didn't know why she'd be so curt.

"Of course I know who you are," she said. "And I assume you know who I am."

"Who are you?" I asked, even though I knew.

"I'm Annali Holmes, lowly servant of the Queen." She stopped wiping the table so she could glare at me. "I'm Finn's mother. And if you came to see him, he isn't here."

My heart would've dropped if I wasn't so confused by the way she was treating me. I felt like she was accusing me of something, and I didn't even know what.

"I—I didn't—" I stuttered. "I went for a walk. I needed fresh air. I didn't mean anything."

"You never do," Annali said with a tight smile.

"You've only just met me."

She nodded. "Maybe so. But I knew your mother, quite well." She turned away, putting a hand on the back of one of the dining room chairs. "And I know my son."

I understood too late where her anger came from. Her husband and my mother had been involved in an affair years ago. Annali had known about it, so of course she'd taken issue with me. I don't know why I hadn't realized it sooner.

Here I was, messing up her son's life, after my mother had almost ruined her life. I swallowed hard and realized I shouldn't have come here. I didn't need to bother Finn or hurt his family any more than I already had.

"Mom!" a girl called from another room, and Annali instantly composed herself, forcing a smile.

A girl of about twelve came into the kitchen carrying a battered schoolbook. She wore layers consisting of a worn dress and wool sweater, looking tattered and cold despite the warmth of the house. Her hair was the same dark mess my hair had always been, and she had a smudge of dirt on her cheek.

As soon as she saw me, her jaw dropped and her eyes widened.

"It's the Princess!" the girl gasped.

"Yes, Ember, I know who it is," Annali said with as much kindness as she could muster.

"Sorry. I've forgotten my manners." Ember tossed the textbook on the table and did a quick, low curtsy.

"Ember, you don't need to do that, not in our own home," Annali chastised her tiredly.

"She's right. I feel silly when people do that," I said.

Annali shot me a look from the corner of her eye, and for some reason, I think agreeing with her made her hate me more. Like I was undercutting her parenting.

"Oh, my gosh, Princess!" Ember squealed and ran around the table to greet me. "I can't believe you're in my house! What are you doing here? Is it about my brother? He's out with my father, but he'll be back soon. You should stay for supper. All my friends at school will be so jealous. Oh, my gosh! You're even prettier than Finn said you were!"

"Ember!" Annali snapped when it appeared that Ember wouldn't stop.

I blushed and looked away, unsure of how to respond to her. I understood in theory why it might be exciting to meet a Princess, but I couldn't see anything exciting about meeting me.

"Sorry," Ember apologized, but it didn't dampen her delight at all. "I've been begging Finn to let me meet you, and he—"

"Ember, you need to do your schoolwork." Annali wouldn't look at either of us.

"I came out because I didn't understand it." Ember pointed to her textbook.

"Well, work on something else, then," Annali told her.

"But Mom!" Ember whined.

"Ember, now," Annali said firmly, in a tone I recognized from years of Maggie and Matt scolding me.

Ember sighed and picked up her textbook before trudging to her room. She muttered something about life not being fair, but Annali ignored it.

"Your daughter is delightful," I said once Ember had gone.

"Don't talk to me about my children," Annali snapped.

"I'm sorry." I rubbed at my arms, not knowing what to do. I didn't even know why I was here. "Why did you invite me in if you don't want me around?"

"Like I have a choice." She rolled her eyes and went over to the stove. "You came here for my son, and I know I can't stop you."

"I didn't . . ." I trailed off. "I wanted to talk to Finn, not take him away from you." I sighed. "I just wanted to say good-bye."

"Are you going somewhere?" Annali asked, her back to me as she stirred the stew.

"No. No, I can't go anywhere, even if I had somewhere else I wanted to be." I pulled at the sleeves of my shirt and stared down at the floor. "I really didn't mean to upset you. I don't even know why I came here. I knew I shouldn't."

"You really didn't come here to take him away?" Annali turned around to face me, narrowing her eyes.

"He left," I said. "I can't force him to return . . . I wouldn't want to, even if I could." I shook my head. "I'm sorry I bothered you."

"You really aren't anything like your mother." Annali sounded surprised by that, and I looked up at her. "Finn said you weren't, but I didn't believe him."

"Thank you," I said. "I mean . . . I don't want to be like her."

I heard men's voices coming up the road. The cottage walls were startlingly thin, and I looked out the small window next to the door. The glass was warped and blurred, but I could see two dark figures walking toward the house.

"They're home." Annali sighed.

My heart hammered in my chest, and I had to squeeze my hands together to keep them from trembling. I still had no idea what I was doing here, and with Finn rapidly approaching the door, I wished I hadn't come at all. I couldn't think of anything to say to him. There was plenty I actually wanted to say, but this was entirely the wrong place and time.

The door to the cottage pushed open, bringing along a cold wind, and I wanted to escape into it. But a man blocked my path, looking about as shocked and sick as I felt. He stopped right in the doorway, so Finn couldn't get past him, and for a minute he simply stared at me.

His eyes were lighter than Finn's and his skin tanner, but I saw enough of Finn in him to know that he was his father. And yet there was something almost pretty about him, his skin softer and cheekbones higher. Finn was far more rugged and strong, and I preferred that.

"Princess," he said after a lengthy silence.

"Yes, Thomas," Annali said without even trying to hide the irritation in her voice. "It's the Princess, now step inside before you let all the warm air out."

"My apologies." Thomas bowed before me, then stepped aside so Finn could come in.

Finn didn't bow, and he didn't say anything. His expression remained blank, and his eyes were too dark to read. He folded his arms across his chest, and he wouldn't take his eyes off me, so I looked away. The air seemed too thick to breathe, and I did not want to be here.

"To what do we owe the pleasure?" Thomas asked when nobody said anything. He'd gone over to Annali, looping his arm around his wife's shoulders. She rolled her eyes when he did it, but she didn't push his arm away.

"Getting fresh air," I mumbled. My mouth felt numb, and I had to force myself to speak.

"Shouldn't you be getting back?" Annali suggested.

"Yes." I nodded quickly, grateful for an escape from this.

"I'll walk you," Finn said, speaking for the first time.

"Finn, I don't think that's necessary," Annali said.

"I have to be sure she gets home," Finn said. He opened the door, letting in the frosty air that seemed like a wonderful reprieve from the suddenly stifling kitchen. "Are you ready, Princess?"

"Yes." I nodded and stepped toward the door. I waved vaguely at Annali and Thomas, unwilling to actually look at them. "It was lovely meeting you. Tell Ember I said good-bye."

"You're welcome here anytime, Princess," Thomas said, and I could actually hear Annali hitting him in the arm as I walked out of the cottage.

I took a deep breath and walked up the gravel road. The stones dug into my bare feet, but I liked it better that way. It distracted me from the awkward tension hanging between Finn and me.

"You don't have to walk with me," I said quietly as we reached the top of the gravel road. From there, the road turned into smooth tar leading back to the palace.

"Yes, I do," Finn replied coolly. "It's my duty."

"Not anymore."

"It's still my duty to carry out the Queen's wishes, and keeping the Princess safe is her highest wish," he said in a way that was almost taunting.

"I'm perfectly safe without you." I walked faster.

"Does anybody even know that you left the palace?" Finn asked, giving me a sidelong glance as he matched my pace, and I shook my head. "How did you even know where I lived?" I didn't answer because I didn't want Duncan to get in trouble, but Finn figured it out on his own. "Duncan? Excellent."

"Duncan's doing a perfectly adequate job!" I snapped. "And you must think so, otherwise you wouldn't have left me in his care."

"I have no control over whose care you're left under," Finn said. "You know that. I don't know why you're angry with me for that."

"I'm not!" I walked even faster, so I was almost jogging. That didn't bode well for me, because I stepped on a sharp rock. "Dammit!"

"Are you okay?" Finn asked, stopping to see what was the matter.

"Yeah, I just stepped on a rock." I rubbed my foot. It didn't appear to be bleeding, and I attempted to walk on it. It stung a little, but I'd survive. "Why couldn't we take your car?"

"I don't have a car." Finn shoved his hands in his pockets and slowed down.

I hobbled a little, and he didn't offer to help me. Not that I would've accepted his offer, but that was beside the point.

"What do you call that Cadillac you always drive?" I asked.

"Elora's," he said. "She lends me the car for work, the same way she lends all the trackers cars. But we don't own them. I don't actually *own* anything."

"What about your clothes?" I asked, mostly just to irritate him. I assumed he actually owned them, but I wanted to argue with him about something.

"Did you see that house back there, Wendy?" Finn stopped and pointed to his house. We'd gone too far to see it anymore, but I looked at the trees blocking my view. "That's the house I grew up in, the house I live in, the house I will probably die in. That's what I have. That is *all* I have."

"I don't have anything that's really mine either," I said, and he laughed darkly.

"You still don't get it, Wendy." He rested his eyes on me, and his mouth twitched into a bitter smile. "I'm just a tracker. You have to stop this. You have to go be a Princess, do what's best for you, and let me go do my job."

"I really didn't mean to bother you, and you don't need to walk me home." I turned and walked again, more quickly than my foot would've liked.

"I'm making sure you get there safely," Finn said, following a step behind.

"If you're just doing your job, then go do it!" I stopped and whirled on him. "But I'm not your job anymore, right?"

"No, you're not!" Finn shouted and stepped closer to me. "Why did you come to my house today? What did you think that would accomplish?"

"I don't know!" I yelled. "But you didn't even say good-bye!"

"How does saying good-bye help anything?" He shook his head. "It doesn't."

"Yes, it does!" I insisted. "You can't just leave me!"

"I have to!" His dark eyes blazed, making my stomach flip. "You *have* to be the Princess, and I can't ruin that. I won't."

"I understand, but . . ." Tears welled in my eyes, and I swallowed hard. "You can't keep going like you do. You have to at least say good-bye."

Finn stepped closer to me. His eyes smoldered in a way that only he could manage, and the chill in the air seemed to disappear entirely. I leaned in to him, even though I was afraid he'd be able to feel the way my heart hammered in my chest.

I stared up at him, praying he would touch me, but he didn't. He didn't move at all.

"Good-bye, Wendy," Finn said, so quietly I could barely hear him.

"Princess!" Duncan shouted.

I pulled my gaze away from Finn to see Duncan standing a little ways down the road, waving his arms like a maniac. The palace was right around the corner, and I hadn't realized how close we were. When I looked at Finn, he'd already taken several steps away from me, toward his house.

"He can take you the rest of the way home." Finn gestured to Duncan and took another step back. I didn't say anything, so he stopped. "Aren't you going to say good-bye?"

"No." I shook my head.

"Princess!" Duncan shouted again, and I heard him racing

toward us. "Princess, Matt noticed you were missing, and he wanted to alert the guards. I have to bring you back before he does."

"I'm coming." I turned toward Duncan, putting my back to Finn.

I walked with Duncan to the palace, not even looking back at Finn once. I was quite proud of myself. I hadn't yelled at him for not telling me about my father, but I did say some of the things I wanted to say.

"I'm lucky that Matt was the one who saw you were gone, and not Elora," Duncan said as we rounded the bend to the palace. The asphalt road gave way to a cobblestone driveway that felt much better on my feet.

"Duncan, is that how you live?" I asked.

"What do you mean?"

"Like Finn's house." I pointed toward it with my thumb. "Do you live in a cottage like that? I mean, when you're not busy tracking."

"Yeah, pretty much." Duncan nodded. "I think mine's a little bit nicer, but I live with my uncle, and he was a really good tracker before he retired. Now he's a teacher at the mänks school, and that's still not so bad."

"Do you live around here?" I asked.

"Yeah." He pointed up the hill, north of the palace. "It's pretty well hidden in the bluff, but it's right up that way." He looked at me. "Why? Did you wanna go visit?"

"Not right now. Thanks for the invitation, though," I said. "I was just curious. Is that how all the trackers live?"

"Like me and Finn?" Duncan was thoughtful for a moment, then nodded. "Yeah, pretty much. All the trackers that stay around, anyway."

Duncan walked ahead and opened the front doors, but I stopped and stared up at the palace, where intertwined vines grew over a massive white exterior. When the sunlight hit it, it glittered beautifully, but it was almost blindingly white.

"Princess?" Duncan waited at the open doors for me. "Is everything all right?"

"Would you die to save me?" I asked him bluntly.

"What?"

"If I was in danger, would you be willing to die to protect me?" I asked. "Have other trackers done that before?"

"Yes, of course." Duncan nodded. "Many other trackers have given their lives in the name of the kingdom, and I'd be honored to do the same."

"Don't." I walked up to him. "If it ever comes down to a situation between me and you, save yourself. I'm not worth dying for."

"Princess, I—"

"None of us are," I said, looking at him seriously. "Not the Queen or any of the Markis or Marksinna. That's a direct order from the Princess, and you have to follow it. Save yourself."

"I don't understand." Duncan's whole face scrunched in confusion. "But . . . if it's as you wish, Princess."

"It is. Thank you." I smiled at him and walked into the palace.

THIRTEEN

captive

The debris had been cleared from the ballroom, much to Tove's chagrin, but the skylights were still covered with tarps. Tove had liked having all the junk around because it gave me something to practice on, but he decided that the tarps would be easier anyway.

Duncan had stayed away today. I think his brain was getting frazzled from me playing around with it. Since he sometimes got hit with stray brain waves when I tried too hard, we all thought it'd be best if he hung around somewhere else for a while.

I'd been trying for hours to get one of the tarps to move, and all I'd managed was a ripple across it. Even that was questionable. Tove said it was probably me, but I suspected it was a strong gust of wind blowing across it.

My head was actually starting to hurt, and I felt like a jackass, holding my arms up in the air, pushing at nothing.

"Nothing's happening." I sighed and dropped my arms.

"Try harder," Tove replied. He lay on the floor near me, his arms folded neatly beneath his head.

"I can't try any harder." I sat down on the floor with an unlady-like thud, but I knew Tove wouldn't care. I had a feeling he barely even noticed I was a girl. "I'm not trying to whine here, but are you sure I can even do this?"

"Pretty sure."

"Well, what if I give myself an aneurysm trying to do something I can't even do?" I asked.

"You won't," he said simply. He lifted an arm up, and holding his palm out, he made the tarp above him lift up and strain against the bungee cords holding it down. It settled down, and he looked over at me. "Do that."

"Can I take a break?" I asked, almost pleading with him. My brow had started to sweat, and stray curls were sticking to my temples.

"If you must." He lowered his arm and folded it behind his head again. "If you're really having a hard time with this, maybe you need to work up to it more. Tomorrow you can practice on Duncan again."

"No, I don't wanna practice on him." I pulled my knee up to my chest and rested my cheek against it. "I don't want to break him."

"What about that Rhys?" Tove asked. "Can you practice on him?"

"No. He's completely out of the question." I picked at a spot on the marble floor and thought for a minute. "I don't want to practice on people."

"It's the only way you'll get good at it," Tove said.

"I know, but . . ." I sighed. "Maybe I don't want to be good at it. I mean, controlling it, yes, I want to be good at that. But I don't want to be able to use mind control on anyone. Even bad people. It doesn't feel right to me."

"I understand that." He sat up, crossing his legs underneath him as he turned to face me. "But learning to harness your power isn't a bad thing."

"I'm stronger than Duncan, right?"

"Yes, of course." Tove nodded.

"Then why is Duncan guarding *me*?" I asked. "If I'm more powerful."

"Because he's more expendable," Tove replied simply. I must've looked appalled, because Tove hurried to explain. "That's the way the Queen sees it. The way Trylle society sees it. And . . . if I'm being really honest, I agree with them."

"You can't really believe that my life has more value simply because I'm a Princess?" I asked. "The trackers are living in squalor, and we expect them to die for us."

"They're not living in squalor, but you're right. The system is totally messed up," Tove said. "Trackers are born into a lifetime of debt simply because they're born here, and not left somewhere out in the world collecting an inheritance. They are indentured servants, which is just a polite name for slaves. And that is not right at all."

It wasn't until Tove said it that I realized that's exactly what it was. The trackers were little more than slaves. I felt sick.

"But you do need guards," Tove went on. "Every leader in the free world has bodyguards of some kind. Even pop stars have them. It's not a horrible thing."

"Yes, but in the free world, the bodyguards are hired. They choose it," I said. "They're not forced."

"You think Duncan was forced? Or Finn?" Tove asked. "They both volunteered for this. Everyone did. Protecting you is a great honor. Besides that, living in the palace is a sweet deal."

"I don't want anyone getting hurt over me," I said and looked directly at him.

"Good." His mouth curled up into a smirk. "Then learn to defend yourself. Move the tarp."

I stood up, preparing to conquer the tarp once and for all, but a blaring siren interrupted everything.

"You hear that, right?" Tove asked, cocking his head at me.

"Yeah, of course!" I shouted to be heard over it.

"Making sure it wasn't just me," Tove said.

That made me wonder what it sounded like inside his head. I knew he heard things everybody else didn't hear, but if that included things like blaring sirens, I understood why he always seemed so distracted.

"What is that?" I asked.

"Fire alarm, maybe?" Tove shrugged and stood up. "Let's go check it out."

I put my hands over my ears and followed him out of the ballroom. We'd barely made it out into the hallway when the alarm stopped blaring, but my ears kept ringing. We were in the south wing, where business was conducted, and a few of the Queen's associates were out in the hall, looking around.

"Why is that blasted thing going off?" Elora shouted from the front hall. Her words echoed from inside my head too, and I hated how she did that mind-speak thing when she was angry.

I couldn't hear the answer to her question, but there was definitely a commotion going on. Grunting, yelling, slamming, fighting. Something was going down in the rotunda. Tove kept walking without hesitation, so I picked up my pace.

"Where did you find him?" Elora asked, but this time I couldn't hear her inside my head. But we were close enough to the front hall that she sounded quite loud.

"He was hanging around the perimeter," Duncan said, and I hurried at the sound of his voice. I wasn't sure what he'd gotten himself into, but it couldn't be good. "He'd knocked out one of the guards when I saw him."

When I reached the front hall, Elora was standing halfway down the curved staircase. She had on a long dressing gown, so I assumed she'd been lying down with another one of her migraines when the alarm went off. Rubbing her temple, she surveyed the room with her usual disdain.

The front doors were still wide open, letting an early snowfall blow in. A group of guards were in a struggle in the center of the rotunda, and the wind gusted in, shaking the chandelier above them. Duncan stood off to the side, much to my relief, because the fight did not seem to be going well.

At least five or six guards were trying to tackle someone in the middle. A couple of the guards were really huge muscular dudes too, and they couldn't seem to get a handle on this guy. I couldn't get a good look at him because he kept slipping between them.

"Enough!" Elora shouted, and a pain pierced my skull.

Tove put both his hands to his head, pressing against it hard, and continued to do so even after the pain in my head stopped.

The guards backed off as Elora commanded, leaving ample room for the guy in the center, and I finally saw what all the fuss was about. His back was to me, but he was the only troll I'd seen with hair that light.

"Loki?" I said, more surprised than anything, and he turned to me.

"Princess." He gave me a lopsided smirk, and his eyes sparkled.

"You know him?" Elora asked, her words dripping with venom.

"Yeah. I mean, no," I said.

"Come, now, Princess, we're old friends." Loki winked at me. He turned to Elora, attempting to give her his most winning smile, and spread his arms wide. "We're all friends here, aren't we, Your Highness?"

Elora narrowed her eyes at him, and Loki suddenly collapsed to his knees. He made a horrible guttural sound and clenched his stomach.

"Stop!" I yelled and ran toward him. At the same time, the front door slammed shut and the chandelier above shook.

Elora took her eyes off him to glare at me, but fortunately, she didn't cause me to writhe in pain. I stopped before I reached Loki. He'd doubled over, his forehead resting against the marble floor. I could hear him gasping for breath, and he turned his head away from me so I couldn't see how much pain he was in.

"Why on earth would I stop?" Elora asked. She had one hand on the banister, and her knuckles grew white as her grip tightened. "This troll was trying to break in. Isn't that right, Duncan?"

"Yes." Duncan sounded uncertain, and his eyes flitted over to me for a second. "I believe he was, at least. He looked . . . suspicious."

"Suspicious behavior doesn't give you carte blanche to torture someone!" I yelled at her, and her expression only got stonier. I knew I wasn't helping the situation, but I couldn't contain myself.

"He's Vittra, is he not?" Elora asked.

"Yeah, he is, but . . ." I licked my lips and looked over at Loki. He'd sat up a bit and composed himself some, but his face was still drawn. "He was good to me when I was there. He didn't hurt me, and he actually helped me. So . . . we should at the very least show him the same respect here."

"Is that true?" Elora asked him.

"Yes, it is." He sat on his heels so he could stare up at her. "I've found that I get what I want more often with basic decency than unnecessary cruelty."

"What's your name?" Elora asked, unmoved by his statement.

"Loki Staad." He held his chin up high when he said that, as if he was proud.

"I knew your father." Elora's lips moved into a thin smile, but it wasn't a pleasant one. It was the kind someone would have after stealing candy from a small child. "I hated him."

"That surprises me, Your Majesty." Loki smiled broadly at her, erasing any sign that he'd been in agony moments ago. "My father was a stone-cold jerk. That sounds like your taste exactly."

"It's funny, because I was going to say you remind me so much of him." Elora's icy smile remained frozen in place as she descended the rest of the stairs, and Loki did an admirable job of not letting his falter. "You think you can use your charm to get out of anything, but I don't find you charming at all."

"That's a shame," Loki said. "Because, with all due respect, Your Highness, I could rock your world."

Elora laughed, but it sounded more like a cackle when it echoed off the walls. I wanted to yell at Loki, to tell him to stop baiting her, and I wished I could do that mind-speak Elora did all the time.

Right now I had to make sure that Elora didn't kill Loki. He'd helped me in Ondarike, risking his own life. We'd only spoken a little, but he'd put himself in jeopardy for me.

Before we left the Vittra palace, there had been a moment when I'd almost asked him to join us. I hadn't, and I wasn't sure if I'd made the right decision or not. There was something about Loki that I couldn't explain, a connection I shouldn't feel.

Oddly, the thing that struck me the most about what Loki had done when he'd let us escape was that he'd disobeyed orders. He'd been put in charge of keeping guard over me, with insubordination punishable by death.

Yet Loki had chosen me over duty, defying his monarch and his kingdom. That was something that Finn wouldn't even do.

Elora stopped in front of him. Loki remained on his knees, looking up at her, and I wished he'd get rid of that stupid grin on his face. It only antagonized her.

"You are a small, insignificant creature," Elora said, staring down at him. "I can and will destroy you the moment I see fit."

"I know." Loki nodded.

Her dark eyes were locked on his, and she stared at him for some time before I realized she was doing something to him. Saying something or controlling him somehow. He wasn't writhing in pain, but his grin had fallen away.

With a heavy sigh, she looked away from him and motioned to the guards.

"Take him away," Elora said.

Two of the larger guards came up behind Loki and grabbed him by his arms, pulling him to his feet. Loki was out of it after whatever Elora had done to him, and he couldn't seem to stand.

"Where are they taking him?" I asked Elora as the guards

dragged him away. Loki's head lolled back and forth, but he was still awake and alive.

"It's none of your concern where they take him or what happens to him," Elora hissed at me.

She cast a glance around the room, and the other guards dispersed to do their job. Duncan lingered, waiting for me, and Tove stood a few feet back. Tove would never be intimidated by my mother, and I appreciated that about him.

"Someday, I will be Queen, and I should know what is done with prisoners," I said, reaching for the sanest argument I had. She looked away from me and didn't say anything for a moment. "Elora. Where did they take him?"

"Servants' quarters, for now," Elora told me.

She glanced over at Tove, and I had a feeling if he wasn't here, this whole conversation would go much differently. Tove's mother Aurora wanted to overthrow my mother, and Elora didn't want Tove or Aurora to see any sign of weakness or unrest. And as much as I disagreed with her methods, I saw the need to respect her wishes here.

"Why? Won't he just leave?" I asked.

"No, he can't. I saw to it that if he tries to leave, he'll collapse in agony," Elora said. "We need to build a proper prison, but the Chancellor always vetoes it. So I'm left holding him myself." She sighed and rubbed her temple again. "We'll have a meeting to see what should be done with him."

"What will be done with him?" I asked.

"You will attend the meeting to see what being a Queen entails, but you will not speak up in his defense." Her eyes met mine, hard and glowing, and in my mind, she said, *You cannot defend him. It will be an act of treason, and your minor defense of him now could get you exiled if Tove reports this to his mother.*

She appeared even wearier than she had before. Her skin was normally porcelain-smooth, but a few wrinkles had sprouted up around her eyes. She held one hand to her stomach for a moment, as if to catch her breath.

"I need to lie down," Elora said, and she held out her arm. "Duncan, please escort me to my chambers."

"Yes, Your Majesty." Duncan hurried over to help her, but as he dashed past me, he shot me an apologetic smile.

I just shook my head. I don't know what else he could've done. The Vittra had tried to kill me, Finn, Tove, my brother, pretty much every person I cared about, and Loki was one of them. I shouldn't be defending the Vittra at all, but Loki was different.

While I agreed that him turning up here did seem suspicious, he'd done nothing to justify torture. I wasn't for letting him run wild, but I was willing to give him the benefit of the doubt. I wanted to find out what he was doing here before I locked him up and threw away the key.

When Elora left, I took a deep breath and shook my head. I knew I'd gotten myself a top spot on her shitlist, and that couldn't help matters at all.

"That was good," Tove said, and I'd almost forgotten he was there. I turned to see him grinning at me with an odd look of pride.

"What are you talking about?" I asked. "I made everything worse. Elora's mad at me, so she'll take it out on Loki. And I don't even know why he's here or why he came alone. I'm trying to rescue him, and I'm not even sure what his motives are."

"No, that went really bad," Tove agreed. "But I was talking about the door and the chandelier."

"What?" I asked.

"When Elora was tormenting him, you made the door slam and the chandelier shake." Tove gestured to both of them as if that would mean something to me.

"That was the wind or something."

"No, you did that," Tove assured me. "It was involuntary, but you did it. And that's progress."

"So anytime I want to shut a door, I just have to get Elora to torture somebody," I said. "Sounds easy enough."

"Knowing your mother, it would be easy." He grinned.

We went back to train more, but I was distracted and couldn't make anything move for the remainder of the day. After Tove had gone, I headed up to my room. I thought I'd check on Matt first, since the alarm going off had to have freaked him out, and Rhys was at school. I knocked on Matt's door, and when he didn't answer, I ventured inside, but he wasn't there.

With the Vittra breaking in, I felt a little freaked about not knowing where Matt was. Before I decided on an all-out search of the premises, I went to my room to grab a sweater, and I found a note from Matt pinned to the door.

Gone over to Willa's. Be back later.
—Matt

Great. I ripped the note down and went into my room. But I'd told him I'd be training all day, so he didn't need to wait around for me. I could have really used some time to talk to him, since everything felt like absolute chaos, and he was hanging out with

Willa, which didn't even make sense. I couldn't imagine what the two of them would be doing, spending all that time together. They should be hating each other.

I flopped on my bed and fell asleep pretty quickly. I didn't realize I'd been that tired, but I guess using my abilities took a lot out of me.

FOURTEEN

stockholm syndrome

I'd gotten used to the defense meetings after the big Vittra break-in during my christening ceremony.

We met in the War Room in the south wing. The walls were plastered with maps. Red and green patches speckled them, indicating other tribes of trolls.

A huge mahogany table stood at one end, a drawing board behind it. Elora and Aurora, Tove's mother, stood at the far side of the table. For some reason, they always led the defense meetings together. Aurora didn't trust Elora to run the kingdom, but I still didn't know why Elora tolerated Aurora taking any amount of control.

Chairs littered the rest of the room, most of them mismatched because they'd been pulled from other rooms to fill the space. Our mothers commanded the meetings, so Tove and I were always the first people in attendance. It worked to our advantage, and we hid in the back.

The usual twenty or so attendees were here: Garrett Strom, Willa's father and my mother's possible boyfriend; the Chancellor, a pasty, overweight man who stared at me in a way that made my skin crawl; Noah Kroner, Tove's ever-silent father; and a few other Markis, Marksinna, and trackers.

Soon the room started filling up more than normal. People I'd never seen before filtered in, including a lot more trackers. None of the trackers took a seat, because that would have been impolite with limited seating. Duncan stood behind me, despite the fact that I told him to sit down three times.

Willa burst in a few minutes before the meeting was set to start, and she pushed her way through the crowded room. Her bracelets jangled as she stepped over a tracker, smiling brightly at me before flopping into the chair next to mine.

"Sorry I'm late." Willa readjusted her skirt, pulling it down so it hit her knees. She brushed her hair from her eyes and smiled at us. "Did I miss anything?"

"Nothing's happened yet," I said.

"There are a lot of people here, aren't there?" Willa glanced around the room. Her father looked at us, and she waved at him.

"Sure are," I agreed.

The chair directly in front of me was empty, so Tove slid it back and forth with his abilities.

Crowds tended to overwhelm him. It was too much noise inside his head. When he drained some of his power by moving objects, it weakened his capacity to hear things and helped silence the static.

"Is it really a big deal, then?" Willa asked me and lowered her voice. "I heard you knew the Vittra that they caught."

"I don't know him." I shifted in my chair. "I saw him when I was with the Vittra. It's not a big deal."

"Did you subdue him?" Willa asked, looking up at Duncan.

She was asking him directly, and not asking me if my tracker had done something. She—Willa—was treating people with basic human dignity, and it freaked me out.

Duncan puffed up with pride, then seemed to remember that I'd defended Loki. His expression shifted to shame, and he lowered his eyes. "I saw him knock another guard out, and I called for backup. That was all."

"How come he didn't knock you out?" I asked.

I hadn't had a chance to talk to Duncan much since yesterday. I'd been wondering how they'd been able to capture Loki, when he could've rendered them unconscious with a single look.

"He didn't think he had to." Duncan looked proud again, and I let him. "My appearance deceived him, and the other guards tackled him."

"What was he doing when you found him?" Willa asked.

"I couldn't tell exactly." Duncan shook his head. "I think he was peeking through a window."

"He was probably looking for Wendy," Tove said offhandedly, and the chair in front of me slid so far back, it almost hit my shins. "Sorry."

"Careful," I said, pulling my legs up to be safe.

I wrapped my arms around my knees, and Elora glared at me. I didn't move, and I heard Elora's voice in my head: *That is not how a Princess sits.* I was wearing pants, so I decided to ignore her, and I looked over at Tove.

"Why do you think he was looking for me?" I asked. Loki had let me go once. I didn't know why he'd tried to get me now.

"He wants you," Tove said simply.

"You are the Princess," Willa pointed out, as if I'd forgotten.

"On the subject of which, do you want to have a girls' night tonight?"

"What do you mean?" I asked.

"I feel like I haven't seen you much lately, and I thought it'd be fun if we did our nails and watched movies," Willa said. "You've been under so much stress lately, you need to kick back."

"It would help your training if you shut off your mind sometimes," Tove said.

"That sounds really great, Willa, but I was thinking of seeing if Matt wanted to do something," I said. "This all has to be so confusing, and I haven't been able to spend much time with him."

"Oh, Matt's busy." Willa readjusted the clasp on her bracelet. "He's doing something with Rhys tonight. Some brother bonding thing, I guess."

I watched Tove move the chair back and forth, and I tried not to feel anything about what Willa said. Matt and Rhys needed to spend time together, and I had been busy a lot. It was good for them. It was good for me.

Somebody sat down in the chair in front of me, and Tove let out a dramatic sigh. Elora glared at him, but his own mother didn't. That had never made sense to me either.

Aurora was always looking down on Elora and me, but Tove acted out way more than I did. Tove did whatever he wanted, whenever he wanted. I at least tried to have some decorum.

"It is really packed," Willa said again as more Trylle filed in.

It was down to standing room only, so even some of the Markis and Marksinna didn't get chairs. Elora cleared her throat, preparing to start the meeting, when two more trackers snuck into the room.

I could barely see them as they came in, but I recognized them instantly. Finn and his father, Thomas. They found a spot at the edge of the room. Finn crossed his arms over his chest and Thomas leaned on the bookcase behind him.

"Good. They're calling out the big guns," Tove whispered.

"What?" I pulled my gaze away from Finn.

"Finn and Thomas." Tove nodded at them. "They're the best. No offense, Duncan."

"None taken," Duncan said, and I think he meant it.

"We need to get this meeting under way," Elora said loudly, to be heard over the buzz of the crowd.

It took a minute, but the room fell silent. Elora's eyes traveled over the audience, purposely keeping them off Thomas, the same way Finn kept his eyes off me.

"Thank you," Aurora said with a saccharine smile and stepped closer to my mother.

"As you all know, we've had an intruder in the palace," Elora said calmly. "Thanks to our alarm system and the quick thinking of our trackers, he was caught before he could do any damage."

"Is it true that it's the Markis Staad?" Marksinna Laris asked. She was a nervous Trylle who once made a comment about how she loved that I let my hair go untamed, and how she'd never be brave enough to do something that unrefined.

"Yes, it does appear to be the Markis Staad," Elora said.

"Markis?" I whispered. Willa gave me a questioning look, and I shook my head.

Loki Staad was a Markis? I'd assumed that Loki was a tracker, like Duncan and Finn. The Markis and Marksinna were the royals of the community, and they were protected. Or at the very least, they didn't do their own dirty work. Willa was a Marksinna, and she was one of the more levelheaded, unspoiled ones I'd met.

"What does he want?" somebody else asked.

"It doesn't matter what he wants." The Chancellor got up, his face drenched with sweat from the exertion of standing. "We need to send the Vittra a message. We will not be bullied. We must execute him!"

"You can't kill him!" I shouted, and Elora shot me a look that made my ears ring. Everyone in the room turned to look at me, including Finn, and my own conviction even surprised me. "It's not humane."

"We're not barbarians." The Chancellor dabbed at his brow and gave me a condescending smile. "We'll make his death as painless and benevolent as possible."

"The Markis didn't do anything." I stood up, unwilling to sit and let them propose murder. "You can't kill someone without just cause."

"Princess, it's for your own protection," the Chancellor said, sounding baffled by my response. "He's repeatedly tried to kidnap and harm you. That's a crime against our people. Execution is the *only* course of action that makes sense."

"It's not the only course," Elora said carefully. "But it is something we will consider."

"You cannot be serious," I said. "*I'm* the one he kidnapped, and I'm saying he doesn't deserve that."

"Your concerns will be taken under advisement, Princess," Aurora said, that same too-sweet smile plastered on her face.

The crowd erupted with low murmurs. I'm sure I heard the word "treason," but I couldn't tell from where. Someone in front of me muttered something about Stockholm syndrome, followed by a chuckle.

"Hey, she's the Princess," Willa snapped at them. "Show a little respect."

"We can barter with them," Finn said, raising his voice to be heard over the rumblings.

"Pardon?" Aurora raised an eyebrow, and Elora all but rolled her eyes at him.

"We have the Markis Staad," Finn went on. "He's the highest Vittra royal after the King. If we kill him, we have nothing. They'll come after the Princess with even more fervor because we took out their only hope of an heir."

"You're proposing that we work with the Vittra?" Elora asked.

"We don't negotiate with terrorists!" a Markis shouted, and Elora held up her hand to silence him.

"We haven't been negotiating, and look at where it's gotten us," Finn said and gestured toward the ballroom. "The Vittra have broken into the palace twice in the last month. We lost more Trylle in that last battle than we have in almost twenty years."

I sat down again, watching Finn argue his point. He had a way of commanding the room, even if he wouldn't look at me. Moreover, everything he said was right.

"This is the biggest bargaining chip we've ever had," Finn said. "We can use Markis Staad to get them to back off. They don't want to lose him."

"He's not the biggest bargaining chip," Marksinna Laris interrupted. "The Princess is." Everyone's eyes turned to me. "The Vittra have never come after us like this before. All they want is the Princess, and in a way, they have a right to her. If we give the Vittra what they want, they'll leave us alone."

"We're not giving them the Princess." Garrett Strom stood up and held his hands out. "She is *our* Princess. Not only is she the most powerful heir we've ever had, but she's one of us. We won't give the Vittra one of our own people."

"But this is all about her!" Marksinna Laris got up, her voice getting shriller. "This is all happening because of the bad treaty the Queen made twenty years ago, and we're all paying the price!"

"Do you remember what it was like twenty years ago?" Garrett asked. "If she hadn't made that treaty, the Vittra would've slaughtered us."

"Enough!" Elora shouted, and her voice echoed through my head, through all our heads. "I called this meeting so we could discuss the options together, but if you are not capable of a proper discourse, then I will end it. I do not need your permission to conduct my business. I am your Queen, and my decisions are final."

For the first time ever, I understood why Elora could be so hard. The people in this room were openly discussing sacrificing her only child, and thought nothing of it.

"For now, I will keep the Markis Staad at the palace until I decide what to do with him," Elora said. "If I decide to execute him or barter for him, it will be my decision, and I will let you know." She smoothed out nonexistent creases in her skirt. "That is all."

"We need to reinstate Finn," Tove said before the crowd had a chance to disperse.

"What?" I whispered. "No, Tove, I don't think—"

"All trackers need to be on hand right now," Tove said, ignoring me. "All the storks in the field should be called back to roost. Both Finn and Thomas need to be at the palace. I can stay here and help, but I don't think that's enough."

"Tove can stay at the palace," Aurora offered up too quickly. "If that would help."

"We have additional trackers on staff," Elora told him, but I saw her looking at Thomas from the corner of her eye. "A new alarm system is in place, and the Princess is never left unguarded."

"They sent a Markis after her," Tove reminded her. "Thomas and Finn are the best we have. They've both been your own personal guards for the better part of two decades."

Elora seemed to consider this for a moment.

She nodded. "Both of you, report for duty tomorrow morning."

"Yes, Your Grace," Thomas said, bowing.

Finn said nothing, but he gave Tove a wary glance before departing. The rest of the crowd began to dissipate after that, but I remained sitting in the corner with Tove, Willa, and Duncan.

Garrett, Noah, the Chancellor, and two other Marksinna lingered to talk to Elora and Aurora. I could feel Elora seething, and I knew I should get out of the room before she had a chance to chew me out. But I needed a moment.

"Why did you do that?" I asked Tove.

Tove shrugged. "It's the best way to keep you safe."

"So?" I asked in a hushed whisper, since a few people still milling about could overhear. "Why is it so important to keep me safe? Maybe the Vittra should have me. Marksinna Laris is right. If all these people are getting hurt over me, then maybe I should go—"

"Laris is a stupid, uppity bitch," Willa cut in before I could finish that thought. "And nobody's gonna sacrifice you because things are tough. That's insane, Wendy."

"The royals are crazy and paranoid. What's new?" Tove leaned forward, resting his elbows on his knees. "You're going to be good for the people. But you have to live long enough to do it."

"That's comforting." I leaned back in the seat.

"I'll head home and pack," Tove said, standing up.

"You really think you need to stay here to watch out for me?" I asked.

"Probably not," Tove admitted. "But it's better than staying at home, and it'll be easier for me to help you with your training."

"Fair enough," I said.

"So." Willa turned to me after Tove walked away. "You *need* to have a girls' night. Especially since the house is going to be crawling with boys from now on."

I would've agreed to anything if it got me out of the War Room before Elora had a chance to lecture me, but a girls' night actually didn't sound that bad. Willa looped her arm through mine as we left the room.

We camped out in my room all night. I thought Willa would want to play dress-up or something silly, but we both wore comfy pajamas and lounged around.

After the meeting, I'd asked about the history between the Vittra and Trylle, and Willa had found a book in her father's things. She let me read through it, and answered my questions as often as she could. In exchange, I had to do karaoke with her and let her give me a pedicure.

I didn't make it through as much of the book as I would have liked, and I didn't find out all that much. Vittra attacked, Trylle retaliated. Sometimes the body count was quite substantial, other times it was only minor property damage.

I ended up staying up way too late with Willa, and by the end of the night, the book had been forgotten. We resorted to singing along with Cyndi Lauper and dancing.

Willa spent the night, and she was a massive bed hog, so I slept terribly. I stumbled out of the bedroom in the morning, feeling like a train wreck. I wanted to go downstairs, eat something, drink some water, and then not move again for another three or four hours.

Duncan wasn't loitering outside my door when I left my room, and I thought it was good for him that he finally got a chance to sleep in.

I made it a few steps down the hall when I realized why he'd slept in.

Finn walked toward me, his hands clasped behind his back, and I groaned inwardly. He was already dressed, his pants freshly pressed and his hair slicked back. My hair was insane, and I had to look awful.

"Good morning, Princess," Finn said when he reached me.

"Yeah, or something like that," I said.

Finn nodded once, and he walked past me. I looked around, expecting to see another person summoning him, but there wasn't anyone else.

"What are you doing?" I asked.

"My job, Princess." He glanced back over his shoulder. "I'm walking the halls to watch for intruders."

"So you're not even gonna talk to me?"

"That's not part of my job," Finn said and kept walking.

"Excellent," I said with a sigh.

Stupidly, some part of me had been excited about the prospect of Finn being reinstated. But I should've known better. Just because he'd be around all the time didn't mean anything would change between us. It would only make the whole situation more awkward and painful.

capulets & montagues

W hy are you here?" I demanded, and Loki only raised an eyebrow in response.

His room was in the old servants' quarters, and it wasn't quite the cell I'd expected. Duncan had explained that the palace had once been overflowing with live-in help, but the last few decades had seen a drastic reduction in both the mänsklig and the Trylle who stayed around. Meaning there were fewer people to staff the palace.

Even though we didn't have a dungeon, I'd thought Loki would be kept someplace similar to where the Vittra had put me. But this was just a room, similar to the one Finn stayed in when he lived here, except this one had no windows. It was small, with an adjoining bathroom and a twin bed.

To top it off, Loki's bedroom door was wide open. A tracker stood guard a little ways down the hall, but he wasn't even at the door. I had convinced Duncan to distract him because I wanted to talk to Loki alone for a minute, and it hadn't been that hard for Duncan to steer the guard away.

Loki lay on top of the blankets on the bed, his hands folded behind his head and his legs crossed at the ankles. A plate of food sat on the end table, untouched.

"Princess, I didn't know you'd be visiting, or I'd have straightened up the place." Loki smirked and gestured vaguely around his room. There was hardly anything in it, so it wasn't messy at all.

"Why are you here, Loki?" I repeated. I stood just outside the door, my arms crossed over my chest.

"I don't think the Queen would like it much if I left." He sat up, swinging his long legs over the edge of the bed.

"Why don't you leave?" I asked, and he laughed.

"I can't very well do that, now, can I?" Loki stood up and sauntered toward me.

Some rational part of me thought I should step back, but I refused to. I didn't want him to see any weakness, so I raised my chin high, and he stopped at the doorway.

"I don't see anything stopping you."

"Yes, but your mother works best in ways you cannot see," he said. "If I were to leave the room, I'd become so violently ill, I'd be unable to walk."

"How do you know for sure?"

"Because I tried to leave." Loki smiled. "I wasn't going to let a thing like bodily harm stop me from escaping, but I underestimated the Queen. She's very, very good with persuasion."

"How does that work? She used persuasion and told you what would happen if you left the room?" I asked. "And now you can't leave?"

"I don't know exactly how persuasion works." Loki turned away from me, growing bored with the conversation. "It's never been my thing."

"What is your thing?" I asked.

"This and that." Loki shrugged and sat back down on the bed.

"Why did you come here?" I asked. "What were you hoping to gain?"

"Isn't it obvious?" He grinned, that same mischievous way he always did. "I came here for you, Princess."

"By yourself?" I arched an eyebrow. "The last time Vittra came for me here, they sent a fleet, and we still defeated them. What were you thinking, coming here on your own?"

"I thought I wouldn't get caught." He shrugged again, totally nonplussed by the whole thing, as if being held captive were no big deal.

"That's completely idiotic!" I yelled at him, exasperated by his lack of concern over the situation. "You know they want to execute you?"

"So I've heard." Loki sighed, staring down at the floor for a moment. Something occurred to him, though, because he quickly brightened and stood up. "I heard you're campaigning on my behalf." He walked over to me. "That wouldn't be because you'd miss me too much if I were gone, would it?"

"Don't be absurd," I scoffed. "I don't condone murder, even for people like you."

"People like me, eh?" He cocked an eyebrow. "You mean devilishly handsome, debonair young men who come to sweep rebellious princesses off their feet?"

"You came to kidnap me, not sweep me off my feet," I said, but he waved his hand at the idea.

"Semantics."

"But I don't understand why you're a kidnapper," I said. "You're a Markis."

"I am the closest the Vittra have to a Prince," he admitted with a wry smile.

"Then why the hell are you here?" I asked. "The Queen would never let me go on a rescue mission."

"She let that other Markis go after you," Loki pointed out, referring to Tove. "The one that threw me against the wall."

"That's different." I shook my head. "He's strong, and he didn't come alone." I narrowed my eyes at Loki. "Did you come alone?"

"Yes, of course I did. Nobody else would be stupid enough to join me after what happened the last time we paid you a visit."

"That really doesn't explain why you're here," I said. "Why would you volunteer for this, knowing how dangerous it is? *Do* you know how dangerous it is? When I said they wanted to execute you, you laughed it off, but they really mean to do it, Loki."

"I missed you too much, Princess, and I couldn't stop myself from coming." He tried to say it with his usual gusto, but honesty tinged his smile.

"Don't make jokes." I rolled my eyes.

"That was the answer you were looking for, wasn't it? That I chose to come back for you?" Loki leaned against the doorframe, just inside the room, and sighed. "My dear Princess, you think too highly of yourself. I *didn't* volunteer."

"I didn't think that." I bristled and my cheeks reddened slightly. "If you didn't volunteer, then why did they send you?"

"I let you get away." He stared off down the hallway, where Duncan had distracted the tracker. "The King sent me to correct my error."

"Why were you in charge of guarding me in Ondarike? Why you? Why not a tracker or something?"

"We don't have many trackers because we don't have changelings." Loki looked at me. "The hobgoblins do a lot of our dirty work, but you could overpower them without even trying. The Vittra that came after you last time are only slightly more powerful than mänsklig, which is how you managed to defeat them. I'm the strongest, so the King sent me after you."

"Who are you?" I asked, and he opened his mouth, probably to say something witty and sarcastic, so I held up my hand to stop him. "My mother said she knew your father. You're close to the Vittra King and Queen."

"I'm not close to the King." Loki shook his head. "Nobody is close to the King. But I do have history with the Queen. His wife, Sara, was once my betrothed."

"What?" My jaw dropped. "She's . . . she's much older than you."

"Ten years older." Loki nodded. "But that's how arranged marriages work a lot of the time, especially when there are so few of the marrying kind in our community. Unfortunately, before I came of age, the King decided he wanted to wed her."

"Were you in love with her?" I asked, surprised to find myself caring at all.

"It was an arranged marriage!" Loki laughed. "I was nine when Sara married the King. I got over it. Sara thought of me like a little brother, and she still does."

"And what about your father? Elora said she knew him."

"I'm sure she did." He ran a hand through his hair and shifted his weight. "She lived with the Vittra for a while. First, right after they were married, they lived here in Förening, but once Elora became pregnant, Oren insisted she move to his house."

"And she did?" I asked, surprised that Elora had been coerced into anything.

"She didn't have a choice, I suppose. When the King wants something, he can be very . . ." Loki trailed off. "I was in their wedding. Did you know that?"

When he looked at me, he smiled at the memory, and his cocky demeanor slipped. There was something disarmingly honest about his smile, missing his usual snark, and when he looked like that, he was almost impossibly handsome. He was truly one of the best-looking guys I'd ever laid eyes on, and for a moment I felt too flustered to say anything.

"You mean my mother and my father's?" I asked when I found my words.

"Yes." He nodded. "I was very young, maybe two or three, and I don't remember it much, except that my mother took me, and she let me stay up all night dancing. I walked down the aisle and threw petals, which is a very unmasculine thing to do, but there were no other children of royal blood to be in the wedding."

"Where were the children?"

"The Vittra didn't have any, and the Trylle were all gone as changelings," Loki explained.

"You remember Elora and Oren's wedding? And you were only a toddler?" I asked.

He smirked. "Well, it was the wedding of the century. Everyone was there. It was quite the spectacle."

I realized that he was constantly using sarcasm and humor to keep me at a distance, much the same way that Finn protected himself with a hard exterior. A moment ago, as he remembered his mother, I'd seen a glimmer of something real, the same glimmer I'd seen in Ondarike when he'd empathized with me about being a prisoner.

"Do you know why they got married?"

"Oren and Elora?" His eyebrows furrowed. "Don't you know?"

"I know that Oren wanted an heir to the throne and Vittra can't have kids, and Elora wanted to unite the tribes," I said. "But why? Why was it so important that the Vittra and Trylle unite?"

"Well, because we've been warring for centuries." Loki shrugged. "Since the beginning of time, maybe."

"Why?" I repeated. "I've been reading the history books, and I can't find a clear reason why. Why do we hate each other so much?"

"I don't know." He shook his head helplessly. "Why did the Capulets hate the Montagues?"

"Lord Montague stole Capulet's wife from him," I answered. "It was a love triangle thing."

"What?" Loki asked. "I don't remember Shakespeare saying that."

"I read it in a book somewhere." I waved Loki off. "It doesn't matter. My point is—there's always a reason."

"I'm sure there is one," Loki agreed.

For a moment, he let his gaze linger on me, his caramel eyes almost seeming to stare right through me. I became acutely aware of how close he was to me, and that we were hidden away in the privacy of his room.

Lowering my eyes, I took a step back from him and demanded that my heart stop racing.

"Now the principals have become too different," Loki said at last. "The Vittra want more, and the Trylle want to hang on to their crumbling empire for dear life."

"If anyone has a crumbling empire, it's the Vittra," I countered. "At least we can procreate here."

"Ooh, low blow, Princess." Loki put his hand to his chest with false hurt.

"It's the truth, isn't it?"

"So it is." He dropped his hand and returned to his usual sly grin. "So, Princess, what's your plan for getting me out of here alive?"

"I don't have any plan," I said. "That's what I've been trying to tell you. They want to kill you, and I don't know how to stop them."

"Princess!" Duncan called from the end of the hall.

I looked back to see him standing in front of the irritated tracker. I didn't know what Duncan had said to hold him off from guarding Loki, but Duncan had clearly exhausted that avenue.

"I have to go," I told Loki.

"Your tracker is summoning you?" Loki glanced down the hall. Duncan gave me a sheepish smile as the guard walked toward us to resume his post.

"Something like that. But listen, you need to be good. Do what they say. Don't cause any trouble," I said, and Loki gave me an exaggerated innocent look, like, *What, me?* "It's the only chance I have to convince them not to execute you."

"If it's as you wish, Princess." Loki bowed before turning his back to me and walking to his bed.

The guard returned, giving me a deeper bow than Loki had, and I smiled at him before hurrying down the hall. I'd wanted to talk to Loki a bit more, although I wasn't sure that it would've accomplished anything. Because the guard was my subordinate, I could've pushed the issue, but I didn't want it going around the palace that I was spending time with Loki. As it was, I had taken a risk that I shouldn't have.

"Sorry," Duncan said when I reached him. "I tried to stall him, but he was afraid of getting in trouble or something. Which is silly, because you're the Princess and his boss, but—"

"It's fine, Duncan." I smiled and brushed him off. "You did a good job."

"Thanks." He paused for a moment, looking startled by my minuscule bit of praise.

"Do you know where I can find Elora?" I asked and kept walking.

"Um, I believe she's in meetings all day." Duncan checked his watch as he fell into step next to me. "She should be with the Chancellor right now, going over the security precautions in case Loki isn't a solitary incident."

I wasn't completely sure why Loki had come here, but I didn't think it was to hurt me or the people of Förening. He'd seemed upset in Ondarike that Kyra had gotten violent with me, and he hadn't even really hurt any of the guards when they captured him here in the palace. If Kyra or other Vittra had come with him, they'd almost certainly fight harder and probably attack me in the process.

Had Loki come here to protect me? Was this his way of letting me escape from the Vittra again?

"I'm pretty sure Loki is an isolated threat, and he's not even really a threat," I said. "I don't think the Vittra have the numbers to launch a counterattack."

"Is that what he told you?"

I nodded. "In so many words, yes."

"And you trust him?" Duncan asked. His tone carried no hint of sarcasm or irritation, and I had a feeling that he trusted my instincts. If I approved of Loki, then Duncan would too.

"I do." I furrowed my brow, a little surprised to find that I meant it. "I think he helped me escape in Ondarike."

"I understand." He nodded, my reasoning enough for him.

"I need to talk to Elora. Alone," I said as we reached the stairs. "Does she have an opening in her schedule?"

"I'm really not sure," Duncan said. When I started climbing the stairs, Duncan fell a step behind, following me up. "I'd have to check with her adviser, but if you really need to speak to her, I can stress the importance so she can squeeze something in."

"I really need to speak with her," I said. "If you talk to her or her adviser, and she doesn't have time to fit me in, find out any time that she's alone. I'll corner her in the bathroom if I have to."

"All right." Duncan nodded. "Do you want to me to run and do that now?"

"That would be fantastic. Thank you."

"No problem." He smiled broadly, always so happy to be of service, and dashed back the way we'd come to find Elora.

I continued back to my room to think. Between the kidnapping, my parentage, Tove's training, and now my attempts to save Loki, my head was spinning. Not to mention that my own people were so eager to throw me under the bus at the defense meeting yesterday.

I wondered if this was the place for me. I really didn't care to rule a kingdom, so in a way, it didn't matter what crown I ended up wearing. Sure, Oren seemed evil, but Elora wasn't far off from that herself.

If I left with the Vittra, they would leave the Trylle alone. Maybe that would be the best move I could ever make as Princess.

"Wendy!" Matt shouted, drawing me from my thoughts. I'd

been passing his room on the way to my own, and he had his door open.

"Matt," I replied lamely as he rushed out of his room to meet me. He was in such a hurry that he carried the book he'd been reading with him. "Sorry I haven't seen you much lately. I've been busy around here."

"No, I understand," he said, but I wasn't sure he did. He held the book to his chest and crossed his arms in front of it. "How are you? Is everything still okay? Nobody's really telling me any-thing, and with the attack the other day—"

"It wasn't an attack." I shook my head. "It's just Loki, and he's—"

"Is that the guy that kidnapped you?" Matt asked, his voice hard.

"Yeah, but . . ." I tried to think of some excuse to rationalize a kidnapping, but I knew Matt wouldn't buy any of it, so I stopped. "He's only one guy. He can't do that much. They have him locked up, and everything's fine. It's safe."

"How is it safe if there's still people breaking in?" Matt coun-tered. "The reason we're staying here is because it's the best place for you, but if they can't keep you safe—"

"It's safe," I insisted, cutting him off. "This place is crawling with guards. We're better off here than we would be out in the real world."

I didn't know if that was true exactly, but I didn't want Matt going off to find out for himself. Oren knew how protective I was over Matt now, and he was definitely the type of guy who would use that against me if he had the chance. Matt's best bet was stay-ing here, under the watchful eye of the Trylle.

"I still don't completely understand what's happening here or who these people are," Matt said finally. "I have to trust you on this, and I need to know that you're safe."

"I'm safe. Honest. You don't need to worry about me anymore." I gave him a sad smile, realizing that was true. "But how have you been? Have you been finding stuff to keep you busy?"

"Yeah, I've been spending some time with Rhys, which has been nice," Matt said. "He's a good kid. A little . . . weird, but good."

"I told you."

"You did." He smiled.

"And I see you found something to read." I pointed to the book he held.

"Yeah, Willa found this for me, actually." Matt uncrossed his arms so he could show me the book. It was hand-bound in faded leather. "It's all the blueprints and designs for the palaces over the years."

"Oh, yeah?" I took it from him so I could leaf through the yellowed pages. They showed the ornate designs of all the lush homes the royalty had lived in.

"I told Willa I was an architect, and she tracked down this book for me." Matt moved closer to me so he could admire the drawings with me. "Her dad had it, I guess."

I instantly felt stupid. Matt's only real passion in life was architecture, and we lived in a luxurious palace perched on the edge of a bluff. Of course he would love this, and I couldn't believe it hadn't occurred to me sooner.

Matt started pointing things out in the drawings, telling me how ingenious they were. I nodded and sounded amazed when it seemed appropriate.

I talked to Matt a bit longer, then headed down to my room to take a break. No sooner had I flopped down on my bed than I heard a knock at the door. Sighing, I got out of bed and threw it open.

Then I saw Finn, standing in my bedroom doorway, his eyes the same shade of night they always were.

"Princess, I need you," he said simply.

métier

B eg pardon?" I said when I found my voice.

"The Queen has found time to see you," Finn said. "But you need to hurry."

With that, he turned to walk down the hall. I stepped out and shut my bedroom door behind me. When Finn heard it, he slowed a bit, so I assumed I was supposed to catch up to him.

"Where is she?" I asked. I didn't hurry to catch him, so he glanced at me. "Where am I meeting Elora?"

"I'll take you to her," Finn replied.

"You don't need to. I can find her myself."

"You're not to be left alone." He paused until I reached him, then we continued side by side.

"This place is swarming with guards. I think I can manage walking down the hall to see Elora," I told him.

"Perhaps."

I hated that I had to walk down the halls with him and pretend like I didn't care about him. The silence felt too awkward between us, so I struggled to fill it.

"So . . . what's it like working with your father?" I asked.

"It's acceptable," Finn said, but I heard the tightness in his voice.

"'Acceptable'?" I glanced over at him, searching for any sign that would give away how he really felt, but his face was a mask. His dark eyes stared straight ahead, and his lips were pressed into a thin line.

"Yes. That's an apt way to describe it."

"Are you close to your father?" I asked, and when he didn't answer, I went on. "You seemed close to your mother. At least, she cares a great deal for you."

"It's hard to be close to someone who you don't know," he said carefully. "My father was gone most of my childhood. When he started being around more, I had to leave for work."

"It's good that you get to be around each other now," I said. "You can spend some time together."

"I could give you the same advice in regard to the Queen." He gave me a sidelong glance, something teasing in his eyes that played against the ice in his words.

"Your father seems much easier to know than my mother," I countered. "He seems at least vaguely human."

"You know that's an insult here," Finn reminded me. "Being human is something we strive against."

"Yeah, I can tell," I muttered.

"I'm sorry for the way things went at the defense meeting." He'd lowered his voice, speaking in that soft, conspiratorial way he did when it was only the two of us.

"It's not your fault. In fact, you came to my aid. I owe you a debt of gratitude."

"I don't agree with the things they said in there." Finn slowed to a stop in front of a heavy mahogany door. "The way they blamed you and your mother for what's happened here. But I don't want you to hold it against them. They're just afraid."

"I know." I stood next to him, taking a deep breath. "Can I ask you something, honestly?"

"Of course," he said, but he sounded hesitant.

"Do you think it would be better for me to go with the Vittra?" I asked. His eyes widened, and I hurried on before he could answer. "I'm not asking if it's best for me, and I want you to put your feelings aside, whatever those may be. Would it be in the best interest of the Trylle, of all the people living here in Förening, if I went with the Vittra?"

"The fact that you are willing to sacrifice yourself for the people is exactly why they need you here." His eyes stared deeply into mine. "You need to be here. We all need you."

Swallowing hard, I lowered my eyes. My cheeks felt flushed, and I hated that simply talking to Finn could do this to me.

"Elora's inside waiting," he said quietly.

"Thank you." I nodded, and without looking at him, I opened the door and slipped inside her office.

I'd never been in the Queen's private study before, but it was about the same as her other offices. Lots of bookshelves, a giant oak desk, and a velvet chaise lounge poised in front of the windows. A painting of Elora hung on one wall, and from the looks of the brushstrokes, I'd guess it was a self-portrait.

Elora sat at her desk, a stack of papers spread out before her. She had an ivory dip pen in her hand, complete with an inkwell to dip it in, and she held it perilously over the papers, as if afraid of what she might sign.

She hadn't lifted her head yet, and her black hair hung around her face like a curtain, so I wasn't sure if she knew I was there.

"Elora, I need to talk to you." I walked toward her desk.

"So I've been told. Spit it out. I don't have much time today." She looked up at me, and I almost gasped.

I'd never seen her look haggard before. Her normally flawless skin appeared to have aged and wrinkled overnight. She had defined creases on her forehead that hadn't been there yesterday. Her dark eyes had gone slightly milky, like early cataracts. A streak of white hair ran down the center of her part, and I don't know why I hadn't noticed it when I first came in.

"Princess, really." Elora sighed, sounding irritated. "What do you want?"

"I wanted to talk to you about Lo—uh, the Vittra Markis," I stumbled.

"I think you've already said quite enough on that." She shook her head, and a drop of ink slipped off the pen onto the desk.

"I don't think you should execute him," I said, my voice growing stronger.

"You made your feelings perfectly clear, Princess."

"It doesn't make sense, policywise," I went on, refusing to let this go. "Killing him will only incite more Vittra attacks."

"The Vittra aren't going to stop whether we execute the Markis or not."

"Exactly!" I said. "We don't need to antagonize them. Too many people have died over this already. We don't need to add anyone else to the death toll."

"I can't keep him prisoner for much longer," Elora said. Then, in a rare moment of honesty, her façade slipped for a minute, and

I saw how truly exhausted she was. "What I'm using to hold him is . . . it's draining me."

"I'm sorry," I said simply, unsure how to respond to her admittance of frailty.

"It should please Your Young Majesty to know that I'm right now searching for a solution," Elora said, sounding particularly bitter when she referred to me as *Majesty*.

"What are you planning to do?" I asked.

"I'm looking over past treaties." She tapped at the papers in front of her. "I'm trying to come up with an exchange agreement, so we can give back the Markis and buy ourselves some peace. I don't know that Oren will ever stop coming after you, but we need some time before he launches another attack."

"Oh." I was momentarily disarmed. I hadn't expected her to do anything to help me, or Loki. "What makes you think that Oren can mount another attack? The Vittra seem too damaged to fight right now."

"You know nothing about the Vittra or your father," Elora said, simultaneously weary and condescending.

"And whose fault is that?" I asked. "If I'm left in the dark about things, it's because you're the one who left me there. You expect me to rule this place, yet you refuse to tell me anything about it."

"I don't have time, Princess!" Elora snapped. When she looked at me, I could've sworn I saw tears in her eyes, but they disappeared before I could be certain. "I want so much to tell you everything, but I don't have time! You're on a need-to-know basis. I wish that it could be different, but this is the world that we live in."

"What do you mean?" I asked. "Why don't you have time?"

"I don't even have time for this discussion." Elora shook her head and waved me off. "You have much you need to do, and I have a meeting in ten minutes. If you want me to save your precious Markis, I suggest you get on your way and let me do my job."

I lingered in front of her desk for a moment longer before I realized I had nothing more to say to her. For once, Elora was on my side, and she didn't plan to execute Loki. It would actually be better if I left before I ended up saying something that would change her mind.

I expected to find Finn waiting in the hall to take me to my room, but instead I saw Tove. He leaned against the wall, absently rolling an orange between his hands.

"What are you doing here?" I asked.

"It's nice to see you too," Tove said dryly.

"No, I mean, I wasn't expecting you."

"I was coming to see you anyway, so I let Finn go." Tove smirked and shook his head.

"Am I supposed to train today?" I asked. I enjoyed training with Tove, but he'd thought it best that I take a day or two off so I didn't get burned out.

"No." Tove tossed the orange up in the air as we started walking away from Elora's study. "I'm staying here now, and I thought I should check up on you."

"Oh, right." I'd forgotten that Tove would be living here for a while, helping to ensure the palace was safe. "Why should you check up on me?"

"I don't know." He shrugged. "You just seem . . ."

"Is my aura off-colored today?" I asked, giving him a sidelong glance.

"Yeah, actually." He nodded. "Lately it's been a sickly brown, almost a sulfur-yellow."

"I don't know what color sulfur is, and even if I did, I don't know what that means," I said. "You talk of auras, but you never explain them."

"Yours is usually orange." He held the fruit up as if to illustrate, then began tossing it from hand to hand. "It's inspiring and compassionate. You get a purple halo when you're around people you care about. That's a protective and loving aura."

"Okay?" I raised an eyebrow.

"At the meeting yesterday, when you stood up and you were fighting for something you believed in, your aura glowed gold." Tove stopped walking, lost in thought. "It was dazzling."

"What does gold mean?" I asked.

"I don't know exactly." He shook his head. "I've never seen it quite like that. Your mother's tends to be gray tinged with red, but when she's in full Queen mode, she gets flecks of gold."

"So gold means . . . what? I'm a leader?" I asked skeptically.

"Maybe." He shrugged again and started walking.

Tove walked downstairs, and even though I'd wanted solitude, I went with him. He proceeded to explain all he knew about auras and what each color meant.

The purpose of an aura still eluded me. Tove said it gave him clarity into another person's character and that person's intentions. Sometimes if the aura was really powerful, he could feel it. Yesterday at the meeting, mine had felt warm, like basking in the summer sun.

He stopped at the sitting room and flopped down in a chair by the fireplace. He began peeling the orange and tossing its skin into the unlit hearth. I sat on the couch nearest him and stared out the window.

Autumn was beginning to give way to an early winter, and heavy sleet beat down outside. As it fell against the glass, it sounded like it was raining pennies.

"How much do you know about the Vittra?" I asked.

"Hmm?" Tove took a bite of the orange, and he glanced at me, wiping the juice from his chin.

I rephrased the question. "Do you know much about the Vittra?"

"Some." He held out an orange slice to me. "Want some?"

"No, thanks." I shook my head. "How much is 'some'?"

"I meant like a slice or two, but you can have the rest if you really want." He extended the orange to me, but I politely waved him off.

"No, I meant tell me what you know about the Vittra," I said.

"That's too vague." Tove took another bite, then grimaced and tossed the remainder of it into the fireplace. He rubbed his hands on his pants, drying the juice from them, and looked about the room.

He seemed distracted today, and I wondered if the palace was too much for him. Too many people with too many thoughts trapped in one space. He normally only visited for a few hours at a time.

"Do you know why the Vittra and the Trylle are fighting?" I asked.

"No." He shook his head. "I think it's about a girl, though."

"Really?" I asked.

"Isn't it always?" He sighed and got up. He went over to the mantel and pushed around the few ivory and wood figurines that rested on it. Sometimes he used his fingers, sometimes he used his mind to move them. "I heard once that Helen of Troy was Trylle."

"I thought Helen of Troy was a myth," I said.

"And so are trolls." He picked up a figurine depicting an ivory swan intertwined with wooden ivy, and he touched it delicately, as if afraid of damaging the intricate design. "Who's to say what's real or not?"

"Then, what? Troy and Vittra are the same thing? Or what are you saying here?"

"I don't know." Tove shrugged and put the figurine back on the mantel. "I don't put much stock in Greek mythology."

"Great." I leaned on the couch. "What *do* you know?"

"I know that their King is your father." He paced the room, looking around at everything while looking at nothing. "And he's ruthless, so he won't stop until he gets you."

"You knew he was my father?" I asked, gaping at him. "Why didn't you tell me?"

"It wasn't my place." He looked out the window at the sleet. He went right up to it and pressed his palm to the glass, so it left a steamy print from the warmth of his skin.

"You should've told me," I insisted.

"They won't kill him," Tove said absently. He leaned forward, breathing on the glass and fogging it up.

"Who?" I asked.

"Loki. The Markis." He traced a design in the fog, then rubbed it away with his elbow.

"Elora says she's going to try to—"

"No, they *can't* kill him," Tove assured me and turned to face me. "Your mother is the only one powerful enough to hold him, aside from me and you."

"Wait, wait." I held up my hand. "What do you mean, nobody's strong enough to hold him? I saw the guards contain him in the hall when he was captured. Duncan even helped bring him down."

"No, Vittra work differently from us." Tove shook his head and sat down on the opposite end of the couch. "Our abilities lie in here." He tapped the side of his head. "We can move objects with our minds or control the wind."

"Loki can knock people out with his mind, and the Vittra Queen can heal them," I said.

"The Vittra Queen has Trylle blood in her, back a generation or two in order for her to be Queen. Loki has our blood, actually. His father used to be Trylle."

"Now he's Vittra?" I asked, remembering what Elora had said about knowing Loki's father.

"He was for a while. Now he's dead," Tove said matter-of-factly.

"What? Why?" I asked.

"Treason." Tove leaned forward, and using his mind, he lifted a vase up off a nearby table. I wanted to snap at him and tell him to pay attention, but I knew that was actually what he was trying to do.

"We killed him?" I asked.

"No. I believe he tried to defect back to Förening." He bit his lip, concentrating as the vase floated in the air. "The Vittra killed him."

"Oh, my gosh." I leaned back on the couch. "Why would Loki support the Vittra still?"

"I don't know Loki, nor did I know his father." The vase floated down, landing gently on the table. "I can't tell you their reasoning for anything."

"How do you know this stuff?" I asked.

"You would know it too, if it weren't for the state of things." Tove exhaled deeply, seeming calmer after moving the vase. "It's part of the training you'd be undergoing now, learning our history.

But because of the attacks, it's more important that you be prepared for battle."

"How do Vittra powers differ?" I asked, returning to the topic.

"Strength." He flexed his arm to demonstrate. "Physically, they're unmatched. Even their minds are more impenetrable, which makes it harder for people like you and Elora to control them. It even makes it more difficult for me to move them. And like us, the more powerful the Vittra, the higher the ranking, so a Markis like Loki is awfully strong."

"But you threw Loki like he was nothing at the Vittra palace," I reminded him.

"I've been thinking about that." His brow furrowed in confusion. "I think he let me."

"What do you mean? Why?"

"I don't know." Tove shook his head. "Loki let me subdue him then, and he let them capture him here. Elora's power over him is real, but the other guards . . ." He shook his head. "They don't stand a chance against him."

"Why would he do that?" I asked.

"I have no idea," Tove admitted. "But he's much stronger than all of us. Elora wouldn't be able to hold him long enough for them to kill him."

"Could you?" I asked tentatively.

"I believe so." He nodded. "I mean, I'm capable, but I wouldn't do it."

"Why not?" I asked.

"I don't think we should. He hasn't done anything to hurt us, not really, and I want to see what he's up to." He shrugged, then glanced over at me. "And you don't want me to."

"You would go against Elora's wishes if I asked you to?" I asked, and he nodded. "Why? Why would you do something for me and not her?"

"My loyalty lies with you, Princess." Tove smiled. "I trust you, and other Trylle will learn to trust you, once they see what you can do."

"What can I do?" I asked, feeling oddly touched by Tove's admission.

"Lead us to peace," he said, with so much conviction, I didn't want to argue with him.

numb

After hearing what Tove had to say about Loki, I wanted to talk to him. He hadn't been very forthcoming with me, but I had to know why he'd come here. What did he hope to gain from breaking into the Trylle palace alone?

But, much to my disappointment, Loki's guards had gotten stricter.

Word of my talk with him had gotten out, and the guards decided they needed to work twice as hard to keep me away from him. Duncan had gotten his butt chewed for letting me see Loki at all, and when he finally returned to fulfill his duty as bodyguard, he refused to let me go near the prisoner.

I could've used persuasion on Duncan, but I'd already screwed with his brain enough while practicing on him. I'd also sworn off using persuasion on anyone, though I hadn't told Tove about it.

Besides, it would be good for me to actually use my day off to relax. Tomorrow, I'd go back to training, and I could try to see Loki after that. I was sure I could find a way around the guards without using persuasion on anybody.

I didn't spend much time by myself, though. Duncan escorted me to my room, and I'd barely been in it for five minutes when Rhys got home from school. He made a pizza and invited me over to his room for bad movies and relaxation with him, Matt, and Willa.

Since I felt like I hadn't been spending enough time with any of them, I agreed and made Duncan tag along. I sat on the couch and made sure to keep a safe distance from Rhys, but I didn't have to try that hard because Matt was chaperoning.

Although Matt seemed to be letting his big-brother duties slide. He seemed preoccupied with Willa, teasing her and laughing with her. She surprised me more than anybody, though. She actually ate the pizza. Even I wouldn't eat pizza, but Willa ate it with a smile.

Unlike the last time I watched movies in Rhys's room, I made sure to leave before I fell asleep. I excused myself while everybody was in the middle of watching *The Evil Dead*.

On my way to my room, I saw Finn making his rounds. I said hello to him, but he wouldn't even nod or acknowledge my presence. Duncan apologized on Finn's behalf, which only made me angrier. Finn shouldn't need other trackers to make me feel better.

The next morning, Tove woke me bright and early. With him living in the palace, he no longer had to commute here. It felt way too early to get up, but Tove's insomnia had gotten worse since moving to the palace, so I didn't complain.

After I got ready, we spent a long day training. We went to the kitchen, which was ordinarily deserted, but with all the guards and people in the palace, the cook was on full time. Much to the chef's dismay, Tove had me practicing on moving pots and pans.

I was hoping for something like *The Sword in the Stone*, with all the dancing dishes, but it didn't work out that way. I did get a couple cast-iron pans to float, and I nearly took off Duncan's head when I flung a saucepan across the room using only my mind.

Part of me was ecstatic that I'd finally gotten stuff to move. Tove thought it had something to do with me slamming the door when Elora was hurting Loki. It had unlocked whatever had been preventing me from harnessing my potential.

The part of me that was thrilled was eventually drowned out by the part of me that was exhausted. By the time we finished, I'd never felt so drained in all my life. Duncan offered to help me up the stairs to my room, and while I could've used it, I refused to let him. I had to learn to master this stuff on my own.

I didn't want people like Duncan and Finn, and even Tove, risking their lives to protect me. Or even if they weren't risking their lives, I didn't want to *need* them. I was stronger than the rest of them, and I had to take care of myself.

I knew I couldn't master everything overnight, but I'd work as hard as I needed to until I was as strong as everyone believed I could be.

After a long stretch of training, I took a short break, and then we had a defense meeting. Tove, Duncan, and I went, along with a few select guards, and Elora. Both Finn and his father Thomas were already in the room when we arrived. I said hello to them, and while Thomas responded, Finn ignored me. Again.

The meeting didn't amount to much. Elora filled us in on what was happening. No more Vittra had broken in. Loki hadn't escaped. She went over the guard shifts with the trackers. I wanted to ask about her plan to barter with the Vittra over Loki, but Elora shot me a warning gaze, and I knew now wasn't the time to bring it up.

When the meeting ended, I wanted to head to my room, take a

long hot shower, and go to sleep. Just before I hopped in the shower, I realized I was out of body wash and went to the hall closet for more.

My brain felt numb and seemed to be short-circuiting. For some reason, I could barely feel my extremities, like my fingers and toes. A migraine pulsed at the base of my skull, and the vision in my left eye was a little blurry.

Training today had been harder on me than I had allowed myself to admit. Tove offered several times to take a break, but I'd refused, and it was catching up with me now.

I think that's why I lost it when Finn walked past me again without saying hello. I'd walked down the hall, wrapped in my robe, to get the body wash, and Finn happened to be making his rounds once again. He walked by, I said hello, and he wouldn't even nod or smile at me.

And that was it. That was the final straw.

"What the hell, Finn?" I shouted, whirling on him. He stopped, but only because I'd startled him. He looked at me, blinking and slack-jawed. I don't think I'd ever seen him look so caught off-guard before. "Of course you won't say anything. Just stare blankly at me like you always do."

"I–I—" Finn stammered, and I shook my head.

"No, really, Finn." I held up my hand to stop him. "If you can't be bothered to even acknowledge my existence, you shouldn't start now."

"Wendy." He sighed, sounding exasperated. "I'm simply doing my job—"

"Whatever." I rolled my eyes. "Where exactly in your job description does it say be a dick to the Princess and ignore her? Is that in there somewhere?"

"I am merely doing my best to protect you, and you know it."

"I get that we can't be together. And it's not like I'm so weak-willed that the simple act of saying hello to me will cause me to jump your bones in the hall." I slammed the closet door. "There is absolutely no reason for you to be so rude to me."

"I'm not." Finn's expression softened, looking pained and confused. "I . . ." He lowered his gaze to the floor. "I don't know how I'm supposed to act around you."

"Why would you think that ignoring me would be the best way to go?" I asked, and to my own surprise, tears brimmed in my eyes.

"This is why I didn't want to be here." He shook his head. "I begged the Queen to let me go—"

"You begged her?" I asked, and that was too much.

Finn did not beg. He had too much pride and honor to beg for anything. And yet he'd wanted to be away from me so badly, he'd resorted to begging.

"Yes!" He gestured to me. "Look at you! Look at what I'm doing to you!"

"So you know that you're doing it?" I asked. "You know and you're doing it anyway?"

"I have so few options, Wendy!" Finn shouted. "What do you want me to do? Tell me what it is you think I should do."

"I don't want anything from you anymore," I admitted, and I walked away.

"Wendy!" Finn called after me, but I shook my head and kept going.

"I'm too tired for this, Finn," I muttered and went into my room. As soon as I closed the door, I leaned against it and started to cry. I don't even really know why, though. It wasn't that I missed Finn. It was as if I couldn't control my emotions. They just poured out of me in epic sobs.

I collapsed in bed and decided the only cure for this was sleeping.

secrets

I t took Duncan twenty minutes to wake me up the next morning, or so he told me later. He tried knocking first, but I didn't hear that at all. When he moved on to shaking me, it still didn't wake me. He'd been convinced I was dead until Tove showed up and splashed cold water in my face.

"What the hell?" I shouted, sitting up.

Water dripped down my face, and I blinked it away to see both Tove and Duncan holding their heads. My heart pounded in my chest, and I pushed my hair out of my eyes.

"You did it again, Princess," Tove said, rubbing his temple.

"What?" I asked. "What's going on?"

"That brain-slap thing you do." Tove grimaced, but Duncan had already dropped his hand. "We scared you into waking up, so you lashed out in your sleep. But it's fading now."

"Sorry." I got out of bed in my drenched pajamas. "That doesn't explain the water, though."

"You wouldn't wake up." Duncan explained what had happened with wide, nervous eyes. "I was afraid you were dead."

"I told you she wasn't dead." Tove cast a pointed look at him and stretched his jaw wide, working out the aches from the slap I'd accidentally given him.

"Are you okay?" Duncan moved closer to me, inspecting for injuries.

"Yeah, I'm fine." I nodded. "Other than being wet. And I'm still tired."

"We'll skip training today," Tove informed me.

"What?" I turned sharply to him. "Why? I'm just starting to get stuff down."

"I know, but it's too draining," Tove said. "You'll pull a muscle or something. We can practice more tomorrow."

I tried to protest, but it was only halfhearted, and Tove wouldn't hear of it anyway. Even after a good night's sleep, I still felt drained and exhausted. One whole side of my head felt strangely numb, like half of my brain had fallen asleep. That wasn't true, obviously, since I wasn't having a stroke, but I did need a break.

Tove left to do whatever it was that Tove did with his free time, and Duncan promised me a relaxing day, whether I liked it or not.

First order of business was changing out of my wet clothes and taking a shower. After I came out of the bathroom, I found Duncan planted on my unmade bed. He started listing all the low-key, quiet things we could do that day, but none of them sounded like fun.

"Would you say talking with friends is relaxing?" I asked, running a towel over my wet curls. Since my head hurt, I wanted to leave my hair down for a change.

"Yeah," Duncan said hesitantly.

"Great. Then I know what I can do." I tossed the towel on a nearby chair, and Duncan moved to the edge of the bed.

"What?" Duncan narrowed his eyes at me. I hadn't sounded excited about any of his ideas, so he clearly didn't trust whatever I wanted to do.

"I'm going to talk to a friend," I said.

"What friend?" Duncan got off the bed and followed close behind me as I opened my bedroom door.

"Just a friend." I shrugged and went out into the hall.

"You don't have that many friends," Duncan pointed out, and I pretended to be offended. "Sorry."

"It's okay. It's true," I said as we walked past Rhys's and Matt's rooms.

"Oh, no." Duncan shook his head as he caught on. "Princess, you're supposed to be relaxing. And that Vittra Markis is certainly not a friend."

"He's not exactly an enemy either, and I only want to talk to him."

"Princess." He sighed. "This is a bad idea."

"Your concerns have been noted, Duncan. And I don't mean to pull rank on you here, but I am the Princess. You can't really stop me."

"You're not supposed to be talking to him at all, you know," Duncan said, falling in step behind me. "The Queen talked to the guards after your last visit."

"If you don't approve, you don't have to come with," I pointed out.

"Of course I'm going to come with." He bristled and quickened his pace. "I'm not about to let you talk to him alone."

"Thanks for your concern, but I'll be all right." I looked over at him. "I don't want to get you in any trouble or anything. If you need to stay, that's okay."

"No, it's not okay." He gave me a hard look. "It is my job to protect you, Princess. Not the other way around. You need to stop getting so caught up in my safety."

We reached the staircase at the same time a booming knock came from the front door. Nobody ever knocked. They always rang the doorbell, which sounded like very loud wind chimes.

Stranger still, Elora came into the rotunda and walked toward the door, the long black train of her dress dragging on the marble floor behind her.

We were still on the second floor, and Elora was directly below us. I ducked down behind the banister before she saw me, and Duncan did the same. Through the wooden lattice, I saw Elora clearly.

She was by herself, and before she opened the front door, she paused and glanced behind her. Her face was smoother and younger than when I had seen her the other day, but her hair had two additional streaks of bright white running through it.

"Why is she answering the door?" Duncan whispered. "And she's without a guard."

"Shh!" I waved a hand to shush him.

With the coast appearing clear, Elora opened the front door. A gust of icy wind blew inside the hall, and Elora had to grip the door tightly to keep it from slamming back.

A woman slid inside as Elora pushed the door back, fighting it with as much grace as she could muster. A dark green cloak hung over the woman's head, shielding her face from us. Her burgundy dress appeared to be satin, and the hem pooled around her feet, looking tattered and wet from the elements.

"So good of you to make it in this weather." Elora gave her a smile, the tight condescending one.

She smoothed her hair, making it lie so it covered up the white streaks better. The woman said nothing, and Elora gestured to the second floor, which didn't make sense. The south wing on the main floor was where all business was conducted. Elora was directing the guest to her private quarters.

"Come," Elora said as she and the woman started walking. "We have much to discuss."

I grabbed Duncan's arm and dashed across the hall before Elora began ascending the stairs. The only thing at the top of the stairs was a small broom closet, and I opened the door as silently as it would let me.

Once inside, I shut the door almost all the way, leaving a small gap for me to peer through. Duncan was pressed against my back, trying to peek out the crack too, and I elbowed him in the stomach so I could have some room to breathe.

"Ouch!" Duncan winced.

Quiet! I snapped.

"You don't need to shout," Duncan whispered.

"I di—" I was about to tell him I hadn't shouted when I realized I hadn't said anything at all. I'd merely thought it, and he'd heard me. I'd done the mind-speak trick that Elora always did.

Duncan, can you hear me? I asked in my head, trying it out, but he didn't say anything. He just stood on his tiptoes and looked over my head.

I would've tried again but I heard Elora reaching the top of the stairs, and I turned my attention to her. Elora stood between her guest and the broom closet, so I couldn't see the other woman's face. Besides that, she still had that green cloak up.

I waited a few beats after they passed before pushing the door open. I leaned out, looking down the hall at their diminishing figures. They walked past the tracker standing watch outside of Loki's cell, but that was the only guard on the second floor.

The main floor was crawling with guards. I usually had one or two in my vicinity, but otherwise, the second floor was empty.

"Why would Elora bring someone up here?" Duncan asked, stepping out from behind me to watch them.

"I don't know." I shook my head. "Do you know where they're going?"

"No, the Queen doesn't invite me into her personal space," Duncan said.

"Yeah, me neither."

I decided that I needed to trail the Queen and find out why she was being so secretive. I slunk along the wall, staying as close to it as I could. Duncan came with, and we looked like a couple of *Looney Tunes* characters trying to hide behind skinny trees and small rocks.

Elora pushed open the massive doors at the end of the hall, and I froze. That was her bedroom, or at least that's what I'd been told. I'd never actually been there before. I pressed myself as flat as I could against the wall, and when Elora turned to shut the doors behind her, she didn't look up.

"What the hell is she doing?" I asked.

"I could ask you the same thing," Loki said, catching me off guard.

His room was only a few doors down from where Duncan and I attempted to hide. Loki leaned on the doorframe, as far out as he dared go anymore, and his guard glared at him when Loki spoke to me.

With all my attention on Elora, I'd forgotten Loki was up here. I stepped away from the wall and stood up straighter, smoothing out my damp curls as best I could.

"That's really none of your concern." I walked closer to him slowly and with purpose, and he smirked at me.

"It's all the same to me, but you and your friend there"—Loki nodded to Duncan—"look like a couple of Acme Spy School drop-outs."

"I'm glad it's all the same to you." I crossed my arms over my chest.

"But I am curious." Loki's forehead crinkled with genuine in-terest. "Why are you stalking your own mother?"

"Princess, you needn't answer his questions," the guard said, giving Loki a sidelong glance. "I can shut the door, and you can be on your way."

"No, I'm quite all right." I gave him a polite smile before turning a severe gaze on Loki. "Did you see who my mother was with?"

"No." Loki's smile grew broader. "And I'm guessing neither did you."

"Princess, this really doesn't seem all that relaxing," Duncan interjected.

"Duncan, I'm fine."

"But Princess—"

Duncan! My mind-speak kicked in again, surprising me, and I hurried to use it while I still could. I turned to face him. *I'm fine. Now please escort this guard somewhere else.*

"Fine." Duncan sighed. He turned to the guard. "The Prin-cess needs a moment alone."

"But I have strict orders—"

"She's the Princess," Duncan said. "Do you really wanna ar-gue with her?"

Both Duncan and the guard seemed reluctant to go. As they walked away, Duncan stared at me, and the guard continued to sputter about how much trouble he'd be in if the Queen found out.

"I see you learned a new trick." Loki grinned at me.

"I've got more tricks than you'll ever know," I said, and Loki arched an approving eyebrow.

"If you want to show me a few tricks, my door is always open." He gestured to his room and moved to the side, in case I wanted to step in.

I don't know exactly what I was thinking, but I took him up on the offer. I went inside his room, narrowly brushing past him as I did. I sat down on his bed, since he didn't have any chairs, but I sat up as straight as possible. I didn't want to look comfortable or give him the wrong impression.

"Make yourself at home, Princess," Loki teased.

"I am at home," I reminded him. "This is my house."

"For now," Loki agreed and sat down on the bed. He made sure to sit close to me, and I scooted away, leaving two feet of space between us. "I see how it is."

"Tove told me about you," I said. "I know how powerful you are."

"And yet you come into my room, alone?" Loki asked. He leaned back, propping himself up with his arms and watching me.

"You know how powerful I am," I countered.

"Touché."

"The King assigned you to guard me because of how strong you are," I said. "You let me go."

"Is that a question?" Loki looked away and picked a piece of lint off his black shirt.

"No. I know that you did." I kept looking at him, hoping it would make him give something away, but his expression only grew sullen and bored. "I want to know why you let me go."

"Princess, when you came into my room, I thought you wanted to play, not talk politics." He pouted and rolled onto his side, so he could stare up at me despondently.

"Loki, I'm being serious," I scoffed.

"So am I." Loki sat up straight again, using the opportunity to move closer to me. One of his hands rested right behind me, so his arm brushed against my back.

"Why won't you tell me why you let me go?" I asked, forcing my voice to stay even as I looked into his eyes.

"Why do you want to know so badly?" he asked, his voice deep and serious.

"Because." I swallowed. "I need to know if you're playing some kind of game."

"And what if I am?" He kept his eyes locked on mine, but he raised his chin, defiant. "Will you have them kill me?"

"No, of course not," I said.

He tilted his head, examining me, then realization dawned. "You're actually appalled by the idea."

"Yes, I am. Now will you tell me why you let me go?"

"Probably for the same reason you don't want to kill me."

"I don't understand."

I wanted to shake my head, but I was too afraid to break eye contact with him. I wasn't using persuasion on him or anything, but I was keeping his attention, and if I lost that, he might stop talking.

"I think you do, Princess." He swallowed hard and took a deep breath before speaking again. "I know what it's like to be a prisoner, and I thought it would be nice to see somebody escape for a change."

"I believe that," I admitted. "But why come after me again? Why let me go just to track me down?"

"I already told you. King's orders."

"He sent you here alone?"

"Not exactly." Loki shrugged, but never looked away from me. His eyes were almost piercing through me. "I asked to go alone. I told him you trusted me, and I could get you to leave with me."

My heart skipped a beat, and I knew I should be nervous or upset with him, but I wasn't. "Do you really believe that?"

"I don't know. But I hadn't planned on trying. I just knew that if Oren sent others along with me, they wouldn't stop until they got you, and that didn't seem fair."

"So you're not going to try to drag me back to Ondarike?" I asked.

He narrowed his eyes a little, as if really considering it. "No. It'd be far too much trouble."

"Too much trouble?" I said doubtfully. "Couldn't you just knock me out again and throw me over your shoulder? Or at least you could've when you first got here, before you let yourself become a prisoner."

"I didn't *let* myself." He laughed. "Sure, I didn't fight as hard as I could, but there wasn't a point. I didn't really want to take you away. I just wanted it to look like I did, so the King wouldn't have any reason to kill me."

I tilted my head, studying him. "So you're only here to save your own neck?"

"It seems that way, doesn't it?"

"Have you done something to me?" I asked.

I felt a little light-headed, and my pulse was racing. His caramel eyes almost seemed to hypnotize me, and my stomach fluttered. The only time I'd felt something like this before had been around Finn, and I didn't want to believe that I might feel something like that for Loki, that I might be attracted to him. So I hoped that Loki had put me under some kind of spell, maybe the same way that he'd rendered me unconscious before.

"Like what?" Loki raised a curious eyebrow.

"I don't know. Like that knockout trick you did on me before."

"No, I haven't." He let out a long sigh, almost sounding regretful. "And I doubt that I ever will again."

"Why not?" I asked.

The corner of one side of his mouth curled a bit, and he leaned in closer to me. For a moment I was afraid he might kiss me, and as my heart hammered in my chest, I realized that I was more afraid that he wouldn't.

His eyes were still locked on mine, but I pulled my gaze away, searching his face. His tanned skin was smooth and flawless, his jaw strong and yet somehow delicate. Loki was quite stunning in his own right, and I think I'd been trying to ignore that since I met him.

Just before his lips touched mine, he stopped short. I could actually feel the warmth of his breath on my cheek.

"I want to know that when you're with me, you're here because you want to be, not because you're forced." He paused. "And right now you're not moving."

"I—I—" I tried to stutter out some kind of response, and I looked away and jumped up off the bed.

"Now who's the one playing games?" Loki sighed. He leaned back on the bed and watched me.

I took a deep breath and crossed my arms over my chest.

"Wendy!" Duncan shouted from down the hall, and I turned to see Finn standing in the doorway, glowering at both Loki and me.

"Princess, you need to leave his room immediately," Finn said. His voice sounded even, but I could hear the rage seething beneath.

"What is that about, by the way?" Loki asked, giving me a confused look. "Why are these trackers telling you what to do all the time? You're almost Queen. You have dominion over everything."

"I suggest you keep your mouth shut before I shut it for you, Vittra." Finn glared at Loki, and his eyes burned. Loki, for his part, didn't appear even mildly threatened, and he yawned.

"Finn—" I sighed, but I left the room anyway. I couldn't talk to Loki in front of Finn, and I didn't want to fight with Finn in front of Loki.

"Not now, Princess," Finn said through gritted teeth.

As soon as I came out of the room, Finn grabbed the door and slammed it shut. I faced him, preparing to yell at him for overreacting, but he grabbed my arm and started yanking me down the hall.

"Knock it off, Finn!" I tried to pull my arm from him, but physically he was still stronger than me. "Loki is right. You are my tracker. You need to stop dragging me around and telling me what to do."

"Loki?" Finn stopped so he could glare suspiciously at me. "You're on a first-name basis with the Vittra prisoner who kidnapped you? And you're lecturing *me* on propriety?"

"I'm not lecturing you on anything!" I shouted, and I finally got my arm free from him. "But if I were to lecture you, it would be about how you're being such a jerk."

"Hey, maybe you should just calm—" Duncan tried to interject. He'd been standing a few feet away from us, looking sheepish and worried.

"Duncan, don't you dare tell me how to do my job!" Finn

stabbed a finger at him. "You are the most useless, incompetent tracker I have ever met, and first chance I get, I'm going to recommend that the Queen dismiss you. And trust me, I'm doing you a favor. She should have you banished!"

Duncan's entire face crumpled, and for a horrible moment I was certain he would cry. Instead, he just gaped at us, then lowered his eyes and nodded.

"*Finn!*" I yelled, wanting to slap him. "Duncan did nothing wrong!" Duncan turned to walk away, and I tried to stop him. "Duncan, no. You don't need to go anywhere."

He kept walking, and I didn't go after him. Maybe I should have, but I wanted to yell at Finn some more.

"He repeatedly left you alone with the Vittra!" Finn shouted. "I know you have a death wish, but it's Duncan's job to prevent you from acting on it."

"I am finding out more about the Vittra so I can stop this ridiculous fighting!" I shot back. "So I've been interviewing a prisoner. It's not that unusual, and I've been perfectly safe."

"Oh, yeah, 'interviewing,'" Finn scoffed. "You were flirting with him."

"Flirting?" I repeated and rolled my eyes. "You're being a dick because you think I was flirting? I wasn't, but even if I was, that doesn't give you the right to treat me or Duncan or anybody this way."

"I'm not being a dick," Finn insisted. "I am doing my job, and fraternizing with the enemy is looked down on, Princess. If he doesn't hurt you, the Vittra or Trylle will."

"We were only talking, Finn!"

"I saw you, Wendy," Finn snapped. "You were flirting. You even wore your hair down when you snuck off to see him."

"My hair?" I touched it. "I wore it down because I had a head-ache from training, and I wasn't sneaking. I was . . . No, you know what? I don't have to explain anything to you. I didn't do anything wrong, and I don't have to answer to you."

"Princess—"

"No, I don't want to hear it!" I shook my head. "I really don't want to do this right now. Just go away, Finn!"

I turned my back on him so I could catch my breath. I could feel him, standing behind me, but eventually he walked away. I wrapped my arms around myself to keep from shaking. I couldn't remember the last time I'd been this angry, and I couldn't believe the way Finn had talked to Duncan and me.

Elora's bedroom door creaked open at the end of the hall, pull-ing me from my thoughts. I looked up to see her opening the mas-sive doors, but I didn't even bother to hide.

The woman with the cloak stepped out, and she had her hood pushed down so I could see her face. She smiled at Elora, that same dazzling, saccharine smile she always had. When she saw me, the smile never changed.

It was Aurora, and I had no idea why she'd be sneaking around with my mother.

arrangements

It took some convincing, but I finally managed to talk Duncan into staying. I'd found him practicing his resignation speech. He was terrified of letting the Queen or me down, but once I got him to see that he wasn't, he agreed not to leave.

I spent the rest of the day going along with every one of his suggestions, including that I relax quietly. Which meant, even though my mind raced a mile a minute, I had to lie still in bed and watch a marathon of *Who's the Boss?* on the Hallmark Channel with Duncan.

But the break was good for me. When I got up the next day, I still didn't feel like I had all my energy back, but I looked refreshed enough for Tove to resume training.

During our session, I told Tove about how I'd done mind-speak on Duncan, but it only worked when I was irritated. Using that logic, Tove spent most of the morning trying to irritate me into using it. Sometimes it worked, but most of the time I just got pointlessly annoyed.

We were getting ready to break for lunch when Thomas came

down. Since coming back to the palace, he'd been guarding Elora, and she had sent him to retrieve me.

"So . . ." I began, filling the silence with small talk as we walked to her drawing room. "How is being back in the palace?"

I looked up at him. His brown hair had been slicked down, making him look more like Finn, but there was something much softer about his features. The oddest thing crossed my mind just then, that he looked like a kept man.

"It looked different when I lived here," Thomas replied in the same cool way Finn always answered my questions.

"Did it?" I asked.

"The Queen likes to redecorate," Thomas said.

"She never seemed much like a decorator to me," I said honestly.

"People aren't always what they seem."

I didn't have a response to that, so we walked the rest of the way to the parlor in silence. Thomas held open the door for me, and when I entered the room, I found Elora lying on a chaise lounge.

"Thank you, Thomas." Elora smiled at him, and it might have been the most sincere I'd ever seen her look.

Thomas bowed before leaving, but he didn't say anything. I found something almost sad in that. Or would've, if I'd approved of my mother having an affair with a married man.

"You needed to see me?" I asked Elora and sat down on the couch nearest to her.

"Yes. I'd hoped to meet you in my study, but . . ." She shook her head and trailed off, as if I'd know what that meant. She looked worn, but not as bad as I'd seen her the other day. She seemed to be on the mend.

"Have you made any progress with the Vittra?" I asked.

"Yes, actually." Elora had been lying back, but she moved so she was sitting up a bit. "I've been in contact with the Vittra Queen. She's quite fond of the Markis Staad for reasons that remain a complete mystery to me, but she's willing to do an exchange for him."

"That's great news," I said, but my cheer felt a bit forced. I was happy that Loki wouldn't be executed, but I was surprised to find that I felt a bit sad to see him go.

"Yes, it is," Elora agreed, but she didn't sound happy. She only sounded tired and melancholy.

"Is something the matter?" I asked gently, and she shook her head.

"No, actually, everything's . . . as it should be." She smoothed out her dress and forced a thin smile. "The Vittra agreed to no more attacks until after the coronation."

"The coronation?" I asked.

"The coronation where you become Queen," Elora elaborated.

"I'm not going to be Queen for a while, am I?" I asked, feeling nervous at the prospect. Even with as much training as I'd done lately, I still felt completely unprepared to rule. "Like a long while, right?"

"Not for a while, no." Elora smiled wanly. "But time has a way of creeping up on you."

"Well, I'm in no rush." I leaned back on the couch. "You can keep the crown as long as you'd like."

"I will." Elora actually laughed at that, but it sounded hollow and sad.

"Wait. I don't understand. The King agreed to peace until *after* I'm Queen?" I asked. "Won't that be too late to kidnap me?"

"Oren's always believed he can take anything he wants," Elora said. "But he wants valuable things, and you're far more valuable as a Queen. I imagine that he thinks you'll be an even greater ally then."

"Why would I be his ally?" I asked.

"You are his daughter," she said, almost regretfully. "He sees no reason that you won't come around to his way of thinking." She looked up at me, her dark eyes distant. "You must protect yourself, Princess. Rely on the people around you, and defend yourself by any means you can."

"I'm trying," I reassured her. "Tove and I have been training all morning, and he says I'm doing quite well."

"Tove is very powerful." Elora nodded in agreement. "That's why it's essential to keep him close to you."

"Well, he's staying down the hall from me," I said.

"He is powerful," Elora reiterated. "But he's not strong enough to lead."

"I don't know." I shrugged. "He has good insight."

"He's scatterbrained and often irrational." She stared off at nothing for a moment. "But he is loyal, and he will stand by your side."

"Yeah . . ." I didn't understand what she was getting at. "Tove's a great guy."

"I am relieved to hear you say that." Elora exhaled and rubbed her temple. "I didn't have it in me to fight with you today."

"Fight with me about what?" I asked.

"Tove." She looked at me like it should be obvious. "I didn't tell you?"

"Tell me what?" I leaned forward, totally confused.

"I thought I just told you. A moment ago." Her brow furrowed, showing even more wrinkles. "It's all going so fast."

"What is?" I stood up, feeling real concern for her. "What are you talking about?"

"You only just got here, and I thought I'd have more time." She shook her head. "Well, anyway, it's all been arranged."

"What?" I repeated.

"Your marriage." Elora looked up at me, wondering why I didn't understand what she meant already. "You and Tove are to be married as soon as you turn eighteen."

"Whoa." I held up my hands and took a step back, as if that would defend me somehow. "What?"

"It's the only way." Elora lowered her eyes and shook her head, as if she'd done everything she could to prevent it. And considering how much she loathed Aurora, she probably had done everything she could. "To protect the kingdom and to protect the crown."

"What?" I repeated. "But I turn eighteen in three months."

"At least Aurora will be planning it all," Elora said wearily. "She'll have the wedding of the century ready by then."

"No, Elora." I waved my hands. "I can't marry Tove!"

"Why ever not?" She batted her dark lashes at me.

"Because I don't love him!"

"Love is a fairy tale that mänks tell their children so they'll have grandchildren," Elora said, brushing me off. "Love has nothing to do with marriage."

"I . . . You can't really expect me . . ." I sighed and shook my head. "I can't."

"You must." Elora stood up, pushing herself up with her arm. She steadied herself on the chaise for a moment, as if she might fall. When she was certain she was steady, she stepped toward me. "Princess, it is the only way."

"The only way to what?" I asked. "No. I'd rather not be Queen than marry someone I don't love."

"Don't say that!" Elora snapped, and the familiar venom returned to her words. "A Princess must *never* say that!"

"Well . . . I can't do it! I refuse to marry him! Or anyone, unless I want to!"

"Princess, listen to me." Elora gripped my arms and looked directly in my eyes. "The Trylle already think you should be shipped to the Vittra because of who your father is, and that is all the ammo Aurora needs to get you overthrown."

"I don't care about the crown," I insisted. "I never did."

"Once you're overthrown, you'll be exiled to live with the Vittra, and I know that you don't think the Markis Staad seems that bad," Elora went on. "Maybe he isn't. But the King is. I lived with him for three years, but when you were born, I left him, knowing what that would mean for our kingdom. But I had to leave him, that's how bad a man he is."

"I won't go back to the Vittra," I said. "I'll move to Canada or Europe or something."

"He will find you," Elora said. "And even if he doesn't, if you left, it would be the end of our people. Tove is powerful, but he is not strong enough to run a kingdom or stand up to Oren. The Vittra would attack and destroy the Trylle. He would kill everyone, especially the ones you love."

"You don't know that." I backed away so she wasn't touching me.

"Princess, yes, I do." Her eyes locked with mine, her sincerity unmistakable.

"You saw it?" I asked and looked around the room for a painting. One that would show me the devastation that she'd seen.

"I saw that they need you," Elora said. "They need you to survive."

I'd never seen her look desperate before, and it scared the hell out of me. I liked Tove, but not romantically, and I didn't want to marry someone I didn't love. Especially when I might love someone else.

But Elora was pleading with me to do this. She believed everything she was saying, and I hated to admit it, but she had a compelling argument.

"Elora . . ." My mouth felt dry, and it was hard to swallow. "I don't know what to say."

"Marry him, Princess," Elora commanded. "He'll protect you."

"I can't marry someone so he'll be my bodyguard," I told her quietly. "Tove deserves to be happy. And I would like a chance at it too."

"Princess, I'm not . . ." She squeezed her eyes shut and pressed her fingers to her temple. "Princess."

"I'm sorry. I'm not trying to argue with you," I said.

"No, Princess, I . . ." She reached out, grabbing the back of the couch to catch herself.

"Elora?" I rushed over to her and put my hand on her back. "Elora, what's wrong?"

Blood seeped from her nose, but it was no simple nosebleed. It was like an artery had opened up. Her eyes rolled back in her head, and her body went limp. She collapsed, and I barely caught her in my arms.

"Help me!" I shouted. "Somebody! *Help!*"

TWENTY

dynasty

Thomas rushed in first. I'd already lowered Elora to the floor, where she twitched like she was having a small seizure.

I'd crouched down next to her, but Thomas pushed me out of the way to tend to her. I leaned against the couch while he attempted to revive her, praying my mother would be okay.

"Wendy," Finn said.

I hadn't even heard him come in. I looked up at him with tears blurring my vision, and he held out his hand to me. I took it, and let him pull me to my feet.

"Get Aurora Kroner," Thomas told Finn. "*Now.*"

"Yes, sir." Finn nodded.

He still had my hand, and he pulled me out of the room. He walked fast because time was of the essence. My legs felt numb and rubbery, but I pushed them to hurry.

"Go find Tove or Willa. Even Duncan," Finn said when we reached the main hall. "I'll come and get you later."

"What's wrong with Elora?" I asked.

"I don't have time, Wendy." Finn shook his head, his eyes pained. "I'll get you when there's anything to tell you."

"Go," I said, nodding to hurry him along.

Finn raced out the front door, leaving me in the hall, alone and scared.

Duncan found me exactly as Finn had left me. He'd heard about Elora's collapse from the other trackers, who'd gone into lockdown mode. I heard them bustling about the palace, but that was secondary. My mother might be dying.

Duncan suggested we go up to my room, but I didn't want to be that far away. I needed to be close in case something happened. We sat in the living room, and he tried to comfort me, but it was futile.

Finn came back a few minutes later with Aurora, and they rushed down the hall. Her dress billowed out behind her, and her hair had come loose from its bun, blowing back as she ran.

Garrett and Willa came shortly after. Garrett went down to check on Elora's progress while Willa sat with me. She put her arm around my shoulders and kept reminding me how strong Elora was. Nothing could stop her.

"But . . . what if she dies?" I asked, staring blankly at the unlit fireplace in front of me.

The living room had a horrible chill from the icy wind beating against the windows. Duncan knelt in front of the fireplace. He had been trying to light a fire for the past few minutes.

"She won't die." Willa squeezed me tighter.

"No, Willa, I'm being honest," I said. "What happens if the Queen dies?"

"She's not going to die." Willa forced a smile. "We don't need to worry about that right now."

"I've almost got this fire lit," Duncan lied to change the subject.

"It's gas, Duncan," Willa told him. "You just turn a knob."

"Oh." Duncan did as she said, and a bright flame roared up through the fireplace.

Staring down at Elora's blood that had gotten on my shirt, I was surprised to find how scared I felt. I didn't want her to die.

She always seemed so strong, so composed, and it made me wonder how much pain she was in. We'd met in the drawing room today, and she'd wanted to meet me in the study. She wasn't well enough to move, I realized. She shouldn't have been standing or exerting herself at all, let alone arguing with me. I'd made her already frail condition even worse.

Why hadn't she told me about how debilitated she was? But I already knew the answer. Her sense of duty came before everything else.

"Princess," Finn said, pulling me from my thoughts. He stood at the entrance to the living room, his face drawn.

"Is she okay?" I jumped up at the sight of him, pulling away from Willa.

"She's asked to see you." Finn pointed toward her drawing room and wouldn't meet my eyes.

"So she's awake? She's alive? Is she okay? Does she know what happened? Did Aurora fix her?" I asked. My questions came out too rapidly for him to answer, but I couldn't seem to slow myself.

"She'd rather tell you everything herself," Finn said simply.

"That sounds like her." I nodded. She was awake and wanted to see me. That had to be a good sign.

Willa and Duncan gave me reassuring smiles, but they couldn't mask their anxiety. I told them I'd be back soon, and that I was sure everything would be fine. I didn't know if that was true or not, but I had to ease their fears somehow.

I walked with Finn down the corridor to the parlor. Finn kept his pace slow and deliberate. I wanted to run to Elora, but I forced myself to stay with him. I wrapped my arms around myself and rubbed my hands along them.

"Is she angry with me?" I asked him.

"The Queen?" Finn seemed surprised. "No. Of course not. Why would she be?"

"I was arguing with her when she . . . If I hadn't been antagonizing her, she might not have gotten so . . . sick."

"No, you didn't do this." He shook his head. "In fact, it's good that you were with her. You got her help right away."

"What do you mean?" I asked.

"You called for help using your thoughts." He tapped his forehead. "We were too far away, and we wouldn't have known if you hadn't done that. Elora might be in a lot worse shape if you hadn't been there."

"What's wrong with her?" I asked him directly. "Do you know?"

"She'll need to tell you."

I thought about pushing Finn for more information, but we were almost to her. Besides, it didn't feel right to argue with him now.

His whole demeanor had changed, seeming softer and more somber. He'd let some of his guard down around me again, and while I wasn't in the mood to take advantage of that, I did enjoy the familiar feel of being with him without a giant wall between us. I missed him.

Aurora came out of the parlor just before we reached it. Her normally flawless skin had gone gray. Her dark eyes were glossed over, and her hair hung in unruly waves around her face. She leaned up against the wall, supporting herself, and struggled to catch her breath.

"Marksinna?" Finn quickly went to her, putting his arm around her to steady her. "Are you all right?"

"I'm only tired," Aurora said as Finn helped her to a chair in the hallway. She moved like an old woman, and her bones creaked as she eased herself down in the chair. "Will you get my son? I need to lie down, and I want him to help me home."

"Yes, of course," Finn said, and he gave me an apologetic look. "Princess, will you be all right seeing the Queen alone?"

"Yes." I nodded. "Go get Tove. I'll be fine."

Finn hurried away to retrieve Tove for his mother, and I went on to the room. I felt guilty for leaving Aurora alone in the hallway looking so completely drained, but I had my own mother to attend to.

The door to the parlor was still open, and I stayed in the hall for a moment, watching.

Elora lay on her chaise lounge, the way she had when I arrived, but she had a black fur blanket over her. Her raven hair had gone even whiter, so it now appeared to be white streaked with black and not the other way around. Her eyes were closed, and the blood had been wiped from her face.

Garrett had pulled up a chair so he sat right next to her head. He held one of her hands in both of his, and gazed at her with worry and adoration. His tousled hair was even more unkempt than normal, and some of her blood stained his shirt.

On the other side of the chaise lounge, Thomas stood keeping watch. He had the same stoic stance all the trackers did when they were on guard duty, but his eyes rested heavily on Elora. They weren't filled with the same intensity as Garrett's, but something glimmered in them, some faint remembrance of whatever had transpired between Thomas and Elora years ago.

When she opened her eyes, it was Thomas that Elora looked up at. Garrett's jaw flexed as he clenched his teeth, but he said nothing. He didn't even drop her hand.

"Elora?" I said timidly and stepped inside the room.

"Princess." Her voice sounded weak, and she made a poor attempt at a smile.

"You wanted to see me?" I asked.

"Yes." She tried to sit up, but Garrett gently placed his hand on her shoulder.

"Elora, you need to rest," Garrett told her.

"I am fine." She waved him off but lowered herself back down. "I need to speak privately with my daughter. Can you both leave us for a moment?"

"Yes, Your Majesty." Thomas bowed. "But for your sake, please take it easy."

"Of course, Thomas." She offered him a tired smile, and he bowed again before leaving.

"I'll be right down the hall if you need me," Garrett said, but he seemed hesitant to stand. He wouldn't even walk toward the door until Elora glared at him. "If you need anything, call for me. Or send the Princess. Okay?"

"If it will get you to leave quicker, I will agree to anything." Elora sighed.

Garrett paused as he passed me, and he looked like he wanted to say something, probably remind me to take it easy. Elora said his name, and he hurried along. He closed the door behind him, and I took his seat next to Elora.

"How are you feeling?" I asked.

"I've been better, obviously." She readjusted the blanket over her, getting more comfortable on the chaise. "But I will live to fight another day, and that's what matters."

"What happened?" I asked. "Why did you just collapse?"

"How old do you think I am?" Elora asked, turning so her eyes met mine. A few days ago they'd been almost black, but now they had the gray haze of cataracts.

Her age was a hard question to answer. When I'd first met her, I'd have pegged her for fifty-something. A very beautiful fifty, but even then, she'd had an aged quality under her stunning features.

Now, lying on the chaise, frail and tired, Elora looked even more advanced in age than that. She looked like an old woman, but I didn't want to say that to her, of course.

"Um . . . forty, maybe?"

"You're kind, and a bad liar." She pushed herself up, so she was sitting up a bit. "That's something you'll need to work on. The horrible reality is that being a leader involves a lot of lying."

"I'll practice my poker face later," I said. "You look good, though, if that's what you're asking. Just tired and run-down."

"I am tired and run-down," Elora admitted wearily. "And I'm only thirty-nine."

"Thirty-nine what?" I asked, confused, and she propped her head on her hand so she could look at me.

"Thirty-nine years old," she said, smiling wider. "You seem shocked. I don't blame you. Although I'm surprised you didn't catch on sooner. I told you that I married your father when I was very young. I had you when I was twenty-one."

"But . . ." I stammered. "Is that what's wrong with you? Are you aging too fast?"

"Not exactly." She pursed her lips. "It's the price we pay for our abilities. When we use them, they drain us and age us."

"All the stuff you do—like the mind-speak and holding Loki prisoner—that's killing you?" I asked.

She nodded. "I'm afraid so."

"Then why do it?" I wanted to shout at her, but I kept my voice as even as I could. "I can understand defending yourself, but calling Finn with mind-speak? Why would you do something if it's killing you?"

"The mind-speak doesn't use as much." Elora waved it off. "The things that are really draining I only do when I have to, like housing a prisoner. But what uses it the most is the precognitive painting, and that I can't control."

I glanced at several paintings Elora had leaned up against the windows. Across the hall, she had a locked room filled with these paintings.

"What do you mean, you can't control it?" I asked. "Just don't do it."

"I can't see the visions, but they fill my head." She gestured to her forehead. "It's an agonizing blackness that takes over until I paint and get them out. I can't stop them from coming, and it's too painful to ignore them. I would go insane if I tried to keep them all inside."

"But it's killing you." I slumped in the chair. "Why even teach other Trylle how to use their abilities, if it means they'll grow weak and old?"

"That's the price." She sighed. "We go mad if we don't use them, we age if we do. The more powerful we are, the more cursed we are."

"What do you mean?" I asked. "I'll go crazy if I stop?"

"I don't really know what will happen to you." Elora rested her chin on her hand, eyeing me. "You're your father's daughter too."

"What?" I shook my head. "You mean because I have Vittra blood too?"

"Precisely."

"Tove told me about them. He said they're very strong, but I'm not strong." I remembered all the fights I'd been in throughout my illustrious school career, and how I'd taken a beating as often as I'd given one. "I'm not like that."

"Some are physically strong, yes," Elora clarified. "That Loki Staad, I believe, is very strong. If I recall correctly, he could lift a grand piano by the time he could walk."

"Yeah, I can't do that."

"Oren isn't that way. He is . . ." She trailed off, thinking. "You met him. How old do you think he is?"

"I don't know." I shrugged. "A few years younger than you, maybe."

"When I married him, he was seventy-six, and that was twenty years ago," Elora said.

"Whoa. What?" I stood up. "You're telling me that he's nearly a hundred? He's over twice your age? So you look older, and he looks younger? How?"

"He's something like immortal."

"He's immortal?" I gaped at her.

"No, Princess, I said he's something *like* immortal," Elora said carefully. "Oren ages, but at a much slower rate, and he heals very quickly. It's hard for him to be hurt. He's one of the last pure-blooded Vittra to be born."

"That's what makes me so special, and that's why you weren't worried when I told you that my host mother almost killed me." I rested my hands on the back of the chair, supporting myself with it. "You think I'm like him."

"The hope is that you're like us both," Elora said. "You'll have the Trylle abilities to move and control things, and the Vittra abilities to heal and be strong enough to handle them."

"Holy hell." My hands trembled, and I sat down. "Now I know how a racehorse feels. I wasn't conceived. I was bred."

Elora bristled a bit at the accusation. "That's not exactly how it was."

"Really?" I looked over at her. "That's why you married my father, wasn't it? So you could make me—your perfect little biological weapon. Once you did, you left him and tried to keep me all for yourself. That's what this whole feud is about now, isn't it? Who can control me?"

"No, that's not right." Elora shook her head. "I married your father because I was eighteen and my parents told me to. Oren seemed kind at first, and everyone told me it was the only way we could stop the fighting. I could stop the bloodshed if I would only marry him, so I agreed to it."

"What bloodshed?" I asked. "What were the Trylle and the Vittra fighting over?"

"The Vittra are dying. Their abilities are fading, they're running out of money, and Oren's always believed that he's entitled to anything he wants." Elora took a breath. "What he wanted was everything we had. Our wealth, our population.

"But what he wanted most was *my* power," she went on. "My mother's, originally. When she refused his advances, he waged endless battles against us. We used to be a great people with cities all over the world, but now he's left us with a few isolated pockets."

"And you married that? A man who killed your people because your mother wouldn't have him?" I asked.

"They didn't explain it all to me when we became engaged, but Oren agreed to peace in exchange for my hand in marriage," Elora said. "My parents believed they didn't have a choice, and Oren turned on the charm. He might not have telekinesis, but Oren can be very persuasive when he wants."

"So you married him and united the people. What went wrong?" I asked.

"Some of the cities revolted, refusing to mix with the Vittra," Elora said. "My parents were still King and Queen, and they wanted to reason with them. They sent Oren and me as ambassadors, to sway them to our way of thinking.

"In the very first city, people questioned us. Him in particular," Elora continued. "He managed to charm them, and using some of my own persuasion, we convinced even the most ardent doubter to join the Vittra alliance. Later, this would prove to be a fatal mistake.

"I never loved Oren, but in the beginning of our marriage, I cared for him. I thought I might one day grow to love him. What I didn't realize was how hard he had to work to be that way, and as we went on our tour, his mask began to slip.

"We stopped in a village in Canada, and we had a town hall meeting with all the Trylle, the way we had in the other cities." Elora paused, staring out the window at the icy weather. "Everyone was there. Even the mänsklig children, all the trackers and their families.

"Someone asked Oren what he hoped to gain from all this, and for some reason, it was more than Oren could bear." She let out a deep breath and lowered her eyes. "He began yelling and attacking them, and the villagers began fighting back. So . . . Oren killed them all. We were the only two survivors.

"He spun the story, and I went along with it because I didn't know what else to do. My parents had convinced me that we needed him for peace. Oren was my husband, and I had been complicit in the murders of our own people because I didn't stand up to him. If I had, I would've been killed too, but that didn't change the fact that I did nothing to save them."

"I'm sorry," I said, unsure how else to respond to her confession.

"Oren was labeled a war hero, and I . . ." She trailed off, picking absently at the fur that covered her.

"Why did you stay with him?" I asked.

"You mean after I realized that I'd married a monster?" Elora asked with a sad smile. "I didn't used to be the way I am now. I was much more trusting, much more willing to hope and believe, and follow. That is one thing I can thank your father for. He made me realize that I had to be a leader."

"What made you finally leave?" I asked.

"Oren made an effort after we got back. He tried to be kind, or as kind as he could manage. He didn't beat me or call me names. He would be patronizing to my every thought or word, but we had peace. No war. No deaths. A bad marriage seemed worth it to me. I could handle that if no one else had to die.

"Then I became pregnant with you, and it all changed." Elora rearranged herself on the chaise. "What I didn't realize then was that you were all he ever wanted. A perfect heir to his throne. We tried for nearly three years before I conceived, and the wait had worn on him as it was.

"As soon as he found out he was having a child, it was like a switch flipped inside him." Elora snapped her fingers. "He was even more domineering. He never let me leave the room. He didn't even want me to leave the bed, in case it would risk losing you.

"My mother and I began looking into families for you to go to. I knew I had to leave you as a changeling, not because it was what we did, but because I couldn't let Oren raise you." She shook her head. "Oren did not want that. He wanted you all for himself.

"So when my father, the King, decreed that you must be a changeling, the way all heirs to the throne had been, Oren took me, and we left. We lived in Ondarike, where he had me locked up as a prisoner.

"Two weeks before you were due, my mother and father broke me out of his palace. My father was killed in the fight, along with many other brave Trylle. My mother took me away to a family she'd been secretly researching—the Everlys. It was a hasty switch, but they seemed to have everything you would need.

"After I had you, I . . ." She stopped, completely lost in thought.

"You what?" I prompted when she didn't say anything.

"It was the best thing for you," she said. "I know you had problems with your host family, but I didn't have time to pick or be choosy. I just needed you hidden from Oren."

"Thank you," I said lamely.

"As soon as you were born, I left. Your grandmother held you, but I didn't have the chance. We had to run to keep the Vittra off your scent. We went to a safe house, a chalet in Canada. When Oren had lived here, we hadn't trusted him enough to tell him of all our secret places." She closed her eyes and took a breath. "But he found us in the chalet.

"That Markis you're so fond of?" Elora gestured in the direction of Loki's room. "It was his father that led Oren to us. He's the one who got everyone killed.

"Oren killed my mother in front of me, and he vowed to get you as soon as you returned." Elora swallowed. "He let me live because he wanted me to see him follow through on his promise. He wanted me to know that he'd won."

confessions

I wanted to ask Elora more questions, but she already looked so worn. She would never admit to being exhausted, but it was painfully clear that she should've been sleeping instead of speaking to me in the first place.

We talked for a bit more, and then I excused myself. I paused when I reached the door and looked back. Elora had already sunk down on the chaise, and she held her hands over her eyes.

Garrett waited outside the door, pacing the hall. Thomas stood a few yards down, giving him space, and Aurora and Finn were long gone.

"How is she?" Garrett asked.

"She's . . . good, I think." I really wasn't sure how Elora was doing. "She's resting, and that's what counts."

"Good." Garrett nodded. He stared at the closed drawing room door for a moment, then turned his concern to me. "Your talk went well, then?"

"Yeah." I rubbed the back of my neck. I didn't know what to make of it all.

Elora had been so cold to me since I'd met her, to the point where I'd been certain she hated me, but now I wasn't so sure. I had no idea how she must feel about me.

Elora hadn't been much older than me when she married a man over three times her age, a man she didn't even know. He turned out to be ruthless and cruel, but she sacrificed her happiness and well-being for her kingdom.

Then, to defend her unborn child, to save me, she risked everything. Both her parents lost their lives in a matter of months, killed by her own husband, for a child she couldn't even be around.

I wondered if she hated me, if she blamed me for her parents' deaths, for all the trouble Oren had caused her since I'd been born.

I didn't know how close Elora had been with her parents, but before the christening ceremony, she suggested that I take the name Ella, after her mother.

And Elora had spared Loki. His father had gotten her mother killed and nearly cost both Elora and me our lives, yet when given the chance for vengeance, Elora hadn't taken any on Loki. I was starting to think I had misjudged her completely.

Elora's insistence on perfection and on me being Queen became much clearer. So much had been lost for me, to ensure that I would someday take the Trylle throne.

My stomach twisted with shame as I realized how ungrateful I must have seemed to her. After everything she and her family and the entire Trylle population had done for me, I had given them so little in return.

When I looked up into Garrett's worried eyes, I realized something else. His wife—Willa's mother—had died long before Willa had come home. I wondered if she had died in one of the battles my father had waged against the Trylle. If Garrett had lost someone he loved because of me.

"I'm sorry," I told him with tears stinging my eyes.

"What on earth for?" Garrett moved toward me, surprised by my display of emotion, and put his hand on my arm.

"Elora told me everything." I swallowed the lump in my throat. "Everything that happened with Oren. And I'm sorry."

"Why are you sorry?" Garrett asked. "All of that was before you were even born."

"I know, but I feel like . . . I should've been better. That I *should* be better," I corrected myself. "After everything you went through, you deserve a great Queen."

"That we do," Garrett admitted with a small smile. "And you know that, so we should be on the right track." He lowered his head to meet my eyes. "I'm certain you'll be a great Queen someday."

I wasn't sure if I believed him, but I knew that I had to do everything I could to make that happen. I would not let my kingdom down. I couldn't.

Garrett needed to tend to Elora, so I left him to it. Thomas stayed outside the door, still standing guard but giving them alone time.

Duncan, Willa, and Matt were waiting for me by the stairs. As soon as I saw Matt's face, I couldn't hold it together any longer. Tears spilled down my cheeks, and Matt wrapped his arms around me.

Once I calmed down, we went up to my room. Duncan got us all hot tea, and I made him sit down and pour himself a cup. I hated when he acted like a servant. Willa curled up next to me on the bed, comforting in a way that made me miss my aunt Maggie.

"So she's dying?" Matt asked. He leaned against my desk, rolling the empty teacup between his hands.

I wasn't sure how much Duncan or Willa knew about my parentage or about how the Trylle abilities hurt us. I didn't want to tell them too much, especially Matt, and make them worry. So I left out all the major plot points, and only let them know that Elora was sick.

"I think so," I said. She hadn't said that exactly, but she had aged so rapidly. She looked to be in her seventies now, and that was after Aurora Kroner had healed her.

"That really sucks," Duncan said, sitting on the chest at the foot of my bed.

"You were talking to her and she just collapsed?" Willa asked. She rested her elbow on the pillow next to mine and propped her head up so she could look at me.

"Yeah." I nodded. "The worst part is I was arguing with her right before it happened."

"Aw, sweetie." Willa reached out and touched my arm. "You know it wasn't your fault, right?"

"Did she say what she's dying from?" Matt asked. The crease on his forehead deepened; he knew I had left something out.

"You know Elora." I shrugged. "She's vague on details."

"That's true," Matt said with a sigh, and that answer seemed to satisfy him. "I just don't like mysterious illnesses."

"Well, nobody does, Matt," Willa said with a teasing lilt to her voice.

"What were you and the Queen arguing about?" Duncan asked. He was changing the subject, which I would've been grateful for, until I remembered the answer to his question.

I was supposed to marry Tove Kroner.

"Oh, hell." I leaned my head back so it thudded against the headboard.

"What was that for?" Willa asked.

"Nothing." I shook my head. "It was just a stupid disagreement. That's all."

"Stupid?" Matt came over and sat on the bed by my feet. "Stupid how?"

"You know, normal stuff," I floundered. "Elora wanted me to be a better Princess. More punctual and stuff like that."

"You do need to be more punctual," Matt agreed. "Maggie was always on you about that."

Another reminder of Maggie stung my heart. I hadn't spoken to her since we'd returned to Förening. Matt had a few times, but I'd been avoiding her calls. I had been busy lately, but the real reason I put off talking to her was because hearing her voice would only make me miss her too much.

"How is Maggie?" I asked, ignoring the ache in my chest.

"She's good," Matt said. "She's staying in New York with friends, and she's really confused about everything that's going on. I keep telling her that everything's fine, that we're safe, and she needs to lay low."

"Good."

"You need to talk to her, though." Matt gave me a hard look. "I can't keep being the go-between."

"I know." I picked at chipped paint on my teacup and lowered my eyes. "I don't know how to answer her questions. Like, where we are and when we're coming back and when I'll see her again."

"I don't know how to answer them either, but I make do," Matt said.

"Wendy's had a long day," Willa said, coming to my rescue. "I don't think now is the time to lecture her on things she should be doing."

"You're right." Matt gave her a small smile before looking at me apologetically. "I'm sorry. I didn't mean to get on your case, Wendy."

"No, it's fine," I said. "You're just doing your job."

"I don't really know what my job is anymore," Matt said wearily. Someone knocked at the door, and Duncan jumped up to get it.

"Duncan, stop it." I sighed. "You're not the butler."

"Maybe not, but you're still the Princess," Duncan said, and he opened my bedroom door.

"I hope I'm not disturbing anything," Finn said, looking past Duncan at me.

As soon as his dark eyes landed on mine, my breath caught in my throat. He stood at the door, his black hair mussed a bit. His vest was still neatly pressed but it was marred with a dark stain from Elora's blood.

"No, not at all," I said, sitting up farther.

"Actually, we were—" Matt began, his voice hard.

"Actually, we were leaving," Willa cut him off. She scooted off the bed, and Matt shot her a look, which she only smiled at. "We were just saying that we had something to do in your room. Weren't we, Matt?"

"Fine," Matt grumbled and stood up. Finn moved aside so Matt and Willa could walk out of the room, and Matt gave him a warning glare. "But we'll just be right across the hall."

Willa grabbed Matt's hand to keep him moving. Finn, as usual, seemed oblivious to Matt's threats, which only made Matt angrier.

"Come on, Duncan," Willa said as she pulled Matt from my room.

"What?" Duncan asked, then caught on. "Oh. Right. I'll be . . . um . . . outside."

Duncan closed the door behind him, leaving me alone with Finn. I sat up straight and moved to the edge of the bed so my legs dangled over. Finn stayed by the door and didn't say anything.

"Did you need something?" I asked carefully.

"I wanted to see how you were doing." He looked at me in that way that went straight through me, and I lowered my gaze.

"I'm good, considering."

"Did the Queen explain things to you?" Finn asked.

"I don't know." I shook my head. "I don't know if I'll ever really understand this world."

"She told you she's dying?" Finn asked, and hearing him say it made it worse.

"Yeah," I said thickly. "She told me. And she finally told me what makes me so special. That I'm the perfect blend of Trylle and Vittra. I'm the ultimate bloodline."

"And you didn't believe me when I said you were special." That was Finn's attempt at a joke, and he smiled ever so slightly.

"I guess you were right." I pulled down my hair, which had gotten messy from lying on it, and ran my fingers through it.

"How are you taking that?" Finn asked, coming closer to the foot of my bed. He stopped by the bedpost and absently touched my satin bedding.

"Being the chosen one for both sides in an epic troll battle?"

"If anybody can handle it, you can," he reassured me.

I looked up at him, and his eyes betrayed some of the warmth he felt for me. I wanted to throw myself into his arms and feel them wrap around me, protecting me like granite. To kiss his temples and cheeks, to feel his stubble rubbing against my skin.

Despite how badly I wanted that—I wanted it so much I ached—I knew that I had to become a great Princess, which meant that I had to use some restraint. Even if the restraint killed me.

"Elora wants me to marry Tove," I blurted out. I hadn't meant to tell him that way, but I knew it would ruin the moment. Break the spell we were under before I acted on it.

"So she told you?" Finn said with a heavy sigh.

"What?" I blinked at him, startled by his response. "What do you mean, she told me? You knew? How long did you know?"

"I'm not sure, exactly." He shook his head. "I've known for a long while, before I met you or Tove."

"*What?*" I gaped at him, unable to find the words that matched the confusion and anger inside me.

"The marriage had been arranged for some time, the Markis Kroner and the Princess Dahl," Finn explained calmly. "I believe it was only finalized a few days ago, but it was what Aurora Kroner had always wanted. The Queen knew it was her best chance to secure the throne and keep you safe."

"You knew?" I repeated, unable to get past that part. "You knew that she wanted me to marry somebody else, and you never told me?"

He appeared confused by my reaction. "It wasn't my place."

"Maybe it wasn't your place as a tracker, but as the guy making out with me in this bed, yeah, I think it was your place to tell me that I'm supposed to marry someone else."

"Wendy, I repeatedly told you we couldn't be together—"

"Saying we shouldn't be together isn't the same thing, and you know it!" I snapped. "How could you not tell me, Finn? He's your friend. He's *my* friend, and you never thought to tell me?"

"No, I didn't want to interfere with the way you thought of him."

"Interfere with what?" I asked.

"I was afraid you might hate him to spite your mother, and I didn't want that. I wanted you to be happy with him," Finn said. "While you wouldn't be marrying for love, you are friends. You could have a happy life together."

"You . . . what?" My heart felt like it had been ripped in half. For a moment, I didn't speak. I couldn't make my mouth work. "You expect me to marry him."

"Yes, of course," Finn said, almost wearily.

"You're not even gonna try to . . ." I swallowed back tears and looked away from him. "When Elora told me, I fought with her. I fought for you."

"I am sorry, Wendy." His voice had gotten low and thick. He stepped closer and raised his hand as if he meant to touch me, but dropped it instead. "But you will be happy with Tove. He can protect you."

"I wish everyone would stop talking about him that way!" I sat back on the bed, exasperated. "Tove is a person! This is *his* life! Doesn't he deserve better than being somebody's watchdog?"

"I can imagine worse things in life than being married to you," Finn said quietly.

"Don't." I shook my head. "Don't joke. Don't be nice." I glared up at him. "You kept this from me. But worse still, you didn't fight for me."

"You know why I can't, Wendy." His dark eyes smoldered, and

his fists clenched at his side. "Now you know who you are and what you mean to the kingdom. I can't fight for something that isn't mine. Especially not when you mean so much to our people."

"You're right, Finn, I'm not yours." I nodded, looking down at the floor. "I'm not anybody's. I have a choice in all of this, and so do you. But you have no right to take my choice away from me, to tell me who I should marry."

"I didn't arrange this marriage," Finn said incredulously.

"But you think I should marry him, and you've done nothing to stop it." I shrugged. "You might as well have arranged it yourself."

I wiped at my eyes, and he didn't say anything. I lay down on my bed and rolled over so my back was to him. After a few minutes, I heard him walk away and the door shut behind him.

accord

S ara Elsing, Queen of the Vittra, was set to arrive at three the next afternoon to collect Loki Staad, so the morning was filled with a series of defense meetings. I attended with Tove, Aurora Kroner, Garrett Strom, the Chancellor, and a select few trackers, like Finn and his father.

Elora was noticeably absent. She didn't have the strength for it, and she wouldn't be able to regain her strength until after Loki left.

When we stopped for lunch, Tove invited me to join him, but I declined. I liked Tove as much as I always had, but I felt weird around him knowing that we were expected to marry.

Also, I wanted to get in a moment alone with Loki before he left. It might be the last chance I ever got to speak with him.

This time, I didn't use Duncan to do my dirty work. I sent the guards away myself. They protested, but with an icy glare I reminded them I was the Princess. I didn't care if anyone talked about it. Loki was leaving anyway. There would be nothing left to gossip about.

"Ooo, I love it when you're feisty," Loki said after I made the guards leave. He leaned on the footboard of the bed, his usual cocky grin plastered on his face.

"I'm not being feisty," I said. "I wanted to talk to you."

"You've come to say good-bye, I take it?" He arched an eyebrow. "You'll miss me terribly, I know, but if you want to avoid all that, you can always come with me."

"That's quite all right, thank you."

"Really?" Loki wrinkled his nose. "You can't actually be excited about the upcoming nuptials."

"What are you talking about?" I asked, tensing up.

"I heard you're engaged to that stodgy Markis." Loki waved his hand vaguely and stood up. "Which I think is ridiculous. He's boring and bland and you don't love him at all."

"How do you know about that?" I stood up straighter, preparing to defend myself.

"The guards around here are horrible gossips, and I hear everything." He grinned and sauntered toward me. "And I have two eyes. I've seen that little melodrama play out between you and that other tracker. Fish? Flounder? What's his name?"

"Finn," I said pointedly.

"Yes, him." Loki rested his shoulder against the door. "Can I give you a piece of advice?"

"By all means. I'd love to hear advice from a prisoner."

"Excellent." Loki leaned forward, as close to me as he could before he'd be racked with pain from attempting to leave the room. "Don't marry someone you don't love."

"What do you know of love or marriage?" I asked. "You were all set to marry a woman ten years older than you before the King stole her away."

"I wouldn't have married her anyway." Loki shrugged. "Not if I didn't love her."

"Now you've got integrity?" I scoffed. "You kidnapped me, and your father was a traitor."

"I've never said a nice word about my father," Loki said quickly. "And I've never done anything bad to you."

"You still kidnapped me!" I said dubiously.

"Did I?" Loki cocked his head. "Because I remember Kyra kidnapping you, and me preventing her from pummeling you to death. Then, when you were coughing up blood, I sent for the Queen to help you. When you escaped, I didn't stop you. And since I came here, I've done nothing to you. I've even been good because you told me to be. So what terrible crimes have I committed against you, Princess?"

"I—I—" I stammered. "I never said you did anything terrible."

"Then why don't you trust me, Wendy?"

He'd never called me by my name before, and the underlying affection underneath it startled me. Even his eyes, which still held their usual veil of playfulness, had something deeper brewing underneath. When he wasn't trying so hard to be devilishly handsome, he actually was.

The growing connection I felt with him unnerved me, but I didn't want him to see that. More than that, it didn't matter what feelings I might be having for him. He was leaving today, and I would probably never see him again.

"I do trust you," I admitted. "I do trust you. I just don't know why I do, and I don't know why you've been helping me."

"You want the truth?" He smiled at me, and there was something sincere and sweet underlying. "You piqued my curiosity."

"You risked your life for me because you were curious?" I asked doubtfully.

"As soon as you came to, your only concern was for helping your friends, and you never stopped," Loki said. "You were kind. And I haven't seen that much kindness in my life."

He looked away from me then, staring at an empty spot down the hall. I think he was trying to hide the sadness in his eyes, but I saw it just the same—a strange loneliness that looked out of place on his strong features.

Loki shook his head, trying to shake off whatever he'd been feeling, and gave me a crooked smile that looked surprisingly dismal. "I thought for once that acting decent ought to be rewarded. That's why I let you go, and that's why I didn't bring you back to the King."

"If it's so horrible there, why don't you stay with us?" I asked without thinking.

"No." He shook his head and lowered his eyes. "Tempting though the offer may be, your people wouldn't allow it, and my people . . . well, let's just say they wouldn't react well if I didn't come home. And whether I like it or not, it is my home."

"I know that feeling all too well." I sighed. Though Förening was starting to feel more like home, I wasn't sure that it ever would completely.

"See? I told you, Princess." Loki's smile returned more easily. "You and I aren't all that different."

"You say that like it means something."

"Doesn't it?"

"No, not really. You're leaving today, going home to my enemies." I let out a deep breath, feeling an ache inside my chest. "If

I'm lucky, I'll never see you again. Because if I do, that means we're at war, and I'd have to hurt you."

"Oh, Wendy, that's perhaps the saddest thing I've ever heard," Loki said, and he looked like he meant it. "But life doesn't have to be all doom and gloom. Don't you ever see the silver lining?"

"Not today." I shook my head. I heard Garrett summon me from down the hall, which meant that lunch was over and the meetings were about to start up. "I have to get back. I'll see you when we make the exchange with the Vittra Queen."

"Good luck." Loki nodded.

I turned to walk away, and I hadn't made it very far when I heard Loki calling after me.

"Wendy!" Loki leaned out into the hall, so far it made him grimace with pain. "If you're right, and the next time we see each other is when our kingdoms are at war, you and I never will be. I'll never fight you. That I can promise you."

The meetings continued on, each one with the same grueling pace. The participants kept repeating the same information. What to do if the Vittra reneged on the deal. What to do if the Vittra attacked. What to do if the Vittra tried to kidnap me.

And it all boiled down to one answer—fight back. Tove and I would use our abilities, the trackers would use their strength and skill, and the Chancellor would cower in the corner.

Our last step before the Vittra Queen officially arrived was to sign the treaty. It'd already been sent over to the Vittra first, so Oren's name was scribbled across the bottom in blood red. Garrett had to take it up to Elora in her room, and she added her own signature. Once he came back down with it, all we had to do was wait in the War Room for Sara to arrive.

At two-thirty, Elora released Loki, and he promised to be on his best behavior. Just the same, Thomas and Finn treated him like they thought he was a bomb about to explode.

Since we were meeting the dignitary of an enemy nation, I thought I'd better look the part of the Princess, especially since Elora was unable to join us. I dressed in a dark violet gown, and I'd enlisted Willa to help me with my hair.

"If I'd known you'd look so beautiful, I would've gotten dressed up," Loki teased when Finn and Thomas brought him into the War Room. Finn shoved him into a seat unnecessarily hard, but Loki didn't protest.

"Don't get familiar with the Princess," Duncan told him, giving him a stony look.

"My apologies," Loki said. "I wouldn't want to get familiar with anyone."

Loki looked about the room. Duncan, Finn, Thomas, Tove, the Chancellor, and I were the ones set to meet Sara. The rest of the house was on standby, should we need them, but we didn't want to look like we were ambushing Sara when she arrived.

"Did you change your mind and decide to execute me?" Loki asked, looking us over. "Because you all look like you're going to a funeral."

"Not now," I said, fidgeting with my bracelet and watching the clock.

"Then when, Princess?" Loki asked. "Because we only have about fifteen minutes until I leave."

I rolled my eyes and ignored him.

By the time the doorbell chimed, I'd taken to pacing the room. I nearly jumped when I heard it. The exchange was supposed to be clean and simple, but I wasn't sure what to expect. My father had lied and betrayed the Trylle before.

"Here we go," I said and took a deep breath.

I carried the treaty in my hands, a tube of paper rolled up and tied with a red ribbon, and I led the way down the corridor to the front hall. Duncan followed directly behind me on my left side, and Tove was at my right. Finn and Thomas each took one of Loki's arms, in case he decided to struggle or fight, and the Chancellor brought up the rear.

Two other guards had let the Queen in, and they waited with her. She stood in the center of the rotunda, flakes of snow sticking to her crimson cloak. She'd pushed the hood down, and her cheeks were rosy from the cold. She'd arrived alone, except for Ludlow, the small hobgoblin I'd seen in the Vittra palace.

"Princess." Sara smiled warmly when she saw me. She did a small curtsy, and I returned it, making sure to keep it equally small.

"Queen. I trust you traveled well," I said.

"Yes, though the roads were a bit icy." She gestured to the doors behind her with velvet-gloved hands. "I hope we didn't keep you waiting."

"No, you arrived on time," I assured her.

"She's here now," Loki said, but I didn't look back to see if he was pulling at Finn and Thomas. "Can you let me go?"

"Not until the agreement is finalized," Finn said through gritted teeth.

"My Queen, can we settle this, please?" Loki called to her, sounding irritated. "This tracker is getting handsy."

"The Markis hasn't been too much trouble?" Sara asked, her cheeks reddening with embarrassment.

"Not too much," I replied with a thin smile. "When we return him to you, you agree to peace until my coronation. Is that correct?"

"Yes." Sara nodded. "The Vittra will not attack you as long as Elora is Queen. But as soon as you become Queen, the cease-fire is over."

I handed the treaty over to her. I'd expected her to unroll it and double-check it for accuracy, but she simply nodded again, apparently deciding to trust us.

"Now they can let me go?" Loki asked.

"Yes," I said.

I heard a skirmish behind me, and then Loki walked past me, smoothing out his shirt. Sara gave him a disapproving look, and he took his place at her side.

"It's all settled, then?" Loki asked.

"It appears that way," Sara said. "Princess, you know you are always welcome at our palace."

"I do," I admitted.

"The King wanted me to extend an invitation to you," Sara said. "If you return to the Vittra to take your rightful place at his side, he will offer amnesty to Förening and everyone who lives here."

I faltered for a moment, unsure how to respond. I didn't want to go there, and I certainly didn't trust the King, but it was hard to pass up. It would protect everybody I cared about, including Matt and Finn.

I glanced at Loki, expecting him to be grinning or teasing me to join him, but instead, his cocky smile had faltered. He swallowed, and his caramel eyes were almost frightened.

"Princess." Tove touched my arm, just above my elbow. "We

have other business to attend to this afternoon. Perhaps we should see our guests out."

"Yes, of course." I smiled thinly. "If you'll forgive me, I do have things I need to do."

"Of course." Sara smiled. "We don't need to take up any more of your time."

"It's just as well." Loki looked relieved and smiled at me. "Ondarike is no place for a Princess."

"Markis," Sara said coolly.

She did another curtsy, which I reciprocated, then turned away. Ludlow the hobgoblin never said anything, but he gathered up her train so it wouldn't drag on the ground. As they walked to the door, Loki started to say something, but Sara silenced him.

He glanced over his shoulder once, his eyes meeting mine, and I was surprised to find how much my heart ached at seeing him go. We hadn't spent that much time together, but I'd felt oddly connected almost since the moment I met him.

Then he was gone out the door, and out of my life, and I actually wanted to cry.

Once they were gone, I let out a deep breath.

"That wasn't so bad," I said. It wasn't bad at all, really. The nerve-racking buildup had been the worst part.

The Chancellor was sweating like a pig, but this was nothing new. I smiled gratefully at Tove. It had been nice having him at my side. Backup and support were never a bad thing.

"Those little hobgoblins freak me out." Duncan shuddered at the thought of Ludlow. "I don't know how they can live with them."

"I'm sure they think the same thing about you," Finn muttered.

"I think we all know what we have to do," the Chancellor said, wringing his pudgy hands together.

"What?" I asked, since I had no idea what we had to do.

"We need to attack them while the truce is still in play," the Chancellor said. Sweat dripped down into his beady eyes, and his white suit had wet circles all over it.

"The whole point of the truce is that we have peace," I said. "If we attack them, we negate that, and we're back at war."

"We need to get a drop on them when they're not expecting it," the Chancellor insisted, his jowls shaking. "This is our only chance to have the upper hand!"

I shook my head. "No, this is our chance to rebuild after the last attack and find ways to handle this conflict peaceably. We need to work on uniting the Trylle and being as strong as we can be. Or coming up with something we can offer the Vittra to get them off our back."

"Well, we know what we can offer them." The Chancellor eyed me.

"We're not negotiating with them," Finn interjected.

The Chancellor glared at him. "Of course, *you're* not negotiating with anybody for anything."

"We can't cross negotiations out," Tove said, and before Finn could protest, he went on. "Obviously, we're not giving them the Princess, but we can't rule out other options. Enough people have died already. And after fighting for all this time, nobody has won. I think we need to try something different."

"Exactly," I agreed. "We should use this time to figure out what that might be."

"You want to find something new to barter with?" the Chancellor scoffed. "We can't trust the Vittra King!"

"Just because he plays dirty doesn't mean we have to," I said.

"And the only reason we won this last fight is because it happened on our turf and they left their strongest players at home," Tove said. "If we meet them at their house, they have the advantage. They would crush us the way they have every other time. We need to learn from our mistakes."

"Fine!" The Chancellor threw up his hands. "Do what you want! But the blood will be on your hands, not mine."

The Chancellor stalked off, defeated. I smiled up at Tove.

"Thanks for backing me up," I said.

Tove shrugged. "It's what I do."

proposal

After Sara and Loki left, I went up to report to Elora how I'd done. Garrett was sitting with her in the drawing room, where Elora was lying down. Her skin color had brightened, but she was still out of it.

I kept my explanation brief, but they both seemed proud of me. It had been my first official duty as a Princess, and I'd passed. Elora actually said I did well. When I left, I felt surprisingly good.

I met Tove on my way back from the room. He came from the kitchen, and he had a handful of grapes. He offered me one, but I didn't feel much like eating, so I shook my head.

"Do you feel like a real Princess yet?" Tove asked me as he munched on a grape.

"I don't know." I pulled off the heavy diamond necklace I'd worn to look the part. "But I don't know if I ever will. I think I'll always feel like an imposter."

"Well, you definitely look like a real Princess."

"Thanks." I turned to him and smiled. "And you did really well today. You were focused and very regal."

"Thanks." He tossed a grape in his mouth and grinned. "I spent a lot of time rearranging my furniture before the meeting started. It seemed to help."

"It did."

We walked in silence for a bit, him eating his fruit and me fiddling with the necklace. The silence between us didn't feel awkward, though, and I thought about how nice it was. Being able to be with someone without it feeling forced or weird or agonizingly restrained.

I also started to understand what Elora and Finn meant. Tove was strong and intelligent and kind, but his abilities made him too frazzled to be a leader. He did an amazing job of backing me up and supporting me, and I knew that no matter what, he'd be at my side.

"So." Tove swallowed the last grape and stopped. He stared down at the floor and tucked his tangled hair behind his ears. "I'm sure that the Queen has told you of the arrangement that she and my mother made." He paused. "You know, about us getting married."

"Yeah." I nodded, feeling strangely nervous to hear him bring it up.

"I don't agree with them sneaking around and plotting things, like we're pawns in a game and not people." Tove chewed the inside of his cheek and looked down the hallway. "It's not right, and I told Aurora that. She needs to stop treating me like a . . . I don't know. A pawn."

"Yeah," I agreed, and I kept nodding.

"She thinks she can control me all the time, and I know your mother tries to do the same stuff with you." He sighed. "It's like they had all these ideas of who we would be before we got here, and they refuse to adjust them even when they see we're not what they expected."

"Yeah, that's true," I said.

"I know about your past." He glanced over at me, resting his eyes on me only for a second. "Aurora told me about your father and how you're at risk of losing the crown because of him, because of your parents' mistakes. That's stupid because I know how powerful you are and how much you care about people."

"Thank you?" I said uncertainly.

"You need to be Queen. Everyone who knows anything knows that, but most people don't know anything, and that is a problem." He scratched at the back of his head and shifted his weight. "I would never take that away from you. No matter what happens, I'd never take the crown from you, and I'd defend you against anybody who tried."

I didn't say anything to that. I'd never heard Tove talk so much before, and I didn't know what he was getting at.

"I know that you're in love with . . . well, not me," he said carefully. "And I'm not in love with you either. But I do respect you, and I like you."

"I respect and like you too," I said, and he gave me a small smile.

"But it's a number of things, and it's none of them." He let out a deep breath. "That didn't make sense. I mean, it's because you need somebody to help you keep the throne, and somebody on your side, and I can do that. But . . . it's just because I think . . . I want to."

"What?" I asked, and he actually looked at me, letting his mossy eyes stare into mine.

"Will you . . . I mean, do you want to get married?" Tove asked. "To me?"

"I, um . . ." I didn't know what to say.

"If you don't want to, nothing has to change between us," Tove said hurriedly. "I asked because it sounds like a good idea to me."

"Yeah," I said, and I didn't know what I would say until it was coming out of my mouth. "I mean, yes. I do. I will. I would . . . I'll marry you."

"Yeah?" Tove smiled.

"Yes." I swallowed hard and tried to smile back.

"Good." He exhaled and looked back down the hall. "This is good, right?"

"Yeah, I think so," I said, and I meant it.

"Yeah." He nodded. "I sorta feel like throwing up now, though."

"I think that's normal."

"Good." He nodded again and looked at me. "Well, I'll let you go . . . do whatever you need to do. And I'll go do what I do."

"Okay." I nodded.

"All right." He randomly patted me on the shoulder, then nodded again, and walked away.

I had no idea what I'd just agreed to. I wasn't in love with Tove, and I really didn't think he was in love with me.

Tove and I understood and respected each other, and that was something. But more important, it was what the kingdom needed. Elora was convinced that marrying Tove was the best thing for me and for the Trylle.

I had to do what was best for our people, and if that meant marrying Tove, then so be it. There were a lot worse people I could end up married to.

I changed out of my gown, then I took Duncan with me to the library. He helped me find some good history texts about the Trylle, and I began reading through them. Finn had had me skim some things before my christening ceremony, but if I planned to rule these people, I needed to understand who they were.

I spent the rest of the evening in the library, getting as much information as I could. Duncan ended up passed out and curled up in one of the chairs. It was late when I woke him up to walk me to my room. I wasn't sure how much protection groggy Duncan really offered, but I doubted I needed it anyway.

The next morning, Tove and I went to the atrium to do some training, and I enjoyed getting back in a routine. Duncan went along, and if things seemed awkward between Tove and me, Duncan didn't say anything. It did feel weird being newly engaged, but Tove did a good job of keeping me on task.

I was getting a better mastery of my abilities, and they were becoming stronger. I lifted the throne off the floor, with Duncan sitting in it, and it didn't require as much concentration as it had before. Right behind my eyes pain throbbed dully, but I ignored it.

When Tove moved a chair, levitating it in a circle to demonstrate what he wanted me to do, I couldn't help but think of Elora. How weak and frail she looked from being drained by her powers.

I knew that we needed to use our powers to keep from going crazy, and with Tove especially, draining his abilities was the only thing that kept him sane. But it made me nervous. I didn't want him to end up like my mother, dying of old age before he was even forty.

When we'd finished practicing, I felt tired, but in a pleasant way. I was becoming stronger and more self-reliant, and I liked that.

Elora was still in her drawing room, recuperating, so I went down to see her. She'd gotten off the chaise, which was a good sign, but she'd taken to painting again.

She sat on a stool facing the windows, an easel in front of her. The shawl wrapped around her had slipped off one shoulder, but she didn't seem to notice. Her long hair hung down her back, shimmering silver now more than black.

"Are you sure you should be doing that?" I asked as I came into her room.

"I've had a terrible migraine for days, and I need to get rid of it." She made a sweeping stroke across the canvas.

I walked up behind her so I could get a better look at it, but so far it was only dark blue sky. Elora stopped painting and set her brush down on the easel.

"Is there something you needed from me, Princess?" Elora swiveled around to face me, and I was relieved to see that the milkiness had vanished from her eyes.

"No." I shook my head. "I just wanted to see how you're doing."

"Better," she said with a heavy sigh. "I will never be quite the same again, but I'm better."

"Better is something."

"Yes, I suppose it is." She turned to the window and the overcast day.

The sleet and wind had finally let up, but the skies remained gray and murky. The maples and elms had given up most of their leaves and stood dead and barren for winter. The evergreens that populated the bluff looked brittle after the beating they'd taken lately, and ice clung to their branches, weighing them down.

"Tove asked me to marry him," I told her, and she whipped her head to face me. "And I agreed."

"You've accepted the arrangement?" Elora raised her eyebrow, in wonder and approval.

"Yes." I nodded. "It's . . . it's what's best for the kingdom, so that's what I must do." I nodded again, to convince myself. "And Tove is a good guy. He'll make a good husband."

Immediately after I'd said it I realized that I had no idea what would make a good husband. I'd spent almost no time around married couples, and I'd never had a boyfriend. I didn't know what category Finn and I fell into, but it couldn't count for much.

Elora was still watching me, so I gulped and forced a smile. Now wasn't the time to worry about what I'd agreed to. I had time to learn what it meant to be a wife before we were wed.

"Yes, I am certain he will," Elora murmured and turned to her painting.

"Are you really?" I asked.

"Yes," she said, with her back still to me. "I won't do to you what was done to me. If I thought you needed to do something terrible, that it was in the best interest of the Trylle, I would still ask it of you. It would still be your duty, but I would tell you exactly what you were doing. I'd never let you go in blind."

"Thank you," I said, meaning it. "Do you regret marrying my father?"

"I try not to have any regrets," Elora said wearily and picked up her paintbrush. "It's unbecoming of a Queen to have misgivings."

"How come you never married again?" I asked.

"Who would I marry?"

I nearly said Thomas, but that would only enrage her. She couldn't have married him. He was a tracker, and he was already married. But that wasn't where her anger would come from. I was sure she'd be incensed that I had learned of the affair.

"Garrett?" I asked, and Elora made a noise that sounded like a laugh. "He loves you, and he's a distinguished Markis. He's eligible."

"He's not that distinguished," she said. "He is kind, yes, but marriage isn't about that. I told you before, Princess, that love has nothing to do with marriage. It's an alignment between two parties, and I have not had any reason to align myself with anyone else."

"You don't want to marry for the sake of doing it?" I asked. "Don't you ever get lonely?"

"A Queen is many things, but alone is never one of them." She held the brush, poised right above the canvas as if she meant to paint, but she didn't. "I don't need love or a man to complete me, and someday you'll find that's true for yourself. Suitors will come and go, but you will remain."

I stared out the window, unsure of what to say to that. There was something noble and dignified in that idea, but something about it felt a bit tragic. Believing that I would end up alone, that I would die alone, was never comforting.

"Besides that, I didn't want Willa in line for the crown," Elora said and began painting again. "That is what would've happened if I'd married Garrett. She would've become a Princess, a viable option for the throne, and I could never have that."

"Willa wouldn't be a bad Queen," I said, and I was astonished to find that I actually did think that.

Willa had really grown on me since I'd been here, and I think she'd grown up as well. She had kindness and insight I'd initially thought her incapable of.

"Nevertheless, she won't be Queen. You will."

"Not for a long time, hopefully." I sighed.

"You need to be ready, Princess." She looked over her shoulder at me. "You must be prepared for it."

"I am trying," I assured her. "I've been training and going to all the meetings. I've even been studying in the library. But I still don't feel like I'll be ready to be a real Queen for years."

"You don't have years," Elora told me.

"What do you mean?" I asked. "When will I be Queen? How long do I have?"

"Do you see that painting?" Elora gestured to a canvas I'd seen in her room before, resting against a shelf.

A close-up of me looking much as I did now, except wearing a white gown. On my head, I had an ornate platinum crown filled with diamonds.

"So?" I asked. "I'll be Queen someday. We both know that."

"No, look at that picture." She pointed at it with the handle of her brush. "Look at your face. How old are you?"

"I'm . . ." I squinted and crouched in front of it. I couldn't be sure exactly, but I didn't look a day older than I did now. "I don't know." I stood up. "I could be twenty-five, for all I know."

"Perhaps," Elora allowed, "but that's not the feeling I get."

"What is the feeling you get?" I asked. She turned her back to me, not giving anything away. "How do I become Queen anyway?"

"You become Queen when the reigning monarchs are deceased," Elora said matter-of-factly.

"You mean I'll be Queen after you die?" I asked, and my heart thudded in my chest.

"Yes."

"So you think . . ." I had to take a fortifying breath before I could continue. "You're dying soon."

"Yes." She painted on, as if I'd just asked her about the weather instead of her impending death.

"But . . ." I shook my head. "I'm not ready. You haven't taught me everything I need to know!"

"That is why I have been pushing you, Princess. I knew we didn't have much time, and I needed to be hard on you. I had to be sure you could do this."

"And now you're sure?" I asked.

"Yes." She faced me again. "Don't panic, Princess. You must never panic, no matter what obstacle you face."

"I'm not panicking," I lied. My heart wanted to race out of my chest, and I felt light-headed. I sat on the couch behind me.

"I'm not dying tomorrow," Elora said, sounding slightly annoyed. "You have more time to learn, but you need to focus on all your training. You need to listen carefully to everything I say, and do as you're told."

"It's not that." I shook my head and stared at her. "I only just met you, and we've finally started getting along, and now you're dying?"

"Don't get sentimental, Princess," Elora chastised me. "That we do not have time for."

"Aren't you sad?" I asked, tears stinging my eyes. "Or scared?"

"Princess, really." She rolled her eyes and turned away from me. "I have painting to do. I suggest you go to your room and compose yourself. A Princess must never be seen crying."

I left her alone to finish her painting. The one consolation I had was that Elora said a Princess must never be *seen* crying, not that I must never cry. I wondered if that was why she had me leave. Not so I could cry, but so she could.

TWENTY-FOUR

tryllic

I f Loki had already known about my arranged marriage, it was only a matter of time before everybody else found out. I thought it would be better if my friends learned about it from me, so I gathered them all together.

Willa and Duncan would probably be excited, but I didn't know how Matt or Rhys would take it. Probably not quite as well.

We met in the upstairs living room, which had been Rhys's old playroom. The ceiling had a cloud mural on it, and there were still old toys stacked up on shelves in the corner. Matt sat between Rhys and Willa on the sofa, and Duncan sat on the floor with his back against the couch.

"I have something to tell you all." I stood in front of them, twirling my thumb ring, and swallowed back my nerves.

The suspicious look Matt gave me wasn't helping matters. On top of that, Rhys grinned like an excited fool. He'd been so happy when I invited him here, since we'd hardly seen each other lately.

He'd been busy doing stuff with Matt, and I'd heard that he'd started dating Rhiannon.

"What is it?" Matt asked, his voice already hard.

"It's good news," I insisted.

"Spit it out, then," Willa said with a confused smile. "You've been killing me with suspense." She'd tried getting it out of me before everybody had arrived, but I wanted to tell them all at once.

"I wanted you all to know that I, um . . ." I cleared my throat. "I'm getting married."

"What?" Matt growled.

"Oh, my gosh!" Willa gasped, her eyes glittering. "To who?"

"So it's true?" Duncan gaped at me. Apparently he'd heard the rumor too.

"To Tove Kroner," I said.

Willa squealed and clapped her hands over her mouth. I didn't think she could've been more excited if she was the one getting married to Tove.

"Tove?" Matt asked, looking unsure. "That guy's a spaz, and I didn't even think you really liked him."

"No, I like him," I said. "He's a good guy."

"Oh, my gosh, Wendy!" Willa yelled and jumped off the couch, nearly kicking Duncan in the head. She ran over and hugged me enthusiastically. "This is so exciting! I am so happy for you!"

"Yeah, congratulations." Rhys nodded. "He's a lucky guy."

"I can't believe you guys didn't tell me," Duncan said. "I was with you both this morning."

"Well, we hadn't really told people yet." I untangled myself from Willa's embrace. "I'm not sure if we're supposed to tell people, but I thought you should know."

"But I don't understand." Matt stood up, clearly disturbed by the news. "I thought you were all hung up on that Finn guy."

"Nope." I shook my head and lowered my eyes. "I'm not hung up on anybody." I let out a deep breath. "That's all behind me."

I was surprised to find that that might be true. I wasn't over Finn exactly, but I had begun to realize that we would never be together. And it wasn't because of our social standings any-more. That I could fight with, argue against, try to legislate.

But Finn's unwillingness to ever try or give me credit or make any effort at all to be with me had left me exhausted. I couldn't be in love by myself.

"Your wedding is going to be so fabulous!" Willa held her hands together in front of her chest to keep from hugging me again. "When is the big day?"

"I don't know exactly," I admitted. "After I turn eighteen."

"That's less than three months away!" Matt shouted.

"We hardly have any time to plan!" Willa paled. "We have so much to do!" Then she grimaced. "Oh, Aurora's gonna have her hand in all of it, isn't she?"

"Oh. Yeah." I scowled too when I realized that I was going to have the mother-in-law from hell. "I guess she is."

"I'm so glad I'm a guy and I don't have to plan any of these things," Rhys said with a lopsided grin.

"The planning is the best part," Willa insisted and looped an arm around my shoulder. "Picking out the colors and dresses and flowers and invitations! That's the funnest!"

"Wendy, are you really okay with this?" Matt asked, looking at me directly.

"Of course she is, Matt," Willa said with an exaggerated eye roll. "This is every little girl's dream. To be a Princess and marry a Prince in a big grand wedding."

"Technically, Tove's a Markis and not a Prince," I pointed out.

"You know what I meant," Willa said. "It's a fairy tale come true."

"Willa, stop for a second." Matt's icy stare rested on her, and she shrank back, retracting her arm from my shoulders. He turned to me. "Wendy, is this really what you want? To marry this guy?"

I took a deep breath and nodded. "Yes. This is what I want."

"Okay," Matt said reluctantly. "If this is what you want, then I'll support you on it. But if he hurts you, I will kill him."

"I wouldn't expect any less from you." I smiled. "But I'll be all right."

Willa continued her excited prattling, telling me all the amazing things we had to plan, but I tuned her out. Rhys and Matt didn't really want or need to hear all of that, so they escaped to do something vastly more fun. Duncan was my bodyguard, so he couldn't leave, but he was actually more involved in Willa's conversation than I was.

Eventually, she exhausted herself. She said she would go home and get a few things, so she could come back bright and early in the morning to plan. We left the room with her listing everything she would bring with her.

"I'll see you tomorrow, okay?" Willa squeezed my arm.

"Yeah."

"This is exciting, Wendy," she reminded me. "Act like it."

"I'll try." I forced a smile.

She laughed at my weak attempt as she departed. I leaned against the wall outside the living room door. Duncan was next to me, but he didn't say anything.

Willa was right. This whole thing was like a fairy tale. So why didn't it feel like one?

I glanced down the hall and saw Finn, doing his evening rounds. He was walking toward me to inspect the north wing, but when he saw me, he stopped. His dark eyes rested on mine for a moment, then he turned and walked in the other direction.

I woke up the next day excited to train and get my mind off the engagement, but I'd only been awake for ten minutes before Aurora burst in. She arrived even before Willa did and stole the whole thing from her. Willa was not happy about it when she found out, but she did her best to be polite around Aurora.

We met in the grand dining room because Aurora had so many papers she wanted to spread out all over the long table. She had guest lists and seating charts and color swatches and fabric material and magazines and dress designs and books and everything anyone would ever need for a wedding.

"We need to have the engagement party this weekend, obviously, since the wedding is only a few months away," Aurora said, tapping a calendar on the table.

I sat in a chair at the head of the table with Aurora standing on one side and Willa on the other. Aurora bent over the table, her green dress flowing around her. Willa had her arms crossed over her chest, and she glared down at Aurora.

"Before the engagement party, we need to have your color scheme and have the bridal party picked out already," Aurora said.

"That's too soon." Willa shook her head. "There's no way we can have all that ready, plus plan a party. It's only a few days away."

"We need to get the wedding invitations out as soon as possible. We will hand them out at the engagement party," Aurora said. "When is your birthday, Princess?"

"Uh, the ninth of January," I said.

"Why do we have to hand out the invites?" Willa asked. "Why can't we mail them like normal people?"

"Because we're not normal people." Aurora shot her a glare. "We're Trylle, and we're royalty. It's customary that we hand out the invitations at the engagement party."

"Fine, but if we have to do that, we should wait at least another week for the party," Willa said.

"I'm not going to argue with you about this." Aurora straightened up and rubbed her forehead. "As the mother of the groom, I'm throwing the engagement party. It's none of your concern. I'll plan it and set it up whenever I feel is best."

"Fine." Willa held up her hands like she didn't care, but I could tell she still was irritated. "You do what you want. That is your right."

"Let's work on the wedding for now." Aurora looked down at me. "Who did you want in your wedding party?"

"Um . . ." I shrugged. "Willa should be my maid of honor, obviously."

"Thank you." Willa gave Aurora a smug smile.

"Of course." Aurora smiled thinly at her and scribbled down Willa's name on a piece of paper. "What about the rest of your party?"

"I don't know." I shook my head. "I don't really know that many people here."

"Excellent. I've compiled a list for you." Aurora grabbed a three-page list from off the table and handed it to me. "Here are upstanding eligible young Marksinna that would make perfect bridesmaids."

"This is just their names and a few random facts," I said, looking over the list. "Kenna Tomas has black hair, freckles, and her father is the Markis of Oslinna. That means nothing to me. I'm supposed to pick strangers off a list based on their hair color?"

"If you'd like, I can pick them for you," Aurora offered. "But I did list them from most desirable to least desirable to make it easier for you, although they are all acceptable choices."

"I can help her," Willa said, taking the list from me before Aurora had a chance to. "I know a lot of these girls."

She immediately flipped to the end of the list, and I felt a small satisfaction in knowing she'd pick the ones that Aurora liked least.

"Can't I just have Willa?" I asked. "I'm sure Tove doesn't have that many friends for groomsmen either. We could have a small wedding."

"Don't be ridiculous," Aurora said. "You're a Princess. You can't have a small wedding."

"Aurora is right," Willa said, sounding sad to be agreeing with her. "You need to have a huge wedding. You have to let them know that you're a Princess to be reckoned with."

"Don't they already know that?" I asked honestly, and Willa shrugged.

"It doesn't hurt to remind them."

"Since your father is out of the picture, Noah can walk you down the aisle," Aurora said, writing something else on her paper.

"Noah?" I asked. "Your husband?"

"Yes, he's a suitable choice," Aurora replied offhandedly.

"But I barely know him," I said.

"Well, you can't walk down alone," Aurora said, giving me an annoyed look.

"Why can't Matt walk me down?" I asked. "He practically raised me anyway."

"Matt?" Aurora was confused, and when she remembered who he was, she wrinkled her nose in disgust. "That human boy? Absolutely not. He shouldn't even be living in the palace, and if others were to find out he was here, you'd be the laughingstock of the kingdom."

"Then . . . fine." I scrambled to think of someone other than Noah. "What about Garrett?"

"Garrett Strom?" Aurora was appalled, but I think it was because he was actually an acceptable candidate.

"He is nearly her stepfather," Willa pointed out with a sly smile. Having her father walk me down the aisle would give her and her family more prestige.

That wasn't why I picked him, though. I actually liked Garrett, and he was the closest thing I had to a decent father figure around here.

"If it is as the Princess wishes," Aurora said, and grudgingly she crossed out her husband's name and wrote Garrett's instead.

They continued that way for a while, and eventually I had to excuse myself. I needed a break from their subtle jabs and bickering. I wandered down the hall. My plan only went so far as to be anywhere that they weren't.

As I got closer to the War Room, I heard voices. I stopped and poked my head inside. The pasty Chancellor sat at the desk with a stack of papers spread out before him. Finn and Tove stood on the other side of the desk, talking, and Thomas was at the bookshelves, searching for something.

"What are you guys doing?" I asked as I came into the room.

"The boys here have an idiotic plan, and I'm indulging them," the Chancellor said.

"It's not idiotic," Finn said, glaring at the Chancellor, who was too busy dabbing sweat from his forehead to notice.

"We're trying to find a way to extend the truce," Tove explained. "We're going through old treaties with the Vittra and any other tribes to see if we have a precedent."

"Have you found anything?" I asked.

I went over to the desk and touched some of the papers. Most of them were written in a language I didn't understand. It was all symbols, almost like Russian or Arabic. When I looked in the library, I'd found that to be common of the older documents.

"Nothing useful yet, but we only just started," Tove said.

"You won't find anything useful." The Chancellor shook his head. "The Vittra never extend their deals."

"What kinds of things could extend the truce?" I asked, ignoring the Chancellor.

"We don't know, exactly," Tove admitted. "But often there are loopholes in the language that we can use against them."

"Loopholes?" I asked.

"Yeah, like Rumpelstiltskin," Finn said. "They usually throw in something clever like that when they make a deal. It seems impossible, but sometimes you can break it."

"I heard the deal. They didn't say anything like that," I said. "Except that the peace only lasts until I become Queen. What if I never become Queen?"

"No, you need to be Queen," Finn said and picked up a stack of papers.

"But that would make indefinite peace, wouldn't it?" I asked. "If I was never Queen."

"I doubt it," Tove said. "The King would find a way around it eventually, and it would only make him more pissed when he finally did."

"But . . ." I trailed off and sighed. "So he'll find his way around anything, including an extension. Why are you even bothering?"

"An extension isn't our goal." Tove met my eyes. "We'll settle for a temporary fix if it's all we can find, but we want to find something that will end this."

"Do you think something like that exists?" I asked.

"The only thing that King will listen to is violence," the Chancellor sputtered. "We need to attack them with everything we have, as soon as we can."

"We have tried that," Tove said, exasperated. "Over and over again! The King is immune to our attacks! We can't hurt him!"

It suddenly hit me when he said that. When Tove had talked about Loki, he'd said that only he, Elora, and I were strong enough to hold him, and he wasn't even sure if we could execute him. The King was even stronger than Loki.

Nobody had ever been able to stop him. Elora wasn't strong enough, and Tove was too scatterbrained. But I had the King's strength and Elora's power.

"You want me to kill the King," I said. "You want to extend the deadline so I have more time to train."

Tove and Finn wouldn't meet my eyes, so I knew I'd gotten it right. They expected me to kill my father.

TWENTY-FIVE

fairy tale

Thomas grabbed a large book from the bookshelf and dropped it on the desk with a heavy thud. Dust rose from the leather cover. Tove had been so busy avoiding my gaze that he jumped when the book banged.

"That might be of some help." Thomas motioned to the book. "But it's written in Tryllic."

"What's Tryllic?" I asked, eager to change the subject to something that wasn't patricide.

"It's the old Trylle language," Finn explained, and pointed to the papers I'd seen written in a symbolic language. "Only Tove is any good at reading it."

"It's a dead language," the Chancellor said. "I don't know how anyone knows it anymore."

"It's not that hard." Tove reached for the book. He opened the pages, letting out a musty odor. "I can teach you sometime, if you'd like."

"I should learn it," I said. "But not right now. We're trying to find a way to extend this thing, right? How can I help?"

"Look through the papers." Finn sifted through some on the table and handed me a small stack. "See if you can find anything about treaties or truces, even if it's not with the Vittra. Anything that might help."

Tove sat in one of the distressed leather chairs to read the book. I sat down on the floor with my stack of papers, preparing to dig into Trylle legalese. It always seemed to be written in riddles and limericks. A lot of it was hard to understand, and I had to ask for interpretations.

I didn't feel so bad about that, though, when Tove called Finn over to help him understand a passage. Finn leaned over the chair so he could peer down at the page, and he and Tove discussed what it meant.

I thought about how strange it was that Finn and Tove got along so well. Finn seemed to turn into a jealous freak whenever I flirted with a guy, but I was engaged to Tove, and he seemed perfectly okay with him.

Finn looked up from the book, and his eyes met mine, only for a second before he looked away. I saw something in them, a longing I missed, and I wondered again if I had made the right decision.

"Princess?" Aurora called from the hallway.

I'd only been sitting on the floor, reading pages, but she probably wouldn't approve of it. I jumped to my feet and set the papers on the desk to avoid a lecture about ladylike behavior.

"Princess?" Aurora said again, and she poked her head into the room. "Ah, there you are. And you're with Tove. Perfect. We need you to go over engagement details."

"Oh. Right." Tove set the book aside and gave me an awkward smile. "Wedding stuff. We have to do that now."

"Yeah." I nodded.

I glanced over at Finn. His expression had hardened, but he didn't look up. Tove and I followed Aurora out as she talked about the things we needed to do for the wedding, and I looked over my shoulder at Finn.

Aurora held Tove and me hostage for far too long, and Willa couldn't lighten the mood. It would've been so much easier if Aurora and Willa were just marrying each other. By the time Aurora let us go, even Willa was relieved to escape.

Duncan was waiting for me, and we went down to the kitchen to eat supper together. Tove went to the War Room to work, and Willa said she had plans. I knew I should be helping Tove, but I was starving. I had to get something to eat first.

I talked to Duncan about what Tove and Finn were researching, and how some of the papers were written in Tryllic. Duncan said he thought he'd seen a book on Tryllic upstairs in Rhys's living room, which made sense because he'd explained that a lot of mänks went through a phase where they tried to learn it.

I didn't really need to learn it this second, but I wanted to get a feel for the language. As soon as we were done eating, I headed up to the living room. The door was shut, but most doors in the palace were kept closed, and I opened it without knocking.

I hadn't been trying to be sneaky, but since Matt and Willa didn't hear me, I must've been awfully quiet. Or maybe they were too caught up in the moment.

Willa was lying on her back on the couch, and Matt was on top of her. She had on a short dress, the way she always seemed to, and Matt had his hand on her thigh, pushing her hem up. Her other leg was wrapped around his waist, and she buried her fingers in his sandy hair as they kissed.

"Oh, my god!" I gasped. I didn't mean to, but it just came out.

"Wendy!" Willa shrieked, and Matt jumped off her.

"What's going on?" Duncan asked from behind me and tried to push past me, so he could protect me if he needed to.

"Quiet!" Willa hissed, fixing her dress so all her parts were a bit more covered. "Shut the door!"

"Oh, right." I pulled the door shut and averted my eyes from Willa and Matt.

They weren't doing anything particularly graphic, but I'd never seen Matt in any compromising situations before. He hardly ever dated, and he almost never brought girls home. It was bizarre thinking of him getting sexy with someone.

When I glanced up at Matt, his cheeks were red, and he wouldn't lift his head. His hair was messed up, and he kept smoothing out the wrinkles in his shirt. Some of Willa's lipstick had rubbed off on his cheek and mouth, but I didn't have the guts to tell him about it.

"Wow. You two?" Duncan grinned at them. "Bravo, Matt. I didn't think Willa would ever date anyone out of her class."

"Shut up, Duncan." Willa glared at him and readjusted her ankle bracelet.

"Don't be crude," Matt growled, and Duncan took a step back, as if he expected Matt to hit him.

"And you can't say anything to anybody about this," Willa warned him. "You know what would happen if this got out."

Willa was a Marksinna, and even though her abilities were nowhere near as strong as mine, she was still one of the most powerful ones left. Matt was a human from a host family, relegating him to an even lower class than trackers and mänks. If Matt was caught defiling Willa's important bloodline, they'd both be exiled.

Considering they were two of my closest friends, I didn't want that to happen. Not only would I miss them terribly, but the Vittra might go after them to get to me. They needed to stay in Förening, where they were safe.

"Of course I won't say anything." Duncan crossed his heart to prove his sincerity. "I never told anyone about Finn and the Princess."

"Duncan, shut up," I snapped. I didn't need Matt to be reminded of that right now.

"Please don't be mad," Willa said, incorrectly thinking my irritation was with her. "We didn't want you to find out this way. We've been waiting for the right time to tell you, but you've had so much going on lately."

"And this doesn't change the way we feel about you," Matt rushed to explain. "We both care about you a lot." He gestured to himself and Willa, but he didn't look at her. "That's one of the things that drew us together. We didn't want to hurt you."

"You guys, I'm not hurt." I shook my head. "I'm not mad. I'm not even that surprised."

"Really?" Willa tilted her head.

"No. You've been spending so much time together, and you're always flirting," I said. "I kinda knew something was going on. I just didn't expect to walk in on you like *that*."

"Sorry." Matt's blush deepened. "I really didn't mean for you to see us that way."

"No, it's okay." I shrugged it off. "It's not a big deal."

I looked from one of them to the other. Willa's dark eyes were worried, and her light brown waves of hair cascaded down her side. She was very beautiful, and she'd already shown how kind and loyal she could be.

"You guys make sense," I said finally. "And I want you both to be happy."

"We're happy." Willa smiled, and she and Matt exchanged a look. It was one of those sweet loving ones, and it even made Matt smile.

"Yeah, we're happy." Matt nodded and pulled his gaze away from her to look at me.

"Good. But you two have got to be careful. I don't want you getting caught and banished away from me. I need you both."

"Yeah, I know you need me," Willa said. "Aurora would eat you alive without my help."

"Don't remind me." I grimaced and flopped on one of Rhys's old beanbag chairs. "And I've only been engaged for like forty-eight hours. Everyone's all afraid of the Vittra, but I swear, this wedding is going to be the death of me."

"If you don't want to marry him, don't marry him," Matt said. He sat down on the couch next to Willa, but he'd turned on his disapproving big-brother voice. "You don't need to do anything you don't want to."

"No, it's not Tove." I shook my head. "I'm fine with marrying Tove."

"You're 'fine' with marrying him?" Willa laughed and looped her arm through Matt's. "How romantic."

"You should've seen the proposal," I said.

"Where is the ring, by the way?" Willa asked, looking at my hands. "Is it out getting sized?"

"I don't know." I held my hands out to look at them, as if I expected a ring to magically appear. "He didn't give me one."

"That's horrible!" Willa rested her head on Matt's shoulder.

"We have to correct that right away. Maybe I'll say something when we're with Aurora tomorrow."

"No!" I said fiercely. "Please don't say anything to her. She'd force me to pick out something hideous."

"How can she force you to do anything?" Duncan asked. He sat cross-legged next to me on the floor. "You're the Princess. She's your subordinate."

"You know Aurora." I sighed. "She has ways."

"That's weird." Duncan looked at me as if seeing me in a new light. "I thought life would be so much different for royals. That you had total freedom."

"Nobody's really free." I shook my head. "You spend like twenty hours a day with me. You know how much of my time is free."

"That's really depressing." Duncan's shoulders sagged as he thought about this. "I thought your life was like this because you were new, but it's always gonna be like this, isn't it? You'll always have to answer to people."

"So it would seem," I agreed. "Life isn't a fairy tale, Duncan."

"And you know what they say," Willa chimed in. "Mo' money, mo' problems."

"Well, *that* was embarrassing to hear you say that, so I'm good." I stood up. "I've got lots of studying to do tonight. I'm going to squeeze in some training before I meet with Aurora tomorrow. Do you think you can keep her busy until I get there?"

"If I must," Willa groaned.

"Don't overwork yourself," Matt said as I was leaving the room. "You've got to make time to be a kid. You're still young."

"I think my days of being a kid are over," I said honestly.

overture

W illa bailed early on in the planning. She said she had to have supper with her father, but I suspected that she couldn't take Aurora anymore.

We were in the ballroom. The skylights were finally fixed, but a layer of snow covered the top of them, making the ballroom dark and cavelike. Aurora assured me that the snow would be removed in time for my engagement party, as if I were worried about that.

She flitted about the room, mapping out where the tables and decorations would be. I helped as often as she let me, which wasn't very often. Her poor assistant was running around like mad to do everything Aurora asked.

When she finally let her assistant go for the night, I was sitting at the grand piano, playing the opening to "Für Elise" repeatedly, since it was the only bit I knew.

"You'll have to take piano lessons," Aurora said. She had a thick black binder filled with all the wedding information, and she dropped it on the piano, making the instrument twang. "I can't believe you didn't already have them. What kind of host family did you live with?"

"You know what kind of host family I had." I continued playing the same bars, louder now since I knew it was getting on her nerves. "You've met my brother."

"About that," Aurora said. She pulled a few bobby pins from her hair, letting her loose curls fall free. "You need to stop referring to him as your brother. It's in poor taste."

"I'm aware," I said. "But it's a hard habit to break."

"You have many habits you need to break." She ran her fingers through her hair. "If you weren't the Princess, I wouldn't bother to help you break them."

"Well, thank you for your time and consideration," I muttered.

"I know you're being facetious, but you are welcome." She opened her binder, leafing through it. "We don't have time for Frederique Von Ellsin to make you a gown for the party, so he's bringing over some of his best pieces tomorrow at noon so you can be fitted."

"That sounds fun," I said, and I wasn't lying. Frederique had made my gown for the christening ceremony, and I enjoyed meeting him.

"Princess!" Aurora snapped. "Will you stop playing that song?"

"Of course." I closed the piano cover. "All you had to do was ask."

"Thank you." Aurora smiled thinly at me. "You do need to work on your manners, Princess."

"My manners are fine when they need to be." I sighed. "But right now I'm tired, and we've been at this all day. Can we regroup tomorrow?"

"You are so *lucky* I'm letting you marry my son." She shook her head and slammed the binder shut. "You are rude and ungrateful and so unladylike. Your mother has almost gotten us killed repeatedly, and my son should be next in line for the crown, not you. If he didn't have some unfounded fondness for you, he would overthrow you and take his rightful place."

"Wow." I stared at her with wide eyes. I really had no idea what to say to that.

"It's a disgrace that he's marrying you." She clicked her tongue. "If anybody found out the way that tracker Finn tainted you, he'd become the laughingstock of the kingdom." She touched her temple and shook her head. "You are just so lucky."

"You are absolutely right." I stood up, clenching my hands at my side. "I am so lucky that your son is nothing like you. I'm going to be Queen, not you. Know your place, *Marksinna*."

She looked up at me, her skin blanched and her dark eyes startled. She blinked, as if she couldn't believe what had just happened. The planning had been as daunting for her as it had been for me, and for a moment she'd forgotten her role.

"Princess, I am truly sorry," she stammered. "I didn't mean that. I've been under so much stress."

"We all have," I reminded her.

Aurora finished gathering her things and mumbled several more apologies. She hurried out of the ballroom, saying she was needed at home. I don't think she'd ever left so quickly before. I didn't know if I'd done the right thing standing up to her, but right then I didn't care.

What I did know was that I had a rare moment when I was completely alone. No guards around me. No Duncan or Tove or Aurora. And I could really use some fresh air.

I hurried before someone found me. If I waited, I knew someone would come along and want something from me. Probably a conversation, but I didn't want to talk. I wanted a moment to breathe.

I ran down the hall of the north wing, bursting through the side door onto a narrow gravel trail lined with tall hedges. It curved around the house, leading down to the bluffs before it opened onto a beautiful garden.

Snow covered everything, making it glitter like diamonds under the moonlight. The wintry weather should've killed off all the plants, but the blue, pink, and purple flowers were in full bloom. The frost on their petals only made them more beautiful.

The vines of ivy and wisteria that grew over the wall remained green and vibrant. Even the small waterfall that ran through the orchard of blossoming trees still flowed, instead of freezing solid the way it should have.

A thin blanket of snow crunched cold under my bare feet, but I didn't care. I ran down the side of the bluff, slipping in a few places, but I never fell. Two curved garden benches stood next to the pond, and I sat down on the nearest one.

The garden was a little piece of magic, and I loved it for that. I leaned back, breathing in the cold night. My breath came out in a fog, and the moon sparkled off the ice crystals in the air. I'd been locked in the house for far too long.

A snap of a twig behind me pulled me from my thoughts, and I whirled around. I couldn't see anyone, but I saw shadows moving along a hedge near the brick wall.

"Who's there?" I asked.

I assumed it was Duncan or another tracker sent to fetch me. When nobody answered, I began to worry that I'd made a rash decision coming out here alone. I could defend myself, but I didn't want there to be a need for it.

"I know somebody's here." I stood up. I walked around the bench and peered through the trees.

I saw a figure standing by the wall. He was too far away to get a good look at his face, but the moon shimmered on his light hair.

"Who's there?" I repeated. I straightened up and tried to look as imposing as possible, which is quite hard for a Princess in a dress, alone in a garden at night.

"Princess?" He sounded surprised and stepped closer to me. When he ducked around a tree and walked toward me, I finally got a good look at him.

"Loki?" I asked, and I felt joy swell inside me, immediately followed by confusion. "What are you doing here?"

"I came for you." He seemed just as bewildered as I was. "What are you doing out here?"

"I needed fresh air. But I don't understand. How did you know I'd be out here?"

"I didn't. This is how I come in." He gestured to the wall behind him. "I scale the wall. You should really get security on that."

"Why are you here?" I asked.

"Don't pretend like you're not happy to see me." His cocky grin returned, lighting up his face. "I'm sure you've been miserable since I left."

"Hardly," I scoffed. "I've been planning my engagement party."

"Yes, I've heard about that dreadful business." He wrinkled his nose in disgust. "That's why I've come to save you."

"Save me?" I echoed.

"Yes, like a knight in shining armor." Loki spread his arms wide and bowed low. "I'll throw you over my shoulder and scale the wall with you like Rapunzel."

"Rapunzel used her hair so a prince could climb into a tower, not escape it," I told him.

"Forgive me. The Vittra don't believe in nursery rhymes or fairy tales."

"Neither do I," I said. "And I don't need to be rescued. I'm where I'm supposed to be."

"Oh, come, now." Loki shook his head. "Princess, you can't believe that. You're not supposed to be locked away in a horrible castle, engaged to a boring fool, forced to sneak out in the night for a chance to breathe."

"I appreciate your concern, Loki, but I'm happy here." Even as I said it, I wasn't sure if that was true or not.

"I can promise you a life of adventure." Loki grabbed a branch and swung over, so he landed on the bench with astonishing grace. "I'll take you to exotic places. Show you the world. Treat you the way a Princess really ought to be treated."

"That all sounds well and good." I smiled up at him. I was flattered by his invitation, even if I didn't trust it. "But . . . why?"

"Why?" Loki laughed. "Why not?"

"I can't help but feel like you're only trying to get me to shirk my responsibilities as a Trylle Princess so I can aid your cause," I said honestly.

"You think the King put me up to this?" Loki laughed again. "The King loathes me. Despises me. Threatens to behead me on a daily basis. The Queen had to go against his wishes to get me. He wanted you all to execute me."

"Now I really wanna go back to that," I said with a smirk.

"Who said anything about going back? I'm asking you to run away from all of this, from all the Trylle and the Vittra, the silly royals and their silly rules." He gestured widely around us.

"Is that why you looked upset when Sara suggested I come back with you?"

"That was dreadful," he admitted. "For one horrible minute, I thought you would accept, and that would be the end of everything."

I cocked my head at him. "The end of everything?"

"The King would never let you get away again," Loki explained. "And you couldn't survive there."

"Why are you so certain I wouldn't survive against the King?" I asked. "I'm strong and smart, and sometimes I'm even brave."

"That's exactly why. Because you're good and brave and kind and beautiful." He jumped down from the bench, landing right in front of me. "The King destroys anything that's beautiful."

"Then how have you survived for so long?" I meant to keep my tone teasing, but as soon as I asked it, his eyes flashed with pain, and he lowered them quickly.

"That story is too long for tonight, Princess, but I can assure you that my survival has come at a price." He swallowed hard, then cleared his throat, and his smirk returned. "Wait. Did you just call me brave and beautiful?"

"Hardly." I laughed and stepped away from him, all too aware of his presence next to me. He seemed to exude heat as well as charm. "So, what would happen if I took you up on this offer? Where would we go? What would we do?"

"I am so glad you asked." His whole face lit up. "I have some money. Not a lot, mind you, but I've hidden some of my mother's old jewelry. I could pawn it, and then we could go anywhere. Do anything your heart desired."

"That doesn't really sound like much of a plan."

"The Virgin Islands," Loki answered quickly and took another step toward me. "We wouldn't need passports to get there, and there's no trolls of any kind. We could spend all day in the ocean, and all night on the beach." He paused, his smile painfully sincere. "Just the two of us."

"I can't." I shook my head, and I hated how tempting the idea was. To run away from all the pressure and stress of the palace. "I can't let the kingdom down. I have a duty here, to these people."

"You have a duty to yourself to be happy!" Loki insisted.

"No, I don't," I said. "I have too much here. And let's not forget that I have a fiancé."

"Don't marry him." He scoffed at the idea. "Marry me instead."

"Marry you?" I laughed. "You told me that I should only marry for love."

"That I did." In that rare moment of honesty, Loki looked almost stunningly handsome. He stepped toward me, moving so close we were nearly touching. "Wendy, marry me."

"That's . . ." I shook my head, astounded by his proposal. "That doesn't even make sense, Loki. I barely know you, and you're . . . you're my enemy."

"I know I haven't known you that long, but I've felt . . . a connection from the moment I saw you, and I know you felt it too."

I floundered, wanting to deny him, but unable to. "Loki, a connection isn't enough to build a life on."

"I don't care where I come from or who your people are," he said simply. "I can make you happy, and you make me happy. We could have a happily ever after."

His eyes were on mine, and even in the dim light they glimmered gold. A slow wave started to wash over me as relaxation flowed through me. Just when I realized that Loki was trying to knock me out, the sensation stopped.

"What happened?" I asked, as the fog lifted from my mind. Loki stood inches in front of me, and I knew I should move away, but I didn't.

"I'm not going to do that to you," he said quietly. "What I told you before is still true. I want to know that when you're with me, it's because you want to be, not because you have to be."

"Loki—" I started to protest.

He put his hands on my face, and they felt warm on my skin, even though they should've been cold from scaling the wall. He leaned in to me, but he paused before his lips touched mine. His eyes met mine, searching them for any resistance, but I didn't have any.

His mouth covered mine, and warmth stirred inside me. He tasted sweet and cool, and his skin smelled of fresh rain. My knees felt weak, and my heart battered against my chest. His hands moved back, tangling in my hair and pressing me to him.

I wrapped my arms around him, and he felt strong and powerful against me. I could actually feel his muscles, like warm marble, and I knew he could crush me if he wanted to. But the way he touched me was passionate and delicate all at once.

I wanted to give in to him, to his invitation, but a voice of reason gnawed at me. My stomach fluttered with butterflies, then twisted with knots.

"No, Loki." I pulled my mouth from his, gasping for breath. I put my hands on his chest and took a step back. "I can't. I'm sorry."

"Wendy." Loki watched me walk backward away from him.

His expression was so desperate and vulnerable, it made my chest ache.

"I'm sorry. But I can't."

I turned and ran to the palace, afraid that I would change my mind if I hesitated any longer.

TWENTY-SEVEN

sacrifice

The next few days were a blur. I did everything I could to keep my mind off the kiss with Loki, or the horrible ache inside me that I knew I might never see him again. I just had to put it behind me and move forward with my engagement.

The training with Tove left me with a constant dull headache in the back of my skull. Making arrangements with his mother left me with pain in the remainder of my head. Willa tried her best to work as an intermediary, but Aurora didn't seem ready to let our earlier conflict go.

Elora was feeling better, so she joined us one afternoon. I thought having her there would help dispel the tension, but it didn't. When Aurora wasn't busy picking at me, she was picking at Elora. And when she wasn't doing that, they were both picking at me.

I spent most evenings in the library with Duncan, studying as much as I could about the Trylle way of life. I'd found a Tryllic dictionary, and I had to keep leafing through it as I looked through older documents. It was impossible to guess what it meant, since Tryllic didn't use the English alphabet. For example, the word *Tryllic* looked like this—Трыллиц.

With the small desk lamp as the only light in the room, I sat at the desk with my nose buried in a book. Duncan was at the shelves, combing through the acres of books to find ones that he thought would be best. He did know more about Trylle history than I did, but not much more.

"Burning the midnight oil?" Finn asked, scaring me so much I nearly screamed. He stood at the edge of the desk, and I hadn't even heard him come in.

"Yeah, I guess." I stared down at the faded pages of the book, keeping myself focused on them instead of Finn.

I hadn't talked to him since I'd kissed Loki. In a bizarre way, I felt as if I'd cheated on him. That was really silly, considering I was engaged to Tove, and what little Finn and I had together was long over.

"I have something I need to go check on," Duncan said, taking his cue to exit.

He didn't need to, since I doubted that Finn and I needed privacy, but it was nice that he tried. He gave me a hopeful smile before he slipped out, leaving me alone with Finn.

"What are you looking up?" Finn asked, nodding to the stacks of books on the desk.

"Anything. Everything." I shrugged. "I figured it was about time I got to know my history."

"It's a very large history," Finn said.

"Yeah. That's what I'm finding out." I leaned back in my chair so I could look up at him. The dim light from the lamp left most of his face in shadow, but his expressions were so unreadable any-way, it didn't really matter.

"The engagement party is tomorrow," he said. "Shouldn't you be upstairs primping and preening with Willa?"

"Nope. I get to do that in the morning." I sighed, thinking of the long day ahead of me tomorrow.

"On that note, a congratulations is in order."

"Really?" I closed the book I'd been reading and stood up.

I didn't want to be that close to Finn anymore, so I went over to a shelf and put the book away. I wasn't sure if it was the right spot, but I needed an excuse to move.

"You're getting married," Finn said, his voice cool and even. "Congratulations is appropriate."

"Whatever." I shoved the book hard in the bookcase and turned around to face him.

"You can't be mad at me for being supportive," Finn said, let-ting disbelief tinge his words.

"I can be mad at you for whatever I want." I leaned against the bookcase. "But I don't get you at all."

"What is there to get?" Finn asked.

"You practically ripped my arm off because you thought I was flirting with Loki. But I'm getting married to Tove, and you treat us both like nothing's happening."

"That's entirely different." Finn shook his head. "The Vittra was bad for you. He would hurt you. Tove is your intended."

"My intended?" I scoffed. "Were you protecting me for him? Making sure that nobody else tainted me until Tove got me?"

"No, of course not. I was merely protecting *you*. Your good name, your image."

"Right. That's what you were doing when you had your tongue down my throat?"

"I don't know why you always resort to being so crude." He lowered his eyes in disapproval.

"I don't know why you always have to be so proper!" I shot back. "Can you tell me how you really feel for once? I'm marrying somebody else! Don't you care at all?"

"Of course I care!" Finn yelled, his eyes blazing.

"Then why aren't you doing something?" I asked as tears filled my eyes. "Why don't you at least try to stop me?"

"Because Tove will take care of you. He will defend you." Finn swallowed hard. "He will be able to do things for you, *with* you, that I never could. Why would I take that away from you?"

"Because you care about me."

"It's because I care about you that I *can't*!"

"I don't believe you." I shook my head. "You don't even care when I'm with him. How could you get so angry when I was with Loki? You admitted you were jealous when I hung out with Rhys. But when I'm around Tove, you're fine."

"I'm not fine." He sighed in frustration. "But it doesn't feel the same when you're with Tove. It doesn't bother me as much."

"How can it not bother you?" I asked, totally dismayed.

"Because he's gay, Wendy!" Finn said finally, sounding exasperated.

For a moment I was too stunned to say anything. I just played over every moment I'd ever shared with Tove until I realized that what Finn had said made sense.

"He's gay?" I asked quietly.

"Don't tell him I told you, okay?" Finn grimaced and looked

apologetic. "I shouldn't be doing that. It's his private thing, and it's not my job to be airing his business."

"Then why is he marrying me?"

"What did he tell you when he proposed?" Finn asked.

"He said . . . because he believed in me and wanted me to be the leader." I thought back to the conversation. "He did it to support me, to save our people. For the same reasons I accepted the proposal.

"He's gay," I repeated. After that sank in, something new hit me, and I shook my head. "That's why you don't care. You know that I don't love him, that I never will, so you'd rather me marry him? But you thought I loved Loki, or that I could."

"It's more than that, Wendy." Finn shook his head. "Loki would hurt you."

"But that's not why you got mad. You were jealous because I might love somebody else." Anger surged through me. "You'd rather I live a lie than find happiness with someone else."

"You think you'd find happiness with a Vittra Markis?" Finn scoffed. "He's dangerous, Wendy. I didn't trust him around you."

"You didn't trust him because you knew I cared about him!"

"Yes!" Finn shouted. "And you shouldn't. He's a bad guy!"

"You don't even know him!" I yelled back.

"Do you want to go run off with him?" His face went stony, trying to hide any hurt he might feel. "Is that what you're saying? That I prevented you from living a fairy tale with him?"

"No, that's not what I'm saying." I swallowed my tears. "I prevented myself from running off with him because I knew what was best for the kingdom was me staying here. But I can't believe how selfish you are. You say everything you do is for me, but if that were true, you'd encourage me to go after happiness, instead of trapping me here with you."

"How have I trapped you here?" Finn asked.

"This!" I gestured between the two of us. "I can't have you, and I can't be without you. And I'm stuck in it with no way out. I care about you, and I can't stop, and you don't even care!"

"Wendy." His expression softened, and he moved toward me. I stepped back and ran into the bookshelf, so I couldn't go any farther. He reached out to touch me, and I pushed him off.

"No!" I shouted, with tears streaming down my face. "I hate that you do this me. I hate how crazy you make me. I hate *you*!"

He reached out, brushing hair back from my forehead. I jerked my head away, but he didn't move his hand. He'd moved right in front of me, so his body was against mine. I tried to push against him, but he stayed firm. He wouldn't move. His hand rested on my face, making me tilt my head up toward him.

His eyes were so black and deep, and they took my breath away, the way they always had. With his fingers, he traced along my hairline. The fight inside me disappeared, but the passion still lingered.

He leaned in, kissing me. His mouth pressed hungrily to mine. An intense quivering started in my heart but radiated out all over me, so my whole body shuddered. His stubble scraped against my skin as he kissed me desperately.

His lips traveled to my neck, and I moaned, burying my fingers in his hair. His weight sent us crashing against the shelves, and books tumbled out around us. We went with them, collapsing in a pile.

"Finn!" Thomas's voice boomed, interrupting us.

Finn stopped kissing me, but he remained on top of me. His breath came out in ragged gasps, and he continued to stare down at me. Passion smoldered in his eyes, but behind that, I saw terror. He realized that he'd done something terrible and didn't know how to undo it.

"Finn!" Thomas yelled again. "Get off her before someone sees you!"

"Yes, sir." Finn clambered off me, tripping over books as he got to his feet. I pulled down my dress, and got up much more slowly than him.

"Get out of here!" Thomas barked at him. "Get yourself cleaned up!"

"Yes, sir. Sorry, sir." Finn kept his eyes on the ground. He tried to cast a fleeting glance back at me, but he was too ashamed and simply darted out of the room.

"I'm sorry," I mumbled, unsure of what else to say. I could still taste Finn on my lips, feel his stubble on my cheek.

"You don't need to apologize to me," Thomas said, and the expression he gave me was much softer than the one he'd given his son. "You need to protect yourself, Princess. Go to your room, forget this ever happened, and pray that nobody ever finds out."

"Yes, of course." I nodded quickly and stepped carefully over the books. I'd almost made it out when Thomas stopped me.

"My son doesn't tell me much about his life," Thomas said, and I paused at the doorway, looking over my shoulder at him. "We've never been close. This job is a hard one. It keeps you isolated, and that is something that you and I have in common."

"I don't feel that isolated," I said. "I'm always surrounded."

"You've been fortunate, but it won't always be that way." He licked his lips and paused. "Sometimes you have to choose between love and duty. It's a hard choice, the hardest you'll ever make, but there is only one right answer."

"And you're saying that it's duty?" I asked.

"I'm saying duty was the right answer for me," Thomas explained carefully. "And duty will always be the right answer for Finn."

"Yes." I nodded, lowering my eyes. "That I know all too well."

"Trackers are often looked down upon." He held up his hand to silence me before I could argue. "Not by everyone, but by many. We're pitied. But it's an honorable life, living in service of people. Knowing that we are essential to creating a better world for the kingdom.

"The Queen lives in service as much as a tracker, maybe even more so. Your mother's whole life has been given to the people here. There is no greater honor than that. No greater deed. That is going to be your honor, Princess."

"I know," I said, feeling even more overwhelmed by the prospect.

"In the end, you find that with sacrifice, you receive more than you give," he said. "I've enjoyed talking with you, Princess, but I will let you get to your room."

"Yes, of course," I said.

Thomas bowed before me, and I turned away. I ran all the way up to my room, lifting my dress so I wouldn't trip on my hem. My hair had come loose so it fell around my face, and I was grateful for it. I didn't need anyone to see the shame in my expression or the tears that stained my cheeks.

honor

"Y ou look amazing," Willa assured my reflection for the hundredth time.

I stood in front of the mirror. Willa was at my back. I was sure I appeared as if I were admiring my white gown, but I barely even recognized myself.

Only days before my engagement party, I'd kissed two different guys. It was odd because, of the two kisses, I found myself replaying Loki's more often. His kiss felt oddly refreshing, breathing new life into my soul. Even though Finn's had felt amazing at the time, once it was over, it only seemed to drain me of the energy I had. Loki had asked me to marry him, and Finn had pushed me away, the way he always did. The way he always would.

After everything that happened, I'd wanted to cry, but in the end, the way I felt about either Loki or Finn didn't matter. Not anymore. I was a Princess, with a duty to her kingdom and her fiancé. Tove and Förening deserved more, so I had to be more. I had to become what they needed.

"Come on, Wendy." Willa grabbed my arm, pulling me away.

"The party is about to start. We don't have time for you to keep staring at yourself."

I nodded and followed her, thinking I'd have time to compose myself, but as soon as I stepped out of my room, I found Tove waiting by the door.

"Sorry," he said when he saw my expression. "I didn't mean to startle you."

"No, it's okay." My mouth felt numb, and it was hard to speak.

"I'll leave you two lovebirds alone." Willa winked at me as she walked away.

"I hope it's not bad luck to see you before the engagement party." He dug in his pocket. "I'm not sure what the protocol is, but I had to give you something. I thought it'd be better to do it before the party."

"You didn't need to get me anything."

"Yeah, I did." Tove pulled a ring box out of his pocket. "It's kinda my job. I should've given it to you when I proposed, but that was kind of a lame proposal."

"I liked it." I smiled at him. "It was sweet."

"Well, I hope you like the ring." He held it out to me, the velvet lid still closed. "My mom hates it."

"I'm sure I'll love it, then," I said, and he laughed.

I took the box from him, and with trembling hands, I opened the lid. It was a thick platinum band, designed to look like ivy wrapped around the giant emerald inlaid in the center. A few small diamonds were dotted around the band.

"Oh, Tove, it's beautiful." As I slid it on my finger, I was actually getting choked up. It was a lovely ring, and such a lovely gesture.

Even though he hadn't told me, and I didn't plan on calling

him out on it, I knew Finn was right. Tove was gay. We would never be in love with each other, but we were friends, and we could find some kind of happiness together. Hopefully.

"Yeah?" Tove had a relieved lopsided grin and ran a hand through his hair. "Good. I was really worried. I had no idea what you would think."

"No, it's absolutely perfect." I smiled up at him with tears in my eyes.

"Good." He bit his lip. "You look really beautiful today."

"Thank you. You look really good yourself." I motioned to his nice suit pants and vest. "You clean up good, Markis."

"Thank you, Princess." He held out his arm so I could take it. "Shall we head down to our engagement party?"

"We shall," I said and looped my arm through his. We walked toward the ballroom to become the leaders the Trylle needed.

ascend

To all the readers—thank you for all your support.

ONE

amnesty

I had my back to the room as I stared out the window. It was a trick I'd learned from my mother to make me seem more in control. Elora had given me lots of tips the past few months, but the ones about commanding a meeting were the most useful.

"Princess, I think you're being naive," the Chancellor said. "You can't turn the entire society on its head."

"I'm not." I turned back, giving him a cool gaze, and he lowered his eyes and balled up his handkerchief in his hand. "But we can't ignore the problems any longer."

I surveyed the meeting room, doing my best to seem as cold and imposing as Elora always had. I didn't plan to be a cruel ruler, but they wouldn't listen to weakness. If I wanted to make a change here, I had to be firm.

Since Elora had become incapacitated, I'd been running the day-to-day activities of the palace, which included a lot of meetings. The board of advisers seemed to take up a lot of my time.

The Chancellor had been voted into his position by the Trylle people, but as soon as his term was up, I planned to campaign against him as hard as I could. He was a conniving coward, and we needed somebody much stronger in his position.

Garrett Strom—my mother's "confidant"—was here today, but he didn't always attend these meetings. Depending on how Elora was doing that day, he often chose to stay and care for her instead.

My assistant Joss sat at the back of the room, furiously scribbling down notes as we talked. She was a small human girl who grew up in Förening as a mänsklig and worked as Elora's secretary. Since I'd been running the palace, I'd inherited Joss as my own assistant.

Duncan, my bodyguard, was stationed by the door, where he stood during all the meetings. He followed me everywhere, like a shadow, and though he was clumsy and small, he was smarter than people gave him credit for. I'd grown to respect and appreciate his presence the last few months, even if he couldn't completely take the place of my last guard, Finn Holmes.

Aurora Kroner sat at the head of the table, and next to her was Tove, my fiancé. He was usually the only one on my side, and I was grateful to have him here. I didn't know how I would manage ruling if I felt completely alone.

Also in attendance were Marksinna Laris, a woman I didn't

particularly trust, but she was one of the most influential people in Förening; Markis Bain, who was in charge of changeling placement; Markis Court, the treasurer for the palace; and Thomas Holmes, the head guard in charge of security and all the trackers.

A few other high-ranking officials sat around the table, all of their expressions solemn. The situation for the Trylle was growing increasingly dire, and I was proposing change. They didn't want me to change anything—they wanted me to support the system they'd had for centuries, but that system wasn't working anymore. Our society was crumbling, and they refused to see the roles they played in its breakdown.

"With all due respect, Princess," Aurora began, her voice so sweet I could barely hear the venom underneath, "we have bigger issues at hand. The Vittra are only getting stronger, and with the truce about to end—"

"The truce," Marksinna Laris snorted, cutting her off. "Like that's done us any good."

"The truce isn't over yet," I said, standing up straighter. "Our trackers are out taking care of the problems now, which is why I think it's so important that we have something in place for them when they return."

"We can worry about that *when* they return," the Chancellor said. "Let's deal with saving our asses right now."

"I'm not asking to redistribute the wealth or calling to abolish the monarchy," I said. "I am simply saying that the trackers are out there risking their lives to save us, to protect our changelings, and they deserve a real house to come back to. We should be setting aside money *now* so that when this is over, we can begin building them real homes."

"As noble as that is, Princess, we should be saving our money for the Vittra," Markis Bain said. He was quiet and polite, even when he disagreed with me, and he was one of the few royals whom I felt actually wanted to do what was best for all the people.

"We can't pay the Vittra off," Tove interjected. "This isn't about money. This is about power. We all know what they want, and a few thousand—or even a few *million*—dollars won't matter to them. The Vittra King will refuse it."

"I will do everything in my power to keep Förening safe, but you are all correct," I said. "We have yet to find a reasonable solution for the Vittra. That means this might very well turn into a bloody fight, and if it does, we need to support our troops. They deserve the best care, including adequate housing and access to our healers if they're injured in wartime."

"Healers for a tracker?" Marksinna Laris laughed, and a few others chuckled along with her. "Don't be ridiculous."

"Why is that ridiculous?" I asked, working to keep the ice from my voice. "They are expected to die for us, but we aren't willing to heal their wounds? We cannot ask more of them than we are willing to give ourselves."

"They are lower than us," Laris said, as if I didn't understand the concept. "We are in charge for a reason. Why on earth should we treat them as equals when they are not?"

"Because it's basic decency," I argued. "We may not be human, but that doesn't mean we have to be devoid of humanity. This is why our people are leaving our cities and preferring to live among the humans, letting their powers die. We must offer them some bit of happiness, otherwise why would they stay?"

Laris muttered something under her breath, keeping her steely eyes locked on the oak table. Her black hair was slicked back, pulled in a bun so tight her face looked strained. This was probably done on purpose to draw attention to her strength.

Marksinna Laris was a very powerful Trylle, able to produce and control fire, and something that strong was draining. Trylle powers weakened them, taking some of their life and aging them prematurely.

But if the Trylle didn't use them, the abilities did something to their minds, eating at their thoughts and making them crazy. This was especially true for Tove, who would appear scattered and rude if he didn't find constant outlets for his psychokinesis.

"It is time for a change," Tove said, speaking up when the room had fallen into annoyed silence. "It can be gradual, but it's going to happen."

A knock at the door stopped anyone from offering a rebuttal, but from the beet-red color of the Chancellor's face, it looked like he had a few words he wanted to get out.

Duncan opened the door, and Willa poked her head in, smiling uncertainly. Since she was a Marksinna, Garrett's daughter, and my best friend, she had every right to be here. I'd extended an invitation for her to attend these meetings, but she always declined, saying she was afraid she would do more harm than good. She had a hard time being polite when she disagreed with people.

"Sorry," Willa said, and Duncan stepped aside so she could come in. "I didn't mean to interrupt. It's just that it's after five, and I was supposed to get the Princess at three for her birthday celebration."

I glanced at the clock, realizing this had dragged on much longer than I'd originally planned. Willa walked over to me and gave the room an apologetic smile, but I knew she'd pull me out kicking and screaming if I didn't put an end to the meeting.

"Ah, yes." The Chancellor smiled at me with a disturbing hunger in his eyes. "I'd forgotten that you'll be eighteen tomorrow." He licked his lips, and Tove stood up, purposely blocking the Chancellor's view of me.

"Sorry, everyone," Tove said, "but the Princess and I have plans this evening. We'll pick up this meeting next week, then?"

"You're going back to work next week?" Laris looked appalled. "So soon after your wedding? Aren't you and the Princess taking a honeymoon?"

"With the state of things, I don't think it's wise," I said. "I have too much to get done here."

While that was true enough, that wasn't the only reason I'd skipped out on a honeymoon. As much as I'd grown to like Tove, I couldn't imagine what the two of us would do on one. I hadn't even let myself think about how we would spend our wedding night.

"We need to go over the changeling contracts," Markis Bain said, standing up in a hurry. "Since the trackers are bringing the changelings back early, and some families decline to do changelings anymore, the placements have all been moved around. I need you to sign off on them."

"Enough talk of business." Willa looped her arm through mine, preparing to lead me out of the room. "The Princess will be back to work on Monday, and she can sign anything you want then."

"Willa, it will only take a second to sign them," I said, but she glared at me, so I gave Bain a polite smile. "I will look them over first thing Monday morning."

Tove stayed behind a moment to say something to Bain, but he caught up with us a few moments later in the hall. Even though we were out of the meeting, Willa still kept her arm through mine as we walked.

Duncan stayed a step behind us when we were in the south wing. I'd gotten talked to many, many times about how I couldn't treat Duncan as an equal while business was being conducted and there were Trylle officials at work around us.

"Princess?" Joss said, scampering behind me with papers spilling out of her binder. "Princess, do you want me to arrange a meeting on Monday with Markis Bain for the contracts?"

"Yes, that would be fantastic," I said, slowing so I could talk to her. "Thank you, Joss."

"You have a meeting at ten A.M. with the Markis of Oslinna." Joss flipped through the appointment section of the binder, and a paper flew out. Duncan snatched it before it fell to the floor and handed it to her. "Thank you. Sorry. So, Princess, do you want to meet Markis Bain before or after that meeting?"

"She'll be going back to work just after getting married," Willa said. "Of course she won't be there first thing in the morning. Make it for the afternoon."

I glanced over at Tove walking next to me, but his expression was blank. Since proposing to me, he'd actually spoken very little of getting married. His mother and Willa had done most of the planning, so I hadn't even talked to him about what he thought of colors or flower arrangements. Everything had been decided for us, so we had little to discuss.

"Does two in the afternoon work for you?" Joss asked.

"Yes, that would be perfect," I said. "Thanks, Joss."

"All right." Joss stopped to hurriedly scribble down the time in the binder.

"Now she's off until Monday," Willa told Joss over her shoulder. "That means five whole days where nobody calls her, talks to her, or meets with her. Remember that, Joss. If anybody asks for the Princess, she cannot be reached."

"Yes, of course, Marksinna Strom." Joss smiled. "Happy birthday, Princess, and good luck with your wedding!"

"I can't believe how much of a workaholic you are," Willa said with a sigh as we walked away. "When you're Queen, I'll never see you at all."

"Sorry," I said. "I tried to get out of the meeting sooner, but things have been getting out of hand lately."

"That Laris is driving me batty," Tove said, grimacing at the thought of her. "When you're Queen, you should banish her."

"When I'm Queen, you'll be King," I pointed out. "You can banish her yourself."

"Well, wait until you see what we have planned for you tonight." Duncan grinned. "You'll be having too much fun to worry about Laris or anybody else."

Fortunately, since I was getting married in a few days, I'd gotten out of the usual ball that would happen for a Princess's birthday. Elora and Aurora had planned that the wedding would take place immediately after I turned eighteen. My birthday was on a Wednesday, and I was getting married on Saturday, leaving no time for a massive Trylle birthday party.

Willa insisted on throwing me a small party anyway, even though I didn't really want one. Considering everything that was happening in Förening, it felt like sacrilege. The Vittra had set up a peace treaty with us, agreeing not to attack us until I became Queen.

What we hadn't realized at the time was the specific language they had used. They wouldn't attack *us*, meaning the Trylle living in Förening. Everyone else was fair game.

The Vittra had started going after our changelings, the ones that were still left with their host families in human society. They'd taken a few before we caught on, but as soon as we did, we sent all our best trackers to bring home any changeling over the age of sixteen, including most of the trackers serving as palace bodyguards. For anyone younger than that, our trackers were supposed to stand guard and watch them. We knew the Vittra would avoid taking them because they couldn't do so without setting off an Amber Alert. Still, we felt that every precaution must be taken to protect the most vulnerable among us.

That left us at a horrible disadvantage. To protect the changelings, our trackers had to be in the field, so they couldn't be here guarding the palace. We would be more exposed to an attack if the Vittra went back on their part of the deal, but I didn't see what choice we had. We couldn't let them kidnap and hurt our children, so I sent every tracker I could out into the field.

Finn had been gone almost continuously for months. He was the best tracker we had, and he'd been returning the changelings to all the Trylle communities. I hadn't seen him since before Christmas, and sometimes I still missed him, but the longing was fading.

He'd made it clear that his duty came before everything else and I could never be a real part of his life. I was marrying someone else, and even though I still cared about Finn, I had to put that behind me and move past it.

"Where is this party happening anyway?" I asked Willa, pushing thoughts of Finn from my mind.

"Upstairs," Willa said, leading me toward the grand staircase in the front hall. "Matt's up there putting on the finishing touches."

"Finishing touches?" I raised an eyebrow.

Someone pounded violently on the front door, making the door shake and the chandelier above us tremble. Normally people rang the doorbell, but our visitor was nearly beating down the door.

"Stay back, Princess," Duncan said as he walked over to the entrance.

"Duncan, I can get it," I said.

If somebody hit the door hard enough to make the front hall quake, I was afraid of what they would do to him. I made a move for the door, but Willa stopped me.

"Wendy, let him," she said firmly. "You and Tove will be here if he needs you."

"No." I pulled myself from her grip and went after Duncan, to defend him if I needed to.

That sounded silly, since he was supposed to be my bodyguard, but I was more powerful than him. He was really only meant to serve as a shield if need be, but I would never let him do that.

When he opened the door, I was right behind him. Duncan meant to only partially open the door so he could see what waited for us outside, but a gust of wind came up, blowing it open and sending snow swirling around the front hall.

A blast of cold air struck me, but it died down almost instantly. Willa could control the wind when she wanted to, so as soon as it blew inside the palace, she raised her hand to stop it.

A figure stood before us, bracing himself with his hands on either side of the doorway. He was slumped forward, his head hanging down, and snow covered his black sweater. His clothes were ragged, worn, and shredded in most places.

"Can we help you?" Duncan asked.

"I need the Princess," he said, and as soon as I heard his voice, a shiver shot through me.

"Loki?" I gasped.

"Princess?" Loki lifted his head.

He smiled crookedly, but his smile didn't have its usual

bravado. His caramel eyes looked tired and pained, and he had a fading bruise on his cheek. Despite all that, he was still just as gorgeous as I remembered him, and my breath caught in my throat.

"What happened to you?" I asked. "What are you doing here?"

"I apologize for the intrusion, Princess," he said, his smile already fading. "And as much as I'd like to say that I'm here for pleasure, I . . ." He swallowed something back, and his hands gripped tighter on the door frame.

"Are you all right?" I asked, pushing past Duncan.

"I . . ." Loki started to speak, but his knees gave out. He pitched forward, and I rushed to catch him. He fell into my arms, and I lowered him to the floor.

"Loki?" I brushed the hair back from his eyes, and they fluttered open.

"Wendy." He smiled up at me, but the smile was weak. "If I'd known that this is what it would take to get you to hold me, I would've collapsed a long time ago."

"What is going on, Loki?" I asked gently. If he hadn't been so obviously distressed, I would've swatted him for that comment, but he grimaced in pain when I touched his face.

"Amnesty," he said thickly, and his eyes closed. "I need amnesty, Princess." His head tilted to the side, and his body relaxed. He'd passed out.

birthday

Tove and Duncan had carried Loki up to the servants' quarters on the second floor. Willa went back to help Matt so he wouldn't worry, and I sent Duncan to get Thomas because I had no idea what we should do with Loki. He was unconscious, so I couldn't ask him what had happened.

"Are you going to give him amnesty?" Tove asked. He stood next to me with his arms folded over his chest, staring down at Loki.

"I don't know." I shook my head. "It depends on what he says." I glanced over at Tove. "Why? Do you think I should?"

"I don't know," he said finally. "But I will support any decision you make."

"Thank you," I said, but I hadn't expected any different from him. "Can you see if there's a doctor that will look at him?"

"You don't want me to get my mother?" Tove asked. His

mother was a healer, meaning she could put her hands on someone and heal almost any wound that person might have.

"No. She would never heal a Vittra. Besides, I don't want anyone to know that Loki is here. Not yet," I said. "I need an actual doctor. There is a mänks doctor in town, isn't there?"

"Yeah." He nodded. "I'll get him." He turned to leave but paused at the door. "You'll be okay with the Vittra Markis?"

I smiled. "Yes, of course."

Tove nodded, then left me alone with Loki. I took a deep breath and tried to figure out what to do. Loki lay on his back, his light hair cascading across his forehead. Somehow he was even more attractive asleep than he was awake.

He hadn't stirred at all when they'd carried him up, and Duncan had jostled and nearly dropped him many times. Loki had always dressed well, and while his clothes looked like they had once been nice, they were little more than rags now.

I sat down on the edge of the bed next to him and touched a hole in his shirt. The skin underneath was discolored and swollen. Tentatively, I lifted his shirt, and when Loki didn't wake, I pushed it up more.

I felt strange and almost perverse undressing him, but I wanted to check and make sure there weren't any life-threatening contusions. If he was seriously injured or appeared to have any broken bones, I would summon Aurora and make her heal him, whether she wanted to or not. I wouldn't let Loki die because she was prejudiced.

After I pulled his shirt over his head, I got my first good look at him, and my breath caught in my throat. Under ordinary circumstances, I was sure his physique would be stunning, but that wasn't what shocked me. His torso was covered with bruises, and his sides had long, thin scars on them.

They wrapped around, so I lifted him a bit, and his back was covered with them. They crisscrossed all over his skin, some of them older, but most of them appeared red and fresh.

Tears stung my eyes, and I put my hand to my mouth. I'd never seen Loki shirtless before, but I knew there had never been scars on his forearms. Most of this had happened since I'd seen him last.

Worse still, Loki had Vittra blood. Physically, he was incredibly strong, which was how he'd pounded at the door so hard it shook the front hall. That also meant he healed better than most. For him to look this terrible, somebody really had to have beaten the hell out of him, over and over again, so he wouldn't have time to heal.

A jagged scar stretched across his chest, as if someone had tried to stab him, and it reminded me of my own scar that ran along my stomach. My host mother had tried to kill me when I was a child, but that felt like a lifetime ago.

I touched Loki's chest, running my fingers over the bumps of his scar. I didn't know why exactly, but I felt compelled to, as if the scar connected us somehow.

"You just couldn't wait to get me naked, could you, Princess?" Loki asked tiredly. I started to pull my hand back, but he put his own hand over it, keeping it in place.

"No, I—I was checking for wounds," I stumbled. I wouldn't meet his gaze.

"I'm sure." He moved his thumb, almost caressing my hand, until it hit my ring. "What's that?" He tried to sit up to see it, so I lifted my hand, showing him the emerald-encrusted oval on my finger. "Is that a wedding ring?"

"No, engagement." I lowered my hand, resting it on the bed next to him. "I'm not married yet."

"I'm not too late, then." He smiled and settled back in the bed.

"Too late for what?" I asked.

"To stop you, of course." Still smiling, he closed his eyes.

"Is that why you're here?" I asked, failing to point out how near we were to my nuptials.

"I told you why I'm here," Loki said.

"What happened to you, Loki?" I asked, my voice growing thick when I thought about what he had to have gone through to get all those marks and bruises.

"Are you crying?" Loki asked and opened his eyes.

"No, I'm not crying." I wasn't, but my eyes were moist.

"Don't cry." He tried to sit up, but he winced when he lifted his head, so I put my hand gently on his chest to keep him down.

"You need to rest," I said.

"I will be fine." He put his hand over mine again, and I let him. "Eventually."

"Can you tell me what happened?" I asked. "Why do you need amnesty?"

"Remember when we were in the garden?" Loki asked.

Of course I remembered. Loki had snuck in over the wall

and asked me to run away with him. I had declined, but he'd stolen a kiss before he left, a rather nice kiss. My cheeks reddened slightly at the memory, and that made Loki smile wider.

"I see you do." He grinned.

"What does that have to do with anything?" I asked.

"*That* doesn't," Loki said, referring to the kiss. "I meant when I told you that the King hates me. He really does, Wendy." His eyes went dark for a minute.

"The Vittra King did this to you?" I asked, and my stomach tightened. "You mean Oren? My father?"

"Don't worry about it now," he said, trying to calm the anger burning in my eyes. "I'll be fine."

"Why?" I asked. "Why does the King hate you? Why did he do this to you?"

"Wendy, please." He closed his eyes. "I'm exhausted. I barely made it here. Can we have this conversation when I'm feeling a bit better? Say, in a month or two?"

"Loki," I said with a sigh, but he had a point. "Rest. But we will talk tomorrow. All right?"

"As you wish, Princess," he conceded, and he was already drifting back to sleep again.

I sat beside him for a few minutes longer, my hand still on his chest so I could feel his heartbeat pounding underneath. When I was certain he was asleep, I slid my hand out from under his, and I stood up.

In the hall, I wrapped my arms around myself. I couldn't shake the heavy feeling of guilt, as if I somehow shared responsibility for what had happened to Loki. I'd only spoken to Oren once, and I had no control over what he did. So why did I feel like it was my fault that Loki had been so brutally beaten?

I wasn't in the hall for long when Duncan and Thomas approached. I'd wanted to alert as few people as possible to Loki's presence, but I trusted Thomas. Not just because he was the head guard and Finn's father. He'd once had an illicit affair with Elora, so I thought he was good at keeping secrets.

"The Vittra Markis is in there?" Thomas asked, but he was already looking past me into the room where Loki slept.

"Yes, but he's been through hell," I said, rubbing my arms as if I had a chill. "He's going to be out for a while."

"Duncan said he asked for amnesty." Thomas looked down at me. "Are you going to give it to him?"

"I'm not sure yet," I said. "He hasn't been able to talk much. But I'm letting him stay here for now, at least until he heals and we can have a conversation."

"How do you want us to handle this?" Thomas asked.

"We can't tell Elora. Not right now," I said.

The last time Loki had been here, he'd been held captive. We didn't have a real prison, so Elora had used her telekinesis to hold him in place, but that had weakened her so much it nearly killed her. In fact, she hadn't recovered from it yet, and there would be no way she could do it again.

Besides that, I didn't think Loki was really capable of causing trouble. Not in his present state, at least. And he'd come to us of his own free will. We didn't need to hold him.

"We need a guard stationed outside his door at all times,

just to be safe," I said. "I don't think he's a threat, but I won't take any chances with the Vittra."

"I can stand watch now, but somebody will have to relieve me of my post eventually," Thomas said.

"I can take over later," Duncan offered.

"No." Thomas shook his head. "You stay with the Princess."

"Do you have any other guards you can trust?" I asked.

Most of the guards seemed to be gossips, and when one of them heard something, they all knew it. But there were very few guards around to tell anymore, since most of them were out protecting changelings.

Thomas nodded. "I know of one or two."

"Good," I said. "Make sure they know they cannot tell anybody about this. This all needs to stay quiet until I figure out what I'm going to do. Is that clear?"

"Yes, Your Highness," Thomas said. It always felt strange hearing people refer to me as *Highness*.

"Thank you," I told him.

Tove arrived shortly after that with the mänks doctor. I waited outside the room while he examined Loki. He woke up for it, but offered very little explanation for his injuries. When the doctor was done, he concluded that Loki didn't have any serious ailments, and he gave him medication for pain.

"Come on," Tove said, after the doctor had gone. "He's resting now. There's nothing more you can do. Why don't you go enjoy your party?"

"I'll let you know if there's any change with him," Thomas promised.

"Thank you." I nodded, and walked down the hall toward my room with Tove and Duncan.

I hadn't felt like having a party before Loki crashed the palace, and I felt even less like having one now. But I had to at least try to have fun so I wouldn't hurt Willa's or Matt's feelings. I knew they had gone to a lot of trouble, so I would play the part of the happy birthday girl for them.

"The doctor thinks he'll be okay," Duncan said, responding to my solemn expression.

"I know," I said.

"Why are you so worried about him anyway?" Duncan asked. "I know that you two are friends or something, but I don't understand. He's a Vittra, and he kidnapped you once."

"I'm not worried," I said, cutting him off and forcing a smile. "I'm excited for the party."

Duncan directed me to the upstairs living room. It had been Rhys's playroom when he was little, and they'd converted it into a place to hang out when he became a teenager. But the ceilings still had murals of clouds and childish things, and the walls were lined with short white shelves that still held a few of his old toys.

When I opened the door, I was bombarded by streamers and balloons. A banner with the words "Happy Birthday" in giant glitter letters hung on the back wall.

"Happy birthday!" Willa shouted before I could step inside.

"Happy birthday!" Rhys and Rhiannon said in unison.

"Thanks, guys," I said, pushing a helium-filled balloon out

of my face so I could go in. "You guys know my birthday isn't actually until tomorrow?"

"Of course I know," Matt said, his voice a little high from inhaling helium. He had a deflated balloon in his hands, and he tossed it aside to walk over to me. "I was there when you were born, remember?"

He'd been smiling, but it faltered when he realized what he'd said. Rhys and I had been switched at birth. Matt had actually been there for Rhys's birth, not mine.

"Well, I was there when you came home from the hospital anyway," Matt said and hugged me. "Happy birthday."

"Thank you," I said, hugging him back.

"And I definitely know your birthday," Rhys said, walking over to us. "Happy birthday!"

I smiled. "Happy birthday to you too. How does it feel to be eighteen?"

"Pretty much exactly the same as it does being seventeen." Rhys laughed. "Do you feel any older?"

"No, not really," I admitted.

"Oh, come on," Matt said. "You've matured so much in the past few months. I hardly even recognize you anymore."

"I'm still me, Matt," I said, shifting uneasily from his compliment.

I knew that I'd grown up some. Even physically I'd changed. I wore my hair down more now because I'd finally managed to tame my curls after a lifetime of struggling with them. Since I was running a kingdom now, I had to play the part and wear dark-colored gowns all the time. I had to look like a Princess.

"It's a good thing, Wendy." Matt smiled at me.

"Stop." I waved my hand. "No more seriousness. This is supposed to be a party."

"Party!" Rhys shouted and blew into one of those cardboard horns they use on New Year's.

Once the party got under way, I actually did have fun. This was much better than if I'd had a birthday ball, since most of the people here wouldn't be able to go.

Matt wasn't even supposed to live in the palace, and since Rhys and Rhiannon were mänks, they would never be allowed to attend a ball. Duncan would be let in, but he'd have to work. He wouldn't be able to laugh and goof around like he did now.

"Wendy, why don't you help me cut the cake?" Willa suggested while Tove attempted to act out some kind of clue for charades. Duncan had guessed everything under the sun, but judging by Tove's comically frustrated response, he wasn't even close.

"Um, sure," I said.

I'd been sitting on the couch, laughing at everyone's failed attempts, but I got up and went over to the table where Willa stood. A cake sat on a brightly colored tablecloth, next to a small pile of gifts. Both Rhys and I had specifically asked for no gifts, but here they were.

"Sorry," Willa said. "I didn't mean to drag you away from the fun, but I wanted to talk to you."

"Nah, it's okay," I said.

"Your brother made the cake." Willa gave me an apologetic

smile as she sliced through the white frosting. "He insisted that it was your favorite."

Matt might be a very good cook, but I wasn't sure. I dislike most foods, especially processed ones, but Matt had been trying hard to feed me for years, so I pretended to like a lot of things I didn't like. My annual chiffon birthday cake was one of them.

"It's not horrible," I said, but it kind of was. At least to me, and Willa and all the other Trylle.

"I wanted to let you know that I didn't tell Matt about Loki." Willa lowered her voice as she carefully put pieces of cake on small paper plates. "He would just worry."

"Thank you," I said and looked back over at Matt, laughing at the ridiculous miming Tove was doing. "I suppose I'll have to tell him eventually."

"You think Loki will be around for a while?" Willa asked. She'd gotten some frosting on her finger, and she licked it off, then grimaced.

I nodded. "Yeah, I think he will be."

"Well, don't worry about it now," she said quickly. "This is your last day to be a kid!"

I tried to push all of the fears and concerns I had about the kingdom, and Loki, from my mind. And eventually, when I let myself, I had a really good time with my friends.

scars

My dreams were filled with bad winter storms. Snow blowing so hard I couldn't see anything. Wind so cold I froze to the bone. But I had to keep going. I had to get through the storms.

Duncan woke me up a little after nine the next morning. Usually I got up at six or seven to get ready for the day, depending on what time my first meetings were. Since it was my birthday, I'd slept in a bit, and it felt nice but strange.

He wouldn't have woken me at all, except Elora had requested to eat breakfast with me today since it was my birthday. I didn't mind being woken up, though. Sleeping in that late made me feel surprisingly lazy.

I didn't even really know what I would do with the day. It'd been so long since I'd had a full day that was free of plans. Either I was working on things for the kingdom, helping Aurora with the wedding plans, or spending time with Willa and Matt.

I met Elora in her bedroom for breakfast, which was usually where I saw her. She'd been in decline for a while, but even before Christmas she'd been on bed rest. Aurora had tried healing her a few times, but she was only staving off the inevitable.

On my way to Elora's chambers in the south wing, I walked past the room Loki was staying in. His bedroom door was closed, and Thomas stood guard outside. He nodded once as I walked by, so I assumed everything was still going all right.

Elora's bedroom was massive. The double doors to her room were floor-to-ceiling, so they were nearly two stories high. The room itself could easily fit two of my bedrooms in it, and my room was quite large. Making the room look even larger was a full wall of windows, although she kept the shades drawn most of the time, preferring the dim light of a bedside lamp.

To fill the space, she had several armoires, a writing desk, the largest bed I'd ever seen, and a sitting area complete with a couch, two chairs, and a coffee table. Today she had a small dining table with two chairs set up near the window. It was all laid out with fruit, yogurt, and oatmeal—my favorite things.

The last few times I'd visited with her, Elora had been in bed, but she sat at the table today. Her long hair had once been jet-black, but it was now silver-white. Her dark eyes were clouded with cataracts, and her porcelain skin had wrinkled. She was still elegant and beautiful, and I imagined she always would be, but she'd aged so much.

She was pouring herself tea when I came in, her silk dressing gown flowing behind her.

"Would you like some tea, Wendy?" Elora asked without looking up at me. She'd only recently begun calling me Wendy. For a long time she refused to call me anything but Princess, but our relationship had been changing.

"Yes, please," I said, sitting across from her at the table. "What kind is it?"

"Blackberry." She filled the small teacup in front of me, then set the teapot on the table. "I hope you're hungry this morning. I had the chef whip us up a feast."

"I'm quite hungry, thank you," I said, and my stomach rumbled as proof.

"Go ahead." Elora gestured to the spread. "Take what you'd like."

"Aren't you eating?" I asked as I got myself a helping of raspberries.

"I'm eating some," Elora said, but she made no move to get a plate. "How is your birthday?"

"Good, so far. But I haven't been awake that long."

"Is Willa throwing you a party?" Elora asked, picking absently at a plum. "Garrett told me something about it."

"Yeah, she had a little party for me last night," I said between bites. "It was really nice."

"Oh, I assumed she would have it today."

"Rhys had plans today, and I don't have that many friends, so she thought it would be better to do it last night."

"I see." Elora took a sip of her tea and said nothing more for several minutes. She only watched me as I ate, which would've made me self-conscious before, but I was starting to realize that she just enjoyed watching me.

"How are you feeling today?" I asked.

"I'm moving about." She gave a small shoulder shrug and turned to look out the window.

The shades were open slightly, letting the brilliant light shine in. The treetops outside were covered in a heavy blanket of snow, and the reflection made the sun twice as bright.

"You look good today," I commented.

"You look nice today too," Elora said without turning back to me. "That's a lovely color on you."

I glanced down at my dress. It was dark blue with black lace designs over it. Willa had picked it out for me, and I did think it was really beautiful. But I still hadn't gotten used to Elora complimenting me.

"Thank you," I said.

"Did I ever tell you about the day you were born?" Elora asked.

"No." I'd been eating vanilla yogurt, but I set the spoon down on a plate. "You only told me that it was hasty."

"You were early," she said, her voice low, as if she were lost in thought. "My mother did that. She used her persuasion, and convinced my body to go into labor. It was the only way we could protect you, but you were two weeks early."

"Was I born in a hospital?" I asked, realizing I knew so little about my own birth.

"No." She shook her head. "We went to the city your host

family lived in. Oren thought I was interested in a family that lived in Atlanta, but I'd chosen the Everlys, who lived in northern New York.

"My mother and I stayed in a hotel nearby, hiding out in case Oren came after us," Elora went on. "Thomas watched the Everlys closely until he saw the mother go into labor."

"Thomas?" I asked.

"Yes, Thomas went with us," Elora said. "That's how I met him, actually, when we were on the run from my husband. Thomas was a new tracker, but he'd already proven to be very resourceful, so my mother chose him to help us."

"So he was there when I was born?" I asked.

"Yes, he was." She smiled at the thought. "I gave birth to you on the floor of a hotel bathroom. Mother used her powers on me, induced labor, and made it so I wouldn't scream or feel pain. And Thomas sat at my side, holding my hand and telling me it would all be fine."

"Were you scared?" I asked. "Giving birth like that?"

"I was terrified," she admitted. "But I had no choice. I needed to hide you and protect you. It had to be done."

"I know," I said. "You did the right thing. I understand that now."

"You were so small." Her smile changed, and she tilted her head. "I didn't know you would be so tiny, and you were so beautiful. You were born with a dark shock of hair, and these big dark eyes. You were beautiful and you were perfect and you were mine."

She paused, thinking, and a lump grew in my throat. It felt

so strange to hear my mother talking about me the way a mother talks about her children.

"I wanted to hold you," Elora said at length. "I begged my mother to let me hold you, and she said it would only make it worse. She held you, though, wrapping you in a bedsheet and staring down at you with tears in her eyes.

"Then she left," she continued. "She took you to the hospital to leave you with the Everlys, and brought home another baby that wasn't mine. She wanted me to hold him, to care for Rhys. She said that it would make it easier. But I didn't want him. *You* were my child, and I wanted you."

Elora turned to look at me then, her eyes looking clearer than they had in a while. "I did want you, Wendy. Despite everything that happened between your father and me, I wanted you. More than anything in the world."

I didn't say anything to that. I couldn't. If I did, I would cry, and I didn't want her to see that. Even as open as she was being, I didn't know how she would react to me weeping outright.

"But I couldn't have you." Elora turned back to the window. "Sometimes it seems to me that that's all my life has been, a series of things that I loved deeply that I could never have."

"I'm sorry," I said in a small voice.

"Don't be." She waved it off. "I made my choices, and I did the best I could." She forced a smile. "And look at me. This is your birthday. I shouldn't be whining to you."

"You're not whining." I wiped at my eyes as discreetly as I could and took another sip of my tea. "And I'm glad you told me."

"Anyway, we need to talk about switching the rooms around," Elora said, brushing her hair back from her face. "I plan to leave most of my furniture in here, unless you'd like to change it, which is your prerogative, of course."

"Switching what rooms?" I asked, confused.

"You're taking my room after you get married." She motioned around us. "This is the wedding chamber."

"Oh, right. Of course." I shook my head to clear the confusion. "I've been so busy with everything else that I'd forgotten."

"It's no matter," she said. "It shouldn't be much work to move things around, since it will only be personal items we're moving in and out. I'll have some of the trackers move my things out Friday, and I'll be staying in the room down the hall."

"They can move my things in then," I said. "And Tove's things too, since he'll be sharing the room with me."

"How is that going?" Elora leaned back in her chair, studying me. "Are you prepared for the wedding?"

"Aurora is certainly prepared for it." I sighed. "But if you're asking if I'm prepared to be married, I'm not sure. I guess I'll wing it."

"You and Tove will be all right." She smiled at me. "I'm certain of it."

"You're certain?" I raised an eyebrow. "Did you paint it?" Elora had the ability of precognition, but she could only see her visions of the future in static images.

"No." She laughed, shaking her head. "It's mother's intuition."

I ate a little more, but she only picked at the food. We talked, and it was strange to think that I'd miss her when she was gone. I hadn't actually known her for very long, and most of that time our relationship had been cold.

When I left, she was climbing back in bed and asked me to send someone up to clean the mess from breakfast. Duncan had been waiting outside the door for me, so he went in to take care of it.

While Duncan was busy with the dishes, I stopped by Loki's room to see how he was feeling. If he was better, I wanted to find out what was going on.

Thomas was still outside, so I knocked once and opened the door without waiting for a response. Loki was in the middle of changing clothes as I came in. He'd already traded his worn slacks for a pair of pajama pants, and he was holding a white T-shirt, preparing to put it on.

He had his back to me, and it was even worse than I'd thought.

"Oh, my god, Loki," I gasped.

"I didn't know you were coming." He turned around to face me, smirking. "Shall I leave the shirt off, then?"

"No, put the shirt on," I said, and I closed the door behind me so nobody could see or overhear us talking.

"You're no fun." He wrinkled his nose and pulled the shirt over his head.

"Your back is horrific."

"And I was just going to tell you how beautiful you look today, but I'm not going to bother now if you're going to talk that way." Loki sat back down on his bed, more lying than sitting.

"I'm being serious. What happened to you?"

"I already told you." He stared down at his legs and picked at lint on his pants. "The King hates me."

"Why?" I asked, already feeling indignation at my father for doing this to him. "Why in god's name would he do something so brutal to you?"

"You clearly don't know your father," Loki said. "This isn't that brutal for him."

"How is it not brutal?" I sat down on the bed next to him. "And you're nearly a Prince! How can he treat you this way?"

"He's the King." He shrugged. "He does what he wants."

"But what about the Queen?" I asked. "Didn't she try to stop him?"

"She tried to heal me at first, but eventually that became too much for her. And there's only so much Sara can do to counter Oren."

Sara, the Queen of the Vittra, was my stepmother, but she'd once been betrothed to Loki. She was more than ten years older than him, and it was an arranged engagement that ended when he was nine. They were never romantic, and she had always considered Loki more of a little brother and protected him as such.

"Did he personally do that to you?" I asked quietly.

"What?" Loki looked up at me, his golden eyes meeting mine.

He had a scar on his chin, and I was certain he hadn't had that before. His skin had been flawless and perfect, not that the scar detracted in any way from how handsome he was.

"That." I touched the mark on his chin. "Did he do that to you?"

"Yes," he answered thickly.

"How?" I moved my hand, touched a mark he had on his temple. "How did he do this to you?"

"Sometimes he'd hit me." Loki kept his eyes on me, letting me trace my fingers on his scars. "Or he'd kick me. But usually he used a cat."

"You mean like a living cat?" I gave him an odd expression, and he smiled.

"No, it's actually called a cat-o'-nine-tails. It's like a whip, but instead of one tail, it has nine. It inflicts more damage than a regular whip."

"Loki!" I dropped my hand, totally appalled. "He would do that to you? Why didn't you leave? Did you fight back?"

"Fighting back wouldn't do any good, and I left as soon as I was able," Loki said. "That's why I'm here now."

"He held you prisoner?" I asked.

"I was locked up in the dungeon." He shifted and turned away from me. "Wendy, I'm glad to see you, but I'd really rather not talk about this anymore."

"You want me to grant you amnesty," I said. "I need to know why he did this to you."

"Why?" Loki laughed darkly. "Why do you think, Wendy?"

"I don't know!"

"Because of you." He looked back at me, a strange, crooked smile on his face. "I didn't bring you back."

"But . . ." I furrowed my brow. "You asked to go back to the Vittra. We bartered with the King so he could have you."

"Yes, well, he still thought you would come around." He ran a hand through his hair and sat up straighter. "And you didn't. It was my fault for letting you go in the first place, and then for not bringing you back." He bit his lip and shook his head. "He's determined to get you, Wendy."

"So he tortured you?" I asked quietly, trying to keep the tremor from my voice. "Over me?"

"Wendy." Loki sighed and moved closer to me. Gently, almost cautiously, he put his arm around me. "What happened isn't your fault."

"Maybe. But maybe this wouldn't have happened if I'd run away with you."

"You still can."

"No, I can't." I shook my head. "I have so much I need to do here. I can't just leave it all behind. But you can stay here. I will grant you amnesty."

"Mmm, I knew it." He smiled. "You'd miss me too much if I left."

I laughed. "Hardly."

"Hardly?" Loki smirked.

He'd lowered his arm, so his hand was on my waist. Loki was incredibly near, and his muscles pressed against me. I knew that I should move away, that I had no justifiable reason to be this close to him, but I didn't move.

"Would you?" Loki asked, his voice low.

"Would I what?"

"Would you run away with me, if you didn't have all the responsibilities and the palace and all that?"

"I don't know," I said.

"I think you would."

"Of course you do." I looked away from him, but I didn't move away. "Where did you get the pajamas, by the way? You didn't bring anything with you when you came."

"I don't want to tell you."

"Why not?" I looked sharply at him.

"Because. I'll tell you, and it will ruin this whole mood," Loki said. "Can't we just sit here and look longingly into each other's eyes until we fall into each other's arms, kissing passionately?"

"No," I said and finally started to pull away from him. "Not if you don't tell me—"

"Tove," Loki said quickly, trying to hang on to me. He was much stronger than me, but he let me push him off.

"Of course." I stood up. "That's exactly the kind of thing my fiancé would do. He's always thinking of other people."

"It's just pajamas!" Loki insisted, like that would mean something. "Sure, he's a terrifically nice guy, but that doesn't matter."

"How does that *not* matter?" I asked.

"Because you don't love him."

"I care about him," I said, and he shrugged. "And it's not like I love you."

"Maybe not," he allowed. "But you will."

"You think so?" I asked.

"Mark my words, Princess," Loki said. "One day, you'll be madly in love with me."

"Okay." I laughed, because I didn't know how else to respond. "But I should go. If I've given you amnesty, that means I have to go about enacting it, and getting everyone to agree that it's not a suicidal decision."

"Thank you."

"You're welcome," I said and opened the door to go.

"It was worth it," Loki said suddenly.

"What was?" I turned back to him.

"Everything I went through," he said. "For you. It was worth it."

FOUR

fiancé

My relaxing birthday turned into a meeting frenzy because I'd granted Loki amnesty. Most people thought I was insane, and Loki had to be brought in for questioning. They had a big meeting in which Thomas asked him lots of questions, and Loki answered them the same way he had for me.

But truthfully, he didn't have to explain much after he lifted his shirt and showed them the scars. After that, they let him go lie down.

I did have a nice, quiet dinner with Willa and Matt, and that was something. My aunt Maggie called, and I talked to her for a while. She wanted to come see me, but I'd been stalling the best I could. I hadn't explained to her what I was yet, but she knew I was safe with Matt.

I'd wanted her to come out for Christmas, and I'd planned on telling her about everything then. But then the Vittra started going after the changelings, and I thought they might go after her to get to me, so I postponed seeing her again.

She'd been traveling a lot, which was good, but it didn't keep her from wondering what was going on with me. I couldn't wait until this all calmed down so I could finally have her in my life again. I missed her so much.

After dinner, I went back to my room and watched bad eighties movies with Duncan. He had to stay with me sixteen hours a day, then the night watchman took over. I'd wanted to study, since Tove was teaching me Tryllic, but Duncan wouldn't let me. He insisted I needed to shut off my mind and relax.

Duncan fell asleep in my room, which wasn't unusual. Nobody said anything, since he was my guard, and it was better that he was with me. He probably wouldn't be able to sleep in my room after Saturday, which made me a little sad. I slept sprawled out in my bed, and Duncan was curled up on the couch, a blanket draped over him.

"It's Thursday," I said when I woke up. I was still in bed, staring at the ceiling.

"It certainly is." Duncan yawned and stretched.

"I only have two days until I get married."

"I know." He got up and opened the shades, letting a wall of light into my room. "What are you doing today?"

"I need to stay busy." I sat up and squinted in the brightness. "And I don't care what anybody says about me needing to relax and take time off. I have to keep active. So I think I'll train with Tove today."

Duncan shrugged. "At least you're spending quality time with your fiancé."

Whenever I thought about the wedding I got a sick feeling in my stomach. Sometimes, if I thought about it too much, I actually threw up. I don't think I'd ever been so afraid to do anything in my life.

I showered and ate a quick breakfast, then I went down to Tove's room to see if he wanted to do any training. I'd mostly gotten the hang of my abilities, and they weren't something I wanted to lose, so I practiced often to keep them strong.

Tove had moved into the palace after the Vittra had kidnapped me, to help keep things safe. He was actually much stronger than any of the guards here, and he may have even been stronger than me. His room was down the hall from mine, and the door was open when I stopped by.

A few cardboard boxes were scattered around the room, some of them empty, one with books overflowing from it. Another sat on the bed, where Tove was putting a few pairs of jeans in it.

"Going somewhere?" I asked, leaning on the door frame.

"No, just getting ready for the move." He pointed down the hall toward Elora's room—our new room. "For Saturday."

"Oh," I said. "Right."

"Do you need help with anything?" Duncan asked. He'd followed me down to Tove's, since he followed me everywhere.

Tove shrugged. "Sure, if you want."

Duncan went in and pulled out some of Tove's clothes from the drawer. I stayed where I was, hating how awkward everything felt between us. When we were training or talking politics, everything was good with Tove and me. We were almost always on the same page, and we talked openly about anything having to do with the palace or work.

But when it came to our wedding and our actual relationship, neither of us could ever find the words.

This may have had something to do with what Finn had told me a few months ago—namely, that Tove was gay. I had yet to bring this up with Tove, so I couldn't say that it was true for certain, but I believed that it probably was.

"Did you want to train today?" I asked Tove.

"Yeah, that'd be great, actually." Tove sounded relieved.

Training helped him a lot too. The palace was so full of people, and Tove could sense their thoughts and emotions, creating loud static in his head. Training silenced that and focused him, making him more like a normal person.

"Outside?" I suggested.

"Yeah." Tove nodded.

"But it's so cold out," Duncan lamented.

"Why don't you stay in here?" I asked. "You can finish packing up some of Tove's stuff." Duncan looked uncertain for a second, so I went on, "I'll be with Tove. We can handle ourselves."

"Okay," Duncan said, sounding reluctant. "But I'll be here if you need me."

Tove and I headed out back to the secret garden behind the palace. It wasn't really secret, I guess, but it felt that way since it was hidden behind trees and a wall. Even though a strong January storm had been blowing the last few days, the garden was peaceful.

The garden was magic. All the flowers still bloomed, despite the snow, and they sparkled like diamonds from the frost. The thin waterfall that flowed down the bluff should've frozen over, but it still ran, babbling.

A drift of snow had blown over the path. Tove simply held out his hand, and the snow moved to the sides, parting like the Red Sea. He stopped in the orchard under the branches of a tree covered with frozen leaves and blue flowers.

"What shall we do today?" Tove asked.

"I don't know," I said. "What are you in the mood for?"

"How about a snowball fight?" he asked with a wicked grin.

Using only his mind, he threw four snowballs at me. I held up my hands, pushing them back with my own telekinesis, and they shattered into puffs of snow from the force. It was my turn to sling a few back at him, but he stopped them just as easily as I had.

He returned fire, this time with even more snowballs, and while I stopped most of them, one of them slipped by and nicked me in the leg. I ran back, hiding behind a tree to make my counterattack.

Tove and I played around, throwing snow at each other, but it became increasingly hard as it went on. It looked like a game, and it was fun, but it was more than that. Stopping a slew of snowballs helped me learn to quickly stop multiple attacks from different directions. I tried to return fire even before I stopped the snowball, and that helped me learn how to fight back while defending myself.

Those were two completely different tasks, and they were difficult to master. I'd been working on this for a while, but couldn't get it down. In my defense, neither could Tove, but he didn't really think it was possible. My mind would have to be able to hold something back and throw something at the same time, which it could do, but doing both things at the *exact* same time was impossible.

When we were both sufficiently frozen and exhausted, I collapsed back in the snow. I'd worn pants and a sweater today because I knew we were training, but all that exertion always left me overheated, so the snow felt good.

"Is that a truce, then?" Tove asked, panting as he lay down in the snow next to me.

"Truce," I said, laughing a little.

We both lay back, our arms spread out wide as if we meant to make snow angels, but neither of us did. Catching our breath, we stared up at the clouds moving above us.

"If this is what our marriage will be like, it won't be so bad, will it?" Tove asked, and it was an honest question.

"No, it won't be so bad," I agreed. "Snowball fights I can handle."

"Are you nervous?" he asked.

"A little." I turned my head to face him, pressing my cheek into the snow. "Are you?"

"Yeah, I am." He furrowed his brow, staring thoughtfully at the sky. "I think I'm most scared of the kiss. It will be our first time, and in front of all those people."

"Yeah," I said, and my stomach twisted at the thought. "But you can't really mess up a kiss."

"Do you think we should?" Tove asked, and he looked over at me.

"Kiss?" I asked. "You mean when we get married? I think we kind of have to."

"No, I mean, do you think we should *now*?" Tove sat up, propping himself up with his arms behind him. "Maybe it will make it a bit easier on Saturday."

"Do you think we should?" I asked, sitting too. "Do you want to?"

"I feel like we're in the third grade right now." He sighed and brushed snow off his pants. "But you're going to be my wife. We'll have to kiss."

"Yeah, we will."

"Okay. Let's do it." He smiled thinly at me. "Let's just kiss."

"Okay."

I swallowed hard and leaned forward. I closed my eyes, since it felt less embarrassing if I didn't have to see him. His lips were cold, and the kiss was chaste. It only lasted a moment, and my stomach swirled with nerves, but not the pleasurable kind.

"Well?" Tove asked, sitting up straighter.

"It was all right." I nodded, more to convince myself than him.

"Yeah, it was good." He licked his lips and looked away from me. "We can do this. Right?"

"Yeah," I said. "Of course we can. If anybody can, it's us. We're like the most powerful Trylle ever. And we're neat people. We can handle spending the rest of our lives with each other."

"Yeah," Tove said, sounding more encouraged by the prospect. "In fact, I'm looking forward to it. I like you. You like me. We have fun together. We agree on almost everything. We're going to be the best husband and wife ever."

"Yeah, totally," I chimed in. "Marriage is about friendship anyway."

"And it's not like people in our positions get to choose who they want to be with," Tove added, and I think I heard a hint of sadness in his voice. "But at least we get to be with someone we enjoy."

We both lapsed into silence after that, staring off at the snow, lost in our own thoughts. I wasn't sure exactly what Tove was thinking. I wasn't even sure what I was thinking.

I guess it didn't make much of a difference that Tove was gay. Even if he wasn't, it didn't change my feelings for him. We could still form a strong union and have a meaningful marriage in our own way. He deserved nothing less, and I could give that to him.

"Should we go in?" Tove asked abruptly. "I'm getting cold."

"Yeah, me too."

He got up and then took my hand, pulling me to my feet.

He didn't need to, but it was a nice gesture. We went into the palace together, neither of us saying anything, and I twisted at my engagement ring. The metal was icy from the snow, and it suddenly felt too large and heavy on my finger. I wanted to take it off and give it back, but I couldn't.

plans

I snuck in a copy of the Tryllic workbook Tove had gotten for me so I had something to do while Aurora went over all the last-minute details. It was the day before the wedding, so I hoped everything was on track. We didn't have time for anything else.

I sat in a chair with the book open on my lap while Aurora and Willa went over a checklist with about twenty wedding planners. Aurora had even put Duncan to work counting table centerpieces to make sure we had enough.

Sometimes they asked for my help, and I gave it, but I think Aurora was happier when I didn't have input so she could run the show.

All my bridesmaids were there, and most of them I'd never even met. Willa was my maid of honor, and she'd chosen the rest of the wedding party because she knew them. Aurora insisted that this had to be huge, so I had ten bridesmaids.

"It's the wedding of the century, and you're studying," Willa said with a sigh as the day drew to a close. Aurora had checked everything twice, and the only people left in the room were me, Willa, Aurora, and Duncan.

"I need to know this." I gestured to the book. "This is essential to being able to decipher old treaties. I don't need to know about lavish party planning. You and Aurora have that covered."

"That we do." Willa smiled. "I think everything's all set. You're going to have a fantastic day tomorrow."

"Thank you," I said and closed the book. "I really do appreciate everything you've done."

"Oh, come on, I loved it." She laughed. "If I can't have a fairy-tale wedding, at least I can plan one, right?"

"Just because you're not a Princess doesn't mean you can't have a fairy-tale wedding," I said and stood up.

She gave me a pained smile, and I realized what I'd said. Willa was a Marksinna dating my brother Matt, a human, and if anybody found out, she'd be banished. She wasn't even supposed to date him, let alone marry him.

"Sorry," I said.

"Don't be." She waved it off. "You're doing the best you can, and we all know it."

She was referring to my efforts for more equality among the Trylle, trackers, and mänks. We were losing a lot of our population because they fell in love with humans and then they were exiled. Nobody was staying around.

From any standpoint, it made more sense to let people love

who they loved. They were going to anyway, so if we stopped making it illegal, they would stick around more often and contribute to society.

I hadn't done much to convince people of this yet, because I was too busy struggling with the Vittra problem. Once we got it fixed (*if* we ever got it fixed), I would make equal rights for everyone in Förening my top priority.

"Are we all done here, then?" I asked.

"Yep," Willa said. "You've got nothing left to do except get some rest, and get pretty tomorrow before the wedding. Then you just have to say 'I do.'"

"I think I can handle that," I said, but I wasn't sure I could.

"Are you all right by yourself, Aurora?" Willa asked as we headed to the door.

"I'm just finishing a few things up," Aurora said without looking up from the papers she was going over. "Thank you, though."

"Thanks," I said. "I'll see you tomorrow, then."

"Sleep well, Princess." Aurora glanced up to smile at me.

Duncan and I walked Willa out, and she kept trying to convince me tomorrow would be fun. At the front door, she hugged me tightly and promised that everything would work out the way it was meant to.

I didn't know why that was supposed to be comforting. What if everything was meant to be a disaster? Knowing that it was meant to be horrible wouldn't make it any better.

"Do you want me to go in with you?" Duncan asked when we got to my bedroom.

"Not tonight." I shook my head. "I think I need some time to myself."

"I understand." He smiled reassuringly at me. "I'll see you in the morning, then."

"Thank you."

I shut the door behind me and flicked on my light, and I stared down at the giant ring on my finger. It signified that I belonged to Tove, to somebody I didn't love. I went over to my dresser to take off my jewelry, but I kept staring at the ring.

I couldn't help myself, and I pulled it off. It was really beautiful, and when Tove gave it to me it had been so sweet. But I'd begun to hate the band.

When I took it off, I glanced in the mirror behind the dresser, and I nearly screamed when I saw the reflection. Finn was sitting behind me on the bed. His eyes, dark as night, met mine in the mirror, and I could hardly breathe.

"Finn!" I gasped and whirled around to look at him. "What are you doing here?"

"I missed your birthday," he said, as if that answered my question. He lowered his eyes, looking at a small box he had in his hands. "I got you something."

"You got me something?" I leaned back on the dresser behind me, gripping it.

"Yeah." He nodded, still staring down at the box. "I picked it up outside of Portland two weeks ago. I meant to get back in time to give it to you on your birthday." He chewed the inside of his cheek. "But now that I'm here, I'm not sure I should give it to you at all."

"What are you talking about?" I asked.

"It doesn't feel right." Finn rubbed his face. "I don't even know what I'm doing here."

"Neither do I," I said. "Don't get me wrong. I'm happy to see you. I just . . . I don't understand."

"I know." He sighed. "It's a ring. What I got you." His gaze moved from me to the engagement ring sitting on the dresser beside me. "And you already have one."

"Why did you get me a ring?" I asked tentatively, and my heart beat erratically in my chest. I didn't know what Finn was saying or doing.

"I'm not proposing to you, if that's what you're asking." He shook his head. "I saw it and thought of you. But now it seems like poor taste. And here I am, the night before your wedding, sneaking in to give you a ring."

"Why did you sneak in?" I asked.

"I don't know." He looked away and laughed darkly. "That's a lie. I know exactly what I'm doing, but I have no idea *why* I'm doing it."

"What are you doing?" I asked quietly.

"I . . ." Finn stared off for a moment, then turned back to me and stood up.

"Finn, I—" I began, but he held up his hand, stopping me.

"No, I know you're marrying Tove," he said. "You need to do this. We both know that. It's what's best for you, and it's what I want for you." He paused. "But I want you for myself too."

All I'd ever wanted from Finn was for him to admit how he

felt about me, and he'd waited until the day before my wedding. It was too late to change anything, to take anything back. Not that I could have, even if I wanted to.

"Why are you telling me this?" I asked with tears swimming in my eyes.

"Because." Finn stepped toward me, stopping right in front of me.

He looked down at me, his eyes mesmerizing me the way they always did. He reached up, brushing back a tear from my cheek.

"Why?" I asked, my voice trembling.

"I needed you to know," he said, as if he didn't truly understand it himself.

He set the box on the dresser beside me, and his hand went to my waist, pulling me to him. I let go of the dresser and let him. My breath came out shallow as I stared up at him.

"Tomorrow you will belong to someone else," Finn said. "But tonight, you're with me."

His mouth pressed against mine, kissing me with that same rugged fierceness I had come to know and love. I wrapped my arms around him, gripping him as tightly as I could. He lifted me up, still keeping his lips on mine as he carried me over to the bed.

Finn lowered me down, and he was on top of me within seconds. I loved the feel of his body on mine, the weight of it pushing against me. His stubble scraped my skin as he covered my face and neck with kisses.

His hands went to the straps of my dress, pulling them

down, and I realized with some surprise how far things might actually go tonight. He'd always put the brakes on things before they got too heated, but his hands were cupping my breasts as he kissed me.

I reached up, unbuttoning his shirt so fast, one of the buttons snapped off. I ran my hands over his chest, delighting in the smooth contours of his muscles and the pounding of his heart. He leaned down, kissing me hungrily again, and his bare skin pressed to mine.

His skin smoldered against me, his mouth searched mine, and his arm was around me, holding me tighter still.

As we kissed, my heart swelled with happiness, and a surge of relief washed over me when I realized my first time would be with Finn. But that thought was immediately darkened when I realized something else.

My very first time might be with Finn, but it would also be my last time with him.

I still had to marry Tove tomorrow. And even if I didn't marry him, I could never be with Finn.

The last time I had really seen Finn was the night before my engagement party, nearly three months ago, when we kissed in the library. He'd been horrified by what he'd done, that he'd let himself choose a moment with me over duty, even for a second. He'd left the palace as soon as he had a chance.

He'd volunteered for the mission to track down the other changelings, and part of me knew it was to get away from me. We'd barely said a word to each other in months. I had been taking over the palace, making the most difficult decisions of my life, and I'd done it all without him.

If I slept with Finn now, that was exactly what would happen again, the same thing that always happened whenever we got close. He would vanish immediately afterward. He'd hide away in disgrace and avoid me.

And I couldn't bear that this time. He was asking me to give myself to him completely, and he'd never be willing to do the same. He would only disappear from my life again. I needed him to be here with me, by my side, instead of leaving in shame. I needed Finn to choose me over honor, and the best he could offer me was one night.

Even if I spent the night with him, it wouldn't mean anything. He would be gone tomorrow, I would marry Tove just as Finn would want me to, and I'd be even more heartbroken than before.

"What's wrong?" Finn asked, noticing a change in me.

"I can't," I whispered. "I'm sorry, but I can't do this."

"You're right. I'm sorry." Finn looked ashamed, and he scrambled to get off me. "I don't know what I was thinking. I'm sorry." He stood and hurriedly buttoned his shirt.

"No, Finn." I sat up, adjusting my dress. "You don't have to be sorry, but . . . I can't do this anymore."

"I understand." He smoothed out his hair and looked away from me.

"No, Finn, I mean . . ." I swallowed hard and let out a shaky breath. "I can't love you anymore."

He looked up at me, his eyes startled and hurt, but he said nothing. He only stood there for a moment.

"You said that I belong to somebody else tomorrow but you tonight, and that's not how it works, Finn." Tears slid down my cheeks, and I wiped them away. "I don't belong to anyone, and you don't get to just have a part of me when you can't help yourself."

"And I know that's never what you meant to do," I said. "Neither of us meant for things to end up this way. We were together when we could be. Hidden moments and stolen kisses. I get that. And I don't blame you or anything, but . . . I can't do it anymore."

"I hadn't . . ." Finn trailed off. "I never wanted this for you. I mean, this thing we've had going on, whatever it's been. You deserve more than I would ever be able to give you, more than I would ever be allowed to love you."

"I'm trying to change things," I said. "And I'll admit that part of it has been selfish. I wanted to repeal the laws so maybe someday we could have a chance to be together. But . . . I can't count on that. And even if I could, I am marrying somebody else tomorrow."

"I wouldn't expect any less of you, Princess," he said quietly. "I'm sorry to have disturbed you." He walked to the door and paused before leaving, but he didn't look back at me. "I wish you all the best for your marriage. I hope the two of you find nothing but happiness."

After Finn left, I tried not to cry. Willa would be so upset with me if my face was red and puffy tomorrow. I went into my closet, fighting back tears as I changed out of my gown and put on pajamas. On my way back to my bed, I noticed the small box on my dresser, the present from Finn.

Slowly, I opened the box. It was a thin silver band with my birthstone, a garnet, in the center of a heart. And for some reason, the sight of it broke me down. I lay down on my bed and sobbed, mourning a relationship I'd never even really been able to have.

altar

I wanted Matt to walk me down the aisle. He'd been the closest thing I had to a real parent for most of my life, but the other Trylle officials would have had a field day if he did. Marksinna Laris would probably get me overthrown on the grounds of insanity.

But at least Marksinna Laris and the other Trylle had no control over who I allowed in my dressing room. Duncan had been waiting outside my bedroom all morning, shooing anybody away who wasn't Willa or Matt. Everybody else could wait to see me until I was in the ballroom, with Willa's father Garrett giving me away.

I'd been ready for hours. After ending things with Finn, I hadn't really been able to sleep, and the sun hadn't even risen by the time I got up and started getting ready. Willa had come over early to help me, but I'd learned how to do my hair and makeup on my own. She really only helped button up my wedding gown, and she tried to comfort me, but that was all I needed.

"You're so pale," Willa said, almost sadly. "You're almost as white as your wedding dress."

She sat next to me on the chest at the foot of my bed. The long satin train of my gown swirled around us, and Willa continuously rearranged it to make sure it wouldn't get wrinkled or dirty. Her dress was lovely too, but it should be, since she picked it out. It was dark emerald with black embellishments.

"Stop fussing over her," Matt said when Willa once again tried to smooth out my dress. He'd been pacing the room, fiddling with his cuff links or pulling at the collar of his shirt.

"I'm not fussing." Willa gave him the evil eye but left my dress alone. "This is her wedding day. I want her to look perfect."

"You're making her nervous." Matt gestured to me, since I'd been staring off into space.

"If anyone's making her nervous, it's you," she countered. "You've been pacing around this room all morning."

"Sorry." He stopped moving but didn't look any less agitated. "My kid sister's getting married. And it's a lot sooner than I expected." He ruffled his short blond hair again and sighed. "You don't have to do this, Wendy. You know that, right? If you don't want to marry him, you don't have to. I mean, you shouldn't. You're too young to make a life decision like this anyway."

"Matt, she knows," Willa said. "You've only told her that exact same thing a thousand times today."

"Sorry," Matt repeated.

"Princess?" Duncan cautiously opened the door and poked his head inside the room. "You asked me to get you at a quarter to one, and it's a quarter to one now."

"Thank you, Duncan," I said.

"Well?" Willa looked at me, smiling. "Are you ready?"

"I think I'm going to throw up," I told her honestly.

"You won't throw up. It's just nerves, and you'll do fine," Willa said.

"Maybe it's not nerves," Matt said. "Maybe she doesn't want to go through with this."

"Matt!" Willa snapped, and she looked back at me. Her brown eyes were warm and concerned. "Wendy, do you want to do this?"

"Yes," I said firmly and nodded once. "I want to do this."

"Okay." She stood up. Smiling, she held her hand out to me. "Let's get you married, then."

I took her hand, and she squeezed it reassuringly when I got up. Duncan stood by the door, waiting for us, and when I started walking, he came over to gather the train so it wouldn't drag on the ground.

"Wait," Matt said. "This is the last moment I'll have to talk to you before this, so, um, I just wanted to say . . ." He fumbled for a minute and pulled at his sleeve. "There's so much I wanted to say, actually. I've watched you grow up so much, Wendy. And you were a brat." He laughed nervously at that, and I smiled.

"And you've blossomed right in front of me," he said. "You're strong and smart and compassionate and beautiful. I couldn't be more proud of the woman you've become."

"Matt." I wiped quickly at my eyes.

"Matt, don't make her cry," Willa said, and she sniffled a little.

"I'm sorry," Matt said. "I didn't mean to make you cry, and I know you've got to get down there. But I wanted to say that no matter what happens, today, tomorrow, whenever, you'll always be my little sister, and I'll always be on your side. I love you."

"I love you too," I said, and I hugged him.

"That was really sweet," Willa said when he let me go. She gave him a quick kiss on the lips before ushering me out of the room. "But I wish you'd said that sometime in the past hour when we were doing nothing. Now we really have to book."

Fortunately, we never wore shoes, which made it easier to jog down to the ballroom. Before we even reached it, I could hear the music playing. Aurora had a live orchestra playing "Moonlight Sonata," and I heard the murmurs of the guests accompanying it.

The bridesmaids and groomsmen were lined up outside the doors, waiting until I arrived to enter. Garrett smiled when he saw me. He'd always been kind to me, so I'd chosen him to walk me down the aisle.

"Be gentle with her, Dad," Willa said as she handed me off to him. "She's nervous."

"Don't worry." Garrett grinned, looping his arm through mine. "I promise I won't let you fall or stumble all the way down the aisle."

"Thank you." I forced a smile at him.

One of my bridesmaids handed me my bouquet of lilies. I felt a bit better gripping on to something, as if it kept me anchored.

As the wedding party walked down the aisle, I kept swallowing, trying desperately to fight back the nausea that overwhelmed me. It was only Tove. There was nothing to be afraid of. He was one of the few people in the world I actually trusted. I could do this. I could marry him.

Willa gave me a small wave before she turned down the aisle. Duncan was behind me, straightening my train out the best he could, but the music hit a crescendo, and it was my turn to go. Duncan stepped back from my dress, and he and Matt gave me encouraging smiles. They didn't want to sneak into the service now, so they'd have to wait outside the ballroom, watching from the back.

I stepped out on the green velvet carpet running down the aisle, littered with white rose petals from a flower girl, and I thought I might faint. It didn't help that the carpet seemed to go on for miles. The ballroom was packed with people, and they all stood and turned to face me when I entered.

Rhys and Rhiannon were in the very back row, and Rhiannon waved madly when she saw me. I'd met many of these people while running the palace, but I had so few friends here. Tove stood at the altar, looking almost as nervous as I felt, and that made me feel better somehow. We were both scared, but we were in this together.

Elora sat near the front, the only person in attendance not standing, but she was probably too weak to stand. I was just happy that she'd been able to make it here, and she smiled at me as I walked past. It was a genuine smile, and it pulled at my heart.

I walked the two steps up the altar, away from Garrett, and Tove took my hand. He squeezed it and offered me a subtle smile as I stood next to him. Willa moved around behind me, smoothing out my dress again.

"Hey," Tove said.

"Hey," I said.

"You may be seated," Markis Bain said. On top of being in charge of changeling placement, he was certified to perform Trylle weddings. He stood in front of us, dressed in a white suit, smiling nervously, and his blue eyes seemed to linger on Tove for a moment.

The guests sat down behind us, but I tried not to think of them. I tried not to think about how I had scanned the crowd, but I'd been unable to see Finn in their numbers. His father was here, standing guard near the door, but Finn had probably left again. He had work to do, and things were over between us.

"Dearly beloved," Markis Bain said, interrupting my thoughts. "We are gathered here to join this Princess and this Markis in holy matrimony, which is commended to be honorable among all Trylle. Therefore it is not to be entered into unadvisedly or lightly—but reverently, discreetly, and solemnly."

He opened his mouth to say more, but a loud banging sound shook the palace. I jumped and looked back at the door, the same way everyone did. Matt was standing just outside the open doors, but Duncan had run down the hall.

"What was that?" Willa asked, echoing the thoughts of everybody in the room.

"Princess!" Duncan yelled, and he appeared in the doorway. "They're coming for you."

"What?" I asked.

I tossed my bouquet aside, gathered my skirt, and raced from the altar. Willa called my name, but I ignored her. I'd only made it halfway down the aisle when I heard the gravelly boom of Oren's voice.

"We're not coming for anyone," Oren said. "If this were dirty work, I wouldn't be here."

I stopped in the aisle, unsure of what to do next, and Oren stepped into view. Duncan and Matt rushed at him, but the two Vittra guards Oren had with him grabbed them both. As soon as the guards touched Matt, I raised my hand and, using my abilities, I sent them flying backward. They slammed into the back wall, and I kept my hand up, holding them in place.

Oren smiled. "Impressive, Princess."

He clapped his hands at that, the sound muffled by his black leather gloves. His long, dark hair shimmered the way Elora's once had, but his eyes were black as coal.

I hadn't meant to leave him standing. I'd wanted to send

him falling back, so he could feel the force of what I could do, but he hadn't. The Vittra were stronger than the Trylle, Oren especially, and Tove had warned me that my abilities might be useless on him.

Matt and Duncan stood up, dazed by the immediacy of my response. Sara, Oren's wife, stood to his side but a bit behind him. She lowered her eyes and kept still. Both she and Oren wore all black, an odd choice for a wedding.

"What do you want?" I asked.

"What do I want?" Oren laughed and held his arms out to the side. "It's my only daughter's wedding." He took a step forward, and I let the guards go, so they fell to the floor. I wanted to be able to focus all my energy on Oren if need be.

"Stop," I commanded, holding my hand palm-out to him. "If you take another step, I will send you soaring through the ceiling."

The ballroom ceiling was made entirely of glass, so that wasn't as remarkable as it sounded, especially since I wasn't even sure I could do it. I could feel Tove standing a few feet behind me, though, and that gave me more confidence.

"Now, Princess." Oren made a *tsk* sound. "Is that any way to greet your father?"

"Considering you've kidnapped me and tried to kill me, yes, I think this is the only appropriate greeting," I said.

"*I* never did anything." Oren put his hands to his chest. "But look at me now. I've come without an army. Just my wife and two guards to help me travel. Nothing else. I assure you, Princess, I plan to uphold our treaty as long as you do.

I will refrain from attacking you or any of your people on the Förening grounds. Provided, of course, that you do the same."

His eyes sparkled at that. He was taunting me. He wanted me to launch an attack, to hurt him, so they could fight back. If I did this, I would start an all-out war between the Vittra and Trylle, and we weren't ready.

I might be able to defend myself and a few of the people, but most of our guards and trackers were gone. If Oren had any other Vittra waiting in the wings outside of Förening, the Trylle would be slaughtered. My wedding would turn into a bloodbath.

"In standing with our treaty, I ask that you leave the grounds," I said. "This is a private affair, and you were not invited."

"But I came to give you away," Oren said, pretending to be hurt. "I traveled all this way just for you."

"You're too late," I said. "And I was never yours in the first place, so you have no right to give me away."

"So who here has possessed you so much that they have a right to give you away?" Oren asked.

"Oren!" Elora shouted, and everyone in the room turned to look at her. "Leave her alone." She stood at the other end of the aisle, near the altar, and Garrett stood behind her. I'm sure it was to catch her in case she collapsed, but it looked like he was merely being supportive.

"Ah, my Queen." Oren smiled wickedly at her. "There you are."

"You've had your fun," Elora said. "Now be on your way. We've tolerated you enough."

"Look at you." He chuckled to himself. "You really let yourself go, didn't you? Now you look like the old hag I always knew you were."

"Enough!" I snapped at him. "I've asked you kindly to leave. I will not ask you again."

He sized me up, gauging my sincerity, and I kept my expression as hard as I could. Finally, he shrugged, as if it were nothing to him.

"Suit yourself, Princess," he said. "But by the looks of your mother, it won't be much longer until you're Queen. So I will be seeing you soon."

He turned to leave, and I lowered my hand, then he stopped.

"One more thing, Princess." Oren looked back at me. "I believe a piece of my trash has washed up here. He's been a horrible pain, but he does belong to me, so I would like him returned."

"I'm certain I don't know what you're talking about," I said, knowing that I would never turn Loki over to him. I'd seen what he'd done to Loki, and I wouldn't let it happen again.

"If he should turn up," Oren said, and I couldn't tell if he believed me or not, "send him my way."

"Of course," I lied.

Oren turned and stalked out, not even waiting for Sara. She gave me an ashamed smile before chasing after him. His guards finally picked themselves up off the floor and hurried to catch up. I heard him say something as they disappeared, but I couldn't understand him.

Duncan stayed in the doorway, and using my mind-speak I told him to make sure that Oren and Sara were really gone.

Everyone else was looking to me, waiting to see my reaction. I wanted to wilt, to let out a sigh of relief, but I couldn't do that. I couldn't let them know how rattled I was, that I'd been terrified that my father would kill us, and I would be unable to do anything to stop him.

"Sorry about the interruption," I said, my voice astonishingly even, and I gave all my guests my most polite smile. "But with that over, I believe we have a wedding to get on with." I turned to Tove, still smiling. "Assuming you'll still have me."

He returned my smile. "Of course."

He held out his arm, and I took it. As we walked back down the aisle, the orchestra began playing "Moonlight Sonata" again.

"How are you holding up?" Tove asked quietly as we climbed the altar stairs.

"Good," I whispered. "Getting married doesn't seem all that scary anymore."

We stood in front of Markis Bain, and I glanced back over my shoulder. Duncan stood in the doorway, and he mouthed the words *All clear.* I smiled appreciatively at him and turned back to the Markis.

"Shall we start with the vows, then?" Markis Bain asked. "Princess, Markis, turn and face each other."

I turned to Tove, forcing a smile and hoping he couldn't hear the pounding of my heart. With a few simple words and an exchange of rings, I vowed to take him as my husband until death. We sealed it with a quick kiss, and the guests erupted in applause.

interlude

Thankfully, between the wedding and the reception there was a brief interlude in which they cleared out the chairs and set up the tables and the dance floor. I wasn't sure where new brides were supposed to spend that time, but I spent mine locked in the nearest bathroom with Willa.

I splashed cold water on my face, and that helped clear my head, even if it did drive Willa nuts. I dried off my face with a paper towel once I felt better, and she frantically reapplied my makeup.

We left the bathroom in time for Tove and me to make our grand entrance as husband and wife. When we walked in, Garrett stood up and introduced us as Prince Tove and Princess Wendy Kroner, and everyone applauded again.

I wasn't sure how they'd done it in such a short time, but the ballroom looked amazing. If I'd been the kind of girl to imagine a fairy-tale wedding, this was exactly how I would've pictured it. The chandeliers that were lit during the ceremony had been shut off, so the room twinkled with fairy lights strung everywhere. Candles glowed on the tables. The whole room smelled of lilies from all the flowers.

While everyone watched, Tove and I danced our first dance to "At Last" by Etta James. I'd let him choose it, and he was an Etta James fan. We did dance well together, thanks to the countless lessons Willa made us go through to be sure we were perfect, but we didn't twirl around the room like magic.

When we finished the dance, the orchestra resumed, playing something by Bach. I would've been happy to spend the night dancing with Tove, but as soon as the song ended, everyone gathered on the floor. I would have to dance with anyone who asked.

Garrett stole the next dance with me, and Aurora danced with Tove. My own mother probably wouldn't dance with him, but she was still here for the reception. I imagined she would stay all night, no matter how weak or tired she got. After that comment Oren had made, she had to prove that she still had it, even if she really didn't.

Willa cut in to dance with me once, which was nice. She made me laugh, and that felt really good. I carried all my tension in my shoulders, and I knew they would ache like mad by the end of the night.

I caught sight of Matt, Rhys, Rhiannon, and Duncan sitting at a table in the back when a Markis was spinning me about. I wanted to escape from the dance to spend a few moments with them, but if I stopped dancing, it only meant I'd have to go table to table and talk to people. That was the only thing I could think of that would be worse than dancing.

I was annoyed and surprised to find out how many people used this opportunity to talk to me about some bill they wanted to pass, what family they wanted their child placed with, or to complain about taxes. Even though everything in my life had become politically motivated, it would've been nice to have a few dances where I could pretend that it wasn't.

The Chancellor cut in to dance with me, naturally, and I did my best to stay at arm's length, but he kept trying to press me to him. It was hard to stay away from his sweaty torso anyway, because his belly was so rotund. His massive hand would probably leave a sweat stain on my back from trying to hold me to him.

"You look very, very lovely tonight, Princess," the Chancellor said, and I hated the hungry way he looked at me. It made my skin crawl.

"Thank you." I smiled only because I had to, but it was difficult.

"I do wish you would've taken me up on my offer, though." He licked his lips, which were already damp with perspiration. "Remember? The last time we danced together, I suggested that you and I—"

"Excuse me," Tove said, appearing at my side. "I'd like to dance with my wife, if you don't mind."

"Yes, of course." The Chancellor bowed and stepped away, but he didn't bother to mask the irritation on his blubbery face.

"Thank you," I said as Tove took my hand in his.

"Do not dance with him anymore," Tove said, sounding exasperated. "I beg of you. Stay as far away from him as you can."

"With pleasure," I said and gave him an odd look. "Why?"

"That man is insufferable." He grimaced and glanced back at the Chancellor, who was already shoving another piece of wedding cake in his mouth. "He has the most perverse, vile thoughts I've ever heard. And he gets so much louder when he's close to you. The disgusting things he would do to you . . ." Tove actually shivered at that.

"What?" I asked. "How do you know? I thought you couldn't read thoughts."

"I can't," Tove said. "I can only hear when people are projecting, and he projects when he's excited, apparently. What makes it worse is that I spent all day moving things so my abilities would be weak. I can barely hear anything. But I hear him loud and clear."

"He's that bad?" I asked, feeling grossed out that I had let the Chancellor touch me.

Tove nodded. "He's horrible. As soon as we get a chance, we have got to get him out of office. Out of Förening, if possible. I don't want him anywhere near our people."

"Yes, definitely," I agreed. "I've already been working on a plan to get rid of him."

"Good," Tove said, then smiled at me. "We're already working together."

A murmur ran through the crowd, and I looked around to see what all the fuss was about. Then I saw him, walking past table after table as if everybody weren't stopping to stare at him.

Loki had ventured down from where he'd been hiding in the servants' quarters. Since I'd granted him amnesty, he was no longer being guarded and was free to roam as he pleased, but I hadn't exactly invited him to the wedding.

As Tove and I danced, I didn't take my eyes off Loki. He walked around the dance floor toward the refreshments, but he kept watching me. He got a glass of champagne from the table, and even as he drank his eyes never left me.

Another Markis came over and cut in to dance with me, but I barely noticed when I switched partners. I tried to focus on the person I was dancing with. But there was something about the way Loki looked at me, and I couldn't shake it.

The song had switched to something contemporary, probably the sheet music that Willa had slipped the orchestra. She'd insisted the whole thing would be far too dull if they only played classical.

The murmur died down, and people returned to dancing and talking. Loki took another swig of his champagne, then set the glass down and walked across the dance floor. Everyone parted around him, and I wasn't sure if it was out of fear or respect.

He wore all black, even his shirt. I had no idea where he'd gotten the clothes, but he did look debonair.

"May I have this dance?" Loki asked my dance partner, but his eyes were on me.

"Um, I don't know if you should," the Markis fumbled, but I was already moving away from him.

"No, it's all right," I said.

Uncertainly, the Markis stepped back, and Loki took my hand. When he placed his hand on my back, a shiver ran up my spine, but I tried to hide it and put my hand on his shoulder.

"You know, you weren't invited to this," I told him, but he merely smirked as we began dancing.

"So throw me out."

"I might." I raised my head defiantly, and that only made him laugh.

"If it's as the Princess wishes," he said, but he made no move to step away, and for some odd reason, I felt relieved.

"You didn't hear about the ceremony, then?" I asked, hoping to keep him from running off. "Oren came to wish me well."

"I heard one of the guards talking about it," Loki said, his caramel eyes growing serious. "They said you did well and that you stood up for yourself."

"I tried to anyway." I shrugged. "He's looking for you."

"The King?" Loki asked, and I nodded. "Are you going to hand me over to him?"

"I haven't decided yet," I teased, and he smiled again, erasing his momentary seriousness. "So, where'd you get the suit?"

"Believe it or not, that lovely friend of yours, Willa," Loki said. "She brought me a whole slew of clothes last night. When I asked her why she was being so generous, she said it was out of fear that I would run around naked."

I smiled. "That does sound like something you would do. Why are you wearing all black, though? Didn't you know you were going to a wedding?"

"On the contrary," he said, doing his best to look unhappy. "I'm in mourning over the wedding."

"Oh, because it's too late?" I asked.

"No, Wendy, it's never too late." His voice was light, but his eyes were solemn.

"May I cut in?" the best man asked.

"No, you may not," Loki said. I'd started to move away from him, but he held fast.

"Loki," I said, and my eyes widened.

"I'm still dancing with her," Loki said, turning to look at him. "You can have her when I'm done."

"Loki," I said again, but he was already twirling me away. "You can't do that."

"I just did." He grinned. "Oh, Wendy, don't look so appalled. I'm already the rebel Prince of thine enemy. I can't do much more to tarnish my image."

"You can certainly tarnish mine," I pointed out.

"Never," Loki said, and it was his turn to look appalled. "I'm merely showing them how it's done."

He began spinning me around the dance floor in grand arcs, my gown swirling around me. He was a brilliant dancer, moving with grace and speed. Everyone had stopped to watch us, but I didn't care. This was the way a Princess was supposed to dance on her wedding day.

The song ended, switching to something by Mozart, and he slowed, almost to a stop, but he kept me in his arms.

"Thank you." I smiled. My skin felt flushed from dancing, and I was a little out of breath. "That was a wonderful dance."

"You're welcome," he said, staring intently at me. "You are so beautiful."

"Stop," I said, looking away as my cheeks reddened.

"How can you blush?" Loki asked, laughing gently. "People must tell you how beautiful you are a thousand times a day."

"It's not the same," I said.

"It's not the same?" Loki echoed. "Why? Because you know they don't mean it like I do?"

We did stop dancing then, and neither of us said anything. Garrett came up to us. He smiled, but his eyes didn't appear happy.

"Can I cut in?" Garrett asked.

"Yes," Loki said, shaking off the intensity he'd had a moment ago, and grinned broadly at Garrett. "She's all yours, good sir. Take care of her."

He patted Garrett on the arm once for good measure and gave me a quick smile before heading back over to the refreshment table.

"Was he bothering you?" Garrett asked me as we began to dance.

"Um, no." I shook my head. "He's just . . ." I trailed off because I didn't know what he was.

I watched Loki as he drained another glass of champagne, and then he left the ballroom just as abruptly as he'd entered.

"Are you sure?" Garrett asked.

"Yes, everything is fine." I smiled reassuringly at him. "Why? Am I in trouble for dancing with him?"

"I don't think so," he said. "It's your wedding. You're

supposed to have a little fun. It would've been nice if it was with the groom, but . . ." He shrugged.

"Elora's not mad, is she?" I asked.

"Elora doesn't have the strength to be mad anymore," Garrett said, almost sadly. "Don't worry about her. You've got enough to deal with."

"Thank you," I said.

I looked around the dance floor. Willa was dancing with Tove again, and when she caught my eyes, she gave me a what-the-hell look. I assumed it was in reference to my dance with Loki, but Tove didn't seem upset. That was something, at least.

morning after

Even though I wore a wedding gown that had to weigh at least twenty pounds, I'd never felt so naked in my life.

I stood at the foot of my new bed in my new bedroom. These had been Elora's chambers, but they were mine now, mine to share with my husband. Tove was next to me, and we both just stared at the bed.

When the reception started winding down, Tove's parents, my mother, Willa, Garrett, and a few other ranking officials, including that disgusting Chancellor, had ushered us up to the room. They were all laughing, talking about how magical this would be, then they shut the door behind us.

"On wedding nights, when a Prince or a King were married, they used to close the curtains around the four-poster bed," Tove said. "Then the family and officials would sit around all night, so they could be sure that they were having sex."

"That is really disturbing," I said. "Why on earth would they do that?"

He shrugged. "To ensure they would produce offspring. That is the only reason why they arranged marriages."

"I guess I should be happy they're not doing that with us."

"Do you think they're listening outside the door?"

"I really, really hope not."

We kept staring at the bed, refusing to look at each other. I don't think either of us knew what to do. I had planned to wait long enough until I was certain everyone had grown bored and left, but past that, I had no idea how this night would go.

Tove and I would never have a normal marital relationship, but for some reason, I did assume we would consummate our union on our wedding night. We would have to eventually, because we would be expected to produce an heir to the throne, regardless of whether we were attracted to each other. Or in Tove's case, even attracted to my gender.

"This dress is really heavy," I said finally.

"It looks like it." Tove glanced at my dress and the piles of train that had been tacked up on the back so I could dance. "The train itself has to weigh like ten pounds."

"At least," I agreed. "So . . . I'd like to get out of it."

"Oh, right." He paused. "Go ahead. I guess."

"Well . . . I need your help." I gestured to the back of it. "There's like a thousand buttons and snaps to undo, and I can't reach them."

"Oh, right, of course." Tove shook his head. "I should've known."

I turned my back to him and stood patiently while he undid all the buttons and snaps. It seemed ridiculous when I thought about it. This dress was meant to come off, but it took him at least fifteen minutes to get them all undone. And the whole time, neither of us said anything.

"There you go," he said. "All done."

"Thank you." I held the dress in the front to keep it from falling off, and I turned to face him. "Should I . . . do I need to put pajamas on?"

"Oh." He rubbed his hands on his pants. "Um, if you want to."

"Are you going to?" I asked.

"I . . . yeah." He bit the inside of his cheek and lowered his eyes. "We don't have to. I mean, you know, have sex. We can if you want to. I guess. But we don't have to."

"Oh," I said, because that seemed like the only thing to say.

"Do you want to?" Tove asked, looking at me.

"Uh . . . not really, no," I admitted. "But we could try kissing, maybe."

"No, that's okay." He scratched the back of his head and looked around the room. "We can take this slow. Tonight's only the first night. We have our whole lives to . . . figure out how to sleep with each other."

"Yeah," I said, and laughed nervously. "So, I'll go put on pajamas?"

"Yeah, me too."

Still holding my dress around me, I went into the closet only to find a problem. I had no clothes here. None of Elora's clothes were even in here. The closet was bare.

"Do you have any clothes?" Tove asked from the bedroom. "Because these dressers are empty."

"Oh, hell, I bet they did that on purpose." I sighed and walked back out.

"They didn't give us clothes because . . ." He trailed off and smiled thinly.

"So I have nothing to sleep in."

"You can wear my T-shirt," Tove offered. He undid the top buttons of his dress shirt, then pulled it over his head, revealing a plain white T-shirt. "Do you want to?"

"Yes, thank you," I said.

He took off his shirt, then handed it to me. I turned around, so my back was to him, and I pulled on his T-shirt. I stepped out of my dress, and it felt amazing to be free of it. Everything about me felt lighter.

When I'd finished, I saw that Tove had taken off his pants, so he was wearing only his boxers. I went around to my side of the bed and sat down on the edge. I peeled off the jewelry I'd been wearing, except for my new wedding ring with a giant diamond.

I climbed into bed, sliding underneath the mounds of covers. The bed was massive, so even after Tove got in it, there was still plenty of room between us. I waited until he was settled, then I leaned over and turned off my bedside lamp, submerging the room in darkness.

"Is it okay?" Tove asked.

"What?"

"That I don't love you."

"Uh, yeah," I said carefully. "I think it's okay."

"I wasn't sure if I should tell you. I didn't want to hurt your feelings, but I thought you should know." He moved in the bed, and I felt a subtle motion on my side.

"No, it's okay. I'm glad you told me." I paused for a minute. "I don't love you."

"And that's okay?"

"I think so."

"It was a nice wedding," Tove said, somewhat randomly. "Except for the part with your dad."

"Yeah. It was really nice," I agreed. "Willa and Aurora did a good job."

"They did."

The day had been exhausting, and I hadn't slept much the night before. So it didn't take long for sleep to overtake me. I fell asleep on my wedding night, still a virgin.

The doors burst open, startling me awake. I nearly jumped out of bed. Tove groaned next to me, since I did this weird mind-slap thing whenever I woke up scared, and it always hit him the worst. I'd forgotten about it because it had been a few months since the last time it happened.

"Good morning, good morning, good morning," Loki chirped, wheeling in a table covered with silver domes.

"What are you doing?" I asked, squinting at him. He'd pulled up the shades. I was tired as hell, and I was not happy.

"I thought you two lovebirds would like breakfast," Loki said. "So I had the chef whip you up something fantastic." As he set up the table in the sitting area, he looked over at us. "Although you two are sleeping awfully far apart for newlyweds."

"Oh, my god." I groaned and pulled the covers over my head.

"You know, I think you're being a dick," Tove told him as he got out of bed. "But I'm starving. So I'm willing to overlook it. This time."

"A dick?" Loki pretended to be offended. "I'm merely worried about your health. If your bodies aren't used to strenuous activities, like a long night of lovemaking, you could waste away if you don't get plenty of protein and rehydrate. I'm concerned for you."

"Yes, we both believe *that's* why you're here," Tove said sarcastically and took a glass of orange juice that Loki had poured for him.

"What about you, Princess?" Loki's gaze cut to me as he filled another glass.

"I'm not hungry." I sighed and sat up.

"Oh, really?" Loki arched an eyebrow. "Does that mean that last night—"

"It means that last night is none of your business," I snapped.

I got up and hobbled over to Elora's satin robe, which had been left on a nearby chair. My feet and ankles ached from all the dancing I'd done the night before.

"Don't cover up on my account," Loki said as I put on the robe. "You don't have anything I haven't seen."

"Oh, I have plenty you haven't seen," I said and pulled the robe around me.

"You should get married more often," Loki teased. "It makes you feisty."

I rolled my eyes and went over to the table. Loki had set it all up, complete with a flower in a vase in the center, and he'd pulled off the domed lids to reveal a plentiful breakfast. I took a seat across from Tove, only to realize that Loki had pulled up a third chair for himself.

"What are you doing?" I asked.

"Well, I went to all the trouble of having someone prepare it, so I might as well eat it." Loki sat down and handed me a flute filled with orange liquid. "I made mimosas."

"Thanks," I said, and I exchanged a look with Tove to see if it was okay if Loki stayed.

"He's a dick," Tove said over a mouthful of food, and shrugged. "But I don't care."

In all honesty, I think we both preferred having Loki there. He was a buffer between the two of us so we didn't have to deal with any awkward morning-after conversations. And though I'd never admit it aloud, Loki made me laugh, and right now I needed a little levity in my life.

"So, how did everyone sleep last night?" Loki asked.

There was a quick knock at the bedroom doors, but they opened before I could answer. Finn strode inside, and my stomach dropped. He was the last person I'd expected to see. I didn't even think he would be here anymore. After the other night I assumed he'd left, especially when I didn't see him at the wedding.

"Princess, I'm sorry—" Finn started to say as he hurried in, but then he saw Loki and stopped abruptly.

"Finn?" I asked, stunned.

Finn looked appalled and pointed at Loki. "What are you doing here?"

"I'm drinking a mimosa." Loki leaned back in his chair. "What are you doing here?"

"What is he doing here?" Finn asked, turning his attention to me.

"Never mind him." I waved it off. "What's going on?"

"See, Finn, you should've told me when I asked," Loki said between sips of his drink.

"Hey, did you guys . . ." Duncan was saying when he walked into my room. Apparently, since Finn had left the door open, he thought he could waltz on in.

"Sure, everybody just walk on in. It's not like I'm a Princess or anything and this is my private chamber." I sighed.

When Duncan saw the bizarre scene, he stopped and motioned to Loki. "Wait. Why is he here? He didn't spend the night with you two, did he?"

"Wendy is into some very kinky things that you wouldn't understand," Loki told him with a wink.

"Why are you here?" Finn demanded, and his eyes blazed.

"Will somebody please tell us what the hell is going on?" Tove asked, exasperated.

"I would, but this is a private conversation." Finn kept his icy gaze locked on Loki, who looked completely unabashed.

"Come, now, Finn, there are no secrets between us." Loki grinned and gestured widely to Tove and me.

"Is it private as in Tove, Loki, and Duncan should leave?" I asked carefully. I didn't know if Finn's visit was about me. If it was, I wasn't sure if I should let him have a moment alone with me.

"No." Finn shook his head. "It's about the kingdom, and I don't trust the Markis Staad."

"I have amnesty, you know." Loki leaned forward, sounding irritated. "That means she trusts me. I'm an accepted member of your society."

"No one will ever accept you," Finn said coolly. "And I sincerely doubt that—"

"Just spit it out!" I snapped. "I'm very tired. I've had a very long weekend. So if there's something I need to know, you should hurry up and tell me."

"My apologies." Finn lowered his eyes. "I was in a security briefing this morning with my father. Apparently there's been a Vittra attack on Oslinna, and it was brutal."

"Oslinna?" I asked. "I have a meeting with their head Markis tomorrow morning."

"Not anymore," Finn said quietly. "He's dead."

"They killed him?" I gasped, and I heard Tove swear under his breath. "When did this happen? How many others were killed?"

"We're not certain of the total loss yet," Finn said. "It

happened sometime during the night, and we're still getting word on it. But so far, the death toll is high . . . and mounting."

"Oh, my god." I put my hand to my mouth, wanting to throw up or cry.

Scores of people had been killed while I was dancing. My people, who I was sworn to protect. And it might have been my father after he left the wedding. It was a ten-hour drive to Oslinna from here, but it would be possible for him to get there. He could have slaughtered them all because he was angry with me.

Or maybe not. This might have been his plan all along. He agreed to peace with Förening, and then went after our changelings, and now apparently was following it up by attacking other Trylle communities. This could be his first step toward total war.

I swallowed back any emotion I had, because that would only get in the way. I needed a clear head if I wanted to help what was left of the Oslinna people.

"We have to do something," I said numbly.

"My father is arranging a defense meeting now," Finn said.

"Is that why he didn't come to get me?" I asked. Finn's father, Thomas, was head of security, and he was the one who usually reported the problems to me.

"No." Finn gave me an apologetic look. "He didn't want to inform you. He thought we should wait until we knew more, since you'd just gotten married."

"I'm still the Princess!" I stood up. "This is still my duty. It doesn't stop because of a silly party."

"That's why I came to get you," Finn said, but he'd looked away, and I didn't think that had been his only motive for retrieving me this morning.

"Is this why you're here?" I asked Duncan.

He nodded. "Yeah. I was downstairs getting breakfast, and I heard a couple of guards talking about the Oslinna attack. I thought you'd want to know."

"Thank you," I said. I held my hand to my stomach, trying to ease my nerves. I had to be cool and calm. "Get the defense meeting set up. We need to get moving on this as fast as we can."

Finn nodded. "Of course."

"Duncan, can you run and get Willa?" I asked, and, using mind-speak, I said, *She's down in Matt's room.* She'd spent more nights with him than at her home lately.

"Yes, of course." Duncan made a quick bow and started walking out.

"Oh, and can you run to my room and grab some clothes?" I asked. "They didn't seem to make it in the move yesterday."

"Sorry about that." Duncan's cheeks reddened. "It was Willa's idea. She thought it would be—"

"Never mind that." I waved it off. "Just grab me something to wear. And make sure Willa comes. I want her at this meeting."

"Yes, Princess." He rushed out of the room, hurrying to complete his tasks, but Finn stayed where he was.

"What?" I asked.

"What about him?" Finn's eyes went to Loki.

"What about him?" I asked, annoyed.

"He's Vittra," Finn said.

"He's not—" I stopped and turned back to Loki. "Did you know about the attack on Oslinna?"

"No, of course not," Loki said, and he did seem genuinely distressed about it. His smirk was gone, his eyes were pained, and his skin was ashen. "The King would never tell me of his plans."

"See?" I turned to face Finn again. "He didn't know anything."

"Princess." Finn gave me a hard look.

"I don't have time to stand here and argue with you, Finn," I said. "You need to get down to the meeting and make sure nobody does anything stupid before I get there. Don't let the Chancellor decide *anything*. I'll be in the War Room in ten minutes, okay?"

"Yes, Princess." Finn didn't look happy, but he nodded and left the room.

"I need to get clothes too," Tove said and pushed back his chair. He got up and tossed his napkin on his half-eaten meal. "Do you have any idea how you want to handle this, Wendy?"

"Not yet." I shook my head. "But I don't entirely know what's happened."

"We'll figure this out." Tove walked over to me and touched my arm gently. "I'll meet you in the War Room."

"Okay." I nodded. "Hurry."

I ran a hand through my hair. My mind raced. An attack meant that people had been killed, but it also meant that many were injured and their homes might be destroyed. We had to help the survivors somehow, as well as figure out how to deal with the Vittra.

"I should probably let you get ready," Loki said, rising.

"What?" I turned back to face him. I'd forgotten he was there.

"I am truly sorry for what happened," Loki said solemnly. "Your people didn't deserve that."

"I know." I swallowed hard. He turned away to leave and I asked, "Would you have done it?"

"What?" Loki paused at the door.

"If you were with the Vittra still?" I asked, and I looked at him directly. He stood a few feet from me, his golden eyes looking dark and sad. "Would you have attacked Oslinna? Would you have killed them?"

"No," he said. "I have never killed anyone."

"But you fought with them."

He shook his head. "I never fought for my King. That's why I ended up in the dungeon."

"I see." I looked down at the floor, understanding dawning. "Stay out of sight. Nobody else will trust you."

"I will."

"Loki," I said just before he slipped out the door, and I turned to him, so he could see I was serious. "It seems to me that the King has wreaked as much destruction on your life as he has on mine. But if I find out you knew anything about the attack, I will bring you to the King myself."

"Yes, Your Highness." He bowed, then left my chambers.

repercussions

Duncan came in a few minutes later, and I dressed quickly. I smoothed out my hair the best I could, because I couldn't look a fright at this meeting, but I didn't have time to make sure I looked top-notch.

I practically ran down the hall with Duncan at my heels, and I reached the top of the stairs at the same time as Willa. Her dress was a bit askew, and her hair was tangled, so she'd obviously gotten dressed in a hurry too. I was happy to see that she'd listened.

"Duncan said you wanted me to come to the meeting?" Willa asked, sounding confused as we went down the stairs.

"Yes," I said. "I need you to start getting involved with this."

"Wendy, you know I'm not good at this kind of stuff," Willa said.

"I don't know why you say that. Public relations is your forte. And even if it wasn't, this is your job. You are one of the highest Marksinna we have. You should be helping shape the kingdom instead of letting others destroy it."

"I don't know." She shook her head, and when we reached the bottom of the steps, I stopped to face her.

"Look, Willa, I need you on my side," I said. "I'm going into a room full of people who think I'm an idiot and a liability. People are in trouble in Oslinna, *our* people. I don't have time to fight with them, and they are fond of you. I need you to help me. Okay?"

"Of course." Willa smiled nervously. "I will help you in any way I can."

Before we even reached the War Room, I could hear them arguing. There were too many voices to clearly understand what they were fighting about, but they were upset.

"We all need to calm down!" Finn was shouting to be heard over them when Willa, Duncan, and I arrived. Finn stood at the front of the crowded War Room, but nobody paid attention to him.

Tove leaned on the desk, watching them all. The Chancellor, his face beet-red, was yelling so much at poor Markis Bain that spittle flew from his mouth. Marksinna Laris was standing up and screaming at Garrett, who tried to keep his expression neutral, but I knew he wanted to smack her.

"Excuse me!" I shouted, but nobody even noticed me.

"I've been trying to get them to calm down." Finn looked at me apologetically. "But they're in a complete frenzy. They think we're next."

"I got this," Willa said.

She climbed up onto the desk behind Tove, carefully because she was wearing a short dress, and she put two fingers in her mouth and let out a loud whistle. So loud that Tove actually covered his ears.

Everybody stopped talking and looked up at her.

"Your Princess is here, and she'd like to talk to you, so you should give her your attention," Willa said with a smile.

Duncan walked over to the desk and gave Willa his hand to help her to the floor. She thanked him, then smoothed out her dress, and I walked over to stand between her and Tove.

"Thank you, Marksinna," I said, then turned my attention to the angry mob. "Who knows the most about the attack on Oslinna?"

"I do," Thomas said, stepping forward from behind Aurora Kroner.

"Tell me everything you know," I said.

"We've already gone over this," Marksinna Laris said before he could say anything. "We shouldn't be rehashing the same things. We should be plotting our attack."

"I am sorry to be wasting your time, but nobody is making any decisions until I know what's going on," I said. "This will all go much faster if you simply let Thomas tell me what happened."

Laris muttered something and looked away. When I was certain she was done, I turned back to Thomas and nodded for him to continue.

"Sometime late last night, the Vittra attacked Oslinna," Thomas said. "It's one of the Trylle's larger compounds located in northern Michigan. Reports vary, but we believe it started around ten-thirty P.M."

"Are we certain it was the Vittra?" I asked.

"Yes," Thomas said. "The King wasn't there, but a message was sent on his behalf."

"And the message was?" I prompted him.

" 'This is only the beginning,' " Thomas said.

Whispers filled the room, but I held up my hand to silence them.

"Do we know how many Vittra they had with them?" I asked.

Thomas shook his head. "It's hard to say concretely. They've begun using hobgoblins in their battles. In previous attacks on Trylle, they rarely used them, preferring to keep them hidden. So we are assuming the numbers of actual Vittra are running low."

"Ugly little creatures," Laris snorted at the mention of hobgoblins, and a few chuckled in response.

"So the hobgoblins comprise most of the Vittra army?" Tove asked dubiously. "How are they a threat? They're small and weak."

"They may be small, but they're still Vittra," Thomas said. "Physically, they have tremendous strength. They seem to be slow mentally and more susceptible to Trylle abilities than most trolls, but not that many of the Trylle in Oslinna even have abilities anymore."

"These hobgoblins caused real damage to Oslinna, then?" I asked.

"Yes," Thomas said. "The town is completely devastated. We don't have an exact figure of how many lives were lost, but we suspect the number to be at least two thousand, and they only had a population of three thousand to begin with."

Someone in the back gasped, and even Willa made a sound, but I kept my face blank. Here, compassion would be a sign of weakness.

"Do we know what kind of casualties we caused the Vittra army?" I asked.

"No, but I don't think it was substantial," Thomas said. "Possibly a hundred. Maybe more."

"So they killed thousands of our people, and we killed maybe a handful of them?" I asked. "How is this possible? How did this happen?"

"They were sleeping or getting ready for bed," Thomas said. "It was an ambush during the night. They might have underestimated the hobgoblins. We had no idea exactly how strong they were until this attack."

"What kind of strength are we talking about?" I asked. "Stronger than me? Stronger than Finn? What?"

"Strong enough to lift a house from its foundation," Thomas said, and the room erupted in more nervous chatter.

"Quiet!" I snapped, but it took them longer to silence themselves.

"We're next," Laris said and stood up. "You heard the King's threat. They are coming for us, and we're completely exposed! We can't stand up to that."

"There's no need for hysteria." I shook my head. "We have

the most powerful Trylle in the world, the most powerful of any creature on earth. Marksinna, you can create fire. Tove and I can move anything. Willa can harness the wind. We have more than enough power here to defend ourselves."

"What about those of us who can't?" the Chancellor asked. "We're defenseless against little monsters that can throw our homes!"

"We are not defenseless," I said, and I looked over at Finn.

"We should call the trackers in," Finn said, understanding my gaze. "We need the guards at home."

As much as I hated to do it, we would have to. That left our changelings unprotected, and they were just kids. We had no idea what the Vittra did with them when they took them, but we had no choice. We couldn't waste manpower protecting individual children when we had a whole kingdom to worry about.

"Do it," I said, and he nodded. "Before they get here, we need to figure out what to do about Oslinna."

"Why would we do anything with Oslinna?" Laris looked confused.

"They were just attacked," I said, speaking as if I were talking to a small child. "We need to help them."

"Help them?" the Chancellor asked. "We can barely help ourselves."

"We don't have the resources," Aurora agreed.

"We have more resources than any other compound," Tove said. "How can you even say that?"

"We need our resources for us," Laris said. "This is what

I've been saying all along. We knew this day would come. Ever since that bastard Princess was born—" She gestured to me.

"Marksinna!" Willa snapped. "She is your Princess. Remember who you're speaking to."

"How can I forget?" Laris asked. "She's the one that will get us all killed!"

"Enough!" I held up both my hands before everyone joined her. "This is what we are going to do. First, Thomas will call back all trackers. Every last one of them. When they return, we can work on assembling an army to defend ourselves, but that also means defending the other compounds.

"Second, we will send a team to Oslinna to assess the damage and relocate refugees. While there, the team will help them clean up and also try to learn more about the Vittra so we can prevent further ambushes.

"Lastly, you will all learn to use whatever abilities you have. We are powerful. I am not going to waste a soldier or a guard defending people who can protect themselves."

"You can't expect us to fight in the war!" Laris said, appalled.

"I am not asking you to, although it would be nice if some of you who can fight would offer to," I said.

"This is obscene," Aurora said. "You can't seriously mean for us to fight."

"Yes, I can," I said. "And frankly, I don't give a damn if you don't like it. This is our best hope to protect the kingdom."

"Who do you propose goes on the team?" Garrett asked.

"People who can help," I said. "I will go."

"Princess, it's unwise of you to leave Förening," Finn said.

"The truce with the Vittra King states that he will not attack our people *here*. He says nothing for the ones outside of Förening."

"You shouldn't travel," Willa agreed. "Not during a time of war."

"Why not?" Laris asked. "Let her go and get herself killed! It would save us all the headache! Not that I think she would be killed. She's probably working with them."

"Marksinna Laris," Tove said, glaring at her. "The next time you speak out against the Princess I will have you banished from Förening on the grounds of treason, and we'll see how well you do against the Vittra."

"Treason?" Her eyes widened. "I've committed no such thing!"

"Under the Treason Act, Article Twelve, anyone who plots or imagines the death of our King or Queen or their eldest child and heir has committed treason," Tove said. "And in a room full of witnesses, you just wished for the Princess's death."

"I . . ." Laris began to defend herself, then gave up and simply stared down at her hands.

"Who will go on the team, then?" Aurora asked.

"I would like volunteers," I said. "A high-ranking official needs to go as my proxy, and I will order people if I must."

"I'll go," Finn said. "My father can stay here and get the army ready. I can help lead a team into Oslinna."

"I'll go," Markis Bain offered. "My sister lives there. I should help her."

"Anyone else?" I asked, but I was met with blank stares. "A healer would be particularly useful now."

"Marksinna Kroner?" Willa prompted when Aurora said nothing.

"I'm the Prince's mother." Aurora put her hand to her chest, aghast. "I can't possibly go." Tove gave her a hard look, so she floundered for an excuse. "The Chancellor! He has some healing powers."

"Not as great as yours," he said defensively. "I'm nothing compared to you."

"You're an elected official," Aurora said. "These people voted for you. They deserve your help."

"Why don't you go, Chancellor?" Tove asked. "You can work as my liaison."

"Do I have a choice?" the Chancellor asked, sounding defeated, and Tove answered him with a glare.

The meeting went on for a few minutes longer. Willa gave an impassioned speech about the importance of helping our brethren. A few people seemed moved by it, but nobody else volunteered until Willa pointed out that if we helped them, the people from Oslinna could come back here and fight for us. That got a couple more hands in the air.

In the end, we managed to assemble a team of ten, and that was about the most I could hope for. Everyone dispersed, resolving that the team would depart the palace in two hours. After everyone else had gone, Tove, Willa, Duncan, and I lingered in the War Room.

"I think that went well." Willa leaned back against the desk.

"What if the Vittra start attacking other towns?" I asked. "What are we going to do?"

"There's nothing more we can do," Tove said. "Not right now. We need to get the trackers back. I'm sure that's what the King's plan was. To get all the trackers out after the changelings and leave us exposed."

"And I had to send them out," I said with a sigh. "The Vittra were kidnapping children. I couldn't let them."

"You did the right thing," Willa said. "And you're doing the right thing now. You're bringing the trackers back. You're helping Oslinna."

"Not enough." I shook my head and stepped away from them. "I should be going there. I should be helping. If these hobgoblins are throwing houses, they'll need people like me to move the rubble."

"Princess, you're a leader now," Duncan said. "You need to stay here and give orders. Let other people do the work."

"But that's not how it should be!" I argued. "If I have the most power, I should do the most work."

"Wendy, you are doing work," Willa said. "They wanted to leave the people in Oslinna to die without help. You need to stay here and organize the rescue efforts, and our defense. And if things are safe, maybe you can go out there and help clean up later, okay? The team needs to go out and investigate first."

"I know." I rubbed the back of my neck. "I've been trying

so hard to avoid unnecessary bloodshed, but Oren is determined to bring it on no matter what I do."

"That's not your fault, though," Willa said. "You can't control what he does."

"None of us can control our parents," Tove said. "But at
least I shut Laris up."

"That was nice." Willa laughed.

"That was really nice," Duncan agreed.

"Thank you for that," I said, smiling despite myself. "Were
you really going to banish her?"

"I don't know." Tove shrugged. "I just got sick of her always
bitching about everything."

"What are you going to do now?" Willa asked.

"Now?" I exhaled heavily when I realized what I had to do.
"I have to go tell Elora about this."

TEN

aid

Elora wasn't mad at me, but I hadn't expected her to be. She'd already begun the process of entrusting me with the kingdom, which was overwhelming, but I'd never let on. I asked for advice as infrequently as possible. I had to know how to do things on my own, and she accepted my decisions most of the time.

The news of the attack had upset her, and that was what I had been afraid of. She wanted to get out of bed and go after Oren herself, but simply getting angry tired her out too much to sit up. She'd become so fragile, and it scared me to see her that way.

I left her in Garrett's care and went to find Finn before he left. I wasn't sure how I felt about him leading the team. I had no right to stop him, and I knew that. I wouldn't even ask it of him if I could.

But this might be dangerous. I didn't know what the Vittra's plans might be. I hadn't expected them to start attacking us, so I'd clearly underestimated Oren's determination to destroy us. Or, more specifically, me.

Even though Finn hadn't been home for the better part of a month, his residence was still technically the palace. What few earthly possessions he had were here in his room in the servants' quarters. As I went to his room, I passed Loki's, and I was pleased to see that the door was shut. He'd taken my advice to lay low.

Finn's bedroom door was open, and he was packing a few clothes to take with him. I wasn't sure how long he'd be gone, but it had to be at least a few days. It depended on how badly damaged Oslinna was.

"Are you about packed?" I asked. I stood in the hall just outside his door, too afraid to go any farther.

"Yeah." Finn glanced back at me. He shoved a pair of boxers in the duffel bag and zipped it up. "I think so."

"Good." I twisted the wedding band around my finger. "Are you sure you want to do this?"

"I don't have much of a choice." Finn picked up his bag and turned to face me. He kept his expression blank, and I hated that he did it so well. I hated that I never knew what he was really thinking or feeling.

"Of course you have a choice," I said. "I'm not forcing you to go."

"I know that. But they need somebody experienced, someone who isn't an idiot, to go along. My father has to stay here, and I'm the next logical choice."

"I could go," I offered. "I should. I can be of more help."

"No. What I said at the meeting is still true," Finn said. "You're needed here."

"I'm not doing anything here except waiting until you get back." I didn't like the way that sounded, so I lowered my eyes.

"We won't be gone that long," Finn said. "We'll probably bring the survivors back to Förening. They can have shelter here."

"I should ready the palace for extra guests, then," I said, and I hated that. He would be out at battle, and I would be at home, making sure the beds were made. "I should be going with you. This is ridiculous."

"Princess, this is the right place for you," he said, almost tiredly. "But it's time for me to go. I don't want to make them wait for me."

"Yes, sorry." I stepped aside so he could walk past me. His arm brushed against me, but he didn't even notice. As he walked by, I said, "Be careful."

"You say that as if you care," he muttered.

"I do care," I said defensively. "I never said that I didn't. That isn't fair."

He stopped with his back to me. "The other night, you made your intentions perfectly clear."

"So did you," I said, and he pivoted to face me. "And you made your choice." He'd chosen duty time and time again, and if he had to sacrifice something, it had been me.

"I never had a choice, Wendy," Finn said, sounding exasperated.

"You *always* did. Everybody does. And you chose."

"Well, so did you," he said finally.

"That I did," I agreed.

He stared at me for a moment longer before turning and walking away. I hadn't wanted that to be my last conversation with him before he left. Part of me still feared that something might happen, but at the same time, I knew Finn could handle himself.

There were going to be survivors coming, and I needed to get the palace ready. I had never considered myself domestic, but Willa and Matt would be good at that sort of thing.

I found them together in Matt's room, where Willa was trying to explain what had happened in Oslinna without freaking him out too much. That was our general approach to telling Matt stuff. We didn't want to keep him completely out of the loop, but he would have had an aneurysm if he understood exactly what we were up against.

"The Vittra killed people?" Matt asked. He sat on his bed watching Willa straighten her hair. We may have been in crisis mode, but that didn't mean her hair had to look like it. "They actually killed people like you?"

"Yes, Matt." Willa stood in front of the full-length mirror across from him, running the straightener through her long hair. "They're the bad guys."

"And they're doing this because they're after you?" Matt asked, turning to me.

"They're doing it because they're bad people," Willa answered for me.

"But that Loki guy, he's one of them?" Matt asked.

"Not exactly," I said carefully. I stood off to the side of the room, and I leaned back against the wall.

"He was, though," Matt said. "He kidnapped you before. So why are you always hanging out with him?"

"I'm not."

"Yeah, you are," Matt insisted. "And the way you danced with him at your wedding? That's not the way a married woman acts, Wendy."

"I danced with a hundred guys last night." I shifted my weight and stared down at the floor.

"Leave her alone, Matt," Willa said. "She was having some fun at her wedding. You can't blame her for that."

"I'm not blaming her for anything. I'm trying to understand." He scratched at the back of his head. "Where is your husband, by the way?"

"He's down talking to the team before they leave," I said. "Giving them instructions and words of encouragement."

"You didn't want to see them off yourself?" Willa asked, turning a bit to look at me.

"No." I thought back to my conversation with Finn and shook my head. "No. Tove's got it covered. He's the Prince now. He can share some of the responsibility."

"Wait." Matt furrowed his brow. "An entire town of trolls just got attacked by hobgoblins. How is this not all over the news? How don't people know about this?"

"Oslinna is secluded, hidden in a valley," Willa explained. "All the other Trylle towns are the same. We live off the map, just out of sight, and we keep to ourselves as much as possible."

"But a big fight like that, somebody had to have heard," Matt insisted. "We may be obtuse, but I think people would notice a war in their backyard."

"Occasionally, a human will stumble onto something and find out more than they should," Willa said. "But that's what persuasion's for. If any humans did see or hear what happened in Oslinna—which is unlikely because of its isolation—they were made to forget it."

Matt shook his head, as if he still didn't understand. "But why all the secrecy? Why go to all the trouble of being hidden?"

"Think back to everything you've ever been told about trolls." Willa leaned forward, inspecting her hair in the mirror, and then she turned around. "Humans believe us to be horrible little creatures. In the past, when we've been discovered, they've called us demons and witches. We've been locked up and burned at the stake. And as powerful as we are, the humans still outnumber us by the millions. If they found out about us, they could destroy us. So we stay hidden, keeping our battles private."

After a pause, Willa changed the subject.

"When do you think the refugees will get here?"

She set the straightener down on the nearby dresser, and I could see burn marks on it from her doing the same thing many times before. She must pretty much live here now.

"I'm not sure," I said. "Maybe in a day or two or six. But we should have the rooms ready, just to be safe."

"Well, we can definitely help you with that," Willa said. "Where are the extra blankets and cleaning supplies?"

Most of the second floor of the south wing were servants' quarters, along with the Queen's chamber, which was now Tove's and my room. I wasn't sure exactly why the Queen resided with the servants, except that the south wing was where the more formal business took place.

Since we had almost no live-in servants anymore, other than two maids, a chef, and a couple of trackers, most of the bedrooms were empty. They hadn't been used in ages, so they were musty and needed freshening, but they weren't exactly dirty.

Each room had extra bedding in it, so we just needed to dust and vacuum. We raided the supply closet at the top of the stairs, and Duncan came up to meet us. He'd been with Tove sending the team off.

Tove stayed with Thomas to work on calling all the trackers in. It was a long and arduous task, and I thought about helping them, but I felt better doing physical work. It felt more like I was accomplishing something.

Duncan helped carry supplies down to the rooms, and I decided to enlist Loki to help us. I wanted to keep him out of sight, but nobody would be checking the servants' quarters. And if he was staying here, he might as well be of some use.

While we cleaned the first room, I asked Loki again if he

knew anything about the Vittra plans. He insisted that he didn't know anything about it, other than that Oren wanted me all for himself. His only advice was to stay the hell out of Oren's way when he was pissed off.

Matt and Willa took a room of their own to clean, while Duncan, Loki, and I cleaned a different one.

"Are you sure I shouldn't have gone with them?" Duncan asked. He'd gathered up the dirty bedding to throw down the laundry chute, while Loki helped me smooth out the fresh blankets on the bed.

"Yes, Duncan, I need you here," I told him for the hundredth time. He felt guilty about not going with the others to Oslinna, but I refused to let him go.

"All right," Duncan said with a sigh, but he still didn't sound convinced. "I'm going to go throw this down. I'll meet you in the next room."

"Okay, thank you," I said, and he left.

"What do you need him for?" Loki asked quietly.

"Shh!" I fixed the corner of the sheet and glared at Loki.

"You just don't want him to go." Loki smirked. "You're protecting him."

"I'm not," I lied.

"Don't you trust him in battle?"

"No, not really," I admitted and picked up a dust rag and glass cleaner. "Grab the vacuum."

"But you sent off that Flounder fellow," Loki said, and I rolled my eyes.

"His name is Finn, and I know you know that," I said as I left the room. Loki grabbed the vacuum and followed me. "You called him by his name this morning."

"Fine, I know his name," Loki admitted. We went into the next room, and he set down the vacuum as I started peeling the dusty blankets off the bed. "But you were okay with Finn going off to Oslinna, but not Duncan?"

"Finn can handle himself," I said tersely. The bedding got stuck on a corner, and Loki came over to help me free it. Once he had, I smiled thinly at him. "Thank you."

"But I know you had a soft spot for Finn," Loki continued.

"My feelings for him have no bearing on his ability to do his job."

I tossed the dirty blankets at Loki. He caught them easily before setting them down by the door, presumably for Duncan to take to the laundry chute again.

"I've never understood exactly what your relationship with him was, anyway," Loki said. I'd started putting new sheets on the bed, and he went around to the other side to help me. "Were you two dating?"

"No." I shook my head. "We never dated. We were never anything."

I continued to pull on the sheets, but Loki stopped, watching me. "I don't know if that's a lie or not, but I do know that he was never good enough for you."

"But I suppose you think you are?" I asked with a sarcastic laugh.

"No, of course I'm not good enough for you," Loki said, and I lifted my head to look up at him, surprised by his response. "But I at least *try* to be good enough."

"You think Finn doesn't?" I asked, standing up straight.

"Every time I've seen him around you, he's telling you what to do, pushing you around." He shook his head and went back to making the bed. "He wants to love you, I think, but he can't. He won't let himself, or he's incapable. And he never will."

The truth of his words stung harder than I'd thought they would, and I swallowed hard.

"And obviously, you need someone that loves you," Loki continued. "You love fiercely, with all your being. And you need someone that loves you the same. More than duty or the monarchy or the kingdom. More than himself even."

He looked up at me then, his eyes meeting mine, darkly serious. My heart pounded in my chest, the fresh heartache replaced with something new, something warmer that made it hard for me to breathe.

"But you're wrong." I shook my head. "I don't deserve that much."

"On the contrary, Wendy." Loki smiled honestly, and it stirred something inside me. "You deserve all the love a man has to give."

I wanted to laugh or blush or look away, but I couldn't. I was frozen in a moment with Loki, finding myself feeling things for him I didn't think I could ever feel for anyone else.

"I don't know how much more laundry we can fit down the

chute," Duncan said as he came back in the room, interrupting the moment.

I looked away from Loki quickly and grabbed the vacuum cleaner.

"Just get as much down there as you can," I told Duncan.

"I'll try." He scooped up another load of bedding to send downstairs.

Once he'd gone, I glanced back at Loki, but, based on the grin on his face, I'd say his earlier seriousness was gone.

"You know, Princess, instead of making that bed, we could close the door and have a roll around in it." Loki wagged his eyebrows. "What do you say?"

Rolling my eyes, I turned on the vacuum cleaner to drown out the conversation.

"I'll take that as a maybe later!" Loki shouted over it.

We worked all afternoon, and by the end we were all tired and cranky. Somehow, that felt good. It meant we'd done something today, and while it hadn't helped anybody in Oslinna yet, it would.

When suppertime came around, I wasn't hungry, so I retired to my room. I was exhausted, and I should've slept, but I couldn't. Tove came in shortly after I got in bed, and we didn't say much. He just crawled in bed, and both of us lay awake for a long time.

I wasn't sure I'd even fallen asleep when Duncan burst through the door. He didn't knock, and I was about to yell at him when I saw how he looked. He wore pajamas and his hair was mussed from sleep, but he was positively panicked.

"What is it, Duncan?" I asked, already throwing my legs over the side of the bed so I could get up.

"It's Finn," Duncan panted. "They were ambushed on the way to Oslinna."

defeat

I don't remember moving or running. It was all a blur of nothing until I was in the front hall with Finn. A small crowd had gathered around, including Thomas, but I pushed them out of the way to get to him.

Finn was sitting on the floor, and I fell to my knees next to him. He was alive, and I almost sobbed at the sight of him. Blood covered his temple, and his clothes were disheveled. His arm hung at a weird angle, and it took me a moment to realize it had to be broken.

"What happened?" I asked, and I touched his face with trembling hands, mostly to be sure he was real.

"We caught them off guard," Finn said. He stared off at nothing, and his eyes were moist. "They were going home, I think, and we happened to run into them. We thought we could get the best of them. But they were too strong." He swallowed hard. "They killed the Chancellor."

"Oh, shit," Tove said, and I turned to see him standing behind me. He'd been tending to Markis Bain, making sure that he'd made it through all right.

"Tove, go get your mother," I said. Tove nodded once and left, and I turned back to Finn. "Are you okay?"

"I'm alive," he said simply.

Finn was in shock, so I didn't push him for details. Markis Bain ended up filling in the blanks about what had happened. They were on their way to Oslinna when they saw the Vittra camped out. The way he described it, it sounded all very Rumpelstiltskin. The hobgoblins had a fire going, and they danced around it, singing songs and telling tales of how they had defeated Oslinna.

The Chancellor thought they should get the drop on the hobgoblins. They could end the fight right there in the woods. Finn was initially against the idea, but he soon decided that if they had a chance to stop the Vittra before they hurt anybody else, they had to take it.

The only reason any of the team had survived was because they had surprised the Vittra, but the Chancellor wasn't the only one who died. Another Markis had been killed, and a second tracker was severely injured.

All of them were battered and bruised. When Aurora came over to heal them, Bain kept saying it was amazing that any of them were alive. Aurora healed Finn's arm, but that was all she'd heal on him. She wouldn't waste her energy on a tracker, no matter what I said.

Duncan and I helped Finn up to his room to rest, and Tove

stayed behind. He wanted to make sure the others had gotten home okay, although he seemed particularly interested in making sure that Bain was fine. We'd have to plan another way to help Oslinna, but we couldn't do it now.

"I don't need to lie down," Finn insisted as Duncan and I helped him sit on his bed. "I'm fine." He winced when I bumped his arm, and I sighed.

"Finn, you are not fine," I said. "You need to rest."

"No, I need to figure out how to stop those damned hobgoblins," Finn said. "They're going to come after us all eventually. We need to find a way to beat them."

"We will," I said, even though I wasn't sure that was true. "But we aren't going to do anything right now. It can wait until the morning, when you've slept some."

"Wendy." He looked up at me, his eyes stormier than usual. "You didn't see them. You don't know what they're like."

"No, I don't," I admitted, and the tone of his voice made my stomach twist up. "But you can tell me all about it. Tomorrow."

"Let me at least talk to Loki," Finn said, almost desperately.

"Loki?" I asked. "Why would you want to talk to him?"

"He has to know how to handle these things," Finn said. "There's got to be some secret to defeating them, and if anyone knows it, it would be a Vittra Markis."

"He's probably sleeping—"

"Then wake him up, Wendy!" Finn yelled, and I flinched. "People are dying!"

I twisted my ring around my finger and relented. "Fine. If you promise to lie down, I'll let Loki talk to you. But once he's done, you have to rest until tomorrow. Is that clear?"

"Fine," Finn said, but I had a feeling he'd agree to anything to be sure I got Loki.

"Duncan?" I looked back to where he waited in the doorway. "Can you get Loki? Tell him I asked for him."

Duncan left me alone with Finn. I motioned for Finn to lie back. He sighed but did it anyway. I sat next to him, and he stared at the ceiling, looking annoyed. His shirt was torn and bloody, and tentatively I reached out to touch a cut on his arm.

"Don't," he said firmly.

"Sorry." I dropped my hand. "And I'm sorry about what happened. I should've gone with you."

"Don't be stupid. If you'd gone with us, you'd only have gotten yourself killed."

"I'm a stronger fighter than you are, Finn."

"I'm not going to argue with you," he said, his eyes still staring straight up. "You don't even need to be here. I'm fine. I can talk to Loki alone."

"No, I'm not leaving you alone with him." I shook my head. "Not when you're weak."

"You think he'd hurt me?" Finn asked.

"No, but I don't want you getting all riled up."

Finn scoffed. I hated how strained things had become between Finn and me, but I didn't know how to fix it. I wasn't even sure it could be fixed. We sat in silence until Duncan came back with Loki.

"This is not at all what I had in mind when the Princess summoned me in the middle of the night," Loki said with a sigh, standing in the doorway to Finn's room. His light hair stood up all over, and he had red marks on his face from sleeping.

"Thank you for getting up," I said. "Did Duncan tell you what happened?"

"Obviously not," Loki said.

"The team we sent out to help Oslinna was overwhelmed by hobgoblins," I said. "Some of our people were killed."

"You're lucky not all of them were killed," Loki said.

"Good men died tonight," Finn growled and tried to sit up in bed, but I put my hand on his chest and pushed him back. "They fought to protect the people here! To protect the Princess! I would think that was something that mattered to you!"

"That wasn't a slam against the lives you lost," Loki said, managing to sound apologetic and irritated at the same time. "The hobgoblins are hard to beat. And from what I heard about the damage to Oslinna, it's astonishing to me that anyone in your rescue team lived."

"We caught them by surprise." Finn settled back down in bed again.

"That does help," Loki said. "The hobgoblins may be strong, but they're stupid."

"How do we defeat them?" Finn asked.

"I honestly don't know. I've never tried defeating them."

"You must know how it's done," Finn insisted. "There must be a way."

"Maybe there is," Loki admitted. "But I've never even fought beside them. The King usually doesn't let hobgoblins leave the grounds. He's afraid that humans will catch on to what we are if they see them."

"Why is he letting them out now?" Finn asked.

"You know why he is." Loki sighed and sat down in a chair in the corner of Finn's room. "The King's fixated on Wendy. He'll do anything to get her."

"How do we stop that?" Finn looked over at him.

Loki stared thoughtfully at the floor, biting his lip, then shook his head sadly. "I don't know."

"What if we can't stop him?" I asked.

"We'll find a way," Finn assured me, but he wouldn't look at me when he said it.

"The hobgoblins aren't very bright," Loki added quickly. "And they're helpless against abilities. Any power you have works twice as well on them as it does on humans."

"What do you mean?" Finn asked.

"Like persuasion or any of Wendy's abilities." Loki gestured to me. "It works on them like that." He snapped his fingers. "That's why I was in charge of guarding her at the Vittra palace. She could've convinced the hobgoblins to do anything for her."

"So the Markis and Marksinna, they can defeat the hobgoblins?" Finn asked. "But I can't?"

Loki shook his head. "Not in hand-to-hand combat, I wouldn't think."

"We're not going to get a Markis or Marksinna to fight in

the war," I said. "Especially not when a Markis was killed to-night, along with the Chancellor. They'll be too afraid."

"We can convince them," Finn said. "If it's the only way we can stop the Vittra, they'll have to do it."

"It's not the only way," I said, but both Loki and Finn ignored me.

"Your people are spoiled," Loki said. "You can't convince them to do anything."

"*We're* spoiled?" Finn scoffed. "That would mean something if it weren't coming from a brat Prince."

"I don't know why you find my comment so offensive." Loki sat up straighter. "I've seen the way these people treat Wendy, and she's their Princess. They're insolent."

"They don't know her," Finn said. "It takes time, and it doesn't help that she spends so much of it with Vittra prisoners."

"I'm not a prisoner." Loki looked disgusted. "I'm here on my own."

"I do not understand that." Finn shook his head in disbelief.

"Finn, he asked for amnesty, and I granted it," I said.

"But your motivations completely baffle me," Finn said. "We're fighting with the Vittra, and you let him stay without consequence."

"It really pisses you off that much that she wants me around?" Loki asked, and Finn glared at him.

"I don't—" I stopped myself and shook my head. "It doesn't matter why Loki's here, but he is here now, and he's trustworthy—I assure you of that. Plus, his intimate knowl-edge of the Vittra is invaluable."

"I'll tell you as much as I know, but I don't know very much that can help you, Wendy," Loki said. "If you want information about policies and procedures, I can help. But if I knew a way to stop the King, I would've done it myself."

"Why?" Finn asked. "Why would you stop the King?"

"He's a bastard." Loki lowered his eyes and pulled at something on his shirt. "Beyond measure."

"But hasn't he always been one?" Finn asked. "Why did you defect now? Why here? There are other troll tribes and hundreds of cities that aren't at war with your King."

"But only the Trylle have Wendy." Loki's smile returned but his eyes were pained. "And how could I pass on that?"

"She is married, you know," Finn said. "So it might be a good idea if you stopped trying to flirt with her. She's not interested."

"It's up to her to decide who she's interested in," Loki said, with an edge to his voice. "And it's not exactly like you're following your own advice."

"I am her tracker." Finn sat up in bed, but this time I didn't try to stop him. His eyes were burning. "It's my job to protect her."

"No, Duncan is her tracker." Loki pointed to where Duncan stood in the doorway, staring wide-eyed at their confrontation. "And Wendy's stronger than the both of you combined. You're not protecting her. You're protecting *yourself* because you're a lovesick ex-boyfriend."

"You think you have everything figured out, but you don't know anything," Finn growled. "If it were up to me I'd have you sent back to the Vittra in a flash."

"But it's not up to you!" I snapped. "It's up to me. And this conversation is over. Finn needs to rest, and you are not helping anything, Loki."

"Sorry," Loki said and rubbed his hands on his pants.

"Why don't you go back to your room?" I asked Loki. "I'll be over to talk to you in a minute."

He nodded and got up. "Feel better," Loki said to Finn, and he actually did sound sincere.

Finn grunted in response, and Loki and Duncan left. I wanted to reach out and touch Finn, comfort him in some way, because I felt like he needed it. Maybe I needed it too.

"Get some sleep," I told Finn, since I could think of nothing better to say to him. I got up, but he reached out and grabbed my wrist.

"Wendy, I don't trust him," he said, referring to Loki.

"I know. But I do."

"Be careful," Finn said simply and let go of me.

It was well after midnight, and the rest of the palace had fallen silent. The morning would bring endless meetings, but for now, everyone had returned to their beds. The hall was dark, and I could see the warm glow of the lamp in Loki's room.

He didn't hear me in the hallway, so I stood outside, watching him. He was making his bed, and when he'd finished, he chewed his thumb and stared down at it. He shook his head and pulled back the blanket a bit, so it looked more unmade. Then he changed his mind and smoothed out the bedding again.

"What are you doing?" I asked.

"Nothing." He looked startled for a second, then smiled and ran a hand through his hair. "Nothing. You wanted to talk? Why don't you come in?"

"Were you just straightening up the room for me?" I asked.

"Well . . ." He ruffled his hair again. "Whenever I have a Princess stopping by, I try to make my room presentable."

"I see." I went into his room and shut the door behind me, which only delighted him.

"Why don't you have a seat?" Loki gestured to his bed. "Make yourself comfortable."

"I need to ask you a favor."

He smiled. "For you, anything,"

"I want you to take me to Ondarike," I said, and his smile fell away.

"Except that."

"I feel horrible asking, because I know what Oren did to you, and I wouldn't expect you to go inside or anything," I said quickly. "I don't know how to get there or how to get inside, but you could tell me and drop me at the door. I'd never put you in danger or risk your life."

"But you expect me to risk yours?" Loki smirked and shook his head. "No way, Wendy."

"I can promise you your safety," I said. "Once I am there, I doubt he'd even care about you. You don't have to go anywhere near the palace even. Just tell me how to get there."

"Wendy, you're not listening," he said. "I'm not worried about me. I won't let you do that."

"I'll be fine," I insisted. "He's my father, and I'm strong enough to handle myself."

"You have no idea what you're up against." Loki laughed darkly. "No. This is completely ludicrous. I'm not even going to entertain the idea."

"Loki, listen to me. Finn almost died tonight—"

"Your boyfriend gets hurt, and suicide becomes the only viable option?" Loki asked.

"He's not my boyfriend," I corrected him.

"Fine. *Ex*-boyfriend," he said. "That doesn't make this better. And as much as I hate to admit it, Finn was right. We can find a way around this. I know I didn't help very much tonight, but I'm sure, if given time, I can come up with something."

"But we don't have time, Loki!" I took a deep breath. "I'm not saying that I'll give myself to Oren as a peace offering, but I have to talk to him at least. I have to do something to postpone the war a little longer. We need more time to get an army ready. And he's out there killing our people *now*."

"So you want me to take you to the Vittra palace so you can have a little meeting with the King?" Loki asked. "While you're in there, I'll wait outside, and after the meeting is done, you'll come out, and we'll drive back here? Is that the plan?"

"Not exactly, but sorta," I said.

"Wendy!" Loki sounded exasperated. "Why would he let you go? He is doing all of this for *you*. Once he has you there in the palace, why would he ever let you leave?"

"He can't stop me, for one thing," I said. "I can defend myself against him and the hobgoblins and anything else he might have. I can't fight an entire war on my own and defend every person in the entire kingdom all at once. But if I'm alone, I can take care of myself."

"Even if that's true, it's still too great a risk," Loki said. "If you try to leave, he could kill you. Not just hold you hostage. Not just threaten you. Actually *murder* you. He would rather do that than see you return here."

"No, not yet." I shook my head. "Someday, yes, that's true. But he wants me to be Queen. That's why he agreed to the truce. He wanted to ensure that I would be the Trylle Queen."

"He wants both kingdoms," he said quietly. "You're going to give him what he wants?"

"Yes." I nodded. "I will agree to rule alongside him over both the Trylle and the Vittra if he stops the bloodshed until I am crowned Queen."

"He won't rule 'beside' you. He'll take it from you."

"I know, but I would never let him rule anyway," I said. "I don't plan to follow through with it."

Loki whistled and shook his head. "If you went back on your deal, he would destroy everything—and I do mean *everything*—that you have ever cared about."

"I won't go back on it," I said. "It will never get to that point. I'm only buying us time to build up the army, and then we'll attack the Vittra, take them down, and I will kill Oren."

"You'll kill him?" He raised an eyebrow. "Do you even know how to kill him?"

"No. Not yet," I admitted. "That's why I haven't killed him. But I will."

"I don't even know if he can be killed," Loki said.

"Everyone can be killed."

"Many, many people have tried," he said. "And they've all failed."

"Yes, but none of those people have his blood pumping through their veins," I said. "I think I'm the only one strong enough to do it."

Loki studied me a moment before asking, "What if you can't? What if you do all this, and you can't find a way to stop him?"

"I don't know," I said. "I will have to find a way. He's going to keep coming until he has me. I would gladly hand myself over to him if I thought that would be enough, but I'm not sure that it is anymore."

Loki stared down at the floor, his golden eyes wide as he thought it through. I didn't know what he was thinking, but he didn't look happy.

"So, will you take me?" I asked.

He licked his lips and let out a deep breath. "You don't know what you're asking."

"I know perfectly well what—"

Loki cut me off, sounding exasperated. "No, Wendy, you don't. You have no idea what it's really like to live in Ondarike, under the rule of a truly merciless King. You don't understand what he's capable of. He—"

He stopped abruptly and stepped closer to me, his expression solemn and his eyes dark.

"Oren killed my father when I was a child. He hung him

from the ceiling by his ankles and slit his neck, letting him bleed out like a pig." Loki's eyes never wavered from mine as he spoke. "And it takes much longer than one would think. Or maybe it just seemed that way to me, since I was only nine, and Oren made me watch. He told me that's what happens to people who betray him."

"I'm so sorry," I whispered, unable to think of anything else to say.

"I'm not telling you this so you'll feel sorry for me," he said. "I want you to know what you're up against. This man has no soul."

"I know he's a monster." I lowered my gaze, trying to break the intensity of the moment. "Why did you stay in Ondarike after the King did that?"

"I was a child, for one thing. I had nowhere else to go."

"What about when you weren't a child?" I lifted my head cautiously, all too aware of how close Loki was to me. "Why did you wait so long to leave?"

"I stayed for Sara," Loki said simply. "She's been like a sister to me, and she's the only family I have. The King was as cruel to her as he was to me, if not worse, and I didn't want her to go through that alone."

"But now you don't care if she does?" I asked.

"No, I still care. But I can't do anything to protect her anymore. I was trapped in a dungeon, unable to help her in any way."

"So that's why you left?"

"No." He smiled as he stared down into my eyes. "I left for

you." I didn't know what to say to that, but he spoke before I could anyway. "And you're asking me to go back."

"No." I shook my head. "I won't force you to go back if you don't want to. I'll find someone else to take me there."

"Who?" Loki asked. "Who else would possibly take you?"

"I don't know." I floundered for a minute. "I'll find the way on my own."

Tove and a few trackers probably knew how to get to the Vittra palace, but they didn't know the intricacies of it like Loki did. But if I had to, I could take a map from the War Room.

"You can't go by yourself," he said.

"I am sorry the King hurt you, I truly am. I know what a terrible man he is, but you telling me how horrible he is only emphasizes why I need to go. I have to stop him from doing to my people what he's done to his own. I have to go."

I turned to reach for the door handle, but Loki stopped me before I could. He grabbed my wrist and stood right in front of me.

"Loki." I sighed and looked up at him. "Let go of me."

"No, Wendy, I won't let you do this," Loki said.

"You can't stop me."

"I'm much stronger than you."

I tried to shove him out of my way, but it was like pushing on concrete. He pressed me back against his bedroom wall and put an arm on either side of me. His body didn't touch me, but it was so close I couldn't move away.

"You may be physically stronger than me, but I can have

you on the floor writhing in pain in minutes. I don't want to hurt you, but I will if I have to."

"You don't have to," Loki said emphatically. "You don't have to do this."

"Yes, I do. I will do whatever it takes to save lives," I said. "If you can't, that's fine. But get out of my way."

He bit his lip and shook his head, but he didn't move away from me.

"It's the middle of the night, and you want to run away with me," Loki said. "What will you tell your husband?"

"Nothing."

"Nothing?" Loki raised an eyebrow. "The Princess goes missing without a word? It would be total pandemonium."

"I'll have Duncan tell them in the morning where I've gone," I said. "That'll buy us a few hours to get there before somebody comes after us."

"If the King doesn't let you leave, he'll kill the rescue party that they send," Loki pointed out. "That would be Finn, Tove, Duncan, maybe even Willa. You're willing to risk them on this?"

"This might be my only chance to save them," I said thickly.

"I can't talk you out of this?" he whispered, his eyes searching mine.

"No."

He swallowed and brushed back a hair from my forehead. His hand lingered on my face, and I let it. His eyes were strangely sad, and I wanted to ask him why, but I didn't dare speak.

"I want you to remember this," he said, his voice low and husky.

"What?" I asked.

"You want me to kiss you."

"I don't," I lied.

"You do. And I want you to remember that."

"Why?"

"Because." Without further explanation, he turned away from me. "If you want to do this, hurry and put some clothes on. You don't want to see the King in your pajamas."

rendezvous

Loki liked alternative country, and the satellite radio in the Cadillac had been playing Neil Young, Ryan Adams, the Raconteurs, and Bob Dylan since we left Förening. He sang along with it sometimes, in an off-key way that was strangely endearing.

It was still dark out, and snow was falling around us, but Loki didn't seem to mind. The car slid in a few places, but he always corrected it. I'd put my makeup on in the car, and he'd managed to keep it steady enough so I didn't poke myself in the eye with liner.

Loki had teased me about the makeup and my choice of clothing. It was a long, dark violet gown, covered in lace and diamonds, with a black velvet cloak over it. I'd chosen it because I knew reverence would go a long way with Oren.

After they'd kidnapped me, Sara wouldn't let me see him without wearing a gown. Respect was important to him, and making sure I looked nice when I saw him would show him that I respected him.

I'd actually been lucky that I'd been able to find something this nice to wear. Most of my clothes had been moved from my old room into the Queen's chambers that I shared with Tove, but some had been left behind. I'd gone to my old room to get dressed because I didn't want to see Tove and tell him what I was doing.

After I had changed, I went to Duncan's room. He'd freaked out when I told him what my plans were, and I knew he'd run to tell Tove as soon as I'd gone, if he didn't *before* I left. I'd used persuasion to get him to hold off as long as possible, which I estimated to be until roughly eight A.M. Maybe longer if my persuasion lasted.

Since I was the Princess, I had access to everything. I'd gone to the garage and taken the keys to a black Cadillac. We'd left Förening without anybody else seeing us, except for the guard at the gates. I used persuasion on him to keep him from alerting anyone, and we were on the road.

"You can sleep," Loki said as I stared out the window at the snowflakes landing against the glass. "I will get us there."

"I know, but I'm fine." Even though I hadn't really slept last night, I wasn't tired. My nerves had me on edge.

"We can always turn back," he reminded me, not for the first time.

"I know."

"I thought I would offer," he said, sounding disappointed.

He sat in silence for a minute before singing along to the radio.

"Your father was Trylle, wasn't he?" I asked, cutting off his singing.

"My father was born in Förening," Loki answered carefully. "But he was more closely related to a snake than Trylle or Vittra."

"You're being metaphorical, right?" I asked. "Your father wasn't literally a reptile?"

"No." Loki laughed a little. "He wasn't an actual snake."

"How did he end up with the Vittra?" I asked. "Did he leave for your mom?"

"No." He shook his head. "He was the Chancellor in Förening, and he met your father when Oren came around courting your grandparents for Elora's hand in marriage."

"I didn't realize your father was a high-ranking official," I said.

"That he was." Loki nodded. "In arranging the marriage, my father had to work with Oren a lot, and Oren's lust for power appealed to him. Evil attracts evil, apparently."

"So he left to join the Vittra?" I asked.

"Not exactly," he said. "The plan at the time was to unite the kingdoms. Oren would rule both of them, once your mother was Queen. This was before she'd even come back to Förening, when she was still living with her host family, but they had already begun working on the deal. As Chancellor, my father was sent to the Vittra kingdom as the Trylle ambassador. That's how he met my mother."

"I thought you said he didn't leave for her," I said.

"He didn't. She was a means to an end. He married her so he'd have a reason to leave, not the other way around," Loki said.

"So he didn't love her?" I asked.

"No, he couldn't stand her. Though she was beautiful." He paused, thinking of her. "But I don't think he even cared. She was a powerful Marksinna. My father wanted power, and she had it.

"For a time, he was both the Trylle Chancellor and a Vittra Prince," he went on. "I'm not technically a Prince, and neither was he, but since we have the title as the highest-ranking Markis, they refer to us that way."

"Your father committed treason against the Trylle, didn't he?" I asked tentatively, remembering how he'd told me that Oren had executed his father.

"Do you know?" Loki glanced over at me. "Did they tell you what my father did?"

"Elora said that your father told Oren where my grandmother and she were hiding," I said. "Because of that, Oren found them and killed my grandmother."

"He did," Loki said. "He did more than that, actually. He tried to tell Oren where you were, but you were too well hidden, so my father was never able to find out.

"But because of his efforts, he became Oren's right-hand man," Loki continued with a bitter smile. "He got everything he ever wanted, and you'd think that would make him happy, but no."

"What happened?" I asked.

"When I was nine, Oren married Sara, and my father was furious," Loki said. "There was a chance they might produce a healthy child, and my father didn't want that. Without a child, I was the only viable heir to the throne."

"But Sara can't have kids?" I questioned.

"We didn't know that at the time," Loki explained. "She has some Trylle blood in her, two generations back, and that's how she has the ability to heal. But the Vittra blood must have thinned out the Trylle in her too much, because she's been unable to have kids."

"But when she married Oren, your dad thought they might have a child?" I asked.

"Right." He nodded. "My father wanted nothing more than for me to be King. It didn't matter that I had no urge to be King, or that Oren might live forever and I would never be King anyway."

"Why did he want you to be King so badly?" I asked.

"He wanted power, more power," Loki said. "He thought if I became King, we could rule the world or something. He never got specific about his plans, but he just wanted more."

"So what happened?" I asked. "I heard he tried to defect back to Förening."

"Yes, that was after everything went to hell," Loki said. "My father came up with some plan to kill Sara. I don't know exactly what it was, but I think he meant to poison her. My mother found out about it, and she . . ." He stopped and shook his head.

"My mother was kind," Loki went on. "I'd been betrothed to Sara, so she'd become like a member of our family. My mother invited her for supper regularly and treated her as a daughter. Even after Sara married Oren, my mother remained close to her."

"And your father was going to kill her?" I asked.

"Yes, but my mother wouldn't let him." He chewed the inside of his cheek and stared straight ahead at the snow coming down. "So he killed her."

"What?" I asked, thinking I'd misunderstood. "Sara's alive."

"No, my father killed my mother," Loki said flatly. "He hit her in the head with a metal vase, over and over. I was hiding in the closet, and I saw the whole thing."

"Oh, my god," I gasped. "I'm so sorry."

"The King found out, and he didn't care that my father had murdered someone," he said. "But then I told the King *why* my father killed her, about his plan to assassinate Sara.

"My father tried to make it back to the Trylle," Loki continued. "He offered Elora trade secrets, anything she'd want to know. I've been told that she accepted, but he never made it there. Oren found him and executed him."

"I'm sorry," I said, unsure of what else to say.

"I'm not," Loki said. "But I am lucky that the King didn't kill me too. Sara took pity on me, and I moved into the palace with them."

"The King and Queen raised you," I said, realizing more what Loki had meant about Sara being his only family.

He nodded. "They did. Sara more so. The King's never

been that fond of me, although I don't think he's ever been that fond of anyone."

Silence settled over us, and Loki seemed morose. Bringing up the death of his mother would have that effect.

What had happened to him was horrible, not that I'd had a great childhood myself. I thought back to when he'd arrived in Förening, and I'd put my hand on the scar on his chest. I'd felt like he was a kindred spirit, and the more I thought about it, the more I realized how alike we really were.

We both had a parental figure who hated us, and we were left orphaned at a young age. His father wanted him to be King, even though Loki didn't want it, and my mother wanted me to be Queen, even though I didn't want it. And we both shared a mixed bloodline of Trylle and Vittra.

"Why aren't you like me?" I asked when I thought of it.

"Pardon?"

"Why aren't you as powerful as me?" I asked. "We're both Trylle and Vittra."

"Well, for one thing, you're the product of the most powerful Trylle and the most powerful Vittra," Loki said. "I'm the product of a very powerful Vittra and a fairly weak Trylle. My father was a low-ranking Markis. He had hardly anything. I did get his ability to render people unconscious, though, but mine is much stronger than his ever was."

"But you have more physical strength than I do," I pointed out.

"Your father isn't physically that strong," Loki said. "Don't get me wrong, he is very strong, especially by Trylle standards. But mostly he's just . . . immortal."

"*Just* immortal," I said. "That's good. That'll make killing him so much easier."

"We can turn back," Loki offered again.

I shook my head. "No, we can't."

The car hit a patch of ice and jerked to the side. Loki reached out, putting his hand on my arm to make sure I was safe, before straightening out the car.

"Sorry about that," he said, keeping his hand on my arm.

"It's okay."

His hand felt warm on my bare skin, and I moved my arm so I could take his hand in mine. I don't know why I did it exactly, but I felt better. It helped quiet my nerves and ease the tightening of my stomach.

I stared out the window, almost embarrassed to look over at him, but he said nothing about it. He just held my hand, and eventually he started singing along with the radio again.

The snow had lessened by the time we reached the Vittra palace in Ondarike. I hadn't really had a chance to look at it the last time I was here. Now I saw how much it looked like an old castle. The brick towers and spirals loomed against the overcast sky. Tall trees without any leaves filled the surrounding forest, and I almost expected there to be a moat to cross.

Loki pulled up in front of the massive wooden doors and turned off the car. I gaped at the palace and tried not to let my nerves get the best of me. I could do this.

"How do I find him?" I asked. "Where's the King?"

"I'll show you." Loki opened his car door.

"What are you doing?" I asked as he got out.

"Taking you inside," he said and slammed the door shut.

"You can't go in there," I said once I'd climbed out of the car. "The King could do something to you."

"What kind of tour guide would I be if I didn't show you all the sights myself?" He grinned at me, but it didn't meet his eyes.

"Loki, be serious." I wouldn't walk with him up the path, so he turned back to face me. "The King will throw you in the dungeon again."

"Maybe," Loki agreed. "But I don't think he will if you succeed in making a deal with him, and we're both counting on you to make a deal."

"I don't like the idea of you going in there," I said.

"Yeah, well, I don't like you going in there either." He shrugged. "So we're even."

Reluctantly, I nodded. I didn't want to put him in danger, but he had a point. If Oren agreed with me, which was what I was counting on, I could get amnesty for Loki thrown in along with it.

Loki walked beside me up the pathway to the doors. I tried to open one, but it wouldn't budge. Loki laughed a little and reached around me. He pulled it open like it was nothing, and then we stepped inside the Vittra palace.

THIRTEEN

the truth

I'd forgotten how cavelike it was inside the King's chamber. The room was windowless, and the walls were dark mahogany. The ceilings were high, and candelabras cast a pale glow over us.

We sat in elegant red chairs, the only furniture in the room aside from a bookcase and large desk. Loki, Sara, and I sat, saying nothing, and waited for the King. Loki chewed his thumbnail, and his leg bounced nervously. Sara had her hands in her lap, and she stared off with a blank expression on her face.

As soon as we'd come inside the castle, Sara's little Pomeranian had charged at us, barking. He growled at me, but he was thrilled to see Loki and peppered him with kisses. Sara came right after, responding to the sound of his barking.

When she saw us, she blanched. She only stopped and stared, and Loki asked if she was happy to see him. Instead of answering him, she sent a nearby hobgoblin to get the King, and she led us to his chamber to wait for him.

She handed the dog off to Ludlow, one of the hobgoblins, and motioned for us to sit down. We waited in silence for what felt like a long time but may have been only minutes.

"You shouldn't have come here," Sara said finally.

"I know that," Loki said.

"You shouldn't have brought her," Sara said.

"I know that," he repeated.

"Why did you come back?" she asked.

"I don't know," Loki said, growing irritated.

"*That* you don't know?" Sara snorted. "He's going to kill you."

"I know," he said quietly.

"I won't let him," I said firmly, and Loki turned to look at me.

"Forgive me, Princess, but you are so naive," Sara said.

"I have a plan," I said, sounding more convincing than I felt. "I will make it work."

"He will never let you go," Sara said as if to warn me.

"He will," I insisted. "As long as I offer him something larger than myself in return."

"What do you have that's more than that?" Sara asked.

"My kingdom."

Loki tried to change the subject by pointing out two swords that hung on the wall. He explained that while most metal swords could probably kill the Vittra, Oren had a special set made with platinum and diamonds. He used them for all his executions, to be certain to get the job done.

I wasn't sure how that was supposed to ease the tension in

the room, but it no longer mattered because the double doors to the chamber were thrown open and the King walked in.

Loki's leg immediately stopped bobbing, and he dropped his hand to his lap. Oren smiled at us, and it made my skin crawl. Sara stood when he entered, so I did the same, but Loki was slow to follow.

"So you finally brought her?" Oren asked, giving him a discerning glare.

"I didn't bring her, sire," Loki said. "She brought me."

"Oh?" Oren looked surprised but he nodded approvingly at me. "You found the trash, and decided to return it, like I asked."

"No," I said. "He's coming with me when I leave."

"When you leave?" Oren asked, and his laugh echoed off the walls. "Oh, my dear sweet Princess, you're not leaving."

"You haven't heard what I am going to offer you," I said.

"I already have everything I want in this room." Oren had begun slowly walking around us in a large circle. Loki turned with him, to keep his eyes on him, but I didn't.

"You don't have Förening or any of the Trylle kingdom," I said. "You don't even have the remains of Oslinna. You may have devastated it, but it's still ours."

"I will get your kingdom," Oren said, his voice right behind me.

"Perhaps," I said. "But how long will it take you? Simply possessing the Princess doesn't ensure a victory over the Trylle. In fact, they will only fight you harder."

"What are you proposing?" Oren asked, and he walked around so he was in front of me.

"Time," I said. "Give me time to get the people behind the idea so you can avoid the uprising that happened when you married my mother."

"I quashed that uprising." Oren smiled slyly, probably fondly remembering all the women and children he'd killed.

"But you lost the kingdom, didn't you?" I asked, and his smile faltered.

"What could you possibly do to guarantee me the kingdom?" Oren asked.

"I will be Queen soon," I said. "You saw Elora. You know it won't be much longer."

"And our truce will end," Oren said, his words threatening.

"If you let me have the time from now until I'm Queen to get the people in order and prepared for the transition, we could do it," I said. "I could get them on your side. If I convinced them I was ruling *with* you, not under you, they would go along with me."

"You would not rule with me," he growled.

"I know," I said hastily. "I just need to get them on my side. Get them behind you. Once everything is in place, and you are King of all the Vittra and Trylle, they would bow before you without complaint. They would serve you as you desire."

"Why?" Oren raised a skeptical eyebrow and stepped back. "Why would you do this?"

"Because I know that you're going to keep fighting, and eventually you will win, but at the cost of thousands and thousands of my people's lives," I said. "I would rather work with you to ensure a bloodless takeover now than a brutal one later."

"Hmm." Oren seemed to think it over and nodded. "Smart. Very smart. What do you want in return?"

"No more attacks on any of our towns," I said. "Stop all fighting against us. If you keep slaughtering my people, it will be hard to convince them to trust you. And besides that, if it's all going to be your kingdom, you're destroying your own property."

"Those are valid points," Oren said. He'd taken to walking again, away from us this time, his back to me. "How does Loki play into all of this?"

"He's Vittra," I said. "By being kind to the Trylle, he will help convince them that you're not bad. That this has been a misunderstanding. He'll help gain the trust of the people on your behalf."

"Are you sure you want *him*, though?" Oren turned back to face us. "I could send Sara in his place."

"They already know Loki," I said. "They're beginning to trust him."

"You mean *you* trust him." Oren smiled wider at that. "He didn't tell you, did he?"

"That's too vague," I said. "I can't possibly know what you're referring to."

"Marvelous!" Oren laughed. "You don't know!"

I licked my lips. "Know what?" I asked.

Oren laughed again. "It's a lie."

"It's not all a lie," Loki said quickly. From the corner of my eye I saw the way his skin paled, and I heard the tremor in his voice. "The scars on my back are not a lie."

"Yes, well, you earned those." Oren stopped laughing and gave him a hard look. "You failed me one too many times."

"I didn't fail you," Loki said carefully. "I refused you."

"No, you failed." Oren stepped closer to him, and Loki struggled to keep eye contact with him. "She didn't run away with you. She chose someone else over you. So you failed."

"What?" I asked, and a sick feeling grew inside my stomach.

"I wouldn't have brought her back here," Loki insisted.

"You say that now," Oren said and stepped away from him. "But that's not what you said when you got back."

"I was in the dungeon, and you were beating me!" Loki shouted. "I would've agreed to anything."

"You did agree to anything," Oren said. "You agreed to seduce the Princess, to trick her into falling in love with you so you could bring her back here to me. Isn't that right?"

"That's right, but—" Loki began, but Oren cut him off.

"You went to her palace and got caught on purpose so you could stay with her, spend time with her, manipulate her," Oren said.

"That's not exactly how—" Loki said.

"And when Sara brought you back, you told me you almost had her." Oren smiled, as if telling a funny anecdote. "You told me how she'd nearly kissed you, and the way she blushed when you suggested that she marry you instead of that idiot she's with now."

Loki said nothing. He stared at the floor and bit his lip. A horrible pain grew inside my chest, because I knew it was true.

"Didn't you?" Oren yelled. Loki jumped at the sound, but he kept looking down.

"I had no choice," Loki said quietly.

"That's okay, then, isn't it?" Oren smiled when he looked at me. "Everything that has ever transpired between the two of you is a lie. But he did it because I asked him to, so that makes it okay. Doesn't it? It's okay knowing every word he ever said is a *lie?*"

"That's not true," Loki said and lifted his head. "I didn't lie. I *never* lied."

"How can you trust anything he says?" Oren shrugged.

"Why are you telling me this?" I asked, surprised by how even my voice sounded.

"Because I was hoping you would reconsider," Oren said. "You can go back to your palace, go back to your husband and your kingdom, but leave Loki here with me. You don't want or need him. He's useless. He's trash."

"No," I said, meeting Oren's eyes. "He goes with me. If you want the deal, if you want me and my kingdom as soon as I become Queen, then he goes with me now. Or the deal is off."

"He means that much to you?" Oren asked. He walked up to me, stopping in front of me so close I could feel his breath on my face. "Even knowing how he's betrayed you, you still want him back?"

"I promised I would take him back with me, and I will," I answered deliberately.

"You keep your promises," Oren said. "Good. Because if you don't keep this one, if you don't give me your kingdom as soon as you are Queen, Loki will be the first one I kill. I will do it right in front of you. Do you understand me?"

"Yes," I said.

"Good." He smiled. "Then we have a deal. All of Trylle will be mine."

"And until then, you won't lay a hand on any of the Trylle people or towns," I said. "You will leave us all in peace."

"Agreed," Oren said and held out his hand.

I shook it and I couldn't help but feel like I'd made a deal with the devil.

Sara walked us to the door, and I didn't say anything the entire way. She said very little, but at the door she told us both to be careful. She hugged Loki, and it looked like she wanted to hug me, but I wouldn't have let her.

Loki and I went out to the car, and I refused to even look at him. When we got in the car, I stared out the window.

"Wendy, I know you're upset, but you *must* listen to me. Some of what the King said is true, but he twisted it all up."

"I don't want to talk about it."

"Wendy."

"Just drive," I snapped.

He sighed but said nothing more, and the car pulled away from the Vittra palace.

I should've felt more relief. I'd gone to talk to Oren, and I'd gotten what I wanted. Oren hadn't killed either of us, which had actually been a very real possibility, and I'd bought more time for my people.

I didn't even realize how much I'd cared about Loki until I

found out it had all been a lie. Loki had just been following orders, and in a weird way I didn't blame him for that. But I still felt like a foolish idiot, and I didn't know why he'd continued to play games with me even after he'd left the Vittra.

What hurt the most was that I had been tempted. The night that Loki had come for me in the garden, I had been tempted to run off with him. I'd even felt bad for turning him down. I'd been afraid that I'd hurt his feelings.

But it had all been a lie.

I kept twisting my wedding ring and refusing to cry. I supposed this was what I deserved for cheating on my fiancé, for wanting to cheat on my husband. Regardless of what kind of marriage Tove and I had, that didn't justify whatever I had been feeling for Loki.

This could serve as a wake-up call. I should be concentrating on honoring my wedding vows and my kingdom. Not some stupid boy.

"I know you must think the worst of me right now," Loki said after we'd been driving for an hour or more. I didn't respond, so he went on, "Oren is a master manipulator. He's trying to poison your mind against me, to torture me, to torture us both."

I stared out the window. I hadn't even looked at him since we'd left.

"Wendy." He sighed. "Please. You have to listen to me."

"I don't have to do anything," I said. "I got you out of there alive. I did my part."

"Wendy!" Loki yelled. "I *never* had any intention of bringing you back to Oren. The King is many things, but he is not a stupid man, and he knows full well that I let you, Matt, and Rhys escape. He would have killed me, but he allowed me to go free to retrieve you. I told you that."

I laughed darkly. "You never told me he let you go so you could *seduce* me into coming back."

"Because I never had any intention of doing that. I swear to you, Wendy."

"I don't believe you," I said and wiped at my eyes. "I can never trust anything you say again."

"This is such bullshit." He shook his head, and abruptly he pulled the car over and put it in park.

"How is this bullshit?" I yelled. "You're the one that lied to me! You tricked me!"

"I never tricked you!" Loki shouted. "I never lied! Everything I have ever felt for you has been real! And I went through hell for you!"

"Stop, Loki! You can stop! I know the truth now!"

"No, you don't!"

"I can't do this." I shook my head. "I won't do this."

I had nowhere else to go, so I got out of the car. We'd traveled far enough so that we were in snow again, and I stepped barefoot into the cold. The stretch of highway was deserted, and empty cornfields went for miles.

"Where are you going?" Loki asked, jumping out of the car after me.

"Nowhere. I need fresh air." I pulled my cloak tighter around me. "I need to be away from you."

"Don't do this," Loki begged and walked after me. "You only heard it from him. You don't know what really happened. You have to listen to me."

"Why?" I asked, turning to face him. "Why should I listen to you?"

"He would've killed me. He executes everyone who doesn't follow orders. Surviving under Oren's rule requires saying and doing whatever the King wants to hear, truth be damned. You saw that tonight." He took a deep breath. "When you were first brought to the palace, he saw the way we interacted, and he thought he could use it against you. That you would fall in love with me."

"I will *never* love you," I said bitterly, and he winced.

"I'm only telling you what the King thought," Loki said carefully. "So he told me to get you to willingly come back with me, and I said I would. Because I didn't have a choice.

"But Wendy, I swear to you, I never would've brought you back to him. Otherwise I never would have tried to talk you out of going there tonight. If that were my plan, I would have encouraged you to place yourself in his hands."

"I understand that you had to appease Oren to survive," I said. "I really do. And I can even forgive that. But why didn't you tell me when you broke down my door begging for amnesty?"

He stared at the ground solemnly, then looked up and met my eyes. "Because I was ashamed that I'd ever agreed to it, even in pretense. And I didn't want to change the way you thought of me. I didn't want you to question all the real moments we'd shared together." He smiled sadly. "Like you do now."

"Why did you go back in the first place?" I asked thickly. "Why didn't you refuse to go back with Sara and stay in Förening?"

"Because if I stayed, it would break the truce, or the King could argue it did," Loki said. "He would come and take you. I didn't want to risk that."

"What about what you said in the garden?" I asked, looking down at my feet. For some reason, it was suddenly difficult to meet his gaze. "When you asked me to run away with you, you wouldn't have taken me back to him?"

"No," Loki said vehemently. "I never would have. Not to save my own life. Not for the fate of the entire kingdom. When I kissed you and asked you to marry me, I meant it. I wanted you to be with me."

I sniffled and stared out at the bleak whiteness around us, and the heaviness in my chest began to subside. I could see a car coming, far off down the road, but Loki put his hand on my chin, tilting it so I met his eyes.

"I made a choice between you and the King, and I chose you," Loki said. "In the garden, we were alone. I could've knocked you out and thrown you over my shoulder, then taken you back to the King. He would've spared me if I had.

"But I didn't." He stepped closer to me, and I could feel the heat radiating from his body. "He told me what he'd do to me if I didn't return you to him, but I couldn't do it."

He lifted his other hand, so he held my face in his hands. His skin was warm against mine, and even if he wasn't holding me, I wouldn't have looked away. There was something in his eyes, a longing and warmth, that took my breath away.

"Do you understand now?" Loki asked, his voice husky. "I would do it again for you, Wendy. I would go through hell and back for you. Even knowing how much you hate me right now."

I was so caught up in the moment I didn't even notice how close the passing SUV had gotten until it squealed to a stop next to us, nearly hitting our Cadillac. Loki moved toward me, and Tove jumped out of the driver's seat. Finn ran around the car and charged at Loki.

FOURTEEN

confrontation

Finn punched Loki in the face, and Loki raised his fist like he meant to strike back. That wouldn't have been so bad, except Loki was about fifty times stronger than Finn and would bust his face in.

"Loki!" I yelled. "Don't you dare hit him!"

"You are so lucky." Loki glared at Finn and wiped the blood from his nose.

"What the hell were you doing?" Finn shouted at him. "What's wrong with you? You had no right to take her any-where!"

"Finn," Tove said. "Stop. Calm down. She's fine."

Duncan and Willa climbed out of the backseat of the SUV, and my heart sank. Loki had been right. They had been part of the rescue mission too, and if we'd left Ondarike an hour later, Duncan, Willa, Tove, and Finn would all be dead.

"Like this was my idea!" Loki yelled back at Finn. "She's the Princess. She commanded, and I obeyed!"

"You don't obey a suicide mission!" Finn shouted.

"It wasn't a suicide mission," I said, loud enough to be heard over their yelling.

They stood in front of the Cadillac, staring at each other, and, strangely, I was grateful that Loki was so much stronger than Finn. If they were equally matched, Loki probably wouldn't hold back, and there would be a hell of a fistfight.

"Are you okay?" Willa asked, walking over to me.

"Why are you on the side of the road?" Duncan asked.

"I needed fresh air," I said. "Everything's fine. I got the Vittra to back off until I'm Queen. They won't attack any of us, no matter where we are."

"What the hell did you agree to?" Finn asked, breaking his icy stare-down with Loki to look at me.

"It doesn't matter," I said. "We'll stop them before it comes to that."

"Wendy." Finn sighed and shook his head, then turned back to Loki. "And you, Markis, I lost any respect I had for you."

"She was going to go whether I went with her or not," Loki said. "I thought it would be better if she didn't go alone."

"She shouldn't have gone at all!" Finn yelled.

"Yes, I should have!" I shouted at him. "If I hadn't, the Vittra would still be killing our people. I bought us more time, and I saved lives. That is my job, Finn. I did what I had to do, and I would do it again."

"You didn't have to do it like this," Finn said.

"It doesn't matter," I said. "It's done. Now I've had a very long day, and I would just like to go home."

"Come on, Wendy." Willa put her arm around me.

"Duncan, would you mind riding with Loki?" Tove asked. "I'd like to talk to my wife."

Duncan nodded. "Yeah, sure."

Willa led me around the SUV, and I glanced back over my shoulder at Loki. He was still standing in the road, watching me walk away. Something in his eyes broke my heart, and I looked away from him.

I climbed into the SUV, and Willa got in the seat behind me. Finn stayed outside, and it looked like he wanted to say something to Loki, but Tove sent him to the car. When he climbed in back next to Willa, Finn was still seething and glared out the window.

Tove stayed outside a bit longer, talking to Loki, and I wished I could read lips.

"What were you thinking, Wendy?" Finn asked, barely restraining the anger in his voice.

"I did what was best for the kingdom," I said simply. "Isn't that what you always told me to do?"

"Not at your own peril," Finn said.

I looked in the rearview mirror so I could meet his eyes. "You've told me over and over again that I shouldn't make decisions because of you. That I should think of the greater good of the kingdom. You were right, but this isn't about me either."

"I'm glad you're safe," Willa said, breaking the tension.

"And I know that you're badass and all that, but you don't have to do this alone. You could've asked for help."

"I had help," I said, watching Loki out the car window. "Loki was with me."

Finn scoffed at that, but at least he didn't say anything.

Outside, I saw Loki nod and get in the driver's side of the car. Tove walked back to the SUV and got in. Loki's Cadillac sped off down the road, and Tove made a U-turn and drove behind him.

"You didn't tell me," Tove said at length.

"I'm sorry," I said. "But I did what—"

"Don't," Tove cut me off. "This isn't about what you did or why you did it or if it was the right thing to do."

"What is this about, then?" I asked.

"We're married, Wendy." Tove glanced over at me. "Do you know why I asked you to marry me?"

"No," I said, and I could feel Finn and Willa watching us from the backseat.

"So we could be a team," Tove said. "I thought you needed someone to support you and stand by your side, and I know I needed the same thing."

"We are a team," I said meekly.

"Then why did you go behind my back?" Tove asked.

"I didn't think you would understand," I said.

"When have I not understood?" Tove asked. "When have I not trusted you? When have I even tried to stop you from do-ing something?"

"You haven't," I admitted quietly. "I'm sorry."

"Don't be sorry," Tove said. "Just don't do it again. I want us to work. But to do that, you have to tell me what's going on. You can't risk your life or make major decisions about the kingdom without at least letting me know."

"I'm sorry," I repeated and stared down at my lap.

"Loki told me what you did," Tove said, and I lifted my head.

"What?"

"What you exchanged for the peace now," Tove said. "He told me the plan, and it's a good one. But we have our work cut out for us."

"What?" Willa leaned forward between the seats. "What's the plan?"

I didn't say anything, because I didn't want to talk anymore. I was exhausted, and I knew how much work we had ahead of us if we were going to stand a chance against the Vittra. But right now, all I wanted to do was sleep.

Thankfully, Loki had told Tove enough that he could explain it to Willa and Finn. I rested my head against the cold glass of the car window and listened to them talk about what we needed to do.

Some of the trackers had already made it back to Förening, and the rest would be there in the next few days. Thomas had already begun a boot camp for them.

Trackers had some combat training to help protect the changelings and other Trylle, but they weren't soldiers. Thomas was charged with turning them into an army, but they were going up against a powerful enemy they didn't know how to defeat.

Thanks to the extended peace agreement, we were now free to go to Oslinna. When we got back to Förening, we could set up another team and head out the next day. This time, Willa volunteered to go. I would go, whether anyone liked it or not, but I didn't say that during the car ride. I didn't have the strength to argue.

The hardest part would be convincing other Markis and Marksinna to join the fight. Loki thought the only thing stronger than the hobgoblins were Trylle abilities, so the ones best equipped to a fight them were the higher-ranking Trylle.

Willa said that we shouldn't tell the other Trylle what I had exchanged to get our new peace agreement. They would revolt if they thought I'd risked the kingdom. I would tell them that I had seen Oren and extended the agreement by offering to go with him voluntarily in six months.

The Trylle still wouldn't like that, but they would feel much better if they only lost me. In the meantime, we would rally them for a fight against the Vittra and hope that it worked when it came time for war.

We all had a mission when we got back to Förening. Willa was to start working on the Markis and Marksinna. They all seemed to like her, and she might be able to convince some of them to fight with us. She'd also been working on her own abilities, and she could train those who had let their abilities atrophy.

Finn would work with his father and the trackers to build up the army. He even grudgingly agreed to enlist Loki to help him. Loki was physically as strong as a hobgoblin, so at the very least, the trackers could practice fighting him to get an idea of what that kind of strength could do.

Tove had to figure out who to appoint as temporary Chancellor until an election could be held. He'd volunteered to fill the Chancellor position because he felt responsible for sending our old Chancellor to die. I assured him that it wasn't his fault, but he said he already had Markis Bain in mind for the role.

And I had what sounded like the easiest job but felt like the most impossible. I had to find a way to kill the King.

When we got back to the palace, there was a flurry of defense meetings going on. Tove had purposely not told anyone that I had left with Loki, out of fear of starting a panic, but I called a meeting as soon as we were back to let them all know.

Loki planned to head off to his room, but I asked him to go with us. I needed the Trylle to trust him. He had the most knowledge of the Vittra, so he would be the best-equipped to help us fight.

The meeting went about as well as I'd expected. Lots of yelling and disagreeing, although the Marksinna Laris was quiet since Tove had threatened to banish her. Once I got them calmed down and explained what I was going to do and what had to be done, they took it a bit better. A clear plan helped ease their fears.

I ended the meeting by telling them that we were going on a recovery and fact-finding mission to Oslinna. Without even asking them, I volunteered myself, Willa, Tove, Loki, and Aurora to go. I was trying to ease the Trylle population into the idea that Markis and Marksinna could do actual work, and hopefully they would when I called upon them.

Afterward, we all dispersed to complete our tasks. As desperately as I wanted to sleep, I didn't have time. I had to go to the library and find every book on the Vittra I could. There had to have been other immortals before Oren, and there had to be ways of killing them.

Of course, all the old texts were written in Tryllic in an attempt to disguise them from the Vittra. That was where the most useful information would be kept on how to stop them. My Tryllic had gotten better, but it wasn't fantastic. It took me ages to read a single page.

"Wendy," Tove said, and I looked up to see him standing in the doorway of the library. My vision was blurry, as I'd spent too long staring down at old texts.

I was sitting on the floor among a pile of books near the far wall. I'd started out carrying books over to the desk before deciding that was a waste of time, and I had no time to waste. We were leaving for Oslinna in the morning, and we would be gone for a few days, so I wouldn't be able to research then.

"Did you need something?" I asked.

"It's late," Tove said. "Very late."

"I have a few more documents to go through."

"When was the last time you slept?"

"I don't know." I shook my head. "It doesn't matter. I don't have time to sleep. There's so much to do, and I don't know how we can possibly do it. I don't know how we can be ready, unless I'm working every minute."

"You need sleep." He came into the room and walked over to me. "We need you to be strong, and that means you need to rest sometimes. It is a necessary evil."

"But what if I can't do this?" I asked, staring up at him with tears in my eyes. "What if I can't find a way to stop Oren?"

"You will," he assured me. "You're the Princess."

"Tove." I sighed.

"Come on." He held out his hand to me. "Sleep now. We can look more in the morning."

I let him take my hand and pull me to my feet. He was already in his pajamas, and his hair was even more disheveled than normal. I guessed he'd tried to sleep without me, but he'd gone looking for me when I hadn't come to bed.

My mind was racing, thinking of all the things I had to do. I didn't think I'd ever really be able to sleep, but as soon as my head hit the pillow, I was out.

FIFTEEN

oslinna

It looked like a bomb had gone off. Oslinna was a small town, even smaller than Förening. It was settled in a valley at the base of several low mountains. I'd never seen it before the attack, but by the looks of what was left of some of the buildings, it had been quite beautiful.

All of the trackers' homes were smashed. Trackers lived in small cottages, most of them nestled in trees or the mountains, and the floors were usually just dirt. They were very easily destroyed. But the nicer homes of the Markis and Marksinna were decimated too, with large sections of the roofs missing and entire walls collapsed.

The palace in the center was the only thing still standing. It was like a version of my own palace, except on a smaller scale and with fewer windows. While the back of my palace overlooked the river, this one was built into the mountain behind it.

Half of the palace had crumbled, and it was blackened, as if burned. The other half looked okay, at least from the outside. There had been some obvious damage, like broken windows and a destroyed fountain, but it looked much better than the rest of the town.

We'd driven slowly through the town, in awe of the carnage, and Tove had to swerve a few times to miss debris in the road. He stopped in front of the palace, parking next to an uprooted oak tree.

"This is too much for us to handle," Aurora said from the backseat. She'd been complaining about helping the entire way here, but we'd left her without a choice. She was the strongest healer, and the people of Oslinna had been hurt.

"We'll do all that we can," I said. "And if we can't do any more, then so be it."

I got out of the car before she could voice any more complaints, and Duncan pulled up in another Cadillac behind us. He had Willa, Matt, and Loki with him. Finn had wanted to come too, but he was still healing and Thomas needed him to help with the trackers. Matt had insisted on coming along, and at first I'd been against it, but we really could use all the hands we could get.

"This is even worse than I thought it would be," Willa said. She wrapped her arms around herself and shook her head.

"This is who you're fighting?" Matt asked, looking around. "The people who did this?"

"We're not fighting anyone right now," I said, cutting off his train of thought. "We're cleaning this up, helping the survivors, taking back refugees, and that's the only thing we need to worry about."

Loki lifted up a heavy branch and moved it off the path to the palace. The path had been cobblestone, but many of the stones were missing, tossed about on the lawn.

Tove and I approached the palace, trying to look both dignified and empathetic. The empathy part wasn't hard. Seeing that much damage was devastating.

Before we got to the palace, the door was thrown open. A girl not much older than me came out, her dark hair pulled up in a tangled mess, and smudges of dirt and ash covering her face and clothes. She was small, even shorter than I was, and she looked as though she might cry.

"Are you the Princess?" she asked.

"Yes, I'm the Princess from Förening," I said, then gestured to Tove. "This is the Prince. We are here to help you."

"Oh, thank god." She burst into tears and actually ran toward me and hugged me. "I didn't think anybody would come."

"We're here now." I patted her head because I wasn't sure what else to do and exchanged a look with Tove. "We'll do everything we can for you."

"Sorry." She pulled herself away from me and wiped at her eyes. "I didn't mean to do that. I've . . . There is much that needs to be done." She shook her head. "My father would be angry at me for behaving this way. I'm sorry."

"There's no need to apologize," I said. "You've been through so much."

"No, I'm in charge now," she said. "So I should act like it."

"Kenna Tomas?" I asked, hoping I remembered her name correctly. She'd once been a bridesmaid candidate and Willa had told me some about her. The only reason Kenna had not made it into my wedding party was because Aurora approved of her. Otherwise, she sounded like a nice girl.

She smiled. "Yes, I'm Kenna, and with my parents dead, I'm now the Marksinna of Oslinna."

"Do you have any survivors here?" I asked. "Any people who need medical treatment? We brought a healer."

"Oh, yes!" Kenna nodded. "Come with me."

As we followed her into the palace, Kenna explained what had happened. While the townspeople were sleeping, the hobgoblins had come in and started tearing the town apart. As far as she could tell, that was their main goal. People got hurt because the hobgoblins happened to be destroying homes with people in them, or throwing trees that would land on bystanders. It was like a tornado hitting a town in the middle of the night, without any sirens to give warning.

They had very few trackers here when the attack started, but the trackers hadn't lasted long. Kenna saw a tracker go up against a hobgoblin, and the hobgoblin snapped him in half. But the hobgoblins retreated pretty quickly after the Markis and Marksinna started defending themselves.

In the Oslinna palace, a small ballroom had been turned into a makeshift care unit. Some of the more injured Trylle had left to go to nearby hospitals, but most of them would rather die than be treated by humans.

It was horrifying to see. Cots were set up all over for survivors, and most of them were bloody and battered. Mänsklig children with broken arms and dirty faces were crying as their host parents held them.

Aurora immediately went to work without any prompting from me, which was nice. Willa and I went around talking to the people and giving them water, helping them if we could.

Kenna took Tove, Duncan, Loki, and Matt outside to show them where the most work needed to be done, and I wanted to go out with them. I would be much more useful lifting heavy objects than Matt or Duncan, because I could move them with my mind.

But I felt like I needed to be inside with the people, at least for a little while. Most of them I couldn't help, other than handing out bottled water, but I think some of them just wanted to talk, to know that somebody cared.

Their stories were heartbreaking. Wives had lost their husbands, children had lost their parents, and most trackers had lost everything. I wanted to cry, but I couldn't. It felt wrong and selfish. I needed to be calm and assure them that we would fix this, that *I* would make everything better.

I paused when I passed a young woman sitting on a cot. She couldn't have been more than a year or two older than me, if that, and even covered in dirt and bruises, she was still devastatingly beautiful. Her long brown hair had warm undertones, like a burnt umber.

It was her eyes, though, that caught me. They were an endless shade of brown, and stared vacantly at nothing. Tears fell from them without a sound.

In her arms she cradled a small child, less than a year old. The little girl had pudgy arms, and she clung to the young woman, reminding me of the way a monkey will cling to its mother. Based on the baby's appearance—her tanned skin, her dark wild curls—I'd say she was Trylle, meaning she was a tracker baby.

"How are you doing?" I asked. When she didn't look up at me, I knelt down in front of her. "Are you all right?"

"I'm okay," she said numbly, still staring off at the floor.

"What about the baby?" I touched the child tentatively. I'd never really interacted that much with babies, but I felt like I should do something.

"The baby?" She seemed confused at first, then looked down at the little girl in her arms. "Oh. Hanna is fine. She's sleepy, but she doesn't understand what's happened."

"That's probably for the best," I said.

Hanna stared up at me, her eyes seeming almost too large for her small face. Then she reached out and grabbed my finger, almost latching on to it, and smiled dazedly at me.

"Hanna's a beautiful little girl," I said. "Is she yours?"

"Yes." She nodded once. "Thank you." She swallowed hard and tried to force a smile at me. "My name is Mia."

"Where's her father?" I asked, hoping against hope that he'd been away when the attack happened.

"He . . ." Mia shook her head, and the silent tears fell faster. "He was trying to protect us, and he . . ."

"I shouldn't have asked." I put my hand on Mia's arm, hoping to comfort her.

"I just don't know what we'll do without him." She began sobbing.

I sat on the cot next to her and put my arm around her, because that was all I could think to do. There was something about her, something so sweet and helpless, and I wanted to fix her problems and ease her pain. But I couldn't.

She looked too young to be a wife, let alone a mother and a widow. I couldn't imagine what she was going through, but I would do anything I could to help her.

"You'll be all right," I tried to reassure Mia as she wept onto my shoulder. Hanna began to wail, most likely because she saw her mother crying. "It will take time, but you and Hanna will be fine."

Mia struggled to stop her tears and rocked her baby. Hanna stopped crying almost as soon as Mia did, and she let out a deep breath.

"I'm sorry to be like this, Princess," Mia said, looking at me. "I shouldn't be crying on you like this."

"No, don't worry about it." I waved it off. "But Mia, listen, when we leave Oslinna, I want you to come back to Förening with us. We'll have a nice place for you to stay, and we'll figure out what you'll do there. Okay? But you and Hanna will always have a place at the palace."

"Thank you." Her eyes were brimming with fresh tears, and I was afraid I would send her sobbing again, so I left her alone to cuddle her daughter.

Something about Mia lingered with me. Even as I went around the room, I couldn't shake the image of her heartbroken eyes. There was a warmth and kindness about her that I could see underneath the devastation, and I hoped that someday she would be happy again.

I stayed long enough to talk to every person in the room, but then I had to move on. I could be of more help to them outside than I could in here. Willa went with me for the same reasons, leaving Aurora alone to heal them as much as she could.

As we were leaving, Willa was tearing up. She had a small, dirty teddy bear clutched in her hands, and she wiped at her eyes.

"That was pretty rough in there," I said, holding back my own tears.

"A little tracker boy gave me this." She held up the bear. "His whole family died. His parents, his sister, even his dog. And he gave me this because I sang him a song." She shook her head. "I didn't want to take it. But he said it was his sister's, and she'd want another girl to have it."

I put my arm around her, giving her a half hug as we walked down the hall toward the palace door.

"We have to do more for these people," Willa said. "That little boy isn't hurt, but if he was, Aurora wouldn't heal him. She wouldn't want to waste her energy on a tracker."

"I know." I sighed. "It's insane."

"That's got to change." Willa stopped and pointed back to the ballroom. "Every one of those people in there has been through hell, and they all deserve help just as equally."

"I know, and I'm trying to make it better," I said. "When

I'm going to all those meetings, this is what I'm trying to do and why I want you to help me with them. I will change this, and I will make it better. But I need help."

"Good." She sniffled and played with the teddy bear. "I will start going to the meetings. I want to be a part of what it is you're doing."

"Thank you," I said, feeling some small bit of relief in that. "But right now, the best way to help these people is to get this place cleaned up so they can start rebuilding their homes."

Willa nodded and walked with me again. Outside, I could see some improvement. Half of a roof had been on the palace lawn, but it was gone now, as well as the uprooted oak by the cars. I could hear the men a few houses down arguing about what to do with the debris.

Matt suggested they make a pile in the road for now, and they could worry about moving it later. Loki started to argue against it, but Tove told him to just do it. They didn't have time to waste fighting.

Willa and I joined them, and we all went to work. Loki, Tove, and I did most of the lifting, while Matt, Duncan, and Willa tried to clean things and straighten up the houses. Just moving the garbage out of the way wouldn't solve the towns-people's problems, but it was the first step in being able to go back and fix it up.

As the day wore on, I started to feel exhausted, but I pushed through it. Loki had to move everything physically, so despite the chill, he ended up warm and sweaty. He took off his shirt, and the ordinarily pleasing sight pained me. The marks on his back looked better than they had before, but they were still there. Reminders of what he'd gone through, for me.

"What happened to him?" Willa asked me while we cleaned out one of the houses. A tree had gone through the window. I got it out, and she cleaned up the glass and branches.

"What?" I asked, but I saw her staring out the open window at Loki as he tossed a destroyed couch on the garbage pile in the road.

"Loki's back," she said. "Is that what the King did to him? That's why he has amnesty?"

"Yeah, it is."

Wind came up around me, blowing my hair in my eyes, as Willa created a small tornado in the middle of the living room. It circled around, sucking all the glass and little bits of tree into the funnel, so Willa could send it out to the garbage.

"So what's going on with you and him?" Willa asked.

"Who?" I said. I tried to pick up one of the couches that had been tipped over, and Willa came over to help me.

"You and Loki." She helped me flip the couch back on its feet. "Don't play dumb. There's something major there."

I shook my head. "There's nothing anywhere."

"Whatever you say." She rolled her eyes. "But I've been meaning to ask you, how's the marriage going?"

"The past three days have been fantastic," I said dryly.

"What about the wedding night?" Willa asked with a smile.

"Willa! This isn't the time to be talking about that."

"Of course it is! We need to lighten the mood," she insisted.

"And I haven't had a chance to talk to you about any of this yet. Your life has been all drama since the wedding."

"You're telling me," I muttered.

"Take five minutes." Willa sat down on the couch and patted the spot next to her. "You're visibly exhausted. You need a break. So take five and talk to me."

"Fine," I said, mostly because my head was beginning to throb from all the objects I'd moved. That last tree had been hard to get going. I sat down next to her, and a bit of dirt billowed up from the couch. "This is never going to be clean."

"Don't worry about that," Willa said. "We'll get this place picked up, and then we can send out all the maids in Förening to help them with the finishing touches. We're only focusing on getting them on the path to recovery right now. We can't do the entire recovery in one day, but eventually we'll get it all taken care of."

"I hope so."

"But Wendy, how was your wedding night?" Willa asked.

"You really wanna talk about this?" I groaned and leaned my head on the back of the couch.

"Right now there's nothing else I'd like to talk about."

"You're in for a real disappointment," I said. "Because there's nothing to tell."

"It was that bland?" she asked.

"No, it was nothing," I said. "And I mean literally nothing. We didn't do anything."

"Wait." She leaned back on the couch as if to look at me better. "You mean that you're married and still a virgin?"

"That is what I mean."

"Wendy!" Willa gasped.

"What? Our marriage is weird. Really weird. You know that."

"I know." She looked disappointed. "I was hoping you could have a happily-ever-after is all."

"Well, it's not ever after yet," I pointed out.

"Wendy!" Matt yelled from outside the house. "I need your help with something!"

"Duty calls." I stood up.

"That was barely even a minute," Willa said. "You do need to take a break, Wendy. You're running yourself ragged."

"I'm fine," I said as I walked out of the house. "I'll sleep when I'm dead."

We worked well into the night and ended up getting most of the big debris cleared out and piled up. I might have pressed on to do more work, but it was clear that everybody else couldn't.

"I think we need to call it a night, Wendy," Loki said. He rested his arms on an overturned refrigerator, leaning on it.

Matt and Willa were sitting on a log next to the pile, and Tove stood next to them, drinking a bottle of water. Only Duncan still helped me as we struggled to pull a shredded mattress from a tracker house. I had to stop using my powers, because it killed my head every time I did.

Only three streetlights in the entire town still worked, and Matt, Willa, Tove, and Loki had taken their break near one. They'd stopped working about fifteen minutes ago, but I insisted that I keep going.

"Wendy, come on," Matt said. "You've done as much as you can do."

"There's more stuff to do, so clearly I haven't," I said.

"Duncan needs a break," Willa said. "Let's quit. We can do more tomorrow."

"I'm fine," Duncan panted, but I stopped pulling on the mattress long enough to look up at him. He was filthy, his hair was a mess, and his face was red and sweaty. I'd actually never seen him look so terrible.

"Fine. We're done for the night," I relented.

We walked back over and sat down on the log next to Matt and Willa. She had a small cooler of water and handed a bottle to each of us. I opened mine and drank greedily. Tove paced in front of us, fidgeting with his bottle cap. I don't know how he had the energy to walk that much.

"We're getting this cleaned up, and that's good," Matt said. "But we're not doing anything to rebuild. We're not even qualified."

"I know." I nodded. "We'll have to send another team down that can rebuild and do more specialized cleaning. After we get back to Förening, we'll really have to get people down here."

"I could work on some blueprints, if you want," Matt offered. "I can design stuff that's quick and easy to build but doesn't look cheap."

"That would be fantastic," I said. "It'd be a great step in the right direction."

Matt was an architect, or at least he would've been if I hadn't dragged him to Förening with me. I wasn't entirely sure how he spent his days at the palace, but it would be good for him to work on something. Not to mention that it would be good for Oslinna.

"The good news is that the damage seems to support what Kenna was saying," Loki said. He stopped leaning on the fridge and walked over to sit next to me.

"What do you mean?" I asked.

"The hobgoblins aren't vicious or mean, not really," Loki said. "They're destructive and irritating, sure, but I've never known them to kill anybody."

"They have now." Willa gestured to the mess around us.

"I don't think murder was their ultimate goal, though," Loki said. "They were trying to destroy the town. And even when they fought with that team the other night, they didn't kill most of them."

"How does that help anything?" I asked.

"I don't know." Loki shrugged. "But I think they aren't as hard to defeat as we once thought. They're not fighters."

"I'm sure that will be real comforting to all the dead people here," Tove said.

"All right." Willa stood up. "That's enough for me. I'm ready to go inside and get cleaned up and get some sleep. What about you guys?"

"Do we have places to sleep?" Duncan asked.

"Yes." Willa nodded. "Kenna told me that most of the bedrooms in the palace weren't that damaged, and they have some running water if we want to wash up."

"Well, I definitely want those things." Loki got up.

We all walked back to the palace, but Tove lagged behind. I slowed down to walk with him, and he twitched a lot. He kept swatting at his ear, like there was a mosquito or a fly buzzing by, but I didn't see any. I asked if he was okay, but he just shook his head.

Kenna showed us to the extra rooms in the palace, and I felt bad taking them when there were so many people without homes. She pointed out that there were too many people for the bedrooms, so she didn't want to divvy them up among the survivors because it would only create discord and add misery to a difficult situation.

Besides that, the rooms she showed us weren't in such great shape. They were small, and while they didn't have major damage, they were in disarray. Our whole room seemed to slant slightly to the side, and books and furniture were tossed all over.

I straightened up the room and let Tove shower first down the hall. Something seemed off with him, and I thought it would be better if he had a chance to rest instead of doing more work.

"What are you doing?" Tove asked. He came back to the room after the shower, his hair all wet and a mess.

"I'm making the bed." I was smoothing out the sheets but I turned to face him. "How was your shower?"

"Why are you making the bed?" he snapped and rushed over to it. I moved out of the way and he pulled down the sheets.

"Sorry," I said. "I didn't know it would upset you. I thought it would be—"

"Why?" Tove whirled around to face me, his green eyes burning. "Why would you do that?"

"I just made the bed, Tove," I said carefully. "You can un-make it if you want. Why don't you get into bed? Okay? You're exhausted. I'll go shower, and you get some sleep."

"Fine! Whatever!"

He ripped the sheets off the bed and muttered to himself. He'd done too much today and overloaded his brain. My head was still buzzing, and I was stronger than him. I couldn't imagine how he felt.

I grabbed the duffel bag I'd packed in Förening and went to take a shower. Leaving him alone to rest would probably be the best thing I could do for him. I wanted to take a long hot shower, but by the time I got to it, the water was cold, so I showered quickly.

Even before I made it back to the room, I could hear Tove. His mutterings had gotten louder.

"Tove?" I said quietly and pushed open the bedroom door.

"Where have you been?" Tove shouted, his eyes wide and frantic. All the cleaning I had done in the room had been un-done. Everything was strewn about, and he was pacing.

"I was in the shower," I said. "I told you."

"Did you hear that?" He froze and looked around.

"What?" I asked.

"You're not even listening!" Tove yelled.

"Tove, you're tired." I walked into the room. "You need to sleep."

"No, I can't sleep." He shook his head and looked away from

me. "No, Wendy." He ran his hands through his hair. "You don't understand."

"What don't I understand?" I asked.

"I can hear it all." He put both his hands to the sides of his head. "I can hear it all!" He kept repeating that, and he held his head tighter. His nose started to bleed, and he groaned.

"Tove!" I rushed over to him and I reached out, just to comfort him, but when I did, he slapped me hard in the face.

"Don't you dare!" Tove turned on me and threw me back on the bed. I was too startled to do anything. "I can't trust you! I can't trust any of you!"

"Tove, please calm down," I begged him. "This isn't you. You're just tired."

"Don't tell me who I am! You don't know who I am!"

"Tove." I slid to the edge of the bed, so that I was sitting, and he stood in front of me, glowering down at me. "Tove, please listen to me."

"I can't." He bit his lip. "I can't hear *you*!"

"You can hear me," I said. "I'm right here."

"You're lying!" Tove grabbed me by my shoulders and started shaking me.

"Hey!" Loki shouted, and Tove let go of me.

I'd left the bedroom door open when I came in, and Loki had been on his way back to his room from his own shower. He was still shirtless, and his light hair was dripping water onto his shoulders.

"Go away!" Tove yelled at him. "I can't have you here!"

"What the hell are you doing?" Loki asked.

"Loki, it's not him," I said. "He's used his abilities too much, and it's done something to him. He needs to sleep."

"Stop telling me what I need to do!" Tove growled. He raised his hand like he meant to slap me again, and I flinched.

"Tove!" Loki shouted and ran over to him.

"Loki!" I yelled, afraid that he would hit him, but he didn't.

Loki grabbed Tove by the shoulders, making Tove look at him. Tove tried to squirm away, but within seconds he was unconscious. His body slacked, and Loki caught him. I moved out of the way so Loki could lay him back down on the bed.

"Sorry," I said, unsure of what else to say.

"Don't be sorry. He was about to hit you."

"No, he wasn't." I shook my head. "I mean, he was. But that's not Tove. That's not who he is. He would never hurt anybody. He just . . ."

I trailed off. I wanted to cry. My face stung from where Tove had slapped me. But that wasn't even why I wanted to cry. He was sick, and he was only going to get sicker. Tomorrow he'd be better, but eventually his powers would eat away at his brain. Eventually, there wouldn't be any Tove left.

Loki leaned in, staring at my cheek with a pained expression. My cheek began to throb, and I realized there must be a red mark. I turned my face away, embarrassed.

"Thank you," I said, "but I'm fine."

"No, you're not," Loki said. "I don't care if he's your husband, and I don't care if he's lost his mind. There's no excuse for hitting you, and if he does it again . . ." The muscle in his jaw twitched, and his eyes flashed with a protective anger.

"He won't do it again," I assured him, even though I wasn't entirely sure if that was true.

"He better not," Loki said, but his anger seemed to lessen, and he touched my arm tenderly. "Now come on. You can't stay here with him tonight."

SIXTEEN

one night

I'd gotten Aurora and sent her in to stay with Tove for the night. I felt guilty for leaving him, but she would be better equipped to handle him if he got out of control again.

Since she was staying with Tove, I took her room. The four-poster bed sat in the corner, draped with red curtains and sheets. One of the walls was very crooked, practically leaning on top of the bed, and it made the room feel even smaller.

"Are you going to be all right now?" Loki asked. He'd walked me over here, and he waited just inside the doorway.

"Yeah, I'm great," I lied and sat down on the bed. "The entire kingdom is falling apart. People are dying. I have to kill my father. And my husband just went crazy."

"Wendy, none of that's your fault."

"Well, it feels like it's all my fault," I said, and a tear slid down my cheek. "I only make everything worse."

"That's not true at all." Loki walked over and sat on the bed next to me. "Wendy, don't cry."

"I'm not," I lied. I wiped at my eyes and looked at him. "Why are you even being nice to me?"

"Why wouldn't I be nice to you?" he asked, looking confused.

"Because." I pointed to the scars covering his back. "That's because of me."

"No, it isn't." Loki shook his head. "That's because the King is evil."

"But if I had gone with him in the first place, none of this would've happened," I said. "None of these people would've died. Even Tove would be better."

"And you would be dead," Loki said. "The King would still hate the Trylle, maybe even more so if he blamed them for brainwashing you. He would eventually attack them and take the kingdom for himself."

"Maybe." I shrugged. "Maybe not."

"Stop." He put his arm around me, and it felt safe and warm. "Not everything is your fault, and you can't fix everything. You're only one person."

"It never feels like enough." I swallowed and looked up at him. "Nothing I do is ever enough."

"Oh, believe me, you do more than enough." He smiled and brushed a hair back from my face.

His eyes met mine, and I felt a familiar yearning inside of me, one that got stronger every time I was with him.

"Why did you want me to remember?" I asked.

"Remember what?"

"When we were in your room, you said you wanted me to remember that I wanted you to kiss me."

"So you admit you wanted me to kiss you?" Loki smirked.

"Loki."

"Wendy," he echoed, smiling at me.

"Why didn't you just kiss me?" I asked. "Wouldn't that have been a better thing to remember?"

"It wasn't the right time."

"Why not?"

"You were on a mission. If I kissed you, it would've only been for a second, because you were in a rush to go," he said. "And a second wouldn't be enough."

"So when is the right time?" I asked.

"I don't know," he whispered.

He had his hand on my cheek, wiping away a tear, and his eyes were searching my face. He leaned forward, and his lips brushed against mine. Delicately at first, almost testing to see if this was real. His kisses were soft and sweet, and so very different from Finn's.

As soon as I thought of Finn, I pushed him from my mind. I didn't want to think of anything else. I didn't want to feel anything except Loki. The exhaustion of the night was pushed away as something surged through, something warm and intense.

Loki kissed me more deeply and pushed me back on the bed. He wrapped an arm around my waist, lifting me up and pulling me farther onto the bed. I clung to him, my hands digging into his bare back. The scars felt like braille under my fingers, scars he'd gotten to protect me.

"Wendy," he murmured as he kissed my neck, his lips trailing all over my skin and making me tremble.

He stopped kissing me long enough to look at me. His light hair fell into his eyes. Something about the way he looked at me, his eyes the color of burnt honey, made my heart beat faster.

It was like I'd never truly seen him before. All his pretenses had fallen away; his smirk, his swagger, were all gone. It was just him, and I realized that this might be the first time I was really seeing him.

Loki was vulnerable and kind and more than a little frightened. But more than that, he was lonely, and he cared about me. He cared about me so much it terrified him, and as much as that should've scared me too, it didn't.

All I could think about was that I'd never seen anything more beautiful. It felt strange thinking of a guy that way, but that's what he was. Looking down at me, waiting for me to accept him or push him away, Loki was *beautiful*.

I reached for him and touched his face, almost astonished that he could be real. He closed his eyes and kissed the palm of my hand. One of his hands was on my side, and his grip tightened, sending hot shivers all through my body.

"I hate to even ask this, but . . ." Loki trailed off, his voice husky. "Are you sure you want to do this?"

"I want you, Loki," I said before I could let myself think about anything.

I wanted him, *needed* him, and for one night I refused to think about the consequences or the repercussions. I just wanted to be with him.

Loki smiled, relieved, and he almost seemed to glow. He bent down, kissing me again, only deeper and more fervently.

His hand slid under my nightgown, strong and sure on my thigh. I loved his strength and power, and the way I could feel it in even his smallest touches. He tried to hold back so he wouldn't hurt me, but when he tried to slide off my panties, he tore them in half.

I took off my nightgown, slipping it up over my head, because I didn't want him ripping that too. He tried to be gentle with me, and some part of me did want him to be, because that was the way I thought my first time should be. But we were both far too eager.

He started out slow, trying to ease himself in me, but I moaned in his ear, gripping tightly on to him, and any pretense of restraint was gone. It hurt, and I buried my face into his shoulder to keep from crying out. But he didn't slow, and very soon the heat grew inside me. I was glad he didn't slow. Even the pain felt like pleasure.

Afterward, he collapsed on the bed next to me, both of us gasping for breath. We'd knocked the bed off-kilter, and I vaguely remembered hearing the sound of a board cracking, so we might have broken it. The red curtains of the four-poster bed had been tied open, but they had come loose, so they fell around the bed and closed off the world around us.

A few candles lit the room, and we were shrouded in a warm

red glow as their light flickered through the curtains. I felt sheltered, like I was wrapped in a warm cocoon, and I didn't think I'd ever felt more content or safe in my life.

I lay on my back, and Loki moved next to me, almost encircling me. One arm was behind my neck, and the other one was draped over my belly. I wrapped my arms around his so I could hold him closer to me.

Because I was nestled in his arms this way, the scar on his chest was right next to me. I'd never seen it this close before. It looked so jagged and rough. It slashed at an angle, starting right above his heart, and stopping below his other nipple.

"Do you hate me?" I asked quietly.

"Why on earth would I hate you?" Loki asked, laughing.

"Because of this." I touched his scar, and his skin trembled around it. "Because of what my father did to you over me."

"No, I don't hate you." He kissed my temple. "I could never hate you. And it's not your fault what the King did."

"How did you get this?" I asked.

"Before he decided to punish me, the King considered execution," Loki said, almost wearily. "He used a sword before deciding that torture might be more fun."

"He almost killed you?" I looked at him, and the very thought of Loki dying made me want to cry.

"He didn't, though." He brushed back my hair, his fingers running through the tangles of it, and he smiled down at me. "The King couldn't, no matter how hard he tried. My heart refused to give up. It knew I had something to fight for."

"You shouldn't say things like that." I swallowed back tears and lowered my eyes. "Tonight was . . . beautiful and amazing, but it was only for tonight."

"Wendy." Loki groaned and rolled onto his back. "Why did you have to say something like that now?"

"Because." I sat up and pulled my knees to my chest. The sheets hung over my legs, but my back was bare to him. "I don't want you to . . ." I sighed. "I don't want to hurt you any more than I already have."

"It looks like I hurt you, actually." Loki sat up and touched my arm. "You have a bruise."

"What?" I looked down and saw a purplish blotch on my arm. "I don't remember you doing that." I'd probably have bruises on my thighs, but Loki didn't grab my arms. "Oh. This isn't from you. It's from Tove."

"Tove." Loki sighed. He didn't say anything for a minute, then looked over at me. "You're going back to him tomorrow, aren't you?"

"He is my husband."

"He hit you."

"He wasn't in his right mind. Once he's back to himself, he'll feel terrible. It won't happen again."

"It better not," he said firmly.

"Anyway, I married him for a reason, and that hasn't changed."

"What reason is that?" Loki asked. "I know you don't love him."

"The Trylle don't want me to be Queen," I said. "They don't trust me, because of who my father is, among other things. Tove's family is very influential and helps balance it out. If I wasn't married to him, his mother would be leading the campaign to get me overthrown. Without Tove, I'd never be Queen."

"Why is that a bad thing?" Loki asked. "These people don't trust you or like you, and you're sacrificing everything for them. How does that make sense?"

"Because they need me. I can help them. I can save them. I'm the only one who can stand up to my father, and I'm the only one that cares enough to fight for the rights of the trackers and the less powerful Trylle. I have to do this."

"I wish you didn't say that with such conviction." He put his arm around me and moved closer. He kissed my shoulder, then whispered, "I don't want you to go back to Tove tomorrow."

"I have to."

"I know," he said. "But I don't want you to."

"You can have me for tonight, though." I gave him a small smile, and he lifted his head so his eyes met mine. "That's all I can give you."

"I don't want only one night. I want *all* the nights. I want all of you, forever."

Tears swam in my eyes, and my heart yearned so badly it hurt. Sitting there with Loki, I didn't think I'd ever felt quite so heartbroken.

"Don't cry, Wendy." He smiled sadly at me, and I saw the heartbreak in his eyes mirroring my own. He pulled me to him and kissed my forehead, then my cheeks, then my mouth.

"So, if this is all you'll let me have, then I will take it all," Loki said. "No talking or even worrying about the kingdom or responsibility or anyone else. You're not the Princess. I'm not Vittra. We're only a boy and a girl crazy about each other, and we're naked in bed."

I nodded. "I can do that."

"Good, because I'm determined to make the most of it." He smiled and pushed me down on the bed. "I think we broke the bed a little bit last time. What do you say we see if we can destroy it?"

I laughed, and he kissed me. Tomorrow I might regret this. Tomorrow I might have hell to pay. But for one night, I refused to think or worry. I was with Loki, and he made me feel like the only thing in the world that truly mattered. And in that night, he was the only thing that truly mattered to me.

A knocking woke me in the morning, and I was surprised that I'd even slept at all. The night washed over me in a hazy, happy blur. Everything felt like a wonderful dream, and I'd never known that I could feel that close to another person or that . . . *happy*. Loki's arms were strong around me, and I snuggled deeper into them. I wanted to stay curled up next to him forever.

"Princess?" Aurora called from outside my bedroom, and it was like a cold slap pulling me from my dream. "Are you up? I need to get my clothes." Loki's arms tensed around me, and before I could answer, the bedroom door creaked open and Aurora walked into the room.

SEVENTEEN

consequence

The curtains were still drawn around the bed, but if Aurora pulled them back, she would find me naked in bed with a guy who was not her son. I heard her moving about the room, and I was too scared to speak or even breathe.

My mind raced to remember what had become of our clothes. Were Loki's pajama pants on the bedroom floor? And what became of the panties he'd torn off me?

"Princess?" Aurora said again, and I could see her silhouette through the curtain. She was right outside. "Are you in here?"

"Yeah," I said, afraid that she would open the curtain if I didn't answer. I tried to quiet the panic in my voice. "Uh, yeah. Sorry. I'm really . . . out of it. Yesterday was . . . exhausting."

"I understand," Aurora said. "I'll take my bag so I can get ready and give you time to wake up."

"Okay. Thank you."

"Of course." Aurora's footsteps went toward the door, then she stopped. "Tove feels terrible about what happened last night. He never meant to hurt you."

"I know that." I winced at the mention of Tove. The warm memories of last night turned into cold truths. I'd cheated on my husband.

"He'll want to apologize for himself, but I wanted to be sure you knew," Aurora said. "He'd never hurt you on purpose."

That was like a knife to my heart, and it cut so deep I could barely breathe for a second. I knew that Tove didn't love me, but I doubted he'd be happy about me having sex with another guy. And he deserved so much better than that.

"I will see you downstairs for breakfast," Aurora said.

"Yes," I said, my voice tight to keep back tears.

The bedroom door shut behind her, and I let out a long shaky breath. I pulled away from Loki and sat up. I'd never felt so conflicted in my life. I wanted nothing more than to lay with him forever, but being with him made me feel guilty and horrible.

"Hey." Loki put his arm around my waist, trying to pull me back to him. "You don't have to rush away. She left."

"We have a lot to do today." I pushed his arm off me, hating that I had to reject him, and grabbed my nightgown from where it lay crumpled at the end of the bed.

"I know," Loki said, sounding a little hurt. He sat up as I pulled the nightgown on. "I'd never try to keep you from your work, but can't you spend five more minutes in bed with me?"

"No, I can't." I shook my head and refused to look back at him. I didn't want to see the look on his face or think about what we'd done. I could still taste him on my lips and feel him inside me, and I wanted to sob.

"So . . . that's it, then?" Loki asked.

"I told you that last night was all we could have," I said.

"That you did." He breathed deeply. "I guess I was hoping that I could change your mind."

I got out of bed and found my torn panties sticking out from under the dust ruffle. The bed creaked as Loki got out after me. I turned back to face him. He'd pulled on his pants, but he hadn't worn a shirt here.

"You'll have to sneak back to your room," I told him. "Nobody can see you."

"I know. I'll be careful."

We stood there, staring at each other and not saying anything. There were only a few feet between us, but the distance felt like miles. There was so much that I wanted to say but couldn't. Any words would only make it worse.

If I said aloud how much last night had meant to me, it would make it too real.

Loki walked toward the door but stopped next to me. His hands were balled up into fists, and I could see him struggling with something. Without saying anything, he grabbed me suddenly and pulled me toward him.

He kissed me so passionately, my knees felt weak. I wasn't sure I would be able to stand when he let go, but I did.

"That was the last time," I breathed when we stopped kissing.

"I know," he said simply. Then he let go of me and walked
out of the room.

As soon as he was gone, I folded my arms across my chest,
hugging myself. My stomach lurched, and I was certain I would
throw up for a moment, but it passed. *Don't cry, don't cry, don't
cry.* I repeated it over and over in my head, but I couldn't use my
own persuasion on myself. I reached behind me and grabbed
the bedpost, afraid that my legs would give out.

What had I done? To Loki? To Tove? To myself?

"Princess?" Duncan knocked on the door, but I couldn't
form the words to answer him. The lump in my throat was too
great. "Princess?" He opened the door, and I did my best to
compose myself. "Wendy, are you okay?"

"Yes." I nodded and swallowed back tears. "I'm tired. Yesterday was too much."

"Yeah, I know," Duncan said. "I slept like the dead, but I
had all these weird dreams about banging noises. Did you
hear anything last night? My room was right next to yours."

"No." I shook my head. "Sorry."

"I just wanted to check on you," Duncan said. "Are you
sure you're okay?"

"I'm fine," I lied.

"I talked to Kenna this morning, and she'd like to send
those whose homes are unlivable to Förening for now," Duncan said. "Willa suggested that we all return today and get the
survivors settled in at the palace. Then we can send back

people that actually know how to rebuild Oslinna, since none of us really know how to build a house."

"Um, yes, I think that sounds good," I said. "I'll have to speak with Kenna first." I realized something and looked back at him. "Is everyone up, then?"

"Yeah, everyone but you, Tove, and Loki," Duncan said. "But I just saw Loki in the bathroom, so I guess he's up now. What happened with Tove last night? Aurora said that he was sick or something?"

"Yes," I said quickly. "He's . . . sick." I rubbed the bruise on my arm, trying to cover it up. "I need to talk to him. Is he in his room?"

"As far as I know," Duncan said.

"Thank you," I said. "I'll go talk to him and get dressed, and then I will meet everyone downstairs. Does that sound all right?"

"Yeah, that sounds great," Duncan said. "And, Princess, you should really take it easy today. You look like you're coming down with something."

I waved him off, and he left. As I walked down to Tove's room, I kept trying to think of what I wanted to say. Should I tell him about Loki?

Not here. Not now. We had too much to do for the people here. I didn't want to waste time on a fight.

Timidly, I knocked on the door. I still hadn't come up with what I was going to say to Tove. He opened the door, and the sight of him made it worse. He looked like hell. His hair was always disheveled, but not this bad. I knew he'd slept, but he still had bags under his eyes. His normally mossy-tan skin had paled, and worst of all, he appeared to have aged a few years overnight.

"Wendy, I am so sorry" were the first words out of his mouth, and for a second I didn't understand what he had to be sorry for. "I never meant to hit you. I'd *never* do that. Not if I was thinking clearly."

"No, it's okay," I said numbly. "I know. Yesterday took a lot out of everybody."

"That's no excuse." Tove shook his head. "I should've . . . done something."

"You couldn't have," I said. "And I understand."

"No, you don't. What I did, it wasn't okay. It's never okay to hit a woman, let alone my wife."

The word *wife* made me flinch, but I didn't think he noticed. I didn't want to have this conversation anyway. I couldn't handle listening to him apologize to me after what I'd done. I didn't condone hitting women either, but that wasn't Tove. He hadn't been in his right mind.

And I'd done something just as bad by sleeping with Loki. I hadn't exactly been clearheaded myself when it happened, but if I was being honest, I *wanted* to, even when I wasn't drained from my powers. Yesterday's overload of work had only weakened my inhibitions, so I was more willing to give in to something I wanted.

I still wanted to be with Loki, and that was why my crime far outweighed Tove's.

I brushed past Tove and went over to my suitcase to get a change of clothes. He tried apologizing again, and I reiterated that he had nothing to be sorry for. Before he could bring up last night again, I changed the subject to talk about all the things we had to get done today.

We had gotten all of the major cleaning done, so there was nothing more we personally could do for Oslinna.

I got dressed and went down to start figuring out how to get people out of here. Some vehicles were still in working order, but not enough for everyone. We'd have to send out more cars once we got back to the palace.

As we helped organize the transport, deciding who would go and who would stay, Willa commented on how strange I seemed. I was acting as close to normal as I could, except any-time Loki came near me, I left in a hurry. It was hard to even be around him.

Once everyone was loaded up, we drove home. Kenna stayed behind to run what was left of Oslinna, but I promised her that more help would be on the way soon. Rebuilding the town would be my top priority. Well, right after protecting the kingdom from Vittra domination.

Willa and Matt rode with Tove and me to Förening, and I was grateful. I didn't think I would've been able to handle a long car ride with just Aurora and Tove. Matt sat in the back-seat, sketching architectural designs and talking about all the things we could do for Oslinna.

When we got back, we helped get the refugees set up in the

spare rooms of the palace. It would be weird having so many people living here, but it might be good too. I personally helped Mia and her daughter Hanna get settled in a room, and they both seemed to be a bit happier.

I tasked Willa with getting the resources together to rebuild Oslinna, and Matt was more than happy to take over the reconstruction plans.

As soon as the people from Oslinna were taken care of, I went down to the library to continue my research. I still had to find a way to kill Oren and stop the hobgoblins. Eventually we would be up against the Vittra, and I needed to know how to defeat them.

Besides that, it would do me good to immerse myself in work. I didn't want to think about the mess I'd made of my personal relationships.

I spent most of the evening searching through old Tryllic texts to no avail. None of them mentioned anything about immortal trolls, or at least not that I could understand. I went back over to search for a different book. When I looked up, I saw Finn standing in the doorway to the library.

I didn't think my guilt could get any deeper until I saw him. Despite the fact that Finn and I had never even really been together, not to mention that whatever we had was officially over, I knew how disappointed he would be in me if he knew that I'd slept with Loki.

"Are you all right, Princess?" Finn narrowed his eyes in concern and came into the library.

"Um, yeah, I'm great." I lowered my eyes and walked back

to the desk I'd been studying at. I wanted space between us, and a huge wooden desk would definitely help out.

"You look so pale," Finn said. "The trip must've taken a lot out of you."

"Yeah, we all worked really hard there," I said and flipped open a book so I would look busy. Anything to keep me distracted from Finn and his dark eyes.

"That's what I heard." He leaned on the desk in front of me. "Loki came to see me today."

"What?" My head jerked up, and my stomach dropped. "I mean, did he?"

"Yeah." Finn gave me an odd look. "Are you sure everything is okay?"

"Yeah, it's all great," I said. "What did Loki say?"

"He told me what he learned about the hobgoblins from your visit to Oslinna," Finn said. "All of the damage was focused on property, and any casualties were people who just happened to get in the way. He seems to think the hobgoblins aren't particularly bloodthirsty, but he's still coming down to help me train the trackers tomorrow."

"Oh." I fidgeted with my wedding ring and lowered my eyes again.

"I'm starting to think he might not be quite as bad as I thought he was," Finn said, almost grudgingly. "But you still spend too much time with him. You have to be careful about appearances."

"I know." My mouth suddenly felt very dry. "I'm working on it."

Finn stood on the other side of the desk, as if waiting for me to say something, but I had nothing to say. I stared down at the book, almost too nervous to breathe.

"I just came to see how the trip went," Finn said.

"It went well," I said quickly, nearly cutting him off.

"Wendy." He lowered his voice. "Is there something you're not telling me?"

"Oh, Princess, sorry to bother you," Mia said, and I'd never been so relieved to have an interruption.

She stood in the doorway, holding Hanna against her side. Since they'd been here at the palace, they'd both had time to get cleaned up, and Mia looked even lovelier than she had at Oslinna, and I hadn't thought that was possible.

"No, no, Mia, you're no bother," I said quickly.

"I was just trying to find the kitchen." She gave me an apologetic smile. "Hanna's hungry, and I've been wandering around this place, but I keep making wrong turns. It's so much bigger than the one in Oslinna."

"The palace does take some time to get used to," Finn said, returning her smile. "I could show you to the kitchen if you'd like."

"That would be great." Mia smiled wider, appearing relieved. "Thank you." Then her expression fell, and she looked worried. "I'm not taking him away from you, Princess, am I?"

"No, not at all." I shook my head. "Finn would be glad to help."

"Yes, of course I would," he said. "Mia, is it?"

"Yeah." Mia smiled at him again, then motioned to her baby. "This is Hanna."

"It will be my pleasure to show you both around the palace." He started to leave with them, but he turned back to me before he left, his lips pursed together, and nodded once.

After he left with Mia, I let out a shaky breath.

I buried myself in the books, although it didn't do much good. I still hadn't found anything useful yet.

It was getting late when Willa knocked on the open door.

"Wendy, I know you're really busy, but you need to come see this," Willa said. "The whole palace is talking."

"About what?" I asked.

"Elora's new painting." Willa pursed her lips. "It shows everyone dead."

EIGHTEEN

future

E lora had the "gift" of precognitive painting, although she'd be the first to tell anyone it was more of a curse. She would paint a scene from the future, from an event yet to happen, and that was it. No context, no preceding actions—just one solitary scene from the event.

Since she'd been so weak lately, she'd hardly painted anything. It drained her too much, but if Elora had a powerful vision, she couldn't hold it in. The precognition caused her terrible migraines until she painted these visions and got them out.

Also, Elora tried to keep her paintings as private as possible, unless she thought they had some value that everyone should see. And this one definitely did.

The painting sat on an easel at one end of the War Room. Elora had tried to keep the gathering small, so only the people who needed to know would see it, but as Willa said, word of the painting was spreading through the palace like wildfire.

Garrett stood by the door, keeping the riffraff from sneaking a peek. When Willa and I entered, Marksinna Laris, Markis Bain, Thomas, Tove, and Aurora were gathered around it. A few others were sitting at the table, too stunned to say anything.

I pushed Laris to the side so I could get a good look, and Tove stepped back. The painting was even more horrifying than Willa had let on.

Elora painted so well it looked like a photograph. Everything was done in exquisite detail. It showed the rotunda, its curved stairwell collapsed in the middle. The chandelier that normally hung in the center had crashed and lay destroyed on the floor. A small fire burned at the top of the stairs, and gold detailing was coming off the walls.

Bodies were everywhere. Some of them I didn't recognize, but others were startlingly clear. Willa was hanging off the destroyed stairs, her head twisted at an angle that she couldn't survive. Duncan was crushed underneath the chandelier, broken glass all over him. Tove lay in a pool of blood spilling out from him. Finn was crumpled in a mess of broken stairs, his bones sticking through his skin. Loki had a sword run straight through his chest, pinning him to the wall like an insect in an entomologist's display box.

I lay dead at a man's feet. A broken crown lay smashed near my head. I died after I'd been crowned. I was Queen.

In the painting, the man's back was to the viewer, but his long dark hair and black velvet jacket were unmistakable—it was Oren, my father. He had come to the palace and caused all this carnage. At least twenty or more bodies littered the scene Elora had painted, including my own.

We were all dead.

"When did you paint this?" I asked Elora when I found the strength to speak.

She sat in a chair to the side of the room, staring out the window at the snow falling on the pines. Her hands were folded in her lap, the skin gray and wrinkled. She was dying, and this painting had probably pushed her to the edge.

"Last night, while you were gone," Elora said. "I wasn't sure if I should tell anyone. I didn't want to start an unnecessary panic, but Garrett thought that you all should know."

"It might help change things," Garrett said, and I glanced back over at him. Worry tightened his expression. His daughter was dead in the picture too.

"How can you change things?" Laris asked, her voice shrill. "It is the future!"

"You can't prevent the future," Tove said. "But you can alter it." He turned to me for confirmation. "Can't you?"

"Yes." I nodded. "That's what Elora told me. She said the future is fluid, and just because she paints something, it doesn't mean it will happen."

"But it might happen," Aurora said. "The course we are on now is set so that this will be our future. That the King of the Vittra will destroy the palace and take over Förening."

"We don't know that he'll take over Förening," Willa said, futilely attempting to help. "We only see that some of us are dead."

"That is a great consolation, Marksinna," Laris said snidely, and Tove shot her a look.

"Aurora has something," I said. "All we have to do is change the course."

"How can we possibly know that we're changing the course the right way?" Laris asked. "Maybe whatever action we take to prevent this scene is the action that will cause it."

"We can't simply do nothing." I stepped back from the painting. I didn't want to see everyone I loved dead anymore.

I leaned back against the table and ran my hands through my hair. I had to think of something to stop this. Something to change it. I couldn't let this happen.

"We have to take out an element," I said, thinking aloud. "We have to change something in the painting. Make something in it go away. Then we'll know we've changed it."

"Like what?" Willa asked. "You mean like the staircase?"

"I can go get rid of that right now," Tove offered.

"We need the staircase," Aurora said. "It's the only way to the second floor."

"What we don't need is the Princess," Laris muttered under her breath.

"Marksinna, I told you that if you said—" Tove began but I stopped him.

"Wait." I stood up straighter. "She's right."

"She's right?" Willa was confused.

"If we get rid of the Princess, the whole scene changes," Aurora said as it occurred to her. "The King has been coming for her this whole time, and in the painting, he finally succeeds. If we give her to him, the painting goes away."

Nobody said anything, and by the confused, worried expressions on both Willa's and Tove's faces, I'd say that even they were considering it. It was hard not to. If it was only one of them dead, they probably would still fight to keep me here, but everyone was dead. My life was not more valuable than all of theirs.

"But even if we give the King the Princess, he still wants the Trylle kingdom," Bain pointed out. "He'll still keep coming after us even if he has her."

"Maybe," I agreed.

"More like certainly," Tove said, giving me a knowing look. "Getting you is just a means to an end for the King. He wants you so he can have the kingdom."

"I know you're right, but . . ." I trailed off. "I'm not saying that surrendering myself to the King will prevent a war between the Vittra and the Trylle, because it won't. What I am saying is that it will prevent that painting."

"So?" Tove shrugged. "We won't die that way, that day. But the King will still kill us."

"No," I insisted. "I can hand myself over and buy more time for you to fight back. I can prevent the painting, and you can prepare the Trylle army to conquer him."

"He's just going to kill you, Wendy," Tove said. "And you know it."

"Tove," Aurora said gently. "If she's with the King, then she won't be in that painting. She'll have changed the course, and it might be the only way to prevent all those deaths. That's something we need to consider."

"You're not giving him my daughter," Elora said firmly. She grabbed the back of the chair and pushed herself up. "That is not an option."

"If I'm going to end up dead anyway, at least I should spare the people," I said.

"You will find another way," she insisted. "I am not sacrificing you for this."

"You're not sacrificing anything," I said. "I am willingly doing this."

"No," Elora said. "That is a direct order. You will not go to him."

"Elora, I know the thought of losing your child is unbearable," Aurora said as gently as she could. "But you need to at least consider what's best for the kingdom."

"If you won't, then we'll have you overthrown," Laris said. "Everyone in the kingdom would stand behind me if you were going to lead us all into certain death."

"Death isn't certain!" Elora snapped. "Overthrow me if you want. Until then, I am your Queen, and the Princess isn't going anywhere."

"Elora, why don't you sit back down?" Garrett said gently and walked over to her.

"I will not sit down." She slapped his hands away when he reached out for her. "I am not some feeble old woman. I am the Queen, and I am her mother, and I have a say in what happens here! In fact, I have the *only* say!"

"Elora," I said. "You're not thinking this through. You always told me that the good of the kingdom came first."

"Maybe I made a mistake." Elora's once-dark eyes, looking almost silver now, darted around the room. I wasn't sure she could really see anything anymore. "I did everything for this kingdom. *Everything.* And look what's become of it."

She stepped forward, although I didn't know where she intended to go. Her legs gave out under her, and she fell to the floor. Garrett tried to catch her, but he moved too late. She was unconscious by the time she hit the floor.

I rushed over to her side, and Garrett was already pulling her from the floor into his lap. Her white hair flowed around her, and she lay still in his arms. A thin line of blood came from her nose, but I doubt it came from her hitting her face on the floor. Bloody noses seemed to be a result of abilities being overloaded.

"Is she all right?" I asked, kneeling beside her. I wanted to touch her, but I was too afraid to. She looked so frail.

"She's alive, if that's what you're asking," Garrett said. He pulled a tissue from his pocket and wiped at the blood. "But she hasn't been doing well since she painted that."

"Aurora," I said, looking back over my shoulder at her. "Come heal her."

"No, Princess." Garrett shook his head. "It's no use."

"What do you mean, it's no use?" I asked, incredulous. "She's sick!"

"There's nothing more that can be done for Elora." Garrett stared down at my mother, his dark eyes swimming with love.

"She's not sick, and she cannot be cured. Her life has been drained from her, and Aurora can't give that back to her."

"She can do something, though," I insisted. "Something to help."

"No," he said simply. Still holding Elora in his arms, he got to his feet. "I'm taking her to her room to make her comfortable. That's all we can do."

"I'll go with you." I stood up and looked back at the room. "We will continue this discussion tomorrow."

"Hasn't it already been decided?" Laris asked with a wicked smile.

"We'll discuss it tomorrow," Tove said firmly, and he draped a cloth over the picture to cover it.

I went with Garrett to my mother's room and pushed thoughts of the painting from my mind. I wanted to see Elora while I still had the chance. She didn't have much time left, not that I even knew what that meant. Her time could be a few hours, a few days, maybe even a few weeks. But the end was drawing near.

That meant I'd be Queen soon, but I couldn't think of that either. I only had a little time left to spend with my mother, and I wanted to make the most of it. I didn't want to be distracted by thoughts of what would become of the kingdom or my friends or even my marriage.

I sat in the chair beside her bed and waited for her to wake up. It took longer than I'd expected it to, and I ended up dozing off. Garrett actually alerted me when she woke up.

"Princess?" Elora asked weakly, sounding surprised that I was there.

"She's been waiting by your side," Garrett said. He stood at the end of the bed, staring down at her looking so small beneath her blankets.

"I'd like a moment alone with my daughter, if that's all right," Elora said.

"Yes, of course," Garrett said. "I'll be right outside if you need me."

"Thank you." She smiled at him, and he left the two of us alone.

"How are you feeling?" I asked and scooted my chair closer to the bed. Her voice was hardly more than a whisper.

"I've seen better days," she said.

"I'm sorry."

"I meant what I said before." Elora turned her head to face me, but I didn't know if she could see me. "You shouldn't give yourself to the Vittra. Not for anything."

"I can't let people die over me," I said gently. I didn't want to argue with her, not when she was like this, but it seemed like sacrilege to lie to her on her deathbed.

"There has to be another way," she insisted. "There has to be something more than sacrificing you to your father. I did everything right. I always thought about what was best for the kingdom. And all I asked for in return is that you would be safe."

"This can't be about my safety," I said. "You never cared this much about it before."

"Of course I cared." Elora sounded offended. "You are my

daughter. I have always cared about you." She paused, sighing. "I regret making you marry Tove."

"You didn't make me marry him. He asked. I said yes."

"I shouldn't have let you, then," Elora said. "I knew you didn't love him. But I thought if I did the right thing, I could protect you. You could end up happy, but now I don't think I've ever done anything that will help you be happy."

"I'm happy," I said, and that wasn't a complete lie. Many things in my life made me happy. I just hadn't been able to enjoy them much lately.

"Don't make the same mistakes I did," she said. "I married a man I didn't love because it was the right thing for the kingdom. I let the man I did love slip away because it was the right thing for the kingdom. And I gave away my only child because it was the right thing for my kingdom."

"You didn't give me away," I said. "You hid me from Oren."

"But I should've stayed with you," Elora said. "We could've hidden together. I could've protected you from all this. That is my biggest regret. That I didn't stay behind with you."

"How come you're talking like this now?" I asked. "How come you didn't say any of this to me sooner?"

"I didn't want you to love me," she said simply. "I knew we didn't have much time together, and I didn't want you to miss me. I thought it'd be better for you if you never even cared at all."

"But you changed your mind now?" I asked.

"I didn't want to die without you knowing how much I love

you." She held out her hand to me. I took it in mine, and her skin felt cool and soft as she squeezed my hand. "I have made so many mistakes. I only wanted you to be strong so you could protect yourself. I am so very sorry."

"Don't be sorry." I forced a smile at her. "You did everything you could, and I know that."

"I know you'll be a good Queen, a strong, noble leader, and that's more than these people deserve," she said. "But don't give too much. You need to keep some of yourself for you. And listen to your heart."

"I can't believe you're telling me to listen to my heart," I said. "I never thought I'd hear that from you."

"Don't act on everything your heart says, but make sure you listen to it." Elora smiled. "Sometimes your heart is right."

Elora and I stayed up talking for a while after that. She didn't tell me much that I didn't already know, but in a weird way, it felt like the first real conversation we'd had. She wasn't talking to me as a Queen talking to the Princess, but rather as a mother talking to her daughter.

Too soon, she grew tired and fell asleep. I sat with her for a while after that anyway. I didn't want to leave her. What little time I had left with her felt precious.

NINETEEN

relief

I don't know, Wendy." Tove shook his head. "I don't want you to die, but I don't know what else to tell you."

"I know." I sighed. "That's where I'm at too."

Tove sat on the chest at the end of our bed, and I stood in front of him, chewing on my thumbnail. We were both still in pajamas, and I wasn't sure how well either of us had slept the night before. I woke him early in the morning, when it was still dark out, and immediately began asking him what he thought I should do about Elora's painting.

"You still don't know how to kill the King," Tove pointed out. "And you did promise him our kingdom when you're Queen."

"I won't be Queen if I'm with him."

"But he won't let that slide," Tove said. "Even if you go to him, he might reject you simply because he wants the kingdom."

"I can tell him that you all booted me out when you found out my plan to combine with the Vittra," I said. "Then he'll have me."

"But he still wants the kingdom," Tove said. "He'll still come after it, even if he has you. At best, you're postponing the inevitable."

"Maybe so," I admitted. "But if that's the best I can do, then that's what I have to do."

"But what then?" Tove asked, staring up at me. "What happens after the King has you?"

"You'll become the Trylle King," I said. "You'll protect our people."

"So that's it?" Tove asked. "You'll go, and I'll stay?"

I nodded. "Yes."

Loki threw open the bedroom doors, making them bang against the walls. I jumped, and Tove got to his feet. Loki's eyes were fixed on me as he stormed in, ignoring my husband.

"What are you doing?" I asked, too startled to sound angry.

"I knew it!" Loki shouted, and his eyes never wavered from me. "As soon as Duncan told me, I knew you would immediately jump to suicide. Why are you so intent on being a martyr, Wendy?"

"I'm not a martyr." I straightened my shoulders for a fight. "What did Duncan tell you? And what are you doing bursting into my room at six in the morning?"

"I couldn't sleep, so I came down to see if you were awake," Loki said. "I heard the two of you talking, but I already knew that's what you would do. Duncan told me about the painting, and I knew you'd try to go back to the Vittra."

"You were eavesdropping?" I narrowed my eyes at him. "I'm in my personal chambers! You have no right to spy on me or come into my room without being invited!"

Loki rolled his eyes. "I wasn't spying on you. Don't be so dramatic, Princess. I paused outside your door to see if you were awake, and you clearly were, so I came in."

"You still can't just barge in." I crossed my arms over my chest.

"Would you like me to go back out and knock?" Loki gestured to the doors behind him. "Would that make you feel better?"

"I would like you to leave and go back to your room," I said.

I hadn't really talked to Loki since we'd slept together, and I could see Tove from the corner of my eye, watching us. Loki wouldn't look away from me, and I refused to look away first, putting us in some kind of staring contest that I was determined to win.

"I will," Loki said. "As soon as you admit that giving yourself to the King is completely preposterous."

I bristled. "It's not preposterous. I know it's not ideal, but it's the best we can come up with. I can't let that painting come true."

"How do you know that going with the King will change anything?" Loki countered.

"You didn't see the painting. You don't understand."

"The only way to truly stop the painting is to kill the

King," Loki said. "And you're the only one strong enough to do that."

"But I don't know how to," I said. "And you're strong. You can do it. I need to do something to divert the outcome of the painting until you can figure out how to stop him."

"Wendy, if I could kill him, I would've done it by now," Loki said. "You know that."

"It doesn't matter." I waved my hands and stepped away from him. "This isn't open for discussion. I've decided what I'm going to do."

"And you think I'll just let you go?" Loki asked.

"*Let* me?" I glared at him. "You don't 'let' me do anything."

"You know I can stop you." His eyes met mine evenly, and he stepped toward me. "I will do everything in my power to keep you from him."

"Loki, he will kill us all," I said emphatically. "The King will kill Tove and me and *you*. This is the only way I can protect us."

"I don't care," Loki said. "I would rather die fighting him. I would rather see *you* die fighting, than know that you surrendered to him. You can't give up."

I lowered my eyes and swallowed. Tove stood off to the side. I'd hoped he would jump in, say something, but he didn't.

"What do you propose I do?" I asked quietly, still staring at the floor.

"We've still got time until he comes for you," Loki said. "Learn how to kill him, and when he comes, fight him."

"What if we lose?" I asked. "What if I can't stop him?"

"If you can't stop him later, then you can't stop him now," Loki said. "Giving up now doesn't mean you can stand up to him later. It just means you're dead."

I glanced over at Tove, who still kept silent, and I thought about what Loki had said. I hated that I didn't know what the right thing was. All I wanted to do was keep everyone safe, and I was terrified that if I made the wrong decision I would get us all killed.

"Okay," I said finally and turned back to Loki. "I'll stay for now. But you need to work twice as hard with Finn. The trackers must be prepared for whatever happens."

"As you wish, Princess." Loki smiled slightly, a corner of his mouth turning up.

But something glowed behind the usual sparkle in his eyes, something deeper, burning. When he looked at me like that, my heart pounded so loudly I was certain he could hear it.

I became acutely aware of how close Loki was to me. He could reach out and touch me if he wanted, and I made sure to keep my arms firmly folded across my chest so I wouldn't be tempted to do the same.

With all the chaos in the palace, I hadn't had a chance to think about Loki, but with him standing here, I could think of nothing else but the night we'd spent together.

More than the things we'd done, the imprints burned into my skin from where he touched me, was the memory of what we'd actually shared. A moment when I'd never felt closer to anyone, as if the two of us had become one.

The painting flashed in my mind, the image of Loki skewered

at the hands of my father, and I knew that I would do whatever it took to save him, even if it went against Loki's wishes. I could not let him die.

"I trust you have much to do, Markis," I said numbly, and my cheeks flushed when I realized we'd been staring at each other for some time. With my husband watching.

"Of course." Loki gave a quick nod and turned to leave.

Tove walked after him, closing the double doors behind Loki. Tove stood in front of them for a moment, leaning his forehead against the wood. When he turned back around to face me, he didn't look at me. His mossy eyes flitted around the room, and he pushed up the sleeves on his pajama shirt.

"Is everything all right?" I asked carefully.

"Yes." He furrowed his brow and shook his head. "I don't know. I'm happy that you're not going off to die. I don't think I would like it if you died."

"I wouldn't like it if you died either," I said.

"But . . ." Tove trailed off, staring intently at a spot on the floor. "Are you in love with him?"

"What?" I asked, and my heart dropped to my stomach. "Why would you . . ." I wanted to argue, but the strength had gone out of my words.

"He's in love with you." He lifted his head and looked up at me. "Do you know that?"

"I—I don't know what you're talking about," I stammered. I walked over to the bed, needing to do something to busy myself, so I pulled up the sheets. "Loki is merely—"

"I see your auras," Tove interrupted me, his voice firm but

not angry. "His is silver, and yours is gold. And when you're around each other, you both get a pink halo. Just now you were both glowing bright pink, and your auras intertwined."

I stopped and didn't say anything. What could I say to that? Tove could physically see how we felt about each other. I couldn't deny it. I kept my back to him and waited for him to go on, for him to yell at me and accuse me of being a slut.

"I should be mad," he said at length. "Or jealous. Shouldn't I?"

"Tove, I'm sorry," I said and looked back at him. "I never meant for this to happen."

"I am jealous, but not the way I should be." He shook his head. "He loves you, and I . . . I don't." He ran a hand through his hair and sighed. "The other night, when I had the break-down, and I hit you—"

"That wasn't your fault," I said quickly. "That never changed the way I felt about you."

"No, I know." He nodded. "But it got me thinking. I only have so much time before I completely lose it. These abilities, they're going to keep eating at my brain until nothing is left."

"No matter what happens, I'll be by your side." I stepped closer to him, trying to reassure him. "Even if I care for . . ." I paused, still not wanting to admit how I felt about Loki. "Other people don't matter. You are my husband, and I am with you in sickness and in health."

"You really would, wouldn't you?" Tove asked, almost sadly. "You would take care of me if I lost my mind."

"Of course I would." I nodded.

It had never occurred to me to leave Tove, at least not because of what had happened the other night, or if he became sick and frail like Elora. Tove was a good man, a kind man, and he deserved as much love and care as I could give him.

"That makes what I'm about to say so much harder." He sighed and sat down on the edge of the bed.

"What?" I sat next to him.

"I've realized how little time I have," he said, "before my mind completely goes. Maybe twenty years, if I'm lucky. And then it's gone.

"And I want to fall in love with somebody." Tove took a deep breath. "I want to share my life with somebody. And . . . that somebody isn't you."

"Oh," I said, and for a moment I felt nothing. I didn't know how to feel about what he was saying, so my body just went numb.

"I'm sorry," Tove said. "I know what you've given up to be with me, and I'm sorry that I'm not strong enough to do the same for you. I thought I was. I thought because we were friends and I believed in you as Queen that would be enough. But it's not."

"No, it isn't," I agreed quietly.

"Wendy, I'm . . . ." He paused, staring down at the floor. "I'm gay."

I swallowed hard. "I thought you might be."

"Did you?" He lifted his head to look at me. "How?"

I shrugged. "It was just a feeling." That was a lie. Finn had pointed it out to me, but once he did, it seemed rather obvious.

"So . . . I guess I'm sorry for marrying you. I shouldn't have let you, not when I knew that this would never be happy for you."

"Well, I didn't exactly think it'd be happy for you either." He rubbed the back of his neck. "In my defense, I didn't realize how strongly you felt for Loki until the wedding. When you danced with him, you both glowed so brightly . . ."

"So you knew?" I asked. "You always knew?" He nodded. "Did you . . . did you know that I slept with him?"

"You did?" Something flashed in his eyes then, something that might have been hurt. "When?"

"In Oslinna, after . . . we fought," I said, choosing my words carefully.

"Oh." He stared off and didn't say anything else for a moment.

"Are you mad?" I asked.

"Not mad." He shook his head. "But . . . I can't say that I'm happy either." He furrowed his brow. "I don't know how to explain it. But I'm glad you told me."

"I am sorry for that. I never meant for it to happen, and I'd never want to hurt you." I smiled wanly at him. "And it won't happen again. I promise you that."

"I know. Because, Wendy, I think . . ." He paused, taking another deep breath. "I want a divorce."

And then it happened. I started to cry. I'm not sure why exactly. A combination of relief and sadness and confusion, and so much else that I'd been struggling to hold in. I was happy and relieved but sad and frightened, and a million other things all at once.

"Wendy, don't cry." Tove put his arm around me to comfort me, the first time he'd really touched me since we'd been married. "I didn't want to make you sad."

"No, I'm not sad, but . . ." I sniffled and looked up at him. "Is this because I slept with Loki?"

He laughed a little. "No. I'd made a decision before you told me that. It's because we don't love each other, and I think we should have a chance to spend time with the people we do love."

"Oh. Good." I shook my head and wiped at my eyes. "Sorry. I'm overwhelmed. And you're right. We should get an annulment." I nodded and stopped crying almost as soon as I had started. "Sorry. I don't know where that came from."

"Are you sure you're okay with this?" Tove asked, eyeing me carefully.

"Yes, I am." I smiled weakly at him. "It's probably the best thing for us both."

"Yeah, I hope so." Tove nodded. "We're friends, and I'll always have your back, but we don't need to be married for that."

"True," I agreed. "But I want to wait until after this is all over with the Vittra. In case something happens to me, I want you to be King."

"Are you sure you want me to be King?" Tove asked. "I'm going to go crazy someday."

"But until then, you're about the only person I trust that has any power," I said. "Willa would be a good ruler someday, but I don't think she's quite there yet. She can take over for you, if you need her to."

"You really think something's going to happen to you?" Tove asked.

"I don't know," I admitted. "But I need to know that the kingdom will be in good hands, no matter what."

"All right," he said. "You have my word. We'll stay married until after the Vittra are defeated, and if something happens to you, I will rule the kingdom to the best of my ability."

I smiled at him. "Thank you."

"Good." Tove dropped his arm and stared straight ahead. "Now that that's out of the way, I suppose we should get ready. We have the Chancellor's funeral at eleven."

"I haven't prepared my speech yet." I sighed and Tove stood up. "What should I say about him?"

"Well, if you plan to say anything nice, you're going to have to lie," Tove muttered as he walked over to his closet.

"You shouldn't speak ill of the dead."

"You didn't hear what he wanted to do to you," Tove said, talking loudly to be heard from the closet. "That man was a menace to our society."

I sat on the bed, listening to my husband gather his clothes before he went to shower, and despite everything that was still going on, I felt as if an immense weight had been lifted from my shoulders.

I still had no idea how to stop the Vittra and save everyone I cared about, and I had to write a eulogy for the Chancellor. But for the first time in a long time, I felt like there might be life after this. If I could defeat the King, if I could save us, there might really be something to live for.

TWENTY

orm

Willa wore all black, but the hem of her skirt only came to the middle of her thigh. At least she had classed it up a little for the funeral. My eulogy had gone over well, or about as well as a eulogy could go over. Nobody had cried for the Chancellor, and that seemed sad to me, but I couldn't bring myself to cry for him either.

His funeral had been held in one of the larger meeting rooms in the palace. Black flowers and black candles decorated the room. I wasn't sure who had planned the funeral, but it looked like a Goth kid at a Cure concert had thrown up here.

After they took the Chancellor away to bury him in the palace cemetery, most of us stayed behind. He didn't have any family or friends, and I wasn't entirely sure how he got elected in the first place.

The mood was decidedly somber, but I didn't think that actually had much to do with the funeral. All the guests in attendance were muttering, whispering, huddled in corners talking quietly, and they kept glancing at me. I heard the word "painting" floating through the air like a breeze.

I stood off to the side of the room, talking mostly with Willa and Tove. Ordinarily, any of the royals would be eager to make some kind of small talk with me, but today they all avoided me. Which was just as well. I didn't have much I wanted to say to any of them.

"When is it polite for us to leave?" Willa asked, swirling her champagne around in her glass. I think she'd already had a couple glasses more than she should have, and she hiccupped daintily before covering her mouth with her hand. "Excuse me."

"I think we've been here long enough." Tove scanned the room, which had already thinned out. His mother and father hadn't been able to make it at all, and my mother could barely move, so she was still on bed rest.

"Whenever is fine with me," I said.

"Good." Willa set her glass on a nearby table, some of the bubbly pink liquid sloshing over the top. She looped her arm through mine, more to steady herself, and we left the room.

"Well, that went great." I sighed, plucking a black flower from my hair as we went down the hall.

"Really?" Tove asked. "Because I thought it went horribly."

"I was being sarcastic."

"Oh." He shoved his hands in his pockets as he walked beside me. "It could've been worse, I guess."

"You should've drunk more," Willa said to me. "That's

how I made it through that thing. And you're lucky you're my best friend, or I wouldn't have gone at all."

"You need to start doing more stuff like this, Willa," I told her. "You're so good at handling people, and someday you might need to do it officially."

"Nope, that's your job." She smiled. "I lucked out. I'm free to be the naughty drunk friend."

I tried to argue with Willa about the merits of being a good Trylle citizen. She schmoozed much better than I ever could, and she was a great ally, when she put her mind to it. But right now she was too tipsy to see reason in anything.

She was giggling at something I'd said when we reached the rotunda. Garrett was coming down the stairs, but he stopped halfway when he saw us. His hair was a mess, his shirt was untucked, and his eyes were red-rimmed.

As soon as his eyes met mine, I knew.

"Elora," I breathed.

"Wendy, I'm sorry," Garrett said, his voice thick with tears, and he shook his head.

I knew he wasn't lying, but I had to see it for myself. I pulled my arm from Willa's and lifted my black gown so I could race up the stairs. Garrett tried to reach out for me, but I ran past him. I didn't slow at all, not until I got to my mother's room.

She lay utterly still in bed, her body little more than a skeleton. The sheets were pulled up to her chest, and her hands were folded neatly over her stomach. Even her hair had been brushed and smoothed, shimmering silver around her. Garrett had arranged her the way she would've wanted him to.

I knelt down next to her bed. I wasn't sure why, except I felt compelled to be near her. I took her hand, cold and stiff in my own, and that was when it hit me. Like a wave of despair I hadn't even known I was capable of, I began to sob, burying my face in the blankets beside her.

I hadn't expected to feel this much. Her death felt as if the ground had been pulled out from under me. Epic blackness stretched on forever to catch me.

There were things her death would signify, consequences I wasn't ready for, but I didn't even think about that. Not at first.

I clung to her, sobbing, because I was a daughter who had lost her mother. Despite our rocky relationship, she did love me, and I did love her. She was the only person who knew what it was like to be Queen, to give me advice, to shepherd me into this world, and she was gone.

I allowed myself an afternoon to really feel the loss, to feel the new hole that had been torn inside of me. That was all the time I had to mourn Elora, and then I had so much more I needed to do. But for that one afternoon, I let myself cry over everything we'd never been able to have, and the moments we'd shared that were worth treasuring.

Willa eventually pulled me away from Elora's body so Garrett could begin the funeral arrangements, and she took me to Matt's room. He hugged me and let me cry, and I'd never been more grateful for my brother. Without him, I'd feel like an orphan.

Tove stayed with me in Matt's room, not saying anything,

and eventually Duncan joined us. I sat on the floor with my back leaning against the bed, and Matt sat beside me. Willa had sobered up rather quickly, and she sat on the bed behind me, her long legs draped over the edge.

"I hate to leave you like this, but I think I should go help my father." Willa touched my head when she stood up. "He shouldn't be doing this alone."

"I can help him." I started to push myself up, but Matt put his hand on my arm.

"You can help tomorrow," Matt said. "You're going to have a lot to do. Today, you can be sad."

"Matt's right," Willa said. "I can handle this for now."

"All right." I settled back down and wiped my eyes. "We need to keep this to ourselves if we can. Keep her death quiet, and hold off on the funeral for as long as possible. I don't want the Vittra King to find out."

"He will eventually," Willa said gently.

"I know." I rested my elbows on my knees and turned to Tove. "How long do I have until I'm Queen?"

"Three days," Tove said. He leaned back against Matt's dresser, his legs crossed at the ankles. "Then somebody has to be coroneted."

"So we have three days." I let out a deep breath, my mind racing with all the things that had to be done.

"We'll keep this quiet," Duncan said. "You can arrange a private funeral."

"We can't keep the death of the Queen secret forever," I said. "We have to begin to prepare now."

"I'll be back as soon as I can." Willa offered me an apologetic smile. "Take care, okay?"

"Of course." I nodded absently.

She gave Matt a quick kiss before leaving. Duncan came over and crouched down in front of me. His dark eyes were sympathetic, but I saw a fierce determination in them too.

"What do you need me to do, Princess?" Duncan asked.

"Duncan, not now," Matt said sternly. "Wendy just lost her mother. She's not in the right frame of mind."

"I don't have time to get in the right frame of mind," I said. "We have three days before I'm Queen. If we're lucky, we have four or five days until Oren comes to claim his prize. I've already taken too much time crying over Elora's death. When this is all over with, I can mourn her. But now I need to work."

"I should tell Thomas," Tove said. "He needs to have the trackers ready."

I nodded. "When Willa gets back, she needs to talk to the refugees from Oslinna. I'm sure some of them will want to fight against the Vittra that killed their families and destroyed their town."

"What are you going to do?" Tove asked.

"I still have to find a way to stop the King," I said, and I looked up at Duncan. "And Duncan's going to help me."

Matt tried to protest. He thought I needed to process what was happening, and maybe he was right. But I didn't have the time. Duncan took my hand and helped me to my feet. Tove opened the bedroom door to leave, but then he stepped aside, letting Finn come into the room.

"Princess," Finn said, his dark eyes on me. "I came to see if you were all right."

"Yes." I smoothed out my black dress, wrinkled from sitting on the floor for so long.

"I'm going to talk to Thomas." Tove glanced back at me, checking to see if that was still okay, and I nodded.

"I'll wait outside for you," Duncan offered. He gave me a small smile before hurrying out after Tove.

Matt, however, stood next to me. His arms were crossed firmly over his chest, and his blue eyes were like ice as he stared at Finn. I was actually grateful for Matt's distrust. It used to be that I would kill to get a moment alone with Finn, but I had no idea what to say to him anymore.

"I'm sorry to hear about your mother," Finn said simply.

"Thank you." I wiped at my eyes again. I'd stopped crying a while ago, but my cheeks were still sticky and damp from tears.

"She was a great Queen," Finn said, his words carefully measured. "As you will be."

"We have yet to see what kind of Queen I will be." I ran a hand through my curls and gave him a thin smile. "I have much to do before I am to be Queen, and I'm sorry, but I really must get to it now."

"Yes, of course." Finn lowered his eyes, but not before I saw the hurt flash in them for a moment. He'd grown accustomed to me turning to him for comfort, but I didn't need him anymore. "I didn't mean to keep you."

"It's quite all right," I said and turned to Matt. "Will you accompany me?"

"What?" Matt sounded surprised, probably because I hardly asked him to do anything with me anymore. So much of what I did involved palace business, and I couldn't let a mänsklig tag along with me.

"I'm going down to the library," I clarified. "Would you come with me?"

"Yeah, sure." Matt nodded, almost eagerly. "I'd love to help you any way I can."

Matt and I left his room, but Finn walked with us because he was going in the same direction, presumably back to train our army. The trackers were doing most of their training in the first-floor ballroom, since it had the most space.

Tove had already left to find Thomas, but Duncan had waited for us, following a step behind as we went down the hall.

"How is the training coming?" I asked Finn, since he was beside me, and I needed to fill the space with something.

"It's going as well as can be expected," Finn said. "They are learning quickly, which is good."

"Is Loki being of any help?" I asked, and Finn stiffened at the mention of Loki's name.

"Yes, surprisingly." Finn scratched at his temple and seemed reluctant to say anything nice about Loki. "He is much stronger than our trackers, but he's done a fine job of teaching them how to maneuver. We will be unable to beat the Vittra hobgoblins with our strength, but we have the upper hand with our wits."

"Good." I nodded. "You know we only have a few days until the Vittra will come."

"Yes," Finn said. "We will work overtime until then."

"Don't overwork them," I said.

"I will try not to."

"And . . ." I paused, thinking of exactly how I wanted to phrase it. "If they can't do it, if you don't honestly believe they stand a chance against the Vittra, do not let them fight."

"They stand a chance," Finn said, slightly offended.

"No, Finn, listen to me." I stopped and touched his arm, so he would stop and face me. His dark eyes still smoldered with something, but I refused to acknowledge it. "If our Trylle army cannot win against the Vittra, do not send them to fight. I will not let them go on a suicide mission. Do you understand?"

"Some lives will be lost, Princess," Finn answered cautiously.

"I know," I admitted, hating that it was true. "But it is only worth losing some lives if we can win, otherwise lives will be lost for nothing."

"What do you propose we do, then?" Finn asked. "If the troops aren't ready to fight the Vittra, what will you have us do?"

"You will do nothing," I said. "I will take care of this."

"Wendy," Matt said. "What are you talking about?"

"Don't worry about it." I started walking again, and they followed more slowly behind me. "I will handle things if it comes to that, but until then, we will continue with the plan. We will ready ourselves for war."

I marched ahead, walking faster so I didn't have to argue with Matt or Finn. Both of them wanted to protect me, but they couldn't. Not anymore.

On the way to the library, we went past the ballroom. Finn

went inside to finish the training, and I glanced in. All the trackers were sitting on the floor in a semicircle around Tove and Loki. They were both talking, explaining what would need to be done.

"Should I go in with them?" Duncan asked, gesturing to the room of trackers.

"No." I shook my head. "You come with me."

"Are you sure?" Duncan asked, but he followed me down to the library. "Shouldn't I be learning how to fight with the rest of them?"

"You won't be fighting with the rest of them," I replied simply.

"Why not?" Duncan asked. "I'm a tracker."

"You're my tracker," I said. "I need you with me." Before he could argue, I turned my attention to my brother. "Matt, we're looking for books that have anything in them about the Vittra. We need to find their weaknesses."

"Okay." He looked around at the ceiling-high shelves filled with books. "Where do I start?"

"Pretty much anywhere," I said. "I've barely made a dent in these books."

Matt climbed one of the ladders to reach the books at the top, and Duncan dutifully went along to start collecting books for himself.

While the history of the Vittra was interesting at times, it was irritating how little we knew about stopping them. So much of the Trylle past had been about avoiding them and making concessions. We'd never actually stood up to them.

By all accounts, Oren was the cruelest King the Vittra had had in centuries, maybe ever. He slaughtered the Trylle for sport and executed his own people for simply disagreeing with him. Loki was lucky to even be alive.

"What's this say?" Matt asked. "It doesn't even look like words." He was sitting on one of the chairs on the far side of the room, and he pointed to the open book on his lap.

"Oh, that?" Duncan was nearest to him, so he got up and leaned over Matt, looking at the book. "That's Tryllic. It's our old language to keep secrets from the Vittra."

"A lot of the older stuff is written in Tryllic," I said, but I didn't get up. I'd found a passage about the Long Winter War, and I hoped it would give me something useful.

"What does it say?" Matt asked.

"Um, this one says . . . something about an 'orm,'" Duncan said, squinting as he read the text. He didn't know very much Tryllic, but since he spent so much time researching with me, he'd picked up more.

"What?" I lifted my head, thinking at first that he'd said Oren.

"Orm," Duncan repeated. "It's like a snake." He tapped the pages and straightened up. "I don't think this will be helpful. It's a book of old fairy tales."

"How do you know?" I asked.

"We grew up hearing these stories." Duncan shrugged and sat back down in his chair. "I've heard that one a hundred times."

"What is it?" I pressed. Something about that word, *orm*, stuck with me.

"It's supposed to explain how trolls came to be," Duncan said. "The reason we split up into different tribes. Each of the tribes is represented by a different animal. The Kanin are rabbits, the Omte are birds, the Skojare are fish, the Trylle are foxes, and the Vittra are tigers, or sometimes lions, depending on who tells the story."

The Kanin, Omte, and Skojare were the other three tribes of trolls, like the Trylle and Vittra. I'd never met any of them. From what I understood, only the Kanin were still doing reasonably well, but they hadn't thrived as much as the Trylle or even the Vittra. The Skojare were all but extinct.

I'd only heard of five tribes, and all of the tribes were accounted for, yet Duncan had mentioned the orm.

"What about the orm?" I asked. "What tribe does that represent?"

"It doesn't." He shook his head. "The orm is the villain of the story. It's all very Adam and Eve in the Garden of Eden."

"How so?" I asked.

"I can't tell it with the same flourish as my mom did before I went to bed," Duncan said, "but the basic idea is that all the animals lived together and worked together. It was peace and harmony. Orm, which was this big snakelike creature, had lived for thousands of years, and he was bored. He watched all the animals living together, and for fun, he decided to mess with them.

"He went to each of the animals, telling them that they had to watch out for their friends," Duncan went on. "He told the fish that the birds were plotting to eat them, the birds that the fox had set traps to ensnare them, and the rabbits that the birds were eating all their clover.

"Then the orm went to the tiger and told him that he was bigger and stronger than all the other animals, and he could eat them all if he wanted to," he said. "The tiger realized he was right, and he began hunting the other animals. None of the animals trusted one another anymore, and they scattered.

"The orm thinks this is all funny and great, especially when he sees all the other animals struggling without their friends," Duncan continued. "They had all been working together, and they couldn't make it on their own.

"One day, the orm comes across the tiger, who is starving and cold," Duncan said. "The orm begins to laugh at how pitiful the tiger is, and the tiger asks him why he's laughing. When the orm explains how he tricked the tiger into betraying his friends, the tiger becomes enraged, and using his sharpest claw, he cuts off the orm's head.

"Usually the ending is told more dramatically than that, but that's how it goes." Duncan shrugged.

"Wait." I leaned forward on my book. "The Vittra killed the orm?"

"Well, yeah, the tiger represents the Vittra," Duncan said. "Or at least that's what my mom told me. But the tiger is really the only animal capable of cutting off the snake's head. At best, a fox could just bite it and the birds could peck out its eyes."

"That's it, isn't it?" I asked, and it suddenly seemed so obvious to me. I pushed aside my book and jumped up.

"Wendy?" Matt asked, confused. "Where are you going?"

"I have an idea," I said and ran out of the room.

preparation

In the ballroom, all the trackers were busy practicing moves on each other. Loki stood near the front, teaching a young tracker how to block. I tried not to think about how young that kid looked or about how he'd fight in battle soon.

"Loki!" I yelled to get his attention.

He turned toward me, smiling already, and his attention dropped from the tracker. Seizing the opportunity, the tracker moved forward, punching Loki in the face. It wasn't hard enough to really hurt him, but the tracker looked both frightened and proud.

"Sorry," the tracker apologized. "I thought we were still training."

"It's fine." Loki rubbed his jaw and waved him off. "Just save the good stuff for the hobgoblins, all right?"

I smiled sheepishly at Loki as he made his way across the ballroom over to where I stood at the door. I couldn't see Finn or Thomas, but I knew they had to be somewhere in the room, working with the other trackers.

"I didn't mean to distract you like that and get you sucker-punched."

"I'm all right," Loki assured me with a grin and stepped out into the hall, so we could have some privacy from onlookers. "What can I do for you, Wendy?"

"Can I cut off your head?" I asked.

"Are you asking for my permission?" Loki tilted his head and cocked an eyebrow. "Because I'm going to have to say no to this one request, Princess."

"No, I mean, can I?" I asked. "As in, am I capable of it? Would you die if I did?"

"Of course I would die." Loki put one hand against the wall and leaned on it. "I'm not a bloody cockroach. What's all this about? What are you trying to find out?"

"If I cut off Oren's head, would that kill him?" I asked.

"Probably, but you'll never get close enough to him to do that." He put his other hand on his hip and stared down at me. "Is that your plan? To decapitate the King?"

"Do you have a better plan?" I countered.

"No, but . . ." He sighed. "I've tried that before, and it didn't work. You can't get close enough to him. He's strong and smart."

"No, *you* can't get close enough to him," I clarified. "You don't have the same abilities as I do."

"I know that, but I can't knock him out," Loki said. "His mind is impenetrable. Even your mother couldn't use her powers on him." His eyes softened when he mentioned my mother. "I'm sorry about that, by the way."

"No, don't be." I shook my head and lowered my eyes. "It's not your fault."

"I wanted to see you, but I knew you'd have your hands full," Loki said, his voice quiet. "I thought you'd rather I be here, helping the Trylle."

I nodded. "You're right."

"But I still feel like a dick," he said. I could feel him studying me, his eyes all over me, but I didn't lift my head. "How are you doing with all this?"

"I don't have time to think about it." I shook my head again, clearing it of any thoughts of Elora, and looked up at him. "I need to find out how to stop Oren."

"That's a noble goal," Loki said. "Cutting off his head may do it, or running him through with a sword. It's never been a matter of killing him. It's getting close enough to do it. He'd have you on the floor before you could even draw your weapon."

"Well, I can do it," I insisted. "I can find a way. I have tiger blood, so I'm strong."

"Tiger blood?" Loki arched an eyebrow. "What are you going on about, Wendy?"

"Nothing. Never mind." I smiled thinly at him. "I can stop Oren. And that's what matters, right?"

"How?" he asked.

"Don't worry about it." I took a step back, walking away from him. "You concentrate on getting them ready. I'll deal with Oren."

Loki sighed. "Wendy."

I hurried back to the library, where Duncan and Matt were still waiting. I didn't let Matt know of my idea, because he would only disapprove. The last few days felt epic and long, and I told Matt to get some rest. We could pick things up in the morning.

I did need to rest myself. One thing I had learned from Tove was that my powers weakened and got more uncontrollable if I was overly tired. I'd been so completely exhausted lately that I wouldn't stand a chance against Oren.

Everything was so simple it was almost infuriating. Everyone had made it sound so difficult to kill Oren, but it would be the same as killing any other Vittra. I thought I'd need a magic spell or something. But all I had to do was get close to him.

I knew Loki was right, and it was easier said than done. Physically, Oren was still much stronger than me, he healed quickly, and his mind was virtually immune to my abilities. When he had interrupted my wedding, I'd tried to throw him back against the wall, and I'd only ruffled his hair.

Stopping him would be difficult, but it would be possible.

But I'd need my abilities to be up to full strength, which meant that I needed to rest. It felt lazy going to bed when so much was happening in the palace, but I didn't have a choice.

I went upstairs to go to my room, and I heard Willa rallying the displaced Trylle from Oslinna. She'd gathered them in one of the larger bedrooms and told them how they could make a difference, how they could avenge their loved ones.

I paused outside the door, listening for a moment. Something in the way she spoke always sounded seductive. It was hard saying no to Willa.

Willa was doing well with them on her own, so I continued down to my room. A rustling sound came from inside my chambers, so I cautiously pushed open the door. I poked my head in, and by the dim light of the bedside lamp I saw Garrett rummaging through my nightstand drawer.

"Garrett?" I asked, stepping inside the room.

"Princess." He immediately stopped what he was doing and stepped away from my nightstand. His cheeks reddened, and he lowered his eyes. "I'm sorry. I didn't mean to go through your things. I was looking for a necklace I gave Elora. I couldn't find it in her new room, and I thought it might have gotten left in here."

"I can help you look," I offered. "I haven't seen any necklaces, but I haven't been searching for any either. What did it look like?"

"It was a black onyx stone with diamonds and silver wrapped around it." He gestured to his own chest at about the spot a necklace would hang. "She used to wear it all the time, and I thought it would be good for . . ." He stopped, choking up for a second. "I thought she'd like to be buried with it."

"I'm sure she would," I said.

He sniffled and shielded his eyes with his hand. I had no idea what to do. I stayed frozen in place, watching Garrett as he struggled not to cry.

"I'm sorry." He wiped his eyes and shook his head. "You don't need to deal with me being like this."

"No, it's okay," I said. I took a step closer to him, but I didn't know what to do, so I didn't move forward any farther. I twisted my wedding ring and tried to think of something comforting to say. "I know how much you cared for my mother."

"I did." He nodded and sniffled again, but he seemed to have stopped crying. "I really did care about her. Elora was a very complicated woman, but she was a good woman. She knew she had to be Queen first, and everything else came after."

"She told me she regretted that," I said quietly. "She said she wished she'd made different choices and put the people she cared about first."

"She meant you." Garrett smiled at me, and it was both sorrowful and loving. "She loved you so much, Wendy. Not a day went by that she didn't think about you or talk about you. Before you came back, when you were still a child, she'd sit in her parlor and paint you. She'd focus all her energy on you, just so she could see you."

"She used to paint me?" I asked, surprised.

"You didn't know?" Garrett asked.

I shook my head. "She never mentioned it."

"Come on. I'll show you."

Garrett headed down the hall, and I went with him. I'd seen the room where Elora kept her precognitive paintings locked away in the north wing, and I thought about telling Garrett that. But I hadn't seen any paintings of me as a child. She'd only had a few of me as a teenager.

He led me all the way down the hall. At the very end, across the hall from my old bedroom, Garrett pushed on a wall. I didn't understand what he was doing, and then the wall swung forward. It was a door built to blend in seamlessly with the walls.

"I didn't know that was there," I said in dismay.

"Once you're Queen, I'll show you all the secrets of the palace." Garrett held the door open for me. "And believe me, there are quite a few."

I stepped through the door to find a small room. Its only purpose was to house a narrow spiral staircase. I glanced back at Garrett, but he gestured for me to go ahead. He stayed a step behind me as I went up the creaking iron stairs.

Before we even reached the top, I could see the paintings. Sky-lights in the ceiling lit the room, and I stepped onto the hard-wood floor. It was small, a hidden attic room with a peaked roof. But the walls were covered with paintings, all of them hung carefully a few inches apart. And all of the paintings were of me.

Elora's meticulous brushstrokes made them almost look like photographs. They showed me in all stages of my life. At a birthday party when I was young, with cake on my face. A scraped knee when I was three, with Maggie helping me put on a Band-Aid. At a failed dance recital when I was eight, pulling at my tutu. In my backyard, on the swings, with Matt pushing me. Curled up in my bed, reading *It* by flashlight when I was twelve. Caught in the rain when I was fifteen, trudging home from school.

"How?" I asked, staring in awe at all the paintings. "How did she do this? Elora told me she couldn't choose what she saw."

"She couldn't, not really," Garrett said. "She never picked *when* she saw you, and it took a lot of her energy to focus on you, to see you. But . . . it was worth it for her. It was the only way she could watch you grow up."

"It took a lot?" I turned back to him with tears in my eyes. "You mean it aged her a lot." I gestured to the walls. "This is the reason why she looked fifty when I met her? This is why she died of old age before she even turned forty?"

"Don't look at it like that, Wendy." Garrett shook his head. "She loved you, and she needed to see you. She needed to know you were all right. So she painted these. She knew how much it cost her, and she did it gladly."

For the first time, I truly realized what I had lost. I'd had a mother who loved me my entire life, and I hadn't been able to see her. Even after I met her, I didn't get to really know her, not until it was too late.

I began to sob, and Garrett came over to me. Somewhat awkwardly, he hugged me, letting me cry on his shoulder.

After I'd gotten it all out, he walked me back down to my room. He apologized for upsetting me, but I was glad he had. I needed to see that, to know about the paintings. I went to bed and tried not to cry myself to sleep.

In the morning, I knew I had much to do, so I rose early and went down to the kitchen to grab breakfast. I only made it as far as the stairs when I heard arguing in the main hall. I stopped and peered down over the railing to see what the fuss was about.

Thomas was talking to his wife, Annali, and their twelve-year-old daughter, Ember. They were Finn's mom and sister, his family, but Finn wasn't around. Thomas kept his voice hushed, but Annali was insistent. Ember kept trying to pull away, but Annali had a firm grip on her arm and wouldn't let her go.

"Thomas, if it's that dangerous, you and Finn should come with us," Annali said, staring up at him. "He is my son too, and I don't want him in harm's way because of some misplaced sense of duty."

"It's not misplaced, Annali." Thomas sighed. "This is to protect our kingdom."

"Our kingdom?" Annali scoffed. "What has this kingdom ever done for us? They barely pay you enough to feed our children! I have to raise goats to keep a roof over our head!"

"Annali, hush." Thomas held his hands up to her. "People will hear you."

"I don't care if they hear me!" Annali shouted. "Let them hear me! I hope they banish us! I want them to! Then finally we can be a family instead of being ruled by this awful monarchy!"

"Mom, don't say that." Ember squirmed and pulled away from her mother. "I don't want to be banished. All my friends are here."

"You'll make new friends, Ember, but you only have one family," Annali said.

"Which is exactly why you need to go away," Thomas said. "It's not safe here. The Vittra will be coming very soon, and you need to be hidden."

"I will not go away without you or my son," Annali said

firmly. "I have stood by you through much worse, and I will not lose you now."

"I will be safe," Thomas said. "I can fight. So can Finn. You need to protect our daughter. When this is all over, we can go away together, if that's what you want. I promise you I will leave with you. But right now you need to take Ember."

"I don't want to go!" Ember whined. "I want to help you fight! I'm as strong as Finn!"

"Please," Thomas begged. "I need you safe."

"Where do you expect us to go?" Annali asked.

"Your sister is married to a Kanin," Thomas said. "You can stay with them. Nobody will look for you there."

"How will I know when you're safe?" Annali asked.

"I'll come for you when it's over."

"What if you never come?"

"I will come for you," Thomas said firmly. "Now go. I don't want you traveling at the same time as the Vittra. They're not something you want to mess with."

"Where is Finn?" Annali asked. "I want to say good-bye to him."

"He's with the other trackers," Thomas said. "Go home. Pack your things. I'll send him down to talk to you."

"Fine," Annali said reluctantly. "But when you come for me, you better bring my son with you, alive and intact. If not, you might as well not come at all."

He nodded. "I know."

Annali stared up at her husband for a moment, not saying anything.

"Ember, say good-bye to your father," Annali said. Ember started to protest, and Annali pulled at her arm. "Now, Ember."

Ember did as she was told. She hugged Thomas, and he kissed her cheek. Annali cast one more look at Thomas over her shoulder, and then she and Ember left through the front door. Thomas stayed behind for a moment, his whole body sagging.

He'd sent his family away to protect them. He'd seen the painting the same as I had, and he knew the destruction that was set to befall the palace. It was no place for innocent bystanders.

But then something occurred to me. I had been trying to find a way to change the outcome of the painting, to do something that would alter the course of events and make it so we wouldn't all die, and I finally figured it out.

offense

W e take the fight to them," I said, and I was met with five blank stares.

Thomas, Tove, Willa, Finn, and Loki stood across from me, none of them looking pleased with what I proposed. I'd called them all into the War Room to discuss things, but so far I'd done most of the talking.

"That's your grand idea?" Loki asked, looking vaguely bemused, and that was the most positive response I'd gotten. "Get killed there instead of here?"

"The idea is not to get killed anywhere," I said and leaned back against the table behind me.

"Well, if this is what you want to do, Wendy, I'll support it," Willa said, sounding reluctant. "But I don't know how much it will help. The Vittra will have home-field advantage."

"Loki knows his way around the Vittra palace." I gestured to Loki, who grimaced when I volunteered him to lead the way.

"And we'll surprise them. That was how Finn survived the hobgoblin attack before."

"I barely survived that, Princess," Finn reminded me. "And we don't have much of an element of surprise. The Vittra are about to come here and take the kingdom. As soon as they get word of your ascension to the throne, they'll be on their way."

"That's why we need to move *now*," I said.

"Now?" Finn and Willa said in unison, both shocked.

"Yes." I nodded. "I've arranged to have my coronation in two hours. Then I'm Queen, and my first order as the ruling monarch will be to declare war against the Vittra. We will go to them, we will attack, and we will win."

"You want to hit them tonight?" Tove asked.

"Yes, when they're sleeping," I said. "It's the best chance we have."

"Princess, I don't know if that's possible." Thomas shook his head. "We can't plan a full-scale attack in a few hours."

"As soon as the King finds out I'm Queen, he will be at our door with an army of hobgoblins." I pointed toward the door to emphasize my point. "We are talking a matter of days here. What more can we do in the next two days that will be superior to attacking the Vittra when they're unprepared?"

"I don't know," Thomas admitted. "But it doesn't mean we should embark on a suicide mission."

"You're talking suicide?" I asked. "You saw the painting. Your son is dead. Everyone in this room, except for you, is dead." I paused, letting that sink in. "We have to do something to change that."

"Attacking the Vittra palace will only change the location of where we die," Finn said.

"Maybe so," I agreed. "But so what? I have read book after book of Trylle history. And you know what it says? We concede. We wait. We avoid. We only defend. We never stand up and fight for ourselves.

"And now is the time to fight. This is our last chance. Not just ours, as in the people in this room, but our entire kingdom's last chance to stand up and fight against the Vittra. If we don't do this now, they will conquer us."

"That's a shame," Willa said, looking awed.

"What is?" I asked.

"That you used that speech now instead of saving it to help me convince the Markis and Marksinna to go fight with us tonight," Willa said.

"So it's agreed, then?" I asked.

"You know that I'll always have your back," Tove said. "No matter what."

Loki nodded grimly. "I almost hate to say it, but yes, I'm with you. I'll attack the Vittra tonight."

"I still think there's a better way," Thomas said. "But I don't know what it is. If this is the best we have, then this is what we must do."

"Is there nothing that can convince you to stay?" Finn asked.

I shook my head. "This is my fight as much as it is yours, if not more. I will be there."

"Fine." Finn sighed. "Then I'm in too."

I wanted to smile. I felt like I should, to seal the deal somehow, but I didn't. My stomach was twisted too much.

"We have a few hours until we leave, then?" Thomas asked.

"Yes," I said. "After my coronation."

"I suppose that I need to brief everyone on the layout of the
Vittra palace," Loki said.

"That would be helpful, yes," I said.

Loki scratched the back of his neck and looked over at Finn.
"Let's get to it, then."

Loki, Finn, and Thomas went to deal with the schematics
of the attack, and Willa had the harder job of convincing the
higher Trylle to fight today. Tove had to go with me, because
he had to be crowned King.

We waited in our chambers, and we discussed the Vittra a
bit, but mostly we said nothing. There was so much to do and
so little to say.

Markis Bain came in to officiate the coronation. It was normally a large ceremony, a huge spectacle for the entire kingdom to attend, but we didn't have time for that. Duncan was
on hand to witness, and Bain swore us in.

With a few simple words and a quick signature on a piece of
paper, we were King and Queen.

Tove immediately left to talk to his mother. He needed to
convince her to join the attack on the Vittra. Her healing powers would be invaluable in battle. Duncan went down to work
with the trackers. I would follow him soon, but first I needed
to take a moment to breathe.

I stared out the window. The snow had taken a break. It was

just above freezing, and the air was thick with winter fog. Heavy white frost covered all the branches, like they had been wrapped in it.

"My Queen," Loki said from behind me, and I turned around to see him smiling.

"You're the first one to call me that."

"How does it feel?" he asked, sauntering over. He touched a vase sitting on the table, then looked at me. "Do you feel like Your Royal Highness yet?"

"I'm not sure," I admitted. "But I don't know that I ever did."

"You'll have to get used to it," Loki said with a smirk. "I predict a long reign ahead of you. Years of being referred to as Your Majesty, Your Grace, Your Excellence, My Liege, My Queen, My Lovely."

"I don't think that last one is a formal title," I said.

"It should be." Loki stopped in front of me, his eyes sparkling. "You are a vision, especially with that crown."

"The crown." I blushed and took it off. "I forgot I was wearing it." It was truly stunning, but I felt ridiculous in it. "I had to wear it for the ceremony, but . . . that's over now."

"It is a beautiful crown." Loki took it from me, admiring its intricacies for a moment, before setting it aside. He stepped closer to me, so we were nearly touching, and I stared up at him.

"How are things going?" I asked. "Does our army understand the layout of the Vittra palace?"

"No."

"No?"

"No, I'm not going to do this," Loki said, his voice firm but low. His hand went to my waist, feeling warm even through the layers of fabric. "Everything is about to go to hell very quickly, so I want one moment where we don't talk about that. We pretend it doesn't exist. I want one last quiet moment with you."

"No, Loki." I shook my head, but I didn't pull away. "I told you that was one night and it could never happen again."

"And I told you that one night wasn't enough."

Loki leaned down, kissing me deeply and pressing me to him. I didn't even attempt to resist. I wrapped my arms around his neck. It wasn't the way we had kissed before, not as hungry or fevered. This was something different, nicer.

We were holding on to each other, knowing this might be the last time we could. It felt sweet and hopeful and tragic all at once.

When he stopped kissing me he rested his forehead against mine. He breathed as if struggling to catch his breath. I reached up and touched his face, his skin smooth and cool beneath my hand.

Loki lifted his head so he could look me in the eyes, and I saw something in them, something I'd never seen before. Something pure and unadulterated, and my heart seemed to grow with the warmth of my love for him.

I don't know how it happened or when it had, but I knew it with complete certainty. I had fallen in love with Loki, more intensely than anything I had felt for anyone before.

"Wendy!" Finn shouted, pulling me from my moment with Loki. "What are you doing? You're married! And not to him!"

"Nothing slips by you, does it?" Loki asked.

"Finn," I said and stepped away from Loki. "Calm down."

"No!" Finn yelled. "I will not calm down! What were you thinking? We're about to go to war, and you're cheating on your husband?"

"Everything's not exactly the way it seems," I said, but guilt and regret were gripping my stomach.

My marriage might be over, but I was still technically wed to another man. And I should be worrying about things more important than kissing Loki.

"It seemed like you had your tongue down his throat." Finn glared at us both.

"Well, then, everything is exactly as it seems," Loki said glibly.

"Loki, can you give us a moment alone?" I asked. He sighed and looked like he was about to protest. "Loki. Now."

"As you wish, my Queen," Loki muttered.

He walked past Finn as he left the room, giving him one more discerning glare, but they said nothing to each other. Loki shut the doors behind him, leaving Finn and me alone in my room.

"What were you thinking?" Finn asked, sounding at a loss for words.

"I was thinking that we're about to go to war, and my mother just died," I said. "Life is so very, very short, and I . . . I love him."

Finn winced. He looked away from me, and he chewed the inside of his cheek. It broke my heart to hurt him, but he needed to hear the truth.

"You barely know him," Finn said carefully.

"I know." I nodded. "I don't know how to explain it. But . . . it is what it is."

"It is what it is?" He laughed darkly and rolled his eyes. "Your love must not mean much, the way you throw it around. It wasn't that long ago you pledged it all to me, and here you are—"

"Here I am married to another man because you wouldn't fight for me," I said, cutting him off. "I did love you, Finn. And I still care about you. I always will. You are good and strong, and you did the best you could by me. But . . . you never really wanted to be with me."

"What are you talking about?" Finn asked. "I wanted nothing more than to be with you! But I couldn't!"

"That's it right there, Finn!" I gestured to him. "You couldn't. We can't. I mustn't. You always took everything at face value, and you never even tried."

"I never tried?" Finn asked. "How can you even say that?"

"Because you didn't." I ran my hands through my hair and shook my head. "You never fought for me. I fought *so* hard for you. I was willing to give up everything to be with you. But you gave up *nothing*. You wouldn't even let me give up anything."

"How is that a bad thing?" Finn asked. "I only wanted what was best for you."

"I know that, but you're not my father, Finn. You were supposed to be my . . ." I trailed off. "I don't know what. You were never my boyfriend. You refused to be anything more to me, unless you saw me interested in another guy."

"I was only trying to protect you!" Finn insisted.

"That doesn't change anything." I took a deep breath. "I have been fighting to change things around here, to make the kingdom better for trackers and all the Trylle. And you have been fighting to keep things the same. You are content to live in this ridiculous hierarchy."

"I am not *content*," he said fiercely.

"But you're not doing anything to change it! You're just taking it, and that I could live with. You're willing to simply accept your fate. But you expected me to do the same, and that I can't stomach, Finn. I want more. I *need* more."

"And you think Loki will give that to you?" Finn asked, and most of the sarcasm had fallen away from his voice. He actually wanted to know if I thought Loki was good for me.

"Yes, he will."

"And how does your husband feel about all of this?" Finn asked.

"I don't know exactly," I said, which was true. Tove seemed to actually know more about the way Loki and I felt about each other than we did, but I wasn't entirely sure how he felt about it. "But once everything is settled with the Vittra, Tove and I are getting our marriage annulled."

"You're leaving him for Loki?" Finn asked, his voice astonished.

"No, actually," I said. "Tove is leaving me. He wants to

share his life with someone he actually loves, and that's not me."

His whole body slacked, and he stared at the floor. Finn ran a hand through his hair, and I realized that I would never again run my fingers through his hair. Whatever had happened between Finn and me, it was over. He was no longer mine. And for the first time, I was okay with that.

"I'm sorry," Finn said quietly.

"Pardon?" I asked, thinking I'd heard him wrong.

"You're right, and I'm sorry." He looked up at me, his eyes stormy. "I never fought for you. If anything, I fought to uphold a system that kept me from you. And . . . I am sorry for that." He swallowed. "I will always regret that."

"I'm sorry too." I bit my lip to keep tears from falling.

"But . . ." Finn sighed and looked away from me again. "At least he does love you."

"What?" I asked.

"Loki." He said his name bitterly and shook his head. "At first I thought it was a trick, but I've been around him enough now and heard him talk about you." Finn shifted his weight, seeming uncomfortable with the conversation. "And he does love you."

He nodded his head, but I wasn't sure why. He let out a shaky breath, and I think he was trying not to cry.

"So . . . I guess I can live with that." He rubbed his forehead.

I stepped over to him and put my hand on his arm, attempting to comfort him in some way. We were so close to each other, but I didn't feel that pull the way I did before. When he lifted his head, I smiled weakly at him.

"This really is for the best," I said. "Me and you never would've worked out anyway. You need someone that you can protect and shelter. And I need someone to push me to take risks, so I can pull this kingdom forward."

"There is more truth in that than I'm ready to admit," he agreed.

I swallowed, realizing something I'd never realized before. "I never could've really made you happy. I would've fought you at everything, frustrated by your attempts to keep me safe and hold me back. We would've made each other miserable."

"Had we ever really had a chance to be together." He exhaled again.

"I'm sorry," I told him again.

Finn shook his head. "Don't be. You're right. This is the best for both of us. And . . ." He paused. "As long as you're happy."

"I am." I smiled. "And you'll be much happier without me than you ever would've been with me."

He nodded, but I wasn't sure if he really believed it or not. "But if you'll excuse me, I should go down to finish getting ready to leave."

"Right, of course. I have much to do myself."

Finn smiled at me once before he left, and as soon as he was gone, I let out a deep breath. I can't say I felt good about ending things with Finn. It was more bittersweet than that. But I did feel better knowing that he finally knew the truth. Things between us were truly over—for both of us—and I could move on with my life. Assuming I still had a life to move on with after tonight.

TWENTY-THREE

time

Throughout the long drive to Ondarike, we said hardly anything. I rode with Tove, Loki, Duncan, and Willa, and the fear was almost palpable. I had no idea if we were doing the right thing. I had sounded so confident when I talked to them, but that was because this was the best I could come up with.

Before we left, I'd gone over the plan of attack with the heads of the teams. Loki thought it would be best to break up our army into several smaller teams that would sneak into different places in the Vittra palace.

Around two hundred trackers had joined our army, and most of the Trylle from Oslinna. Mia had tried to come along, but Finn had convinced her it would be better for her to stay behind and care for her baby, which I was grateful for. I didn't want Hanna to end up an orphan.

Maybe two or three dozen Markis and Marksinna had come

along, including Marksinna Laris. I promised myself to be nicer to her when we got back to Förening. *If* we got back.

A few mänks had even volunteered. I'd sent Rhys and Rhiannon away this morning, and I tried to send Matt away, but he refused to leave Förening. Matt had even wanted to fight with us, but I'd convinced him that he would only distract Willa and me, and he agreed to stay behind.

Willa would be leading her own team of twenty trackers and two Markis. They would be going in a side door off the kitchen, and Loki thought there would be hobgoblins in there getting a midnight snack. But Willa could blow around the pots and pans, and Markis Bain could control water, so maybe he could flood the place.

Finn and Thomas led two different teams, but they would be doing about the same things. They were coming up through the dungeon. Loki had escaped through a section of the cellar that connected with the dungeon. The cellar sprawled beneath the whole palace like a long maze, and through its long tunnels, Finn, Thomas, and their teams would be able to sneak up and deflect a lot of hobgoblins.

Tove had volunteered for the most dangerous mission. Bain had tried to go along with him, but Tove had insisted Bain go on Willa's team. Tove would go through the front doors, leading a team of fifty trackers. His objective was to make noise and alert the hobgoblins that he was there. That way, the other teams could sneak up behind the hobgoblins while they were busy trying to ward off Tove and his team.

Duncan had wanted to be on Tove's team, but I reassigned

him to Willa's team. So far, hers sounded about the safest. Not that any of this was really safe.

Loki's job was to get me into the palace and lead me to Oren, and then he would go help Tove fight. He wasn't thrilled about the idea, but he knew that I had to do this, and I had to do it on my own.

In the long history of the Trylle, we had never attacked. No matter how provoked we might be. This was the one thing Oren would never expect, and it might give us enough of an advantage to stop him.

Loki knew the palace best, so he drove our SUV and led the rest of the Trylle. We had a caravan of Cadillacs that we drove to Ondarike. When we got near the palace, he cut the headlights, and the cars behind us did the same. He parked at the bottom of the hill, so we were hidden behind the forest of dead wood, and that was as close to the palace as he felt comfortable.

"Are you sure you want to do this?" Loki asked me quietly after we got out of the car.

"Yes," I said. "Are you?"

"Not as much as I'd like," he admitted.

"Just get me to Oren."

I looked back behind me, at all the other Trylle getting out of their cars. Finn was already directing a few of them up the hill, telling them how to get inside. Loki had gone over detailed maps with the team leaders before we left, but we hadn't had enough time to show all the Trylle.

"Everybody knows what to do?" I asked and looked over at Willa, Tove, and Duncan.

"Yeah, we'll be okay." Willa reached out and squeezed my arm. "Just stay safe."

"We got it," Duncan said, flashing a nervous smile.

"Don't be a hero," I told him sternly. "Protect yourself."

"Take care of her," Tove said to Loki.

"I'll do my best," Loki said.

Most everyone else had started up the hill, with Loki and me going in an entrance on the far side of the palace, away from them. We were going a different route, sneaking around the hobgoblins and going directly to the King.

We went through the trees, slipping through snow and branches cracking under our feet. When we reached the palace, Loki led me to a small wooden door almost completely buried under vines. The vines looked brown and dead, but they were covered with sharp thorns that cut Loki's hand when he pushed them back.

He opened the door, then slid inside, and I followed. We stepped into a narrow, dimly lit hall. The floors were covered with red velvet carpets, and they helped silence our footsteps. As he led me through the back halls of the palace, I heard banging and yelling from far away. The fighting had started.

I jumped when something slammed into the wall right next to us, leaving a large crack in the wood.

"What's on the other side of that wall?" I asked, pointing to the crack.

"The front hall." Loki took my hand and looked at me. "If you want to do this, we need to hurry. He's going to hear the fighting."

I nodded, and we walked faster. The back hallways turned and twisted a few times before we came across a very constricted stairway. I almost had to turn sideways to climb up, and the steps themselves were so thin I had to stand on my tiptoes.

At the top of the stairs was a door, and when Loki pushed it open, I knew exactly where we were. Right across from us were the doors to Oren's chamber. Vines, fairies, and trolls were carved into the oak, depicting a fantasy scene. The hall was deserted, and the cacophony of fighting sounded farther away.

I heard a scream that sounded too much like Tove, and the entire palace shook.

"Go," I told Loki.

"I don't want to leave you to face the King alone."

"No, I can do this." I put my hand on his chest and faced him. "They need you downstairs. I can handle the King myself."

He shook his head. "Wendy, no."

"Loki, please. You must help them. You're strong. They need you," I said, but I knew that wouldn't convince him. "I will send you flying down the hall myself, but that will drain my abilities. I don't want to do it, but I will if I have to."

His eyes searched mine, and I knew he didn't want to leave me. But I couldn't let him come with me. I wanted him safe, or at least safer than he would be around Oren. And more important, my friends needed him to help fight against the hobgoblins.

"I can do this," I repeated. "I was born for this."

He didn't want to, but he finally relented. He kissed me, quickly and fiercely on the mouth.

"I will help them, and then I will be back for you," he said.

"I know. Now go."

He nodded and dashed down the hall. Taking a deep breath, I turned around to face the doors. I went down the hall, prepared to kill my father.

TWENTY-FOUR

beginning of the end

I pushed open the doors, and I wasn't exactly sure what I expected, but it wasn't this. Oren was awake, sitting on his throne. He wore black satin pants, and his robe hung open, revealing his shirtless torso, so I assumed he had been sleeping recently.

He sat casually in the chair, turned slightly to the side so one of his legs hung over the arm. His fingers were bedazzled with heavy silver rings, and he held a glass of red wine in one hand, sipping it slowly.

I glanced around the room, searching for the swords Loki had told me about. The platinum ones that could cut through anything. We had our own swords back in Förening, but Loki didn't think any of them would be powerful enough to use on Oren. Even his flesh and bone were stronger than the average Trylle or Vittra. I'd have to use the King's own weapons on himself.

"My child." Oren smiled at me in that way that made the hair stand up on the back of my neck. "You've come home."

"This isn't my home," I said, my voice as strong and sure as I could make it.

I spotted the swords, their handles glistening with diamonds from where they were mounted on the wall, and that helped give me a bit more confidence.

Oren ignored my comment. "It sounds as though you've brought guests." He twirled his glass, watching the wine swirl about in it. "You're supposed to wait until your parents go out of town to throw a party."

I grew irritated with his attempts at humor. "I'm not throwing a party. You know why I've come."

"I know why you *think* you've come," he clarified. He stood up, and in one quick swallow drained his glass. When he'd finished, he tossed it to the side, making it shatter against the wall. "But if I were you, I would seriously reconsider."

"Reconsider what?" I asked.

"Your plan." Oren walked toward me in that same stealthy gait he always had. "There is still time to follow through on the terms we agreed to. There is still time to save yourself and your friends, but not much.

"I'm not a patient man," he said, walking around me in a large circle. "If you weren't my daughter, you would already be dead. I have given you more than I've given anyone else. And it's time you show me some gratitude."

"Gratitude?" I asked. "For what? Kidnapping me? Killing my people? Overtaking my kingdom?"

"For letting you live," he said, his gravelly voice behind me, right in my ear, and I didn't know how he got that close to me so fast.

"I can say the same thing about you," I said, surprised by how even my voice sounded. "I've let you live thus far, and I will let you continue to live. If you call this off. Let us go. Leave us alone. Forever."

"Why would I do that?" Oren laughed.

"If you don't, I will have no other choice," I said as he strolled back in front of me, facing me as I spoke. "I will kill you."

"Have you forgotten our deal?" Oren asked, a twisted smile on his lips and something dark sparkling in his eyes. "Have you forgotten what you agreed to when you gave me your kingdom?"

"No, I haven't forgotten."

"You've merely decided to back out on it?" he asked, smiling wider. "Knowing what it would cost you."

"It will cost me nothing," I said firmly. "I will defeat you."

"Maybe you will." Oren seemed to consider this for a moment. "But not until you lose everything."

"Is that your answer, then?" I asked.

"You mean will I give up, let you and all your friends live happily ever after?" he asked, his tone condescending, but that changed instantly. "*I* get the happily ever after, and I will not concede to a spoiled brat like you." His face was hard, and his words were filled with venom.

"Then you leave me no choice."

I summoned all my power, concentrating and focusing on

everything I had been practicing. I held my hands out toward him, palms out, and, using everything I had in me, I began to push. I knew I couldn't kill him this way, but I hoped to get him incapacitated enough that I could get close to him.

His hair ruffled, his robe even blew back, but nothing else happened. I used everything inside me, and a buzzing sound started in the back of my head, growing more painful as I strained to use all my energy.

But Oren never even moved. He only smiled wider.

"Is that all you've got?" He threw back his head and laughed, the sound reverberating through the room. "I have highly overestimated you."

I pushed and pushed, refusing to give up, even when the pain in my skull became excruciating. Everything else in the room, the furniture, the books, began flying around like there was a tornado, but Oren remained unmoved.

I could feel something warm and wet on my lips, and I realized my nose had begun to bleed.

"Oh, Princess, darling," Oren said, as sweetly as he could. "You're exhausting yourself. I hate to see you in so much pain." He sighed, attempting to sound regretful. "So I'll put you out of your misery."

He stepped forward and raised his hand. He struck me across the face, backhanding me so hard I flew across the room and slammed into a wall. Everything that I had sent flying in the air collapsed to the floor around me.

Loki had tried to warn me about how strong Oren was, but

I hadn't understood until now. It was like being hit with a wrecking ball. My side ached terribly where I'd crashed into the wall, and some of my ribs must have been broken. My leg screamed in pain and I was lucky I hadn't broken my neck.

"I hate to do this to you," Oren said, and at least he wasn't smiling when he said it. "But I told you what would happen if you went against me."

I pushed myself up so I was sitting, still leaning back against the wall. He towered over me, and I steeled myself, waiting for him to hit me again. But instead, he went over to his chamber doors and opened them.

"Bring him to me!" Oren shouted out into the hall. He left the doors open and returned to me. He crouched, his black eyes meeting mine. "I warned you. I gave you every chance to join me. I wanted you with me, not against me."

"I would rather die than serve you," I said.

"I see that." He reached out, meaning to wipe the blood from my forehead, but I pulled away from him, even though it sent shooting pain through me. "Well, the good news is you won't die alone."

He rose and stepped back from me. At the same time, Kyra—the Vittra I'd tangled with before—and another Vittra came into the room, carrying Loki with him. I hadn't seen the other Vittra before, but he was huge, a barbarian of a man.

They were literally dragging Loki. They held him by each arm, and his legs trailed limply on the floor. His head hung down, and blood dripped from his temple.

"No!" I shouted, and Loki lifted his head at the sound of my voice. He looked over at me, and it was clear they had beaten the hell out of him.

"I'm sorry, Wendy," he said simply. "I tried."

"No," I repeated and struggled to my feet. My body didn't move the way I wanted it to, but I ignored the pain. "No, don't hurt him. I'll do whatever you ask."

"It's too late." Oren shook his head. "I promised you that I would make you watch him die. And I am a man of my word."

"No, please," I begged him. I stumbled over to a chair and leaned against it, holding myself up, because I couldn't stand on my own. "I will do anything. *Anything.*"

"I am sorry," Oren said again.

He walked over to the wall where the two long swords still hung, the only things still intact in the room after I had sent it into a flurry. He pulled one down, the diamond-encrusted bell guard covering his hand.

I tried to use my powers to stop him. I held out my hand, pushing out what energy I had left. Some of the lighter things in the room stirred, like papers and a curtain, and Kyra winced. But Oren was unruffled.

"Loki's met with this blade before," Oren said, admiring the sword. "And it's the same one I ended his father with. It seems fitting that it will be the one to finish him."

"Please." I let my hand fall to the side. "I will do your bidding. I will do anything."

"I've already told you." Oren walked back, stopping in front of Loki. "It's too late."

Kyra and the other Vittra held Loki higher, and Loki grunted. Tears streamed down my face, and I could think of nothing to do to stop Oren. My powers weren't working on him. I wasn't strong enough to fight him. I had nothing to barter.

Still staring at me, Oren lifted up his sword, and with one quick move, he stabbed Loki straight through the heart.

mortality

Kyra and the other Vittra instantly let go of Loki, and he collapsed on the floor. They both held their heads, clutching at them, and at first I didn't understand.

I couldn't really think or feel anything, except that I had been ripped in two. It felt as if Oren had torn my heart from my chest. I had never felt such consuming pain or anger as I did then.

Blackness surged through me with an intense heat. I didn't even really know what was happening around me. Everything felt like a hazy blur.

Then I saw Oren, squinting and touching his own head, and I remembered.

I could do something with my mind when I was frightened or angry. I'd done it to Tove when he tried to wake me, and I'd even done it on a smaller scale when Elora had been torturing Loki.

That feeling—that intense fear or anger—unlocked a power inside me. I did something to people inside their heads, causing great agony. It usually only lasted a few seconds, but I had never been as pissed off before.

As soon as I realized what I was doing, I harnessed it and directed it at Oren. At first he looked confused and simply started backing up. He kept squinting and tilting his head, as if he were staring at a very bright light.

In the back of my mind, I knew my body should hurt, but I felt nothing. I'd blotted out any pain. I walked evenly toward Oren, and he began to hold his head. He fell to his knees. He was moaning and begging but I couldn't understand anything he was saying.

Both Kyra and the other Vittra were curled up on the floor, and Kyra was actually sobbing. I went over to Loki, refusing to let myself actually see him, to really believe he was dead, and I pulled the sword from his chest.

I walked over to where my father was slumped on his knees, bent forward. His hands were clamped to his ears. He was muttering at first, but when I raised the sword over my head, I heard him begin to shout.

"Make it stop!" Oren yelled. "Please! Make the pain stop!"

"I'll put you out of your misery," I said, and I swung the sword down, slicing through his neck.

I turned away so I didn't have to see it, but I heard his head fall to the floor.

I stood there, still holding the sword, and looked around the room. The haze had faded away, and pain returned to my body. My body screamed in agony, and my legs threatened to give out beneath me. Kyra and the other Vittra had stopped writhing and they both sat up.

"Go," I said, struggling to catch my breath. "Tell them the King is dead."

Kyra looked at Oren's corpse with widened eyes, and she didn't question my orders. She and the other Vittra scrambled to their feet and ran out of the room, leaving me alone with Loki.

I dropped the sword and rushed to his side as quickly as my body would allow. I knelt next to him, and pulled his head onto my lap, but it lolled to the side. Blood stained the front of his chest, and I put my hand over the wound, trying to press the life back into him.

"No, Loki, please," I said as tears streamed down my face. "Loki, stay with me. Please. I love you. You can't leave me like this."

But he didn't move. He didn't breathe. I bent down, kissing his forehead as I sobbed, and I didn't even have words for the pain I felt. With nothing else to do, I began to wail.

"My god, I'm too late," someone said, and I turned to see Sara standing in the doorway. She looked at the dead King, her husband.

Loki had saved her life once, and she was a healer. She would be the only chance I would have at saving him.

"Help me," I begged and tried to hold Loki up to her. "Please. You have to help him."

"I . . ." Sara didn't answer for a second, and then she ran

over to us, kneeling on the other side of Loki. "I don't know that I can. He might already be gone."

"Please," I cried. "You have to try." She took a deep breath and nodded.

"Do you have any energy left?" Sara asked.

"I don't know," I admitted. I felt weak and drained. Fighting Oren had taken everything out of me.

"Well, help me, if you can," she said. She put her hand on top of mine, the one that covered the hole in Loki's chest. "Give me any energy you have. I need all I can get."

I nodded and closed my eyes, focusing on her and Loki. A warm tingling went through my hand, a sensation I was familiar with from being healed before. But something else happened. I felt it in my veins, flowing through me, being pulled from me. Like hot liquid escaping out through my fingertips.

Then I heard it. Loki gasped loudly, and I opened my eyes.

He took deep breaths, and tears of relief slid down my cheeks. Sara's hand was still over mine, and her skin had become wrinkled and loose. Her hair suddenly had gray in it, and her face had aged noticeably. She'd given Loki a lot of her life force to save him.

"Loki," I said.

"Hey, Princess." He smiled dazedly as he looked up at me. "What's wrong?"

"Nothing." I smiled and shook my head. "Not anymore."

"What's this?" He took my hair and held it out so I could see. A curl near the front had gone completely silver. "I take a nap, and you go gray?"

"You didn't take a nap." I laughed. "Don't you remember what happened?"

He furrowed his brow, trying to remember, and understanding flashed in his eyes.

"I remember . . ." Loki touched my face. "I remember that I love you." I bent down, kissing him full on the mouth, and he held me to him.

TWENTY-SIX

home

W endy!" Willa was nearly screaming, and I rushed to
try to get to my feet. The panic in her voice made me
forget about how weak I was, and I would've fallen to the floor
if Loki hadn't caught me.

"Easy, Princess," Sara said, looking up at me from where
she knelt on the floor. Loki had gotten to his feet and had an
arm around my waist, holding me up. "You used much of your
life force today."

I wanted to thank her for helping me and ask her exactly
why she had. Loki'd already explained to me how close he'd
been to Sara, but I had no idea how she might feel about the
fact that I'd just killed her husband.

Before I had a chance to say anything to her, Willa appeared
in the doorway to the King's chambers. Her clothes were wet,
her hair was a mess, and she had blood on her cheek.

"Wendy!" Willa shouted again and ran to me, throwing her

arms around me. She would've knocked me over if Loki hadn't been there.

"Willa, settle down." Loki gently pushed her off me, so she wouldn't smother me.

"I'm so glad you're okay." She stepped back from me and scanned the room, her eyes landing on the King's head on the floor, his long hair lying over it like a blanket. "So it's true, then? The King is dead? The war's over?"

"The King is dead." I nodded and turned to Sara to see how she would respond. She was Queen of the Vittra, after all, and she could continue this war if she wanted to.

Loki followed my gaze and his eyes met hers. "The war is over," he said, but I wasn't sure if he was simply telling her or declaring it.

"The King's reign of terror has lasted long enough," Sara said. She got to her feet slowly and smiled wanly at us. "Our war is over, and I'll be happy if I never see another one again."

"Good." Willa smiled in relief. "When that tracker came down and said the King was dead, the hobgoblins started retreating. A lot of them ran outside."

"They're happier in the woods than living indoors anyway," Sara explained.

"So how did we do?" I asked Willa, my heart tightening at the thought of how our army had fared in the battle. "Did everyone survive?"

Willa's expression fell. She pursed her lips and shook her head. "I don't know for sure. As soon as I heard the King was dead, I went to find you. But . . . I know not everyone made it."

"Who?" I demanded.

She hesitated before answering. "A few trackers. I don't know for sure."

Since Willa wouldn't answer me, I had to see for myself. I started walking away, again forgetting that my legs barely worked. This time, when they gave out under me, Loki scooped me up, carrying me in his arms.

I wanted to protest and insist I could walk, but I couldn't really. So the best I could do was direct him to take me down to the main hall, where Willa had told me the worst of the carnage was.

Loki carried me out of the room, with Willa at our side and Sara following a few steps behind. The upstairs didn't look that bad, but I doubted the fighting had really made it this far. We did pass a small table with a hobgoblin hiding underneath it, and when he saw us, he took off running the opposite way, his little legs moving as fast as they could.

When we reached the top of the stairs, I asked Loki to stop and put me down. From here, I had the best vantage point to view the front hall. The top of the stairs were over twenty feet above it, and I could survey the entire scene.

"Wendy, I don't think—" Loki tried to hang on to me, but I squirmed away from him, and he reluctantly set me down.

I grabbed the banister to steady myself and stared down. The room itself had once been lovely—plush red rugs, paintings on the wall, and all the furnishings dark mahogany, matching the walls.

Everything had been destroyed, and I do mean everything.

The paintings were shredded, the chairs broken, the rugs burned. Even the walls were cracked. Most of the crystals on the chandelier had been shattered, but it still hung from the ceiling, casting the room in light.

Bodies littered the floor, most of them Trylle, but there were a few hobgoblins. Fortunately, they mostly appeared to be wounded, but not all of them had survived. I knew all of the dead—not well, but I knew them. They were mostly trackers and mänks, those least equipped to fight the hobgoblins, and I wondered if I had done the right thing by allowing them to come into this war.

Aurora was going around tending to the injured, and I was pleased to see her moving from Markis to tracker without appearing to care about their standing. She was going to whoever had the worst injuries and helping them first.

Laris had no visible wounds, so she was helping organize those who had been hurt and helping treat those with the least serious injuries, like wrapping an arm.

Bain was leaning against one of the walls. His clothes were drenched, and he had blood on his shirt, but he was talking to Tove, so he must've been all right. Tove was crouched in front of him. He'd torn off the sleeve of his shirt and was wrapping it around Bain's leg, but other than that, Tove appeared to be no worse for the wear.

As I scanned the room, accounting for everybody, taking in the losses with a pained heart, I realized that Finn was absent from the room—not among the living or the dead.

"Where is everyone else?" I asked Willa without taking my eyes off the front hall.

"Um, I'm not sure," Willa said. "We told everyone to meet in the front hall once the fighting had stopped."

"So what does that mean if they're not here?" I asked, already fearing the worst about Finn.

My heart had already begun to panic when the door to the dungeon swung open. Finn came up the stairs, walking into the hall, with his father's arm looped around his shoulders. Thomas didn't look so good, but he was supporting some of his own weight, so that was a good sign.

Finn's face was bloodied and bruised, but when he glanced up at me at the top of the stairs, I saw a mixture of pride and relief in his eyes. I smiled down at him, happy to see him alive. Just because I'd ended things with him didn't mean I could handle him being dead.

Finn and Thomas hobbled past a tipped-over buffet table on their way over to where Aurora was treating people. My eyes were following them, and that was when I saw legs sticking out from underneath the table. They were clad in skinny jeans, and I only knew one person ridiculous enough to wear skinny jeans into battle.

"Duncan!" I shouted and raced down the stairs. Fortunately, adrenaline had kicked in, propelling my legs to move despite the pain.

I tripped when I reached the bottom step anyway, but Loki was right there, pulling me back up to my feet. When I reached the table, I collapsed next to it and immediately tried lifting it up. Obviously, I didn't have the strength for it, but Loki lifted it easily.

And it was just as I feared. Duncan had been crushed underneath it. As Loki moved the buffet table away, I scrambled over to Duncan's head, kneeling next to him. His chest was bloodied, and I could actually see a bone sticking out of his side.

"Duncan," I breathed, with tears sliding down my cheeks. I brushed the hair back from his forehead and tried not to sob. I'd tried to protect him, and I'd made him promise that he would do everything he could to save himself. And all of that had been in vain.

Suddenly he coughed, blood coming out of his mouth.

"Aurora!" I shouted and looked back over my shoulder for her. "Aurora, I need you!"

"Princess?" Duncan opened his eyes and smiled dazedly at me. "Did we win?"

"Yes." I nodded fervently, cradling his head in my hands. "Yes, we won."

"Good." He closed his eyes again.

"Duncan, stay with me," I begged, trying not to cry so my tears wouldn't land on his face. "Duncan. That's an order. You have to stay with me."

"Aurora!" Loki was yelling for her now, since she wasn't coming fast enough.

Duncan coughed again, harder this time, and finally Aurora appeared at my side. Her hands were already covered in blood from helping the other Trylle, and she pressed them against the bone protruding through his skin.

He groaned loudly when she did that and tried to jerk away, but I held him still. Aurora pushed on his side, and once the bone was back in, with the skin healed over it, she pulled her hands away.

"I can't heal him completely," Aurora said as Duncan took a deep breath. "I need to save my energy to help the others."

"Thank you." I smiled at her. "I understand."

"Do you need my help?" Aurora asked, holding her hands out toward me, but I shook my head. "Are you sure?"

"I'll be all right," I insisted. "You go take care of them."

She nodded and left to do just that. Duncan stirred a bit, but I told him to rest. She'd fixed him enough so he wouldn't die, but that didn't mean he was in good shape.

Willa had gotten some bandages from Sara, who had apparently joined our effort to care for the injured, and she took over the care of Duncan, wrapping up his wounds.

When I had been yelling for Aurora, Tove left his post next to Bain to see if he could help. Once Duncan was stable, I turned my attention to Tove. He held out his hand and pulled me to my feet. I had to lean on him for support, and Loki was nearby, in case I needed more.

"You know, it's almost a shame we don't love each other," Tove said, with his arm around my shoulders. "We make an awfully good team."

"I don't know about that." I looked around the room, at all the Trylle and even the Vittra hobgoblins that had been hurt.

"Wars have casualties," Tove said, understanding what I meant. "And that's not to say I'm not sad about the lives we lost tonight, but we managed to stop a centuries-old war. Imagine how many lives that will save in the future."

I realized he was right. I mean, I had known it—that was why I'd wanted to go to war in the first place—but the devastation of it all had a way of blocking that out.

But now, standing there with Tove, I felt good. Despite the losses and the damage, we had done what we had set out to do. We'd freed ourselves, and the Vittra people, from Oren's oppressive rule. We were free.

"We did the right thing." I looked up at him, and his mossy eyes looked unusually light.

"We did." He squeezed my shoulder and kissed me gently on the temple. "I'm proud of what we accomplished."

"Me too."

"But what do you say we get out of here?" Tove asked. "Let's get our people fixed up as best we can and get them back home."

"That sounds fantastic."

"I'm going to go see if my mother needs any help." Tove let go of me and started stepping back toward his mother.

I managed to stand by myself, but Loki was only a few feet away, helping Willa set another tracker's broken leg, if I needed him.

"Hey, Tove," I said as he walked away, and he paused, turning back to me. "Just because we won't be married anymore doesn't mean we can't still be a team. I still expect you to work with me back at the palace."

"I wouldn't have it any other way." Tove grinned. "And trust me, I have *plenty* of ideas on how to run things."

I helped as much as I could with our people, but I really didn't have the strength to do much. Fortunately, Loki was working at 110 percent, and he managed to help out quite a bit. Aurora healed as much as she could, focusing on the worst cases, and the rest of the injuries were wrapped and set until we could get back to the palace and enlist more help.

As soon as we were able, we started to load up the vehicles, and began sending the caravan of Trylle back to Förening. We were careful to take those we'd lost with us, since they deserved a proper burial back home.

Even though I was hurt, I insisted on waiting to be last to leave. I wanted to make sure we saw everyone off.

I talked with Sara briefly before we departed, and she assured me that there would be no more attacks on the Trylle, not by any of the Vittra. We would convene in a few days to sign a new peace treaty, but for now, we both needed to rest up and get our communities in order.

Willa drove us home to Förening, with Duncan sitting in front beside her, sleeping soundly. Tove had decided to ride home in Bain's car, and they left right before we did. Tove had stayed until the end with us, making sure we'd gotten everyone out safely.

The sun was just beginning to rise as we made the trek back

home, and the sky above the horizon looked more pink and purple than blue.

I curled up in the back next to Loki, his arm around me, and my head resting on his shoulder. My body ached all over, but it felt good being with him. He kissed the top of my head, and I snuggled up closer to him. He'd been helping me at the palace, but we'd waited until we were alone in the car to be affectionate. Willa had raised an eyebrow at us, but she said nothing. Later on, back in Förening, I'd have a thousand questions from her. But for now, she let us have our moment together.

"I can't wait until we get home," I said.

"*Home*," Loki said and laughed a little.

"What?" I lifted my head to look up at him. "What's funny about that?"

"Nothing." He shook his head. "I just . . . I don't think I've ever really felt like I had a home before." He smiled down at me. "Not until I met you."

Loki leaned down, kissing me gently on the mouth. I'm sure he wanted to kiss me more deeply, but he was afraid of hurting me. He continued to kiss me tenderly, and I clung to him as tightly as I could as heat swirled through me.

When he stopped, he rested his forehead against mine and breathed in deeply. "I cannot wait to get home with you, Princess."

"I'm the Queen now, you know," I teased, and he laughed and kissed me again.

epilogue:
four months later

The first few weeks after the battle were rough. I'd broken several ribs and dislocated my shoulder. So many of our people needed Aurora and Sara's healing powers that I refused to use any on myself. I had to heal the old-fashioned way.

Everyone was quick to point out that I healed much more quickly because of my Vittra blood, but it was still a rough couple of weeks. Some good things came out of it, though. Like Loki waiting on me hand and foot. Truth be told, he barely left my side.

As soon as I was well enough to attend, we had my mother's funeral. The entire kingdom turned out, and to my surprise, the King and Queen of the Kanin came, as well as the Queen of the Omte. They came to pay their respects but also to thank us for ending the tyranny of the Vittra.

Oren had set his sights most fervently on the Trylle, but we weren't the only ones. It wasn't until the funeral, when so many people came that the crowd overflowed into the street, that I realized what exactly we'd accomplished.

I also got to hear from other Trylle and even other tribes what my mother had done to protect them. The deals she had made, the things she gave up, and all the work she put into keeping the peace. Elora had given so much to the people, and it was deeply moving to see how much they appreciated it.

Losing Elora made me understand even more the importance of having a mother, and what had been taken from Rhys. Despite the way my "host" mother, Kim, had treated me, I knew she'd done everything out of love, love for a child she'd never even met.

Matt took Rhys to see Kim, where she's still locked up in an asylum. Matt's still resistant to the idea of repairing his relationship with her, but being willing to see her at all is a huge step.

Rhys plans to go to college near the asylum in the fall, so he can begin getting to know her. Matt says that Kim is doing a bit better, and if she continues on the road to recovery, she might be released one day.

Matt came back to Förening, though. He says his home is here, and for that I'm grateful. I know I'm an adult with my own kingdom now, but I don't think I'm ready to live that far away from my brother.

Oslinna is still rebuilding, and Matt has spent a great deal of time helping them with the process. His designs are gorgeous, and it's been really good for the Trylle people to see a mänks do something so well.

We're still working against prejudice, and I know it will be a while before they completely give in to the idea that it's okay for people to marry whoever they love, no matter if they're Trylle or not. But we're on the right road.

Before I hang up my crown as Queen, I'm certain we'll make it legal for anyone to marry whoever they love. Willa's hoping that it's sooner rather than later, of course, but she's been shopping around for a wedding dress since she was eight.

She's taken a much more active role in our society. Since I was on bed rest when we first came back, she stepped up to handle a lot of the day-to-day work with Tove. He is still one of my smartest and most trusted confidants, and he works alongside me all the time.

Shortly after the funeral, Tove and I had our marriage annulled. He insisted on it, because he said my and Loki's auras were blinding him. It turned out to be a rather complicated process, but thanks to our recent defeat of a major enemy, the Trylle people were much more willing to go along with our ideas.

Tove seems to be taking our annulment better than our marriage. Thanks to his efforts on the campaign, he managed to get Bain elected as Chancellor, which is a drastic improvement from our last Chancellor. Both Tove and Bain are working hard to improve the entire Trylle community.

Tove's met someone, although he's been very tight-lipped about who it is. Though he won't name names, I have an idea who the special someone might be. He's still afraid of how the community will react to him being gay, but I don't think it will be long before he's able to be open about it.

After we defeated the Vittra, Thomas left, joining his family in the Kanin tribe, and I don't think he'll be coming back. Finn stayed behind, taking over his father's duties as head tracker.

It's still a bit strange seeing Finn around the palace. I don't love him anymore, not like I did, although I don't think I can ever truly stop caring for him. He was my first love, and he was immensely important to me becoming the Queen I am today.

At first he was cold and distant, but the ice between us seems to be melting. We're on the path to becoming friends again, and that's something.

I've seen Finn talking with Mia, spending time with her and her small daughter. When he's around them, he seems relaxed in a way that he never was around me. Even though he did care for me, I don't think he was ever able to really relax or be himself with me. But when he's holding Hanna and laughing with Mia, I've never seen him happier.

She's giving him something that I never could, and for that I'm forever grateful. Finn deserves to be happy and to truly love someone who can love him back.

And Loki . . . well, Loki has hardly left my side since we came back, but I wouldn't let him into my bed again until he made an honest woman of me. So he did.

Two weeks ago in the garden, beneath the spring flowers, we had a small wedding, much different from my first one. This time, it was only my closest friends in attendance, including my aunt Maggie. I actually had a hand in planning it, and it was exactly as I wanted it.

But its greatest difference was that I wanted this wedding, and I married a man I desperately love.

Maggie's been staying with us for a few weeks, and it's mostly been wonderful. She still hasn't completely wrapped her mind around everything that's going on here, but she took to Rhys immediately. Thankfully, he's spent the last week keeping her entertained so Loki and I can have a little bit of time to ourselves.

Unfortunately, there's never enough time. The nights seem too short, and the sun always seems to come up too early when I'm still snuggled in bed with him. Usually he wants to sleep in as much as I do, but not today.

He opens the shades, so the morning light shines in too brightly, and I squeeze my eyes shut and bury my face in the pillow.

"Aw, Wendy." Loki kneels down on the floor next to the bed and brushes the hair back from my eyes. "You knew today was coming."

"I know, but I didn't want it to come." I open my eyes so I can look at him, smiling at me even though his eyes are pained. "I shouldn't have let you agree to this."

Loki laughs. "You don't 'let' me. I'm the King. Nobody tells me what to do."

"That's what you think," I scoff, making him laugh harder.

"But seriously, my love, are you going to get up and see me off today?" Loki asks. He takes my hand in his, kissing it. "You don't have to, of course. I can do the ceremony myself, and I know how mornings have been for you lately."

"No, if you're going to leave, I want to say good-bye." I sigh. "But you better hurry back."

"As quickly as I can." He smiles. "Nothing in the world will keep me from my Queen."

I throw off the covers and go into the closet to get dressed. We're having a ceremony to see Loki off, so I have to choose a nice gown, and I even have to wear my crown. I avoid it for the most part, since it makes me feel silly, but I have to put it on for formal occasions.

Loki is already dressed for the day. I'd felt him get up about an hour ago. I kept sleeping, though, since I've been so tired lately. I'd like to say it's because of how worn out Loki had left me after our honeymoon, and while that is definitely part of the reason, it isn't all of it.

"How are you feeling this morning?" Loki asks. He leans against the closet door, watching me as I pull on a dark emerald gown.

"Other than being sad, I'm okay." I slip the dress on, but I can't zip it up myself, so I turn my back to him. "A little help, please."

"You really ought to get a lady-in-waiting or something," Loki says as he struggles with the zipper. "These things are impossible to get on."

"That's what husbands are for," I tease.

He continues to yank at the zipper, and it finally goes up. But I know what the problem is, why my dresses are so hard to get on anymore.

From behind me, Loki reaches around, holding his hand against the snugness in my middle, and he kisses my shoulder.

"We're going to have to tell them soon," Loki says, hugging me.

"I know." I sigh. "But not until you get back, okay? I don't want to have to deal with all the talking and questions unless you're with me." I turn around so I'm facing him. "That means you'll have to hurry back soon."

"As if I need another reason to do that." He smiles and playfully tugs at my silver curl, the lock of hair that always refuses to stay in place.

Loki kisses me deeply, holding me to him, and he still makes my knees go weak. I keep expecting that feeling to fade, but every time he touches me, I feel it all the same.

We go down to the throne room for the ceremony. Sara is already waiting for us, along with Finn working as head guard and Bain working as the Chancellor. Tove is there too, mostly for moral support. Sara has been here since last night, so she can ride with Loki in a gesture of solidarity.

Loki and I sit on our thrones, waiting until everyone else arrives before beginning the ceremony. I had met with Chancellor Bain last night, and he had gone over all the right words I should say. Uniting kingdoms happens so rarely in our history, but apparently there is still a script I should follow.

Once everyone is here, Loki and Sara take their places in front of me. I stand up and do my best to recite the words that Bain taught me. I think I muddle up the middle part, but the basic idea is that we are uniting the Vittra and Trylle, pledging to work together and all that.

As part of the deal, Loki is going back to the Vittra to help them rebuild. Their society has begun to crumble since I killed the King. Sara has been doing her best to hold it together, but without intervention, it will soon fall apart.

"Since you both agree to work together in peace and respect, I say this union is complete," I say, finishing up the ceremony. "You may now . . . work together."

"Thank you." Sara gathers her skirts and curtseys to me.

"Thank you." Loki bows with a smile on his face.

"And you'll only be gone for two weeks?" I ask him.

"Two weeks is the absolute maximum, and then I'll be right back at your side," Loki assures me.

"I promise not to keep him any longer than I need him," Sara adds.

Her eyes are warm when she smiles at me. I didn't want to lend my husband out to her, but she had saved his life. And it's better if the Vittra work to become our allies instead of our enemies.

Loki kisses me, even though it isn't polite. A King and Queen are never supposed to show public affection, but Loki breaks that rule as often as he can. Although, to be honest, I don't do much to enforce it.

"Hurry back to me," I whisper.

Loki smiles. "As you wish."

As he turns to leave, I feel that familiar flutter in my stomach. Not the one out of love for Loki, but something different, something alive inside of me. I put my hand on my stomach, holding it as if to calm the baby.

The night Loki and I had spent together while I was still married to Tove had resulted in a small surprise. I'd told Loki weeks ago, and even though we were both frightened, we were both really excited. We're first-time parents, but we will also be the first royal Trylle parents. My child won't be a changeling.

I know that the idea of changelings can't go away overnight. Our society still needs a lot of restructuring before things are different and we can stop being dependent on the money the changelings bring in.

But we are working on it every day, Loki and I, and Willa, Tove, and even Finn. We are going to turn the Trylle community into something it should've been all along. A great people with a great appreciation for each other and for life.

I will make this world a better place, whether they like it or not. That's the fun of being Queen.

GLOSSARY OF TRYLLE TERMINOLOGY

aura—A field of subtle, luminous radiation surrounding a person or object. Different-colored auras denote different emotional qualities.

changeling—A child secretly exchanged for another.

Förening—The capital and largest city of Trylle society. A compound in the bluffs along the Mississippi River in Minnesota where the palace is located.

hobgoblin—An ugly, misshapen troll that stands no more than three feet tall.

host family—The family that the changeling is left with. They are chosen based on their ranking in human society, with their wealth being the primary consideration. The higher-ranked the member of Trylle society, the more powerful and affluent the host family their changeling is left with.

Kanin—One of the more powerful tribes of trolls left. They are considered quiet and peaceful. They are known for their ability to blend in, and, like chameleons, their skin can change color to help them blend into their surroundings. Like the Trylle, they still follow the practice of using changelings, but not nearly as frequently. Only one in ten of their offspring are left as changelings.

mänsklig (often shortened to *mänks*)—The literal translation for the word *mänsklig* is "human," but it has come to describe the human child that is taken when the Trylle offspring is left behind.

Markis—A title of male royalty in Trylle and Vittra society. Similar to that of a Duke, it's given to trolls with superior abilities. They have a higher ranking than the average Trylle, but are beneath the King and Queen. The hierarchy of Trylle society is as follows:

> King/Queen
> Prince/Princess
> Markis/Marksinna
> Trylle citizens
> Trackers
> Mänsklig
> Host families
> Humans (not raised in troll society)

Marksinna—A title of female royalty in Trylle and Vittra society. The female equivalent of the Markis.

Omte—Only slightly more populous than the Skojare, the Omte tribe of trolls are known to be rude and somewhat ill-tempered. They still follow the practice of using changelings but pick lower-class families than the Trylle. Unlike the other tribes, Omte tend to be less attractive in appearance.

Ondarike—The capital city of the Vittra, and site of the royal palace. It is located in northern Colorado.

persuasion—A mild form of mind control. The ability to cause another person to act a certain way based on thoughts.

precognition—Knowledge of something before its occurrence, especially by extrasensory perception.

psychokinesis—Blanket term for the production or control of motion, especially in inanimate and remote objects, purportedly by the exercise of psychic powers. This can include mind control, precognition, telekinesis, biological healing, teleportation, and transmutation.

Skojare—A more aquatic tribe of trolls that is nearly extinct. They require large amounts of fresh water to survive, and one-third of their population possess gills so they are able to breathe underwater. Once plentiful, only about five thousand Skojare are left on the entire planet.

stork—Slang term for tracker; derogatory. *"Humans tell little kids that storks bring the babies, but trackers bring the babies here."*

tracker—A member of Trylle society who is specifically trained to track down changelings and bring them home. Trackers have no paranormal abilities, other than the affinity to tune in to one particular troll. They are able to sense danger to their charge and can determine the distance between them. The lowest form of Trylle society, other than mänsklig.

Trylle (pronounced *trill*)—Beautiful trolls with powers of psychokinesis for whom the practice of using changelings is a cornerstone of their society. Like all trolls, they are ill-tempered and cunning, and often selfish. Once plentiful, their numbers and abilities are fading, but they are still one of the largest tribes of trolls. They are considered peaceful.

Tryllic—An old language that Trylle wrote in to disguise their important documents from humans. Its symbols are different from those of the standard Greek alphabet, and are similar to Arabic or Cyrillic in appearance.

Vittra—A more violent faction of trolls whose powers lie in physical strength and longevity, although some mild psychokinesis is not unheard of. They also suffer from frequent infertility. While Vittra are generally beautiful in appearance, more than fifty percent of their offspring are born as hobgoblins. They are one of the only troll tribes to have hobgoblins in their population.

Return to the beloved world of Trylle with

THE KANIN CHRONICLES

AVAILABLE MAY 2015

AVAILABLE AUGUST 2015

Book 1   Book 2   Book 3

"Amanda Hocking knows how to tell a good story
and keep readers coming back for more."

—*KIRKUS REVIEWS*

St. Martin's Griffin